AMANDA BROWN OMNIBUS

Family Trust
Legally Blonde

AMANDA BROWN OMNIBUS

Family Trust
Legally Blonde

AMANDA BROWN

timewarner
paperbacks

A *Time Warner* Paperback

This omnibus edition first published in Great Britain by
Time Warner Paperbacks in 2006
Amanda Brown Omnibus Copyright © Amanda Brown 2005

Previously published separately:
Family Trust first published in Great Britain as a paperback original
in 2004 by Time Warner Paperbacks
Copyright © Amanda Brown 2004

Legally Blonde first published in Great Britain as a paperback original
in 2003 by Time Warner Paperbacks
Reprinted 2003 (three times), 2004 (twice)
Copyright © Legally Blonde Productions, LLC, 2003

Grateful acknowledgement is made to
American Broadcasting Companies, Inc. for the use of
lyrics from the song 'Conjunction Junction'.

The moral right of the author has been asserted.

A CIP catalogue record for this book
is available from the British Library.

ISBN-13: 978-0-7515-3776-5
ISBN-10: 0-7515-3776-4

Printed and bound in Great Britain by
Clays Ltd, St Ives plc

Time Warner Paperbacks
An imprint of
Time Warner Book Group UK
Brettenham House
Lancaster Place
London WC2E 7EN

www.twbg.co.uk

Family Trust

For my Lovebug who always makes me smile, my mother who always believed in me, and my husband without whom none of this would be possible. Not to be forgotten: My furry babies Gomez and Underdog.

Acknowledgments

Special thanks to Jim Hornstein, Hillary Bibcoff, Nancy Nigrosh, Michelle Forrest, Daniel Greenberg, and Laurie Chittenden.

Chapter 1

All Business

Becca Reinhart laughed. Her eyes were bright, shining with humor as she listened to her telephone call. Her loose black hair brushed her shoulders as she shook her head in protest. She laughed, but her answer was firm. No way.

She stood leaning against her desk, her long, graceful arms supporting her tall figure as she turned her eyes toward Central Park. In a second she had absorbed the lush view of dewy treetops surrounding the pond. She breathed deeply, adjusting her headset. She began to pace.

Worn into the border of her Turkish carpet was a footpath, the wake of her intense relationship with the telephone. The carpet was rubbed to a vague crushed pattern of scarlet, gold, and cobalt in that rectangular path, once a meticulously designed border, hand-woven and delicate. It was, perhaps, a mismatch from the start. Nothing about Becca Reinhart or her restless, money-drenched world was delicate.

"A thousand times no!" Becca insisted, grinning with amusement. "Listen, I've met him. The guy's rude to his own shadow. Abby Joseph Cohen wouldn't give him a buy."

She stopped in front of her brass-studded leather chair, which functioned mainly as a padded shelf for her incoming files and faxes. To those who knew her, the end of her pacing was a sign that she was ready to end the discussion

1

or the deal. If she had a nickel for every lawyer her mother wanted her to date!

"Not even a hold, Mom," she said firmly. "He's an absolute sell." Becca glanced down at her open desk-calendar, searching it quickly for an excuse. "Anyway, I'm out of town. I'm in Hong Kong next week through Saturday."

Though Becca's feet were still, she kept her hands busy. With a stray pen she scribbled idly on the Saturday block of her calendar.

"I know it's a holy day, Mom," she said. She hung her head.

Her eyes traveled for comfort out the northern window of her West Fifty-seventh Street office, her gaze resting again on the unparalleled extravagance of Central Park. Manhattan's great, enduring, beckoning heart. Inhaling the view like pure oxygen, Becca spoke with renewed confidence.

"I'm meeting with the finance minister, Mom. What was I supposed to do, reschedule?"

She leaned against her desk, staring at its scattered papers. Her hair brushed her chin and her shoulders as she nodded. She glanced at the screen of her computer, which indicated several dozen new messages had arrived. All were first priority.

"All right, Mom. I'll try," she promised.

Becca waved her hand as the quick little figure of Philippe, her secretary, popped his head into her office. His hair, until recently jet black, had been highlighted with some gray, achieving a salt-and-pepper look that people typically paid to erase. With a gesture of welcome, she invited him to take a seat on her couch.

Philippe returned her smile and reclined on the couch to wait. He began to page through an issue of *The Economist,* the only reading material displayed on Becca's coffee table.

Today is the third of September, but it feels like June, thought Philippe. A dull haze hung in the thick, humid air. The sun seemed to have ripened, swelling in intensity as if to remind the city masses that summer held court for another three weeks.

Philippe looked affectionately at Becca, who had resumed pacing as she laughed into the telephone. Her restless energy had made him nervous when he first met her, but Philippe had come to appreciate, even to crave, the warmth of Becca's style. She was an incredible creature.

Between board meetings, speaking tours, conferences, and the usual round of deal negotiations, Becca had been traveling every week this summer. It was natural to her; travel suited her pace. There were days at a time when she was nothing but a blur to Philippe, racing past his desk with her Pullman suitcase bumping and rolling behind her, hurrying to finish the call on her headset before she lost cellular service in the elevator.

Becca had fire, the effects of which he saw reflected in the faces of the clients and hopefuls that revolved through her office. Sometimes their worn lines of anticipatory tension were soothed by her competence, her iron reliability. And other times he ducked to search for imaginary files under his desk, unwilling to meet the violent eyes of the seekers of capital who came away burned.

Philippe was amazed that Becca could survive the physical pressure of travel on top of her intense load of back-to-back meetings. She changed time zones with chameleonlike agility. Every day she met with companies at the make-or-break stage, and handled their urgent pleadings with integrity and dispatch. He wondered, sometimes, what Becca would have done without this demanding career. Would she run marathons? Climb mountains? He knew she was cut out for something extraordinary.

He smiled to see her suitcase by the door, standing at the

ready. Becca prepacked her bags for different climates and labeled each piece of luggage for maximum travel efficiency. A brass-rimmed tag that dangled on the Louis Vuitton rolling bag that leaned against the wall read LONDON, AUTUMN.

Philippe knew she was tightly scheduled as usual. She would hardly have time to adjust to the six hour time change before she was supposed to conduct a meeting to evaluate an offer for the shares of Machovia, a Davis Capital portfolio company in whom she was the single largest private investor. Though they had not put the company up for sale, an unexpected and tempting offer had come in. She would take a helicopter from the city to the Teterboro Airport in New Jersey where the Davis Capital plane would land her at Heathrow at 10 A.M. London time. Most people took at least three days on the ground before returning from business in London. Becca would be three days door-to-door.

She had succeeded quickly in this unyielding world, thanks to the gamble Dick Davis had made on her when he gave her the chance to join the partnership five years ago. She was leading the technology group at Morgan Stanley at the time, a young analyst with a sterling reputation for her exhaustive, diligent research and an iron stomach for risk. Her returns, even in the bear market, were unbeatable.

Dick Davis, the founding partner of Davis Capital, had left Bear Stearns nearly twenty years before to found the venture capital firm. He had seeded it at first with the fortune that his wife inherited from her grandfather's piece of Standard Oil. Today the firm managed eleven billion dollars of invested capital.

Becca would never forget what Dick Davis made possible for her: to enter the elite, private partnership of Davis Capital as a relative *child*. She was twenty-six years old

4

when she started with the firm. Dick's confidence in Becca was aggressive, and she soon proved it to be well-placed.

Though it carried the Davis flag, the name that came to mind when anyone thought of Davis Capital was Becca Reinhart. At thirty-one years old, Becca Reinhart was by far the firm's youngest partner, and on their portfolio compensation scheme, she was also the best paid. Her own portfolio made up nearly forty percent of revenues and over half the profits of the firm. Becca had high visibility from her very first day at Davis Capital.

Her brash entry into the firm was an industry legend. The day she accepted Dick's offer, Becca got his secretary, Philippe, on the phone, asked him what he made, and offered him more money to come and work for her. She wanted somebody who knew the business, she said, and who better than her boss's secretary?

"Poached my secretary," Dick would laugh, pretending to complain about her hard bargaining, "and she didn't blink an eye!" He told the story all over Wall Street. He had wisely chosen not to fight her. With a knowing smile, he told Philippe to pack up his desk. Dick realized at that moment that Becca's confidence was going to make the partnership rich.

Philippe was happy with the switch, as he had never been fond of Dick Davis's overbearing wife. For Becca, as long as he could talk fast, type fast, and schedule every ten minutes precisely for the next three months, he stayed above the water. He managed Becca's calendar, and her travel, copied the reports for her meetings, and trotted in with her faxes, sorted her mail, and kept her files secure. She had another assistant to handle the phones, and the analysts took care of her research. The clippings service prepared its own news summaries.

Becca could have a staff of fifty, Philippe marveled, and she wouldn't know what to do with it. She had never quite learned how to delegate. She put a bear hug on her own companies, and served on dozens of their boards. For travel, however, she had learned to lean on Philippe.

In a moment she was rushing toward the couch to join him.

"Did you get my message?" She held her breath, glancing at the eastern standard clock on the wall. Eleven-thirty. Her eyes, dark and expressive, shone with energy as she turned toward Philippe for his answer.

"Check," he said, nodding simply. "Consider it done."

He stroked his hair, intending to draw her attention to it. This color was a big change for him. Alexander, his partner, who ran a fashionable Upper East Side salon, had worked for days to get just the right silver tone in the gray on his temples.

She paused. "I'm in London till Tuesday; I arrive in New York at six-thirty in the morning. We're doing an eight o'clock meeting at Wasserstein; I won't have time to get back here after the flight."

He ran a hand over his salt-and-pepper hair. "I know, Becca. I scheduled the meeting. I *love* to wait on you in my spare time."

"What *is* spare time?" she shot back with a laugh.

She dug the JFK locker key from her desk drawer, being careful not to confuse it with the La Guardia key, and scribbled down her combination to the electronically secured file room in which she kept the permanent records for her portfolio companies. She began to describe the precise location of the Wasserstein files when Philippe waved impatiently.

"I filed them, sweetie, I know," Philippe assured her. He was practically pointing to his hair with both hands in his eagerness for her to notice it. He tried to catch Becca's nomadic eyes and saw that her glance had passed him already. She was moving again, headed toward the coffee bar.

6

Philippe began to feel a little testy, and paused to console himself that his *hair* was not at fault in her failure to notice him: It was Becca's fundamental lack of attention to appearances. He remembered the day she asked Dick Davis when he had started wearing glasses. It was just a few months ago, when they were working late in his office on the Celex deal.

"Nineteen-ninety two," Dick had informed her, to Becca's enormous surprise. Dick still laughed about that.

Philippe declined the latte that Becca, standing in front of her coffee bar, offered to him. Her imposing black coffee machine, mounted into the wall, featured over thirty small silver buttons that produced on demand an infinite variety of coffees. For herself she pushed the espresso button five times before placing a large mug below the coffee spout.

Philippe broke down. "Look at my hair, Becca," he pleaded.

She turned her head at once. "Philippe," she said, smiling broadly, "it's great!"

"The Old Economy's back in," he boasted, sauntering toward her. "Alexander says people are *rushing* into the salon for gray temples and sideburns. Gravitas is hot, you know. Credibility is back."

Becca put the coffee in the refrigerator to cool so she could drink it quickly.

"Good thing," she said, grinning. "Now how do we sell it?"

She closed the door behind Philippe, turning quickly to answer a call that the secretary had put through. She said hello to David Sheffer and simultaneously pulled on her nylon warm-ups. She had determined that it saved a few minutes for her run if she pulled on the workout clothes at the same time she was undressing. For one second she moved the phone and slid off her shirt and bra. Becca was

7

in a hurry. She had scheduled herself to take a run at twelve-fifteen, and she stuck to her schedule.

Sheffer was the external lending director of the European Investment Bank. Becca had known David when he ran the European equities platform at Morgan Stanley. It was a strange time to call from Luxembourg, she said; he replied that he was in New York. He had a German paper company he wanted to put her on to, which the EIB wouldn't fund because of his family's stake in the business. She agreed to meet with the German CEO next week, if she could get a translator, and appreciated him sending over the company's information. She tapped an e-mail on her computer directing Philippe to adjust her schedule to leave open a half hour next Thursday.

David held for a second while Becca slipped her jogging bra and a T-shirt carefully over her headset. Her eyes roved around her office. There were a half-dozen stacks of paper to read, all before she left for London. The messages and faxes piled up by the minute; if she had an impromptu social conversation in the hall, it knocked her off schedule. Empty mugs lined the coffee machine, alternating with empty Evian bottles. Now and again one pile of mugs would disappear and clean ones would appear in their place.

Becca glanced at the bagels, still untouched, which she had delivered to her office every morning to guard against the real possibility of starvation. She tried to keep a bagel in her purse for the times when she ran to get a cab and felt the sidewalk spinning.

Becca used time as efficiently as she thought it could be used.

Marking the time on the clock, Becca started the treadmill on Alpine Walk, making conclusory remarks into her headset to let David know she had no more business with him. Then David got to the real point of his phone call.

He had a nephew that he would like her to meet for dinner this week.

She cranked the machine up to Hard Jog. Not another nephew!

Becca did her best to listen politely, since she did want to check out the German paper firm as a possible investment, but the setup was difficult to endure. Was she wearing a sign? DESPERATE SINGLE GIRL: MARRY ME PLEASE? She pounded through her workout, fueled by indignity.

"He's thirty-four," David offered, a bit tragically. "Lawyer at Simpson Thatcher, good practice, good prospects. Never married."

"Frankly, David," she told him flatly, "I'm more interested in the business piece. I'll let you know how the paper company looks after we talk." She cut off the call and ran for several minutes as hard as she could.

Becca couldn't understand why capable professionals, with whom she had a solid business relationship, were always trying to get her married. She didn't ask after their prospects. She didn't comment on their divorces, their affairs. Why was her personal life so interesting to them? Didn't they see how busy she was?

It had gotten worse since she turned thirty-one last year. Even her mother, for whom marriage had never done any favors, was constantly after her to give a nice boy like Gary Yahkzen a chance. Everybody had something to offer, her mother would point out, despite apparent shortcomings. Who says it's not nice to be a urologist?

Her father must have found something useful in the state of marriage, Becca reflected, with the spite she reserved for the man who had abandoned her mother. He had tried it twice. When her mother was being treated—successfully, thank God—for her cancer, Becca's father and the chemo nurse began an affair. He eventually married her. Her father's betrayal never lost its bitterness.

He had left her mother when Becca was only ten, and for all practical purposes, she considered her father to be dead. She never spoke of him. But Becca's mother, Arlene, had more than filled the void her father left. To Becca, Arlene was both parents and a dear friend, not to mention a conscience.

Becca tried to get to Brooklyn on Friday for Shabbos dinner with her mom, but these days she only made it every other month or two. Things were all right between them, though, in spite of Becca's absence. Becca and her mother were secure in their love for each other, and both were good friends of the telephone.

Becca was her mother's sole source of financial support, outside of the part-time work Arlene did at her temple, where really she went just to stay in the congregation's loop. Lately Arlene had been hearing about everybody's grandchildren. If Becca had spent an afternoon kibitzing with Arlene's friends, she would understand the logic that motivated Arlene's sudden interest in matchmaking.

She felt the muscles of her calves stretching from the pull of racing with the treadmill. The workout was an extreme one. Becca tried to exhaust her natural intensity before she conducted client meetings. Even the hours of travel, she knew, would not wear her down. She hoped she would appear mellow and reasonable if she conducted the meetings in a state of physical exhaustion. Her feet and her mind raced together as Becca rehearsed the speech she was giving at the Capital Markets meeting next week.

Checking her watch, Becca wound down the treadmill. She kept her exercise clothes on, tugged an Armani pantsuit from her closet, and folded it in a tight sleeping-bag roll. The pantsuit went into her shoulder bag along with shoes, stockings, and an underwear set that would have surprised any of her fellow board members with its sexy, lacy femininity. She intended to shower and change at the airport's VIP lounge.

She combed her hair with her fingers in the small mirror on the office wall, not the least bit aware of the way the sunlight picked up the red tones, all natural, in her dark, glossy hair.

A dab of lipstick and she was off.

"Becca—your mother is on the phone," Philippe said over the intercom.

That was strange. Her mother never called without reason. She sighed—she was already behind schedule.

"Mom?" She cradled the phone on her shoulder and flipped through the messages in her in-box.

"Honey"—her mother jumped right in as though they were in the middle of a conversation—and perhaps they were—a marathon lifelong exchange of ideas and feelings. Becca never understood the problems other women had with their mothers.

"Yes, Mom—what's up?"

"I don't mean to be nosy."

"Yes, you do."

"Okay—so I am. But you don't sound exactly right. Is something making you nervous?"

Only a mother—or maybe only Arlene Reinhart—could look straight through all the froufrou and braggadocio into her daughter's soul.

"Well, not that it's bothering me too much. But the owner of the London company is not a great supporter of women arbitrageurs. And he doesn't know how old I am."

"You mean how young."

"Well, yeah."

"Listen to me, Becca Reinhart. Remember whenever you feel nervous anywhere, anytime, you just turn around and look back to who you come from all the way up the Reinhart line."

11

"You say that all the time."

"So it works every time, am I right?"

Becca's dark eyes shone with the electric heat of her intelligence and joie de vivre. "You got me there, Mom—"

"Okay. So maybe you'll call from there?"

Grrr. Her mother was fabulous—she was also a scholar of those lessons mothers learned from the Secret Mother Rules they all seemed to follow.

"Love you, Mom," Becca blew her a kiss and left her office seemingly while her feet, in their Diesel running shoes, were in midair.

Becca hurried past Sam Wattenberg's office. Sam's door was open.

"Becca," he called, leaping from his desk chair.

She kept moving. Sam followed her.

"Sam, I've got a meeting at the airport at three and a flight at six," she told him over her shoulder.

"I've got a press conference in ten minutes. Any recessionary expectations?"

Stepping sideways toward the elevator, Becca ticked off a few suggestions.

"Venezuela, Peru, and Columbia plunge this year. Russia's always in recession, so throw it in. Egypt looks bad, Czech Republic is slipping. Japan may make it, but I'd put it in the slide category. Argentina probably goes with Peru. I've got to go, Sam!"

Becca blew Philippe a little kiss. The elevator doors closed, and she smiled broadly, taking a deep breath as she dug her hand in her Hogan bag to check for her Palm, her phone, her ticket confirmation, and her wallet.

She could feel her heart beating rapidly as she thought ahead to the meeting in London. Sexist issues aside, the offer for her British company was likely to get approved; Becca would recommend accepting it and she thought she had the votes on her side. She had always liked that company, and she had a good feeling about this deal. It was proving to be a smart investment. She could bet on getting tapped for a spot on the holding company's board of directors, if she wanted one.

She smiled, looking forward to the manicure she would get from the Davis Capital's in-flight spa therapist. Becca felt a surge of enthusiasm as the elevator doors opened in the lobby. The Davis car was waiting to take her to the airport. She could start calling the American directors right away and get a count of their votes. She had assumed the board was accepting proxies, but she should get that into the minutes of the meeting. She'd move for that at once; she'd have to make sure to have a second to back her up. Who should she call? Who had the next largest investment? Her mind began to race: She had little time and much to do.

She barely noticed the sharp, quick, sad, prescient pull at her heart. Later she would understand. Becca Reinhart breathed deeply. She loved her job.

Chapter 2

Accept with Pleasure

Edward Kirkland shaved, splashed his cheeks with 4711, and dashed across Park Avenue from the Racquet Club to the quiet, antique-strewn office of the Kirkland Philanthropic Foundation. If he took care of things at the office in an hour or so, he thought, he might get another squash game together in the afternoon.

A towering stack of unanswered invitations filled the cherry wood "in-box" on the hand-carved mahogany desk in Edward's office. The Tiffany lamp on his desk cast its tinted shadows over the envelopes, spotting them with shapes of blue, green, and purple. An additional pile of envelopes sat in a neat stack on the leather blotter, beside the brass-plated holder for his Montblanc pen and pencil set. The piles of current invitations sat next to a tiny, out-dated globe that was of no earthly use to anyone. Where it had come from, he couldn't exactly say. Probably it adorned one of his father's old desks, like so much else in his office.

Edward's desk was usually organized and clear, as he had little to do.

Still standing, with his back to his work, he looked across the street where the flag of the Racquet Club waved in the crisp, early September sun.

Alice Carter, his private secretary, had entered without his noticing. She sniffed the air critically.

14

"Is it raining aftershave?"

She welcomed him with bright hazel eyes. As was her practice, she took the leather armchair that sat across from his desk, pulled it around carefully so as not to drag the tassels on the Persian area rug, with its rich hues of red and violet that darkened the cozy room, and sat down next to Edward's chair.

"Sit, sit, Edward," she said. "Labor Day's on us already. You have a big weekend."

Edward grinned. "Labor Day! The Union Club opens its private stock this Sunday."

She pointed at the envelopes, which he surveyed with visible deflation.

"Don't tell me I have plans on Sunday?"

"Likely," Alice responded.

"No CPs, I hope."

CPs were command performances—charitable events that involved The Family. They could not be avoided. But everyone would be at the Union Club, he told himself, beaming with anticipation of the great chef's dinner that the club put on twice a year when it dipped into the private stock of wines.

Alice smiled to look at him. What joie de vivre! Edward's fine, clean-shaven face expressed so much. He had such a well-developed instinct for pleasure. His blazing blue eyes shone at the thought of a glass of wine, as the eyes of a schoolboy would shine at a fire engine. And as impetuously as anticipation moved him to happiness, the thought that a prescheduled event would keep him away from his luxury drew a dark cloud of disappointment across his face.

A hopeful flash lit his expression again: Alice knew from experience that Edward would conceive of a method to have it both ways.

"You know, Edward, if you married, you could send

15

your wife to some of these things," she teased him. "Then you could go to the club every Sunday."

"Let's not ruin a good day talking about my death." Edward grinned, shaking his finger at Alice.

"Edward!" she said, laughing warmly. "I'm married. It's not death. Marriage would be good for you. Your mother has been frantic to see you happy since you turned thirty. The only . . ."

"Alice," Edward interrupted her, straightening quickly in his chair. "Have I ever struck you as unhappy?"

The question was rhetorical. She shook her head no, glancing at the ground lest she display too much admiration in the way she looked at him. Edward Kirkland had a limitless capacity to enjoy.

"I still think you'd spend more time at the club," she said, "if you had a wife attending these things in your stead." The morning sun glinted on her modest clear nail polish as she gathered some invitations from the desk. Her hand was stopped by Edward's, who turned her amused face to face his.

He squinted at her like a police investigator. "Alice," he said gruffly, "I'll have to go through your accounts. I'm worried about financial irregularities."

"In *my* accounts?" she asked, catching the bait.

"Absolutely." He let go of her hand. "Anyone who could convince me that I should get married so I can spend more time at the club has got to be on Bunny Stirrup's payroll."

Alice smiled. She was on Edward's payroll, and had grown accustomed to living the details of his fortunate life. She was a knight of the Kirkland table, one of the family's collection of devoted servants. But Alice knew better than to complain. A social secretary accepts the bounds of a modest life lived at the perimeter of a great one.

She found it hard to describe her position precisely to people who did not already understand it. For a social secretary was no more a secretary than the Secretary of State. A lady-in-waiting, a trusted messenger, a well-schooled practitioner of etiquette, a confidante, a conscience, and a person of extraordinary discretion and fine penmanship capable of delivering, when appropriate, unwelcome truths, to an indulged personality, were some of the qualities that fell under the title of social secretary. By and large, they worked in the homes of women who did not work outside of their homes.

Alice came from the Pavilion agency. She had fastidious manners and a clean, polished preppiness. Like the other women who finished with her at Pavilion, Alice had attended private schools and counted among her personal friends several of the well-heeled. She held faithfully to the Social Register crowd, with the knowledge, sealed by her quiet superiority, that she was *among* them without being *of* them. Altogether, Alice was a charming accessory: tactful, dependable, and unthreatening.

She juggled, on Edward's behalf, a busy black-tie life divided between homes in Manhattan, the Hamptons, England, and Bermuda, with parties in season, knotted and proper or shockingly dissolute, depending on the crowd. Technically speaking Alice was the confidential secretary to the Chairman of the Kirkland Philanthropic Foundation. This position gave her the first experience she had known of working in a formal office. Now on her lunch hour instead of being cast into the service kitchen to eat with the maids, she was able to get out and enjoy the city. Frankly, the Philanthropic Foundation was nothing more than a corporate personality thrown like a coat over Edward's shoulders. He was the sun around which Alice revolved, and she treasured him dearly. Ten years her junior, Alice could not help considering Edward like she might a nephew or a younger friend.

Edward Kirkland was a genteel, considerate, and enjoyable

young man, a step up from her former employer, Leslie Davis, she of the Standard Oil fortune and advantageous marriage to the founder of the profitable investment house. Leslie's husband, Dick Davis, had hired Alice after his own secretary had threatened to quit due to Leslie's demands. Quite fairly, Alice's predecessor in the Davis employ claimed it was demeaning for him to have to interview and hire kitchen maids for Leslie and even worse to have to visit St. Bart's ahead of the Davis family to make sure they were on the guest lists for the A-list parties. Leslie had unquenchable needs.

Leslie had set Alice up in her home and was satisfied with the secretary's modest diligence until she heard, from her tennis partner, that a famous founder of a Fortune 500 firm had married his third wife's social secretary. She raced home and fired Alice that day: standing right there in her Fila tennis skirt, her arm outstretched and her finger pointing to the door, she actually *fired* her, which is simply never done. But Alice had landed on her feet.

Edward considered Alice to be indispensable, and trusted her with a confidence that inspired her to care for him.

"Bunny Stirrup has not paid me a nickel," Alice corrected Edward with a wide smile. "And you know it. We'll have to agree to disagree, young Edward. I think you are in need of a wife."

"And I think you are in need of a reminder," Edward said, returning her smile, "that I am perfectly happy to remain as I am."

They laughed together as she directed him to the business at hand.

"Let's get to work," she said, lifting the roof from the tower of envelopes, a move that sent much of the pile sliding across the aged, leather blotter that covered his desk.

They were practiced, and after their first cup of coffee

18

they had moved into an efficient process of invitation review.

"Okay. How about Golfing for Glaucoma. Benefactor, sponsor, or patron?" she asked, holding the engraved card in the air.

"Family on the board?"

"No."

"Did we do it last year?"

"Yes. It's Muffy London's pet charity, remember? Her great-uncle died of glaucoma."

Edward stopped himself from laughing out loud, but couldn't repress his smile.

"You can't *die* of glaucoma. I remember Pepper London. He was about two hundred years old. He just fell out of bed, spilled his last glass of brandy, and that was that."

"Muffy said it was the glaucoma that killed him. He wouldn't have fallen out of bed, she said, if he could see."

"He could see, all right. I think he was in bed with Sharon Leland at the time."

Alice smiled too, remembering old Pepper.

"Well it makes it all the more important to Muffy, you know, to put the emphasis on the glaucoma," she pointed out.

"I see." He paused, considering the sponsoring group and Muffy's interest in the matter. It seemed harmless enough, except that it took an entire day and evening. First the golf, eighteen holes, then the dinner.

He tried to remember anything special about the event, for better or for worse. Last year's gift bags included sterling silver golf club swizzle sticks from Tiffany, designer sunglasses by Gucci, and a Lucite eye chart from the Zapper Laser Eye Clinic.

The Zapper Clinic, which sponsored last year's event, also provided neon orange and blue golf shirts decorated in the style of a Union 76 sign, with the Zapper letters in

19

silver glitter. It was obvious that they were designed with the vision-impaired in mind. You could see the shirts from a mile away.

"What level did we do last year?"

"Benefactor."

"Any reason to change?"

"No."

Edward pushed his Windsor-blue coffee cup, which was empty, out of his sight. The joy of eating and drinking was manifest in him, but he had inherited the patrician's distaste for viewing, even momentarily, the evidence of a well-enjoyed feast.

"How much is benefactor?"

"Ten thousand, twenty for a table."

Alice stood to clear Edward's coffee cup without being asked. She read his facial expression, the quick flash of aversion that Edward reserved for old plates and dates who stayed for breakfast.

"Where is it?"

"Piping Rock," she answered, her back to him as she rinsed the cup.

"Do a table."

She met his order with a nod, trotting back to her seat.

"Eight to a table," she said, with her pen ready.

Edward leaned back in his chair, stretching.

"Eight. All right. Call George and Bonnie Whelan, Clifford and Susie Marks, Arthur Stearns and Amy Kolasky, and . . . for me . . ."

He paused. This was an all-day event.

"I don't know. How about Cricket Quinn?"

Alice wrinkled her brow. "Well, she's on the LPGA tour. Do you think you can bring professionals?"

"Why not?"

Edward Kirkland's job as chairman of his family's charitable foundation had two elements, separated by a little shuffle of other people's steps. He decided what events to sponsor or attend, and with whom; and he showed up appropriately dressed and accompanied.

Between the decision and the attendance, Alice got to work. She would handle the acceptance, and she would call to invite the women he chose to accompany him. She would select the table, invite his guests, select the meals, if she thought it necessary, she would direct the event staff as to the proper order of table service, forms of address for dignitaries, or matters of concern in left-handed and right-handed seating arrangements.

Alice would forward the payment instructions to Milton Korrick, Edward's banker at Morgan Stanley, who handled all his financial obligations and balanced the books. She would call Edward's driver, James, who would put the event on his schedule, and promptly report it to Edward's mother, who insisted on knowing his whereabouts at all times. And finally, before he dashed out the door, Alice would tuck a folded briefing paper into Edward's free hand.

The paper would supply useful information about the charity, and more importantly, talking points for any guests with whom Edward might not be instantly familiar. As a special courtesy, Alice included information that he might find useful about his own date: her place of birth, for example, or food preferences. Edward had a reputation for being extraordinarily thoughtful, a tribute that Alice secretly attributed to her own research skills.

They had moved on to the Tango for Teeth, which would be catered by La Paella, a popular tapas restaurant. Alice was pressing him to name a date.

"Who's on for the night before?" Edward asked, waiting for her to consult his schedule, which she derived by poking a few buttons on some handheld piece of digital equipment. Edward learned of his schedule by poking the buttons of his telephone to call Alice.

"Cricket Pierpont, at the New York Historical Society dinner." Bubbly Cricket would help take his mind off that stuffy crowd, he thought with a smile.

Another Cricket, Alice thought. It was hard to separate out who he was referring to at times because they all seemed to have the same first name.

"Anyone else that week?"

"Bee Frothingham, Bitsy French, Whitney St. Clair. Bee and Bitsy are dinners; Whitney's a lunch event."

"Is Morgan Devonshire back from Wales?"

"Sure is. She's doing a tent at the Harriman."

"Is she? Morgan, then."

"Check," Alice said. "One down." She moved on at once to the next foil-lined envelope.

"Here's a new one. Embalming Awareness Society. Dinner."

Edward winced. "Dinner?"

She shrugged.

"Decline with contribution," he said, shaking his head. He had eaten while doctors described heart transplants, organ donations, and prostate cancer, but slicing into a filet while watching a presentation on the embalming of the dead was a step too far.

"Okay." She shuffled her envelopes, unfolding a gold-edged, rose-tinted paper. It was a personal note to Edward, included in the invitation for the Antibiotic Awareness Gala, from an old girlfriend of his. She had once suffered a bad case of tonsillitis that was resistant to antibiotics. She urged his attendance.

"Strange that she didn't just have her tonsils removed," he said. "But she was a singer. I guess that makes a difference. Anyway, she married her ENT doctor, so all's well that ends well. Where's the event?"

"The River Club."

"White tie?"

22

"As always."

"I'll take Minnie Forehand."

"She's married."

Edward cringed, but lost hardly a step.

"Deb Norwich."

"She's on the board. She once had a resistant strain of mono. So she'll be there already."

He shrugged. "Cricket St. James, then."

"She's in Paris."

"She's always back by Labor Day."

"I'll call her tonight." Alice said, standing to refill her coffee. Edward declined another cup, opting instead for a glass of fresh orange juice, which Alice poured from the crystal pitcher she had filled in the morning. She had the chilled, green bottle of Pellegrino in her hand before he even asked, knowing he liked bubbly mineral water in his freshly squeezed orange juice. If it were afternoon, she would pour the Pellegrino into cranberry and orange juice together, the drink she called his "afternoon virgin."

Not only did Alice not mind performing these little domestic tasks—she actually considered them to be a treat, a perspective that was purely the result of Edward's charm. Anyone who has prepared a meal knows the creator's pride of watching it be eaten with pleasure. Edward received all the gifts of his life—and they were ample—with such cheerful animation that it was a distinct pleasure to bring him anything he enjoyed.

"If you don't mind my asking," she said, handing Edward the cool crystal glass that was half full of juice, and placing the bottle of mineral water on the desk, "why aren't you taking Bunny to any of the parties?"

Edward's face clouded.

Alice persisted. "You were seeing her quite a lot over the summer."

"We're neighbors out at the Hamptons," he said,

attempting to sound casual. "How can I help it? She's practically . . ."

Alice peered closer. Edward studied the floorboards as
he spoke.

"She's practically in the family," he finished quietly.
Averting his eyes from Alice provided him with no relief.
When his eyes caught the wool tassels of the Turkish patterned rug beneath his desk, he could hardly avoid the
thought of Bunny. Her parents' house had a dining room
rug just like that one. Everything there was so much the
same, as if the whole twenty-two room Tudor were an
annex of his own house.

The pictures were hung at the same height, in the same
places. You could count four relatives to a room, the oldest
in the prominent spot over the fireplace. Candelabra held
court from the east and west poles of the mantel, a gilded
rectangular mirror presided over the couch. Either the
upholstery or the curtains would feature an Eastern pattern with flat-capped monkeys jumping through a floral
jungle—but not both. One gigantic oil painting of a familiar landscape would loom in the hall, sporting art would
line the study, all with heavy, gilded frames that would
crush like dull guillotines.

One would find, in Bunny's parents' house, the flattering
debutante pose of an aunt remembered only in her wheel-
chair. Fresh flowers were scattered in vases to catch the
morning and afternoon light that shone predictably, as if
instructed, into regular areas of the house. Persian area rugs
were thrown down geometrically over the polished wood
floors, chair rails shone white against the elegant brick reds
of the plaster walls, grandfather clocks, umbrella stands,
hand-painted lamps sat in the same corners of the same
rooms, as if the families had merely spliced one cell into
two.

Bunny's father, Randall Stirrup, had died. He had been a

business partner of his dad's through at least a dozen profitable ventures. Every summer that he could remember, the Kirklands had spent together with the Stirrups in the Hamptons. Their mothers were so close, they had even put Bunny and Edward under the care of the same nanny one summer.

Thank God Bunny went to Choate for the equestrian program, instead of St. George's, where Edward went, mainly to sail. He at least had had that interlude, high school and college, without Bunny looking over his shoulder. And Bennington was far enough away that he hadn't seen too much of her when he was at Harvard. But she always came home for Thanksgiving and Christmas, and then came the summer.

Edward remained silent, thinking that Bunny had been arranged for him so perfectly, so long ago, he wondered whether she were merely an invention of his parents.

Alice, saying nothing, poured the Pellegrino into his drink.

"Thanks."

"You have an event with Bunny tonight," she reminded him gently.

"Can I skip it?" He raised his eyebrows.

"No, sir. You're being honored. And so is Bunny. She's done a bit of work for the charity."

He sighed. There was no way around that.

"What's the event?"

"Armani for Everyone." Alice stifled a laugh as she described an unusual program of high-end closet-cleaning for charity. Bunny Stirrup chaired the committee that collected secondhand clothes by Giorgio Armani, and other participating designers, for distribution to the homeless. The outpouring of goodwill, apparently, was based on the assumption that high fashion was a universal need. In an event designed to coordinate with the Armani retrospective anniversary at the Guggenheim, Bunny and Edward were to be honored for their contributions, hers personal and his financial.

The event had diplomatically overlooked a glitch in the well-meant program. All the donated clothes had fallen in between the American sizes of two and six, because the charitable impulses of the rich only took them so far. People didn't just go and donate Armanis that still *fit* them. Only the very hungriest of the homeless fit into those clothes, and Bunny had personally rejected all photo opportunities with the sorry souls. But the party would proceed as planned.

Edward shook his head. "What's the dress?"

"Armani, of course."

Alice mentioned that Bunny had been by the office this morning. She said she wanted to know which Armani tux he was wearing, and if he were going with his club cummerbund or a vest. It was essential for their outfits to be harmoniously coordinated, as they would be photographed together on the podium for *The New York Times*.

"Did she say anything else?"

"She'll meet you at the Carlyle, promptly at seven, for a drink before you go."

Edward groaned. She wanted to catch him at home so she had time to send him back to his room to change. He tolerated his mother's dominance because he felt sorry for her, but he'd never let Bunny, or any other woman, keep a leash on him.

"Maybe we'll miss each other," he said hopefully.

"She'll be at Bemelmans."

Edward, standing, checked his Patek Phillipe watch.

"Where's the party?"

"It's at the Guggenheim." She smiled, knowing Edward's reaction to the circular museum.

"The Slinky!" Edward buried his face in his hands. He

hated doing events at the Guggenheim. He got so dizzy standing anywhere in the middle of that spiral; everywhere you walked, you were on a ramp, and standing in the middle made you feel like you were spinning down a drain.

"I've got to run out and get some Dramamine." His face did look a little green; whether the Guggenheim or the Bunny factor had spoiled his mood, Alice couldn't say.

He heard the phone ringing, and his muscles tensed.

"Forget it," he said to Alice, indicating the phone. "If it's Bunny, she'll call again in ten minutes."

"Okay. Where shall I tell her you can be reached?"

"I can't be reached," he said. "I'm out for the day."

In response to her disapproving stare, he added, "Don't worry, Alice. I'll be there. I'll meet her. I can *handle* Bunny."

She shook her head imperceptibly. I doubt it, she thought. Bunny was closing in, Alice could feel it. There were forces stronger than Edward's charisma that bore down upon him, forces that were set on connecting his horizontal space of the family tree to Bunny Stirrup in time to perpetuate the Kirkland heritage. Alice wished a way out for him, but knew it was as unlikely as Edward's mother wearing a Betsey Johnson minidress to tea.

What was one tiny personality in the great corridors of Manhattan? His family had been here before the Social Register even had its name. Edward would do as they all had done before him, and Alice felt the time was drawing close. He would marry, and if he didn't face the fact himself, his mother would be likely to get involved. Catherine DeBeer Whitney Kirkland who, personally, since the moment of her birth, had owned eleven percent of South Africa's largest diamond mine, would see to her own agenda soon.

Alice looked at Edward with sympathy, wishing he could stay the same, knowing he could not.

"Cover for me?" he asked her, with the eagerness of

someone for whom asking was merely a necessary routine that preceded the answer yes.

She paused, smiling sadly at him.

"I'll take Jenny Mayfair out for lunch. Will you call Jenny? Please? Ask her to meet me at Balthazar."

"All right, Edward," she agreed. She smiled, watching him relax with a great relieved sigh. It was so easy to be nice to him. "Are you reachable for anyone else?"

He thought a minute, collecting his things to leave.

"Well, Mother, of course."

"Needless to say."

"Nobody else."

She nodded.

"What would I do without you, Alice?" He kissed her cheek quickly before darting for the door.

She grinned. "I don't know, but if I were you I'd take the stairs. You never know who you'll meet in the elevator!"

"You're good!" Edward called from the hall.

Chapter 3

Armani for Everyone

Bunny Stirrup didn't need a mirror. She caught a dazzling image of herself in the admiring eyes of everyone she passed as she circulated in triumph through the stylish crowd at the Guggenheim. The thousand details that Bunny had occupied herself with as chairwoman of Armani for Everyone had blended into an absolutely brilliant event, and she ascended the gallery in awe of her own mastery.

She had worried a bit about the location. The museum's retrospective of designs by Giorgio Armani, Milanese icon of minimalist chic, was the first backdrop she ever felt she might have to fight for prominence. Clusters of mannequins draped in the crisp elegance of Armani's deconstructed gowns occupied the gallery walls in backlit groups of three and four, organized by color. The gallery lighting had been softened to a romantic, night-light tenderness. The exhibit space Bunny had just left, a darkened room filled with shimmering silver gowns, was a vision of flight, dream, and wonder, with a ringing background of Eastern sacred music enhancing its mysterious appeal.

The mannequins were headless, minimizing their visual competition with the event's chairwoman. To be safe, Bunny stuck to the rooms with neutrals, the better to be seen in her silver-sprinkled, flame-red gown. Her tiara, which marked her as chair of the event, she had on loan from Harry Winston. Sixteen carats of diamonds sparkled in her hair like dew on the petal of a perfect rose. After her second glass of wine, she felt the tiara simply *belonged* on her head, and the thought of giving it back to Winston for someone else to wear filled her with indignation.

Where is Edward? she wondered, hurrying her step. If I had done a dinner, I could have kept better tabs on him.

The Guggenheim could do three hundred for dinner, but one thousand for a reception. Bunny couldn't bear to lord it over the lowly former, and opted to do a cocktail reception with heavy hors d'oeuvres. After all, tonight she would stand in the famous rotunda, encircled by the Frank Lloyd Wright spiral that drew the eye upward to a higher consciousness, awash in publicity, receiving her award. Benefactress to the humble homeless, dispenser of fashion riches to them all, Bunny would stand next to the hand-some Edward Kirkland, his Armani tux and tails perfectly coordinated to accent her dazzling gown. She would gleam with diamonds and modesty—after all, this was a charity, and modesty was the appropriate pose—as she was pho-tographed in glory, arm in arm with her catch.

And he would be her catch after tonight, Bunny told her-self. Her talks with Edward's mother had moved from general to specific about the day Bunny Stirrup would marry Catherine Kirkland's son. Having crossed that perilous bridge over *if* to *when*, Bunny was assured that the path to *I do* had been laid. She was steps away from launching the blessed wedding event in all its splendor.

Edward's mother was prepared for greatness. She had assured Bunny that the Kirklands in their majesty would make Charles and Diana look like a couple of frumps. The picture of Bunny and Edward taken tonight would be a perfect crown for the glorious wedding announcement that Bunny's social secretary was composing for the *Sunday Times*. Radiant and glamorous, their well-bred charitable credentials on display, Bunny and Edward would be the world's envy.

So where was he? She grew conscious of her hasty step and paused, enjoying her visible position in front of some deliciously drab men's suits. She decided to search the rooms that housed the museum's permanent collection, where wine bars and appetizers were set up. Edward always seemed to be eating at these things.

Suppressing a frown, Bunny drew in her breath and reminded herself to occupy the moment.

She caught the eye of Morgan Wyeth, the party poser who had worked with her all afternoon on the proper flutter of her eyes when she accepted her award.

"Avoid the big smile, Bun-bun; in the camera it's all chin," he had cautioned. Bunny was stung, but she remembered his tip. "Go with the left shoulder raised, head tipped down toward it. It's a beautiful pose: all innocence—the village girl at the festival—a wreath of flowers in her hair. It's Giselle! You can do it. And turn your eyes toward Edward. Nothing is as photogenic these days as a good, steady look of devotion."

Morgan winked at her, and Bunny felt her power.

Yes, Bunny thought to herself, stroking her tiara, I am in the moment! I've caught the wave!

When Bunny heard that Edward was going to London without her, ostensibly to buy a dog, she had impulsively joined her friend Whitney St. Pierre on a beach vacation in Mexico. Camouflaging themselves under Hermès scarves and Chanel sunglasses, they spoke French to each other in the airport until they were sure that nobody on the flight to Miami knew them. The first-class cabin was safe, and the flight to the Baja peninsula was so anonymous that they even reverted to their native tongue.

Their destination was "Girl in the Curl," a surfing retreat taught by Pacific Paige, motivational speaker and

31

best-selling author of books on improving relationships. Having been conceived on a surfboard (which was then at rest in the sand, he explained to a confused member of the audience), Pacific had the lover's momentum from the start.

Bunny didn't surf, nor did she know anyone who did, but Pacific Paige's retreats were all about conquering the new and unknown. His book, a tattered copy of which Whitney had lent to Bunny, claimed that any woman who could occupy the moment had an aura of irresistibility. This aura would pull friends and lovers in like a wave.

It sounded a little flaky, but Whitney swore that four, count them, four of her friends had gotten engaged within months of attending the retreat. And not just engaged: properly, and profitably. Bunny agreed to go, if only to get a mysterious suntan with which to greet Edward on his return. And it was working. After the weekend in which she waxed a surfboard while chanting, along with twenty other women, an ancient Hawaiian mantra (so effective and covert they had to sign a promise not to repeat the words outside of the retreat facility), she had caught the wave. She returned to New York feeling fearless and magnetic, and began claiming Edward with more authority than she had ever risked in the past. Tonight she would pull him under.

Armani for Everyone, the first big charity event of the fall season, was an important night for a lot of people. Leslie Davis had her husband, Dick, by the arm as she hobnobbed with contemporary sculptor Istvan Grotjan, throwing out as a bone the possibility that she and Dick might fund an important collection of nonobjective art. More than once she carelessly mentioned her interest in serving on the governing board of the Guggenheim. A word from Grotjan would get her into the position just vacated by Armello Canadida's untimely demise.

In the Thannhauser gallery, Isaac Mizrahi was locked in an animated bond of mutual admiration with Phillip Wilson, an experimental theater director known for his boundary-breaking "mod-umentaries." Elia Mercer, a buyer for Bergdorf Goodman, had cornered Polly McGover, the style editor at *Vogue,* and was quietly making the case that Donna Karan, more than any Italian designer, was the proper heir to Armani's minimalism. Judy Armoire, cocurator of ceramics at the Met, pursued Guggenheim board members throughout the spiraling floor plan in her quest to land the open position as curator of the museum's Venice location.

Judy had met Edward Kirkland in Chatham, on Cape Cod, last summer at the MSPCA Shag, an event honoring lifesaving pets of the beach patrol. A former art history major from Connecticut College, Judy honed in on museum events, where she could impress attendees with her depth of analysis. She had dated Edward only once since they met, but felt intensely connected to him on a cultural level. She thought he possessed a deep and sensitive soul, and with his Harvard degree she was sure he would make an excellent lifemate for someone as intelligent as she.

Judy was a D-cup, probably a size thirty-eight even after the reduction. She had trouble finding an Armani to fit, but lucked out when she found his Orient collection at Bergdorf's. A luxuriously embroidered evening jacket and wide-legged pants suited her perfectly, and she walked around the gallery as physically and psychically comfortable as if she were wearing her pajamas. Cradling her chardonnay in a neatly manicured hand, she turned her knowledgeable gaze around the rotunda, deciding which feature of the permanent collection cried out for Italian ceramics as a backdrop. Her eye caught her college classmate, Bunny Stirrup.

"Bunnykins!" she called out, with the false note of sisterhood.

"Jude!" Bunny embraced her.

"You look beautiful," said Judy. "But I didn't know it was a costume party!" She laughed, pointing at Bunny's princess crown.

"Well, why did you dress like a majarishi then?" Bunny said through her teeth.

Judy's face fell.

"It's from Armani's Orient collection," Judy began. She paused to remind herself—I am valuable—as she had learned in her assertiveness training class.

"The maharajas inspired his fall collection, dear," Judy said, gaining confidence as she took a scholarly tone. "With their great spiritual wealth."

"Yes, yes," Bunny chirped. "Blessed are the meek! I've got to run along. Give my best to . . ."

She paused, waiting for Judy to answer.

"Hmm?" she prompted.

"There's nobody," Judy answered at last. She shrugged, looking at the floor.

"I'm *so* sorry," Bunny said, smiling viciously. "Ta ta!"

She hurried away with a dazzling smile. She thought she remembered a shrimp cocktail was set up in one of the tower galleries. No doubt Edward had found it by now.

She found him surrounded, as usual, by attentive ladies whom he charmed and flattered in turn. On the wall just behind him, Vasily Kandinsky's colorful modernist painting *Several Circles* was on display. Bunny smiled with satisfaction. She knew what to say.

Secretly, and under cover of a red wig, Bunny had attended a series of lectures on the Guggenheim's architecture and permanent collection in the eerie Peter B. Lewis amphitheater, a puffy auditorium that felt like the inside of a jewelry box. She had intended to drop her choice bon mots about the museum for Edward's benefit.

"Hello, darling," she said, elbowing through the hen party to kiss Edward's lips.

"Hello, Bunny." Edward smiled affably.

"You know Deb Norwich, Tina Volley," Edward said, smiling at each in turn. Bunny nodded, her face set in a frozen smile.

"And Babs Stern—of course you know Babs," he added, indicating the woman who stood closest to him.

"Dear of you to come and support us tonight," Bunny said. She gathered Babs' hand in her own to give her a little squeeze, then moved the woman away from Edward as she slid next to him, showing her back to Tina and Deb.

"Oh, the Kandinsky frames you wonderfully," she said to Edward, edging backward to behold him in front of the painting, a move that caused the other women to shuffle back a bit further.

"It's so appropriate here in this sensational building! The circle motif is *ingenious,* don't you think? Geometric, but so supple, with such *elegant plasticity*."

"You would know plastic," said Tina, turning to leave.

Ignoring her, Bunny beheld Edward with adoring eyes.

"What do you think of the Kandinsky, darling? Those circles put me in mind of champagne bubbles, rising in a clear, chilled flute. Of course the thought of champagne always leads me to you! We have so much to celebrate," she concluded, fluttering her lashes over a delighted gaze.

"It's nice," Edward said, turning to the painting. "It reminds me of a Lava Lamp."

"A Lava Lamp?" Bunny repeated. Her voice had a scolding tone. Michael Straub, assistant curator for research, said nothing of Lava Lamps.

Babs and Deb, who lingered with their eyes on Edward, giggled.

"I like Lava Lamps," Edward said.

Babs and Deb raced each other to agree.

Bunny smiled.

"That's dear, Edward. We'll put one in your playroom." She stared coldly at his lady friends, who showed no signs of moving. She would have to move first.

"We're clear for departure, darling," said Bunny. She gripped Edward's elbow, and flashed the women a lofty smile.

"We have a little part in the program tonight," Bunny explained, running her free hand around Edward's back, the better to steer him.

Babs and Deb rolled their eyes at each other.

"Ta ta, my darlings," Bunny chirped, "we'll wave from the podium!"

She led Edward out of the gallery, moving with quick steps down the spiral ramp that descended through seven floors of the museum. In the grand, open space of the atrium, more people would see them together.

"Bunny," Edward said, stopping in the hall. "What's the hurry?"

"How could you stand there with that disgusting Babs Stern?"

"What's wrong with Babs? She's a nice girl. I've known her forever. Listen, she's racing her little Boston Whaler this weekend. She invited us out to Newport for the regatta."

"Us?"

"Where I'm invited, you're invited," he said, sidestepping the question with grace. As he had told Alice, Edward knew how to handle Bunny. He put his hands on Bunny's shoulders, and turned her to face him. She looked up into the calm of his eyes.

"Relax, Bunny." He massaged her shoulders with his fingers. "You did a great job putting this all together. Time to declare victory! Settle down, okay?"

She sighed, stretching her neck like a cat. He stroked her shoulders gently.

"I'm just nervous, that's all." She peered up at him, and his smile reassured her.

"You look beautiful, Bunny." Edward's appetite had returned with a vengeance. Ordinarily he would have grabbed something before the party, since it wasn't a sit-down, to tide him over, but he hadn't felt hungry this afternoon. Now all he wanted to do was shake a few hands and then run out to get some dinner.

He left his hand on Bunny's shoulder as his mind scanned the menus he knew by heart from restaurants on the Upper East Side. "Let's just accept the award, stay a few minutes, and skip out together for a bite to eat," he said to her. "Just you and me."

He turned her face to his, smiling with the pleasure of asking too much and expecting to get it, like a boy with his eyes on the dessert cart.

Bunny's heart beat quickly. A tête-à-tête with Edward was nice, but she much preferred to show him off. She had to find a way to keep him here.

"I think we'd better stay," she said. "There was some talk of Giorgio coming in for this himself, and if he does, I promised we'd hand the award over to him. All impromptu, no need for big speeches, but it would be *appropriate* to recognize him."

She used the magic word. Edward always did what was appropriate.

"Well, I suppose that makes sense," he agreed. With a smile, he drew her close to him. "So where are you pulling me? Is there a private room?"

He was so damned *private,* it drove her insane. She shook her head and coyly pulled back.

A telephone rang in his tux.

"Edward!" She glared at him. "Don't you *dare* answer that!"

Edward had no reason to carry a phone when she was

with him. He had a reputation, which though it was of considerable authority, Bunny tried to ignore, of being an inveterate ladies' man. Bunny gamely insisted that Edward's charitable work compelled him to socialize, and the ladies he dated were merely, needless to say, *friends of the family*.

"It wouldn't be polite to use the cell phone here."

"All right," he said, his easy shrug consoling Bunny that the call was a surprise to him. "The voice mail picks up anyway."

"Bunny, darling, can we get a picture?" Mitch Beluga, *Quest's* photographer, pulled Bunny in front of a headless group of gauzy, beige-draped Armani mannequins. "You two are the stars of the night, and we've hardly seen you!"

Bunny took her position a half-step in front of Edward and smiled modestly, her head tilted, her eyes turned upward with tenderness. The flash of the camera brought joy to her heart.

The museum lights flickered off and on, giving Bunny a cue that the program would commence in ten minutes. She grabbed Edward's hand to tug him along to the rotunda. Incredibly, she felt him resist.

"Come on, Edward."

"Bunny," he protested, "I'm *starved*." He had only gotten to a couple of shrimp in the Thannhauser gallery before the ladies got to him. "I'm going to go grab a few appetizers before we get started with this thing."

"Edward!" She looked at him suspiciously. How could he think about wild mushroom pastries at a glamorous opportunity like this one? She gasped to think that something else might be going on. Was it the phone call? That little shrimp Bitsy French was behind it, she thought. She had noticed Bitsy's painted eyes trailing after Edward at too many parties. Behind her smile, she ground her teeth.

She darted toward him and grabbed the phone from his tux.

"No time for calls!" Bunny sang in a pleasant voice. She smiled and teased him, waving the phone in front of him like bait.

Edward shrugged, walked toward Bunny, and kissed her cheek.

"I'll meet you down on the stage in ten minutes," he said before leaving.

Bunny nodded. She knew when not to push him. She swung her hips as on a catwalk down the undulating ramp, rehearsing her acceptance speech.

"Still have work to do, changing people's lives, making the world a better place, dignity through fashion . . ."

She was shocked to hear the phone in her hand ringing.

Stepping back into a shadow behind the display of ladies' accessories, Bunny answered the phone. By now she was positively sure it was a call from Bitsy French.

Before she heard anyone on the line, Bunny hissed, "You little slut, if you *think* about calling Edward again you are *over!*"

She hung the phone up and turned it off. Edward would receive no more calls tonight.

A glimpse of the podium magnificently centered under the skylight gave Bunny a rush of energy. Her stage was set, and her curtains were opening. She smiled and fluttered toward George Weston and Clifford Chase, Edward's friends from the Union Club. Accepting compliments from them both, she evaluated the cut of their tuxedos to determine whether she'd approve of them as groomsmen.

Chapter 4

The Chosen

Thirstan Heston had been trying to reach the concerned parties all night. A wills lawyer has, by and large, a comfortable practice, largely concerning avoidance of federal and state taxes. Unlike his corporate peers at Stearns & Fielding, Thirstan was able to take long and comfortable vacations with his wife and their two children. But the unexpected "death event" was the heart of his business, and when this occurred, professional ethics required his prompt attention to the matter.

When, as in the death of Arthur Stearns, there was a minor child involved, mercy and law joined hands to require his swift action. Under the code of the state of New York, legal guardianship of his client's minor child, whether designated by will or supplied in default by statute, would be established at a hearing within thirty days of the death event. If he got his ducks in a row, he could move the whole estate into probate at the same time. But the child's needs were immediate; she had to come first.

Thirstan had hurried into town from the Vineyard, where his family was enjoying the last weekend at their cottage before they closed it for the season, the children returned to Groton and Miss Porter's, and his life, like that of a closing flower, entered its autumn phase in the city.

At first he had trouble understanding the nanny who

had called him to report the death of her employers. She was frantic, and spoke in torrents of French, spattered with halting and incorrect English that confused him even further. Thirstan's French was sufficient to order any dish that Alain Ducasse prepared, but it was not enough for him to interpret the nanny's outburst, until she got to the heart of it. I work for Arthur Stearns, she had told him in English. He and Emily's mother are dead.

Thirstan went immediately to Arthur's apartment, still dressed in the ancient white sweatpants and sweatshirt with its Yale Law School moniker. He had practiced law with George Stearns, Arthur's father, before Arthur joined the firm as a corporate associate. In the beginning of the young man's tenure, he was skeptical about Arthur's work ethic, for, having prepared his trust instrument, he knew that Arthur would come into hundreds of millions of dollars at the age of thirty-five. But the young man had turned out to be a promising young lawyer who would someday on his own merit achieve partnership.

Would have achieved, Thirstan corrected himself. What a shame. He heard details of the crash on the local news, which he watched in the back of his car to keep from falling asleep on the drive into the city. Prominent environmental activist Amy Kolasky and her partner, the lawyer Arthur Stearns, were presumed dead after the crash of their small plane into the side of a mountain in the Alaskan wilderness, where they had gone on a ten day fly-fishing expedition.

Tragically, the couple's death left orphaned a beautiful four-year-old girl, a golden-haired whippet by the name of Emily, whose picture had thankfully not been acquired by the television stations, because it was obscene to feed this lovely child to the voyeuristic public.

The crash had been big news on the Anchorage stations right away, since the airplane's pilot, Joe Francis, was considered invincible. It had been said of the decorated Vietnam pilot that he could fly between two raindrops and not get wet. He was as good a pilot as ever flew over Alaska, the local broadcasters mourned, before mentioning three other casualties: a young couple on a fishing trip, and their guide. The high winds of a sudden snowstorm had eliminated all visibility; the pilot could not have seen the mountain until the plane struck it. The end, at least, was merciful; all passengers died instantly, according to the salvage crews, who were not even able to search the location until two days later when the storm subsided.

Thirstan had stopped at the law office to collect Arthur Stearns' trust papers from the vault. He had to review the language of the trust to see whether Arthur had forfeited his inheritance or whether any provision was made for his death before the age of thirty-five. Thankfully for little Emily, Thirstan noted, there was an alternate provision that made immediate distribution, in the case of his death, to any children of his blood. He was pleased to see that she was well provided for, and, all the better for tax avoidance, that it was done through the trust, avoiding the slow and taxable will.

He did need to locate a will to determine Emily's guardian, however. When he arrived at the building Thirstan tactfully talked his way past the doorman and put his copy of Arthur's key in the lock only to be startled by a pull on the door from the inside. The nanny was up and already helping the child to dress—or this was what Thirstan discerned from the babble of French mixed with English-as-a-second-language, rapid-fire hysteria. Once inside he began to hunt. He was practiced at finding the location of such papers in the houses of his deceased clients, and had to look no farther than the top drawers of the matching nightstands in the master bedroom before finding, in sealed envelopes, the two separate wills of Amy

42

Kolasky and Arthur Stearns. The wills were simple, hand-written instruments, witnessed by the nanny and perfectly valid, leaving everything to the couple's only child.

Each will named a legal guardian for Emily. Arthur's will named Edward Kirkland as the child's guardian. Amy's will named Becca Reinhart. They were identified as residing at different addresses and they had different home phone numbers.

Thirstan paused, staring at one paper, then another. Did they mean to do this? Though unusual, the twin designations were perfectly valid. Arthur and Amy had never married, and separate wills in that context bore no caution flag. They would be presumed to have died at the same time, and both of their wills would be enforced as written, unless they were in conflict. It was common to name two legal guardians for a child, so the designation of these two individuals presented no difficulty. They simply needed to be notified at different locations.

Though he quickly arrived at what would seem a simple answer, Thirstan's stomach bunched into knots of anxiety. In all his years of practice he had never seen two *unrelated* guardians named to care for one child. It was distinctly odd. Thirty years of practicing trusts and estates law had not instilled in him any desire to execute something unique and original. As a result he shuffled around the apartment, alternately preparing the tax filing and calling the home and office numbers Emily's guardians-to-be to get the matter settled.

He had tried Edward's mobile phone last night but gave up trying after the strange experience he had. He thought he had reached the right number, but twice a woman answered, once calling him a slut and hanging up on him. He had tried again a time or two, in frustration, but the phone seemed to be turned off. Fundamentally cautious, especially in his professional capacity, Thirstan declined to leave a voice mail message for Edward under those peculiar circumstances. He was assuming he might leave word for Becca Reinhart to call him, but her secretary had transferred him to Dick Davis's line. Thirstan and Davis knew each other the way all of a certain caste of global professionals knew each other—distantly but with enough history to allow Thirstan to tell Becca's partner about the accident.

"So you'll have her call me after you've talked to her?" Thirstan pled.

"Don't worry about Becca. She'll take it in stride."

Dick had agreed to tell Becca that her friend had died, but Thirstan kept to himself the second shoe—the information about the child's guardianship.

This morning he had finally also reached Edward's secretary at his office number and related the sad news to her. Alice Carter was her name. He was pleased to find that she knew his wife; or rather, knew the secretary that worked for his wife, so he trusted her implicitly. She had a lovely way about her; very tactful. He had ceased worrying about Edward when he left the matter in Alice's hands.

Working on the probate paperwork at the Stearns' kitchen table, Thirstan acknowledged the nanny's declaration, called from the front hall, that she was taking Emily for her French lesson. They had something called a "playdate" in the park afterward; Thirstan scribbled the word on a manila folder, consulted the dictionary in his Palm computer that did not elucidate its meaning, and finally circled it with a question mark, considering it to be lost in the wide gulf of the nanny's translation abilities.

He had nearly an hour of solid, quiet working time, in which he had arranged most of the couple's simple estate matters to the point where he could delegate the file to an associate. As he was gathering his files, he heard the door open. A second later, he heard a woman call his name.

Becca Reinhart had burst into the apartment, calling for

the lawyer in a faltering, uncertain voice, a voice full of worry. So she knew about the accident, he thought, sighing with relief. He hated to deliver this news ab initio. It was easier when people were prepared. He was surprised that she had gotten into the apartment without calling first, but perhaps she knew the family well. The doorman might have let her up if she were a regular visitor. He entered the morning room, a sunny sitting room with wide western windows overlooking Central Park, where he found Becca, leaning against the worn tapestry of a chair favored by Arthur, breathing in gasps.

His heart went out to the woman, who had quite obviously been crying. There was a scarf around her neck, a cheerful Hermès print, a sort of climbing vine of cabbage roses on columns, printed on the lustrous silk in bold primary colors: fuchsia, aqua, green. The scarf hung around her neck as limp as a rag, wet and crumpled, having been used, he guessed, to wipe the tears from her face.

She turned a surprised expression toward him at once. He introduced himself, and approached her with an outstretched hand. He would like to have been able to console her, but he was incapable of empathy so there was no warmth or sympathy. He was a lawyer first. She lifted frightened eyes to him, her hair loose, framing a sorrowful face drained of color. She did not take his hand; she did not appear to see it.

"She's dead, I know. I heard it on the news," she said. "Amy was a real thrill-seeker, she'd hike miles to get to a creek that was really wild—unspoiled. Arthur loved her for it. They could never push themselves enough, those two. For fish!" Becca sunk her head into her hands. "They would go anywhere to chase a damn piece of swimming lox! It's hard . . . ," she said, pausing to choke back a sob. "It's hard to think that there's any fish in the world that was worth this."

She and Amy, college roommates at Columbia, housed together as freshmen in what they jokingly referred to as the "scholarship dorm," had shared the love of travel, and went out of their way to enroll for summer classes and semesters abroad, taking advantage of cheap student rates to see as much of the world in four years as was practically possible. Before then, Becca could name the islands she had visited on one hand: Long Island, Staten Island, Manhattan Island. But Amy's love of adventure travel was contagious.

The lawyer had no talent for consolation, but plenty of patience. He stood, with a sad half-smile, waiting until he thought Becca was ready.

With a sudden flash in her eyes, Becca stormed across the room and ran down the long hall of the apartment. Thirstan could tell by her direction what was on her mind. He followed her, slowly, on steps as tentative as those of a burglar, to the child's room.

Emily's bedroom, which Thirstan had always considered a bit too overdone, was part Hollywood starlet and part nursery school, but all—one hundred percent—little girl. Amidst this carefully constructed dream of a perfect rose-colored childhood sat Becca, slumped miserably on a gilded pink couch in the dress-up corner. She stared dully at the apricot walls, her eyes following the white rails that traced the walls. At her feet lay a Jean Bourget tutu, Emily's dress-up of choice this morning before she scampered off for her French lessons. The tutu lay together with a hastily discarded marabou stole and a tiny sequined purse. The child's closet door was open, and Becca glanced in the direction of the colorful room, making a note to herself to turn off the light.

Emily's closet had been a sitting room before Amy made it over with hanging bars, covering the window with a sheer pink curtain and standing in front of the wall a striped vanity bench beside a well-lit, oval-shaped standing mirror. A sparkling rainbow of dresses, from frothy Joan Calabrese party dresses in lavender silk and taffeta, to Florence Eiseman jumpers in deep red velvets, hand-smocked cotton dresses in cheerful blues and yellows, and pressed linens in sherbet pastels: All of these lined the walls like hopefuls at the dance of the sugarplum fairies. This was Emily's world.

Without thinking, Becca picked up the feather boa, royal blue in color, and lifted it to her cheek. It was soft, with a clean smell reminiscent of baby powder. She sighed, feeling the tears build behind her eyes as she remembered buying the cherry wood jewelry box she saw on Emily's marble-topped vanity. When the top was open the tiny ballerina inside twirled to the music of *Swan Lake*.

The lawyer walked toward her, slowly, holding a copy of Amy's will in his hand. Without speaking he handed it to Becca, whose eyes spilled over with tears when she recognized Amy's handwriting. Soon she got to the heart of the matter.

She was Emily's legal guardian.

Becca dropped the page, which fluttered to the floor. Her stomach twisted inside her. She clasped her head in her hands, wishing she could shrink, disappear. She sat stone still, terrified.

Until this moment, the biggest thing Becca Reinhart ever had charge of was money. It was millions at a time: It mattered a lot, but in the end it was just money. It fluctuated. It was won and lost in minutes. It didn't look up to you or hold your hand.

A four-year-old girl. Emily had just celebrated her birthday in August. Becca remembered shopping for her gift and the looks she had gotten at FAO Schwartz when she asked for a pink computer desk.

Her eyes were wet with tears; she had simply stopped wiping them dry. She was responsible for Amy's little girl. It was nothing she had prepared for, nothing she could have prepared for, nothing she was *suited for*. How could Amy have done this to her?

"But—Amy's parents—Don't you think they'd want custody of Emily?" Becca knew Arthur's parents were dead.

"Yes. I thought so," Thirstan said. "But I contacted them through the state department's emergency system." He paused. As unemotional as Thirstan was, he had been horrified by how cold was Emily's grandparents' response.

"And?"

"And they were happy to hear Amy had appointed a guardian. They wished you good luck and asked if you might see to the funeral arrangements. Said they'd be in touch when they passed through New York next year."

"You're joking!" Becca's remembrance of her grandmother's love was precious and part of her self-image. In Grandma's eyes Becca was brilliant, gorgeous, like a rare bird or a Stradivarius violin. She had been the reason Grandma kept going until she was ninety-two. Or so she said. There was a reason to cook chicken fricassee (which Becca and her mother laughed about with affection because it was so terrible), a reason to dress up on Fridays, because Becca always came home for Shabbos Eve in those days. And in the end, her grandma told her, she was the reason she could pass on knowing that the future of their family would shine in Becca's hands. What would make the Kolaskys so thoughtless about a child's future—so easily able to discount that child's love? Just thinking about this triggered Becca's motivation to embrace Amy's wishes.

She remembered when Amy got pregnant—it was just about the time Becca went with Davis Capital. She and Arthur couldn't marry—something to do with his trust money—for a while, she said, but her clock was ticking. She was going to have his baby anyway. They would be just like any other family until they were really a family. Emily could be her flower girl, she had laughed, when they finally got married.

Becca had swung her friend into a warm embrace, feeling a flash of joy mixed with defiance. "Of course you'll have a beautiful baby," she had said, as she tugged Amy out the door of her apartment, wondering where she could find a bottle of sparkling cider. "You'll be a great mother. You don't need a new last name for that—you don't need to marry Arthur. Of course you don't! You can count on me to stand by you, Amy."

Becca had been as good as her word. Arlene Reinhart, whom Amy had known since college, had helped Amy get the basics together: strollers, receiving blankets, pacifiers, silver rattles, tiny soft nightcaps.

Becca had gone with Amy to the hospital the weekend Emily was born. She recalled how incredibly strange she thought it was that Arthur had picked that time to go bone-fishing in the Keys.

But four years had intervened since then, and as Becca circled the globe and watched the sun rise from her desk chair, Amy had overseen a Jamaican baby nurse, a pram-pushing English nanny, a ballet-certified French nanny, and a sparkling never-never land of cookies, puppets, and fairy tales that seemed as strange to Becca as sleeping in on the weekends.

Through glassy eyes she looked out Emily's bedroom window at the yellow taxis, the black limousines, the white-gloved nannies already pushing their strollers along Fifth Avenue, this citadel of privilege. She noticed a rocking horse, idle, pushed to the corner of the room. A rocking horse! She wiped her eyes, feeling them well up again, as if years of crying had built up for this moment.

What would she do here? What would the child expect of her? She was so scared.

Abruptly, Becca thought of her mother, and a hopeful

light broke across the sadness of her face. She stood and waved her hand at Thirstan to indicate that, though shaky, she could manage on her own without falling.

"I need a couple of hours," she said, gulping back her tears. More resolutely, she added: "I'll be back, don't worry. I can handle this. I just need some time."

"I understand," he said, though he knew understanding was impossible, and the best thing he could do was to get out of the way. But he had an obligation to tell her everything.

"You're not alone," he said, thinking she would find solace in the promise of someone to lean on. "Arthur named another guardian. I'm sure he and Amy wanted you two to work together, to support each other." Thirstan looked warily at her shocked expression, wondering if he had expressed himself right. "You have a partner, Becca."

"A what?" she said, stumbling back against the wall. Her mind raced wildly. She had no time, no experience, and no talent for child-raising—and now she had no control?

"His name is Edward Kirkland," the lawyer said. "Your coguardian."

The name meant nothing to her. Becca shook her head angrily, her dark hair cascading loosely around her face. She wheeled around to face Thirstan. "Listen," she said, "I don't do partner. I don't do coguardian—co-anything. I'm no team player, all right?"

He nodded uncertainly.

Becca thrust her face into her hands. "Is this some kind of joke?" Her breaths came quickly, in short gasps. She paced the room, her mind whirling with protest.

She looked at her watch and breathed deeply. Her life was coming apart. Her whole, balanced, precisely scheduled footrace of a life was tearing open, and she was alone with a lawyer talking about sudden, terrifying motherhood while her phone rang and her clients waited and her world was somewhere else. What should she do? Where was Emily? Had anybody told her? Becca hadn't even seen Emily since she came to her fourth birthday party, a princess tea-party affair held in the lobby of the Plaza—she thought that was such a scream at the time, weeks ago, or was it months? She felt her hands trembling as she lifted them to her cheeks. Her face was burning.

Thirstan approached her and spoke gently. "Becca, feel free to go and take some time to understand the obligation you have here. We'll talk about what to do if you can't handle this. Having a coguardian gives us some flexibility if you aren't up to the task. I want you to be sure," he said, looking into her eyes, "that you can accept this responsibility."

"Who's with her?" Becca asked suddenly, her eyes darting around the apartment. "Where is she? Is she okay?"

"She's with her nanny. You remind me," he added, "that she didn't handle the news very well. She gave her two weeks notice, and she has already begun to pack. From what I can understand she is moving back to France."

Becca stared at him in disbelief. An inadvertent shudder ran through her shoulders.

"Do you have any other questions?" the lawyer asked her gently.

"Has anybody told Emily about her parents?" Becca asked, her voice trembling.

"No."

She caught her breath, feeling her eyes threaten another storm. What would she say? What do four-year-old children even know?

Becca stepped past the lawyer, out of the room. "I'll be back tonight," she said over her shoulder. She faced away from him, her eyes hot with tears. "But first I have to go to Brooklyn."

Thirstan didn't question this explanation, though it seemed slightly odd.

Her head swimming, Becca staggered to the lobby and hailed a cab. She thought about this day, which until an hour ago had seemed just another ordinary, unbearably busy day. She had deplaned this morning with nothing but the Wasserstein meeting on her mind. That meeting ended before it began, as the firm had already accepted an offer from Deutsche Bank, and Becca headed to the office with what she thought were a few stolen minutes to catch up on her reading. But as soon as she arrived, Dick called her into his office.

She had already missed a breakfast meeting; she needed to reschedule it while the principals were still in town. She had three other meetings today, and no matter what happened, she couldn't get out of the trip to Hong Kong. The whole Asian fund hung around her neck. She had to return dozens of calls, the usual backlog that pooled every morning by the hour.

She knew these things, but as she caught her own reflection in the dull, dirty window of the cab to Brooklyn, Becca nearly choked with the surprise of knowing something different. She looked like a zombie, a pale, empty shell of a person. Oddly, the time change from London was hitting her; she felt unbalanced, and her hands were shaking. She couldn't do anything today. She called Philippe, instructed him to redirect all her calls and cancel her meetings, and directed the cabbie to the shabby little rowhouse in Brooklyn where she knew she would find her mother.

Chapter 5

Bubbe

Arlene Reinhart was cooking when Becca staggered into the house. Without a word her mother rushed to embrace her in the warm, fleshy arms that Becca had to lean down to in order to meet, and tugged her into the kitchen for some food.

With a soft dishcloth she wiped Becca's tear-stained face, poured her coffee without asking, and turned a chair from the small, round dinette table for Becca to sit in. In a flood of emotion, without logic or order, Becca told her mother what had happened to Amy, about Emily, and what it meant for her. She was a mother. She was terrified.

Arlene brushed Becca's loose hair back, cupped her daughter's face in her soft hands, and kissed her on the cheek.

"Becca," she said. "I'm so sorry about Amy. She was a great friend."

Arlene's tears met Becca's in a moment of silence.

"But don't worry about being a mother," Arlene said, rising from her chair to rub Becca on the head. "You're a natural."

"Mom, how can you say that?" The color rose in Becca's white cheeks. "All I've ever managed is money."

"You'll do fine. Trust me," she said, turning from the pot where she was stirring a warm, fat chicken in heavy broth.

It smelled delicious. "There is no such *thing* as a bad mother."

Becca smiled to herself.

"Mom, really," she protested, nodding her thanks at the plate of food her mother plunked in the center of the table. Brown bread, sour pickles, cold veal chops, and honey cake.

"Eat," her mother directed.

Becca felt hungry and ate a little of the cake, but her frustration returned when she thought about how little sympathy she was getting in this, what should be the most supportive quarter of the universe.

"You can't believe the week I have," she said, "the month, the year! Meetings, more meetings, and travel, and in between I'm on the phone. I hardly have time to shower! When will I have time for a four-year-old?"

Arlene finished chewing her pickle. She was on a diet, consisting mainly of choosing pickles over honey cake when she nibbled, drinking Diet Coke by the case, and ordering salad dressing on the side. Her cooking—her mainstay—was unaffected. Who could change what is?

"Make time," she said simply.

"Mom!" Becca complained. "You don't understand. It's not like with you. This just *happened* to me. I'm not ready!"

"Ha!" laughed Arlene, standing to retrieve a Diet Coke from the refrigerator.

She turned an aggrieved face to Becca. "Do you know how long I was in labor with you?"

"I know, Mom," Becca said, nodding her head impatiently. "Thirteen hours. The most difficult thirteen hours—"

"Of my life," Arlene finished, smiling with satisfaction. Becca was a good kid. She would never forget how her mother suffered. "How I suffered!" she added, mopping her forehead at the thought of it. "And even though I was at Beth Israel . . ."

54

"Where they will always choose the mother over the baby if the choice has to be made," Becca chimed in with her mother, knowing this story by heart.

Her mother nodded. "Even so—what suffering! And then! It was a year before I was sure you were all right in the head. You just don't know, with the little ones. Oh, how a mother's heart grieves!"

She began to describe Becca's first fever, her first visit to the emergency room—the suffering!—the first food she refused, the color she always looked best in—the whole life epic for which Becca had to thank her struggling, suffering, giving mother, the rock of every family, who ought to be thanked every day, such a heart!

Becca, warmed by the cadence of these old familiar stories, began to smile.

"Mom," she said, grinning. "You don't cut me any slack."

"Why should I?" Arlene returned vigorously, slapping the table in front of her. "Thirteen hours I labor, a year I worry, my heart grieving over every cough, every fever—just to get you on your feet. And you—you wake up one day with a beautiful little girl—such hair! Such golden hair!—healthy as a cow, a little overdressed, I recall—but she has her health! You're as lucky as Abraham!"

Becca laughed out loud. "Well, when you put it that way," she said, "it sounds great. But I have a job, don't forget."

"Take a few months off. You can live! You can kill your-self with that job later. It will be there."

The support, if you could call it that, from her mother, combined with Becca's natural and reviving confidence, had begun to develop in her the appetite for taking control.

"Maybe I could get my analysts on it," Becca thought out loud. "Cover the current press on four-year-olds, the parent magazines and stuff. Do a little executive summary for this afternoon."

"What are they there for, if not to help you?" Arlene said, throwing her arms into a shrug. She paused, her eyes resting on Becca with affection.

"Get up to speed if it helps you, honey," she said, stroking Becca's hair, "but let me tell you the truth: You have it all inside. Go with your instinct." She patted Becca on the back as if that were the end of it.

Becca sighed, shaking her head.

"I don't know, Mom. It's a big change for me," she said. She looked up at her mother's face, and her gaze melted in the adoration that lit her mother's eyes so tenderly. Becca smiled, her shoulders relaxing as she let out her breath.

"You'll be a great mom," her mother said fondly.

Becca blushed and smiled. "How do you know?"

Arlene parked her hands on her hips and laughed. That was an easy one. "Because you're just like me, Becca."

Becca returned her mother's grin, happy to share the compliment.

"Now if you'll excuse me," Arlene told her, tapping the back of Becca's chair as she hurried behind it, "I have to make a few phone calls. Who would believe it? I'm a Bubbe now!"

Hastening to spread her joy, Arlene walked out to the phone, which she kept on a small table by the front window, where she could see what everybody was up to.

"Bubbe," Becca repeated. She smiled, seeing her mom for the first time as a grandmother. She took a deep breath, comforted by the familiar kitchen. She could do this. Her mother was always straight with her. If this were something to reconsider, she would have heard it from Arlene.

From *Bubbe*, Becca corrected herself, grinning.

Becca did not have a clue what she would do about making arrangements for Emily while she went off to Hong Kong. She certainly wasn't leaving her with her "coguardian," a man she didn't know. Edward Kirkland to her knowledge still had not been located. Great—a coguardian who as far as she could tell was footloose and irresponsible.

She had asked her mother, who came up with the obvious answer.

"Mom—my first weekend as a mother and I'm already in crisis mode. How am I going to do this?"

"It's simple—one crisis at a time. This one is easy. Take her with you."

"To Hong Kong?"

"Why not?"

Why not? Good question. Becca's ability to analyze options kicked in. She had none—except to take Emily with her.

But first, she'd have to see Emily and give her the news that would rock her world.

From her phone in the cab on her way back to midtown, Becca started her analysts on a high-priority research project. She intended to be an expert on child-raising by close of business.

The nanny brought Emily home from her playdate. Becca noticed Emily had replaced the tutu with a Tartine et Chocolat delicate smocked dress. This child of hers was a clotheshorse at four. What would she be like at thirteen?

This child of hers. The concept produced less fear every time she thought it—and more anticipation.

The children's grief psychologist her analysts had consulted had written a sample script for Becca to follow and prepared her with possible opportunities that might present themselves as an opening.

Becca had read the script and dismissed it. Emily was too bright to be fed serious information using canned dialogue. The right time would present itself.

Becca, on automatic pilot, had stopped by her own

apartment to grab the suitcase tagged "Asia, Autumn." She looked around at the sleek furniture, sisal carpet, white on white décor, and realized the place was childproof because no child had ever been there! How quick her perspective had changed.

Once in the Fifth Avenue building, Emily's home, she headed toward the kitchen where Emily sat with her sour-faced nanny.

"Where's the prima ballerina?"

"Aunt Becca!" Cookie crumbs decorated Emily's clothes and her milk moustache made it difficult to imagine her as a dancer. "Are you here to visit Mommy? Because she and Daddy are in . . ."

"Alaska, I know, sweetheart. But I'm here to visit you."

"Wow!" Emily clapped her hands together, standing, whirling around and managing to grab Becca's hand at the same time, pulling her into the playroom. The room was decorated with red carpet and white walls—these made from a washable material designed for crayon scribbles. For that purpose a humongus box of Crayolas stood atop a white metal table, where a puzzle game lay half finished—a puzzle Arthur had started with Emily, Becca was sure, and it looked to her like a life stopped midsentence.

Becca and Emily built a structure out of a futuristic Lego kit Becca had never seen. An hour or more went by.

"I'm hungry." Emily had fallen into a pouty mood as though she knew what was coming.

"Let's go eat, then."

"We call Thai."

"Is that what you want to do?"

"I want to be able to say exactly what I want all the time and then it magically appears!"

"That's asking for a lot of magic."

"My mommy says my life will be filled with magic." They both were now sitting on the floor so Emily's face was just a little lower than Becca's. Which is how Becca managed to catch the shift in the child's expression. Emily wasn't thinking about magic.

"When is Mommy coming home?"

Becca didn't answer at once. Instead she drew the child to her.

Becca looked down into blue eyes, dyed nearly navy by sadness, which shifted to study her face.

"Momma's gone for a long time?"

How did she know? How could she not? There had been comings and goings and phone calls. Who knows what Emily overheard.

Becca nodded. That was all.

"And Daddy too, I bet. He'd want to be with Mommy." When Becca nodded, Emily shuffled on unsteady feet out of the playroom.

Becca stayed stupidly on the playroom floor. Maybe she should bring Emily a little brandy in the glass of water like her mother used to do for her. No—go to her. Becca could hear her mother's voice egging her on, guiding her.

Emily was face down on the bed. Her little arms were by her sides and she sobbed, taking in gasps of air. She wasn't shrieking, as Becca would have done in her place, nor was she banging her fists or stomping on the floor in a tantrum. These sobs were from a broken heart. Becca's own heart shattered in that moment and she reached out for Emily, pulling her to her and rocking her, humming a tune from she didn't know where, perhaps her own childhood. Eventually the sobs turned into quiet weeping. Becca placed one hand on Emily's head. With the other arm she held her close. Emily would never know a greater pain than this. And here she was, responsible for helping her heal. The thought strengthened her, knowing Emily would help her get over her own hurt.

"Mommy's left you and me to take care of each other."

This seemed to intrigue Emily as a concept because she stopped crying, sat up, legs dangling. "Where did they go? Where did Mommy and Daddy go?"

Becca told her the truth. Brushing and braiding the child's golden hair, Becca told her that her parents had flown into the sky and had flown away together forever. Emily would live with Becca and her daddy's friend, Edward, and together they would always remember her mom and dad.

The child had clung to her, crying and afraid. They spent hours upon hours remembering all the wonderful things about her mother, which Emily wrote on special paper with the fanciest letters she could make. The paper that so impressed Emily was nothing but graph paper, and the child's fancy was delighted by nothing more than a pack of four highlighting pens that Becca gave her to decorate the pages. Together they made a special memory book for her mom and dad that flew away, and Becca, in one sitting, learned as much as she could tastefully manage about how to go about her new life as a parent.

It was a book they could add to forever, Becca thought, wondering all of a sudden what she should do with the rooms full of Amy's things. But necessity and instinct together told her to leave things as they lay, and Emily seemed a little bit sunnier after Becca told her about the adventure they were going on in the morning. She packed the fanciest dresses she could find, and was excited about the exotic dress-ups Becca described they would find.

Chapter 6

Ask Alice

Alice Carter, with the highest degree of tact, had stopped by the Carlyle to inquire if Edward were home. She had not been able to reach him on his mobile phone, and though she had left messages, she was never sure if he checked them. Edward was a simple soul, and he had never really warmed to the idea of carrying a phone.

She found him feeding his crew, the three dogs he kept in his private apartment at the Carlyle. It was one of the reasons he liked to stay there: They not only tolerated dogs, but actually had an excellent dog-care program, in which, by the simple expedient of a phone call or e-mail by nine o'clock each morning, the dogs would be fed, walked, bathed, brushed, and read aloud to from a vast library of dog-oriented literature. For additional charges a whole range of spa services were available to the canines, from manicures to salt scrubs, but Edward kept his dogs for companionship, and was as likely as not to handle all of their care by himself. The dog nannies were useful when he traveled, though, he reflected, having ordered their morning care from George's phone last night.

At a time that was much too late, well after the Armani spectacle, George Whelan, who had sweated and strained with Edward on the crew team at Harvard, and his wife Bonnie, invited everyone who was still standing to their house on Sutton Place. Edward wanted to be out of his tuxedo and alone somewhere, but nobody, including Bunny, seemed to want the party to end. George rolled the bar outside to the wraparound terrace, where the group made a ridiculously clumsy attempt at candlelit croquet. In the early morning hours, the straggling crowd of ten or twelve guests hurried in a great laughing clump to the kitchen for omelets. They fell asleep here and there, on couches, beds and chairs, slumped against pillows, curled like kittens, yawning and full of the joy of rising with nothing in particular to do.

Bunny had found a suitable bedroom, of course, and rose early to get the newspaper. She had a way of looking after her interests.

Edward greeted Alice warmly, offered her a drink, and walked with her to the balcony, closing the door gently against the wet nose of his old, white-faced golden retriever, who would otherwise give him no peace. With a bedridden tuft of his hair raised in the back like a rooster, Edward blinked his eyes against the sunlight. He yawned, stretching out his arms like a child. He had not an ounce of pretense, Alice thought, dreading what she had to say.

With the balance of sympathy and consideration that was characteristic of her, Alice told Edward about Arthur and about Emily. She was familiar with Thirstan Heston, who was a member of the Union Club, and in fact was, by coincidence, rather friendly with Barbara Kenton, who was the private secretary of Thirstan's wife. She had gotten the whole story from Thirstan and now told Edward that Arthur must have thought highly of him as to honor him with the gift of his child.

It was a long time before Edward spoke. He rubbed his head, squinted at the sun, and suggested they go inside. He took one of the dogs down, in the small, interior elevator that led to a secured extension of his apartment down-stairs, and returned after ten or fifteen minutes to sit with Alice. His eyes were rimmed with red.

If Edward had cried, Alice realized, he had not wanted her to see it. His healthy, broad shoulders were slumped and tired. He walked slowly and evenly to the couch that faced her upholstered chair and leaned into the pillows. Without speaking, he lowered his head into his hands. His breath came with difficulty.

Alice cried, unable to bear for a moment Edward's suffering. She didn't notice him rising from his seat. She started with surprise when Edward rested a kind hand on her shoulder, and with the other hand produced a hand-kerchief from his pocket. He always carried a handkerchief. He was such a dear, kind young man. Alice cried harder.

Edward, his eyes traced with veins of red, leaned his face close to her.

"I've inherited lots of things, Alice," he said gently. "But this is a first."

"Oh, Edward!" she exclaimed, leaping from her chair to wrap him in a big, unabashed hug, like a mother might hold him, Edward thought. His own mother, a reserved and tasteful woman, was not prone to displays of affection.

He pressed his face into her shoulder, and breathed deeply. Then he stepped back, and for a long time, an unforgettable time, he talked to Alice about his old friend Arthur Stearns.

When Edward called the apartment, he was shocked to hear Amy Kolasky's voice lingering on the voice mail, relating the "busy message," as someone was on the other line. It was too eerie and he decided not to leave a message. Nearly an hour passed before Edward tried again to get through. The phone continued to ring busy. Alice had told him that the lawyer mentioned a coguardian but Edward was barely listening, and when he heard the line was busy he assumed the lawyer was at work there. He had no idea that Becca, her computer sitting idle but still on-line, was tying up the phone connection.

In a stroke, Edward had been handed responsibility for a helpless little girl, and by the same stroke had been cut off from the one person he would most naturally turn to for honest advice. Today he had lost his best friend, and before he had even a moment to fathom what life would be like without having Arthur—who understood him in the unconscious manner of someone he had always known, his roommate from St. George's all the way through Harvard—he had become a father.

He had no warmth in his heart for his own father, so fully dominant with the thriving industrial success of his conglomerate as to occupy every field in which Edward might have taken a professional interest. What was the point of learning the shipping business, the chemical business, the cement business, the palm-tickling of corrupt public works ministers that led to sweetheart construction contracts? What was the use of an M.B.A. when his father declared he would run Kirkland Enterprises for twenty more years? Edward saw his choices as working for his father or competing against him, and neither held much appeal. So he had trifled with his studies, finding at last that the field of history provided him with the right combination of escapism, impracticality, and masculine credibility. Ironically, his father had a massive heart attack soon after Edward graduated and the stockholders voted to sell Kirkland Enterprises in pieces. Kirkland Enterprises was no more—but plenty more money had flowed into his mother's coffers.

He saw his father as someone to be avoided. Now he wore the badge. Edward felt utterly alone, a desperate sensation altogether different from the irresponsible solitude he had known and enjoyed. Nobody had ever depended on him before.

He reached the lawyer at his home in the evening, at a phone number that Alice had diligently obtained, and was advised by Thirstan to "keep his powder dry." By that, the lawyer explained, he meant that Emily would be better off sleeping on the changes that had already disturbed her over the course of the day, before Edward's presence delivered a new shock. The lawyer was tired, and had fallen into speaking in the same manner in which he wrote. In this way he advised Edward to cease and desist from visiting, until the morning, when things always looked better.

But in the morning, nothing seemed a scarce bit clearer to Edward, except that he felt in dual measure rejected and negligent to have spent this first night away from his daughter. But he was, to his credit, a man to whom neither self-criticism nor self-pity attached for long, and by the time he arrived at the Stearns' apartment, his heart was beating with anticipation. He longed to hold Emily Stearns, to squeeze her tightly in his arms and promise her that nothing would ever hurt her. He longed to be a father that she would turn to, that she would trust. Though he was apprehensive, and mourned his friend deeply, Edward felt stirring in his heart the first sensation that he might be of use to someone. He hurried his step as he resolved in his heart to handle this situation well.

He had stopped by the Union Club to get the apartment key he knew Arthur left there, and arrived at the apartment in the late morning, though he had woken, by his standards, pretty early, with the alarm ringing at seven-thirty. He had gotten through to the apartment only to reach voice mail, where he left word of his imminent arrival.

The doorman knew Edward and led him upstairs. The apartment was quiet when he stepped inside. He called for

Emily, and, hearing nothing, started slowly toward the library, his feet carrying him on autopilot to the room where Arthur liked to sit. He cleared his throat and called the lawyer's name, but the silence that met him told Edward that nobody was in the apartment. The step of his leather soles creaked on the aged wooden boards of the hallway.

He caught his breath as he turned on the desk lamp and took in the familiar sight of Arthur's library. Sitting down heavily in Arthur's leather reading chair, Edward ran his eyes across the spines of the venerable old books that lined the built-in shelves. His eye traveled over the worn volumes of law and literature, ragged travel guides and large glossy fly-fishing books, the sections of memoirs, biographies, the novels from continental Europe, bound photo albums of mountain hikes and fishing trips with Amy. A tabletop chessboard, little used, was pushed into a corner where it bumped against a brass, standing lamp. A humidor stood on a shelf behind it; Arthur had been proud of that, a gift from Amy that he proclaimed as "the best in its class." The Persian carpet, with predominant hues of burgundy and navy, was worn where Arthur moved an ottoman to rest his feet. Someone's got to settle where all these things go, Edward thought.

Near the window facing Fifth Avenue, he saw a folder marked Alaska. Taking a deep breath, Edward walked toward the window and opened the folder. A receipt fluttered out; just two weeks ago Arthur had bought new chest-high waders from the Cabela catalogue in Amy's size. Amy had laughed at Arthur's waders, Edward remembered, since they had overall-style straps. She called him Farmer Stearns when he wore them. But she had relented, feeling too many times the cold rush of river water over the tops of her thigh-high waders rendering useless their waterproof effect.

On the Stearns & Fielding notepaper that Arthur kept on his desk were notes about flight arrival and departure times, several brochures describing different Alaskan fishing lodges, and a scribbled note that caught Edward's eye: "Big Kodiak bear at FAO Schwartz—holding for Em."

Edward tucked the paper back into the file. This was a life interrupted midstep.

Squaring his shoulders, Edward took a deep breath. Emily could walk in anytime. She would be sad enough, he imagined; it wouldn't help for her to find him stumbling moon-faced around the apartment. He slapped his cheeks with his hands as if he could wake himself from this nightmare and walked down the hall to the kitchen.

A note addressed to him, written in an unfamiliar hand, lay on the table. At the top, underlined several times, was scribbled the name "Eddie." He smiled. Nobody called him Eddie. It was signed by Becca Reinhart. It was hastily written, and the sentences tilted across the page in long collapsed lines. He noticed some flowers had been colored around the edges in crayon. Emily!

He leaned into the dim light cast by the hanging lamp in the kitchen to read.

> *Eddie—*
> *we couldn't get in touch with you so i took emily with me to hong kong. i'm there on business until sunday. Thirstan—the lawyer—says we have an expedited hearing monday am with judge jones. talk to him about where to go.*
>
> *FYI i'm emily's other guardian—thirstan will explain. it was a big surprise to me too.*
>
> *i hope you're doing okay, eddie. i heard how close you were to arthur. don't worry about em. she's a real trooper. she's going to be fine.*
>
> *sincerely—becca reinhart*

*PS—doorman knows to let nobody but thirstan up—
already sent two PI lawyers and a dozen real estate
agents packing! thirstan says the apartment's in trust in
emily's name—she can stay here. she has more than
enough to live on.*

*PS—will you talk to the nanny? i can't understand a
thing she says. Thanks.*

Edward closed his eyes and rubbed his temples slowly.
Matters were growing stranger and stranger. Edward felt a
mild quake run through his body. He was frightened. Or
was he mad? He had wanted to get going with his new
relationship with Emily. And shouldn't this Becca, his
coguardian, have consulted him before she took the child
to the bottom of the globe? He re-read the note, then folded
it and put it in the pocket of his khakis. He glanced at the
refrigerator, where was posted the office number of
Thirstan Heston. The lawyer was with Stearns & Fielding,
Edward noticed, Arthur's firm.

He should stop by Arthur's office and get his matters in
order. Alert his clients, have his papers filed, take his pictures down and bring them back to the apartment: final
matters. There were funeral arrangements to be made, he
thought, feeling his eyes burn. It didn't sound like there
was anything left to bury, but somebody had to handle the
obituary, put together a memorial service at least.

Edward felt no better suited to the task at hand than a
cat contemplating the feel of a deep-sea dive, but he didn't
know if anyone else would see to it. Arthur's dad, who had
suffered from heart trouble, had died several years ago, followed quickly by his mother. There was only a step-sister,
Edward recalled. Perhaps Thirstan had already informed
her.

Instinctively, Edward opened the refrigerator. Inside he
found several yellow boxes with animated Pokemon

characters, containing cherry-flavored drinks, presumably for Emily. The back and the shelves of the refrigerator were full of useless condiments: capers, Kalamata olives, balsamic salad dressing, several types of mustard, and the like. There was a large pitcher of thick melon-colored juice that smelled a bit sickly, a shrivelly couple of apples, a package of hot dogs, and a box of Thai takeout.

He withdrew a Pokemon box drink, poked the straw into its top, and immediately squirted his shirt with a flood of cherry punch. Edward sighed, rubbing the stain on his shirt with his hand as if he could hide it, which only succeeded in spreading it out until it bled over most of the left side of his oxford. He moved to the bathroom to take a look at the damage, feeling miserable and stupid.

Edward caught sight of himself in the mirror of the Jazz Age bathroom, a convenience no larger than a stall that was made to feel confiningly small by the tiny tiles of black and white, which the mirror repeated endlessly, in every direction, like an Escher print. He was a pitiable thing to see. His tired eyes drooped with exhaustion, his face was unshaven. His cherry-stained shirt, reflected in the checkerboard headache of the walls, gave him the surreal feeling of posing for a pop art postcard.

Welcome to parenthood, Edward thought to himself. He felt composed, though ruefully so, when he considered the task he had assumed upon himself. He would pay his respects to Arthur by handling all of the matters left undone by his and Amy's deaths. And then he would make arrangements for the memorial service.

A noise coming from the front of the apartment shook him out of his own thoughts. He heard a woman calling, "Hello, is anybody here?"

Edward walked to the foyer where he found a middle-aged woman, nicely dressed in a black pantsuit. She had a big gold heart suspended from a chain around her neck and a number—a lot—of gold chain bracelets, each a different style, on her left wrist. She was removing a bright red Pashmina shawl. This woman probably wouldn't be on any A-list he knew about—she was too colorful.

"Edward Kirkland?" Her eyes seemed electrified, lit from a source within. Her double chin was beginning to sag. But his eyes didn't rest there. He was drawn back to her eyes.

"I am Edward Kirkland." As he drew closer, he saw her looking at his shirt.

"You have to put seltzer on that stain immediately—come, let's see what's in the refrigerator. Where's the kitchen?"

"There is no seltzer," he said without thought.

"I am Arlene Reinhart." The somewhat stocky woman held out a pudgy hand and he noticed she wore a sedate diamond ring on her right ring finger, but no wedding band. Then it hit him.

"Reinhart? Then you are . . ."

"I'm Becca's mother."

"Oh—how nice to meet you," he hesitated, hoping she'd explain this visit.

The silence was growing just a pinch too long. So he said, "Would you like to sit down?"

"Yes."

"I can't offer you anything to drink."

"I brought water, juice, a little instant coffee."

Edward looked behind Mrs. Reinhart, but there was no indication she'd brought a bag or tote with her.

"I left it with Frank."

Edward looked blank.

"Frank—the doorman. Such a great guy. He has a cooler in the employees' locker room. He offered to leave the sandwiches and other stuff there."

"You have visited here?"

"No, I just met him downstairs and one thing led to another. If you want, I'll ring for him."

"No, that's all right. You must have quite a gift for chatting people up quickly, if you discovered there was a cooler in the locker room in such a short time."

"Why don't we see about my gift of gab. Let's sit."

He led her to Arthur's library. "This is not the sunniest room in the house," he apologized as they made themselves comfortable. "But I'm just familiarizing myself with the apartment."

"I imagine so." Arlene's eyes swept over the shelves of books, the sculptures in brass and clay. There were two paintings. One, a small oil, was obviously a portrait of Arthur fishing. It was inscribed "To Arthur—Safe Passage—Wherever you roam," and it was signed "Laura." Well, that was pretty eerie. The other painting was abstract and very futuristic. It looked like an important piece. Also expensive.

"So, where are all their things going? Who's taking care of the packing?" Arlene Reinhart had an expressive stare. Edward determined from just a moment of her glance that this was something of a priority in her opinion.

"Well, I was thinking about that myself. And I thought either the lawyer had some instructions that he hadn't had time to convey, or perhaps Ms. Rein—I mean, your daughter and I should make decisions about these things together." This wasn't exactly true. Edward had thought about this, but never considered the logistics. "I guess I thought my assistant could take care of organizing things."

"Are you crazy?"

Edward considered this statement thoughtfully. Certainly nobody had ever talked to him in quite that way. Nor questioned his sanity.

"I don't think so. I wasn't when I walked in here this morning. It's conceivable that I lost my mind since I've been here. Why do you ask?"

"Obviously no one you love has ever died before. Because these things are personal treasures. This place is like a museum of Amy and Arthur's stuff. And someday that little girl is going to start making trips to visit this museum. These objects have to be organized so that she doesn't look at everything too reminiscent right away nor anything too valuable, because she's young and she'll just take it and put it in her plastic purse and that will be that. And then there are things she can have as soon as she asks."

This made sense to Edward. He just didn't have a clue how this could be accomplished.

"I have to admit, Mrs. Reinhart—"

"Arlene."

"I know nothing about this—any of it. Handling personal effects, planning memorial services."

"Looks like you have a tough time drinking juice from a box too." Arlene kept a straight face.

Edward looked down at his shirt and, pulling it away from his body, said, "I'm still at the drinking glass stage, but I'm learning."

Arlene liked this. She was relieved that he wasn't totally uptight. Becca had asked her to check at the apartment, make sure everything was all right. She imagined hordes of lawyers, reporters, auction house representatives, real estate agents swarming and circling like insects and man-eating fish. It was a huge bonus that Kirkland was here, that she got to meet him. She might call Becca tonight.

"Let me call for Frank. I'm sure there's a washer and dryer here."

Edward held up his hand. "It's a shirt, Arlene. I've got many. I want to spend time talking about your daughter— I assume that's why you're here—"

"Why?"

"To learn what you can about me."

72

Arlene sat back against the arm of Arthur's well-worn leather couch, took her shoes off, and put her stockinged feet up. "I had no idea you would be here. I live in Brooklyn. Do you think I'd come into the city just in case there was a chance you'd be here?"

Good point. He had spent too many years as the center of everybody's universe. This was refreshing—Arlene Reinhart was refreshing—strong with a positive attitude—not like his mother, who seemed to bring the dark with her wherever she went.

"I'm here because my daughter asked me to make sure vultures stayed away." Arlene paused but it was clear she wasn't finished with this thought. "You'll find she has a mind like a shooting star."

"I don't understand."

"She's brilliant. She is always in motion. And she is rare."

Edward mulled this over—stripped of a mother's tendency to blow her child's assets out of proportion, Edward heard that Becca Reinhart thought ahead, was either hard to pin down or had lots of energy, or both. The rare part seemed one hundred percent mother's love.

"Does she know anything about raising children?"

"No."

Edward's stomach grabbed at his chest. "Neither do I."

Arlene didn't even turn her head to look at him. She was studying a painting. "Sounds like an interesting experience awaits both of you."

And that was that. No advice, no suggestions about what to do when he first saw Emily, not a word of direction about how he and her daughter might work this out together.

"Are you hungry?" she asked. Without waiting for an answer, she walked barefoot over hardwood herring-patterned floors and pushed the call button. A voice came on and Arlene asked if Frank might send someone up with her package.

"Let's move to the kitchen, shall we? God forbid I drop a crumb on that Persian rug. I'll kill myself."

"That seems a little extreme," Edward said.

"You don't know anything about Jewish mothers—I can tell."

So she told him the joke about how the Jewish mother tested her son's love and wasn't satisfied until he gave her his heart—then she took poison because her son was dead and she didn't want to live without him. And Edward threw his head back and laughed, so she told him another joke about a Jewish mother, and one about a Jewish grandmother. Then he started telling her jokes that he did not even know he remembered. And Edward, who always considered himself one of those people who couldn't deliver a punch line, had Arlene screaming with laughter.

Edward laughed so hard that tears ran down his face and Arlene had to excuse herself to go to the bathroom.

And then they ate—turkey breast sandwiches, pickles, a plastic container of vegetable soup (some people can make more than just chicken soup, Arlene said), babka, a little salad for Arlene's diet. While they ate they planned how to store Amy and Arthur's possessions—and still keep them in the apartment. Edward called Alice and Arlene called her nephew Brian, who needed money ("Come, help the new Bubbe," is what she said). And soon enough the two ersatz packers had their instructions.

Arlene put on her shoes and shawl and at the door she patted Edward's cheek and stood on tiptoe to give him a kiss.

"Where to next?" she asked.

"I'm going to Thirstan Heston's office and then I'm going to see what we should put in our museum from Arthur's office."

74

The elevator came. She blew him a kiss.

Edward left Arthur's apartment, determined to handle this matter well. He hailed a cab to the offices of Stearns & Fielding. He forgot all about the stain on his shirt.

Chapter 7

Tell It to the Judge

On Monday morning, Edward was waiting at the courthouse to meet Becca Reinhart. He had arrived fifteen minutes early, knowing she was planning to come straight from the airport, and he had spent the time watching a regular stream of people enter the courthouse. Most of them he judged to be lawyers. And everyone seemed to be talking on the phone. The sun was deceptively bright, shining over a temperature that had dropped into the forties, but Edward was comfortable in his warm tweed jacket. With his back to the wall of the courthouse, Edward saw the lean, muscular calf of a woman stretching her leg out of a taxi. He kept his eye on the dark-haired woman, who struck him at once as being in a hurry. She ran around to the trunk to move several pieces of luggage to the sidewalk, carrying them energetically, with dispatch, but without display of effort. The driver made a move to assist her, but she brushed him off courteously, handing him a couple of bills with a quick smile. He noticed one of the two rolling suitcases, a shiny, pink patent bag, was unusually small and featured a picture of Airport Barbie.

He smiled. This must be her.

He watched the lady lean toward the backseat of the

taxi, offering her hand to a child inside. She stood, tossing back her loose black hair, and guided Emily Stearns to the sidewalk.

"Emily!" Edward called out.

Emily wore no coat over her red silk kimono, and gave a little shiver when she felt the cold air. She stood in place, her hand raised slightly. Edward watched her, knowing she had not heard his voice over the busy street noise.

"What?" asked Becca, standing next to the gesturing child. "You want to hold my phone again?"

"Hands!" said Emily, shaking hers. "Watch out for cars!"

Nodding, Becca took the child's hand. Imitating Becca, Emily slung her purse strap across her chest, Rambo-style, and used her free hand to carry her rolling Barbie suitcase. The ladies were just in from Hong Kong, and Emily felt very important.

Spending the weekend abroad with her new child had taught Becca right away that little Emily Stearns had a constant need for amusement. She talked all the time, interrupting thoughtlessly, eagerly—and, to Becca's happy surprise, endearingly. Her perspective was hilarious. In the thick of a fairy tale stage, Emily saw the world through the romantic spectacles of a rose-cheeked princess. She didn't drink from a cup, she sipped from a golden chalice. She didn't sleep in a bed, she crawled under the shade of a flower petal in a magic garden.

At first, eating the vacuum pack of airline peanuts had only made Emily thirsty, but when Becca suggested the peanuts were enchanted seeds, every crunch of which made an e-mail pop up on Becca's laptop, Emily finished the pile in ten minutes. She was amazed to see the messages keep flashing on the computer screen, and would have eaten a mountain of magic peanuts until Becca told her the plane had flown out of range for the magic spell. So they got their nails done together, and Becca told Emily about olden times, when there were no airplanes and people were bored to tears all day long.

Edward called out to the child again, and this time Emily heard him.

"Edward!" she exclaimed, rushing to wrap him in a hug. He lifted her in his arms and twirled her until they both were dizzy. An open lipstick—Chanel's Radical Red—that she clutched in one hand left huge smudges all over the shoulder of his tweed jacket.

Becca cringed, ready to apologize, but she noticed that the man just laughed.

"Becca Reinhart," she said, peering at him as he introduced himself and shook her hand in greeting. He didn't seem even a little bit worried about his jacket.

"Edward Kirkland," he introduced himself. They were even in height, she noticed, returning his gentle smile. His eyes met hers, and then shifted to Emily, whom he held in a long, affectionate embrace. For the past several days he had been exiled in the severest of circumstances, known to nobody but himself and Alice, and he was overjoyed to greet the child he was bound to love and protect. And here, finally, he had lifted her into his arms.

What did Edward Kirkland care, at that moment, about a lipstick stain?

His enthusiasm was extravagant, and Becca relaxed, watching Emily return the warmth of his embrace. The child burrowed her face into his strong shoulder. When she sat back in his arms, Becca saw that the child beamed with the importance of being met at a big building by a friend of her father's. The thought that flashed into Becca's mind surprised her: Maybe Emily needed a dad.

Becca shook her head. What was she thinking? She had done fine without a father. How strange she felt suddenly, how dizzy and unfocused.

"I'm sorry about Amy," Edward said to her. "You must

have been very close." She felt his hand resting on her arm. Confused, she took a step backward. Was she close to anybody?

"It's sad," she stammered, keeping her voice low so Emily would be unaware. "It's really sad." She glanced at Emily, who was talking incessantly, describing really fancy dresses and dragons and sticks in the hair and airplane lockers and magic peanuts.

"Does she know?" Edward spoke only loud enough to bridge the distance Becca kept between them.

"Yes—as much as she can grasp, I think."

Edward perceived that Becca knew exactly how to handle the truth with Emily. He dropped the subject. Bending down, he caught hold of Becca's luggage to carry it inside. In an instant Becca had pulled it out of his hand.

"What?" She squinted at him in the sunlight. "Do you need something?"

Surprised, Edward shook his head. Setting Emily down on the ground, he picked up the Barbie suitcase and reached for her hand. "Come on, Em," he said, turning to give Becca a smile. "I'll carry your Barbie bag."

Uncertainly, Becca joined them, her bag bumping behind her as they ascended the courthouse steps together. She let Edward carry her bag when he offered again inside the building, feeling the strange pressure of Emily's eyes upon her, as if seeming to ask, "*Why not?*"

At once, Becca reached for Emily's hand. She realized how anxious she was because her free hand felt empty, lifeless without a phone to dial or a suitcase to lug behind her. She had no business with Edward, and at the same time they were about to begin the most personal job-share in the world. She felt awkward, and walked without speaking.

"I like your dress," Edward complimented Emily.

"It's called a kimo-jo," Emily bragged, sticking out her

stomach to show Edward the purple embroidered dragon that chased the princess with the sticks in her hair.

They laughed, letting Emily's neutrality relax them. Together the threesome entered courtroom eleven. Becca and Emily sat down while Edward found a place to put the suitcases. Becca's phone rang, but she left it alone. She cringed to hear it ring unanswered, biting her lip with frustration. The judge might start any minute. For this, she thought, looking at the judge's austere wooden bench, her call would have to wait.

Emily stuck out her hand to answer the phone, but Becca shook her head. She smiled, seeing her own impatience mirrored in the child's demand to know who was calling. Did she act like a four-year-old, she wondered? She was going to find out. Hopefully she turned off the phone, leaving the vibrating signal off.

"Later," she promised. "We have our special meeting first, remember?"

Emily rolled her eyes, but Becca had promised her candy, and she smiled with anticipation when Becca tapped her bag of sugary treats.

"For well-behaved little girls," she said.

"When?" asked Emily.

"Soon," Becca promised.

Emily thought of the lollipops. "A rainbow one?"

Becca nodded. "Two," she whispered, smiling. Emily was so easy to be nice to. While Emily clapped her hands and promised to be perfect, Becca handed her a Ziploc bag of crayons and a pad of graph paper.

"Draw funny pictures of everybody in the room," she whispered to Emily.

Emily giggled and looked around for a good target.

Edward returned from the back of the courtroom, where he had stowed the suitcases, and noticed with approval the activities Becca had brought along for Emily. He wouldn't have thought of that. She's four, he reminded himself, feeling some apprehension as he realized that she probably didn't play squash yet. He tickled the back of her neck with his fingers.

Judge Lillian Warfield Jones entered the courtroom.

"Draw the judge with a moustache," Becca whispered to Emily, who giggled and got quickly to work. Becca stood next to Edward as the judge walked across the room, her quick, firm steps echoing on the wood floor. Judge Jones was known for tight control of the courtroom. She disposed of cases quickly and dispassionately.

With a bang of the gavel, Judge Jones called the court into session, and the parties took their seats.

Edward was surprised to feel a wave of apprehension rising within him. The black-robed judge, the seal of New York, the witness stand, the bailiff: The hallmarks of law's binding presence hit him at once with their compulsory force.

He felt suddenly short of breath, and reminded himself he had been chosen for this day. His friend Arthur had believed he was the right person to take care of Emily; he had left his child to him, Edward thought, squaring his shoulders. He really had no excuse not to accept the responsibility. He was old enough, he was rich enough, he had no real personal commitments that would interfere with Emily's needs. He felt Emily's head rest trustingly against his shoulder when he hugged her on the street. He looked back to see her coloring, and the obligation of parenthood hit him like a train.

He glanced nervously at Becca, who flashed him a wide, confident smile.

"Look alive, Eddie, it's our big day," she whispered.

He laughed, taking strength from her self-assurance.

The guardianship matter was scheduled to be heard and decided first. The wills were not contested, and the guardians, whose identity was not questioned, were present. The judge moved directly to the next step, parental fitness testing by a court-appointed psychologist. Setting aside forty-five minutes for testing and evaluation, a half hour for lunch, and another half hour for the discussion session with the counselor, the judge adjourned the proceeding. Boom.

Becca was impressed as she exited the courtroom. This was drive-through justice at its best. Her inner taxpayer was well satisfied.

Together in the hallway, Edward and Becca walked for a minute in silence. Emily had an interview scheduled with the court psychologist. After that her temporary nanny was coming to sit with her while Edward and Becca saw the court psychologist.

She turned toward Edward with a sudden smile. He wore a distant expression and walked without noticing her.

She shrugged, reached into her Hogan bag and withdrew her mobile phone.

He smiled then, noticing her. Digging his hands into the pockets of his wool gabardine trousers, he turned his eyes straight ahead and walked silently into the examining room.

Chapter 8

Sunday Starter

Inside the courtroom, the psychologist, the judge, and the representative from Stearns & Fielding stayed in their seats. Dr. Gail Erikson, the child psychologist, approached the witness chair where Emily was already seated. Emily's eyes were wide and her mind was full of adventure. The location of the witness box was a particular delight to her. She pretended she was trapped in a tower surrounded by a crocodile-filled moat, where she had to answer questions put by an evil princess until her beautiful fairy godmother came to rescue her.

"We need to learn a few things about your friends Becca and Edward," Dr. Erikson began. "Would you mind answering some questions for me, dear?"

"Why?" Emily wanted to know.

"You can help us," cooed the psychologist.

"I can?"

"Sure you can. Your feelings are important to us. We have to decide what's in your best interest."

"What do you mean, 'interest'?"

"What's best for you."

The psychologist changed tactics for a minute, complimenting Emily's purse, her shiny kimono, her beautiful hair. When she felt the child had been lulled by enough small talk, she pounced.

"What do you think of Becca?"

"She's great!" Emily bubbled with enthusiasm. "She's so much fun. She wore a kimo-jo in the hotel that was all purple, like a magical fairy princess! We had a great time. We put feathers in our hair and called room service. She put me on the handles of her bike too, and we went so fast! All over Hong Kong, up and down the hills!" She puffed her cheeks out like a frog. "We ate soooo much rice," she said importantly.

Dr. Erikson moved her hands like waves, inviting the child to go on.

Pausing, Emily remembered the super-cool "first" that Becca had contributed to her life. She puffed out her chest and bragged: "I flew to Hong Kong with her on business. Across the *ocean*. And I wasn't even scared."

The psychologist raised one eyebrow. This was the first clue Dr. Erikson had that Ms. Reinhart might be inclined to take too many risks with this recently traumatized young child. Perhaps Mr. Kirkland should assume the major portion of custody. All she said to Emily was "Lovely."

"It was great," Emily said. "I love peanuts. I think I ate . . . five hundred! Or five hundred five hundred!" Emily bragged, spreading her arms wide.

The judge bit back a chuckle while Dr. Erikson nodded her head with a frozen smile.

"I know you haven't been together for very long," the doctor said gently, "but can you tell us anything you've learned from your friend Becca?"

"Sure. She taught me how to eat with chopsticks. And karate *chop!*" Emily sliced the air and made a scary face to show she was a fierce dragon fighter.

"Wonderful," said the psychologist, but Emily didn't hear her. She was karate chopping the air with wild swats, imagining that the big Chinese dragons were all around, and her chops were turning them into glitter. When she had settled breathlessly into her seat, Dr. Erikson resumed the conversation.

"Has Becca taught you anything else?"

Emily took the bait eagerly. It had been an exciting few days. She wanted to tell them all the cool things Becca had shown her.

"She showed me how to make pictures of myself on the Xerox. Look!" Emily dug around in her Barbie suitcase, which she had pulled up to the witness box with her, in case she got any e-mails, she said. She pulled out several pieces of paper.

"This is my ear. That's my chopsticks in an X. That's my butt!"

Emily laughed and laughed, her shoulders wiggling with delight, as she held up the page. "See? I have a heart on my jeans pocket. See there?"

The psychologist frowned. "How artistic," she attempted.

Emily smiled.

"Has Becca taught you anything, perhaps, in the category of early childhood development?"

"What?" Emily asked.

"In English," Judge Jones reminded her.

"Any big learning ideas?"

"I already told you that," snapped Emily. "When is Becca coming back?"

"Any colors?" persisted Dr. Erikson.

"I already know my colors."

"Okay," the psychologist nodded, "good. Can I do a little game with you?"

Emily nodded.

The psychologist pointed to her yellow-green scarf.

"What color is this?"

"Chartreuse," Emily answered. "And it looks bad with your face."

This time the judge actually released a tiny chuckle as Dr. Erikson stumbled for a moment on her next question.

Emily noticed that she was having an effect with her answer about the colors, so she went on.

"Becca gave me a scarf on the plane. She tied it on me. It was called a sarong. It was tangerine, with melon stripes. She never wears it, she said. She got it at a wedding party. So she gave it to me!" Emily clapped her hands. Her eyes sparkled.

"How charming," said Dr. Erikson, still smarting from the child's comment about her scarf.

"How old are you?"

"I don't know," Emily said with a careless shrug. "How old are you?"

Dr. Erikson gulped.

The psychologist reviewed her file and recalled that the child was four. Some kids do numbers at four, but not all. "How would you like to count to ten with me?"

"I can do my numbers in French. *Un, deux, trois,*" Emily began.

"Good!" The child psychologist beamed. French. That was something.

"Did Becca teach you that?"

"*No!* Becca calls it 'frog talk.' But Eddie knows it. He says I am *très bien.*"

"Charming."

"I can hop like a frog," Emily announced, springing up at once to demonstrate.

"Not here, dear."

"Becca lets me do it wherever I want," the child answered, her arms crossed defiantly.

"How nice. She seems permissive."

"What does that mean?"

"It means she lets you do what you want," Dr. Erikson explained, trying to hide her disapproval under the shallow ring of an affirming, preschool-teacher voice.

"Nuh-uh," said Emily. "I wanted to show everybody at the good-bye dinner my days of the week wheel, but she said I shouldn't."

"Oh, too bad. What's your days of the week wheel?" she prodded.

"It's what Becca gave me to teach me the days of the week."

"That's wonderful. And very advanced for four."

"I forget them sometimes," Emily admitted. "But then I check the wheel. Becca says I can have the wheel until I get them all in my mind. Then I don't need it anymore. Anyway I can't hurt anything with it, she says. It's all empty."

"Empty?"

"Yeah!" Emily dug around in her Barbie suitcase, glad she brought it to the stand. She had so much to show off. She pulled out a round, green birth-control dispenser. The pills were all gone, but the days of the week were prominently featured on stickers.

"See?" Emily said, holding the dispenser in the air with a proud smile.

"This kind is a 'Sunday Starter,' " Emily said importantly. "So we start with Sunday as the first day. Ready? Sunday, Monday, Toosday, Wens-day, Tursday, Friday, Sataday, and then"—she twisted the wheel—"see—it goes back again. I can read the letters, so that's my hint. I see an S . . ." she explained her method, but her little voice fell on deaf ears.

Dr. Erikson stared wide-eyed at Emily's day-counting device. The courtroom had fallen quiet, except for the bailiff, who had trouble stifling his laughter.

"A birth-control dispenser," Judge Jones whispered under her breath. "How unorthodox."

Marge Hannock, the court reporter, had heard worse in thirty years of witness testimony. She shrugged her wise, square shoulders.

"What's the big deal?" she said to the bailiff. "It's empty."

Emily was still explaining her method.

"Also I can use the colors if I forget. On Becca's full one, the yellow ones are in Monday . . ."

"Enough, please," the psychologist said, in a firmer tone than she intended. More gently, she added, "Becca won't want you to tell *all* her secrets."

"Oh, she won't care," replied Emily with a happy shrug. "She doesn't care what people think about her. That's what she told me in Hong Kong, when I wanted my food plain."

The psychologist saw an opening to gather more information.

"I see. Can you tell us what happened? Did you get your food 'plain'?"

"Sure did. Rice, rice, rice. And then fortune cookies. It was great!"

"Anything else?"

"Well, on the airplane Becca said I didn't have to eat the chicken. Becca says airplane food is . . . I forgot the word."

Dr. Erikson gasped. "You don't mean 'shit,' do you?"

The judge's eyes fastened on the little girl seated beneath her. Lillian Jones took a measured approach in custody cases. But there were boundaries. Four-year-olds should not hear profanity.

"No—it began with *druh*."

Stumped, the psychologist prepared to move on.

"Dreck," the woman from Stearns & Fielding volunteered.

"That's it, dreck," Emily clapped her hands. This was fun, like twenty questions.

The adults in the courtroom shared a congenial laugh. Everyone but Dr. Erikson, who pressed on. "I'm sorry, Emily. I didn't express myself very clearly."

"What's 'express'?" the child interrupted.

Dr. Erikson paused. "I mean I didn't say that right. Here,

let me try again. Has Becca taught you anything else? Any nursery rhymes? Any songs?"

"No. I already know those."

Emily began singing "Old MacDonald" until the judge stopped her with a deft compliment.

"What a beautiful voice," she praised Emily. "And you've used it quite a bit today, with all these questions. Can we bring this to a close, Gail?" she said, in a voice that directed the psychologist rather than asking her.

"Yes, Your Honor. I have the Rorschach test, and that's all."

"Any questions about the male guardian, Gail?"

"No," she answered. Judge Jones looked puzzled, so the psychologist explained.

"Edward has significant income. All our research tells us that a male guardian will be sufficient based on income. It's the maternal influence that really counts, from a *psychosocial* point of view."

"How progressive," quipped the judge.

"We have one more little game to play, Emily. We're going to look together at some shapes."

Emily looked scared.

"I want Becca," she announced.

"No, this game is not for Becca," answered Dr. Erikson, trying to sound enthusiastic. "It's for you!"

Quickly, she held up the first picture. To help Emily feel better, she promised her that there were no "right answers" for this game.

"What's the point of it, then?" Emily asked. The judge, laughing, agreed.

"I'm going to call a recess," she decided. "Give our little lady here a break."

Chapter 9

No Wrong Answers

After the break for lunch, Edward returned to the room where earlier he and Becca had taken the parental fitness personality test. He took his seat to wait for Becca and the court-appointed psychologist to return. Refreshed by the quick walk he had taken, his spirits raised by the first chill of autumn, Edward relaxed in his chair, stretching his legs out in front of him and folding his arms behind his head.

When Becca rushed into the testing room, Edward rose. The simple courtesy of standing when a lady entered the room was so ingrained in Edward that he acted automatically.

Becca pulled the phone away from her ear.

"What?" she flung at him. "Where are you going? Are we switching rooms?"

Smiling, he shook his head no, and took his seat.

"Good," she said. "Every minute counts."

She ended her call quickly, then sat down and checked her watch.

He saw her annoyance that the evaluation did not start promptly at one, as scheduled. She really ought to relax, he thought. For a minute he watched her tap her fingers on the bag in which she carried her BlackBerry. And already he could read her well enough to know she was deciding whether she would have enough time to check her e-mail.

"I've never had my personality tested before," Edward

said to Becca, who turned toward him with evident surprise. "Have you?" he asked.

"Sure," Becca answered casually. "All the time. It's a staple at corporate retreats," she said. "Old hat."

He raised his eyebrows. "Well? How do they go? Do you learn anything exciting?"

At that minute Becca's phone rang, and she hurried to answer it.

"Forget the CAD," she said gruffly. "Forget the Basle standard. Even if they adopt it, they'll never implement it. Just go forward." She paused. "Yeah, right. In Poland and Hungary too. I've got to go."

She listened to her caller, shaking her head with frustration that increased the longer she listened. "What?" she said finally. "Forget it. I'm out!" She paused to listen, and Edward saw her nod her head yes. He smiled, thinking she had gotten what she wanted.

"That's right," she said. "Exactly. It's the only right way."

She hung up and noticed Edward was watching her, waiting for something.

"The CAD is a capital adequacy directive," she explained.

He shrugged, uninterested. "What about your personality tests? I'm curious—I've never done this."

She laughed dismissively. "Oh, they're all stupid, Eddie. Always come out the same. First, a totally ridiculous bunch of questions. You know, 'do you get angry when you are kept waiting, try to do everything yourself, race through the day, get too little rest, think there is only one right way to do something, blah blah blah,' and of course it's all yes yes yes, and then the management consultant people freak out and say you're in the danger zone, and you all laugh with the CEOs and see who got farthest into the danger zone, and that's how you bond, you know? Then you go rappelling."

91

"I see," Edward said. He stretched his arms behind his head and was overpowered by such a relaxing yawn that he forgot to cover his mouth. Even though she hadn't seen her father the dentist in twenty years, she reflexively noticed he had no fillings. Not one. She raised her eyebrows.

Dr. Ben Honeywell, bow-tied and prim, entered the room clucking like a hen.

"Tsk, tsk, friends," he said, wagging his finger.

They looked at him without speaking.

"I heard a phone ringing. No no no no no." Bizarrely, he introduced them to his index finger.

"This is Mr. No," he said, moving the finger hypnotically, slowly to and fro. "Mr. No says '*no telephone calls during our session.*'" The effect was not nearly as mesmerizing as he had intended.

Becca shot a glance at Edward in time to see him stifle his laugh. She laughed out loud, her shoulders shaking. For a moment she was unable to speak.

"Who *are* you?" Becca finally managed. "I mean, the man behind the finger," she added. At that she and Edward simultaneously put a hand over their mouths in badly concealed laughter, like sixth graders looking at a teacher with a KICK ME sign.

"I'm Dr. Ben Honeywell," he said, keeping calm by speaking softly and slowly, and reminding himself that subjects sometimes expressed their nervous apprehension through juvenile humor. "I'm your evaluating psychotherapist."

"I'm Becca Reinhart." He had not offered his hand to shake—maybe he wanted Mr. No where he could keep an eye on him. "I'll put the phone down, but keep it short, will you please?"

"We can't rush our mental wellness, Ms. Reinhart," he responded in the same artificially calm voice.

"Then don't tell me what to do with my phone," she replied, staring into his face.

The doctor ignored her, diverting his eyes from her stare as he distributed copies to the subjects of their evaluated parental fitness tests. He kept the originals at his desk.

Edward's eyes lingered on Becca, who was rifling through her test, vainly searching for her grade. He felt a jolt of pleasure, enjoying this energetic, colorful personality that had been so abruptly introduced into his life.

An intense woman with a smile like the Mediterranean sun, Becca's expansive personality made her seem as if she were the only person in the room. Yet Edward could see in the first minute that Becca had no consciousness of her own appeal. Obsessively occupied by her work, she didn't give herself a minute's thought. There was something sincere and dependable about her, yet her carefree humor struck playfully at any worthy target.

"Where's my grade, Dr. Honeywell? Did I get an A?"

"You may call me Dr. Ben," he said, mainly to Becca. "And your papers weren't *graded*," he said, adding the words "*per se*" in air-quotes.

Edward hadn't even touched his paper. He closed his eyes, wondering if he could get away with a little catnap. But the doctor was in session.

"I have deep concerns about some of your answers on this parental fitness test, Becca. We need to *discuss* these issues. We must connect, today, to your *essential* personality—the 'why' in Y-O-U."

Becca's phone rang again. Obligingly, she turned it off. "The O in O-F-F," she said, mimicking Dr. Ben with her air-quotes.

Dr. Ben took her imitation as flattery, nodded at her silenced phone and clapped his hands in the air. He seemed to think he needed to speak on two levels, with words and with obvious gestures, like a mime.

"My main concern is the large—chasm—of difference between your answers, Edward and Becca." He sighed, spreading his hands far apart, like airplane wings. "In layman's terms, you're what we would call . . . incompatible personalities."

"To each his own," Edward said simply.

"Who did the best?" Becca asked at the same time.

Dr. Ben frowned at Becca. "You two will need to work together as guardians of this child, and frankly, I'm not very optimistic that two people of your opposing temperaments can get along in such a challenging task."

Becca rolled her eyes. "What's the bottom line, Doc?"

Ignoring her, he turned to the questions.

"Here's an example," he said, pointing to question eleven from the Agree or Disagree section. He read the question out loud.

"When a discussion turns to the subject of my feelings, I change the subject." He turned first to Edward. "Edward, you disagreed. So you don't have any trouble talking about your feelings?"

Edward gave a good-natured shrug. "No." Actually, since he had been raised in a home where nobody expressed anything and the people he was surrounded by never talked about anything personal, the complete answer to that question was that, since Arthur's death and his coming to terms with his instant fatherhood, he was aware of a longing to talk to someone. His brief time with Arlene Reinhart had fulfilled this feeling. But this test left no room for explanation.

Dr. Ben's expression showed his approval, then darkened as he turned to Becca.

"Becca, you didn't answer this question. Why not?"

"I didn't want to talk about it."

He shook his head sadly.

"We had a similar problem here on number twelve: 'It is

easy for me to see things from someone else's point of view.' Edward, you agreed."

Edward nodded his head.

"Becca, you didn't answer this one either. Why not?"

Becca threw her shoulders back and her chin forward, defiantly.

"It's vague."

"How is that vague?"

"What things? Whose point of view?"

Dr. Ben shifted uncomfortably in his seat. "Why does that matter?" he asked.

Becca gave an exasperated sigh. "It matters. End of discussion." She looked at her watch. "Come on, Doc, we don't have all day."

Dr. Ben turned the tables. "You slowed things down yourself, Becca," he said, "by leaving so many answers blank."

She tossed her shoulders carelessly. "They were bad questions," she said. "That's not my fault."

Dr. Ben strongly disagreed. "Number six here is very typical. 'My weaknesses are my own business and I hide them as much as possible.' Your choices were '*strongly agree, agree*'—"

"Okay," Becca interrupted. "I remember that one. Of course I didn't answer it. What kind of question is that?"

Dr. Honeywell set his jaw. "The statement is perfectly understandable. So do you agree, or disagree? 'My weaknesses are my own business—' "

"It's ridiculous!" Becca said, knocking her chair backward as she stood and approached the doctor, whom Edward noticed shrinking back defensively.

"How can I respond to a statement like that?" Becca asked an imaginary audience of supporters. She began to pace across the front of the room, waving her hands in the air excitedly. "First, of all, the statement assumes I *have* weaknesses. I don't buy that. Maybe I *don't* have weaknesses. How would you know?" She looked into Ben's eyes.

He seemed small, seated under her questioning glare. But she didn't press the point. When Dr. Ben made no answer, she returned to her seat. Instantly she began to drum her fingers on her desk, making it clear to all concerned that she had better things to do. She didn't notice that Edward had fixed her overturned chair during her tirade.

Dr. Ben drew a nervous breath before speaking.

"Becca," he said, "even those with great strength have what . . . what I'll call . . . 'lesser strengths.' " Again, he illustrated his concept by hooking his fingers into quotation marks.

"Well you didn't ask the question about my 'lesser strengths,' " she said, making her own air-quotes, "did you? And even so, what business is that of yours?"

"I'll just put you down here for 'strongly agree,' " Dr. Ben said, making a mark on her test paper.

"And I suppose Eddie 'disagreed,' " she said in a mocking tone.

"Yes, in fact, he did," said Dr. Ben.

Edward shrugged. Becca's defiance amused him. He knew his affable nature was getting on her nerves, and he enjoyed the sensation. Edward Kirkland was known all over Manhattan as prime marriage material. He was accustomed to an unending rain of female flattery. Yet her subtle disapproval attracted him.

He admired Becca's graceful, proud neck that she held so confidently. Her shoulders were tight; she seemed to bear a lot of tension, and Edward imagined how a gentle massage would affect her.

She continued to drum her fingers on the desk as Dr. Ben flipped through the test sheets for their next humiliation.

Impatiently, she turned to look at her coguardian, wondering how he was responding to the doctor's inquisition. Edward, who was watching Dr. Ben with a lazy smile, looked positively careless. His legs were extended in front of him, feet crossed at the ankles, hands folded behind his head: He was the picture of ease and contentment. Although the chair was small for him, he seemed to have endless patience to sit in place. He might have been watching ponies run, or boats sail, or children collecting shells, judging from his relaxed poise. Becca shook her head with amazement.

Practically the only movement she saw Edward make was to remove his hands from behind his head to massage the muscles of his neck, or to tip his chair back from time to time. He wore a dark blue polo shirt that fit him comfortably, and when his long, tanned arms hung by his sides, they were calm and motionless.

Becca tapped and rocked in her seat, wondering what calls she had missed.

"Okay, folks," Dr. Ben called out, "a couple more questions here. We asked a simple question about hobbies, Becca. You drew a line through the blank space. Do you mean to tell me you have no hobbies?"

"Bingo!"

"None?"

"Right again!"

"What do you do on weekends?"

Becca squinted at him. "I work," she answered plainly.

He nodded, returning her stare a bit fearfully before picking up Edward's paper.

"Edward," he said, "you have an extensive list of hobbies."

Edward nodded. "I tried to be thorough."

"I was interested in the one you listed first. Dating?"

"Sure," Edward said, grinning. "I enjoy dating."

"It's not exactly a *hobby*, though, is it, Edward?" prodded Dr. Ben.

"What do you mean?"

"Well, establishing . . . personal relationships is a serious matter. It involves emotional interaction of some significant depth."

"Sometimes," Edward said, shrugging his shoulders. "Not always." His eyes were sincere.

Becca nodded. He had something there.

Dr. Ben was dissatisfied. The answer was completely unorthodox. How could he evaluate that?

"I wouldn't put it on a list of hobbies, Edward, as if it's a sport of some kind, like archery or swimming," he argued.

"Okay," agreed Edward, "scratch it, then. But I date just about as often as I swim."

"How often do you swim?" wondered Becca.

"Every day." Edward glanced at her, smiling. She shot him a quizzical look. Who was this clown? Didn't he work?

"Let's move on," said the psychotherapist, clearing his throat. "Edward, you have some other hobbies that are a bit more . . . conventional." His eyes scanned the page, and he smiled. "I should say that your list, Edward, is quite something. It's really . . ." he paused, searching for the right word. "Well, it's really *long*."

Edward shrugged.

"You enjoy fly-fishing?"

"Sure."

"Shooting?"

"Very much."

"Shooting what?" Becca asked, turning around.

"Whatever's in season. Dove, grouse, pheasant."

"You mean you're a hunter?"

"Sure, hunting, shooting, whatever you want to call it. The English call it shooting, and I guess I had that in mind. I'm just back from London."

Becca paused. She knew the CFO of the British Company, the prospective buyer was a renowned equestrienne and shooter. As Becca recalled, he headed a well-known hunting group, right outside the city. She considered; the sad imperative that forced her and Ed Kirkland to become ersatz co-parents might have fringe benefits. Perhaps she'd gain access to a social strata closed to her because of her background.

"Dogs," Dr. Ben was saying, "are another of your hobbies?"

"That's right."

"You described yourself as a stud-dog owner?"

Becca made a sudden snort of laughter. "You're kidding!"

Edward was perfectly composed. "That's right. I own stud dogs. Sporting dogs. I breed them."

"How nice," Becca said, still laughing through her words. "A stud-dog owner. Never in all my time have I met a *stud-dog owner*. Some schleppy dog owners, sure. But this is a first!"

"Great," Edward said, with the same easy smile.

Dr. Ben Honeywell cleared his throat, turning the page to where Edward had continued his list on the back. "Here's an interesting hobby. 'Riding to hounds'? Tell me about that one."

"That's fox hunting," Edward explained. "I go to Virginia for hunts in the late fall. Down around Middleburg, usually." He paused. "It will be really busy this year. They banned it in England. We'll have a big influx, I bet."

Becca's jaw dropped as she turned to look at Edward Kirkland. She was, by now, convinced that she had met the most useless person in the entire universe.

Edward turned to Becca with an enthusiastic smile.

"Emily should come down to Virginia with me this year.

The trees are beautiful, and the hounds love kids. She'd have a great time."

Becca imagined a silver-tray tea party of old Confederate ladies with those gruesome fox stoles clipped around their necks.

"I'm sure," she said, skeptically. She couldn't believe he was serious.

Dr. Ben was still fixated on Edward's hobby list. "Sailing?"

"Sure, I sail. Just recreationally, these days. I don't race anymore."

"And you travel quite a bit?"

"Sure," Edward said. He rubbed his temples, feeling a yawn coming on. He needed to get outside.

"Can you give us some examples?"

"No problem. I mentioned London; I go to England in the fall, to shoot. That's pretty regular. Sometimes I go to the art openings in Paris, but only if it's someone I know. And I keep a yacht off Mykonos. We sail from there to some spots in the Mediterranean."

"You said *we*," Dr. Honeywell shrewdly observed. "Do you travel with a companion?"

"Sure," Edward answered casually. "With a variety of them. I really hate to travel alone." He turned his calm, pleasant eyes toward Becca, who stared straight ahead. She was occupied with a single idea.

"I see," said Dr. Ben. "Mostly European travel, then?" He forgot where he had been going with this, from a psychological standpoint, and hoped by talking to pick up the thread.

"Mostly," Edward agreed.

Becca couldn't hold her fire any longer.

"Do you *work?*" she asked, the disdain in her voice indicating her extreme doubt.

Edward nodded. "I do. I manage the Kirkland Philanthropic Foundation. It's a charitable trust."

"Who does your investing?" she asked in a flash.

"Milton Korrick at Morgan Stanley," he answered.

Becca nodded with approval. Milton was trustworthy: a good old shoe. But she could get better returns than Milton, she was sure of it.

"I'll skip the rest of these hobbies," Dr. Ben said, flipping through several pages, "so we can get on to the essays."

"Listen," Becca interrupted impatiently, "did I pass this test or not?"

"The evaluation has not been completed," Dr. Ben answered evasively.

"Whatever."

"No, it's not 'whatever,' " he rejoined, looking strictly at her. "These questions are designed by experts to evaluate your fitness as a parent."

"I read the statute," Becca answered back. "I know I meet the minimums for parental fitness. I have no drug offenses, no felony convictions, a good employment record, plenty of money, blah blah blah." She picked up her phone to check its LCD display.

"Ten messages!" She held it up. "You see that, Doc? Can we move on?"

"We're almost finished," he finally disclosed to her, not concealing his own relief. "We have just one more topic."

"I'm all ears," Becca prompted.

"You were asked to write short descriptions of your mother and father. Your answers are positively *alarming*."

For the first time, Edward interrupted. "I didn't expect you would read those answers out loud."

"Well, Edward, there is no reason for you two to have secrets from each other—especially about *parental issues*. You will soon be parents. Together." He looked through raised eyebrows at Becca, as if to say "unless I change my mind." She took the cue and turned her impatient glance to the floor.

101

"Ahem. Edward, we'll start with you. You described your mother briefly. I'll quote. You called her 'sweet and needy, like jelly.' "

Becca laughed out loud. "Yikes! What a description! That's great! I never would have guessed it from you, Ed!"

"What is needy about jelly?" Dr. Ben wondered.

"Have *you* ever eaten jelly just plain?" Becca cut in.

"No," he admitted.

"Of course you haven't. You eat it on blintzes. Because it's no use on its own. That's what he meant. Right, Eddie?"

He nodded, avoiding her eyes. He really didn't mean for her to hear that answer.

"Edward," Dr. Ben cut in, "let's talk about your father."

"I'd rather talk about blintzes."

"I'm sure." He turned to read from the test paper.

"Edward, you described your father as, and I'll quote— 'a cross between an executioner and a Stalinist colonel in an occupying army.' "

Edward nodded without emotion.

Becca laughed. "That's great! You have a real way with words!"

Dr. Ben was not so amused. "Do you have brothers and sisters?" he asked.

"Dad executed them on their eighteenth birthdays," Edward said coldly.

Nobody spoke.

"Just kidding," he said, breaking into a grin. His easy laughter relieved the tension. "No executions, no brothers, and no sisters."

"Do you have much contact with your parents?"

"As much as they please."

Becca rolled her eyes. To Dr. Ben, she joked, "I bet he still wears short pants at Easter!"

Dr. Ben sighed, ignoring her comment. These two were hopeless.

"Let's turn to you, Becca. You described your father more briefly."

Becca answered the question herself. "Two words. Sperm donor."

"Not a lot of contact with your dad, then."

"Less than none. And that's too much."

"Okay," he said, "so there you have it. And your mother. You said she is perfect. Do you care to elaborate?"

"Could I *make* that any stronger?"

"Right," he said, making a note on his page. "So we see where your loyalties are, in the parental category."

Becca laughed out loud. "Doesn't take much detective work," she returned.

"No," he conceded, glaring at her. "I suppose it doesn't."

Edward's eyes went from one to the other as Dr. Ben and Becca sparred. The doctor didn't have a chance in this contest. Their eyes met for a moment and she smiled.

Dr. Ben checked his watch, then stood. "Time to head back to the courtroom."

Becca brightened. "Did we make it? Did we pass?"

The therapist's shoulders drooped with misgiving as he nodded yes. He hated to do this; it was so contrary to his clinical judgment, but Becca was right about the statute. The personality test was a chance to talk through some "issues," but on a minimal level both of these oddballs were psychologically fit to serve as child guardians under New York law.

"As a clinical matter," he felt compelled to add, "I have *never* seen anyone named as a guardian whom I consider less fit to become a parent than you, Ms. Becca Reinhart."

Instinctively, Edward rose to her defense. "I think you're wrong. If you knew her . . ." What was he talking about, he asked himself. He had just met her! Still, there was an expansiveness and vitality that drew him to her—and that he hungered for in his own childhood. Edward thought

Becca was a natural. Anyway, what did it matter? They made it!

Becca cracked a ballpoint pen inside her purse with the huge effort it took her to keep quiet.

"Nonetheless," Dr. Ben continued, glad to feel his tension dissipate as he vocalized his anxieties, "you do meet the statutory minimums. How you plan to care for a four-year-old child between your phone calls"—he pointed to Becca—"and your social life," he said, shaking his head at Edward, "is beyond me. But it is literally *beyond* me, because it is up to you two from here." He left the room in an exasperated shuffle.

When he was out of sight, Becca rushed toward Edward, raising her hand for a high-five.

"We did it!" she said happily.

He grinned, slapping her hand.

"Nice job, Ed, you didn't let him rattle you."

"I think *you* rattled *him*," Edward said. "Let's go get our little girl."

Edward waited for Becca to gather her things. He held the door as they left the examination room together.

Chapter 10

Home Sweet Home

Not finding it wise to split the baby, Judge Jones had, for practical purposes, merged her caretakers. When Edward and Becca took Emily home, the child's soft, trusting hands linked her baffled but well-intentioned guardians. Together they stepped from the cab in front of the Stearns' Fifth Avenue apartment to begin an uncertain life. All Becca knew, as she stood facing the apartment building, with one hand on her phone and one hand on her child, was that instinct would have to guide her from here. Edward and Emily were as unfamiliar to her as a couple of kangaroos. Edward especially.

He didn't pay for the cab, she reflected, smiling—his mind seemed already to be elsewhere, as he scooped the radiant Emily in his arms and held the car door for Becca's exit. She slid a ten through the window as she departed. She didn't mention it to him, but she thought it odd. Was he absentminded, or just that accustomed to his private car?

But they were in this together, to some foreseeable extent. It would not help Emily for her new parents to antagonize each other. They had to agree on her care. Becca took a deep breath, glad that he had put Emily down to walk, glad she had the girl's hand to hold. She heard her Jimmy Choo pumps clicking along the sidewalk to the tune of Emily's "Ba-Ba-Black Sheep." Funny she picked that one, Becca thought. It described all of them nicely. Three black sheep.

With the cheerful, flush-faced Emily skipping and singing between them, Becca and Edward proceeded to the Stearns' penthouse apartment. Becca pressed her fingers against the cushioned buttons of her telephone; Edward's free hand rested in the pocket of his wool gabardine trousers. For a minute, as they waited to speak to the doorman, they might have been three passengers at a train station, standing close but disconnected, each occupied with personal thoughts.

The doorman, who was relatively new to the building, recognized Emily. Edward and Becca introduced themselves as her guardians.

"Mr. and Mrs. . . ." asked the doorman, waiting for their name.

"Reinhart," Becca blurted out. She turned toward Edward awkwardly. His laugh did not reassure her.

"And Kirkland," she said, pointing at Edward.

"We're not married," he explained.

"Just legal guardians," Becca added quickly. "Together by accident."

Emily looked up with a sudden gasp. Her blue eyes were wide with worry as she gripped Becca's hand in hers. Was Becca leaving her too? Was she dropping her off with the doorman? The child clung to Becca's arm and spoke in a small voice.

"What's a guardian, Becca? Are you going away? Who had an accident?"

Becca saw Emily's worry, and her heart surged with warmth.

"Did I say accident?" she stammered, leaned toward Emily. "Oops! It was an accident!"

She lifted the child into her arms, tickling and poking her. Emily looked at her skeptically.

"A guardian," she said, thinking fast, "is like a fairy god-mother. I'm specially picked just for you, Emily. By—by the fairies," she added, thinking of her storybooks. "I'll always take care of you. And so will Eddie," she added quickly.

Emily's soft, thin arms grasped Becca's neck. It was like being wrapped in the wings of a bird. She lay her cheek against Emily's hair and looked into the doorman's eyes. Did he need to see anything else?

"Send your names down so I can change them in the book," he said, returning Edward's handshake.

Becca promised to send down the court summons, the only paper she could think of that had all their names spelled together. At Edward's instigation they pretended to be lost, and Emily was proud to take over. She led them into the elevator and pushed the top button, *all by herself.* Then she practiced her numbers, saying each out loud to the rhythm of the beep when the button lit up at each floor. She could count higher than twenty though, as a result of living at the penthouse level, she was under the impression that the number twenty-one was followed by the "number" P.

While Emily counted, Edward leaned toward Becca. "Nice footwork with the guardian thing," he said. "So am I the fairy godfather?" Edward asked with a laugh.

Becca faced him with a smile. "Beats the witch or the frog."

She and Edward swung Emily over the crack between the elevator and the rich, gray-carpeted floor, and she sprinted to the door of the apartment. Becca unlocked the door, noting again that Kirkland didn't budge. So she'd have to teach him how to open a door where there is no butler. Just great. But like so many other points in this guardianship, there were no other options. For a while, and depending on how they arranged things, this building was their home.

She was a *joint custodian:* The awkward term made her laugh, as if she guarded spliffs of marijuana with a push broom in her hand. Judge Jones had concluded the proceedings by awarding Becca Reinhart and Edward Kirkland joint custody of Emily Stearns. She found the parental fitness of the two guardians to be the same, without specifying whether their scores were equally good or bad. She didn't care how they arranged their schedules, but set a few standards to be followed for the care of the child. Even the minimum—and the judge made it clear that she was talking about a minimum—represented a huge change in the lives of both Becca and Edward. Someone was telling them where to sleep.

As an initial matter, Judge Jones would not permit Emily to be moved from her apartment. The judge agreed with the child psychologists. A change of environment would needlessly unsettle the grieving child. She didn't care how the guardians arranged their schedules, but obviously at least one of the two would sleep at the Stearns' apartment, so Emily could rest with the confidence that Becca or Edward would be there when she awoke, even in the middle of the night.

It was *permissible* for them to continue with hired help, during the day, *if need be,* the judge declared; but the way she said it, squinting with narrow eyes through her rectangular reading glasses at Becca, in particular, made her disapproval clear. At another point in the ruling she strongly advised against "contracting out" Emily's care at this crucial moment for her healing heart. She would revisit that issue in three months at their status conference.

The mention of fairy godparents had fired Emily's imagination. "Let's go read the princess stories," Emily said, grabbing Becca's hand to tug her to the playroom. There the fairy tales, in young children's editions, were kept in a white bookcase.

Becca looked helplessly back at Edward, who shrugged, walking to the morning room where he reclined in a soft armchair. "Call me if you need me," he said, just quietly enough to make it possible that nobody heard him. Taking a deep breath, Edward folded his hands behind his head and closed his eyes, intending to give Becca a few minutes alone with Emily before he took the child to her last afternoon lesson.

Becca agreed not to peek while Emily changed into something "fancy," and she took the moment to walk around the playroom. She was struck, noticing the effort someone had taken to put this all together, with a pang of regret at the loss of her friend Amy.

Amy had made this room into everything a little girl could dream, and not out of any egoistical ambition to relive her own childhood either, Becca knew. By Amy's description, her youth in the state department was a makeshift cocktail of anything convenient and available. Her parents were assigned to a different country every two years, and all their houses, even to this day, were rented. But here, in this tribute to a child's imagination, she saw where Amy had channeled her love: The room was an onslaught of twinkling stars and dreams, almost desperate in its desire to please by dazzling.

The walls, meant for coloring, met at the ceiling where there was a mural of abstract forms representing the moon, the sun, clouds, stars. The mural was painted in blue against which the objects of yellow and silver-gray shimmered across the floor, on which lay a green rug with a floral border. Small chairs were set around the table where the puzzle had been opened. At one edge of the rug stood a bright-yellow wooden boat, large enough to hold two adult passengers, where a princess might make her escape from the two-level castle that presided over the room from the corner.

The overall effect of the room was a cross between Romper Room and a New Orleans bordello, which perfectly approximated the dreamy, confused perspective of girlhood.

There was a tea table, nestled in another corner behind hand-painted silk screens, featuring a mini-buffet with small porcelains and a miniature Georgian silver tea set gathering dust on a tiny mahogany sideboard. The tea table was little-used, as was an accompanying dollhouse, so intricate it must have been built to emulate some great manor house to the very last light switch. These items felt out of place.

Becca wondered if Arthur had provided the dollhouse. It would not have come from Amy's nomadic parents. She wondered how it was that she had spent so much time with Amy and so little with Arthur. Edward seemed to know Arthur primarily from the club, and from their old school days together. She didn't remember Amy ever talking about Edward. She wondered if Amy and Arthur had spent much time together at all.

Announcing herself with much fanfare, Emily appeared in a lavender gown of layered silk tulle, wearing a towering, triangular crown, which was secured by a silver sequined chin strap.

Becca's laughter was sincere and bottomless. Emily had relaxed a thousand percent since their trip to Hong Kong, and the child proved an uninhibited performer. Emily had taken a fancy to acting fairy tales out as they were read, so when Becca read "dragon" she bared her teeth and leaped from a rose-colored love seat that sat beside the castle (suede cloth, Becca noticed—Amy was always practical). And when Becca read "princess" she made the blinky eyes of a mooning and helpless damsel, clutching her heart with a hundred sighs.

The painted castle, which demarcated the "fairyland"

corner of Emily's playroom, had an interior staircase leading to its balcony. This fixture drove Emily's imagination to ecstatic heights as she raced up the stairs to be the captured princess. In the next instant, without removing her towering hat, racing down the stairs to charge around on the white hobbyhorse and plan a rescue.

Edward, who instinctively drew toward the sound of frivolity, entered the playroom with a good-natured smile.

"I heard there was a damsel in distress," he said, approaching Emily's castle balcony.

"The damsel is learning to look out for herself," Becca said, turning a devilish eye to Edward. "She's got everything a girl needs, so she's decided to expand her empire."

"Naturally," he returned in the same tone, his eyes meeting Becca's. "But I'll rescue her all the same." With a firm step he swept Emily from the balcony, twirling her helicopter-style until her feet flew inches from a brass coatrack draped with marabou feathers and sequins.

"I promised Emily we'd go to the Carlyle to visit my dogs today," he said, smiling as her eyes brightened with excitement.

"You have a *dog* at the Carlyle?" Becca asked, squinting at him in amazement.

He nodded matter-of-factly. "I have three. Emily's friend is MacDuff. I've had him forever. He used to hang around the marina, where I kept my sailboat, but the marina captain didn't want to take him when he moved back to England. He's really friendly: a golden mix with some setter, I think. We'll take him for a walk, and we can get dinner there together," he offered.

Emily jumped like a puppy, and Becca, unsure whether Edward meant to invite her, looked at her watch. She needed to get to the office, she announced hastily, as if someone had accused her of taking it easy.

"No problem, chief," Edward reassured her. "I'm the

anchor man tonight." He smiled at Emily's gown, thinking how proud he would be to walk his warm, friendly old dog through Central Park with Emily.

Becca squinted at him. What language did he speak?

With Emily's hand in his, Edward turned to leave. Becca hurried a step after them, carrying a tiny faux-fur coat. "She'll need this at night." She kissed Emily good-bye, and promised to leave a surprise in her room if she got home too late to say good night.

"Don't worry about us," Edward called out behind him.

"All right," she answered cheerfully. But as the apartment door shut, leaving her alone, Becca was filled with a sudden sense of apprehension. She hadn't yet left Emily all to Edward. She walked to the window over Fifth, hoping to catch sight of them, and in a minute saw Edward helping Emily get all her skirts into the back seat of the cab.

He was well built, she noticed, as he ducked his head to climb in behind Emily. He had a very individual air about him: She didn't quite have a handle on it yet. She didn't sense any fire, any of the brutal instinct that she saw so often in her business. Instead she noticed in him a calm, unhurried attitude, a sense of comfort with himself. Her eyes widened as she wondered if he had brought any cash for the taxi.

Shaking her head to regain her focus, Becca began to hunt for a place to run her DSL line. She had been plugging in, using Amy's phone line and using an ISP. But now she needed permanency. She surveyed the wood-paneled library first. It was too dark, too warm. She paused to regard the pictures on the bookshelves; fresh-faced Amy and Arthur in active pictures: beautiful sun-dappled waters rippling over rocks, patches of shade, wet, green banks with all their abundance. Amy was holding a fish; Arthur was holding a fish; Amy had a snake on her neck; Arthur had a goose upside-down by the feet. Arthur was holding Amy.

Becca turned away. She noticed a cigar box, a chess table, an eternity of books. It was strange, she thought, pausing curiously. No pictures of Emily.

She moved to the music room, which was lovely, but so formal, with the baby grand piano and the antique wind instruments on a stand by the silk curtains. It felt too stiff, as if it rented out for receptions. Better to keep that as a sitting room, Becca thought, for Edward to use. He probably received guests in rooms like this.

She opened a bedroom full of boxes, and closed it quickly, but not before seeing the names Amy and Arthur written on the boxes. It occurred to her for the first time that someone had packed up the couple's things. She had not been to the apartment before today since leaving for Hong Kong, and Emily had pulled her straight to the playroom.

With a burning feeling in her throat, Becca realized that Edward might have seen to the packing. She felt ashamed to have left that responsibility to him, embarrassed, before this man she knew so little, to reveal what appeared to her as her own immaturity. She had never really *managed* a death before, never picked up the pieces. She realized she had overlooked Edward's relaxed ability to take control and her underestimation of him felt like someone inside her had laughed at him in a cutting way. So much for her judgment of people. Her cheeks colored as she resolved not to think about the matter any further. She drifted around the apartment still looking for a place to hook up the computer. It was then that she saw the note and recognized a familiar handwriting. No—it was impossible. Her mother was a planet away—but it was definitely Arlene's handwriting, or a forgery.

Becca—everything is under control, so don't worry— relax and enjoy your new adventure. Edward and I organized the packing and storing of Amy and Arthur's stuff. Be nice—Edward is wonderful.

—And single, Becca knew her mother meant.

In one of the apartment's six bedrooms she found a wall with a phone jack that would work. She measured the wall with her forearm, marking the length fingertip to elbow with a pencil before measuring again. She knew the length, as measured by her forearm, of her desk and credenza. She could get a computer, printer, and phone along the long wall, a file cabinet and credenza on the short wall, and still have a nice view of the park, if they ran the DSL line through the wall to the rear. On her mobile she called and left a message for the property manager to set a date for installation.

Becca entered a guest bedroom. It was furnished comfortably, and she took the opportunity to sit in a crimson-and-gold upholstered chair. Unplugging the telephone from the wall, she unfolded her laptop on the matching ottoman. It was essential to check in before she set foot in the office. Becca did not like to be caught unprepared by the first person to catch her in the hall announcing, "Did you get my e-mail?"

While she waited for a connection, her mind turned to what the judge had said this morning. The proceeding, after the personality test, had gone pretty quickly and almost without surprise. Almost.

Becca's mind returned to the vexing matter. Of the many surprises of this extraordinary day, the bizarre turn of the proceedings into an inquisition about marital status had, for Becca, been the least expected.

To confirm her findings of fact, Judge Jones had asked Becca and Edward to confirm that they were, in fact, each single. Both confirmed that they had also been single at the time of the Stearns' accident. It was a surreal moment:

Becca remembered having the thought, like a student caught napping, that the judge was just testing them to see if they were paying attention. But it was no joke. Judge Jones followed by asking, on the record, if either of them had any current plans to get married—specific plans, affecting the near future.

Becca took the question first, and in tribute to her long-suffering mother, she replied that she saw no advantage in getting married. She didn't have time to take care of *two* children, she said.

Nobody laughed. She did mention to Judge Jones that Amy, Emily's mother, had never married Arthur, Emily's father, and she felt comfortable that Amy left the child to her knowing that she was likely to follow a solitary path.

Frowning, the judge turned to Edward, who answered simply, with an easy smile.

"No, Your Honor," he replied. "I'm not the marrying type."

Becca had a tendency to resist being denied anything—even something she didn't want—so she asked the judge stubbornly what difference it would make if she did tie the knot.

State law in New York was clear, the judge replied, that where guardianship of a minor is at issue, a two-parent custodial household provides superior opportunities for the child's physical, emotional, and behavioral development over the long term. So where a choice is to be made, a guardian in a two-parent household gets preference over a guardian in a single-parent household, for permanent custody.

"Well, we're both single," asserted Becca, with a glance at Edward, "so we share Em's custody, right?"

The judge nodded, but prudently raised a finger as she hemmed her answer with technicalities.

"Your award of custody is probationary," she cautioned

them. "I'll follow the wills to the letter, for now. But we have a status conference scheduled in three months. If your marital status changes, before then, either of you—*I will reconsider how that affects the child's permanent placement.*"

"What will you consider?" Becca's eyes were suspicious.

The judge made herself clear. "If one of you decides to marry, Ms. Reinhart, it will be in the best interest of the child to move permanently to custody in the two-parent household."

"So whoever marries gets Emily?"

The judge nodded. "It's simply in her best interest."

A peculiar tension clouded Becca's mind. What strange incentives! But Edward was not the marrying type, and she had nothing in view. After the status conference, which was down on the calendar for early December, the judge would award permanent custody. Considering the path her thoughts had taken, Becca paused and took a deep breath. Why was she so tense? The hearing was only three months away. Nobody got married in three months.

Chapter 11

Kosher Is King

Becca, Emily, and Edward arranged to meet for brunch the next morning at Katz's deli, in what Becca considered a "strategic planning" session. She had spent the early morning in the office preparing her agenda. Her analysts had completed gathering helpful information on four-year-olds from scientific journals, pediatric Web sites, and the annual reports of Disney, Fisher-Price, and FAO Schwartz. They could hardly stop laughing long enough to give her their summaries, a fact that raised Becca's stubborn streak. She could do this.

She cancelled a dinner date for that night: some Jack Pearson, a reinsurance executive at AIG. Philippe had called with her regrets, then buzzed her to report that Pearson had drawn his "line in the sand." This was her second cancellation of their long-planned dinner. She would have no third chance.

She laughed, replying to Philippe that it was Pearson who had missed his chance, and resubmerged in the on-line archives of *Parents* magazine. She printed instructions for making an octopus from paper plates and crepe paper, reviewed the basics of the crab walk to confirm that her arms were, in fact, supposed to be straight behind her, and not upside-down in the manner of a backbend; ordered a tiny green set of doctor's scrubs in the hope that she could get Emily past the princess stage by Halloween.

Last night when she returned, Edward was asleep in a guest room. He left a note on the table in the morning room, which had all the indications of becoming the family's bulletin board, to let her know how the night had gone. Emily was asleep by herself in her own bedroom, he reported. They had read the tale of *Sleeping Beauty*, though he had skipped over the scary parts, and Emily lay sleeping softly and peacefully, imagining herself in the lead princess role.

Becca was impressed. It was her experience that Emily, though a sound sleeper, was not a willing one. The first night before they went to Hong Kong, Becca had stayed in the apartment, although the nanny was still in residence, thinking that Emily might wake up looking for her parents. Becca had slept in the master bedroom, and Emily had run to the room in the night, seeming more confused than frightened. Becca's heart warmed as she welcomed Emily to cuddle on her mommy's side of the bed, thinking tenderly that she was the child's security and protection. She drew the letters of Emily's name on her back, talking calmly to lull her to sleep.

It was cute for about five minutes. After that, the restless child flipped around and peppered Becca with stories so odd and unrelated that their only object must have been delaying the onset of sleep. She asked questions without waiting for answers, climbed up to the headboard and plunged down with a jarring bounce, tickled Becca, blew on her face like a wet sea breeze, wiped her nose on the sheets, rolled and tugged at the covers, burrowed underneath like a gopher and then became scared of the dark, and generally made herself a nuisance. When Emily finally fell asleep, as Becca explained to her the concept of current account balances, her head rested like a stone on Becca's outstretched arm. So petrified was Becca of waking Emily that she left her arm in place, not allowing herself to move until the pins and needles tingled so severely she thought she might have lost her hand.

In Hong Kong she had been lucky. Either two beds in the same room made Emily feel more secure or the time change and jet lag were acting in Becca's favor. She got a few nights of sleep.

Emily woke early in the morning when she heard Becca taking a shower. It was five-thirty, but time means nothing to a child who wants to wake up. As she had promised, Becca had left a present—a miniature globe with only one country—Hong Kong and its islands, as seen from the sky. She had hoped the globe might preoccupy Emily for a little while, but no dice.

Since Becca was not available, Emily headed for the nanny's room. On the way she spotted someone else sleeping. There was Edward! Emily pounced on him, so happy that both he and Becca were here with her.

"Get up, get up!" she yelled, so loud Edward thought the decibel level must be higher than at Giant Stadium. "Uncle Eddie, please, I'm hungry. Becca's not here."

Not here? Did Ms. Reinhart go to work at 6:00 A.M.? Now he was in motion. If he was the guardian in charge, then he better snap to.

The child was standing by his bed, singing "Rudolph the Red-Nosed Reindeer" at the top of her lungs. Edward sensed that Emily was grieving in this way—making herself heard and making sure she was the center of attention. He reached out and grabbed her into his arms. This quieted her. He sat on the edge of his bed in his gold-colored silk pajamas and rocked his little girl.

Just then he heard footsteps on the staircase. "Who goes there?" he shouted, and Emily laughed.

"It's Aunt Becca, silly," said Emily.

"But you said she was gone."

"I went to thank her but couldn't find her in her room. She brought me a ball that spins with Hong Kong on it."

A globe? Edward thought. Medicine ball from China?

"It's a globe." Becca was on the staircase, close enough to hear.

"Aunt Becca is here, Uncle Edward is here—and me. We're just like a family."

Becca's heart hurt when she heard this. The poor girl.

"We're the hungry bear family," Edward said, obviously trying to distract her. "I'm baby bear, you're poppa bear."

"That's silly, Uncle Eddie."

"Momma bear says come downstairs for breakfast."

"The refrigerator is empty." What an idiot he was, he told himself. Why hadn't he shopped? There was no reply so he began gathering his clothes from the overnight case he'd brought from the Carlyle. But Emily started tickling him and he tickled back until he heard a strange noise from the phone.

"Who goes there?" Emily imitated Edward. "It's the innercomb."

Innercomb? He ran his fingers through his sleep-tossed hair. The buzz intruded again—Intercom! Becca Reinhart was paging him—practically ordering him to appear in the kitchen. Edward Kirkland wasn't sure how to respond— pick up the phone and ask her politely to slow down? Pick up the phone and with his rarely used icy tone tell her she was not to buzz him ever again—or maybe he should just go along with her for now. Edward picked up the phone and rang back. The handset clattered, obviously having slipped out of her hand.

"Hey," she said eventually. "I have to get to my office. I want to make sure Emily eats breakfast before I go."

"I can take care of Emily." His tone was a challenge.

She hesitated and then Becca said, "I just wanted to see

her, Eddie. Make sure she's okay this morning. I got used to doing that these last few days."

Edward melted. His whole body changed—his posture lost tension, his face dropped the frown and went back to his habitual smile.

"I'm in pajamas."

"I've got to go. The car is downstairs. Both of you meet me for lunch—one o'clock, Katz's deli."

Emily had lost patience entirely and she grabbed Edward's hand, pulling him down to the morning room at breakneck speed. They arrived just in time to see the door close behind Becca. "I'm hungry!" Emily was getting cranky and Edward was at a loss without a hotel catering staff. He guided Emily to the table where they found two glasses of something other than orange juice. Thick yellowy orange. He hoped it wasn't from the pitcher he'd seen before. "Gava—Aunt Becca remembered. It's my favorite."

Guava, he realized. A glance around the kitchen and a peek in the refrigerator told him they weren't going to go hungry after all. Becca had seen to that.

"Sit, drink your juice." He realized Emily had dressed herself before waking him. She must have awoken in the middle of the night. Her overalls were a little crooked and the shirt underneath was a white dress-up shirt, but otherwise, she was fine.

Emily held up her glass, now empty. "You drink yours."

He had no idea what guava juice tasted like, but he was game—so he drank a few sips. It was disgusting, heavy with bits of fruit. On the table was a note: "Boxes of cereal in pantry. Also microwavable oatmeal. Sweet rolls. Milk, etcetera. See you at lunch!" Then there was a P.S.: "I am Arlene Reinhart's daughter. I take it you've already met her. Food is like air—you are never without it." It was signed "B" and then that was crossed out and she'd written "Becca."

His glance at the clock gave him a flashback of the mornings he had spent training for crew. Until now he had never thought of that as a very long time ago. Today it seemed like another life. He was not living only for himself anymore.

After more coffee than he usually drank in the morning, Edward and Emily went downtown. By the time they met Becca for brunch, Edward was carrying a large bag from FAO Schwartz with tutus and sequins poking out of it. Also, Arthur had ordered a four-foot pink teddy bear, which the store was sending over. They reached the restaurant ten minutes late, which, for Edward, was a prompt arrival.

KATZ'S DELI
"Where the Kosher Consumer Is King"

Edward looked inside the deli with anticipation. The only "kosher" he knew was a pickle, but he could smell wonderful food cooking halfway down the block. Though he had eaten already, Edward had a natural tendency to accept pleasant things in life that were offered to him. His appetite was stirred.

Becca, fueled by her coffee, had not eaten a bite. She had covered the hard topic of discipline this morning with the information from her analysts, and was satisfied that four-year-olds were essentially angelic creatures whose main function was to strive for acceptance. The experts recommended using something called a "time out," which was more or less the penalty used for high-sticking in hockey, and she wanted to talk to Edward about where in the apartment they might set up a penalty box.

Barry Katz, the deli's owner, was as friendly as he was round. Becca Reinhart was a regular customer for whom he had much affection. She had arrived early to tell him about

Emily, and Barry was eager to meet the new "daughter." The white-smocked teddy bear emerged from the kitchen after Becca called for him, his arms waving happily, his wide, red face warm and inviting. He invited Emily to dye bagels in the kitchen with kosher food coloring, and nearly collapsed with shock at her answer.

"What's a bagel?" she asked him innocently.

"It's like a doughnut, Em," Edward explained, "but harder, like it's stale."

Becca was sure that Barry would have a heart attack.

"Like a doughnut?" Barry threw his hands out wildly. "Who is this dummkopf?" He pounded his balding head. "He has the brains of a bagel!"

Becca laughed, first at Barry, then at Edward. She reminded Emily about bagels, the heavy bread things that made Becca's purse smell like onions. She stood and whispered something to Barry, who softened, and smiled.

"Be nice," she had whispered. "He just doesn't *know* better." She glanced at Edward's tweed blazer, starched collar, belted khakis, and cordovan loafers, summing him up in a quick wave of her hand.

"All right, Becca," Barry returned, offering his pudgy hand to Emily, who took it after Becca nodded permission. His tone was unconvinced, and he flung Edward a frown before trudging back to the kitchen.

Edward looked around him with curiosity. He felt like a man from the moon.

Becca gave him a sympathetic look. She didn't want to be too tough on Edward. He meant well. She sat down quickly, before he had a chance to politely rise. Soon she'd have to abolish that practice.

"Forget about it, Eddie. Let's get to work." She pulled a red pen out of her roomy black Fendi bag. "The first thing we need to do is to define our mission statement for Emily."

He laughed out loud, but she ignored him.

"We're talking at this stage about her growth as the first priority," she continued, shuffling through a file of hand-written notes, "though moral development is important too. The main contributor to growth is eating. I have a few ideas about that."

She handed him a piece of paper. Grinning, he folded his menu closed and glanced at her bullet points. She had highlighted certain topics: *Protein Builds Muscle, Passing Fruit Off As Dessert, The Benefits of Milk*. He laughed when he saw the circle with exclamation points around *Vegetable Strategies*.

"Very thorough," he complimented her. His bright blue eyes shone as he smiled at Becca; his gaze was steady and calm. What sadness he felt for the past few days, Edward seemed to have internalized into his natural good balance.

"We have Emily's language development to consider too: essential in controlling impressions. We need to build brand identity now."

"Brand identity?"

"Image, personality, whatever you want to call it," Becca fired back, waving her pen in the air as she talked. "It's a highly front-loaded process. Once a positive brand is in place, a kid can go miles. With good image projection and placement, she'll pick up share every year."

"Share? Market share? Of what, the playground?" Edward couldn't finish for laughing.

Becca nodded, making a note with her pen.

"I have a caution flag here. The trusted brands are simple: simple personality, simple message. One look, and you know what you've got. Kleenex. Kellogg's. Xerox." She dropped her eyes to consult her bullet point. "Here's the danger with Emily." Becca looked Edward in the eye to deliver the bad news.

"Confused message."

He shrugged. "What do you mean? I think Emily's a great kid."

"She's great, of course," Becca said, frowning, annoyed that Edward brought up this non sequitur. "Emily's the best. And from what I've read, she's ahead of the game. Early talker: That's a plus. But we have to be careful. The kid is developing a screwed-up language identity. I think we ought to pull her out of the French classes."

Edward gave her a funny look. He had always heard that kids absorbed language best when they were youngest, but he didn't want to argue. Edward was a patient soul. He had long experience of sitting quietly while a monologue whistled past his ears. Without speaking, he looked down at his menu.

The waiter and Becca noticed at the same time that Edward had looked at his menu. The waiter approached at once, and Becca turned vehemently to scare him off. She waved him off like a pigeon.

"I'll tell you when we're ready!" she shouted.

"*Eyngeshparter!*" he shot back.

"Don't *eyngeshparter* me," Becca returned. "You're as stubborn as a ram."

"Am not," she heard him fling over his shoulder.

Turning calmly to Edward, she continued delivering the lecture that had resulted from the past ten hours of her research. The current literature said that kids could suffer in their self-confidence if they lacked a clear language identity.

"When did you pick up your Yiddish?" Edward asked her.

"What?" Becca laughed. "What does that have to do with anything?" She tried to frown at him, but her eyes revealed that she knew she had talked herself into a corner.

"When?" he pressed his point with a frank smile. "When you were little, I'll guess."

She turned her eyes down. "I've always known it."

"I rest my case," he said, lifting her hand from his menu. "Don't worry about the French lessons."

"But French is different," she protested.

"*Je ne suis pas d'accord*." Edward grinned at her blank face. "I disagree," he said with a laugh. "Do you think I've lost my brand?"

She shook her head. "No way. You're still Joe Ivy."

He smiled, offering himself to win his point.

"So she sticks with French?"

"All right," she conceded. "But French is your action item." She handed Edward a blank pad and a pen.

"Thanks." He laughed, returning his pen to the table.

It annoyed Becca that Edward didn't write anything down. What if he forgot? She leaned across the table and wrote his action item on his notepad.

"Before you get too far down your list," Edward interrupted, touching her hand gently, "Let's order."

Jumping at the chance to put Becca in her place, the waiter hurried to the table when he saw Edward motion for him.

"Whaddaya want?" he demanded.

Edward rarely ordered off the menu. He was surprised that the waiter hadn't yet mentioned the day's specials.

"Special service today," snapped the waiter. "We'll bring it right to the table. So whaddaya want?"

Edward gulped, and ordered something ordinary.

"I'll have pancakes, with a side of bacon," Edward tried. "And a latte."

"Ha!" The waiter took his pencil off the pad. "*Chazer!* Is he kidding?"

"He'll have the blintzes," Becca took over, "and potatoes on the side. Eggs too?" she asked, turning to Edward.

He held up two fingers. "Two eggs. No potatoes."

The waiter turned to Becca, scribbling on his pad with his eyes locked on hers.

"What about you? The honey cake?"

"No," said Becca, "A strudel for Emily, and *leber mit tsibeles* for me. Make it hot," she added, lowering her eyebrows. "Last time I had to send it back."

"All right!" the waiter fired at them, slamming his spiral closed. "So I'll be a minute! Who's in such a hurry?"

He stomped off to the kitchen.

"What am I having?" he asked politely. He couldn't remember anybody ever ordering for him. Even when he was little his parents would have told him what to order, then put him on the spot when the waiter arrived, like a little bird taught to sing on demand.

"Oh, the usual. Cheese-filled, crispy pancakes, eggs. The pancakes are called latkes—but actually, forget about it— you don't need to know latkes, the blintzes are better. And don't even say the *word* bacon. No pig. Got it?"

Edward nodded, letting Becca's words roll over his ears. She talked an awful lot. As he watched her turn her eyes back down to the paperwork she had prepared, becoming absorbed, for the moment, in the details of her own thoughts, he stole the chance to watch her thinking. It was only in stolen moments like this one that Edward had gathered his impressions of this blunt beauty. Her hair, shining and dark as a blackbird, fell in loose layers that brushed her shoulders. Her charm had an accidental quality that stunned him: it was different in nature, not in degree, from the powdered and pampered tribe that he knew. She had a practical efficiency about her, a casual grace.

His glance traveled over her tapping fingernails—no polish, he noticed—and he caught sight of the notepad she had brought for him. The only writing on it was hers. The pen she had flung next to the notepad was ordinary and worn. Her pen was the same, a Bic. He had a feeling that they were stuffed chaotically in a crammed desk drawer, dime-store ballpoints next to sleek fountain pens—

Becca's corporate gifts. Why was he so sure that Becca Reinhart got no particular pleasure out of acquiring things? Why did she seem detached from the usual pursuits: self-contained in her intensity?

His gaze had rested on Becca long enough for him to conclude she was paying him no mind. Suddenly, her eyes flashed a welcome. She threw her head back with a merry laugh.

"Emily!" she called.

Emily Stearns skipped from Katz's kitchen toward Becca and Edward, squealing with excitement. Her hand-smocked dress was soaked with green food dye. Becca's eyes met Edward's. She smiled. This was going to be fun.

Chapter 12

So Make Time

Together they ate, and when they had gathered enough bread crumbs from Barry's kitchen for Emily to feed a whole army of ducks, they took a cab to the south entrance of Central Park. While Emily scattered crumbs, taking not a few bites herself, Edward broke the news to Becca.

"Emily already *has* a schedule," he said, sitting on a bench and inviting her with a pat on the seat to join him. "I don't know what we'll do with these action items of yours. Really, she has almost no free time."

Edward reached into his Orvis bag for the copy of the schedule he had gotten from the nanny while Becca and Emily were in Hong Kong. They would not have time to breathe. And since Becca had summarily discharged the nanny, not wanting such a disloyal employee to stay on one minute longer, there were only the two of them.

"We'll have to divide this up between us," Edward reminded her, handing her the schedule to look over. "What days are good for you?"

Becca's face fell. She didn't answer. No day was good for her.

She remembered what her mother had told her, and her cheeks colored with a mixture of shame and resolve. She handed him back the papers.

"Let me rearrange my schedule. I'll make time," she promised quietly.

Edward smiled. He appreciated her willingness.

"I think Emily needs to spend time with us right now," he said. "She needs to trust us."

Becca nodded silently in agreement. Her eyes turned to Emily, who was squealing with excitement as a green-headed mallard waddled close to her. She felt a sudden and surprising sense of relief, as if she had already cleared something, some obstacle to embracing this child, just by declaring that she would make the time. She turned to Edward, and noticed that he, too, was watching Emily with pride and pleasure.

Her eyes rested on his boyish face, and she wondered, suddenly, where he had come from. She had never really known Arthur, having lost so much of her day-to-day contact with Amy since the college days when they traveled together. After Emily was born, she renewed her contact with Amy, but they always met in the park with the baby, or had lunch. Becca had gotten the idea that Amy needed to get out. She had lost the chance to get to know Arthur, and wondered, suddenly, if he were anything like his friend Edward.

She felt at home in Edward's company: a peculiar feeling, as she hardly knew him, and nobody like him. Not personally—if she met someone upper crust through business—boundaries were set, nobody's real self was revealed. He turned, meeting her eye, and she looked away quickly.

"We'll be fine, Eddie. All it takes is scheduling. If we can schedule it, we can get it done."

She probably talked to her staff that way, Edward thought, reclining, to the extent he could, on the wooden park bench. He stretched his arms behind his neck, the chipped bench yielding with a slight bend behind his strong back. With a sigh, he massaged his neck and shoulder muscles, sure that Becca underestimated Emily's schedule. He wondered how bullish she would be when she saw the sheer number of Emily's classes, groups, lessons, and activities. He had a sinking feeling that Becca would have to make more time than she bargained for.

"So, what's on the program?" she asked him, having resumed her coach's voice as she reached for the papers he had withdrawn from his flat envelope-sized, rich, burgundy leather briefcase.

He kept the papers in his hand.

"Her day planner is all in French," he explained. "I didn't have time to copy the whole thing. I'll translate."

"I know some French," said Becca, defensively. But she didn't object when Edward read it to her.

Edward put on his reading glasses, then removed them as a sudden thought occurred to him.

"I forgot to mention this weekend. Sorry, but I'm flat-out booked. You'll have to cover for me."

Becca raised her eyebrows. "What's your conflict, Eddie?"

"It's been scheduled for ages," he said, grinning with anticipation of the event. "I'm playing in the member-guest tournament at the Racquet Club. I already have my times—well, my first round times. The finals are Monday night at seven. Labor Day. So I am out of pocket until Tuesday morning. Probably late morning would be best. There's a great party after the tournament on Monday night. It's a holiday, you know."

Becca's jaw dropped. Was he kidding?

"A holiday," she said, looking down at the table. "You're joking. What's that?"

"No, seriously," Edward said, trying to help. "It's a federal holiday. The markets will be closed."

"Markets closed? The bell-ringers might take the day off," Becca laughed, "but it's a workday for me."

"Why?" Edward asked. She saw innocence in his eyes.

"Every day is a workday for me, Eddie," she answered simply.

They were miles from each other. He saw the determination in her eyes, and he knew that she didn't understand who he was. She was not so open-minded, he thought suddenly: She doesn't know that there is more to life than what she has already concluded. He saw himself, in her eyes, as she must see him: He felt shallow, like his reflection.

She stared into his eyes, searching, for a minute, and as he pondered her expression, he thought he saw her sharp, glittering stare yield to something different. He saw warmth in her eyes, but as soon as he noticed the spark of tenderness, it was gone. The suggestion of her soul had flickered before him like a candle, and gone out. The flint was back when she spoke quickly to him.

"I'll take Emily to work this weekend. Don't worry. She'll have lots of fun. Play your tournament—hats off, or whatever you people say. Talley ho. We'll have a great time." She waited for him to thank her.

Edward gave a simple nod. "Okay. So I'm off for the weekend, and back on board Tuesday."

She stared at him, nodding silently.

"I *am* busy," he heard himself saying. He called out to Emily, patting the bench to invite her to sit with them. Emily declined, finding that the grass in front of the bench, in a little clearing shorn of trees, functioned like a shadow box, with the sun almost directly overhead. She stuck out her arm to point out a snake creeping in the direction of the duck's crumbs, and chattered about the great battle that was in store.

Becca withdrew a large, worn Filofax from her bag and got ready to make notes of Emily's commitments. Edward could see that her pages were already full of notes. Having recently reviewed his swirl of cotillions, benefits, and galas

132

with Alice, Edward had a good sense of his own commitments. He would be flat-out busy once the event season kicked off after Labor Day. Evening galas tended to tie him up until the early morning hours—past the time Emily's day had begun. And the four-year-old's days were booked by the hour.

"How about—you take Monday through Wednesday? I'll do Thursday and Friday, and we'll wing it over the weekends," Edward suggested.

Becca's smile dropped. "Eddie, I can't, not this week," she said. Her tone was gentle, apologetic, but without room for discussion. "I'm out of town Wednesday," she added. She flipped through her Filofax and began to read from it, as if it took the matter out of her hands.

"I'm booked on the early shuttle into Boston to start a day of back-to-back board meetings. Then Thursday afternoon I'm in Pittsburgh to review an RFP proposal for one of my portfolio companies—an aerospace firm. NASA has a big exclusive provider deal up for bid. If we get the nod we'll be in Annapolis to meet with one of the admirals who got us on the approved vendor list. Then we'll do some site testing."

Edward met her eyes with an even stare. He was holding a highlighted page of Emily's day planner. "I don't know what to do, then, Becca," he said. "You've got to cover Wednesdays. Emily has playgroup in the one o'clock slot, and the nanny left word that it's very exclusive—mothers only. She couldn't even go."

"Mothers only?" she repeated in disbelief. Who did that sort of thing? Didn't people work?

He nodded. "It's called My Special Playtime." The sound of the group made him laugh, and Becca laughed with him.

"You're kidding."

"Not even a little," he assured her. "So Wednesdays are all yours."

Becca slumped into the bench, trying to visualize My Special Playtime.

Edward smiled, pointing at Emily, who was wearing on the patience of the ducks by throwing bread crumbs to tempt them and then racing for the prize herself, laughing to see them flurry away, at which point she would throw the bread at them all over again.

"The nanny said most of the playgroup kids are also in Opera for Tots, so you ought to go to that one too. Or the other mothers will think you're avoiding them."

Becca dropped her chin into her hands. "When's the opera class?" she asked.

"It meets Tuesday at five, but there's a voice warm up and soft-drink cocktail reception beforehand at four. The nanny said it's a must."

Becca, uncharacteristically silent, continued to stare ahead.

Edward continued. "The mothers provide refreshments. They rotate. Next week it's your turn. They are studying German opera, so the snack should be culturally appropriate."

"No problem," Becca said, noticing the street address on Edward's schedule. "There ought to be a hot dog stand in shooting range. We'll call them wieners."

Edward laughed. "That ought to do it. The rest of your schedule is pretty well laid out here. French for Tots, Fairy Tales in Motion. . . ."

He handed Becca the schedule, on which he had scribbled the class names.

"Tap for Tippy Toes, Creative Parent-Child Clay Play," she read. "I don't believe this."

Edward gave an accepting shrug. "It could be fun."

Becca nodded, but her eyes were wide with apprehension. Her tone changed from hope to exasperation as she noticed the schedule continued on another page.

"I also get Piano for Pee-Wees and Tiny Tumblers?" Edward nodded.

"What do you get?" She held him in a suspicious glare.

"I knew you'd ask," he laughed, handing her his list.

Becca laughed out loud. "Flipper-Toot Swim Splashers? Little Squaws Singalong? Weaving and Believing?" She tried to imagine Edward taking the lead in "Princess Yoga," and her eyes teared up with laughter.

Birds less desirable than mallard ducks had begun to swarm Emily's crumb feast. As Edward gathered Emily's schedule into his bag, he spotted the file of school applications.

"Emily has some school interviews coming up," he observed casually. "Towards the end of the month. The applications are in, that's the good news. But we pick up right at face-time, you know, when we have to make nice with the admissions people."

Becca stared at her Filofax, unable to close it. The reality of inheriting a child with her own prescheduled life was hitting her hard.

"What's wrong?" Edward asked, leaning down to let Emily climb onto his back. They actually moved faster when he carried Emily piggy-back than when the dawdling dreamer walked on her own, stopping at every tree to search it for angels or elves.

In answer, Becca handed him her calendar page. She recited it from memory.

"I have conflicts. Next week I'm in town on Tuesday, but on Wednesday I'm supposed to testify in Washington, D.C., before the Senate Finance Committee. They have a hearing on volatility in the financial markets."

He breathed in heavily. "We'll figure something out," he said, without much force.

"I'll be back on the shuttle that afternoon." she offered. "But I have meetings until late. Then I'm in town Thursday, but Friday I'm on the red-eye to Paris. I have a meeting with the head of the Bourse to talk about the two companies we'd like to take public in France. Then I'm staying to give a talk at a dinner Saturday night. Topic is the convergence of computing and communications."

Becca stared straight ahead. Her expression was dark. She had left Sunday open, but she was sure the Bourse meetings would go through the weekend. From Paris she had an open ticket; but she had wanted to stop in Stockholm. Hong Kong was fun, with the kimonos and the chopsticks, but she wasn't sure Emily would find Stockholm so interesting, and they'd be on airplanes practically every day.

"Stockholm?" Edward was surprised at the extent of her travel.

She shrugged. "The European Union's finance ministers and central bankers meet there on Monday. They're changing EU law on bank capital adequacy regulation."

She took a nervous breath. She really didn't *have* to go. She was not a participant in the conference, but she was always there for the big meetings.

Make time, she heard her mother's voice echoing. Emily was tapping her shoulder for attention. She was reading letters, trying to sound out the words of a street sign.

"I'll skip it. The weekend will be cleared," Becca muttered. "Sam, one of the partners, was going with me anyway; I'll just ask him to handle the meeting." She swallowed hard. "He can give the convergence speech. I already wrote it."

He looked at her gratefully.

"Forget about it," she said, stopping him before he could speak.

"What are you guys *talking* about?" demanded Emily. She was growing insistent, as she had noticed a bird that seemed to be from dinosaur times and wanted to show off the word *pterodactyl*.

Becca reached over to tickle her.

Edward paused. A good judge of people, he knew how much could be gained with humor when no other avenue looked promising. He leaned down to let Emily show the dinosaur bird to Becca, and impulsively picked up his pen to scribble on the spiral pad Becca had given him. When they resumed their walk he gave the page to Becca.

"What's this?"

"Your new schedule," he told her, grinning.

She read it out loud. "Monday: Cancel Your Other Commitments. Tuesday: Make Friends in Group. Wednesday: Be Nice to Edward."

"I haven't gotten to Thursday, yet. Do you want to cook dinner for us?" he asked, teasing her with his smile.

Her eyes flew open. "Cook?" She laughed, shaking her head no. She couldn't gauge how much he was kidding.

"How about quit your job?" he tried.

She gasped in shock.

"All right," he said. "I'll put you down for ballet."

Becca's beautiful, loose hair swung around her shoulders as she laughed. Take her with you, again her mother spoke from the place Arlene reserved inside Becca's head.

"Why don't we take this week by week? Don't worry, somehow I'll cover my commitments. I wonder if grand-mothers can go to the mothers-only meeting."

Edward took Emily's hand and demanded that Becca go check in at her office. He had resolved to take his little girl to the Racquet Club. He was suddenly hopeful that she had a talent for squash.

Chapter 13

The Zeitgeist

Edward's tournament started that Friday, so Emily went to the office with Becca. She had covered every inch of her dazzling ruby ball gown with yellow and blue tape flags when Dick buzzed Becca's intercom. She scribbled a few edits on a report from her energy sector analyst, then went to meet with Dick. She laughed to see Emily gathering her skirts to make her entrance in the fanciest possible way.

"Congratulations to the new mother!" Dick said. She shrugged off his hug with a friendly smile.

"Thanks," she said, "but here's the real star," she said, lifting Emily, who beamed at the pleasure of meeting new people in all her glorious dress-ups.

Emily smiled and waved one hand silently in the fashion of Miss America. She had learned this move in MiniModels, a premodeling program that she took over the summer. The class was designed to ensure success in preschool social environments. They had, for example, spent a week on strategies for parallel play. Boys were advised to make an impression by lifting large things with ease; girls were taught to lock in a smile and wave blindly to passersby.

"She's a perfect *beccisima*," Dick pronounced, pinching the air to put emphasis on his Italian.

Becca smiled proudly. "That's my girl!"

They had entered Dick's office just as he was celebrating a perfect nine-foot putt, achieved from the low point of his putting green. The golf ball was a lucky one, marked with the crest of St. Andrews. Dick pumped his fist in the air victoriously.

Emily raced to the putting green. "Cool!" she exclaimed.

With a quick switch to a plain, dispensable ball, Dick handed her his putter and let the child try her hand at golf.

"Becca!" He flung one arm around her neck, once again welcoming her with a chummy hug.

"What's with the love-in today?" she asked, brushing contact dust from her sleeves.

"I see motherhood hasn't softened your edges," Dick said, smiling. "Hi, Emily." He extended his hand. "Nice to meet you."

Emily, face down on the putting green, waved her hand.

"Emily, meet my boss, Mr. Davis," Becca said, laughing at the sound of Dick's formal name. "Dick, my fairy goddaughter, Emily Stearns."

Emily's manners class kicked in and she turned, switched the club to her left hand and stuck out the right. Looking way, way up so she could attempt to look Dick directly in the eyes as she'd been taught, Emily shook his hand. Then went back to the green.

"Becca, Becca," Dick sang out. "If you knew what I know," he explained, dancing around her, "you would be singing!" He clicked his heels in the manner of the tin man on the yellow brick road, but without falling down.

"Impressive," Becca said, walking across the room to pour herself some coffee. "Your yoga classes are improving your flexibility."

"Two things, darling Becca," Dick said, gliding to his

desk. "First," he announced, cradling a file folder with an adoring look, as if it were a gift of the Magi, "the Santech deal closed, FDA approval went through, and twenty-four hours later your little New Jersey garage company is up 450 percent!"

He danced over to Emily, who by that time had discarded the golf club to attempt a more accurate, soccer-style putt with her ballet slipper.

Emily followed Dick's antics with eager eyes. "Dance, dance," she urged Becca.

Laughing, Becca agreed to be led in a celebratory waltz to the tune of Dick's own humming, the sight of which transported Emily Stearns into a happy trance. Emily's view of life, outside the oppressive moments when she thought about her parents, was a constant kaleidoscope of twirling, flouncing gowns and falling glitter. All the world through Emily's eyes, overseen from her shining turret, was achirp and aflutter, studded with rubies, galloping with stallions, glowing in magnificent splendor. The loss of her parents would find its place when it was time.

"It isn't easy, being rich," he sang with glee, turning his face upside down in front of Emily's dazzled smile.

Becca shrugged, but she shone with pride. "I told you I liked that company. One of a handful this year."

"It's almost unseemly, really," he returned dryly as he sailed by on the wings of a 450 percent increase in a three-hundred million initial investment. "Only the tax man makes returns like you do. And he puts nothing in."

"Who's the tax man?" Emily asked.

"You're happier not knowing," Becca answered. But Emily did not wait for an answer. She had retrieved the golf club, deciding it functioned more properly as a magic wand, and was pointing it at objects around the room.

Becca removed a book from the center shelf of Dick's perfectly functionless egg-shaped end table.

"Liberating Everyday Genius?"

"I'm mastering gifts I didn't even know I had," came Dick's response. He trotted from his desk with some reading material of his own.

"Which brings me to the second of the twin pillars of my astonishing news, Becca Reinhart."

"Aren't you the wordsmith?" she teased him. She sat on his boomerang couch and laid her espresso carefully on the coffee table in front of her knees. She wanted to be comfortable. From experience she knew that Dick would victimize her for a while with the most fashionable management theory of the moment. He had the virtue of believing so firmly in the jargon of self-improvement that he was unfazed by Becca's skepticism. He regarded her as his teaching opportunity.

Emily, lying on the putting green, was trying to roll golf balls down her arm into the cup.

"Becca," he asked her, shaking pages from a magazine with a flourish, "how is it that you're always on top of the zeitgeist?"

"I don't know zeitgeist," she said, her eyes sparkling, "but whoever he is I swear I wasn't on top of him."

Dick chortled, then sat next to her with the earnest look in his eyes that usually followed a meeting with his executive coach.

"You just *have it,* kid."

"Spit it out," she said, smiling.

He ruffled her hair. "You never could take a compliment. Beautiful thing about you. I met with Christine-Elaine Piper—my executive coach—yesterday."

"How is Coach Piper?"

"She's fine," he said, ignoring her mockery in his earnestness. "And from what she says, you're on to something."

Becca grinned. "Shoot."

Dick glanced at his aquarium, where Emily had dropped a neon golf ball into the water. Gulping back the acid reflux that affected him when his inner nervous old lady surfaced, Dick controlled the impulse to protect his tank.

He walked to the couch and squatted down next to it, so his eyes were staring close to Becca's, like a coach in the huddle.

"Kid, the zeitgeist," he said, speaking in a slow, firm voice, "is creativity."

"What?"

He laughed. "I wouldn't have guessed you a natural for it either. But the big idea now is associative thinking. It's *naturally* creative. It triggers the concepts that we need for more progressive management decision-making."

Becca, who had closed her eyes pretending to fall asleep, made a snoring sound.

He poked her. "Come on. I mean it. This is really influential stuff. The point of more progressive decision-making," he said with emphasis, "is to beat the market. Okay? That's the point."

She stared at him. "Dick," she said, "an efficient, publicly capitalized market works on the basis of all available information. It can't be beat. It can only be survived."

Dick laughed. "And if you believed that, you'd be a librarian."

It was Becca's turn to laugh. "Okay, so you can win on good days. What's your new angle?"

Dick pointed at Emily, who had climbed high enough on a tower of self-help books to peek over the side of Dick's tropical aquarium.

"Who has the most open, spontaneous, creative mind you know?" he asked her, still pointing.

Becca smiled. "The four-year-old with a putter in the fish tank."

"Exactly," Dick answered. His voice wavered as he

glanced toward his prized aquarium. Emily had dug the golf club into the tank's colorful gravel, trying to get her golf ball through the fish bridge.

Dick, in the sway of the creative-thinking hype, clapped his hands to encourage her.

"Eureka! Do you see that, Becca? She's playing through! That's the name of the game, now, Becca. Creativity! It's the zeitgeist! The very *spirit* of executive success."

With a crash, Emily's golf club punctured the glass. The tank shattered in an instant, making an extremely creative sound. The water purifier hummed, spinning dry air, dulling the sound of six dehydrating fish flopping on their last fins.

"I'm told that mothers learn to be experts at crisis management," Dick said to himself, watching Becca race to the fish tank to make sure Emily didn't get cut.

His carpet was littered with broken glass, colored rocks, strange plants, and exotic fish. It looked like the parking lot at a Grateful Dead concert, and smelled worse.

"Don't just stand there," said Philippe, who had heard the crash all the way down the hall and raced in. "Fill the sink!"

The three of them conducted a hasty fish-rescue while Emily watched in awe. The perfect storm left no casualties. While Philippe whisked Emily down to the kitchen to get an orange soda, Dick and Becca held their noses to mop up the carpet.

With most of the damage cleared, Becca sank into Dick's womb-chair.

"To think I came in to ask for a couple of days off," she said, shaking her head. "I have some parenting to do."

Dick smiled generously. "Anything to keep you away from my fish tank."

"What fish tank?" she said. She took a sniff of her wet sleeve and made an awful face.

"The one we're wearing," he said, looking nauseous. With sudden concern for the integrity of his womb-chair, he asked her to stand up and step away from it. Becca hurried toward the door.

"So I'll be in, oh, I don't know, next Thursday?"

"Make that Thursday two months from now," he offered suddenly.

"What?" She squinted at him, unsure if she heard him right.

"Paid leave," Dick explained. "Administrative. Listen, kid, with the Celex deal you're already ahead of your last year numbers. If you don't take a break, you'll personally originate over half our profits! I'll move Philippe over here and we'll be fine."

Becca smiled proudly. "Why would you pull your first string quarterback, if she's having the game of her life?"

"To save her for next season," Dick answered. "And to give your teammates some time on the field."

She nodded. She could trust Dick not to have any hidden agenda. "Full pay?" she asked.

"Of course. Come into the office once a week or so and check in. I'll call a special meeting of the management committee and we'll approve it this week."

Becca paused, shocked by the generosity of Dick's plan.

Emily, who had a sugary orange mustache, rushed to the door to tug at Becca's leg. "Can we play now? Becca? Pleeease?"

Dick raised an eyebrow, indicating it toward Emily with a nod of his head.

"You never know, Becca. I think you'll be busy enough."

"All right," she agreed, "I'll take the time off. Promise me you'll get a new carpet with my year-end bonus. Not to mention a fish tank."

"It's all right," he said, waving casually at the mess on

144

the carpet. "I'm over the fish fad." Becca smiled at him and left the office.

After a minute, Dick stepped into the hall and called out after them. "I wanted to redecorate anyway. The thing now is jungle cats!"

Chapter 14

Le Petit École

Becca, Emily, and Edward stood together in the crisp afternoon air, surveying the red, white, and blue paneled door of Le Petit École, Manhattan's exclusive French-immersion preschool. A nondenominational, international, fully bilingual preschool, Le Petit École was accredited by the International Baccalaureate program's Primary Years Program. It was the Sorbonne of nursery schools.

Though they faced another door into the unknown, Becca and Edward stood undaunted, waiting cheerfully, squeezing Emily's hands and laughing together. The three had grown playfully comfortable together over the past couple of weeks, and they looked upon the school's bright tricolor with a sense of amusement. They knew too little to be afraid.

"Cute playhouse," Becca noticed, looking through the window at a Provençal-style chateau that sat at the far end of one classroom, complete with blooming windowboxes of flowers and wooden chickens that swung slowly on springs to peck for imaginary seeds.

Edward agreed. As they waited, he glanced down at the school's brochure, then gave a quiet laugh.

"What?" Becca asked reflexively. Like Emily, who was tickling the palm of her hand, she hated to be left in the dark.

He showed her the school's preachy "vision statement."

"Whatever they mean by inquiry-based, transdisciplinary learning," Edward read from the English side of the bilingual brochure, "I bet they have great food at parents' night!" Tipping his head back, Edward breathed in the delicious scent of chocolate and croissants that drifted from the building.

Becca still had doubts about dunking Emily headfirst in French, but Dick Davis, whose children had languished on Le Petit École's waitlist until they were almost too old to attend, gave the preschool his highest compliment.

Dick's wife, Leslie, had shepherded their kids through this process not too long ago, he explained to Becca, when she had stopped by his office that morning to see his safari-themed redecoration. She had not yet adjusted to her time off, and was still having a problem not attending meetings. But Dick absolutely insisted that she attend the school visit with Emily. She had to *promise* him.

"Both parents always attend the school interviews," he cautioned her. "It's a given."

"Calm down, Dick," Becca said, laughing at the urgency in his voice. "It's just preschool. We thought she'd have some fun there, make a few friends."

Dick was astounded at her naivete.

"Fun? Friends?" He shook his head emphatically. "You've got it all wrong, Becca. This is the day that will decide the rest of Emily's life! It will virtually guarantee her place in elementary school."

Becca remained unmoved.

Dick felt his blood pressure going through the roof. He thought of Becca as his protégé even though she was often one step ahead of him. The explanation of the realpolitk involved in the process of getting children into New York preschools wasn't exactly something a senior executive was meant to pass on. Nevertheless, Dick felt that his role was to find a teachable moment here.

"Seriously, Becca," Dick said, rubbing his temples with the sudden stress of recalling the preschool rat race. "Take it seriously. Every parent in Manhattan *dreams* of sending a kid to Little Eton! Its yacht racing team wins the fourth grade division every year."

Becca did not conceal her surprise.

"They teach yacht racing to fourth graders?"

"That's only the half of it," he laughed. "Sit down, kid. Let's get rid of that wool over your eyes."

She sat, her arms folded.

"Le Petit École traditionally feeds into Little Eton. You can't miss a shot at Little Eton. It's the best day school in the city. It's hidden in the southeast corner of Central Park, between the zoo and the pond. You can almost see it from your window."

"I didn't know there was a school there."

"It's the only one with a variance. And it's not just a school, Becca. It's Shangri-la."

Becca burst out laughing. "Not you, Dick," she teased him. "Caught up in a flashy image? I don't believe it for a second."

"Listen, Becca," Dick insisted, drawing toward the couch where she sat, "the school is so perfect, at first I thought it was just my delusional fantasy. Let me tell you how it works. It's more than just image."

Becca sunk into the couch as Dick began to regale her with Little Etonite lore. According to Dick, whose kids were Etonites, the place was heaven on earth. Its primary school curriculum was based on the open-ceiling British system, which allowed the brightest children to move ahead of the pack at whatever pace was set by their private tutors. The students' little brass-buttoned blazer jackets and navy wool jumpers, which were designed by Ralph Lauren to feature the school's unique coat of arms, were only the beginning of Little Eton's dapper charm. At sixth grade graduation, the young boys stood straight as arrows to recite Shakespearean sonnets. The little girls, carrying single red roses as they proceeded down the aisle in white lace gowns, wore wreaths of lavender and baby's breath in their hair. Delightful!

The school's behavioral standards were strict. Ten polite, snub-nosed, shiny-combed boys and symmetrically braided young girls stood stiffly by their desks to greet the teacher when he entered the room each morning. (The teachers were all male, in the manner of wine stewards at fine restaurants.)

Onward the footsoldiers marched through their structured days. The little gentlemen wore embroidered beanies on the practice field, where they tried their small hands at morning cricket, and the little ladies donned white gloves for lunch! In art class they designed their own tartans! From the dining hall to the handbell choir, Little Eton was a charmed circle. For parents, anyway, and they paid the checks.

Dick's children had attended Little Eton since kindergarten, which was one triumph he could share with his illustrious style-rival, leverage-buyout wizard Henry Kravis.

Becca scoffed to think of children more concerned with afternoon tea than multiples, but Dick assured her that it was an important step on the road to the Ivy League.

"British, Shmitish," Dick said. "That's all marketing. The best thing about Little Eton is that it feeds to St. George's. You have to start early."

"You can't be serious," Becca protested. Was it this bad?

"Let me put it this way," Dick said, stepping to his putting green. "Le Petit École gets you a tee time. Little Eton takes you down the fairway. Groton gets you up on the green, and 'tap' "—he nudged an imaginary golf ball—"you chip one in for a birdie at Harvard." He pictured Little

Eton's manicured cricket greens, windy yacht races, crew regattas, and for a minute, thought he might cry. Parents had so much to look forward to!

Becca shook her head with sympathy. Poor Dick was always chasing the right image. She promised to go, teasing Dick that she would get a seat in the back and make some phone calls.

She was surprised at how severely his face had clouded. Even for Dick, he seemed incredibly earnest. He warned Becca to take the process seriously. She was walking into a firestorm, and she was treating it like a Sunday stroll in the park.

"Whatever you do, Becca, don't screw up the interview. You're lucky to get it. Make sure the kid is ready. Every step of school competition is more cutthroat than the last. If she blows it at preschool, she's sunk."

Becca shrugged. "I'll be myself, Dick. And so will Emily, I hope. She's a great kid." She checked her watch.

"Where is she?" asked Dick.

"She's playing Hansel and Gretel with my staplers," Becca said, laughing. "They've probably left a pretty long trail by now. Wish us luck!" She turned to leave the office.

Dick shook his head. He had a bad feeling about this.

"Hey," he called after her. "Don't forget, you're being evaluated too."

"Like hell I am!" Becca called back. Did he really think she could care what some Polly Do-Good in a Happy French playroom thought of her? It was already a bad joke to have competition for kids not long out of diapers. But asking her to put on a sash for the parental beauty contest was too much.

Five or six families had assembled at the schoolhouse door to wait behind Becca, who had elbowed the way forward for Edward and Emily, unconscious of the resentments she created in pushing ahead to stand as the "line leader." Though each parent had the stomach of a pit trader, the manners of a tea party were supposed to prevail.

As Dick had predicted, two parents stood with each child. The children were scrubbed, fidgety, and bored. Becca noticed the parents greeting each other warmly, like old friends. They all seemed to know one another.

Edward smiled and waved to several of the mothers, who greeted him with enthusiasm.

"You get around, Eddie," Becca observed under her breath.

He grinned at Becca.

"They're all in French for Tots with Em. I took her last week, when you did the speech at the World Trade Organization. Remember?"

One swarthy, heavyset father threw a shoulder and edged Becca out of the path to the door. A look from Edward suggested that she let it go, and she unclenched her fists in time to clap with the others when the merry doorbell tune of "Frère Jacques" rang in the air.

The parents enjoyed a laugh, a delightful relief in the atmosphere of nervous apprehension.

"Will we have to speak French?" Becca asked Edward.

"Probably," he whispered back. "The brochure says it's a school for the whole family. You speak a little, don't you? I thought you said you spent some time in Paris on a bank deal."

Becca had spent a few months consulting with French banks on their compliance with the Basle capital adequacy framework, but she was pretty rusty.

"No *problemo*," she answered. She noticed Edward cringe slightly before giving her his polite smile.

"It'll come back to me when I hear it," she promised.

The man who had edged Becca out to ring the doorbell made a show of shaking his injured right hand to draw

151

attention to its splint. "My wrist!" he complained loudly. "I sprained it writing checks to the French tutor!"

His unbearable joke drew sympathetic laughs.

His wife spoke up quickly while her daughter dove like a mole into the folds of her coat.

"Nadine sings 'Frère Jacques'—both verses—with the most *authentic* accent. And it's not *all* because of the tutors. The summer we spent in Nice did wonders for her pronunciation. I knew that trip would be a great investment!" An unpleasant thought occurred to her, clouding her eyes like a stage curtain. "You wanted to go to Bali," she spat at the check-writer.

"Not now, dear," he hissed back. "Shut up and be charming."

"Delightful, delightful," she sang to nobody in particular. Young Nadine, for all her pronouncing prowess, had yet to emerge from her mother's coat.

"Are you ready, dear?" her mother coaxed. "Practice makes perfect!"

A shy "*oui, oui*" was spoken into the coat. Nadine appeared to be shaking. Her hands were white.

"She'd better be ready, for what it goddamn cost," her husband snorted, checking the time on his massive gold Rolex.

A woman standing next to him, whose sweet dripping Boucheron perfume attracted the notice of a half-dozen pigeons, pulled her daughter protectively away from the crowd. The child, her fearful eyes blinking back tears, cuddled the mink-lined edge of her mother's jacket and began to suck her thumb. The father followed.

"Work with me, Madeline," her father implored her. "It'll help my Newport Yacht Club application if you get in. Wouldn't you like to play with Babette, in the game room? Wouldn't you like to go sailing with Daddy?"

The child screamed.

Becca's phone rang. Parents stared at her with disapproval.

"Is that me?" she asked with mock surprise. Only Edward gave a polite laugh.

She answered the call in a clear, businesslike voice that echoed loudly, as the other parents had quieted and held her in their hostile stares. Becca, consumed by the topic of her call, was oblivious of the reaction she created.

Edward gently stepped forward to hold her place in line.

"Forget it, Jack," she said.

A cuckoo clock screeched two, and the school door swung open. At once the crowd of parents erupted into an instant smiling contest. A minute later, the children, poked in their little backs, were smiling too. Except Emily. She was pacing behind Becca, imitating her gestures, waiting for her turn to use the phone.

"*Bonjour!*" greeted Penelope Hobnob, director of admissions. She glared at Becca, shaking her finger.

"Rule one on the classroom visit, as you might have read in our handbook," she snipped. "No phones."

Becca nodded without answering. She held up her finger to indicate she'd be finished in a minute. "I'll get to you in a sec," she said in Penelope's direction.

Penelope glared, standing with her hands on her hips. She clearly meant to hold the waiting parents hostage to her silence until Becca put the phone away.

"Listen, this is a bad time, Jack. But the answer is no. And don't you *dare* go around me. If you find anybody at Davis to pony up for this one, I'll have your—" she glanced around "your, you-know-whats on the chopping block! *Capisce?*" She paused, then smiled, laughing out loud.

"Great. I'll call you this afternoon."

Becca handed her phone to Emily, who put it to her ear and began to speak with great animation as they both stepped into line.

"Your name?" the director asked Becca.

"Becca Reinhart," she answered. Emily gave Becca's leg a big hug.

"Charming, Ms. Reinhart. I'll be so interested to get to know you today."

Her eyes approached Edward's and stopped. "Why, Edward Kirkland. What a surprise! How is your dear mother?"

"Wonderful, Nellie. I'll send her your greeting."

Penelope Hobnob smiled warmly, overlooking the fact that the gauche Becca Reinhart was linked to dreamy Edward by the little hands of Emily Stearns.

As they entered the brightly decorated school, Becca's phone rang a second time. Edward volunteered to go in with Emily while Becca finished her call in the hall. Covering the receiver, she explained to him it was important for her to take this one. "I'll just be a minute," she promised, pacing down the flowered hall, which was decorated in the style of a French *jardin*.

Half an hour later, she rushed into the classroom.

Penelope Hobnob tore herself away from Edward's side, where she had been smitten with his colorful tales of the French Riviera, to glare at the hurried entering figure of Becca Reinhart. Emily rushed to greet Becca with a hug.

Monique Pegnoir, who taught the fours class to which Emily had applied, smiled maliciously.

"*Bonjour,*" she said to Becca. "*Comment vous appelez-vous?*"

Edward, pushing his familiarity with Nellie Hobnob a bit, threw Becca a life preserver by taking the question.

"This is Emily's other guardian, Becca Reinhart. Becca has traveled to Paris frequently on business."

Penelope butted in. "Ms. Reinhart, we at Le Petit École believe that parents . . ." she paused, considering Emily's situation, "or . . . parental figures . . . have a great deal to do with our students' language retention."

"Retention! Great! I believe in a very retentive family environment," Becca said with a laugh. "I'm highly retentive myself. That's what my analyst tells me."

Leonardo's father chuckled, earning a severe glare from his wife.

Penelope cleared her throat. She stared at Becca without laughing.

"All joking aside, Ms. Reinhart, it is important for us to ensure that some French will be spoken at home. Edward has done wonderfully in conversation with our group," she fluttered her eyes at Edward, who turned his face down modestly.

"*Enchantée*," remarked Becca, offering her hand to the admissions director.

Penelope paused. "Well, I am pleased to meet you too, Ms. Reinhart."

"*Je m'appelle Becca*," she replied.

Penelope smiled. "Lovely. Becca, while you were in the hall, we took a *pretend* journey. We have arrived in France." Penelope wiggled her fingers as if dispensing magic dust. She was suddenly inhabited by the persona of a small fairy.

"We visited the market, and we've just arrived at the drugstore. Now, I'm behind the counter. Would you like to ask me for anything?"

Becca thought fast. She was last in Paris over a year ago. There was that funny little drugstore. Why had she been there? What had she needed?

Penelope tapped her foot. Edward, behind the waiting figure of Penelope, was mouthing the words "*Je voudrais*— I'd like." Becca caught his eye.

"*Je voudrais*," she began, hesitantly.

"*Oui, madame?*" prompted Penelope.

"*Je voudrais . . .*" Becca repeated. What had she needed in that drugstore? She remembered!

"*Je voudrais un déodorant.*" She smiled.

The room erupted in laughter, but Penelope, with a stern expression, stayed on target. She stared into Becca's eyes.

"*Je regrette, il n'y en a plus. Vous desirez un autre chose?*"

Becca stared without speaking. Who did this lady think she was, anyway, testing the parents? Ridiculous. Becca could show off her expertise too. Is that what a classroom was for? Ready, set, *price this option in front of the class?* How would Penelope like that?

Having regained the upper hand, Penelope felt a wave of noblesse oblige. "If you're a little rusty, Becca, I understand. I said, 'Sorry. None left. Do you want anything else?'"

"*Oui, madame.*" Becca paused, thinking back to the consulting days in Paris. The sound of French being spoken had brought a little of it back to her. She remembered something. She had stayed in that hotel for over a month. She had needed. . . .

Becca smiled. "*Je voudrais des Tampax,*" she pronounced, savoring the silence in the classroom. "What's Tampax?" shouted Leonardo, prompting a chorus of questions from other curious children.

Becca was laughing out loud. "*Puis-je voir le directeur?* Can I see the manager? What kind of drugstore is this, anyway?"

"You may take your seat," Penelope snapped.

Leonardo's father bellowed with laughter. "You're terrific!" he joked. Seated next to him his wife's face had silently colored to a shade somewhere between crimson and violet.

A few other laughs were hastily stifled, and the room grew quiet.

"Ms. Reinhart, I'll see you after class. The rest of you are dismissed. *Au revoir*."

Drawing in her breath, Penelope pulled herself together to face Becca Reinhart. Shame about the kid, she thought, watching Emily skip out with Edward Kirkland. Emily Stearns wouldn't make the waiting list for any decent school in Manhattan after Penelope got the word out about this guardian of hers. The kid was finished.

Chapter 15

What You Don't Know

"I blew it," Becca admitted that night. They had ordered Thai takeout, and after Emily was in bed, Edward had opened a bottle of wine. At his suggestion they had gone to sit in the library, which felt, to Becca, a little too dark and quiet, but since she had no real reason to object, she followed him in and sat down in an oversized, comfortable leather reading chair. Dispensing with the ottoman, she kicked off her shoes and curled her feet beneath her in the chair.

"No, Becca," Edward consoled her with a gentle touch on her arm. "Penelope blew it. She went *mano a mano* with the wrong woman . . ." he broke off, unable to finish his thought as he laughed at the memory of Penelope's shocked face. "What was the deal with the imaginary French drugstore, anyway? And the fairy dust?" He chuckled, moving to an upholstered chair in the corner, where he set his wine glass on the chess table.

"Listen, Becca," Edward continued in a serious tone, "*they* blew it. They lost a great kid. Anyway, maybe you're right. All French at that age might be a little weird." Edward's voice trailed off again, and Becca caught his eye on the humidor.

"You want to smoke a cigar?" she asked him.

He sighed. "I took Arthur's cigars out of there; they're in a box. I couldn't really throw them away, but I couldn't really smoke them either."

Becca nodded. She understood. She wouldn't wear Amy's perfume. There were just some things you had to put a lid on.

"You were at school with Arthur?" she asked him.

Edward nodded. "We roomed together at St. George's, and then again at Harvard." He paused, and his eyes dropped low. "I didn't go to law school, you know," he said, as if it were a confession. "Arthur went to Yale, but, you know, I wasn't really interested."

Becca squinted at him. Who had to explain himself for not being a lawyer?

"Yeah," she said, taking the wrong inference. "I wanted to get right to work too. I got my M.B.A. in night school. I was just sick of having class, you know, *all day*. I wanted to get my feet wet, you know?"

His eyes rested on her affectionately. She was so different. In his mind flashed an image of New York City, a place as much his home, as much his background as it was hers. What a wide city it was. It suited her temperament perfectly: It didn't yield, but it didn't bear a grudge, either: it simply rolled forward. But the pleasures of New York, its abundance, its generosity, the charm of its world of interiors, of interior people: that was his.

Edward sipped his wine. They had another interview coming up with Emily, at another preschool. He forgot the name. He was thankful the application had been sent before the trip to Alaska.

He looked at Becca, whose eyes were shining with a memory of her own. Her hair was lit softly by the brass standing lamp; it was lustrous and dark. He wondered what it would be like to kiss her. What would she taste like? The scent she always brought into a room compelled

159

him to wonder about her, and the memory of it always stayed with him when she was gone.

But these were dangerous thoughts—inappropriate for sure.

"What did you like about school?" he asked her suddenly.

"What?" She looked at him with surprise. "What do you mean?"

"What were you interested in, when you were in school?"

She squinted at him, thinking. Then her eyes lit with the answer.

"I was good at math," she said, stretching her legs to the floor.

He laughed, sipping his wine. The books around them: Arthur's, mostly, reminded him of the reading room in Eliot House. The small, upstairs room, with a quiet perspective of the Charles River, the arched bridges. The books were leather-bound, with gold writing on their spines, so old you feared to open them, lest the pages flutter out and you find yourself responsible for the death of an original Milton.

He noticed that Becca was smiling, proud of herself for some achievement he had brought to her mind. She hadn't answered his question.

"But what were you *interested* in?" he repeated.

Her smile dropped and she scrutinized him. She did not understand.

"I was good at math," she said, in a louder voice.

His expression softened. Of course. She would do what she did well. She was practical: She valued achievement for its own sake. He wondered if she had any real interests. His eyes rested on her face, lovely in its confusion.

"I still am," she said, flushing. "I can do exchange rates in my head."

"Really?" asked Edward, smiling with pleasure. "Show me."

She converted the dollar and pound: the easiest, first, and moved on to the mark, the franc, and the yen. She wasn't sure how the euro would be valued, though that would happen soon. Edward began to test her, making up dollar amounts and watching her think them through to their foreign currency equivalents.

He laughed amiably, standing to refill his wine glass, offering to refill hers first. "You know I can't tell if you're right or not."

She nodded knowingly. "But I *am* right," she assured him.

He grinned. "I know."

He felt disappointed when she declined to have more to drink. She stayed, though, in the library with him, asking about his life, surprising him with the questions she asked. She was curious about his nightlife, the charity galas. Was the food good? What did women wear? And when did he decide if it was time to go to his home in Bermuda or England?

Becca would never have revealed to anyone that this information about the people, whose family had owned for generations the penthouse co-op they now inhabited, was of interest to her. Not even Arlene—actually especially Arlene—would never know that Becca read *Entertainment* and *Details* and, occasionally, *People* when she was traveling.

"Do you 'see' anyone?" she asked.

"That's an incredibly personal question, coming from you." Becca graced him with a teasing smile. He poured the last of the wine before answering.

"I think we're going to be involved in each other's lives for a long time. Forever," she said. "Or until one of us gets married—whichever comes first." There was more to this

161

statement than what she said. There were her nuances, and the challenge written on her stunning face slightly amused, but also searching.

"And that's incredibly probing, coming from you," he said.

"Well, at least it throws you on the defensive."

"And turns the conversation away from you."

"Right."

With this, Becca closed the door to any further personal questions. She was like no other woman he'd ever met before. There was no mess about her, no frightening questions that other women asked. Probing questions designed to discover his availability, was he ready for marriage, did he have access to the family money, and so on.

"Okay, I won't ask anything. When you're ready, tell me anything about your lifestyle that affects our guardianship."

She had scared him off, Becca realized. What was she thinking? She wasn't thinking, she mentally kicked herself. Of course they needed to know each other's personal details. In fact, she wanted to know particularly about his attitude toward dating as a hobby! She checked her watch. "My lord, it's one A.M.!" Becca searched for her shoes, which she'd thrown off when she sat down.

"It's your night, *Edward*." She used his formal name and made it sound amusing. "In fact, any minute Miss Emily will be making her first bid for attention."

"Right. The 'I'm thirsty, Uncle Edward' thing."

She stood, placing her pocketbook across her chest and automatically checking her phone to see how many calls she had. But the thought of going home to respond to calls and queries drained her. She had always felt invigorated by the need to get back to work.

"You look tired," but still shining, he thought. She was infectious with the feeling that a great adventure was about to happen. "Listen, stay here. Tomorrow is your day anyway." The idea seemed totally obvious.

They had both stayed in the apartment for the first week or so until Emily seemed stabilized. She still asked where her mommy and daddy were, though the question meant were they in heaven yet? Could they see her? Now the person on watch stayed and the other went home. In Becca's case, she'd usually go to the couch in her office, which made her feel more at home than her apartment. The weeks of forming an ersatz family and spending time in the Stearns' apartment were changing her, though she did not want to examine how and why.

"The room is calling you, I can hear it."

This was the ridiculous sense of humor he had that always made her shake her head and smile at the same time.

"You don't have to say another word. I'm tipsy and exhausted." She headed for the master bedroom.

Edward took both glasses to the kitchen and washed them in the sink.

Chapter 16

K. K. Will See You Now

Dick had strongly advised Becca to seek the aid of an educational consultant, so Friday, she was waiting to meet Edward in the office of K. K. Meyers, the high priestess of preschool admissions.

"Listen," Becca heard K. K. Meyers boom into her headset. "This is *not* amateur hour. I'm all about the *big five*. If you want to screw around with second-tier preschools then don't waste my fucking time!"

Her office door was open, and from Becca's seat in the waiting room she could see K. K. appearing and disappearing as she moved back and forth like a shark. Her bushy dark hair, graying from front to back, protruded above and behind her headset, which ran in a little ridge over her skull from ear to ear. With her hands on her hips, the consultant marched across her office, scowling. She had the demeanor of mixed cement, moving obsessively as if she would freeze and crack by standing still. From her hips, her hands would shoot up on occasion to wave around in the air, and the walls echoed her shouting voice. She jiggled a bit when she flung her arms around, as she was rather fat, which Becca found curious since she doubted K. K. took much time to eat. But K. K. enjoyed tub after tub of caramel popcorn in her office, so often that the stuffy room had the distinctive fragrance of a circus tent, minus the animals.

Becca sat on the waiting room couch, paging through back issues of *Parents* magazine, but her mind was elsewhere. The candy-smeared couch, upholstered with an April Cornell floral pattern, looked like an Easter dress on a tomboy. Cigarette ash smeared the yellow and rose of the English-garden pattern. K. K. didn't smoke, but the parents who raced to her in desperation were prone to a variety of nervous habits. Next to the ashtray was a jar of mints, a well-worn book of *New York Times* crossword puzzles, and a pen and spiral pad for compulsive doodlers.

K. K. handled her clients with the compassion of a college basketball coach facing a loss at the buzzer. But her intensity got results. So Becca waited, watching K. K.'s vehement concentration with interest, and not without familiarity. IvyBound Educational Consultants was a one-woman show.

Checking her watch to determine just how late Edward was, Becca stood with a smile when K. K. waved her into her office. Uninhibited by Becca's presence, she continued her phone call yelling furiously into her headphone while she pounded both fists on her desk.

Edward, who had found his way to the office, entered quietly and overlooked the mess of Post-Its and caramel corn, his mind on the curve of Becca's neck and shoulders as he watched her lean down to retrieve her phone from her bag. Nobody noticed him, so he walked over to look at K. K.'s ego wall, filled with pictures of K. K. greeting pre-school admissions directors. He noticed the location of one of the prestigious graduation ceremonies.

"That's the lawn at Ocean Edge Resort, on the Cape," he said, turning toward Becca. "Isn't it?" He realized what a faux pas that was and luckily Becca was listening to messages on the phone, and held her finger in the air.

"Hang on, Eddie," she said. She returned her attention to her telephone, leaving Edward to his own thoughts.

He leaned back against the wall, staring out the window. He had just dropped Emily at her MiniMozart listening and puzzle class, in which the children played with blocks and puzzle pieces, developing their spatial reasoning under the influence of Mozart's *Jupiter Symphony*. He was due to pick her up again in two hours: They listened to all four movements.

Money had never been short for Edward and he had therefore not developed much talent for thrift. Becca was different. The millions of dollars she had saved in salary, bonuses, dividends, and stock were attributable to her precise attention to financial detail. She was staggered when she wrote the $1,500 check to IvyBound Educational Consultants; the fee covered two ninety-minute sessions with K. K., an applicant evaluation for Emily, an interview prep session, and advice on completing one preschool application (which, in their case, was unnecessary). That got you in the door. After that it cost three hundred dollars an hour for K. K. to yell at you.

At this time of year, K. K. was dealing with September's dreaded "transitional calls." Parents who weren't happy with the preschool they had selected after their child's first week of attendance called in droves to line up transfer applications for next year. Manhattan parents en masse subscribed to the "feeder theory" of upward mobility, which convinced them that Ivy League admissions depended on scoring the right preschool. A scramble and panic had raged across the Upper East Side since Labor Day, as parents reevaluated their preschool status. K. K.'s telephone blinked and rang like a pinball arcade, with a sound so constant that it dwindled, eventually, into background noise, like street traffic.

"Listen!" K. K. shouted into the suspended microphone

of her headset. "Goddamn it, listen to what I tell you! Stop calling the school!" Her hands waved in the air with her frustration, then shot back to her hips. Becca felt restless, like she should pace too, but the office wasn't big enough.

"Every time you want to call the school, call me," she shouted, her hands flying around in vexation. "That's what you pay me for. If you call the school you're going to piss them off and you'll never get in. Listen, pal, write this down and paste it to your fucking forehead, okay? One call says you're interested. Two calls says you're anxious. Three calls says you're a pain in the ass. You're at two calls. You do it again and you're finished. I can't help you after that."

Shaking with frustration, K. K. crossed the office, putting a visibly impatient Becca off with the "wait a minute" finger in the air. Becca nodded, checking her watch. She liked K. K.'s style, but not enough to wait more than ten minutes.

"How could you let her say that?" K. K. challenged the caller in her gruff voice. "I warned Kingsley not to mention Barbie. That was a loaded question."

Becca stood to leave just as K. K. threw her mouthpiece over her head, disconnecting the call.

She stuck her hand into Becca's. "K. K. Myers. But I'm sure you know that."

At her joke, she gave a self-congratulatory laugh. "And you are?"

"Becca Reinhart," Becca responded. "Call me Becca." Edward approached, taking K. K.'s hand and introducing himself.

K. K. pulled her hand back from Edward impatiently. "Come on, people. Details. Details! *Remind me*," she emphasized, "*who* you are."

Becca took the cue. "Here's the deal, K. K. We're doing

our best for a wonderful little girl who we love like crazy but we don't have a clue. We kind of got dropped into this. We're—"

K. K., interrupting, finished her thought. "The guardians. Heard about the French school. I've been expecting you. Sit down," she directed, turning her frazzled attention to her desk.

"Of course," Becca answered. She liked this process less and less, but she was here, as was Edward, because they felt they owed it to Arthur and Amy and they wanted to give Emily the best education they could manage. If the preschool bar had really been raised so high you couldn't clear it without paying one of these quacks, they'd pay, and get Emily in the door.

"Anything to say for yourselves?" K. K. asked, looking at Edward.

"We're willing to be active, wherever Emily goes to school," Edward attempted.

"We'll give money," Becca added matter-of-factly. "Whatever it takes."

K. K. narrowed her eyes at Becca. "Glad to hear you're ready for the big leagues, Reinhart. It takes a softer sell, I'm afraid. You've got to quit your job."

"What?"

She nodded firmly. "All the top preschools really frown upon working mothers. That's what's hiding under 'parent participation.' "

"And you," she said, pointing at Edward. "You've got to get some credible interests." She paused. "I have to think about you."

"I play squash," he offered.

She turned fiercely towards him. "I'll tell you your interests in a minute!" she shouted.

Wheeling towards Becca, she stopped and pointed at her.

168

"Most of the time," she said, "it comes down to the mother."

Becca sighed, slumping in her chair. "What do I have to do?"

K. K. nodded. "One," she said, counting on her fingers. "Quit your job. Two: Read ten issues of *Parents* magazine. Cover to cover. Three: Ten issues of *Good Housekeeping*. Four: Repeat steps two and three. I want you to know how to make a Halloween costume from a pattern and the challenge of baking a soufflé. Got it?"

Becca was shocked. "What?"

"You don't have to *do* it," K. K. shouted at her. "Just talk like you can do it. You must be comfortable speaking preschool. It's a language. Right?"

Becca looked sullen and unconvinced. She made no answer. She probably could make her hiatus appear to be "quitting her job."

With a vehement motion, K. K. leaped to her office door and flung it open. "You want out?" she shouted. "You want out?"

Becca looked wide-eyed at Edward, and both of them laughed.

"*Do it!*" K. K. boomed.

The phone rang, and Becca cringed to see K. K. answer it. She stood, ready to leave, but remained in place when K. K. handed the phone to Edward.

As he listened, his face grew pale. "It's about Emily," he said to Becca.

He spoke quickly into the phone. "I'll be right there."

He handed the phone back to K. K. and turned to Becca, his face drawn with worry. "They played a symphony in the Mozart class that Amy used to play a lot at home. She's crying her eyes out. She wants her mommy."

Becca stood at once, feeling a whirlpool of emotions rise within her: tenderness, worry, love, and protectiveness. "I'm going with you," she said.

Edward nodded, and the worry on his face lifted a bit. He smiled. "Can you get out of the office this afternoon?"

Her jaw dropped. She had forgotten to mention her meeting with Dick. He didn't even know she was on leave.

"I'm free as a bird," she said. "Got two months off."

Edward, though surprised she had not told him, had an admirable lack of egotism, and took the news without any bitterness as to its mode of delivery. He was thrilled to hear she could devote more time to Emily.

"That's great," he congratulated Becca.

She smiled, nodding at him. She hadn't told him anything about her sabbatical; Edward was tactful, unusually considerate. He had not intruded one step into her privacy since the night at the apartment.

Her eye drifted down to the starched collar of his oxford shirt, one of the well-tended but casual shirts he wore every day, always tucked in. He always tucked his shirts in and he always wore a belt. The sun glinted on his Patek Phillipe watch.

"I'm sorry, K. K.," Edward said in a firm voice. "We have to cut this short. Emily's not feeling well." Becca noticed a more commanding tone than usual in Edward's voice.

Becca took an additional minute or so gathering her things, but really she was gathering herself. She felt struck, suddenly. What was she doing here, in this office, paying through the nose for an obnoxious woman to sentence her to hours of magazine reading so she could talk crochet? She was Becca Reinhart. She could figure exchange rates in her head, assess a rough current account balance, and predict profits for a company (including subs) based on a few pages of revenues and ARs. And now she felt her head swimming, like she was drunk, with images she couldn't fasten anything to. The song at MiniMozart, Emily's pink mohair cardigan, Edward's suntanned neck, the little French playhouse at Le Petit École, Emily's beautiful smile. . . .

Emily. That was her compass point. The thought of her sweet face turning mottled and red, and streaming with tears, gripped Becca's stomach until she thought it would tear. She hurried after Edward, eager to put her arms around Emily, anxious to escape this false world of interview coaches and application strategies. She wanted to hold her daughter.

Chapter 17

Ethical Kiddies

They took it easy for days after Emily's trouble in Mozart class. It felt like they were playing hooky. The night of the Mozart disaster Becca was in bed, lights out, but not able to sleep. The door opened a crack.

"I have to sleep here," Emily said. "If Mommy comes to visit, I think she'll come here."

Becca had more or less moved into the master bedroom. "I think your mommy will come wherever you are," Becca had turned and was leaning on her left side, her face propped up on her chin. This made Emily pause. Becca could see the tiny wheels of her brain working. "But what if she doesn't—what if she can only make one stop, like the express bus."

"Well, if we are both in the same room, then she will definitely arrive there."

With this, Becca opened her sheet to welcome Emily next to her. Becca could not remember the last time she shared a bed with anyone. Actually, she'd rather not think about that too long. Anyway, it was the first time she'd felt a warm little body in her pink flannel nightie curl against her. Becca pulled the girl close, wrapped her arms around her. Nothing was going to hurt this child—nothing or no one, as long as Becca was alive. Becca finally understood what compelled a man or woman to go into harm's way to defend something precious to them. She was trying to finish this thought, but had automatically followed Emily's breathing and soon she was calm, and then she slept.

Without discussing it, Becca and Edward were both staying at the apartment—living there really. Emily needed balance. For a week she slept with Becca. In the morning there was no pouncing, singing, demands. In the night she did not ask silly questions. Emily was becalmed. Slowly the two of them brought her around. One morning Becca felt her slip out of bed with the birds. This marked the beginning of Emily's next step in her healing. She brought the scrapbook she and Becca had started into Becca's room.

"Let's put more stuff in."

"Okay, do you have any more photos?"

"Mommy kept everything. My daddy used to say she was a garbage can." This made Emily giggle, though Becca wasn't so sure that remark was funny.

"Well, where did she put that stuff?"

Emily started walking away, her legs threatening to break out into a run. "Come on, Aunt Becca! Don't be so pokey."

"Who's pokey?" Edward met them in the hallway. He caught up to Becca and placed a warning hand on her shoulder. "She shouldn't go in there." Becca stopped. Emily was at the entrance to a small study tucked into an alcove, the furthest from the stairs.

"Why not?"

"The room is nothing but boxes."

"What's in them?"

"Stuff—memorabilia, maps, photos, pressed leaves and what looks like herbs—you know—stuff."

"Then it's not packed," Becca said.

"What are you talking about?" Sometimes Becca seemed to know an entirely different language—one that had to do with inner guidance.

"Arlene—"

By now Emily had used the doorway to twirl into the study. Edward screwed up his eyes and mouth, like he was waiting for a scream.

"Relax, buddy." Becca walked in to join Emily, who by now was digging into open boxes, all marked and organized. The little girl was pulling out anything that could possibly fit into a scrapbook—and other things besides.

"Aunt Becca—look at all there is!" She dragged out a set of castanets—black, hand-painted. When Becca got closer she could see the painting was a scene—a town with women, probably African, carrying things on their heads. Emily recalled that Amy and Arthur had traveled through East Africa not too long ago.

"It was probably a present Mommy forgot to give me." Emily already had tiny fingers caught in the silk ribbons that kept the wood pieces together.

"Probably," Becca said, sitting on the floor beside her. "We can hang them in your bedroom."

"No—kitchen—so I can see them every day and so can you." She spotted Edward leaning against the door, "And you!" She pointed, giggled, put her hands to her head.

Edward met Becca's eyes. "What did you mean? How could you possibly ascertain. . . ."

" 'Possibly ascertain?' " Becca teased him. "I can possibly always for certain know that my mother has a sixth, seventh, and eighth sense about, well, mothering. She would know Emily would be ready soon to go through it." Becca paused. "Actually, now that I think of it, I would also know." She looked at Edward and said, "And so would you."

All day the three went through boxes that allowed Emily to teach them how to give her what Amy and Arthur did to parent her. There was one whole box filled with bird feathers, odd stones, things that looked like acorns, but were not—animal photos, a bag of reddish dirt. Emily told them that her mommy loved to be outside, walking and hiking and finding animal homes in the trees, where they imagined they could see whole fairylands and friendly chipmunks escaping from nasty old badgers. They hiked all around, sometimes with a place to go and sometimes just for the thing called "exercise" that her mom had to get every day. Her mom had funny names for plants and trees that were really long and fancy-sounding. She also grew little plants called herbs; they used to be lined up on the balcony, and when she needed them for cooking she let Emily cut them into little pieces with her safety scissors.

Her mommy had gone on airplanes too and spoke in lots of languages. She spoke to the nanny in French but it was too fast for Emily to hear it right. She liked faraway places, same as Becca, Emily pointed out, except that Becca went to inside places and her mommy went to outside places. Becca blushed, but remained silent, astonished by this new Emily, until now a lovely but closed little bud. She was opening, and the combination of her vulnerability and her candor was striking to see.

Emily's mommy loved the art that she made, and she took her to art shows so Emily knew already that she was just as good as the famous people. Amy set up her play table in the kitchen sometimes with the watercolor easel. Amy played music all the time in the apartment, music like they played in her music classes—with big sounds and no words—and when the nanny finished taking her to lessons, and Emily could speak English again, she liked to play "kitchen" while Amy did some baking. She was not allowed to wear her dress-ups out of the house, she mentioned, looking at the floor.

Emily's heart seemed to pause until Becca reminded her that her fairy godparents loved her dress-ups, since she was really a princess to them. Emily's courage returned with a flush of her cheeks, and she took a happy step toward Becca. She had naps she was supposed to take a long time ago when she was really little but mostly she painted her fingernails under the covers. When she got in trouble it was no sweets and sometimes it was no dresses but that was just for *really bad* things like when she bit the nanny on her hand.

Becca and Edward both cringed at that image. Emily's independence had been shocked into remission when she lost her parents. She had clung to them from the beginning, with an open heart, as if some defensive sense told her she would be badly served to struggle against her protection in this dangerous world.

But she was walking steady steps on her own now. This child was so much more than a princess in pretty clothes, or a gem waiting for the light to come alive.

Emily was dividing all the objects that had filled four large boxes into piles only she could understand. But each pile was designated to a particular room. And there was no question that these objects would find their way to Emily's dictates.

By noon, Becca was exhausted. Since it was technically "her day," though the schedule was no longer adhered to, she stayed on the floor and Edward went off. Emily didn't even glance up when Edward patted her good-bye on the hand.

Watching her triggered something for Becca. It was painful, whatever it was. Emily would stop every so often to show something to Becca, or to fasten a feather to her clothes, or stand to show off a cloth—one scarf Becca recognized as a particular blue that was the Montengards' mark. Amy and Arthur must have traveled in the north country of Vietnam. How they wandered! Becca got snagged on a memory: a man who had to be her father—a piece of cloth—she went to the room's telephone and dialed.

"Hello," her mother had a way of pronouncing the "o" that made it sound like she was pretending to be a proper lady. It always got a smile out of Becca.

"Mother—what's new with you?"

"What is new is that I can nag you now that I never get to see my granddaughter."

They both laughed with great affection. The preliminaries over, Becca explained what they were doing and then said, "Did my father give me a scarf? Or a piece of cloth that I might remember?"

Her mother got real quiet—not like the quiet when she was listening, but a quiet that was more profound.

Emily had worked her way over to where Becca stood and was tugging on the hem of her pants.

"Aunt Becca!"

Becca was listening into her mother's silence. "Mom?"

"Aunt Becca," the little girl repeated.

"Mom, what?"

Emily screamed one long sound and Becca understood the phrase "screamed bloody murder."

"What's going on, Becca? What's happened?"

"I'll call you back."

"You'll put the phone down and keep me on hold."

Without replying, Becca stooped to Emily's level and saw that she was running little streams of tears—more like creeks.

"What happened, sweetie?"

Emily threw herself into Becca's arms.

"Mommy—I want my mommy. You have her." The sobs came from Emily's soul. She was fractured by her loss and at this moment Becca was powerless. She could only hold Emily and hope the moment passed.

She picked up the phone. Maybe Mom had some advice. Then it hit her that Emily must have heard her address her own mother and stumbled emotionally.

"Did you hear everything?"

"I did."

"Are you thinking what I'm thinking?"

"Probably—does it have to do with you talking to me?"

"Exactly. Now what?"

"Let her cry. Crying is good. When she's done, take her anywhere in the house she wants, give her a treat. Not sweets." Becca laughed—the honey-cake queen was warning against sweets. "Milk—then stay with her—she'll fall asleep—but stay with her."

"Roger."

"Becca, it's important that you stay there."

"Got it, Arlene. Love you."

It wasn't until she hung up that Becca remembered the memory of the cloth.

As the days went on, there was more talk about Emily's parents. They asked about Arthur, but Emily revealed very little in her recollection of her father. Her daddy, she said, loved to lift her up and kiss her on the tummy at the end of the day, and sometimes watch the puppet shows she did in the playroom, but mostly he was at the club until late. She thought that he didn't hear so well, since he missed a lot of what she said to him. Lots of the time he looked somewhere else and said "What?" In that way he reminded her of the nanny who wouldn't listen at all to her questions in English.

It was a sketch, only a hint of her childhood, but Emily had stepped towards them in trust. Edward and Becca's shared gratitude and warmth were mingled.

Becca's gratitude faded, however—and Edward's broadened—when Emily suggested that she and Becca should bake a cake.

Becca cringed at the thought of baking, but was put on the spot, and declared without hesitation that she would love to bake a cake. Emily said that the kind she baked with her mommy was called a box cake and you only poured water into the mix. She knew just where it was in the grocery shelf because it was on the same place as all the sweets and icings.

Both Edward and Becca saw the enthusiasm that rose to Emily's eyes when her mind turned to baking. There was no getting out of it, Becca thought, but a cake in a box couldn't be too much trouble. While Emily flounced importantly down the hall to get her beaded city purse, Becca asked Edward for the location of the closest grocery store.

He laughed, since necessity had driven him to take over ordering their sustenance for delivery from the grocery, the greengrocer, and occasionally, when the maid agreed to cook, from the butcher. Becca admired this survival skill. Like morning glories leaning toward twin suns, they had been drawn in the direction of their differing talents. Becca had expanded Emily's world, taking her to the floor of the stock exchange the way some people take children to the zoo; in fact it was not unlike the zoo, and Emily had squealed with excitement at the frenzied scene. Edward had no innate talent or interest in cooking, but he had a great deal more need for eating, and so by default had been the one to pick up this essential chore.

Emily accepted with a pout that they had to wait until later to bake the cake, since she had another preschool interview in the afternoon, but Edward made her laugh with a ridiculous story of a daddy who ate cake before the interview and then burped at all the teachers. Becca regarded him with admiration as Emily giggled, forgetting what she might have insisted upon, her stubborness washed away in peals of laughter. With Eddie around, Becca thought, things were smooth as silk.

Edward's manner was so naturally pleasant, so smooth

and straightforward, he was the indoor equivalent of a lovely, calm day. He relaxed everyone in the room. So little invested was he in some prearranged course of his own conduct that he simply adapted to Emily's preferences; but when he had a goal in mind, he saw quickly to the child's avenues of persuasion, and moved her gently on what seemed to Emily to be the force of her own decisions. If she had *wanted* to pick a fight with Edward, the child wouldn't have had a chance.

They arrived, that afternoon, at a familiar scene brewing on the sidewalk in front of Ethical Kiddies, a coveted preschool whose aspirational name did not change the essential reason for its large applicant pool. It was a surefire feeder into Chapin and Spence, two of the best elementary schools in the city. The toddler popularity contest came into view as they rounded the corner.

They counted their steps out loud, swinging Emily's feet off the ground on "five." Emily squealed with delight as they gave her a last energetic swing, with Edward pulling her higher and higher to hear the sound of her giggle, and Becca tugging with all her strength to be sure she pulled her own weight. They took their places in line, toward the back this time, as they had not arrived early.

Upper East Side parents congregated nervously before the cheerful red barn-shaped building that housed Ethical Kiddies. Spouses bickered, neighbors compared remodeling contractors, and everyone danced the tricky middle ground between commiserating with each other and exposing any weakness in their child's preschool portfolio.

"Here goes," said Edward, shifting Emily in his arms. She laid her flushed cheek on his shoulder, smiling as Becca obligingly handed Emily her mobile phone. She had decided on this short-term surrender, lest she make the same mistake that got her in hot water at the French toddler lot.

Edward glanced past the crowd at the school's Alice-in-Wonderland-style door, which adults had to duck to enter. Neon orange placards, imitating road signs, surrounded the front entrance with cheery, esteem-enhancing slogans. PRE-LEADERS AT WORK, read one beside the door. CAUTION: CONFIDENCE BUILDING, read another. Edward shook his head, smiling at the aggressive, opinion-forward cuteness of this preschool stage. He couldn't remember preschool, of course, but something told him that this crash of lingo, psychology, and affirmation was a new way of reaching four-year-olds.

Becca glanced at Emily. She was reassured, at the sight of her pure little face, that Emily was oblivious of the pressure building around her among the jockeying parents. She was secure, Becca could see; she knew she was loved. It didn't matter what happened at this school, she thought: They were doing all right with Emily. She felt a surprising sense of accomplishment, though they were only at the gates. Watching Emily point her tiny arms at shapes she imagined in the clouds, rejoicing at the sight of her plump, excited face as she described to Edward the dragons, castles, and monsters in the sky, Becca breathed deeply. She felt a tension had been released from her muscles, from her mind. She was grateful. They had gotten through a little bump in the road with Emily, and she was growing to trust them.

"I like this place," Emily declared suddenly, having noticed the tiny barn door surrounded by pretty orange signs. "Will I go to school here?"

"If it's good enough," answered Becca. "We'll see today if it's a good place for princesses."

Emily's eyes widened. "I hope so," she said. It was a cool fall day, but a brilliantly sunny one, and Becca could almost feel Emily's heart bursting with anticipation.

Edward, who had a sixth sense for impropriety, poked

Becca to draw her attention to some people standing near them in line. She stifled a laugh when she caught view of the situation: a man and woman who were so far gone in their battle of wits that they stood on the verge of pawing the dirt and snorting at each other.

"How could you wear that tie, Nelson?" the woman hissed. "I specifically laid an African Kente cloth out on your dressing table before I left for tennis."

"I *told* you," he snapped back, "I thought the decorator left it there. It looked like a pillow for the game room."

"In our prep session, Hayley told us to go with an indigenous style," the woman snapped at him. She planted her hands on her hips. "Do you consider *that* to be *indigenous?*" Her face was twisted with contempt.

"It's indigenous to Wall Street," he replied stubbornly. "So get off my ass!"

At the notice of eyes upon them, Nelson made a hasty surrender of the offending neckwear. His wife, Cassie, threw it behind a bush, concerned that a school official might see it poking out of her open safari bag. She glared at her husband's clothes and felt herself overcome by panic. Their son, Bowen, had blown three interviews straight. If he didn't get into Ethical, they'd be finished. Finished!

Any tense line that may have broken through the botox disappeared from Cassie's face at the instant the little barn door swung open in welcome. White teeth appeared everywhere, glittering on every parent in the line.

A large woman, wearing an orange housedress that was silk-screened with totem-pole faces, beamed on the assembled crowd.

"Aloha, everybody!" she called out, her arms jiggling as she waved. "I'm Marsha Holt, the team leader of Ethical Kiddies. We're ready to share our inclusive day with all of you, persons of the world!"

Edward's eyes met Becca's, and hiding their laughter,

both of them tried to nod and smile with wide-open earnestness.

"First," Marsha chirped, "we'll get our person identifier tags. People are people, of course, but we rejoice in our diversity! After we project our identities, I'll invite you all in for a simultaneous embrace! Get ready to love!"

Becca glanced at Edward. He looked like he might jump out of his skin.

Marsha turned to a smiling team supporter who stood by her side and took from her a tray of nametags. Each sticker, shaped like a shining sun, read HELLO, MY PERSON IDENTIFIER IS, and the child's and each parent's name was printed in.

"We like to start each day at Ethical Kiddies with a big hug," Marsha announced, as the parents fastened identifiers to their person-children. "We have a hug-invigorator on staff, if anyone feels a little down and droopy this morning!"

Marsha was practically singing her joy as the nametags disappeared from her tray. Though Becca felt the onset of a posthippie hangover, she glanced at Emily and noticed the child's beautiful smile was shining upon Marsha's face. Emily was beaming: She was enthusiastic and excited. She caught Becca's eye with a giggle.

Edward also noticed Emily's enthusiasm, but he was slower to find his sea legs.

"Stand next to me for the group hug, will you?" he asked Becca, pulling Emily close to him as additional family armor.

"Well, heck," sang Marsha, overcome with self-satisfaction, "forget the identifiers! Let's celebrate what unites us: the need to be loved! Everyone line up."

Suddenly the song "Lean on Me" was playing from a Fisher- Price tape player and Becca watched Marsha's toes swaying to the beat in her Birkenstocks. Her thick yellow toenails curved fully over the front of each of her toes, adding probably a full shoe size to her feet. Everyone swayed; everyone toe-tapped, everyone joined the circle and hugged on cue.

"Now, doesn't that feel great!" Cassie exclaimed, hoping Marsha would hear her.

"Lovely," replied Erin Starker. A Park Avenue princess, Erin was dressed down with a vengeance this morning. She had never been so affable, as she swung her daughter's hands to and fro.

"We do the circle-hug every morning at home," she declared in a loud voice. "And we *always* hug bye-bye."

"So do we," several of the other mothers echoed.

"As if they take their children to school themselves," Cassie snipped into Nelson's ear. "The sluts pretend they don't speak nanny."

He shushed her like a child. "Didn't you take your Prozac?"

"Shut up!" She pinched him.

Hastily, they flashed Norman Rockwell smiles at the approaching school director.

Holding hands in a line led by Marsha, the parents were shepherded into a round yoga room for the first activity.

"Everybody grab a mat and make yourselves comfortable," said Marsha, taking two for herself.

A mass experiment with contorting inflexible joints began, and in the midst of the agony, the Rolffs made their mark. A perceptive couple who had engaged the consulting services of Upper East Side yogi Hans Johan, Barbie and Hamish Rolff had precisely this moment in mind when they paid eight hundred dollars for two hourly sessions. They made a splendid display of outstretched limbs in reenactment of the earth, air, fire, and water poses, their hearts beating eagerly as they previewed the joy they would have in describing to Marsha their family yoga hour.

Their admissions consultant had cautioned them, though, to tread carefully when discussing how yoga had improved little Chad's agility. They had to be careful to emphasize that sports, in the winning and losing sense, were not at all important to them. Barbie was no soccer mom. She'd be thrilled to see Chad take up an interest in orienteering, for example, or whittling. The family was simply interested in deep breathing, relaxation, and flexibility for its own sake, and for the unique joy of experiencing oneness in their togetherness.

"Do you do yoga?" Barbie asked Becca, but the disturbance in Barbie's aura that occurred simply by watching Becca tap and fidget on her mat made her doubt it.

"I relax when I sleep," Becca shot back, keeping one cagey eye on Marsha.

The parents' jaws snapped shut as Marsha began to chirp about the school.

As if she has to sell it to this crowd! thought Becca. She was growing restless.

"Ethical's a top-five preschool," Marsha crowed, "but you *know* that." The parents' heads bobbed furiously to show their agreement.

"So what makes us different? Hmmmm?" She looked around the circular room, savoring the quiet, the hopeful, upturned faces, the *power* she had over these rich people.

"Open choice," Marsha concluded, to a chorus of approval.

"That tells me very little," Edward whispered to Becca.

"Shhh!" she said, laughing. "K. K. said we have to score this place!"

Emily had managed to stretch one leg completely behind her head, but lost her balance and rolled into Edward's lap. He held her, brushing her curls, paying attention to anything he could, to keep a straight face as Jabba the Hutt in a housedress numbed his brain with her jargon.

"Open choice is our term for free but ideologically directed play. We love big ideas! Can anybody guess what our biggest idea is here at Ethical Kiddies? Hmmmm?"

Nobody ventured.

"*Fun!* Fun is our biggest idea!" She raised her hands in a hurrah.

A little cheer went up. Edward poked Becca in the back.

"Cut it out!" She meant to scold him with her tone, but in the quick turn of Becca's head, Edward saw that her eyes were bright with humor. He felt a playful impulse to cause some trouble, and restrained it, staying behind Emily and keeping his laughs shielded.

"Open choice means that your child will make decisions for herself. Does she want to play in our organic vegetable garden, or learn about another culture through dramatic play with one of her very diverse classmates? Perhaps he'll build an indigenous necklace with our natural fibers, or break the gender barriers in our dress-up corner?"

Edward shrugged. "I'd go for the Play-Doh," he whispered to Emily, who nodded.

Marsha had grown silent. "We've just been connectors," she said suddenly. "Now let's all be reflectors." She folded her hands as if in prayer, and for thirty seconds all was silent, including the admirably well-coached three- and four-year-olds.

"We're reflecting," she announced, "on what we have just beheld. Let's use all our senses, now, quiet . . . that's right. That's it. When we are reflectors, we learn to cope with what is new to us."

Becca thought the world could hear her heart beating as she made an enormous effort not to laugh. Edward restrained his desire to poke Becca again. They were supposed to be reflectors. What could he do? He was a born connector.

Edward looked around the room, trying to be a reflector, and started with what was in front of him. His eyes scanned its plaster walls, its skylit circularity, and he was suddenly reminded of the Guggenheim, which always made him sick. Bunny had sailed around and through the museum as if she had been born there, he thought, growing dizzy with the memory of that absurd crown-and-glory event. He was glad to be connected with Emily Stearns, who dressed herself up in the magical grace of her childish, flowery innocence. Emily was a tribute to what beauty should be. With Bunny, every jewel was a sharp-edged implement.

Weirdly, as if she had never turned into that meditative person of two minutes ago, Marsha jumped up and hurried to direct the tidying of yoga mats.

"Okay! Next we have a class meeting. We will split up into teams, and discuss our feelings about what we just did. Come on, persons of the world! Let's head for the meeting room. Chop chop! And don't forget our top priority. Let's hear it on three. One, two, three!"

"*Fun!*" remembered a sharp-eyed parent. Marsha's eyes shone with approval.

Edward and Becca shuffled with their fellow participants to the Ethical meeting room, where they followed instructions through the coping session and a musical Ritual of Forgetting. The children had been shown to another room, where, in a switch they enjoyed immensely, they were permitted to spy on their parents, while learning facilitators in a curtained area behind the plant life spied on them. A National Geographic video of tribal dancing drew the attention of some. Like the other scheduled activities, the television program was a hidden test. If the children swayed with the rhythm, they gained points, but if they watched passively, they drew strikes as TV types.

By the time Becca and Edward approached their personal parent interview, they had been completely rattled by the animal imitation session, in which each parent, in front of the group, imitated a wild beast to the rhythm of the partner-parent's maracas. As they waited for the interviewer in their rough seats of unfinished wood, Becca had a second to prep with Edward.

"It's the three *Us*, remember? We're Unmarried, Uncommitted, and Unorthodox."

"How about Unprepared?"

"I think we're doing all right," she said, tapping him affectionately on his strong, square shoulder. His muscles were tense.

"You're nervous, Eddie," she said. "Relax."

"Did you read our copy of the application?"

"Yes."

"It was like a cross between the census and an FBI background check."

She smiled. "Don't worry, Ed. They'll love you. Everybody loves you."

Becca's complexion looked particularly radiant, Edward thought, as his eyes lingered on the shadow created by her sculpted cheekbones. He was encouraged by her confidence, and her humor calmed him. He reclined, to the extent he could, in his chair full of natural knotholes, folding his hands behind his head. With his thumbs he massaged the muscles of his neck, drawing a deep breath into his chest. He smiled as the door opened. Worry did not take hold of Edward for long.

He stood to greet the entering interviewer. Reading his glance, Becca, too, shot up from her chair. Into the room strode a member of the Nez Perce tribe, clad in buckskin that flapped as she walked. Her bodily use of animal skins had caused some offense among the vegan learning facilitators, but her tribal ethnicity created kind of an understood exemption from their usual ban on animal products. Declining to shake hands, she bowed before a plant that had withered in the back of the room, then turned her steely gaze on Edward.

He raised his hand like a Boy Scout, remembering the episode when the Brady Bunch went to the Grand Canyon.

She ignored the salutation. "I am Green Field," she boomed.

"I'm Becca, he's Edward," Becca introduced them both. She paused, wondering why the great chief continued to point her eagle eyes at Edward. She nodded her head to give a little ceremonial bow.

"Have a seat," Becca announced, sitting. Edward stood next to his seat, his eyes locked on the interviewer, who regarded him with a curiously hostile glare.

Green Field also continued to stand. Her eyes blazed like a predator's. She pointed an accusing finger at his face.

"Edward Kirkland," Green Field spat out the name, her face disfigured by a ferocious scowl. "I expected you to look different." Her eyes were from the grave.

"Younger than you thought?" Edward returned. He smiled, but the interviewer clenched her teeth. Only Becca gave a polite laugh. With a sigh, Edward slunk into his seat. He had the feeling he got sometimes in his father's office, that it would be best just to sit and wait it out.

Closing her eyes, Green Field offered a silent sacrifice to the gods of rain and soil, of wind and earth. She stroked her necklace of antelope teeth in a self-soothing ritual.

"Your statistics were never promising," said Green Field, brandishing a paper. "But then we thought of you as a courageous exception."

"Well, I've never been called courageous or exceptional," Edward admitted from his slump. "So there must be some mistake." His voice was controlled.

"Don't be so tough on yourself, Eddie," whispered Becca.

She turned to the interviewer. "I think you have a piece of paper you're not sharing, Miss Field." She stuck her hand out for a copy. "How about a little 'open choice'?"

Green Field ignored her. She was still locked like a snake on Edward.

"Oppressive colonialist background, elitist recreational habits, membership in a Christian organization not known for accepting alternative lifestyles. Welcome in the private men's clubs, I'll guess?"

"The Union Club. The Racquet Club," he responded, casually. "Why? What difference does it make to Emily?"

"Patriarchial slime!" she shrieked, racing for his desk.

Becca stood between them. "Take it easy, there, chief," she laughed, putting out her hand to stop the woman's hostile advance. She turned quickly back to Edward with a whisper.

"Do you think she'll communicate with me?" she asked him.

He shrugged. "It's worth a try," he said, but his tone was doubtful.

The Indian skidded to a stop, bowing to Becca. She took her hand solemnly.

"You, we respect," she announced, raising Becca's fingers to the sky in victory. "Religious Minority, Breaker of Gender Barriers, Shirker of Marriage Conventions, Cohabiting Legal Guardian of a Love-Child." In a lowered voice, she added: "We had some trouble with your capitalist ethic, but we adapted our mission statement to allow that doing well can be channeled to useful ideological interests."

Becca stared with the eyes of a fighter fish. "Is this a joke?"

The Great Spirit had calmed Green Field, but her eyes

still burned with a slow fire when she turned again toward Edward.

"You lied to us," she said, glaring at him. "You lied on your addendum to the application."

His voice was calm, but Becca could hear his annoyance. "It was Emily's application," he corrected her. "And I was perfectly candid with you—there must be some mistake."

Though any addition of an addendum was news to her, Becca instinctively rose to his defense. "Eddie would never do that," she chimed in. "Straight as an arrow."

Watching the moccasined native woman stroke her necklace of antelope teeth, Edward cringed at Becca's choice of words, but appreciated her trust in him.

"Emily was intended to add to our diversity in a very *particular* way," Green Field said sadly. Her eyes sought the solid wooden beams that supported the ceiling and she soaked in the strength of their sacrificed trees.

Becca turned a confused look on Edward. Diversity was supposed to be their selling point. Unmarried and Unorthodox. Too baffled to deliver their stump speech, they sat in silence.

Green Field approached Edward with a hostile glare.

He watched her without speaking. She reminded him more and more of his father.

"You identified your mother as African-American in our schematic, Edward," she spat at him.

"In fact you claimed the reason you were sending the letter was to call attention to all of Emily's 'unique blending of sociological and ethnic strands.' " The chief had pulled a letter from a pouch that looked a little like the Hermès saddlebag.

"That's true," he replied simply.

"You are not black!" Green Field shouted, her clenched fists shaking.

"I'm not," he agreed. He sat back in his seat and folded his arms.

"I did some research," Green Field shot back. "With *all* my senses. My eyes tell me you are whiter than snow, and my reading told me that your father is Horace Kirkland, who produces more chemical pollutants than Three Mile Island, and your mother is Catherine Whitney, of the exclusive bourgeois art museum."

Becca, surprised by all that she heard, turned from Green Field to Edward as if she were watching a tennis match.

"If you had dug deeper, Miss Field," he responded with gentle certainty, "you would have learned that my mother is a DeBeers on her mother's side. She was born in Johannesburg while her parents were consolidating the family's holdings. That's in South Africa, which, last I checked, makes my mother an African."

The interviewer shook with fury. To control the spirit of anger, she began to dance, chanting Ki-oh-*wa*-ji-*nay* maniacally as her feet pounded in place.

Edward, stunned, was making a heroic effort not to laugh.

"Emily's background has changed a great deal since she became my—our—child. I thought that was important," he defended himself.

The interviewer looked for a way to challenge him. Emily Stearns was not so unique. They had national and ethnic categories for Bengalis, Inuits, Kazakis, Acadians. They had cultural slots for children adopted by homosexuals or conceived by surrogate. Green Field was determined to prove that this new-formed family was not unique enough to qualify for an automatic acceptance under the "proves school's stellar ethics" rule.

But Becca had already stood to leave. This place was absurd.

192

"I think we've said all we have to say, today, Green," she announced.

Edward stood and pushed in his chair. He gave the interviewer a last confounded look, and Becca's heart went out to him. She was moved to pity by his perplexed blue eyes. Poor Eddie, she thought, watching him. He didn't do anything wrong.

"Miss Field, I was honest with you," he said, stepping over to Becca's abandoned chair and pushing it back into place. "Maybe you should just make it clear that WASPs should not apply here. That way you could have dropped me right into the rejection pile." He heard Becca laughing next to him, and he smiled.

Green Field scowled. "We'll have no stereotyping in this class!"

"That would be a miracle," said Becca. She walked close to Edward, standing beside him. "It's all I've heard so far."

Smiling cordially at Green Field, then warmly at Becca, Edward turned to leave.

"Shall we?" he said, offering his arm to Becca. "It's a family tradition."

She linked her arm with his, and together they departed.

When they were alone in the hall, Becca became suddenly conscious that they were touching. She dropped her hand to her side hastily, then reached into her bag for her phone. She forgot that Emily had taken it. She rooted around in her bag a little, digging for something or other. She glanced at Edward, leaning against a wall displaying art of the four seasons. Two raindrops cut from recycled tinfoil on the picture behind him looked like earrings dangling from Edward's ears. Becca noticed the fall leaves were colored in oil pastels. She tugged him away from the wall by the sleeve.

"You'll get smudged," she told him.

He nodded thanks. Becca waited, watching Edward. He stood in place for a minute, his hands finding his pockets, his eyes finding hers.

"I wonder where Emily is."

"The open choice room, I think," she said. "Or whatever they call it. Come on, Eddie. Let's go get her."

He stopped her with a hand on her arm. "I'm sorry, Becca," he said. "I should have consulted you before I sent the letter."

"Forget about it, Eddie." She flashed him a bright smile and he felt the warmth of her acceptance.

His smile returned slightly. She was standing close to him. She rubbed his arm, and together they began to walk.

"I wasn't so crazy about the group hugs, anyway," he said with a grin.

"Listen, Ed," Becca said. "Emily won't go to a school where they scatter kids around like lamps to lend color to a room. She'll be better off with us."

They reached the classroom, and Edward held the door. At the sight of her fairy godmother, Emily Stearns dropped her maracas with a crash. Edward watched her make a running leap from Ethical's open choice into Becca's open arms.

He looked at Becca, feeling he should offer to carry her bag while she carried Emily. He reached over to tousle Emily's curls. Poor kid. With bumbling guardians like them, she'd never get into school anywhere.

Becca stroked Emily's hair and her hand met Edward's. It seemed they couldn't help bumping into each other and, if she were honest, she would admit to herself that she didn't mind. She turned toward him, their eyes meeting over the gentle curls of Emily Stearns' soft golden hair. Emily was singing a song, and when Becca told her that the school was not their favorite one, and they thought they'd all stick together and play and learn at home for a while longer, Emily shrugged indifferently, and asked if they could all go for ice cream—a double and with rainbow sprinkles too.

Edward was in awe of Becca's confidence. He watched Becca's lips curve into a smile as she laid her cheek against Emily's soft head.

That was his answer. Becca's eyes and lips spoke what he felt in his own soul. Emily was better off with them.

Edward took his handkerchief and wiped away the ice-cream stains on Emily's face. That's why he didn't hear Becca's whispered warning. When he stood, he was looking straight into Bunny's pinched face. But he hadn't been brought up in a "colonialist" home for nothing. So he immediately collected himself.

"Bunny! Great to see you. Have you met Becca Reinhart? Becca, this is Bunny Stirrup. Bunny, this is Becca, my coguardian."

"Your what?"

But Becca held her hand out to shake and Edward kept talking, stealing time. "And this sugarplum is Emily Stearns—you probably haven't seen Amy and Arthur's little girl since she was a baby. Emily, I want you to meet Miss Bunny Stirrup."

Unfortunately, Emily had apparently forgotten what she'd learned in manners class.

"Bunny is a silly name," she said, and ran behind Becca to hide.

"Emily!" Edward said. But he was certain the child had been rude because she sensed danger. In the last few weeks he'd learned much more about children than the loose-leaf notebook of information Becca's staff had gathered. Observing Emily when she wasn't aware of him proved to be a graduate school course called "Why God Made Kids." Emily was like a canary when it came to assessing situations or judging people's sincerity. She was a lightning rod in any tense situation and right now the sky over Bunny had begun to storm.

Bunny seemed to have regained her equanimity because she dug up a smile made for the stage and said, "I haven't had a good talk with you in weeks, Edward. I heard about poor Arthur and Amy, of course—"

"Be careful what you say." Edward gestured toward Emily.

"Oh yes, of course. Anyway, your dear mother told me you had been named the child's ward—"

"Guardian," Becca said. "Wards went out with the Brontës."

Bunny turned all of her considerable talent for putting other women in their place on Becca.

"You are Ms. Reinhart, of course."

"Becca, Bunny."

This caught Edward unaware and he laughed. Emily inched her way toward Becca's knee. Reflexively, Edward put his hand on Emily's head and she grabbed it and started kissing him, a continual string of pecks all over his hand.

Becca saw that Bunny couldn't take her eyes off the display going on between Emily and Edward. In fact, she seemed to have forgotten what she was saying because she put her hand to her perfectly buffed and blushed cheek and said, "I must tell your mother we ran into each other. She'll want to know all about—" She groped for a moment and then remembered, "Emily."

"If she wanted to know all about Emily, she would have asked to meet her," Becca said. She noted that Bunny was dressed in cashmere Juicy Couture sweats, pink, and on her feet were the Merrell shoes that reminded Becca of Mercury delivering a message.

Sensing that she had stumbled into messy territory, Bunny agilely turned the conversation to what only she

196

and Edward could discuss. "Bitsy was disqualified in the first round of the trials for the garden."

Bunny had managed to both change the conversation into another language and take a swipe at another woman—assuming Bitsy was a woman. She's good, Becca thought—very clever. Becca, who still knew little about Edward's personal life, found herself suddenly ravenous for information about this side of him.

Her attention to the unspoken communication between Edward and Bunny was a mystery to her. Thus far they had never again tiptoed near conversation about their personal lives. Edward left, wearing tuxedos most of the nights he was "off." She knew that though he still kept his rooms at the Carlyle, he had moved the dogs to the Stearns' Fifth Avenue apartment and had virtually not spent one night away from the apartment. If he had a woman in his life, relations between them had to be either relegated to daytime trysts, or chaste. So what claim did this woman have on him that made her desperate to catch Edward's eye?

Emily was standing between Becca and Edward in what had become the threesome's standard, with the child holding a hand of each, the majority of these times claiming much of their attention.

"You go away now, Bunny," Emily said.

"Emily, apologize to Ms. Stirrup," Edward said.

Becca studied Bunny's reaction. For a moment she saw hatred flash through her pale blue eyes. Hatred toward Emily, Becca realized. That's it—they were out of here!

But before she said a word, Edward began to move the three of them past Bunny toward home.

"I think we should get Emily home, Bunny. So if you'll excuse us—it was nice running into you."

"Yes." She turned her body in their direction, trying to detain him for as long as possible. "I'll tell your mother I ran into you and Ms. Reinhart," she repeated again.

Becca was certain she heard a sneer in this. "Becca, Bunny," she said again, knowing it would crack Emily up.

"Becca, Bunny," Emily repeated. Not once, not twice, but like a mantra—if four-year-olds had mantras, Becca thought. As though by prior agreement, Becca and Edward avoided each other's eyes—knowing if they glanced at each other there would be muscle-aching laughter.

"Seriously, Bunny, it was nice to meet you." Becca put her hand out once more and Bunny once more gave her a wet-fish handshake.

"I'll see you at the Glaucoma Evening?" Bunny asked Edward, who by now was past her so she was talking to Edward's back. And what Becca saw was a tigress letting today's prey get away because she wasn't really hungry and she knew there would be a next time.

Chapter 18

Bunny Takes Tea

Bunny Stirrup crossed one modestly covered leg over another as she pressed a lemon against the side of her porcelain teacup. She was visiting Catherine Kirkland in her city residence, a stately mansion furnished with the family's elegant collection of eighteenth-century tapestries, mahogany letter-desks, walnut end tables, and gilded footstools. She arrived at 4:30, in time for afternoon tea. Bunny straightened her spine so as not to touch the Beauvais tapestry that covered the antique armchair in which she sat.

She was visiting Edward's mother to talk about their plans for the wedding. Their union as mother and daughter-in-law had to be accomplished without further delay. The short but significant chance meeting with Edward, his ward, and that woman, had informed Bunny— there was no more time. The three of them were quickly growing into a family and before this afternoon visit was ended she would have landed Edward Kirkland, albeit through a less glamorous way than she had hoped for. And while the delightful young lady made nice, sipping her steaming cup of Earl Grey and agreeing with Catherine's archaic views on everything from the proper scent of sheets to the necessity of chaperones, she was scrutinizing her elder with an unyielding stare, waiting for her moment to pounce.

Bunny felt as confident as a queen. As soon as she and Catherine sent the wedding announcement to *The New York Times*, she had selected everything white from her summer closet, and wore the dazzling color everywhere, glad to stand out against the dark wools that crept out like moss after Labor Day. She was the awe of everyone she knew. That she could be so bold as to wear white after Labor Day was a manifestation of her triumph: Soon she would reign over the Social Register as a bona fide Kirkland. Whatever she did would be glamorous, and her friends knew it. They were finally treating her with the respect and attention she deserved. The only detail left undone was to bring Edward in on the plans.

Of course, to her meeting with Catherine Kirkland, she wore an acceptable winter white. Even in the face of her confidence, Bunny's caution had risen to the magnitude of what she had to lose. She had neither seen nor spoken to Edward since *The New York Times* went to press with their wedding announcement; quite intentionally, she had avoided him. She simply wanted to hear him say "I do." After that, she thought, smiling triumphantly, he could say anything to her that he liked. It wouldn't matter. And she'd decide what to do about the child afterward. As for Ms. Reinhart, Becca, she thought with a malicious mental swipe, she'd amputate Ms. Becca from Edward's life immediately. If not sooner.

She had played this just right. She had gone to the source.

The grande dame herself, chattering with pleasure in her blithe detached absurdity, had given not a moment's thought to Edward's opinion about his marriage. She would as soon have consulted a fish before changing his bowl.

Bunny studied her quarry with a furtive eye, and determined the time was not yet right to strike. She invited Catherine to tell her more about the portrait artist, sighing with satisfaction when she saw Edward's mother quiver with emotion.

If there was one thing to get old Catherine talking, it was the family portraits, Bunny thought, barely concealing her smug attitude. Even the city mansion, small by the Kirklands' standards at a mere twenty-one rooms, had two halls and one gallery expressly for the family portraiture. In their house at the Hamptons, the Kirklands kept two prominent rooms on the wing of the house facing Georgica Pond reserved just for the oil portraits of their dogs. Each dog was painted indoors, posed on a velvet pillow by the fireplace, in the courtly style. Their likenesses were logically arranged beside the family portraits, and apart from the sporting art, to emphasize the devotion of this noble family to its great breeds.

Catherine tittered with laughter. "I want you to know this is a first for me, Bunny," she said, her eyes wide as she smiled to congratulate herself. "Dear old Randolph Kent passed on, you know, and we haven't used anyone else for the oils in *years*." To indicate how dreadfully long they had been using dear old Randolph, Catherine floated a hand across the room as if it had set sail, drawing the word *years* out for a small eternity.

"I took a chance, dear, on someone new for your wedding portrait. So you'll have to credit me with a great deal of whimsy!" She set her teacup down and laughed, giving a lovely shake of her fair head. In a habit of old vintage, she shot a quick glance at the footman who stood by the door. He responded with a hearty laugh and an obsequiously eager nod. Catherine smiled, satisfied. The servants were perfectly devoted to her.

Swallowing the lump in her throat, Bunny followed suit.

"I'll say that takes some spunk!" she cheered at Catherine.

"That it does, that it does, my dear," announced

Catherine with a grand nod. She reclined into her tapes-tried chair with a sigh and set about describing the extent of her spunk and whimsy.

She had hired a portraitist by the name of Quinn Brown, an artist from Newport whom one could not exactly call untried. He had done a half-century of highly regarded work for the Rockefellers, the Mellons, and the Roosevelts, as well as some decidedly lesser pieces that hung in the Frick. He was remarkably talented, and quite a "fanciful character," Catherine insisted with a giddy raise of her eyebrows.

Bunny knew Quinn well by reputation. Jinks Preston, who had been in Bunny's book club until she married five years ago, had hired Quinn to do a mural for the tennis court at her house in West Palm Beach. Quinn was com-missioned to paint spectators in the stands, styled to imitate crowds at Wimbledon, except with the faces changed to portray all Jinks's friends. The mural was com-pleted in short order, to Jinks's delight.

When she noticed the sun-washed mural beginning to fade, however, Jinks invited Quinn back at once to touch up her face. She was well pleased with how her image stood out against her faded mother-in-law, Hester, and directed Quinn to make no further improvements to the mural. Quinn returned every few months to touch up Jinks's image, and Jinks, like a reverse Dorian Gray, grew younger in the mural with each year. By contrast her mother-in-law, whose pathetic appearance had never been improved, developed horrid sunlit cracks that ran directly through her cheeks.

Bunny smiled with amusement. She was sure Catherine didn't know that story. Hester Preston was a dear friend of hers who would certainly be at the wedding. Bunny thought with a laugh that Hester would be the only woman she had met in the Hamptons whose face was an improve-ment over her portrait.

She was glad to know the name of the portrait artist in advance. She'd put a call in to Jinks, inviting her to be a bridesmaid, and drop a hint for Jinks to say a good word about her to Quinn. Quinn could make any face the portrait's high point; he just needed to know who would make it worth his while.

Just the other day, as Catherine Kirkland had forced Bunny to sit though a viewing of her wedding album, she had seen a young picture of Hester Preston in a sherbet-colored gown, attending Catherine Whitney as a bridesmaid in her 1950 wedding to Horace Kirkland. Bunny had her fill of Catherine's going-away pictures: her beaming, starlit smile, her queenly silk-gloved hand emerging from the sleeve of her sumptuous fur jacket, waving ta-ta to the humble onlookers as she left for her glorious honeymoon.

How could she be bothered with Catherine's memory lane when she had courting bouquets arriving every hour at her apartment? This morning's four-hundred-dollar silver-plated urn filled with lush violet-colored sweet peas, pink roses, and baby's breath was as disgusting as a heart-shaped box, she had thought with distaste, throwing it upon the avalanche of free arrangements sent by florists in the hopes that Bunny would use them for the wedding and later for her weekly fresh flowers. Vera Wang, Carolina Herrera, and Badgley Mischka had all sent over dresses and shoes, and Van Cleef & Arpels, Cartier, and Harry Winston had sent over representatives with cases of jewelry they would loan to Bunny to adorn her lovely ears and neck on her wedding day. She sighed with pleasure as she realized it would be the last day she would have to borrow anything.

Returning to her senses, Bunny blinked her eyes and smiled winningly at the grande dame who presided at the floodgate of her riches. Edward was Catherine's only son.

In time, Edward's wife would inherit all her furs, all her diamonds, the houses, the cars! Bunny vowed to find a museum in New Mexico where she could donate the bloody oil paintings, and redo all the houses in her own style. She was so close, so close.

She noticed that Catherine had instructed her servants to draw the curtains on the western window. The sun was bothering her; she appeared to be tired. Bunny caught her breath. Now was the time to strike!

"Do you suggest a wedding portrait or should I have one done later?" she asked, giving Catherine a sweet blink of innocence. She knew she wouldn't have time to sit for a wedding portrait, especially since she wanted to keep her gown a surprise from everyone.

"Oh, a wedding portrait, in your gown, dear," Catherine answered firmly. She instructed a servant to refresh their tea, which was done in the prompt and anonymous fashion of the best houses.

Bunny thought quickly. How could she convince Catherine there was no time for a wedding portrait and make her think it was her idea?

"Will you wear your mother's gown?" Catherine wanted to know. Some of the older heirlooms couldn't be cut to fit a taller bride, but she imagined that Bunny would fit into Eileen's gown.

Bunny nearly choked with surprise. "No!" she gasped. The enormous A-line gown that Mother had worn gave the appearance of concealing a life preserver around the hips.

Catherine's eyes widened.

Bunny caught herself. "I'm afraid," she said, turning her eyes down demurely, "I would be too emotional if I dared to step into the shoes of my own mother at such a time."

Catherine swallowed the lump of her own emotion. She leaned over to pat Bunny's knee. "Dear girl," she said.

"I've actually already commissioned Vera Wang," Bunny said, describing the dress in terms as traditional as she could come up with. She didn't mention that her abdomen would be exposed by the gown; that was going to be a surprise. "One more fitting and we're good to go," she mentioned casually.

"Already?" Catherine asked with surprise. "Whatever for? I suppose you'll have it all tucked and tightened again in a year's time."

Bunny dropped her head in sadness. Her plan was working perfectly. She picked up her tea, made her hand shake, then set it down again as if overcome by emotion.

"Catherine," she began, "I don't know how to say this."

"What, dear?" said Catherine, leaning toward her with concern.

"I need to marry Edward quickly."

Catherine smiled, touched by the urgency of young love.

"Whatever for?" she asked gently.

Bunny stared directly into her face.

"Edward is falling in love with Becca Reinhart."

At this suggestion Catherine frowned with displeasure. "The guardian?"

Bunny nodded, widening her eyes to appear frightened.

Catherine sipped her tea, considering the possibility. A smile slowly stretched across her thin lips, and she shook her head.

"Darling," she reminded Bunny, "she's Jewish."

Bunny's heart beat quickly. Her face flushed as she turned an imploring face to Catherine.

"I know," she breathed, reaching out to grip the slim oval tapestry on the arm of the old lady's chair. "That's just the problem." Her eyes glinted with a fervor that was at odds with the helplessness she intended, and she swallowed hard.

"Whatever do you mean by that?" Catherine asked crossly.

Bunny took a deep breath. "Well, Catherine, I don't know this for sure. But I've been *told*, by certain people familiar with this sort of affair, that, well . . ." She paused again to breathe deeply, as if calming herself. "This is hard to tell you," she admitted.

Catherine made an impatient motion with her hand. "Get on with it," she said sharply.

"Well, they *say* that when a man falls in love with one of those kinds of people . . ." She paused, filling her chest with air as if to draw together the courage to speak.

"Yes?" Catherine tapped on the table with her teaspoon.

Bunny leaned toward Catherine like a conspirator. "The man falls in love with their *whole way of life.*"

Catherine gasped. "You don't mean—"

Bunny nodded gravely. "He'll convert."

Catherine clutched her heart. "Not my Edward!"

Bunny's eyes grew misty. "It could happen, Catherine. I've been told—" She paused again, dropping her head to cover a smile.

"What? What?" Catherine prodded her arm with a monogrammed silver teaspoon.

Bunny raised her head. "That he's taken to eating *blintzes.*"

Catherine remained still, and for a moment all was silent.

"And *latkes*," Bunny added ironically. She had fabricated this.

"What the bloody hell are you talking about?" the old lady snapped.

"They're *ethnic* foods," Bunny explained, raising her eyebrows. "Kosher!"

"God bless you," replied Catherine, clapping for service. The monogrammed linen handkerchief that arrived was so heavily starched it almost cut Bunny's skin when she raised it to her nose.

Catherine, who had a moment to think, reconsidered the matter of the food. Edward had traveled the world, she explained, and had eaten lots of adventurous things. Perhaps he simply had the explorer's palate.

Bunny shook her head. "Catherine," she said, "there's an old saying that comes to mind. The way to a man's heart is through his stomach." She paused, then spoke gravely. "The *blintzes* are only the first step. Those people won't stop until they make Edward *one of them*."

Catherine's eyes widened as she imagined Edward fiddling on the roof. She shuddered, set her teacup down on its saucer, and stared at Bunny's grave face.

Suddenly she shook her head. "I'll have to ask Morton about this. He's been doing our taxes for thirty years, and I can't say he's ever tried to turn us into his kind of people."

Bunny gulped. She had to think fast. "Professional courtesy," she pointed out.

Catherine, who knew nothing of the working world, nodded. "I see."

"I know this is hard for you to face," Bunny urged, "but if Edward doesn't marry me soon, you'll see him next at his bar mitzvah."

The sound of this guttural phrase gave Catherine a shiver, and she hung her head.

"How soon?"

"Two weeks," said Bunny. Hastily, she added, "at my house in the Hamptons."

Catherine raised her eyes to Bunny's, saw that she was serious, and obliged. The new ways were so fast; everyone rushed about these days, with their blinking phones and computers. She supposed it was for the best. But the child would not get away with everything, she thought, noticing Bunny's eyes seemed happier than they should.

Bunny had reached for her teacup to take a drink. Catherine reached her arm across the tea table and set her hand firmly on the gold-rimmed cup, pressing it back into the saucer. Staring stonily at her future daughter-in-law, she kept her hand over the steam that rose from the tea. She held it in place to prevent Bunny from drinking.

With narrowed eyes, she challenged Bunny.

"You may have your wedding in two weeks," Catherine allowed, "but it will be at *my* house in the Hamptons."

Bunny's eyes met Catherine's with a glare. She was the bride!

Catherine stared without flinching, holding the teacup in place even as Bunny reached for it.

"Of course," Bunny managed. "That would be delightful. You have such a lovely home."

Catherine lifted her hand, allowing Bunny to drink her tea.

I'll have to tell Adrian, Bunny sighed to herself. She had already given her wedding coordinator, Adrian Parish, the measurements of all her party rooms. He was so precise he had asked for the grading angle of the lawn down to Georgica Pond. Now Adrian would have to spend a day chasing the Kirklands' house staff for details, just now when they couldn't spare a minute of time! She glared at Catherine, who was staring at her sternly. This was no way to start their relationship. She had to make her own power play.

"I've already engaged a wedding coordinator," she announced.

Catherine's expression told her she had made a mistake.

"What in the bloody hell is a wedding coordinator?"

Bunny recalled that Catherine had been married in 1950, back when a girl counted on her mother's social secretary and private house staff to put the event together.

She swallowed hard. "He's, uh—like a florist."

Catherine's hard blue eyes stared straight at her as she spoke in a low, even voice.

"Thank you, dear, but I have a lovely florist," she said. "We always use him for family events."

Bunny sipped her tea and nodded. She breathed deeply before she spoke.

"Of course, Catherine. I'm sure Adrian and your florist will work together beautifully."

Catherine raised an eyebrow. "Together?"

Bunny gave a warm laugh. "Oh, Catherine, I'm sure I didn't explain myself well. Adrian is not so much a *florist,* really, so to speak: he's more on the *arranging* than the *procuring* side of things, you see. He works with florists all the time."

"With?" Catherine looked at her suspiciously.

Bunny swallowed her pride. "For," she corrected herself, looking at the sumptuous gold-toned Turkomen carpet.

Catherine nodded with satisfaction.

"Fine, dear." She felt an outpouring of graciousness now that she knew her people would be managing Bunny's people. "How appropriate, to have our staff work together," she offered smugly.

"Yes, Catherine, how wonderful." Bunny took the opportunity to notice the grandfather clock in the corner. "Oh dear, the time has just flown! Catherine, I must be off. Thank you for this lovely tea." She stood from her chair and motioned for the servant to clear her tea service.

Catherine motioned for the same servant to stay put.

Swept by the noblesse oblige that accompanied her successful shows of power, Catherine rose from her chair and, following Bunny to the north portrait hall, laid a cool hand on Bunny's shoulder.

"Roberta, darling," she said, surprising Bunny by using the formal name she loathed.

"Yes, Catherine?"

"I'd like you to call me Mum." Catherine beamed as she said this, as if she had just opened a tower door to release a prisoner in a grand show of mercy.

Bunny cringed, but with an effective exercise of control turned her disgust into the little twinkle of nose that precedes a giggle. She laughed merrily.

"Oh, Mum, what an honor!" she said, leaping forward to embrace Catherine, which gave her a quick opportunity to relax the sore smiling muscles of her face.

Chapter 19

Sunday Times

Becca had taken Emily to shop for Halloween costumes, after which they planned to change their clothes for a "girls' dinner" at someplace fancy. The idea of changing her clothes for dinner had Emily absolutely entranced. For a child of only four, she had an astounding mental inventory of her closet.

The simple mention of one of Edward's charity events would send her racing down the hall to her bedroom, in a great show of pretending that she was invited. When she returned, holding her chin high in the air and half-closing her eyes to display her importance, she would invariably be trailing two different outfits in her soft little hands. One would be a sweeping gown—perhaps a lilac taffeta Florence Eisemann, for example, empire-waisted and alto-gether dreamy. In the other hand she would tug her Lily Pulitzer bolero jacket, together with something chic—her magenta pantsuit, perhaps, with the rainbow-beaded ankles.

Emily would sigh a thousand sighs, casting both outfits on the couch in front of the smiling, indulgent eyes of Edward and Becca. "I just can't decide," she would tell them. Emily didn't know the debt her mannerisms owed to this urbane little corner of the world, the unbearably put-upon Upper East Side, but her guardians did, and they laughed tears. She sighed, rolled her eyes, and earned a great deal of sympathy. Emily felt very grown-up and accomplished when she talked about her clothes. Youth reveals its innocence in the modesty of its dreams.

Edward had plans to attend the Tartan Tango, an odd, festival-style medley of kilts and red lipstick that had occupied the same October weekend for so many years that, like the luau for Madagascar's Oyster Growers, repetition had dulled its sheer ridiculousness. It was always held the first Sunday in October; Edward, as usual, had done a table.

Edward had announced his destination to Becca and his straight face earnestly told her he was serious. Her eyes danced as she congratulated Edward for going out at least one night this week in something other than his tux.

Edward met his car downstairs, as arranged. Though he would ordinarily walk to the Carlyle from the Racquet Club, he needed a few minutes to review the briefing papers that Alice had prepared for him. He was surprised to see James pull up in the old black Bentley, one of Kirkland Enterprises' company cars.

Edward experienced a paralyzing moment of dread when he suspected his father would be waiting for him in the car, probably to attend the Knot Tying Dinner or some blustery event at the Union Club, but was relieved to find the car empty of all but a heavy jasmine-scented perfume. Edward could imagine the scenario. His father's driver, Robert, had taken Horace Kirkland home in Edward's green Jaguar, Horace had dispatched his son's driver James to drop his mistress off at La Guardia in the company car, sending James on to his appointment with Edward in the Bentley.

"Who was it this time, James?" Edward asked with a laugh. "Miss Whitshire or Miss Abshire?" Horace insisted on calling his mistresses by their proper names, to rest his laurels with propriety.

"Strike two," smiled the driver, who knew Edward kept his confidence. "Miss Shropshire."

"I don't believe I've met her," Edward admitted. "My junior or my senior?"

"She's a good bit older than you, son," James advised him, and said no more.

Edward opened the window a crack to relieve them both of this sickly floral reminder of his father. He turned to his briefing papers to assess his prospects for tonight. Cricket St. James, he read, unfolding the paper. He thought he could picture her. Blonde, he remembered. Or was that Cricket St. Clair?

He grinned with the sudden memory of the black and green crickets that Becca and Emily had made from pipe cleaners. They had hidden them in his bathtub, trying to scare him. He laughed to himself, recalling that he had rehidden the same creatures in Becca's bedroom. He wondered if she would retaliate.

Unable to sort out his Crickets, he consulted the briefing paper. Cricket St. James, a curator at New York City's Museum of Television and Radio, was a part-time sculptor. He studied the pictures Alice had provided from a press piece describing Cricket's sculpture exhibition at Max Fish last spring. He couldn't get past the exhibition's name: Haiku in Plaster.

Cricket herself looked like twenty other people he knew: he was glad to have arranged to meet her at the Carlyle, as she would be harder to recognize. The event was at the St. Regis, as usual. Proceeds would be donated to fund an airlift of dental supplies to the Balkans.

The air hung thick and misty under the heavy sun. It had rained last night; or so he was told—Edward was not woken by the thunderstorm that sent Emily sprinting into Becca's room for cover. The day had warmed again, but without brightening: Rain seemed again to be imminent, and the air was dense. Edward leaned toward the window of the car, relieved to see the familiar view of the Carlyle. Graceful black and gold canopies shielded the hotel's entrance: It appeared to Edward as welcome as a port.

It was still too early to expect much of a crowd. He had arranged to meet Cricket for a drink at five-thirty, according to Alice. He had just enough time to change.

Edward paused, asking the driver to wait, noticing something strange. His eyes moved past the lush white jardinieres, imported from Versailles, that guarded the entrance, to the crowd that buzzed around them. Who had imported the Junior League, he wondered, puzzling over the glut of heel-clicking bon vivants? The crowd was chaotic, scurrying about, unconnected: a swarm without a hive. He saw some perky pincurled blondes, some sleek brunettes dressed for art openings; a few women in workout clothes, a few in clothes suitable for the office. He could see only women, and many of them were toting things: heavy bags, pictures in frames, folded sweaters.

Where were their dates? Why were they carrying all those things by themselves? Were they shooting an Upper East Side episode of the *Antiques Roadshow*?

Edward leaned closer and recognized Cricket St. James on her way into the lobby. He had just been thinking of her. She seemed upset. What was she holding?

He drew in his breath when he saw the photo collage Alice had prepared for Cricket after their yacht trip. She had set down another crate of things to offer a condescending, drop-fingered hand to an acquaintance. Edward peered from behind the shield of his one-way window into Cricket's crate. He thought he saw the royal blue sailing jacket she had worn in Mykonos, which he remembered letting her keep.

In the crowd he saw little Bitsy French. She was consoling someone. Minnie Forehand? Edward felt a sense of foreboding. He was grateful for the cover that the unknown car provided in this strange circumstance. James called for the concierge, and in minutes, the frantic figure of Dwight Owsley raced to the side of the Bentley.

He poked his head into the back window while it was still opening.

"Quick! Let me in!" He jumped inside and dropped his head to his ankles to hide.

"Pull around to the back entrance!" he ordered the driver.

When they were out of sight, he sat up and flung a pained glare at Edward.

"Mr. Kirkland," he addressed him. "What have you done?"

Edward stared speechlessly.

"The operators are going *mad!* We haven't taken a reservation all morning. Your voice mailbox is full, the hotel's mailbox is full. Everyone is *frantic!* I have been slapped, I have been tackled, I have been cursed in Swabian! Everyone is looking for you! What have you done?"

Edward, stunned, shrugged his shoulders. "I don't know, Dwight."

"Our storage facilities are overflowing. Women have been throwing boxes of things at me all day. Lingerie! Perfume! Bracelets! Men's fishing sweaters, Burberry scarves, umbrellas. And about ten thousand pictures of you smiling on a yacht deck with every girl in Manhattan!"

Edward sunk his head into his hands. His gifts. People were hurling them back at him. When did he get the plague? "What happened?"

"I expected you would tell me that," the concierge snipped, squinting at Edward long enough to determine that the source of this fracas was as baffled as he. Spying his general manager carrying a box from a dark-tinted Mercedes sedan into the hotel, Dwight ducked his head again.

James, circling the hotel, stopped at the back entrance.

Edward prepared himself to be swarmed—which might be all right. At least he'd find out what the commotion was about—the women were beginning to look for sticks and newspapers and that looked like they were going to create his effigy.

"Good luck." When James opened his door, Edward noticed he was smiling. He was beginning to feel like the butt of a joke. He hurried through the kitchen to the service elevator with growing curiosity.

When he got to his tower apartment, Cricket St. Clair was waiting for him. She was slumped against his door: She had been crying. He reached out to her with concern, and was shocked by the sharp, stinging slap that was her answer to his help.

With a sullen look back at her, he unlocked his apartment, leaving her in the hall. He left the door open. She had better explain herself.

By the time he had poured himself a glass of water, she had poured herself onto his carpet, pounding her fists on the Persian rug and shouting in a mixture of apology, anger, and accusation that left him utterly confused.

"Cricket," he said, leaning against the wall to regard her from a distance of several paces. "What the hell is going on?"

The only thing he understood from her torrent of screams, threats, and accusations was that the *Sunday Times* had something to do with it. With a wary eye on Cricket, whom he wanted under no circumstances at his back, he walked to the hall and gathered his unopened edition of the newspaper.

"Enlighten me," he asked her. Petulantly she snatched the Sunday "Vows" section, unfolded it in a huff, and shoved it under his nose.

"Does *this* help you understand why I feel like such an

asshole? Just last week I confirmed our date with your secretary. I talked to Alice *yesterday*. You might have told her to give me a heads-up!"

Edward listened without interrupting, staring at her evenly, trying to understand what had happened. Cricket, finally exhausted, looked back at Edward in a daze. She was furious to find him neither regretful nor angry. He was waiting—inscrutably—regarding her with his quiet composure, with self-control.

"How could you keep this from me?" she shrieked at him.

He looked curiously at the newspaper, surprised she had handed him the "Vows" section. If his father's company was at fault, it was covered in "Business."

She recited from agonized memory what he read from the paper:

Heir to Chemical and Diamond Fortune to Wed
Notable Equestrienne in Private Ceremony

"Well?" She studied his face as he read further: read his own wedding announcement. The strange scene in the lobby became clear to him. In the minds of an angry torrent of women he had behaved badly, last week, last month, last night. He was getting married. Married!

"Cricket." He looked straight into her eyes. "This is a total surprise to me."

Her jaw dropped and for a moment she was too angry to speak. She clenched her fists and trembled. "Don't take me for an idiot!" she hissed at him.

He set his jaw. He had been thinking the same thing.

"Get out," he said, throwing the paper down with frustration.

She shivered, stepping backward toward the wall. She had never seen him angry.

His eyes burned, staring past her, and without another word to Cricket he reached for his tweed jacket. He bent to the floor to retrieve the newspaper, and placed it under his arm. His face was aflame as he stared through her, his eyes fixed, lit with an unutterable intensity. She drew in her breath when he spoke.

"I'll call you a cab," he said, and his voice was like stone. She shook her head, uncertain, hiding her face behind her hands. He pulled a phone from his breast pocket to call for his car.

"Our date is cancelled," he said, holding his arm on the door. "I apologize for the inconvenience to you." Cricket hurried out, as eager to leave as he was to dispense with her.

She sunk against the wall, crying into her hands, unable to grasp the emotions that swung and whistled around her. She was breathless, ashamed, and angry—but she believed him now. The change she had just seen in his blazing eyes! It must be true. She had seen his sudden severity and terrible resolve, his face flushed in streaks. She had seen him become someone else.

She knew Edward was telling the truth. He had been engaged by ambush. And his reaction, she thought, her heart overflowing with pity, was the opposite of joy.

His mother was behind this, Edward thought, dropping his eyes at the thought of her silent force: her presupposition that he would oblige her, the compulsory undertone of her delicate suggestions. His mother.

And Bunny! How devious she was. How could he marry a woman who was taking him hostage?

Edward stood alone in the elevator. He stared fiercely ahead, his eyes burning, the pressure pushing into his brain, the unyielding, uncompromising future he had tried to ignore. So now a wedding was set for him like a tea table.

He read the impeccable prose of his wedding announcement, read and re-read it, the words swimming past his eyes as he lurched through the service kitchen and hurried out to the street. He wondered if he could really say that this engagement took him by surprise. Hadn't he seen it coming? His thoughts kept returning to the Hamptons.

Bunny had visited his mother alone too often this summer. He should have known something was brewing when she actually took up bridge and began to play with Catherine Kirkland and her cousins once a week. His mother had dropped hints for years that it was time for him to get serious with Bunny, but he had never expected her to do more than talk. It was his life.

Wasn't it?

He directed the car to his parents' house in Sutton Place.

Chapter 20

Mother Knows Best

Edward paused in the small half-circle of a Japanese garden that graced the north face of the house. He had lingered outside when he saw Bunny's car in the driveway, and he remained in the shade of a stately old elm tree as he watched her depart.

It was the first time Edward had felt strange in his parents' home. The doorman greeted him with a customary half-bow as he entered from the garden, and Edward returned his stiff politeness with a kind smile, but the cheerful temper that was his natural solace had withered inside him. As he waited, listening to his mother's proper English as she spoke unguardedly into the phone, he regarded the gilded portraits which lined the north hallway.

Edward cast an eye over his great uncle Henry Castor, pictured with a full proud chest as he stood holding the bridle of his Tennessee walking horse; his cousin Margaret Springer Whitney, seated on a red velvet ottoman, was trailing a double-length strand of pearls lazily from her jeweled right hand. He gazed indolently over the faces of a half-dozen more aunts and uncles, feeling no more warmth towards their disdainfully dropped glances than he felt for the woven Turkish carpets painted under their feet or the fur stoles thrown imperiously over their icy shoulders. His own shoulders sank and he kicked the fringe of the Kazaki carpet with the toe of his cordovan loafer. All the people in his life struck him suddenly as absurd decorations, assembled like jewels in a case to dazzle the visitor with the glamour and glory of the House of Kirkland.

He was agreeable with his mother, of course, when she moved upstairs to receive him in the suite overlooking the garden, adjacent to her master bedroom. She had fresh tea and scones brought up from the kitchen for him. Edward stood to hold the door for the maid when she arrived with the tea; he paused to regard the gentle evening that was taking form outside in the dusky garden. He turned to find his mother smiling contentedly at him from where she sat in a tapestry-covered armchair. She tapped her silk slippers on the red and gold Persian rug, squeezing a lemon with the tip of her silver teaspoon over the steam that rose from her porcelain teacup. She nodded to indicate that she was preparing the tea for him.

Edward returned her smile, noticing with shame that he turned his eyes to avoid her blank, contented gaze. He was unable to look at her directly when he could not share her carefully constructed joy. Edward sat beside his mother in a matching chair. He rocked back and forth restlessly, finding himself unable to rest his feet on the finely patterned ottoman for fear of kicking it over. He found that he drew no pleasure from his mother's finery, her gold-rimmed, lemon-scented tea service, her silk curtains, soft bedroom slippers, and the gleaming white façade of her French marble fireplace. His restless spirit felt estranged in the familiar elegance of this room he had visited a thousand times. He felt like a stranger here, and perhaps always had been.

His mother's admission regarding the wedding announcement was immediate and remorseless. So simply did she state her reasons for publishing the announcement without informing him that Edward began to glimpse the totality and depth of her self-deception. She acted as if it all was perfectly normal. She seemed to regard the typical Manhattan society family as a feudal entity whose alliances were forged by parental negotiation and announced to the public at appropriate intervals. Incredibly, he felt sorry for her.

Watching her speak, so simply and ridiculously, he knew his mother had been used. Beautiful illusions had always sparkled before her lovely eyes like frost on a window glass. Edward saw how this innocent frost had somehow preserved his mother, insulated her vulnerability, protecting her like a doll in a case. She had been cheated, he thought, of some necessary interaction with reality. Had he?

It was all a matter of scheduling, according to his mother. His father, who had given up on the pipeline through Turkey and was now negotiating a path through Kazakhstan, had quite a bit of travel coming up that winter. She had to get the date on his calendar before he was committed through next spring. It would be soon, she said, looking at him from beneath a raised eyebrow.

"You won't make any travel plans for the next few weeks, will you, darling? We're rushing a bit, chop-chop, right up to the gate, but Bunny and I have decided there's something fresh and romantic in that, don't you think?"

Edward sat back to catch his breath. A few weeks? She couldn't be serious.

He had no chance to confirm the date, however, before his mother had moved on to the details. The Oxford Boys Choir, as Edward knew, had sung at every Kirkland wedding ceremony for 250 years, and they had to be zipped over on a chartered plane right-o, so they could get back in time for midterm exams. The Esquida trio, a chamber music ensemble that played on original Stradivarius violins, would be perfect for the first day of receptions, if they could squeeze it in before the October festival they played in Salzburg. She was certain that the trio would oblige, since the acoustics in the shell-roofed music room with its original horsehair plaster would ideally suit their original instruments.

She had to think of the minister, and a soloist for the arias. . . . Catherine recalled Bunny's mention of having engaged a flower arranger, and gave a little sigh of pleasure.

"That Bunny is simply the most *considerate* young lady," Catherine exclaimed, smiling proudly. "So *attentive*."

Edward almost spit out his tea with surprise.

"Bunny?" He covered a smile with his hand. She had a great seat, a commanding riding style, nice posture, and an attractive bust, but Bunny was no Florence Nightingale.

"Bunny has chosen a delightful flower arranger who will help us with some of these dreadful little details. Isn't that dear of her? She'll be a lovely wife."

Edward listened patiently, with sympathy, unable to speak. What could he say? His mother lived in a snow globe. A word of opposition now would shatter her.

Before he stood to leave, though, Edward calmly asked her a question.

"How do you know, Mother, if I love Bunny Stirrup?"

She squinted at him without understanding. He had always been intended for Bunny, and Bunny for him.

"Edward, don't be silly," she scolded.

She approached him, laying a hand on his shoulder. "Dear Edward," she began, and her eyes filled with tears.

"Oh, Mother, don't cry," he said, reaching for her hand. He removed her hand from his shoulder and gripped it warmly.

"Edward, please," she said, her voice calm and serious. "This is so important to the family. Bunny has always been meant for you. She's so devoted to you, darling."

She noticed that this news hardly affected Edward, who stared vacantly across the room.

"She keeps an excellent seat," his mother pointed out. "So many riders these days bounce around like cowgirls. Roberta pays attention to the important details. Mark my words, Edward: Roberta Stirrup will never use bad form."

He was amused to hear his mother use Bunny's proper name.

"You call her Roberta now?"

His mother nodded. "And I've *already* asked her to call me Mum," she added.

He sat for as long as he could manage, speaking respectfully to his mother as he felt the warm scones crumble in his fingers. For the first time within the sanctum of his family, Edward felt his impulses separating from his actions. He promised to cooperate, but out of duty, not love.

Edward caught his reflection in the gilded mirror. His blue eyes were empty, as blank as smoke. He stood and leaned forward to kiss his mother's cheek. Just then the butler brought a telephone into the room.

Bunny had put a call in to Catherine Kirkland from her car, to clear up one matter they had overlooked.

Catherine was again touched by the insistence of young love when she considered that Bunny must have stopped somewhere to use a telephone.

"What a surprise, Bunny, dear."

Edward walked away to give his mother privacy. Still he could hear her courteous voice. He cringed to think what subplots Bunny was creating now.

Bunny explained that she'd be hand-delivering invitations in a matter of days, and certainly would include everyone on the list Catherine's private secretary had sent over. They had discussed the sensitive matters presented by a few divorces, and come to amicable conclusions. But what would they do about Becca Reinhart?

Catherine considered the matter with consternation. In her noble graciousness she knew the event gave her an opportunity to reach out to the alienated, but when she put a fine point on it, she realized that she couldn't risk exposing herself to ridicule among her own guests. And she had planned to use her French Regency porcelain table settings, the eighteenth-century Sèvres celestial blue arrangement. She would simply die to see those elegant antiques shattered in the plate-smashing festivities that Ms. Reinhart would find culturally necessary.

"They do tend to smash plates at weddings, don't they, dear?"

"Oh, absolutely," Bunny said in a rush. "It's positively a *rule* for her kind of people."

"All right, then," Catherine decided. "Send her an announcement, but no invitation." Catherine would have said something about how she wished they could be magnanimous, but she had not yet excused Edward and he stood nearby.

"Yes, you're exactly right," Bunny agreed, pumping her fist in the air. She hung up the phone before Catherine could reconsider, and redirected her driver to the Warren-Tricomi Salon on West Fifty-seventh. This day called for Zen music, floating roses, and a full-body massage.

"Good-bye, Mother."

She caught his arm before he reached the door.

"Edward?"

"Yes?" He noticed she looked nervous. She held her hands together, and with a finger and thumb was hastily twisting her large sapphire ring back and forth.

"We'll manage the guest list. All very close friends, intimates and the like."

He sighed. He had tried to hide from this day for ten years.

"Okay, Mother," he said, raising his eyes to hers to nod

with an agreeable smile. Another action separated from feeling. Edward saw his whole life before him, days strung together with lies—lies to appease, lies to deceive, eventually, he supposed, lying got to be the norm. He was eager to leave, and tried again to turn for the door.

"Edward?"

He turned again. "Yes, Mother?"

"We don't want any surprise guests," she said. She had moved an uneasy hand to the pearl clasp on her necklace, which she tapped with her manicured fingernail.

He stared at her, and she turned an evasive glance to the window before forcing herself to look back at him. He saw now what she meant. She didn't want Becca to set foot on the family's sacred ground. And she lacked the courage to tell him that directly.

"None of Emily's grown-up friends, you mean," he said. He did not conceal the bitterness in his voice as he glared at his mother. "No guardians."

"Exactly," she returned coolly.

He nodded, and walked away without turning back.

It seemed to take no time at all for the car to get him through town to the Upper East Side, as Edward sat silently, his senses lulled out of focus by the fleeting lights and sounds of city life.

Emily had just gone to sleep when he walked into the apartment. He went to her bedroom and kissed her cheek, drawing comfort from the rose blush of her cheek and sweet smell in her hair. As he left the room, he turned off the television, which was tuned to CNN Financial. Becca had turned it on to help Emily get to sleep.

He entered the library. He knew to look for Becca there: She liked to sit close to Emily's bedroom, where she could hear her, at least until she was sure Emily had gone to sleep. She was reading the *Sunday Times*, he noticed. Or anyway, it was at her feet. She took a sip from a bottle of Perrier, then held the bottle up to offer him a drink.

He declined her offer. His eyes darted around the room nervously. He remembered a different time in this library, when he had sipped wine and looked inward, discovering himself as he opened to Becca, about Arthur, about college: seeing intimately, in the soft evening light cast by the single brass standing lamp, into Becca's casual beauty, her mysterious self-possession.

His shoulders sank when he saw her lift the newspaper to her eyes. Everyone read the bloody *New York Times,* he thought, feeling a surge of resentment at its uncontrollable circulation. A million Sunday readers and pass-along readers and waiting room readers were now expecting Edward Kirkland to get married. If he made the wire syndicate, his wedding announcement would be news from Tucson to Concord, by way of Duluth. The Harvard alumni magazine would pick it up; St. George's would paste him into their "Milestones" section. He could picture, already, the announcement cut and tacked to the bulletin boards at the Racquet Club and the Union Club; no doubt some piece of buffoonery was scribbled beside the headline: "The Soldier Bows to the Queen."

She squinted at him. "You look pale. Are you all right?"

He forced a smile. "Sure. Why?"

She shrugged. "Maybe it's just the light."

He offered to bring in another lamp for her.

"Don't worry about it," she said, giving him a curious stare. She glanced at her watch. "I didn't expect to see you this early. It's not even ten o'clock. Not much of a tango this year, was it?"

Edward blushed, feeling ridiculous.

"Where's the kilt?" Her grin was playful, but even as Becca toyed with him she could sense his embarrassment. He seemed ashamed.

227

She dropped her chin to the palm of her hand and looked at him, standing there bashfully with his hands in his pockets. Doubt and sympathy mingled in her eyes, and the tender concern that washed over Edward felt stark in relief against the cold hand of duty with which his mother had steered him.

Edward knew he should tell her, but he couldn't find the words. It was supposed to be good news. How would Becca understand the bitterness that would crackle around his words? He couldn't even pronounce the word *engagement* without hostility: without the degraded, dishonorable rage that he felt, guilty and helpless in the vortex of his responsibility to the Kirkland name. It was time for Edward to give back, the delayed price of admission to his golden circle of luxury and ease had finally, unalterably come due.

"Listen," he tried, his eyes on the floor. "I didn't go to the party. I—"

"Are you okay, Ed?" Becca stood and walked close to him. He felt her hand drop down on his shoulder, and his eyes met hers directly. They were the same height.

"Hey, buddy, who moved your cheese?" she asked him in a quiet voice.

His face broke into a smile. Her humor was so kind and open. Becca didn't pause to think much before she talked, unlike his perfectly cultivated mother, with her precious decorum; unlike his shrewd, cunning bride-to-be, who would have a pond measured for ripples before she ventured to toss her pebble in. He smiled, looking at her fondly; but Edward could get no closer to the thing he had to say.

"I forgot something," he began, his eyes searching the room. "I forgot about the kilt. I'll, uh—I've got to get back to the party." He heard himself speaking in a monotone. Here's how lies started. He could not face her. Edward turned with a heavy step and walked out of the room.

"I won't be home tonight," he said, his back to her.

He wondered, as he walked away, why he had called this place his home. He swallowed hard. What was he doing here, anyway? Becca was "on duty" with Emily tonight and tomorrow until lunchtime. He lived at the Carlyle.

Becca shrugged, listening to Edward walking slowly down the hall. She didn't believe him, but he was entitled to have his bad days. Returning to the reading chair, she put her feet up on the ottoman and reclined with the newspaper. She pulled out the "Week In Review" to scan the headlines.

Becca paused when she heard the apartment door close quietly. She smiled, knowing that Edward made an effort not to let the heavy door slam when Emily was asleep. Abruptly she dropped the newspaper, realizing that he had left immediately. He hadn't picked up his kilt—he hadn't picked up anything. What had just happened?

She rubbed her neck, feeling a sudden wave of pity for Edward. And she didn't know why. With a deep sigh, Becca dropped her head into her hands. He had seemed ready to say something, standing there before her, shoving his hands in his pockets, shifting his feet. She reproached herself for failing to listen. Why did she have to do that bit about the cheese? Why did she want to make him laugh all the time?

But Becca warmed, remembering his smile at her little joke. Maybe that was what he needed. Edward was so naturally genial that the sudden cloud over his mood seemed tragic. He was not the kind of guy made for suffering.

What was the matter with Edward?

She shrugged, repeating to herself that she could not let it get to her. It was the same with Emily: Her moods would fly past, and if you allowed yourself to be victim to a foot-stomping moment over mixed-up food at the restaurant, then you would miss all the fun when Emily, forgetting, would crack fortune cookies, poke a paper umbrella in her hair and hide giggles behind her plump hands.

Once again she picked up the heavy Sunday edition of the *New York Times* to set about the long business of reading it. She removed the front page, placed it on top of the business section and dropped the rest of the newspaper to the floor.

Chapter 21

Any Port in a Storm

The next morning began like any other. Emily's footsteps pounded down the hall to the master bedroom, picking up speed as she approached the room where Becca sat in bed, tapping on her laptop. Quickly, Becca pushed her cup of coffee a safe distance away on the walnut nightstand, hid her slim computer under the bed, and in a minute was prepared for Emily's crash landing. The child burst through the door and exploded onto the bed with a great running leap. Eddie's old dog, MacDuff, lifted his head to check out the action, but then returned to his doggy dreams.

With a small shriek and a great act of being surprised, Becca rolled Emily into a burrito in the fluffy duvet that covered the bed like a cloud. Emily squealed with delight as Becca poked her, tickled her, and finally unrolled her to say good morning. She kissed the happy cheek of her red-faced girl, who gasped a breath before burrowing under the sheets for a repeat of the beloved morning ritual. Giggling, diving, and laughing in squeals, Emily alternated between hiding and popping up to startle Becca, who tackled her in a flurry of tickles.

Finally Becca collapsed backward against the wall of pillows that guarded the brass headboard, pretending to fall asleep. Emily pressed her face right into Becca's, her wide, shining eyes not an inch from Becca's closed ones. Her giggling was too much to resist; Becca opened her eyes, encountering Emily's enormous fluttering blue ones. Her face was so close it seemed to float like the moon. The trust she shared with her little angel made her feel warmed. She loved being woken by Emily.

Becca rubbed Emily's pillow-tangled curls.

"Come on, Em. Let's go brush your hair. The early bird catches the worm."

Emily jumped to the floor. Her pudgy feet immediately sought the warmth of the heart-patterned mohair rug, where she wiggled her pink-painted toes in pleasure. The mornings had grown brisk. Emily wrapped a silk kimono, which she insisted was her bathrobe, around herself.

"Can I have some guava juice now?"

"It wouldn't kill you to ask nicely."

"Pleeeease. And please please some truffles from Maison Du Chocolat? I saw the box on top of the refrigerator. Pleeeease?"

Becca softened the answer no with a loving smile. She wrapped herself in one of Edward's plaid flannel robes, which he had lent to her on a chilly morning.

"Eddie gave me a Toblerone," Emily bragged. "I hid it and I know where it is."

Becca laughed, pulling socks on her feet. She lifted Emily to her hip for their speed-skating down the hall to the kitchen. The brushing could wait.

Emily always began her mornings with a glass of guava juice and a plea for candy. Though Becca was perfectly comfortable with an eat-when-you're-hungry approach, adopted during years of working 24/7, as a parent she knew implicitly that she had to draw lines. She could find better things to do with their money than build a third beach house for Emily's pediatric dentist. So Becca decreed that nobody would eat candy at least until after lunch, and then it would be followed by tooth-brushing, plus a

232

rinse with the Water Pik. Emily tried all morning to find ways to sneak candy, and failing that, bided her time until Sunday mornings, when Edward would take her out for sugary donuts after church.

Edward was "on duty" with Emily around eleven, for the rest of the day, and Becca already regretted the time she would lose with her chirpy little bird. But she suspected there were fires to put out at the office: She was used to being needed there, and hovered, even after her leave of absence, like a back-seat driver.

As she poured her coffee into the twelve-ounce mug and Emily's guava juice into a "jewel"-studded goblet, Becca felt her neck and shoulder muscles growing tense. She had not slept well, puzzling about Edward's black mood, and finally gave up trying. Her laptop greeted her with hundreds of unread e-mails, and many gave her cause to worry. She had not checked in at the office for several days, and always paid dearly for inattention.

Her chief concern was an underperforming company to which she had extended one round of bailout funding. (This was the compromise she had carved out for herself— no travel and only one day a week in the office allowed until her "leave of absence" was over.) She had a confab scheduled with their executives—the execs wanted more, and she had to squeeze them harder. She would require between eight hundred and a thousand job cuts as a con- dition of the supplemental loan she offered—and she knew the corporate officers would be shocked at the level of cuts she required in management. The big-screen conversations she looked forward to having with them were not pleasant ones.

The hard tone she would have to take in her meeting seemed a world away, as Becca hid under the waving neon crepe paper legs of Emily's octopus collection. They were playing sharks and minnows, and Emily, as usual, was the shark. She squealed with laughter as she identified Becca's hiding place, then launched a shark attack with delighted fervor. Even before her second cup of coffee, Becca was racing around the apartment, making fins on her head and shoulders, hiding behind doors and chairs to escape the shark. The duality of her life felt peculiar; the playful, loving person of the morning could not simply button a jacket and scowl over the inarguable economics of her spreadsheets. But that was what Becca had to do. And since Edward had not yet returned, she would take Emily with her. Philippe was turning into a high-priced baby-sitter and he loved it!

Frustrated by her inability to control the troubled thoughts she had about Edward, Becca went over this rather routine meeting hundreds of times in her mind, grateful for the chance it gave her to focus on something firm. She felt nervous, though, from the intensity of her thoughts: She had particular trouble waiting for Emily to get dressed, which was challenging for her even on a good day.

The task was one of "enabling" the child to get herself dressed. If parenting magazines had one theme, it was this: Preschool children developed essential independence and self-confidence by learning to do little tasks by themselves.

It sounded simple enough to Becca, from the "give a man a fish" versus "teach a man to fish" perspective that she regularly quoted to companies who wanted money without strings attached. But when she required funded companies to "learn to fish," Becca never had to stand uselessly there in the room while they struggled up the learning curve. Standing in place, straining not to take control while helplessly watching a four-year-old fumble at her shirt buttons could tax the patience of a calm soul. For Becca, it was almost unbearable.

She pressed her head into her hands with regret as

Emily chose, from her closet, a "fancy" dress with about thirty sparkling flower-shaped buttons. Round buttons were hard enough for Emily's pudgy fingers. Flower buttons were the black diamond slope. Why on earth Amy had let Emily pick out clothing with complicated fastenings was at first a mystery, but very soon Becca had learned that Emily was her own "personal shopper."

Becca bit her lip and tapped her feet on the floor, vowing to be a positive, encouraging presence. These were the steps to self-reliance, she reminded herself. Becca checked her watch, then tried to forget what the time was, so as not to put pressure on Emily to hurry.

After a few minutes she stood up. She glanced at Emily, saw no progress, and began to hum a little tune in an attempt to act casual. She straightened some things on Emily's art shelf. She glanced back—nothing. Becca turned to the curtains and fiddled with them for a minute. She looked out Emily's window, becoming occupied in the motion of the street, which had a soothing quality for Becca, as some people feel who regard the passage of a river.

When she turned around she saw that Emily had drawn to the window behind her. She was silent, watching the city scene with a serious face. Becca smiled, for she knew that Emily was imitating her, and that the impulse was one of love. She kissed her round head, retrieved her cup of coffee from Emily's rosewood bureau, and sat down once again on the couch. She sat for what seemed like an eternity, then allowed herself to glance at Emily, intending to cheer her progress.

Emily had given up on buttoning in order to arrange her nail polishes into categories of "glitter" and "pearl." Becca checked her watch. Thirty minutes had passed. She returned to the couch, and pretended she was at an ashram in the Adirondaks, breathing deeply, purifying her city soul. She glanced again to see Emily's progress in getting dressed.

Emily stood entranced by her reflection in the oval standing mirror, making the blinky-eyed faces of a princess in love. Her dress hung in a wide-open triangle from the neck. Becca saw at once that the top button, which was about halfway in, was at that moment in great danger of sliding out of its buttonhole. She shivered with the effort it took not to leap up and fix it. *Encourage, encourage,* she told herself.

"I like that pretty dress you picked, Em. Can you put it on?"

Emily smiled in agreement, then twirled around the room humming the "Dance of the Sugar-Plum Fairy." She fell into a dizzy lump, then picked herself up, and began to twirl again. Becca checked her watch. Forty minutes. Her coffee was cold.

"I'll run and get dressed for work, Em," she said, offering herself an escape. "Meet you back here in a few." Despite her better self, she added: "Let's see who can get dressed first!" Then she ran down the hall, cursing herself for impatience.

In her room, Becca washed her face, brushed and flossed her teeth, slid into a black Gucci pantsuit, and slowed herself down by applying a coat of moisturizer. She was proceeding in as slow a fashion as possible, which was difficult for Becca, who was in the habit of flying through life with a rocket in her pants. She brushed some color on her cheeks, once she determined which of her black Chanel makeup cases contained what. (Becca wore makeup by chance and as time allowed, and as a result she was unfamiliar with her own offerings.) She shrugged at the lipsticks, not knowing how she was supposed to choose. Indifferently, she rubbed a sheer color on her lips. She concentrated on her breathing while checking her watch. She didn't know what else she could do to pass the time.

She walked, as casually as she could, into Emily's room.

She caught the child midcurtsy, and by habit applauded, calling *Encore! Encore!* to Emily's beaming face. Emily had spent the last half-hour perfecting an elaborate ballet dance that followed the patterns of her rug. Her dress hung entirely open. Even the top half-button had come loose.

With a claim that the weather had grown cool, Becca raced to the closet and grabbed a pullover. It was a new one from Baby Prada.

Emily held the Tiffany snow globe in front of her eyes, looking at Becca through the magical mystery flowers that swept through its miniature cityscape.

"What?"

"Here's a pullover for you. A little hooded cashmere. They're *very* fashionable."

Emily peered at the cashmere as if it would bite. "No, thanks," she answered politely. She looked as if she had smelled a dead rat. "It doesn't go with my dress," she added, shaking the snow globe to watch the flowers glitter down and around the tiny buildings inside. "Sparkle!" she whispered, delighted.

Becca nodded. She knew she was at her limit. "Okay, honey," she said, smiling. "I'll be right back."

On her way to refill her coffee, Becca almost bumped right into Edward, who had quietly entered the apartment.

"Hey Ed," Becca greeted him cautiously. She was glad to see him, desperate for a break from getting Emily dressed. Edward had a talent for making games out of those sort of things, and anyway he was better adapted than she to the prospect of sitting still. Also he didn't have to rush to a meeting. He gave her an unreadable smile.

"You look like the bottom of a shoe," she called from the

237

kitchen, where she groaned to see the Betty Crocker cake box still on the counter. She had promised Emily they would bake together, and Becca reproached herself for putting it off. She lifted the box, which contained the raw material of a basic yellow cake, and studied it carefully to be certain of every detail, as if it were her tax return. It was as the child had claimed: you added water (eggs were optional) and then you baked it. There was even a little round icon shaped like a pan. So that was it. The cake was not as formidable a task as she had imagined. When she got home, they would bake it.

Becca saw that Edward had shuffled into the morning room, but he had not sat down in the armchair that was his usual spot. He stood quietly, his back against the wall. When she joined him he turned to greet her and his eyes were tired.

"I can take Em to the office, Eddie, if you need a rest," she said, staring curiously at him. "I've got a meeting at two—unavoidable—but Philippe will be there."

He looked at Becca with affection. In the depth of his melancholy, she could always make him smile.

Becca stepped closer to him. "What do you think? Can you manage her today?"

"Sure," he answered, and the smile that crossed his lips, when he thought about spending the day with Emily, was genuine. Her needs were simple. His eyes rested on Becca, searching her. Did she know? Could she be the only woman in Manhattan who didn't know?

She paused, but he didn't reply, just stood still, watching her. Their yearning to understand each other was evenly matched with their unwillingness to pry, and the silence hung thick.

"Okay, Eddie," she said. She gave him a cautious glance.

He sighed, digging his hands into the pockets of his wool trousers. Their friendship would end like all the others. Every woman he knew had cut him off like a leper when the *Sunday Times* hit the streets with his wedding announcement. It had been just a day ago, but the cancellations had flooded in and Alice made light of it; sweet Alice. She was perfectly decorous, congratulating him simply and formally on the engagement, and not asking any more questions.

He felt wrong about going to the club last night. He had ducked away from Becca, not ready to confide in her, but unwilling to dishonor her with insincerity. The false tone was impossible for him to maintain and his plans for the tango party were erased from his short-term memory, and so he fled to the library at the Union Club. This served to prove how muddled Edward's thinking was, that the club had occurred to him as some sort of haven for his privacy. If his engagement to Bunny was the storm, the Union Club was precisely the opposite of the port he was seeking.

Drinks had been rushed on trays to him with dash and generous wishes, which Edward bore, one by one, filling himself with alcohol as a substitute for warmth, trading cigars and winks and slaps on the back. It was worse than loneliness; it was a lie.

He glanced at the kitchen, into which Becca had trotted impulsively. A sudden flash of hope lit within Edward's heart. Maybe it wouldn't matter to her.

Their friendship was dug in different ground, with Emily's needs at its source. He noticed that Becca was friendly with her boss, a married man. And with her analysts, and her secretary, and the stream of entrepreneurs she had dinner with when they were in town: They were all men, and she had no romantic interest in them. She didn't play those angles. Maybe they could work some visitation agreement out, and get together over the years for Emily's school plays or her ballet recitals.

Even as Edward fantasized, he knew this would be

impossible. He had only cared for Emily in partnership with Becca, and only imagined their bringing her up together. But he had known Bunny all his life, and he had his obligations to her: She would want to applaud at Emily's ballet too, and take pride in "ownership" if nothing else. Becca's candid habits of speech worried him when he thought of her in the same room as Bunny.

Becca pushed a cup of coffee into his hands. "Drink this, Eddie. You'll need it."

He smiled, accepting her gift. Together they went to Emily's room, to change the guard from her authority to his. They found Emily singing merrily, painting the toenails of her Madame Alexander dolls. She had succeeded in covering most of their feet and not a little of her manicure table. Becca said good-bye to Emily with a little kiss.

"I'll come home for lunch," she promised. "And I'll pick you guys up some fruit plates from the Healthy Bite."

Edward gave a grateful nod as he took a seat on Emily's four-poster bed. He felt hungry, but it was apathy, dissipation, and habit that turned him to food. In truth he was lonely, and his emptiness was not the kind that a meal would cure. He welcomed Emily onto his lap, paying no mind to the red nail polish on her fingers, which drew streaks on his sleeves. He sighed with pleasure, rubbing her warm, golden hair. Edward felt his whole body relax. Becca, who was taking her leave with leisure, noticed the change.

"You look better, Eddie," she said gently. "I think I see a daddy who missed his little girl."

He nodded, smiling as Emily hopped off the bed to her manicure table. He felt as if he had held his fists clenched tight for forty-eight hours and now let them fall open. Edward turned to look at Becca, feeling a sudden urge to tell her everything, as a man getting a bad day off his chest might turn to his wife for comfort. But when he looked at her, she had her eye on her watch, and he knew her mind was already on her own life.

Blowing a kiss to the room at large, Becca hurried away. Her smile lingered in his memory as Edward listened to her footsteps in the hall. Contentedly, he reclined on Emily's bed, leaning his head back against the mountain of fluffy lace pillows. He no longer felt as welcome at the Carlyle, where he had made his address for nearly five years, as he did in this apartment at this moment. He couldn't believe he had hardly spent a month here.

With tenderness, as he watched his daughter play, he felt the return of a sense of meaning that escaped him whenever he was away. Emily needed him.

And Becca? He imagined her wide smile, her easy laugh, her energy. Then suddenly, his mind focused on the image of her checking her watch, turning to walk out of the room. People needed *her*. Maybe she had a place in her heart for Emily, but she didn't have time to worry about him.

Still, his thoughts refused to release her. In a short time they had built up a huge bank deposit of memories. Edward realized that the three of them together had history. Between him and Becca, however, it was not so clear. He only knew any room expanded when she entered it. He couldn't recall a single one of her jokes: he couldn't remember any, exactly, as they were all the situational quips of her quick mind, also the serious thoughts they shared eluded him, but he knew when he was with her, he was his best self. Her whole presence was like energy itself. She made him think—and feel.

Edward had not reflected on his connection to Becca like this before. They had been catapulted into their responsibility to Emily. And in the shock of reacting to that, they had simply begun to live with each other. He had not stopped to think about her when he had assumed she would be there the next day. Now that he was losing her, he could think of nobody else.

He turned at the sound of Emily humming to herself as she began to paint McDuff's toes with sparkling nail polish. What would he tell Emily? He had never had to think of other people so much in his life. For years he had been pulled inexorably along the path cut by his family. He had carried on merrily enough, without concern for what lay ahead. Edward had never realized he was surrendering to a scripted future until he met Becca. She didn't ask him a thing about himself, but in the rapid good cheer of her own useful living, the excitement and sense of purpose she lived out had suddenly thrown all of Edward's assumptions into question. She seemed so different from the women he knew, but Edward never felt so much himself as he did in her lively company. Becca put him totally at ease.

If he had any talent for introspection, Edward Kirkland would have been able to identify the feeling that had been clarified. Instead he sat on Emily's bed, playing a game that involved naming fruits. He knew that he belonged here.

Chapter 22

The Last to Know

The place where Dick Davis belonged was in custody, thought Becca, gazing around his office with astonishment.

Gray Nikes and Adidases and soft navy athletic shorts with the Champion logo stitched on them were piled dozens high on the boomerang couch. A rainbow of running gear waved from hangers like a decorative row of windsocks. Running shoes, walking shoes, cross-trainers, and hiking boots were arranged in a little march across his George Jetson chrome-topped desk. The only item of clothing that looked remotely like it might belong to Dick was the soft, fluffy terrycloth robe that hung from the back of his desk chair. The office was buzzing with image consultants.

"So we're taking the NFL public?" she guessed, pointing at a row of tube socks.

He couldn't answer her, as the stylist Kenneth Dapper was holding his mouth closed like a beak, peering through a jeweler's glass to evaluate Dick's upper lip for mustache potential.

"No way," Ken concluded, stepping down from his bench. "But your neck hair looks great. Nothing ingrown; will wax perfectly."

Becca cringed. This was more detail than she wanted to hear.

"I'll come back, Dick, if you're busy," she said.

"No!" Dick clapped his hands to draw the attention of a busy little hive of consultants, several of whom emerged from his closet as if startled.

"People, I need some private time now," he said to the crowd. "Take a break, take a break! There's a Starbucks in the lobby."

The image army grumbled and muttered out the door, leaving Becca and Dick alone in his office.

"Tell me," she guessed, still baffled by the clothes. "Henry Kravis is running a marathon, and you've decided to best him with the triathlon."

Dick shook his head. "*Leslie,*" he said, with a sigh that said his wife's name was enough to explain any intrusion on his dignity. "She's decided I should take on an image that is similar to our president in his leisure."

"So you're exercising now?" she asked him, lifting a gray "Property Of" gym shirt from his desk. This, unlike the other clothing, actually looked worn.

He shook his head no, patting his Buddha-style tummy. "No, Becca—that's just for Fridays. Haven't you gotten the e-mail?"

She laughed out loud. "Even if I had, I'd ignore it. What in God's name is Piloga?"

"A merger of Pilates and yoga."

"I think you mean merging, not merger."

"You need a Berlitz course in real-life English instead of business-ese."

"Your standards are too high," she retorted. The thrust and parry of their banter was such that her strikes to his vanity were usually met with his jabs at her lovelife. But today Dick trod lightly.

He walked to his desk to get his copy of the "Vows" section of the *Sunday Times,* which Leslie had her social secretary fax to him with her explicit instructions to get them an invitation. Did she know? He looked at Becca, who stood smiling casually at him, looking bright, vigorous—perfectly normal, for her. Changing his mind, he dropped on his desk the item about the engagement between the chemical heir and the equestrienne. He wasn't sure how to approach this with Becca. She always had her eyes so wide open; he had never really seen her disappointed. He dreaded what he had to say.

"Tell me how it's going with your coguardian," he asked her, as innocently as he could manage. "Kirkland, right? Real Society Joe, from what Leslie tells me. I'll bet he spends *days* in front of the mirror."

"Eddie?" Becca gave a full laugh as she pictured Edward in a mirror of self-absorption. It was hilarious: so unfitting an image for him. Edward was the most natural, unassuming, easygoing person she knew. Come to think of it, the apartment was full of mirrors, and she had never seen him pause at one.

Dick peered at her for her answer. The light of fondness was in her eyes when she talked about Edward. His shoulders grew heavy. He wished he could spare her from what was coming. He hated to be the one who would put that light out of her eyes.

"No way," she said, "not Eddie. I mean, he's in a tux half the time, but he doesn't give a thought to how he looks in it. He couldn't care less. He lets Emily pick out his bow tie."

"Smart man," Dick mused. "I didn't know that women were supposed to pick my clothes until *after* I got married. I guess he'll be good and ready. He'd better be." He paused, breathed deeply, and said it. "It's going to happen soon."

Becca's smile died on her lips.

"He's engaged to be married, Becca," Dick told her gently.

Becca's loose black hair tossed defiantly behind her as she shook her head no.

"It can't be true," she replied. "Not Eddie. He's not the marrying *type*." She laughed.

"I'm afraid he is, Becca," Dick replied. His voice was kind, but serious; he could see the matter cut straight to Becca's heart. He approached her with the newspaper in his hand. In a minute she was reading the copy of Edward's wedding announcement.

Becca could feel her cheeks flush red with humiliation. She swallowed hard and stared ahead of her intensely. She had been betrayed.

She sat down to catch her breath, a fire roaring in her eyes. Her mind raced over the last few days: This had just happened, she realized, and who would have guessed it from Edward's behavior? He had been so withdrawn, so inaccessible all of a sudden. He was usually so busy at night, but he had been holing up in his room, reading, he said, or answering his mail. He was acting more like a fugitive than a fiancé.

He had told her he had a lot of cancellations. Now she understood why.

Dick broke the silence with a question that went straight to her heart.

"What are you going to do about Emily?"

"Emily!" Becca gasped. Dick was right. This changed everything.

"I want to help you," Dick said, sitting down next to her. "Becca, since Emily's been in your life, you've seemed to me to be better balanced—more fulfilled."

Becca sunk her head into her hands. "Yeah, I know," she remembered. "You told me all about it. The zeitgeist."

Dick nodded. "More creative too. Kid, it's been all good for you. You've been great here, you know, even a day a week. Less demanding, better with the analysts. You're a better manager. They are responding great to your new approach."

Becca looked up without understanding. "I have a new approach?"

He smiled. "I wish I could tell you how much better you are at your job, but I don't want you to get mad at me. You were a sort of freak of nature; a star. You don't know it, but you've changed."

She nodded, but his kindness did not penetrate—she was a slow fire growing frantic. "Dick," she began, and faltered. "I'm not sure what to do."

"Becca, I'm telling you this for a reason. I want you to know my motives. I want to help you keep that kid, and I want you to understand why. I think Emily's been good for you personally, but you're the best judge of that. Anyway I *know* your last month has been good for Davis Capital. The best long-term thing I ever did for this place is make sure you took a little time off with that kid. You're a leader now, Becca."

She nodded, slowly, but her mind was not on analysts. It was on Emily.

"Dick," she said, raising her eyes to meet his, "he'll get custody."

"That's why I wanted to talk to you, Becca. I know a thing or two about custody," he said, making the rare reference to his first wife, who had taken their son after the divorce and immediately remarried the club's golf pro. "His marriage will give him a solid claim for sole custody, no visitation."

Becca was silent, rubbing her head with her hands as her mind raced over what he was saying. Dick was right. Edward would take Emily, and she'd be—an ex-guardian? What was that? She would have no rights, no chance. Forget visitation—she had no blood relationship with Emily. She breathed quickly, realizing that once Edward married, it was possible she would never see Emily again. Not that Edward would ever be that cruel—but that woman . . .

"What can I do?" she asked him.

He smiled. "There's only one thing, Becca. You need to get married."

She laughed out loud.

"You're crazy!" But the joke, so familiar between them, suddenly took on a new light.

He nodded, holding his ground.

She raised her hands like a shield, but her eyes were lit again and dancing. "Not your nephew again!" she pleaded. But her mind had picked up on this possibility. She began to pace, thinking.

Dick grinned, noticing that her whole demeanor had changed. She was circling around the office, thinking as she walked, putting things together, connecting the dots. Becca was confident. She had a job to do.

"Married," she said, pausing to look out Dick's plate glass window at the bustling street below. "All right. That makes sense." She wheeled around with a victorious smile. "So how hard can it be?"

Dick was so glad to see Becca come back to herself that he almost hugged her. But she was staring ahead, tapping her hands against her thighs, thinking of a plan.

"Well, kid," he said, delivering the blow of blows to a control freak: "It takes two."

She shrugged, uninterrupted in her plotting.

"What doesn't?" She was thinking out loud, and grabbed a pen and pad of note paper from Dick's desk to capture her thoughts.

"Getting the Go-Forward Agreement—that's the hurdle, you're right. Not insurmountable," she said, scribbling a bullet point. Her glance at Dick was thoughtful as she paused to think it through. Then she made another note with enthusiasm.

"We've solicited bids for acquisitions plenty of times," she said to him. "I've just got to get an offering circular out there. Dick, get up on the block. I'll bring in the bids, I know I will," she announced, tossing her hair with a confident smile. She dropped her pen to the notebook with a flourish. "So that's it. I merge, consolidate, and move forward."

Dick laughed out loud. "People don't release an offering *circular,* Becca."

But she was already rushing out of his office.

She called Edward, before Emily was asleep, when she knew he would not be busy carrying on a background conversation with the irrepressible four-year-old. She told him simply that she was "buried" and would have to work all night. Some matters needed personal attention, she added, some things she couldn't delegate.

He expressed his understanding, knowing that she had found out.

She needed to stop by her apartment, she mentioned, to check on some things. Would he be able to manage Emily alone for a day or so?

He would, he assured her, reminding her of all his sudden cancellations.

Becca paused, gathering the words to congratulate Edward on his wonderful news. There was an etiquette to that, she thought to herself. Congratulations was outdated, she remembered, offensive to the modern ear. Best wishes was what you said to the groom, wasn't that right? Or to the bride?

Letting her mind become occupied by this little formality, Becca waited, and waited, until Edward finally ended the pause.

"Don't be a stranger, Becca," he said to her.

She caught her breath.

The other line rang, and she said good-bye to Edward. He hung up before her. She listened to the quiet for a minute, with the uncanny feeling that her mind had gone empty.

Philippe was working late for her. He had paged through the archives of While You Were Out notepads that Davis used for phone messages before the system went digital. He had pulled all the messages from Becca's personal calls. He brought them in for her to review.

She was surprised at how scant the pile of messages was. He had checked two years of time: She had thousands of incoming calls, but the calls marked "personal" were few, and when she paged through them she found that they were dominated by calls from her mother. The electronic messages were easy to search, but this exploration yielded only a scarce few marriage prospects. Becca knew she had to try another way.

Her next call was to the Jewish matchmaker.

Chapter 23

Blintzkrieg

"Jeannette Werman & Associates. Please hold!"

Becca bit her lip. If she had to hold more than a minute, she would give this up. Jeannette's advertisement in the classified section of the *Wall Street Journal* had always intrigued her. In more confident times, she had looked at the matchmaker with curiosity from a business perspective, wondering what her margins might be. She had considered calling before, wondering if the matchmaker marketed people any differently than she marketed companies. Like any outsider, she had at one time experienced the devilish impulse to know what kind of people used these degrading services.

Now the degraded one was Becca, and she tapped her fingers as if she could hurry the call. She wanted swift, untraceable action.

Jeannette promised "exclusive introductions to attractive, educated, accomplished Jewish professionals seeking life partners." Becca knew from vetting her own companies for acquisitions that the best deals united compatible corporate cultures of firms with more synergy than duplication in their core businesses. So she had made the decision to go Jewish, but thought it best to avoid venture capitalists and bankers.

"Sorry to keep you waiting," a pleasant female voice said.

"Thanks," Becca said, and while she was about to deliver her story, she realized she was speaking to a recording.

The recorded female voice continued. "If you are a woman, please press one on your touch-tone phone. If you are a man, please press number two."

Becca pressed one and clenched her teeth.

"If you are divorced, please call (212)555-1234 for a second chance with our excellent subsidiary designed for women in your less-than-desirable dating position. If you have never been married, please remain on the line."

Becca perked up as she waited.

"Thank you. If you are under thirty, press one. If you are over thirty, press two."

Becca hung her head and pressed two.

"Thank you. If you are calling to meet a nice Jewish doctor, press one. If you are calling to meet an intense Jewish lawyer, press two. If you are calling to meet a successful Jewish banker, press three. If you have no specific profession in mind, please press four."

Becca pressed four and rubbed her temples where she was getting a headache. She was feeling more humiliated by the second. She knew that this service was a two-way street. Somewhere a pathetic soul was poking his telephone, and the powers behind Jeannette's advertised smile would match his data to hers and stick them in a room together. She felt like a dog waiting for stud service, and the thought reminded her, suddenly, of Edward. She swallowed hard, fighting the swell of conflicting emotions that rose within her when she let her thoughts turn to him. He was a gentleman, anyway, she thought, rubbing her forehead wearily. She could bet he treated his dogs better than this service was designed to treat people.

After a pause, the recording continued.

"If you are calling for Orthodox, press one. If you are calling for Reform, press two. If you are interested in meeting or becoming a Bu-Jew, press three."

More afraid than interested to find out what a Bu-Jew was, Becca pressed two and finally a woman picked up the phone.

"Okay, sweetheart, what's your name?"

"Becca Reinhart. Is this Jeanette?" She heard the operator's gum smacking in her mouth as she talked. This couldn't be the elegant dating guru with her picture, all confidence and repose, emblazoned across the classifieds.

"No, sweetheart, Jeannette doesn't handle the low rungs."

"Oh, thanks," Becca said sarcastically. She sighed into the phone, plunking her chin on her hands.

"Let me ask you a few specifics, honey," the woman went on. "You're over thirty, Jewish, and never married?"

"Right."

"And you live in Manhattan?"

"Yep."

"Oh my God! What does your mother think?"

Becca's cheeks burned with frustration. "What's the difference?" she retorted. "Listen, I've got a kid who needs a father quick. Like in two weeks. I've got to go before a judge to keep custody—"

"Honey, honey, honey," the woman was interrupting her. "Cut it right there. You're barking up the wrong tree, sweetheart. We don't take divorcées. Can't deal with the kids—too messy. It's right up front on the recorded message."

"I'm not divorced," Becca corrected her.

The lady let out a long whistle. "Oh, baby, you're wrong for us. Single mother? That's a tough street to walk. My heart goes out to you."

"Thanks for your sympathy," was Becca's dry reply.

"Really, really, hon, I mean it," the dating operator went on. "What you need is somebody quick, huh?"

"Like yesterday," Becca responded, more hopefully.

"Right, hon, sure. And Jewish? You still want a Jew?"

Becca felt like she was picking out a tie. "Yeah, a Jew would be nice."

"Call Blintzkrieg," the operator said.

"What?" Becca heard herself laughing out loud at this "Yinglish" combination of Jewish pancake and war effort.

"Blintzkrieg, sweetheart, that's what you need. Jewish speed dating. It's in the book. New introductions every seven minutes: It's the fastest dating around." She paused, then added: "But don't tell Jeannette I told you."

Becca nodded, scribbling the name on her open desk calendar. "Thanks," she said, obliged to this anonymous woman.

"Sure, honey, no problem," she said. "And Becca?"

"Yeah?"

"Don't lead with your heart. Be tough out there. Check 'em out solid for yourself. You should see some of the schmoes we call 'quality,' " she added ominously.

"Thanks," Becca said, hanging up the phone. Overcome with pressure, bewilderment, and diminishing hope, she called for the Blintzkrieg listing. She couldn't let any setback throw her off course. Eddie might be married before she had a chance to say her first "Shalom."

Becca got the details quickly, and due to the net annual income she estimated to the operator over the phone, was able to get a standby seat for that very evening's Blintzkrieg dating event.

"Think of it as like flying Southwest," he added hastily. The phones were ringing behind him constantly, creating a nerve-racking, emergency atmosphere.

Becca wrote down the directions and buzzed Philippe to call her a car. Then she flew through the Internet on a research mission, collecting, from sources ranging from the American Academy of Pediatrics to Concerned Citizens for Wooden Toys, a makeshift guide to the best practices of fatherhood. With only seven minutes in which to evaluate each of her potential husbands, she wanted to dive right into the important stuff.

Would he be a good father to Emily? In the end, that was the only criterion she really cared about.

The event was an early one—cocktails before dinner, with the idea that any matches made in the speedy table-swapping event could, like Clara and her nutcracker prince, be swept away in the taxi equivalent of a chariot to whatever delights they desired in enchanted Manhattan.

Chapter 24

Visiting Dinosaurs

While Becca analyzed fatherhood to pieces, Edward was operating beneath the cloud of melancholy that her sudden departure had caused. He knew that Becca had plausible reasons to be in the office—he knew she hosted a busy little beehive up at the top of West Fifty-seventh. He knew it was only reasonable to accept her need to take off a day or two, but he did so sullenly, with resistance.

Edward and Emily decided they would visit the Museum of Natural History. He called to see what time it would open. Then he put the *Nutcracker Suite* on the CD player so she could twirl in her nightgown like Clara while he took a shower.

He had been concerned that the museum would not be open by the time they finished the donuts he had promised to take her for—until he saw what Emily had chosen to wear. "The Old-Fashioned Lady Dress!" she announced excitedly, pirouetting around her room with the high-necked, long-sleeved linen dress.

Eighty buttons stood between Emily's fumbling fingers and the donut shop. Edward made an effort to smile encouragement and caught her beautiful, willful eyes with their fire of determination. She tossed her curls back with a swagger and started, as Becca had taught her, from the bottom, concentrating intensely to show Eddie what a grown-up girl she was. She had been *practicing*, she told him. Edward watched the child fondly, ignoring the growling of his stomach as he sat down to wait.

They ended up delaying the museum until the afternoon. Right after donuts Edward had to take Emily to Tiffany's Tiny Table Manners, a class at which four- to six-year-old girls learned the essentials of social climbing. Emily was delighted at the day's Table Task: She was instructed in the art of holding fresh strawberries by the hulls before dipping them into whipped cream or sugar. This she did admirably well, understanding that if she dropped the berry, the sugar too would be lost. She was less successful using her spoon to lift berries in juice. But the strawberry juice only complemented the chocolate from her donuts, Edward told her, promising to show her a Jackson Pollock at the Met done exactly in the same style.

In the afternoon they had an extraordinary time at the Museum of Natural History. Edward forgot his concerns in the thrill of watching Emily's first sight of a dinosaur skeleton, remembering his own excitement at first encountering the great mysteries of the world. Emily developed her own theory of the dinosaur extinction as they walked together through Central Park. She was certain that the dinos had just become very small one day, tired of being too big to fit through all the doors of the buildings.

According to her theory, the beasts were still alive, so she and Edward looked under clovers and behind bushes for their footprints. Emily found definite evidence of the great T. rex in the tiny hole of a tree, and hurried to protect the baby T. rex from the approaching ducks and geese. Edward realized they had drawn close to the pond. They were right across the street from Becca's office.

Edward mentioned their location to Emily, and she squealed with excitement, forming a plan for a surprise visit that involved each of them covering their eyes and then uncovering them to say *boo!* He wished he was Emily's age, when to cover one's own eyes was to shield oneself from the world. He agreed on the plan of surprise, glad he could say it was Emily's idea.

Becca looked over the familiar, ever-stirring view of the pond with a different attitude. Tonight, she thought with anticipation, I'll get this situation back on my terms. If I can marry before the hearing, then we'll both be hitched, and when things are equal, the judge always goes with the mother. She smiled, her confidence buoyed, rather than challenged, by the immediacy of her speed dating event. There was ordinary time, and New York time, and then there was Becca's time, in a category all its own. Perfect, she thought. She liked the idea so much, she wondered why she had never tried it before. Why waste a whole evening on a date with one person when she could cram in seven? Why go to the trouble of meeting and making small talk when a third party could get them all seated at once, ambitions transparent, résumés in hand?

She knew she had to shine. The clothes in her office had been hanging there, except for their refreshing rotations through the dry cleaner, for the better part of five years. She had some new things at the Stearns' apartment, but couldn't bear the thought of running into Edward. If she ran into him, he might question her about her plans. So she had run over to Prada and bought a purple dark-bordered mini-shift.

She smiled to herself as she shut her door to get dressed. She lifted the dress from its hanging bag, reflecting tenderly on the color Emily had brought into her life. Before she met the little rose-cheeked cherub, she had thrown together a careless, efficient wardrobe of gray and black. She might have been mourning, to look at her back then,

Becca thought, her eyes twinkling with hope. But Emily had changed everything.

She was not going to lose her.

It was already five-thirty. Becca stretched her long legs into her hose and wiggled herself into comfort. She had tried on a new pair of shoes at Prada, but decided that tonight was the wrong time to break them in. She expected to be on her feet quite a bit, jumping from table to table— or was that what the men would do? Smiling, she had a sudden thought of Eddie. If he were there, he would insist on changing tables so the ladies could sit, and he'd give that little half-bow if anyone stood up, and he'd be so quick to offer his handkerchief—he carried a handkerchief!— and get the door for anybody. Becca shook her head sadly, smiling with tenderness for his silly, gallant old customs. She wondered if they'd stay friends, if he'd resent what she was doing to keep Emily. Would he understand? A new life had been handed to her one day: a better one. She couldn't give it up.

Catching a glimpse of the Eastern Standard clock on the wall, Becca shook her head and hurried to her desk for her earrings.

The BlackBerry buzzed at her, but she ignored it, as she ignored the ringing phone, the blinking laptop. A simple pair of diamond studs shone at her from behind a little pile of binder clips on her desk, where she had placed them unmindfully days ago when she was going to use the treadmill. She was prone to leaving things around, as Becca lived at a hurry-to-do-something-more-important-than-tidy-and-file pace. Diamonds, scarves, clunky-heeled shoes, bags full of bagels, and coffee cups were scattered here and there around her office. In the past she had only herself to look after, and if she didn't care, what was the difference?

She scooped up the earrings and put them on, trotting around her desk to give herself a final once-over in the mirror by her sink. Her teeth, freshly brushed and flossed, glittered magnificently. She felt a little strange with the makeup on, like a little girl playing Becca Reinhart rather than Becca herself, but she was satisfied with the overall impression.

"You look beautiful!" came the little voice behind her.

Becca gasped at Emily, bright, happy, and chocolate-stained.

"You forgot to say 'boo!' " reminded Edward, poking her in the back.

Emily giggled. "Oh yeah. *Boo!*" she squeaked. "Surprise!" She rushed toward Becca to feel her soft dress.

Becca's startled eyes turned hastily toward Edward. "Eddie," she stammered. "What . . . what a surprise."

"Becca! We saw the dinosaurs!" Emily exclaimed. She began talking at a wild pace, but Becca, noticing nothing in her shock, merely stood staring at Edward. She didn't even notice he had removed her FAQs from the coffee table.

"Essential Points of Modern Fatherhood," he read, smiling wryly at Becca. "Is this for me?"

Emily was tugging at her dress. "Can we bake the cake? Can we see the dinosaurs again? Hello! Becca!"

She tore from Emily's grip to grab the paper from Edward.

"Eddie!" she exclaimed. "Give me that!"

"Can I see it?" asked Emily. "Becca? What's wrong? Becca!" Emily was tugging at her dress. "You're *purple?*"

Regaining her composure with an extraordinary effort, Becca leaned down toward Emily.

"I'm sorry, Em," she said, wanting to hug her but wary of her sticky dress. With the chocolate and strawberry on her cream-colored linen, Emily looked like a cone of Neapolitan. She leaned down to kiss her instead, stroking her hair for a minute while her mind raced.

"Do you want to play the Dragon Tales game on my

computer?" she offered, walking nervously to her computer to punch in the PBS site.

Emily raced to the keyboard, leaving Becca facing Edward alone.

"Hi," he said, shyly. He was surprised to see her dressed so flamboyantly. What did he really know about Becca? Did she have a different life here?

She returned his greeting with a cautious eye, walking quickly to retrieve the Essentials of Fatherhood. She folded the page and put it in her purse.

"We missed you," he began.

That was it, Becca thought. How could she avoid it? Here he was, the poor *lemishke,* in her office, for her blessing. Should she be happy?

"Yeah," she said, stepping backward, away from him. In front of Emily, she could see the colorful dragons hopping over rainbows on the computer. She looked past it, at Edward, and her heart was heavy. Edward was watching her intently, but he dropped his eyes, suddenly thinking a better thought. Who was he to Becca? She was carrying on because nothing had set her back. So Eddie got engaged. What was the difference to her? Obviously she was in some form of denial and hadn't come to terms with the fact that the married guardian would gain custody of Emily. Once that hit her, she would be less buoyant. Did this make him happy? What was wrong with him? But he couldn't quiet the relentless thought that, if she realized the consequences of his engagement, she would need him. Perhaps she would act in some way that he didn't dare.

As she approached him, her eyes were warm and spoke of the pleasure it was to see him. Or perhaps he was kidding himself. Or maybe she was glad to see Emily. He wanted to stay in her world, on some terms. He wanted her to think the same of him. He couldn't bear, suddenly, to think about a time when they wouldn't stand together like this.

"Congratulations, Eddie," she said, looking right into his eyes. "I hear you're getting married."

"Yeah," he said, shrugging his shoulder. "Don't mention it." And I mean that literally, he thought to himself.

He looked at Becca's dark, loose hair, groomed for whatever she had planned tonight, admiring her radiance, her fire tempered by tenderness. He was making a mistake.

The thought, which had only played at the edges of Edward's mind, occurred to him strongly, but still he fought it. He had always been expected to marry Bunny Stirrup: His mother set her heart on it, and now hundreds of thousands of *New York Times* readers were in on the glorious plan. But he felt that the life he looked ahead to, and that he looked behind at, were secure only at the price of being screened. The only real life he felt he had ever experienced was standing before him, staring deeply at him. And her eyes were pleading for him to explain.

"It was a big surprise," he said, unable to suppress a shrug that communicated his overwhelming detachment.

She dropped her eyes and stepped away from Edward. He had no courage to be straight with her, she thought, seeing his calm, even exterior as a weakness. Edward was too damned polite. He probably thought he'd spare her feelings by keeping his engagement from her, she thought, angered in a flash of pride. Becca never considered the possibility that Edward might have kept the matter to himself to spare his own feelings.

"I guess so," she heard herself saying, walking away from Edward. She needed to displace Emily from the computer, somehow, so she could move on. She had a big night ahead of her.

Edward drew close behind her, and with a gentle touch turned her toward him. His fair hair glinted in the fading sunlight. The Indian summer they had spent together, a sudden gift as suddenly withdrawn, was coming to its

262

inevitable end. Standing before her in the sunshine, his blue eyes so wide and serious, Edward seemed young, and Becca couldn't help the tender smile that crossed her face.

"Becca," he said, his voice earnest, his desire to explain immense. "Becca," he repeated, "it's not the way they said it in the paper."

Becca sighed, leaning gently against her desk. She was supposed to feel sorry for Edward now? She was on her way to a Jewish cattle call so big they had to hold it in a ballroom, with a number pinned to her own chest. Nobody *makes* a guy get married, she thought, folding her arms as she looked at him, trying to understand, but overcome with frustration.

"Hey, Ed," she said, as gently as she could manage. "Here's a tip. If you don't like swimming, don't jump in pools. Okay?"

Edward's cheeks colored with embarrassment. How absurd she must think him! Becca didn't know how things worked in his family. How could she know? He shook his head, his eyes flashing. He reached for her, grasping her forearm with his hand.

"I didn't jump in the pool," he said to her. "That's what I'm trying to tell you."

She laughed out loud. "Sure, Eddie, I should have guessed. Nobody jumps. You were pushed."

He nodded. That was it! "Exactly," he said.

"So who's the culprit?"

"My mother," he answered, and noted that her instant reaction was surprise.

Then she laughed at him. "Your *mother*? What is this, the twelfth century?"

"You haven't met my mother," he said simply. Then he put his hands in his pockets and watched her, saying nothing. It was too hard to explain.

Becca checked the clock, noticing with a gasp that it was

already six, and hurried to gather her purse. She slipped her hand into the Prada bag, making certain her Essentials of Fatherhood notes were in place, and went to Emily, promising her gently that she could play another time, but that Becca had a meeting.

"I'm sorry," Edward said, taking a seat on her couch. "We were hoping to steal you away for a night on the town. The Screening Room is showing *Chitty Chitty Bang Bang*. Can you believe Emily's never seen it?"

"And then we can get ice cream at Rumplemeyer's!" Emily added, jumping away from the computer to tug at Becca's dress. "Please, Becca?"

Becca hesitated. Here was what she was trying to keep. Here, in front of her, tugging her, needing her. She wanted to stay, and she put down her bag.

Suddenly Philippe's voice came over the speakerphone. "Your car is here. Also there's a fax."

"Read it to me."

"Front sheet says it's from—" Philippe paused. "This is weird—the company name is Blintzkrieg: Jewish Speed Dating. The fax says that they can guarantee there will be room for you tonight. . . ."

"Okay, that's enough." Becca had colored to crimson, and stood with her mouth open, about to scream. Her hands flew to cover her mouth, and her eyes, as wide as plates, focused on Edward, who was making a gentlemanly attempt to conceal his glee. But one trill of laughter escaped.

Now Becca did scream. Emily, seeing that a joke had caught on, began laughing too, chasing Becca and tugging on her skirt.

Becca's eyes teared with tattered pride. She leaned down, kissed Emily on the head, grabbed her purse and raced out of her office faster than ever before, too fast to speak to anyone, too fast to be apprehended with questions, with anything. She ran for the elevator, and then hastily, rather than waiting for it, Becca took the stairs.

It was ten or eleven flights before she realized she could exit and take the elevator from a different floor, and so she did, collecting herself as effectively as possible, on her way to meet a new father for Emily. But when she looked at her face in the cab (asking the cabbie to twist his rearview mirror for her since she didn't carry one), Becca looked every bit the shattered, baffled mess that she felt.

"Truth in advertising," she thought with indifference. The cab pulled over in front of the Etoile on Fifty-sixth between Park and Lexington. The ride was quicker than Becca had expected. She paid the driver, breathing deeply at the sight of a crowd forming at the door. Reaching into her purse for the list of Essentials of Fatherhood talking points, Becca stepped out of the cab to meet her match.

Chapter 25

Game, Set, Match

The crowd, as she had feared, was assembled for Blintzkrieg: the mating call of the efficient professional had trumpeted from the hills, and many had heeded it. Though Becca tried to convince herself that quantity worked to her advantage, she felt as unique as a small black ant when a number was pinned on her chest. The women wore odd numbers, the men wore even. She was sixty-one. This number suggested to her that she was in the company of at least one hundred and twenty Jewish date-seekers.

In that assumption, Becca was incorrect. There were two women for every man in the room. The total assembled dating population fell just under one hundred. Becca had a high number because she had signed up late.

The Etoile ballroom looked like a polling center on Election Day. Organizers had set up folding tables and chairs by the score to serve as meeting centers. Each individual center was shielded by a double curtain on a single rod. An open curtain would mean a new date was free to enter; a closed curtain meant an introduction was in session.

Women were to remain seated behind the tables in the curtained spaces, with their chairs facing outward; men were to switch places when the whistle blew every seven minutes. Since there were more women than men, there was the possibility of an idle seven minutes, but as the organizers pointed out, it was a chance for the woman to make notes, assess her approach, or refresh her lipstick.

The whistle would sound every seven minutes, at which time conversations were halted and all men were to stand outside of the curtained spaces, turning, at the second whistle, to the next participant. To guard against liability, there was also a single bell on each table, which a woman could ring if she felt uncomfortable for any reason with the man in her tent. The men had promised, in that extraordinary case, to leave their chairs without another word and exit the space at once.

A dating commando in a headset ran around with flapping arms. Once the women were seated, drink servers circulated carrying heavy trays dripping with cocktails. There were only two choices: gin martinis and vodka tonics. Becca picked a vodka tonic, hoping for inspiration. While the men were organized into approach units, Becca looked over her questions.

> Who is your favorite character in children's literature?
> What is your position on overnight camp?
> Are you more of an Ernie or more of a Bert?
> Do you consider bed-making to be an essential life skill?
> How would you handle a four-year-old vomiting on a plane?

There were more pages, but she kept the less controversial ones on the top sheet, her ice-breaker page.

After reviewing her talking points, she ran her eyes over the regulations. Each person had a name and e-mail address with the registrar, tracked by dating number. The participants were to keep track of the eye-opening dates by number, and make choices at the end of the session. If two people chose each other, the dating facilitators would distribute to both the essential contact information to follow up. If you were picked by anyone you did not choose, your case was closed. Nobody would be contacted who didn't express interest in the contacting party. But allowance was made for serendipity: There was a twenty minute open-chat period, in which the participants could make whatever private arrangements they desired, at the end of the session.

In total, the speed dating session went on for an hour. You could meet up to eight potentials in that time, announced the dating facilitator, who had grabbed his clipboard to get things started.

With a whistle, he called the session to order. "Ladies, remain in your seats. Gentlemen," he said, his voice cracking with laughter, "start your engines!"

Some "vroom!" sounds were met by tittering laughs but Becca kept her eye on her fact sheet.

"Go!"

Number forty-four leaped into Becca's tent. His eyes widened with approval. Good chemistry on the first shot! He stuck his hand forward, but Becca shook her head no.

"No touching," she cautioned him.

Short, slight, and excitable, forty-four withdrew his hand to his lap. He stared at her with contact-lensed eyes of swimming blue, his hand shooting up to cover, and then explain, the hair loss that was making progress from the crown of his head toward his eyes, like the spot of an alleged UFO landing.

"Barry Sidwell," he said, breaking the rule against last names in his eagerness to impress.

Becca nodded without giving her name.

Barry, without thinking to ask about Becca, trumpeted his stats in a hurry. "Multimillionaire software developer," he crowed. "Drive a Porsche, house in the Hamptons, picked number forty-four myself so you can remember my age. Unassuming and warm, sincere, attractive, divorced. Harvard JD; dropped that life, went for the millions in software, and hit it big. Want to share my heart with a leggy—"

Barry paused to look under the table. Becca crossed her legs and tapped her pen on her notepad.

"Whoo!" he exclaimed. "Leggy! Wait a minute—want to share my life with a leggy, well-educated people person."

She smiled at him as he caught his breath.

"What do you mean 'people person,' Barry?" she asked, leaning toward him.

"You know," he attempted. "Like, someone comfortable with people."

"You mean, accessible, like a Teletubby?"

"A what?" His hand flew to cover his head. Was this a bald joke?

Becca slumped in her seat. "Or funny, like a Muppet?"

"A puppet? I'm no puppet," he retorted. "CEO, CFO, and Can't Say No! That's Barry. Total control. Why? You got a thing for puppets?"

Becca eyed him carefully, unsure if he knew the line between humor and idiocy.

"Any kids from the first marriage?"

"Whoa," said Barry, waving her off with his hands. "Don't remind me. Selfish little shits. All they do is take."

Becca dropped her head into the palm of her hand.

"I'm not for you, Barry," she told him simply. She wrote forty-four on her page and marked an X through it. Becca pointed her thumb toward the curtain.

"Out."

"Your loss," he said in a huff, standing to leave. He poked his head back into the curtain, scowling. "I'll do better than you will, with that attitude."

Becca breathed deeply, checking her watch to see how much time she had wasted with Barry. She looked at her

Fatherhood sheet. Seemed perfectly fair. Her attitude was fine. She was here to buy as much as to sell.

A head poked meekly into her curtain.

"Mind if I sit down?" number sixteen asked her. "I'm a minute early, but I sort of abandoned the last one. Not my style, you know?"

Becca, smiling warmly, nodded at the poor lamb.

"I'm Mark," he said, keeping within regulations and concealing his last name. He crossed his legs at the ankle, bumped into Becca's legs under the table, and nearly jumped out of his skin. "Sorry," he said quickly, pulling his legs under his chair. His face was pale.

"I don't know how I got mixed up in this, really. My friends put me up to it, I guess. But in the end it was my decision. I hoped I might meet somebody special."

"I'm Becca," she said, offering her hand. He shook it limply.

"What do you do, Mark?"

He sighed. "I organize eco-friendly tours. It's fun, I guess, if you like to travel. But I sort of thought there'd be more travel. I guess you could say I'm like a desk jockey with a lot of hope."

Becca felt like crying. This guy needed a mother!

She turned to her sheet.

"Do you like to read, Mark?"

"Sure," he said, brightening. "I have lots of time. I sit and read and look at these pictures of the Galapagos and Costa Rica, you know, and I just think: Wow. What an awesome world."

Becca nodded. "Okay, Mark. Who's your favorite character from children's literature?"

He paused, rubbing his soft cheeks a little as he thought about it.

"Oh yeah," he said, a light in his eyes. "Ichabod Crane."

Becca stifled a laugh with her hand. She looked at him

in disbelief. "Ichabod Crane? The skinny bald guy in *The Legend of Sleepy Hollow*?"

He nodded, his eyes wide and sincere.

"Why?"

Mark shrugged his shoulders. "He was always running from something, you know? First out of town, then on the road, from that pumpkin-headed ghost? I guess I feel sort of like that too. I've always been running. From jobs, from roots, from respectability. From relationships."

Becca caught her breath. This guy was no father figure.

"I'm sorry, Mark," she said, scarcely able to hold back tears for him. "You're a dear heart, really, I can see that." She stretched her hand across the table again, and gave his hand an affectionate little rub. "Why don't you just go home? I don't think this game is for you."

"I think you're right," he said, standing. His arms swung loosely, like a monkey's. His shoulders drooped as he turned toward her. "Thanks, Becca. You're a straight shooter. Good luck," he said, and trudged through the curtain.

Becca rubbed her temples, breathing deeply. She was on the verge of leaving to go check on poor little eco-friendly Mark when the whistle blew and her curtain flew back once more.

A stocky, muscular man, who looked to be in his late fifties, entered with a firm step. He lowered himself carefully into his seat: Becca had the idea that he might have broken a few chairs that he sat on with less caution. He had powerful arms, with an anchor tattooed on his forearm. He was covered with hair; she could see the hair bristling around his neck, curling against his collar. He wore a hat with the initials U.S.N.A., so she could not verify whether he also remained hairy at the top of his head.

He tipped his hat slightly as he sat down. He had a composed smile, confident and affable, like one might use with a neighbor. She had to admit that he put her at ease, as he carried himself with sincerity.

"Stu Kornheiser," he spoke, with a coarse kindness. "Served in Korea; picked the right war. Union organizer," he added, "for the past twenty-four years."

He described himself with the simplicity typical of fanatics.

Becca paused.

"What's a pretty girl like you doing here?" he asked her, grinning.

Becca shrugged, holding her cards. "I don't know, Stu. Scoping, I guess."

"Cute," the navy man said, picking up her joke.

Becca studied him carefully. Would he work? More a grandfather figure than a father figure, but he passed the straight arrow test. He reminded her of dozens of neighbors she had known back in Brooklyn.

"What's your interest here, Stu?"

"Marriage," he said, simply. "My cooking is worse than the mess hall. I'm widowed: lost a good one. But I don't dwell on the past. You look like a nice kid," he said, his smile friendly.

Becca shrugged. "Tell me about what you do."

"I've organized everybody I can get to," he said. "A lifelong commitment. I've always had it in me to stick it to the big guy, you know?"

Becca nodded. She could listen, even if she didn't identify.

"Any kids?"

"Nah," he said, shaking his head. He looked at his pants. "Some problems in that department. But I work with them all the time. I talk about unions in schools."

"You do?" she brightened. Maybe Stu was her man.

"They won't let me up the avenue anymore," he said. "Made a big stink in Park when I organized the second grade."

Becca gulped.

"Those Upper East Siders think they're untouchable," he said, his voice growing hostile. "You've got to break them from within. They have their illegals under lock and key: tough conditions; no benefits—vicious people. The power imbalance is incredible. But their kids, they have no control over. You should see what I had those kids asking for! A choice of juice and entrée at breakfast; or they won't dress for school. A computer in their room and an hour of unrestricted access; or they won't do their homework. One elective credit for every foreign language those UN-lovers make them speak!" He had stood and was pacing, gripping his hands into fists as he barked angrily.

Becca, trembling, put her hand over the emergency bell.

"To see those parents quivering in front of the grievance committee!" he recalled, brightening at his triumph. "It was beautiful. Here they were, with their neighbors and their neighbors' kids on the committee, evaluating every grievance before they could even think about punishment. I'll break 'em, I know I will. They send guys like me to fight for their freedom, and then they don't think of the little guy. Well, with Stu Kornheiser against them—"

Becca's hand slammed against the bell.

For the remainder of the session, she met entering dates with her questions right off the bat. The mortician left right away, declaring that she was a "bag and tag." The lawyer tried to turn her questions back against her and trap her with an admission, but she rang the bell on him quickly. The neocon governor's aide lingered, insistent that he could persuade her to boycott Teletubbies on the certainty that the purple, purse-carrying Tinky Winky was gay, but Becca was not interested in the politics of childhood, or the symbolism of learning. As the time wore on, she was not interested in much at all.

*

273

Edward felt the sting of Becca's absence. Her sudden work distractions were not coincidental to his engagement—they were responsive to it, and he felt the reproach of her departure in the hollow, echoing halls of the Stearnses' apartment. He ached to see her.

For the second time that week he rose from bed when he heard Emily shouting Becca's name. Becca was an early bird, and Emily naturally had learned to turn to her first in the mornings. Becca was always smiling and awake; she had cool things to see on the computer, she hugged Emily and talked loud and fast and excited, and tickled her and poked her and rolled her around. Edward in the morning was different.

For two days she had dragged her pudgy feet down the hall to the master bedroom, expecting to find Becca, and for two days the bed had been empty. Her cherished morning ritual had been stolen from her, abruptly and without explanation. Feeling uncertain of herself, confused and worried that someone special might leave her again, she became a bit ornery.

Rubbing her sleepy eyes as she clutched her velvety cotton blanket, Emily stood in place and hollered toward the shower. "*Becca!* I'm *awake!*"

Pulling a robe over his pajama bottoms, Edward hurried down the hallway. He greeted her with the best smile he could manage, but he was fighting his own sullen face. He woke in a cloud, feeling the pressure of his reclusiveness, feeling a grudge against everything. He was as out of sorts as she was. Both felt Becca's abandonment keenly, and she had only slept at home for two nights now.

Chapter 26

Bunny Digs In

Fresh from a rejuvenating morning facial and mud treatment at Elizabeth Arden's Red Door Salon, Bunny stepped into a cab and purred the address of the Sherry-Netherland. She was pleased with herself for turning to her friend at Weil, Gotshal & Manges for ideas on how to dispense with Emily. He had drafted a waiver right in front of her eyes, like a magic act, and the draft, reproduced in triplicate, sat tucked in her Fendi bag like a crown jewel. It was smart to see a lawyer, she thought with satisfaction. She hadn't even anticipated a prenuptial agreement, but the lawyer assured her that even someone as old-school as Catherine Kirkland would drop one in her lap before too long.

Catherine had invited her to the city residence again that afternoon, presumably to go over some last minute changes to the invitation list. If Bunny got hit with a prenup in that situation, her lawyer advised, as long as she was alone with Catherine, she had a silver bullet. She should receive the document in a posture of overflowing generosity. She should not even read it, assuring Catherine, with a look straight in the eye, that she trusted her completely. She would insist that anything Catherine requested of her, would be as noble and fair as the great lady herself. Then she should make a great show of signing her name, and hand it to Catherine with a scoff at the ugly world of lawyers that made them reduce these reasonable family understandings to a piece of paper. Marriage to a Kirkland, she would then assert, is an honor no matter what the terms.

His guess was that Catherine, in that situation, would find it unseemly to look at Bunny's signature. And the signature, which she was to pen next to an accurate date, was very important. She would sign it Bunny Kirkland, a false name in advance of the wedding, and one without legal effect. If Catherine did see it, she would only see Bunny's sweet loving eagerness: She would be charmed by her youth. For security he recommended that she sign with her left hand, to ensure that the signature would not look like hers.

The lawyer was pleased with himself. A marriage that started on this footing would soon explode, and he would naturally get Bunny as a client out of the breakup. For that reason he drafted the waiver without charge, thinking of it as a loss leader in advance of Bunny's big divorce bills.

But Bunny Stirrup had no thoughts of divorce. She fairly floated out of the cab, feeling invincible: Every detail was done. You hire a snake to do the work of a snake, she thought, beaming as she approached the grand Sherry-Netherland, and you hire a peacock to do your wedding.

She saw the flamboyant wedding coordinator and called out to him. "Adrian! Darling!"

Adrian, flipping through the pages of his Franklin planner, was stumbling into passersby like a pinball as he hurried toward the hotel's entrance. Bunny sailed to meet him with the grace that her dreamlike success imparted to her every glorious move. Though she had only met Adrian once before, at the Bow Wow Luau in the Hamptons, she had followed the pictures captured of him in the society pages for as long as she could remember, and greeted him as if he were her old friend. At any rate, Adrian would be hard to miss. He always dressed in feathers.

Adrian's neck, poking out of a Versace suit jacket whose

Nehru collar was adorned with shock-dyed feathers, whipped around at the sound of his name, and his eyes lit to sparkling at the sight of his next moneybag, Bunny. She took his arm and led him through the doors to Doubles, where they had scheduled their first planning meeting over lunch.

I can't lose, she laughed to herself, recalling that she had dreamed of hiring Adrian Parish to do her wedding even longer than she had dreamed of marrying Edward Kirkland. He was simply *it:* a peacock, she thought again, smiling at the feathers that flounced with each of his hasty steps. His weddings were exorbitant affairs: lavish, unembarrassed events that appealed to her vanity with their lush, dazzling scale, sparing no expense for perfect luxury. There had been extensive press coverage of the wedding he designed that recreated New York City for a homesick bride marrying at a Los Angeles hotel, complete with a quaint Central Park including a manmade pond, and a Brooklyn Bridge, which was a float made from ten thousand imported black orchids. He had even taken the trouble to fashion a little Harlem in the corner where they threw their trash.

Adrian would attract acres of paparazzi to Bunny on her wedding day, and if there was one thing she had always hoped to achieve on the day she married, it was splashy publicity. She could trust only someone as accomplished as Adrian to provide a stage worthy of her. It would be easy to make Catherine think her people were in charge. And by the time the staff began to revolt, it would be too late. And anyway, no matter how furious she was, Catherine would never make a scene.

Doubles was the perfect place to meet, Bunny thought, casting air-kisses left and right as she waltzed past the jeweled and manicured socialites who filled the deep red club like canned goods fill a pantry.

"Pathetic bag of hopefuls," she whispered through the clenched teeth of her smile. This club was so Junior League, she thought, recalling her meetings with Lily Pulitzer's advisory committee here, over hors d'oeuvres and tales of promising dates with investment bankers. Those days were already as stale as the memory of her high school prom, thought Bunny, though just a year ago the meetings had been rather a highlight of her social life. She couldn't resist appearing here, one last time, with the wedding coordinator that everyone wanted.

Bunny's white Cerruti suit shone over her silver bustier. Into her cleavage dropped a whimsical rhinestone necklace, its heart-shaped pendant chirping "I Do, I Do!" in pink script lettering.

"*Love* the necklace, darling," Adrian said as he kissed her. Forgetting that Adrian was a professional flatterer, Bunny threw her head back in a laugh of careless vanity. She told him that she hadn't seen him since the doggy luau, and they commenced an opening round of name dropping.

Bunny could tell in a glance that Adrian was vibrating with possibilities. She ordered champagne at once, eager for it to arrive so she could drink it left-handed. Unable to wait, she finally dropped her left hand with an obvious thump on the table, waiting for him to comment on her massive diamond.

The ring, which she had not of course chosen, was an heirloom presented to her by Edward's mother the day she agreed to the text of the wedding announcement. Bunny had known she would be stuck with an heirloom: Really rich WASPs never bought their engagement rings. Still, the 10.3 carat oval diamond set in a platinum, diamond-studded band was impressive. Ten carats. She grew giddy just thinking about it. She needed to work out the muscles of her ring finger to support its weight.

"Waiter, she's wounded!" Adrian shrieked, shielding

himself from the ring. "Somebody get that sharp rock off her hand!"

He was even more obsequious today than was typical for him. In the exhaustion that followed the Michael Douglas and Catherine Zeta-Jones affair, he had escaped to Bali for two months, and needed Bunny's big score to get back on top. He had started to work with some branding executives about marketing "his" weddings a little more aggressively, capitalizing on the inevitable publicity that always followed one of his affairs. The marketing people were talking about a ready-for-production line of the wacky-shaped made-up animal dolls now popular among the wee Barney set, licensed original table settings, and a signature line of honeymoon clothes.

Bunny brought him back to earth when she told him she wanted it done in two weeks.

He attracted laughs and winks from the ladies at lunch when he screamed the word *no*! at Bunny's face.

"I said it would be in October," she told him evenly, smiling at the waiter who arrived with their champagne. Without consulting Adrian, she ordered two shrimp salads and a fruit plate, then scatted the waiter away with her hands.

"I assumed you meant next October," he said, mopping his forehead. "Bun-Bun, I've got to get a set designer, a florist, a name-brand diva, a tent man to raise the Venetian palace, a caterer, my fireworks team, and a few dozen Asian drag queens, sweetie. Two weeks?"

She didn't budge. "Ten days, actually. What's with the drag queens? It's a blueblood affair."

He rolled his eyes. "Let Adrian be Adrian, sweetie. My queens blow kisses in the receiving line: They get things moving, call them my spirit leaders. Right? And I know about Edward. I'd do a club corner, with single malt scotch and cigars. Distressed leather recliners, foot massages, and a jazz combo that would make Billie Holiday blush."

Bunny zipped through the details with approval. "Well, do it fast. And you don't need a florist. My mother-in-law has volunteered hers."

He frowned, leaning over the table until his feathers almost brushed her chest.

"Nobody tells Adrian how to do his weddings."

Bunny nodded. "I'm in for over a million," she said, "and I'll kick your fee from twenty to twenty-five percent."

"Thirty," he proposed, "and your florist can dress me in an orchid."

"Thirty," Bunny agreed, smiling coolly. "But you don't say the word *no* to me again. Got it?"

Adrian cringed under her vicious glare. He was glad to go to the altar quickly with this client. He couldn't imagine a year of singing her tune. But poor Edward Kirkland, he thought, would get this booby prize for life. All the press he had managed to gather on Edward suggested he was a pretty nice guy: Joe Varsity with white-glove manners. He remembered the other family detail he wanted to get out of the way.

"We'll have to get Emily in for a quick fitting, then," he said. "She'll be a charming flower girl, though I should tell you that multiple flower girls are in, so if you have any nieces, or she has any classmates—"

Bunny's hand slapping the table in sudden fury set Adrian aquiver.

"The child will not *be seen* on my wedding day."

He raised his eyebrows and said nothing.

Mistaking his shock for understanding, she lowered her voice. "Listen, Adrian, you've seen it happen, I'm sure. Some wide-eyed Shirley Temple stealing the show from a perfectly beautiful bride."

He nodded, acquiescing. "Okay," he said, making a note in his book. "No kids, no puppies."

She smiled with satisfaction. "Exactly."

He raised his eyebrows with concern. "Where will she be?"

Bunny's face froze into a smile, and for a minute its painted stillness appeared before Adrian like a horrible mask. "Leave her to me," she said, glancing around quickly. "Emily won't be a problem at the wedding," she assured him.

Adrian gulped, nodded, and said no more until the little girl's absence raised a technical question in his mind.

"What do you want to do about flower girls?"

He scooped the floating raspberry from his flute of champagne on a silver teaspoon and savored the little treat as he waited for Bunny's answer.

When she had finished her sip, she told him. "I'll have plenty of flowers. I'll have plenty of girls. That covers it, as far as I'm concerned."

He nodded. One less detail.

"How big are you thinking?" Adrian asked, wondering if now was an appropriate time to announce an increase in the per-person fee.

"About four hundred and fifty people." Bunny said.

"No, no, no," Adrian said, covering his face.

"Don't say *no* to me, Adrian," Bunny snapped at him.

He nodded, giving a weary sigh as he tipped his head back for a long drink of champagne.

"*Non, non, non,* Bunny dear," he said, trying it in French. "It must be smaller."

She looked at him with scorn. "I'm not trying to *elope,* Adrian."

He rubbed his forehead with his hand. She needed a tutorial.

"Bunny, look at it this way," he told her, leaning back to make room for the arrival of his shrimp salad, which was presented in a delightful silver bowl, the watercress salad arranged neatly beside it on the signature silver-rimmed china.

He forgot for a moment this miserable client as he delighted in the neat exquisiteness of his little lunch.

She smiled too, curious to know why Adrian of all people would argue that less is more.

"Weddings are many different things," he began. "They are graceful, formal, memorable, sometimes meaningful, always *exasperating* . . . no doubt your wedding will be all of these. But if you don't limit the guest list, baby, the only time you'll read the word 'romance' in your wedding coverage is in Liz Smith's column—when she tells the world what it *lacked*."

Bunny gasped. It was inconceivable that she would hear the word "lack" in connection with herself.

She was stubborn, though. She had thought hard about the guest list.

"I have messengers ready to hand-deliver everything."

"Bunny," he said, appealing to her vanity. "Think of where you and Edward are going—as a *name*, in your shared public image. People . . . the masses . . ." he glanced at her, taking a soft tone, "your *public*, Bunny."

Bunny's smile glowed with the thought of having a public.

"Your public," he repeated, "wants to see *exclusive* events. I mean the Miller girls. . . ."

She nodded. "I was there."

"Everyone was there, Bunny. That's the point. They invited seven hundred and fifty people to their wedding. Nobody was *left out*—there was nobody left to guess about what happened. Talking about that wedding would be like talking about your day at the post office. Everyone already *knows* what it was like."

Bunny paused, frowning. She hadn't thought of it that way. "All right," she agreed, wondering which of Edward's relatives she could cut without getting too much flack from her mother-in-law. "I'll send you a shorter list."

"Send it to Michaela," Adrian said, handing her a business card. "My Feng Shui consultant. I've sent him the blueprints of your property so he can find harmony among the terrain, the guests, and the land's ancient inhabitants."

"I hate to disturb his harmony," Bunny said with a sneer, "but the wedding won't be at my house!"

Adrian gasped. "Bad karma," he said.

Bunny rolled her eyes. "Tell me about it. But Edward's old bat of a mother insisted on having it at her house in the Hamptons."

Adrian looked around nervously. He wouldn't talk about Catherine Kirkland that way. Twenty people either friendly or beholden to her could be sitting around them right that minute.

Bunny noticed his nervous glance, and quieted her voice a bit. "Don't worry," she said, to assure herself as much as Adrian. "If she's in the city, which I doubt, she's at Astor Court."

"In the St. Regis?"

"Right. The only tea she drinks, other than Fortnum & Mason's Earl Grey, is Astor Court's house blend." Bunny realized as she spoke that afternoon tea was not served for a few hours yet, and chided herself on her carelessness. After all, she only had to keep her seat for ten more days.

Her eyes shining with severity, she leaned toward Adrian and whispered to him.

"You're right, I shouldn't trash the old bat here. Anyway, I'm letting her have the wedding at her house. Why not? It's the last time she'll have any control over what Edward does."

Adrian was quiet. He'd seen pushy brides galore, but this Bunny was something extreme. He laughed to think of her mother-in-law getting the jump on her. Imagining a lion in full roar against a tiger, Adrian began to daydream.

Bunny mistook his quiet moment for interest, and continued, "Do we meet with Michaela?"

Thinking with a smile how Bunny's presence would spike gentle Joy's disharmony scale into the red zone, Adrian said, "He's too busy."

"Too busy for *me?*" Bunny was astounded.

"I told you on the phone," Adrian said, "Rosita Naranja's destination wedding is the same weekend as yours. He's booked for all 'Five Days of Olé.' In fact, he's on my flight to Rio."

"You won't be at my wedding?" Bunny was surprised, but instantly saw the advantage in that.

"No," Adrian answered, hanging his head. "But you'll love my assistant, Jo-Jo. He'll be able to execute the details we've worked out."

Bunny was thrilled to have Adrian Parish at her steering wheel, and even more excited to have one of his minions there for the actual wedding. Adrian was a genius, everyone knew that, but he had said *no* to her, and so she regarded him as lacking in deference. She was sure she would be able to bully his little Jo-Jo around if she wanted any last-minute changes.

As they enjoyed their lunch, making small talk and laughing over the mistakes other people made at their horrendous and unenviable weddings, Adrian asked Bunny again about Emily.

"Do you know my relic of a mother-in-law actually thinks I am going to raise the little brat?" Bunny laughed at the ridiculousness. "She's not even Edward's!"

Adrian recalled the details.

"What will you do?" he asked, concealing his shiver of revulsion with a hasty shrug of the shoulders.

"Pack her suitcases," Bunny answered, laughing. "Actually, not even that—it's a job for the maid. But you get the picture."

"She's moving out?"

Bunny nodded. "Edward doesn't know it yet, but she will. Thank God for lawyers."

"You don't hear that every day," Adrian observed, looking past Bunny to avoid showing his disgust.

"No, no," she sang, "but who else can reorganize your family to rid it of some of the deadweight?" Sipping her champagne, Bunny paused to enjoy the cherished dream that was so nearly her reality. "I just came from Weil, Gotshal & Manges," she told him. "You did a wedding for the managing partner over there, didn't you?"

Adrian nodded. "Both of his wives used me; the second so that I would pull the file and double everything I did for the first."

She smiled indulgently. "To each his own!"

After toasting something to do with this sentiment, she explained, "My lawyer drew up a little paper that terminates Edward's parental rights. Bing bang boom! We'll let her zip over to the other guardian, but just for child care. The papers keep me as trustee: Did you know she sits on a little eight-hundred-million-dollar nest egg?"

Adrian finished his champagne hastily.

"So we won't *abandon* her, exactly. I'll make the decisions regarding her assets, and we snuck into the fine print that the trustee will be the sole decision-maker regarding the child's school."

Adrian was confused. "So what, exactly, does the guardian get?"

"Legal responsibility," Bunny said, laughing with delight at her cleverness. "Liability, of course, if the child breaks anything. And very little else. I've enrolled her to begin right away at a boarding school in Zurich. Thank God they have full-day preschool in Switzerland! I had to call in a favor to get her in the midsemester, but, you know, for the children!" She toasted again, raising her champagne flute high in the air. "Between school and riding camp in the Alps next summer, little Emily will enjoy quite a bit of mountain air! And her French will be delightful."

"Does your fiancé know?"

"Of course not."

"And he doesn't need to sign the papers?"

"Oh—he will—once he's my husband, he will."

Adrian was quiet, sitting in stunned silence.

"Well, enough about that," Bunny said, unsure of his devotion to her.

"I'll need you to gather your bridesmaids for lunch tomorrow," he said. "We have a million details to discuss. And I'll need blueprints of the Kirkland property."

Bunny smiled smugly. "Lunch tomorrow at the Four Seasons," she said. "Twelve sharp, so we get a good table," she added.

Adrian left quickly. He needed to take a shower.

Chapter 27

Blame It on Rio

Becca could not fall asleep in her own apartment. Her mail had piled up, as had her phone messages, but she left the letters lying in a pile and erased her voice mail with the touch of a button. Nobody she wanted to hear from would call her here. The doorman had already forgotten who she was: he never knew her well, with all her travel. Her apartment was hollow; she tossed restlessly in bed with thoughts of another place, uncertain where in the world she could really call home.

She and Edward had begun, first when it was convenient, and then as a matter of practice, to sleep at the Stearns' apartment at the same time. He got home late, usually after she had gone to sleep, and Becca rarely heard Edward let himself in. The bedroom he had chosen was well removed from the rest of the living quarters. But she knew he would be there in the morning, and that helped her sleep.

Edward slept in a small room, formerly the residence of Emily's nanny, a comfortable little nook with an oak floor and a west-facing window. Down a half-flight of stairs from the music room and the library, his bedroom adjoined a full bath and some overflow cedar closets where Amy had stored her furs in cloth bags. He had claimed to find the room easy and welcoming, with its pale-yellow chintz curtains and battered suede reading chair. But it was no more than a changing room for him. As often as not a tuxedo and shirt were thrown across the seat of his reading chair, pant legs draped across the ottoman, as if a man had fallen and evaporated in place. When he was in the apartment, he sought the life of the rooms they used in common.

Becca knew he had chosen the nanny's room for his own to give her privacy in the master bedroom. Edward was flawlessly considerate. She wondered if Emily knew to head down the hall in the morning, to wake Edward instead of her. She found herself hoping that Emily would be careful on the stairs. She felt like calling, suddenly, but knew it was too late. Anyway, she had nothing to say. She wondered if Edward were awake too.

She sighed, lying in her bed, thinking of Edward. What an experience they had shared. She supposed she had learned a little something, for at first she had regarded his lazy, frivolous life with disdain, as she might consider a feather that had drifted into her office: an annoying distraction floating through a humming, productive world. But she met him now with a smile of joy, unable to resist the pleasure of greeting Edward Kirkland. She had grown fond of his ruddy complexion, his cheerful smile, his healthy diversions: squash, yachting, tramping around in the woods behind dogs. She had learned to appreciate the benefits gained by these activities she once dismissed as useless.

Before she met him, she never would have respected a life like Edward's. He seemed content with knocking the dirt off his boots and getting some fresh air in the countryside without achieving a thing from sun to sun. She still didn't know where he lived, in a sense: She knew all his numbers and addresses and she could always find him, but she didn't know where his spirit lived.

But as she tossed in bed under her crisp starched sheets, twirling herself like a pastry, she saw Edward's life in a different light. Whatever it was, whatever it was good for, he had decided to share it with someone. Or he had *consented*, she corrected herself, still a bit baffled by his awkward explanation of being engaged by ambush. And there it was. Emily would have a new mother.

She made herself smile, trying to imagine Emily as a teenager, asking the private steward for a deck chair on board a yacht to Europe, sailing to help her mother open a new house there, in St. Tropez, her golden curls long, then, streaming in the wind. A charmed life, she would have, under the wing of Bunny Stirrup.

Bunny Stirrup. Becca had only a single image to connect with the awful name, but as she replayed the brief encounter she, Emily, and Edward had with Bunny over and over in her head, her midnight imagination produced horrible possibilities all turning their selfish pampered backs on her beloved Emily.

Forget about it, she told herself, forget about it, Becca. You can't do a thing to stop what is happening. Your life will be as it was.

Her mind swam with thoughts without fixing on any in particular. Finally she began to calculate exchange rates, to calm herself. And in time she slept.

Becca met Edward at public places for the next few days when they changed the guard over Emily, finding anything preferable to being confined in the apartment with him there. Only when Edward had made it clear that he would be out for the night did she stay overnight with Emily, and at the morning's first light Becca tugged Emily out of the building with the nervous energy of an animal captured and released. She had found things for them to do early in the morning. New York in October was perfect—they walked, along with what seemed like everybody in the city, on Central Park's runner's path. They collected leaves. Sometimes they stopped at one of the twenty-four-hour greengrocers and bought carob-covered peanut clusters— Becca kept them in their little plastic bag until lunchtime. By eight o'clock, they were planning their day. Edward no longer hung out in the apartment when he had "down" time. He had asked her if he should take MacDuff and the other two dogs back to the Carlyle but this sounded like just another blow to Emily's sense of permanence, and Becca said no. So now when they went back home, or to the Stearns' apartment, or whatever that physical space should be called, they had the dogs to play with. Carmelita, the Bichon Frise, invariably found her way to Becca's lap. MacDuff kept one eye on them, to make sure he was part of the action—with the other eye shut in that funny way dogs have of leaving eyes open while they sleep. The lab did what everybody else did because that was his nature—so they rested a lot these days. And it seemed like a death watch. The wedding was a week away and Becca was counting days—was Edward, she wondered? Or was he caught up in all the prewedding festivities? She didn't want to know.

Edward was shocked to hear her rush into the apartment in the middle of the following week, while he and Emily were playing "duck the boom" in the sailboat in her room. He was "on duty" with Emily until the evening. Their paths had not crossed there for better than a week.

She is here to pack, he thought sadly, noticing that Becca flew past Emily's room down the hall to her bedroom with a hanging bag on her arm.

Edward had mentioned to Becca, or rather to her voice mail, that Emily had been invited to his parents' house for the weekend. She knew without asking that she would not be invited. She was too proud to mention it.

He was still reeling with disbelief at the speed with which his change in course had taken place. One minute he was picking up Emily from Little Ladies Lacrosse, and the next minute, his mother was on the phone telling him to pack his morning coat and vest, his tuxedo, and a dinner suit, and come out to Sternwood with some pretty clothes for Emily to wear to the wedding. Pack for Bermuda too, if you want to honeymoon there, she added. We sent people over to open the house. No point in putting things off any longer.

When Becca peeked into the playroom, Emily directed her at once to remove her shoes. By the serious look on her face, Becca knew she was deeply involved in pretending something, and so she consented at once, kicking her Jimmy Choos into the corner.

"They'll scratch the deck," Emily declared, sliding to Becca in her sock feet.

Edward's heart lifted with pleasure. He was grateful to see her, as a child playing with porcelain dolls would be at the sudden, skidding entrance of a squirming puppy. Becca always called out for Emily first, laughing as she greeted her child with hugs and kisses. Edward watched her lift Emily in the air with pleasure. Then, when she turned her shining eyes and her smile upon him, her laugh ringing in his ears, her sincere joy at hugging her Emily . . . Edward turned his eyes to the floor.

He found himself wondering about her speed dating. Somehow it did not strike him as quite so funny, when he thought about it. He felt protective of Becca. He felt ashamed to have invaded her privacy. But when he watched her laughing with Emily, her eyes bright and confident, Edward felt himself relax. He sighed, smiling too. It was such a relief to be together again.

"Aye, aye, captain," Becca said, saluting Emily as she put her down. Emily giggled, fixing her captain's hat on her head before sliding back to the wooden boat.

"We're playing duck the boom!" she announced to Becca.

Edward had removed the curtain rod from Emily's puppet stage to swing it over Emily's head, making much of the danger of "the boom" as Emily hit the deck with happy shrieks. Becca watched them play, noticing Edward held the curtain rod firmly, well over Emily's head, without apparent exertion even while he kept it still in the air. She smiled at him, admiring both his strength and the imaginative games he played, which Emily loved.

She had come to tell them she was going away, and seeing them together so happily helped her to let them go. Emily would be okay, she told herself, with Edward. He was a natural, as Arlene would say. Her plan was to use the rest of her two months to adjust. Maybe she'd take a trip. Paris was beautiful this time of year. She had standing invitations to visit colleagues who had second homes in Monaco, St. Tropez, St. Lucia—many places. Becca did not make many friends, spending all her time and energy advancing. Her associates and clients had filled this need.

But not anymore. Becca felt that the whole world and every day forever—for the rest of her life—would lack color. She couldn't imagine what it would be like a week from now—four days. This time in her life had altered her. She would have to learn to understand the new Becca. To say the least, it was a challenge.

"Did you have a good event, the other night?" Edward asked her. His smile was devilish, without being unkind, and he brought her back from her reverie.

Becca laughed. "Sure," she said. She tossed her head defiantly, taking a bold attitude. "You bet, Eddie. It was a dream come true."

"Anyone interesting?" he persisted, watching her steadily. When she got defiant like this she'd toss her head so hard that her hair would fan out like one of those shampoo commercials. How he would miss it—how he would miss her—

"For sure! *Top* men, Eddie," she said, cracking a smile as she met his stare. "Really top men. A mortician, even. And an optometrist. Very diverse crowd of professionals. Have you ever met a specialist in grocery shelf arrangement strategies?"

"Not that I remember," he said, looking at her warmly. She could laugh at herself.

"Turns out an inch of shelf space made free by ten degrees of product rotation can save you millions!" She laughed out loud, enjoying the release of talking about the horrific experience. "I met eight men in just under sixty minutes," she bragged.

"I admire your efficiency," he said.

She flashed him a cheeky smile. "I'm a quick one," she told him, brushing an errant strand of hair from her eyes. She looked at him for a minute, then spoke more quietly. "Eddie," she said, "I need to talk to you about something."

He stepped toward her abruptly. "Alone?" His eyes were hopeful.

"No," she replied, glancing at Emily. "Here is fine."

He sat down, and Becca told him about the strange call she had gotten on her cell this morning. Alex McKenzie, an old buddy from her early days in the technology group at Morgan Stanley, was getting married over the weekend. She had been invited ages ago, and as usual had declined with a gift. But something had happened during the week to one of the bridesmaids—she didn't quite get it. His bride had no one else. Her friend needed a sub, so he called Becca.

"To fill in as a bridesmaid?" Edward asked her. Things were happening to them so quickly, he wanted to make sure she wasn't filling in as her friend's bride.

"Yes," said Becca. "Strange but true. Having twelve

293

bridesmaids seemed to be a big deal to his fiancée. She's got consultants in on it."

Edward nodded without speaking. Being up against female insistence in the matter of a wedding was one thing, but when consultants were involved, a guy didn't have a chance. He saw the desperation of the groom's position. In fact, he saw it better than Becca did.

Though she didn't understand what made her buddy Alex tick, she was eager to accept his invitation, just to get away. The "destination wedding" was in Rio de Janeiro. To Becca, the promise of a week away right now was a god-send. She had told him she'd be on the next flight.

"Popular weekend to tie the knot," she observed, glancing at him.

"I guess so." He shrugged, avoiding her eyes. Then, to Emily: "Duck the boom!" With a great burst of energy, alarming in its sudden force, he swung the curtain rod over her head. She squealed and hit the deck.

"I got the sail!" she announced, catching the velvet cloth in her fists.

Edward allowed the sail to fall gently over her, and Emily, laughing, jumped out from under it. "Again! Again!" she pleaded. Edward, nodding to her, turned back to Becca.

"So you're going to be in his wedding?"

"I had no other plans," she returned evenly.

He looked at the floor. He was guilty.

"I know," he said, shifting his feet, preparing to say something.

"The thing is," she interrupted him quickly, "I have to go today. It's in Rio."

"As in Brazil?"

She smiled at him, nodding. "You're a real Magellan."

"You're going today?" His eyes clouded with pain.

"I'd like to," she said, turning a long glance to Emily. She sighed and walked slowly toward her, avoiding Edward's eye, and then kissed her good-bye, wondering if she would see her again before they met in court.

He nodded without speaking.

Emily closed her eyes to give Becca a hug.

"What's going on?" Emily asked, opening her eyes to look from one to the other. "Everybody's so quiet!"

"Nothing," Becca said quickly. "I'm going on a little trip, Em, to a different country, Brazil. I hear the women wear big pretty dresses and flowers in their hair."

Emily's eyes were wide. "Can I come?"

"I'll bring you back a present," Becca answered, turning for the door.

Emily clapped her hands. She remembered something, and tugged at the leg of Edward's pants.

"You said we could play hide the hat."

Edward nodded, rubbing her head. He heard Becca walking down the hall.

"Bye, guys," she called from the hall. "I'll have my phone."

Emily had already closed her eyes and was counting to twenty.

Edward tossed the hat under a seat in the boat and walked quickly across the room.

"This time, Em," he called behind him, "try to find it without clues. Okay? Special prize if you find it all by yourself."

"Okay," she said, peeking between her fingers. She saw Edward walking away, skipped straight from number eleven to twenty, and began to rifle behind the curtains, which was where she found it last time.

Edward hurried after Becca, and caught her at the door.

She smiled at him. "Okay," she said, pulling her bag up to her shoulder. "I'll be back on Sunday or Monday, depending how things go."

He looked straight into her eyes. They both knew he would be married by then.

"I'd walk you to the cab," he said, but nodded toward Emily's room, to explain that he could not.

"Of course," said Becca. She lingered at the door. Despite the surprise of hearing from her friend, just when she was considering a vacation alone, despite a dissolute few days in the tropical heat of Rio, in which she could forget these weeks with Edward and refresh herself to move ahead, despite it all, she lingered there, smiling at him.

He moved to take her hand, which he held firmly.

"Be safe," he cautioned, staring into her eyes.

Before she could answer, he had leaned forward to kiss her. His arms circled her with sudden strength. He ran his hands up and down her back, luxurious and smooth, tangling his fingers in her free, black hair, kissing her deeply and rejoicing as he felt her welcoming him. Edward's heart beat as he felt her arms wrap around his shoulders. He heard her bags drop to the floor. He caressed her neck, her head, her back, feeling her soft mouth press against his. He pulled her tightly to him. He wanted her to stay.

Becca opened her eyes, and she saw that his were open. Her eyes were wet and shining.

They stared at each other without speaking.

Becca broke the silence. "I should go," she whispered, looking away to avoid his eyes, which were burning with the strength of his passion for her. There was no place in the world she wanted to be more than here, more than with him, and it took all her will not to step forward again, and simply laid her head against his chest, listening to his heart.

Edward turned her face to him. She felt the warm palms of his hands cupped under her chin, his fingers resting gently against her neck, gently holding her cheeks. It was how he held Emily, she thought, her eyes filling with tears.

"Becca, can you stay?" His voice was firm, and he stared intensely at her, waiting.

She took a deep breath, collecting herself. Her eye caught the curl of his golden hair on his oxford shirt collar, the half inch of collar that always showed above his jacket. It was frayed, a bit, at the top, from starch. His shirts were always starched. Edward's life was different, would always be different than hers. She had to go.

"Your collar is a little frayed, Eddie," she said, rubbing her hand gently behind his neck. "You'd better clean that up before your big weekend."

His eyes turned to the floor in discouragement. He watched her hands reach down to collect her bags. He watched her feet turn from toe to heel. She was leaving.

"Becca—" he began, raising his eyes to meet hers.

She looked away, crying. "I have to go," she said, and he stood silently. He watched her walk away, hurrying as she headed down the hall. She was crying. Her beautiful shoulders shook as she waited for the elevator. He stood silently, watching her back. She did not turn to look at him again.

The elevator door closed behind her.

Emily had stolen close to him like a mouse. She began to cry.

Edward turned with a start.

"Why did she leave?" she asked him through her sobs.

He smiled gently, with pity for the child who shared his emotion. He held her, rubbing her back, making no answer because he had none.

"How long have you been standing here?" he asked her finally, kneeling down before the child, who had calmed in his arms and stood pouting, catching her breath.

"Long enough to see you kiss," said Emily, giggling into his shoulder.

"You did?" he asked. His cheeks turned red.

"You kissed for a *long time*," Emily added.

"We did?"

She nodded, with wide eyes. He smiled.

"I guess we did." Edward closed his eyes, trying to relive the moment. But holding her, finally kissing her, had answered all his questions and at the same time, spoiled whatever happiness or even contentment he might have found with Bunny, because when he kissed Becca all the restless pieces inside him that no one knew about came together and he knew what it meant to need, love, desire forever. What was he going to do?

"So why is she going away?"

Edward swallowed hard. "She has to, I guess." He took a deep breath. "Come on, Em," he offered, standing. "We're going to take a trip to the country."

He lifted her, and she dropped her head on his shoulder. She was not altogether consoled.

"I wish Becca were here," she pouted.

Edward nodded, rubbing her head. "We can't always get what we want, Em."

She lifted her head and stared into his eyes. A general prohibition was never enough to satisfy Emily's thirst for understanding.

"Why not *this* time?"

He smiled, carrying her to her room to pack her suitcases.

"You'll see, Em. You'll see when you grow up." But as he spoke, he wondered the same thing.

Chapter 28

A Peacock to Do
Your Wedding

In Adrian's fifteen years of business as a consultant in the highly competitive wedding industry, he had never met anyone like Bunny Stirrup. He was actually thankful to Rosita Naranja for the Five Days of Olé, as her destination wedding in Brazil had been tagged. He felt the need to put an actual physical distance between himself and his most demanding client. His poor assistant, Jo-Jo, would earn his stripes this weekend at Bunny's wedding, Adrian reflected, reclining comfortably in his first class seat. It was an event he would put in the category of a funeral for the groom.

He declined the offer of another vodka tonic, feeling a pleasant hum from his first drink, or perhaps simply from the relief of escaping his bionic client, who ate, drank, and slept with images of her own glory impossible for even him to provide in her sprint to the altar.

Compared to Bunny, even the parties he arranged for the sultan of Brunei were a breeze. Before he went on vacation he had organized twenty-five black limos to transport the sultan's wives and daughters to the private discotheque they had rented for a party. One sultana per car. But the sultan's challenges were merely logistical in nature, putting Adrian basically in the shoes of an air traffic controller. Bunny was impossible, to the marrow of her bones.

It wasn't just her constant demands: That was old hat for

Adrian. During wedding season he whittled his sleep down to four hours, which was enough to revive his typical demeanor, that of a happy frog. He expected to take calls and make decisions at any time except his sleeping hours, which he scheduled between six and ten in the mornings, when most of his clients were sleeping or dressing for brunch.

Adrian could hardly believe it himself, but he had come to loathe Bunny Stirrup, privately crossing the line he always drew between himself and his clients, whom he regarded, more or less, as cartoons. Bunny was simply in a different zone of selfishness, ego, and manipulation than anyone else he had known. He had watched the gracious smile she turned on her cowering bridesmaids, dazzling them with her perfection while she salted the wounds of their insecure hearts by prying, with cutting faux innocence, into the progress of their love lives. She dug her heels into the kittens she called her friends with a joy he could only call vicious. Bunny made the poorer girls beholden to her, dangling custom-made black pearl necklaces for them to keep as if pearls were nothing but pebbles to her, in all her extravagant graciousness. The next afternoon she would leave them surprised by the responsibility to pay their own lunch tabs at the Colony Club, simply to remind them that she had the royal prerogative: She could extend opulence, but she could withdraw it at whim.

He saw that Bunny counted Edward as less than nothing in this process, and he saw the mere mention of this same Edward made her friends quiver with longing to their paraffin-waxed knees. And the callous way she treated the poor child, Emily, would have violated the dignity of a turtle.

Adrian guessed it all must wash under the arching bridge of Bunny's beauty. But how could Edward submit to this fate? He supposed that love, in this case, was not blind but rather the opposite, a case of too-vivid sight blocking the effectiveness of reason.

In this manner, Adrian put himself to sleep until the touchdown in Rio. Refreshed by his catnap, the irrepressible bubble bobbed up from his seat, and floated away to begin working his magic.

He could thank Bunny for one thing, he thought, hailing a cab in his travel-book Portuguese. She had trained him hard. He could manage the remaining Day of Olé with his eyes closed. The mishap with Linda Libra, the bridesmaid gored by a bull on Tango Thursday, was an unfortunate setback, but the groom had actually secured a substitute whom he promised was en route. Adrian couldn't believe that Rosita Naranja had a thirteenth friend, but Alex promised him that someone named Becca Reinhart would meet him today for a little nip and tuck session to get Linda's dress hanging on her right.

Everybody was so drunk, asserted Alex with pride, that he didn't believe anyone would care about the slight change in cast. Adrian felt especially thankful to this emergency substitute bridesmaid for filling in at the last moment. He really should have arrived earlier to keep an eye on the olés for all five days. Bunny had kept him too long.

After showering and changing his clothes at the hotel, the eagle-eyed, feather-collared wedding coordinator headed to the Naranja ranch to oversee the dressing of the bridesmaids. He sought first a minute to coordinate with Haze Oolong, a South Beach fashion photographer who had flown in yesterday to shoot the wedding event.

When Adrian entered, Haze was losing a valiant struggle against yards of frothy orange fabric, trying to get a swarm of gigantic bridesmaids' dresses to "hang right" for his picture. The bride had designed the dresses to imitate tutus, only on a much larger scale. Each was appliqued with beaded tangerines, and the overall collision of sparkle and crunch in the fabric was absolutely overwhelming.

Becca's cab was a few minutes behind Adrian's. She was still pinching herself at the incredible good luck of landing in this tropical tangerine parade. What a perfect avenue for escapism! She had even slept on the flight, a better rest than she had gotten for several nights. She laughed, watching the photographer struggle against this tittering circle of fabric models. They were holding as still as a hive of bees. She envisioned herself in this hilarious Minnie Mouse getup. She hoped to keep her picture out of the society pages. Dick Davis would never let her live this one down.

Becca's presence in the dressing room went unnoticed. In her smooth black Donna Karan pantsuit, she moved like a cat behind the blooms of this orange grove. Finally, she spoke up.

"Who's the boss here?" she asked the crowd.

"Idiot!" cursed the bride, furious that Becca didn't recognize her. Spotted tutus quivered with laughter.

"Take it easy," Becca cautioned her, extending her hand in greeting. "I'm the new girl. Alex says you have my dress?"

The bride flung a scowl at Becca.

"She's too tall," Rosita declared. She looked sharply at Haze, expecting his veto.

"She's better than Kitty Meow," Haze hissed at her.

"She's perfect," agreed Adrian, flouncing across the room with the signature, can-do ebullience that Rosita had retained at his premium fees. "So get her dress." He paused, allowing the magenta feathers of his collar to be admired by the assembled wedding army. "Go on, go on," he said, waving his hands away from his body. "Chop, chop, little ladies. The master is speaking to you!"

Rosita clapped her hands and was attended by several

302

nieces, who brought Becca her glorious gown. The dress stood up on its own! Becca felt exhausted, relieved, and bewildered, all at the same time, but when she saw her dress, all her feelings coalesced into a sense of the ridiculous, which she hid until Oolong shot an ironic glance at her—at that point she laughed so hard she cried.

Rosita pointed an orange fingernail at Becca. "Help her with the zipper," she ordered her nieces, ignoring Becca's outburst.

Becca stepped into the polka-dotted tutu with the help of four Ewok-sized nieces chattering in Portuguese. One of them took a moment to massage the muscles of her neck. Now this was a vacation!

"Rosita! *Ayudame!*" Victor Azul, the makeup artist, screamed at Rosita for help.

The maiden of honor, Dolores Mas Dolores, had grabbed the Vixenish Violet eye shadow reserved for the bride. He was battling her for control. Rosita hurried to the scene. When she heard what Dolores had done, she nearly slapped her false friend.

"Betrayer!" she shrieked, holding her hand back with a ferocious effort. She directed the weeping bridesmaid to the corner of the room, to snuffle in shame. Vixenish Violet was the bride's color. The bridesmaids wore Alluring Aqua, like it or not.

She turned to give Victor a tongue-lashing too. "You *upset* her. Don't let it get to this point again. I'll have no tears! No salt streaks!" And then, at the sight of Becca, Rosita herself burst into tears.

Her bridesmaid's dress was too short. "It was supposed to be a ball gown," she shrieked, "floor length!" She pointed at Becca. The gown hung awkwardly in the air at a point just below her knees. She covered her face, wailing miserably. "This ruins everything!"

Adrian came running to control the damage. He

promised to pin some fabric onto Becca's dress to make it hit the floor, if that would make his little *pollito* happy. Becca, who did not help matters by talking on the phone while Rosita hyperventilated, plugged her ear to listen to two new messages.

Emily and Edward, speaking together, left her a cheery hello from the car. They were visiting the kennel, then tomorrow would be off to Sternwood, the Kirklands' house in the Hamptons, for his wedding. Emily was excited to see the horses that Edward's parents kept on the twenty-five-acre property. She laughed that the house had a name, and wanted to know if she could shake its hand. Both of them seemed so carefree, so full of animation and the jolliness of being together. They missed her, Edward said plainly. They wished she would come back soon.

Becca turned off her phone. She didn't check her other message. The giddiness of her escape had been shattered. She felt empty, realizing that she would not be able to let Emily go without suffering. Her face had grown pale, and Becca hardly noticed when Adrian crouched at her knees to pin a swath of fabric around the bottom of her dress.

She felt urgently that she should leave. She longed to be with Emily.

Dully she noticed, as Adrian buzzed around her legs, that he was tickling her.

"Come on, sweetie, don't let the jet lag get you down," he chirped. "Look alive! We all should be glad we're here, and not at Bunny Stirrup's wedding this weekend."

Becca gasped, which Adrian took as a sign she was relaxing with deep breathing exercises. He walked her over to the corner.

"That's it, in and out. Listen, get a load of this, to make yourself feel better," he whispered. "I've met a witch! This ice queen Bunny Stirrup had me working like a slave on her hitch to some rich kid, Kirkland, I think," he said with pity. "Boy is he in for it. I can't even laugh about it—and that's saying something, sweetie, believe me! Poor little lamb, I don't think he'll ever laugh again."

Becca was different from the other girls, a Wall Street friend of the groom, and such a fish out of water that he adopted her naturally as a confidante. She held her breath and listened, not revealing anything she knew. She felt a pressing need to discover all that she could about Edward's wedding.

He had shuttled Becca next to the sewing table where he could reach all the pins stuck in Rosita's custom orange cushion, which the on-site seamstress would alter to fit Becca. They were far from the other girls, who were waiting together for Victor to do their makeup.

Becca laughed, showing Adrian that his story relaxed her. "Go on," she said. "I could use something funny, especially about weddings. And I used to think my job was stressful."

He smiled, gratified that she recognized what he suffered. "Oh, she's typical, in some ways, has a little basket of kittens for bridesmaids, bats them around"—he paused to remove a pin from his teeth—"like that one." He nodded his head to indicate Rosita. "But I hate to think of what she says behind my back, because every time someone leaves the room I see her turn from Yin to Yang, you know what I mean?"

"Not exactly," said Becca, allowing Adrian to turn her feet in a new direction as he traveled the endless circumference of her gown with his pins.

"Like she falls all over the poor guy's mother, calls her Mum and compliments her tea and crumpets, and then as soon as she's in the next room she curses her soul and counts the days until she dies and dumps her fortune of diamonds and furs into Bunny's lap. She says she's got the old bat hoodwinked on the prenup, and I wouldn't put it past her."

Becca's face grew white. She felt nauseous and blinked as if waking from a dream. Edward was walking into that? She squared her shoulders, trying to imagine facts she didn't know, something to better explain it. Edward was a big boy, she told herself, and it was stupid to listen to gossip. He knew his fiancée best, she told herself, but she knew Edward Kirkland better than that. He was as honest as the day is long, and half as innocent.

"Yikes," she managed, to keep Adrian talking.

Adrian withdrew a pin from his mouth. "Oh, she's crass, and she absolutely hates everyone who doesn't bow to her, and even most of the people who do, but it's a shame to have the little kid involved. I suppose it's for the best that the ice princess is shipping her off to Zurich first thing. She'll be safer the farther she is from Bunny."

Becca's heart jumped into her throat. Her impulse was to tackle the feathered Adrian and shake every word of gossip out of him, but she held her place, breathing quickly, pulling her hands close to her, in fists, as she spoke.

"Zurich?"

She heard Adrian laugh. "Oh, you should hear her! She's absolutely delighted with her cleverness. Bunny got the kid in midsemester to some year-round boarding school out in Switzerland. She says they'll visit her in ski season, *maybe*," he imitated her voice, "except the Alps are so *passé*, they simply might not."

Becca was trembling. Her heart had gone cold. She stepped back, her face white. Adrian looked up at her with surprise.

"Oh, dear," he said hurriedly. "My mistake! Sorry, darling. I didn't mean to scare you. I go a little postal on Bunny, I know. I should have waited to unload on my analyst. It's just that I hate her so. The kid will definitely be safer in Switzerland."

He giggled. It felt good to get it out.

Becca staggered backward.

"Why—" she began, faltering on her words. "Why do you think it's good for Emily to go away?"

"You know her name," the wedding consultant said slowly. He took a deep breath. Something more was going on here than he knew. It had probably been wrong to speak that way about a client. But he saw Becca's face suddenly go pale—she obviously cared for children. He realized that telling the truth wouldn't hurt him a bit. Who knew—perhaps the woman could do something to help the little girl. She traveled in Kirkland and Stirrup's circle, obviously, or she wouldn't be here. If telling the truth hurt Bunny, he smiled, what did he care?

"All right. Keep in mind," he said in a low voice, "that I don't know if she was kidding. With her, you know, I really couldn't tell."

Becca supported herself with her hand against the sewing table. Her face, at first drawn and white, became flushed with sudden energy. She had her eye on her Prada bag in the middle of the room. Her mind whirled. The plans she had made, had cancelled, had remade, her assumptions, her values—everything whistled in her ears. She didn't know anything. I have to get to my phone, she thought. Emily needs me. She didn't see the bridesmaids, involved in a heated argument over whose shoes were whose, though all the shoes were exactly the same. She didn't see the makeup artist whiling away his ennui by painting the photographer. Emily needed her.

"I have to go," she cried, shaking.

Becca ran for her bag and was a flash of orange out the door before Adrian could say another word. The last thing he saw was a trail of half-pinned fabric, dangling from her dress as she turned the corner.

She rushed toward the paddock, the first place she

saw with cars. Who could she pay? Who could help her? She saw men leading horses into a convoy of white trailers. She thought how Emily would love to see these horses.

Fearing she might never see her little seahorse again, Becca's mind went into four-wheel drive thinking of a plan. Quickly, she grabbed the mane of the horse that the men were about to load into a trailer. Barging into their conversation, she dangled an American fifty dollar bill in the air and pointed to the trailer keys. The two men hesitated for just a moment, then handed her the keys. They could always say she was dressed like a bridesmaid, so they assumed she was acting on behalf of the bride.

She opened the driver's seat door with a crash, repeating the Spanish word for airport over and over, hoping the Portuguese was something similar. She dug her hand into her purse and thrust more money in front of her. Airport, please, please, quickly, she was saying, in any language that occurred to her, hoping the money would talk. A portly, middle-aged stable worker, wet with perspiration, stepped forward and Becca led him quickly toward the door. He took the wheel, but she pushed him aside, taking the wheel herself. In seconds the trailer skidded away, with a frightened Brazilian polo pony pressed firmly backward against its locked gate.

Becca raced through the dusty, hot streets, flying past signs she didn't understand, pulling her navigator's hands to the wheel as she dialed her phone. She wired cash to the airport in Rio, which she knew would clear her only path home. When she arrived at the airport, she crashed through its crowds scattering dollars like seeds in topsoil. It took three thousand dollars to buy the first class seat of an English-speaking businessman, but everyone believed from her gown that she was a celebrity, and crowds parted with curious faces turned toward her. Tense as a wire, Becca got home.

In Miami she called Philippe as she was changing planes. He had the task of picking up Becca first thing Saturday morning at JFK International Airport. She was heading for the Hamptons, she explained to Philippe, as a surprise for Emily. Her voice was tense: She snapped her answers to his questions. He asked if she were all right, and she finessed the question as best she could without bursting into tears of exhaustion. Everything whistled and ripped past her ears; her eyes were blurry from crying. She could hardly fasten on any thought in her panic about Emily.

But she did remember to ask Philippe one last favor, and he was sure by then that she had gone crazy.

"Bring my mother."

Chapter 29

October Showers

There was a time when Bunny Stirrup, like the other thousand women who turned out in spring silks and broad-brimmed hats for the Conservancy Luncheon, thought that the extravagant celebration marked the pinnacle of Manhattan's midday scene. She had come so far since then, Bunny realized. The champagne brunch that was spread in her honor beneath the gleaming, orchid-filled tent on the Kirkland lawn was easily as important as that B-list affair. It was attended by the most luminous and envied socialites in New York City, maybe even the world, since some of the guests were foreign. She had invited her bridesmaids and fifty of her most photogenic friends to join her for this intimate get-together. Tonight, at the white tie wedding she had always dreamed would be hers, under the soft, lustrous glow of stars and outdoor candles, they would all witness her triumph.

Adrian Parish's plan (implemented by his lovely henchman, Jo-Jo, whom she regarded as her private butler) had organized this reception on the enchanting green front lawn of Sternwood, the Kirkland's twenty-eight-room beach cottage. The home had been built in 1891 for Edward's great-grandfather, who preferred leisure to labor, and consequently had a little railway car built behind the house to move steamer trunks and boxes from the yacht landing to the main quarters. The railway had long since been dismantled, but a few stones of the track remained like ancient ruins in the rolling hill that led down to the water.

The busy photographers were impressed, Bunny could see, at the A-list vintage of her guests. The graceful ladies swept from air-kiss to air-kiss with lovely, shimmering ebullience. The weather was delightfully clear. Everyone had caught the wave.

Both Bill Cunningham from the *Times* and Mary Hillard from *Vogue* were on the lawn shooting hundreds of pictures. Bunny felt giddy from the mere sight of them. She had, after much internal debate, decided to forego her daily pharmaceutical cocktail, and was elated that the sweet mood in which she fluttered this afternoon was actually her own. How could she feel less than total joy? In hours she would be in a position to look down on most of the guests at this brunch. She would luxuriate—by *right,* and not just by invitation—with the *well-bred* rich, the *multi-generational* rich, whose beds were feathered by inherited money and whose culture was bred in the bone.

She had already gotten some good advance press. The *Times* piece was a nice touch; she had to credit Adrian with its execution. He had flown in Yoshi, a wedding proposal specialist, known as a "romance concierge," from the Ritz-Carlton in Osaka. Together, the three of them brainstormed a fabulous story of Edward's proposal to Bunny.

All knew that Edward was an adventurous sailor and fisherman, so Bunny kept him in character, telling the press that he had hired and piloted a seaplane to take them to a secluded part of Peconic Bay. He knelt, of course, no small feat in the cramped quarters of the plane, and proposed with this stunning ring, which simply slid onto her finger as naturally as Cinderella's slipper dropped onto her tiny little foot. Afterward, they enjoyed a picnic of champagne and sandwiches.

311

The *Times* had eaten it up. It went out on the wire service, so Bunny was prominently featured in more second-rate papers across the country than she could count, but it wasn't her job to count. It was her private secretary's job, and Cecil Barnaby had been busy every minute since she engaged his services last week. He would pull her clippings, and she would decide which to frame.

Bunny couldn't tell the story enough, and had actually come to believe it, in a sort of what-*should*-have-been sense. She was extending her hand to show the ring once more to a gasping audience, preparing to tell the delightful tale again, when she noticed Edward's car making its slow progress along the half-mile brick driveway that ended in a horseshoe in front of the graceful house. She scowled when she remembered that Emily was with him.

Seated together in the roomy leather back seat of the Bentley, playing tic-tac-toe and hangman on the spiral notepad that he had discovered on a bookshelf in the car, Edward and Emily turned to the window as the car entered the Sternwood grounds. Fresh and happy from winning all the games she had played, Emily watched with wide eyes as Edward showed her the big house where he had spent time as a little boy. The car passed the grass tennis court and trellises climbing with roses and trumpet vines. When the shingled mansion came into view, Emily shrugged her shoulders.

Hmm, she said. She thought it would be fancier, with turrets and moats or something. Or at least a tower. She yawned, stretching her fists in the air. "Can we play again, Eddie?"

Edward laughed, grateful for the child's honesty. Sternwood, he had been reminded unceasingly by his parents, was the crown jewel of East Hampton. Surrounded by three miles of private roads, the twenty-five-acre estate had water views in all directions across Georgica Pond and out to the ocean. The stables, small enough for family and guest use, consisted of eight stalls with a tackroom, an indoor dressage ring, an outdoor ring with brightly painted practice jump fences and a small cottage for the use of the groomsman and his family in season. Wooded trails wound throughout the estate's acreage, around two of the five fingers of the pond, and above the ocean on one spectacular bluff, which the family's thoroughbred horses knew blind.

Georgica Pond, an area named after a spring-fed tidal pond, had reputation for style and privacy that dated at least from the gilded 1890s. Edward's great-grandfather, Horace Cornelius Kirkland II, was a founding member of the Georgica association, a private group who built the first homes on large lots at the pond and quickly circled the wagons to keep out newcomers. Over one hundred years later, the Georgica association had largely succeeded in its goal of maintaining exclusivity, as the pond's grand surrounding homes still bore the old names of the great families along with a smattering of preapproved clans, such as the Stirrups. Randall Stirrup was not only super, extraordinarily rich, but also the business partner of a founding family heir.

Edward got out of the car and pulled Emily behind him as he led her behind the house to show her the pretty pond. He stopped as he rounded the sun porch, gasping at the sight laid out before him. An invading army had landed. He stared in disbelief, unsure what he could tell Emily about this place that had always represented for him all that was open and solitary. Edward had meant to give her a leisurely walking tour of the grounds, unfolding the magical history of his old family home; he wanted to show her some of the hiding places and climbing trees, take a rowboat out on the pond, and visit the stables to feed the horses carrots and sugar cubes. He had even thought, using Emily as his "family armor," he might avoid some of the guests he saw splashed across the front lawn like scattered dolls. But he was paralyzed by his first glance at the extravagant scale of this prewedding activity for what he'd believed was to be an intimate, at-home wedding.

All this ceremony is for you, he thought with dread. He stooped to explain the gleaming white tent to the child, noticing when he looked at Emily her air of excitement, happiness, and wonder. She was innocent of what came next. It was beautiful to her that this stately old house was tarted up like a wedding planners' trade show.

"When is Becca coming?"

Oh-oh, Edward thought. Dense as he was, or perhaps preoccupied by his own sense of impending doom, he had not thought to explain to Emily what was happening.

The private dock and a gazebo on the water at the yacht landing had been taken over by Adrian Parish's people, a bustling crew of men and women strutting around officiously barking orders, like a hundred spastic roosters. Commandos wearing headsets ranged the grounds dispatching directions to uniformed workers who were scattered everywhere preparing for the evening's ceremony. A crisis had followed the collapse of something electronic at the poolhouse, which was halfway converted into a club complete with DJ for all-night dancing.

Together he and Emily proceeded to the pond to skip some stones. In an attempt to ignore the circus that everywhere had overtaken his house, Edward straightened his neck and stared straight at the pond as if forcing his way through a storm. He couldn't help but glance back at the garden facing the pond, where ten or twelve gardeners worked with painful uncertainty, uprooting half an acre of flowers, one stem at a time. The perennials were being removed and replaced with two-day blooms of white, framing Bunny in the purity she deemed essential for her hallowed wedding ground.

To ensure that the wedding blooms would last through the evening wedding and full day of receptions tomorrow, they were being planted in glass vials. They would be uprooted after the ceremony, allowing Catherine Kirkland to replant her garden in any fresh manner she desired. Mrs. Kirkland had already informed the perplexed garden staff that she wanted her new garden to look exactly like her old one. She directed them to replant exactly the same flowers they were presently pulling, which made the job of pulling them agonizing, each gardener knowing he or she would have to suffer through just the opposite exercise the day after tomorrow.

Edward's mother joined them by the water.

"This is my mother, Emily, Mrs. Kirkland, and Mother, this is my darling Emily." He made certain to claim pride and loyalty for Emily right up front so his mother would hopefully follow his lead and, in doing so, rein Bunny in.

"I am pleased to meet you." His mother surprised him, gesturing for Edward to pick her up so they could shake hands.

Edward must have looked astonished because his mother said, "Why are you so surprised, Edward? This child is my granddaughter, at least until my flesh and blood arrives. And I want you to call me Grandmama," she said, turning back to Emily.

"Okay, Mrs. Grandmama," Emily said. And both Edward and his mother laughed.

Catherine invited Edward with her into the house to discuss his wedding portrait and directed Emily to run along with the servant who had been assigned to watch her and dress her for the tea party with Bunny's friends.

Nervous at first, Emily was consoled by the thought of dressing up fancy, and went into the house uncertainly

315

holding the warm fat hand of Mrs. Carter. She turned her fair, curly head back once at Edward, who nodded his approval to her, after which she skipped in a lighter step, with Mrs. Carter gamely hurrying to keep up. Edward's mother rested on his arm as they took the path up the hill they must have taken a hundred, no a thousand times. In a rare, perhaps even singular show of motherly affection, Catherine stopped halfway up the hill to pat him on the arm that supported her.

"You're a good son, Edward. And you'll see, this will work out just fine."

He said nothing and they began again their leisurely walk up the hill.

Bunny was surprised when Emily joined them in the tea room. A guest of honor must not make herself too accessible, so she had left the reception after taking photographs with the people whose images mattered and ducked inside for a touch-up manicure. Eventually her bridesmaids and a few extras just to fill in spaces joined her. When Emily trotted into the room, alone, dressed to please in her antique Irish linen dress, Bunny read the situation at once.

Her cloying mother-in-law had seized an opportunity to steal Edward away for a little tête-à-tête. The woman's love for her golden son bordered on the romantic, thought Bunny, whose jealous heart hardened at the thought of her mother-in-law getting Edward's ear to herself. She'll criticize me, she thought, I just know it.

Her cold blue eyes regarded the room, of which she was the focal point, in search of an escape. She said not a word to Emily, seeing her for what she was—the hot potato tossed here by Edward's mother. Now it's my move, Bunny thought. So involved was she in plotting her endgame against Catherine's sleight of hand, Bunny failed to notice that Emily, who had drawn close to her when Mrs. Carter pointed out her new mother, was tapping on her arm.

"Where should I sit?" Emily asked in a shy voice. She noticed that all of the chairs were taken.

"There is no place for you here, Emily," Bunny replied coldly.

Emily squinted at her, not sure what that meant. Shrugging her shoulders, she figured she could just as well sit on the floor. She noticed a silver candy dish that had *three* levels, sitting in the middle of the table untouched. Immediately, she forgot about Bunny and rushed to the table for a treat.

Mrs. Carter, who had remained in the doorway making certain Emily was in good hands, stayed put. The bridesmaids, already nervous in their obsessive focus on how they would look in their pictures, became uncomfortably silent.

Penelope Hobnob leaned forward in her chair, indicating Emily with a nod of her head. The child was filling her arms with candy treats as if she had starved for a week.

"Are you going to let her eat all that, Bun-Bun?" Nellie asked, her implication obvious.

Bunny gave a cruel laugh. "What do I care?"

Emily's eyes traveled from Bunny to Nellie and then back to the candy tray. Confident that nobody would stop her, she shoveled more candies into her arms, smearing the linen of her dress with chocolate truffles.

"Bunny," Nellie protested in a loud whisper. "You *are* her mother."

"She *has* no mother," Bunny replied at once.

Emily, caught off guard by the lash of Bunny's comment, coughed on a hard candy. She stumbled backward, her eyes filling with tears. Emily choked harder, her arms waving for help, and finally collapsed forward against the coffee table, coughing and gasping for air.

317

"Bunny!" shrieked Nellie. "Do something!"

Bunny stood up hastily. "I've just gotten manicured for the portrait! I'm not going to stick my finger in her *mouth*!" She shuddered all over with distaste at the idea, looking behind her for the domestic staff. Where was the service bell?

Mrs. Carter, who had run to the child as soon as she saw her in need, by then had dislodged the candy from her throat. She picked Emily up and hurried out of the room with her at once, throwing a fierce glare at Bunny as she left.

Bunny smiled coolly as her bridesmaids, sitting in their polite circle of friendship, stared at her in shock.

"Irish," she said dismissively of the maid. "Probably has eight kids herself. They're always surrounded by children and animals."

Tina's little laugh was followed by a small chorus of titters.

Smiling, Bunny stood next to her chair. She had been looking for an exit. It was time to repossess Edward from his mother.

Chapter 30

The October Revolution

At the gate, wrapping her soft plump arms around her, Arlene let Becca cry. As they stood embracing, passengers and security people moving past them, Arlene tried to think of the last time she had seen Becca cry. Grandma's death—she had been nine years old.

"Cry, my baby . . ."

Becca came up for air, blew her nose and started the sobs which, like labor pains in reverse, would hurt Arlene in her soul, first with very little time between the gut-wrenching pain, and then with longer and longer time between them. Arlene took the opportunity to look her daughter over. What was she wearing?

As Becca's sobs slowed, Arlene led them to an empty waiting room.

"I don't—I have to—where's Philippe?" Becca said, finally, her first complete sentence.

"Calm down. He went to get you coffee and to leave us alone. Now, tell me the story—all of it. Did something happen in Brazil?"

Becca shook her head. "No, it's nothing like that."

Philippe found them and gave Becca a Grande cup of Starbucks Cappuccino. "What is with that dress?" he asked her.

Arlene bit her bottom lip so she wouldn't laugh. Becca

looked down at herself and, starting in her belly first, silently, then moving to her throat, she began to roar with laughter. And also she cried. So she laughed and cried and then, looking at her watch, she stopped abruptly and said, "I gotta go."

"Becca—no—not until I know what's what."

"I'll fill you in. You're coming with me and Philippe."

"Where to?" Arlene placed her hands on her hips while Becca pulled her along. "As if I didn't know." Arlene caught Becca's eye and kept it in her sights for a moment or two. "As if I didn't know everything."

Very few words had to be said. Arlene knew early on what Becca didn't—how her daughter's heart had found its home. She had just waited until Becca caught up—but then, this wedding thing happened and Arlene was devastated for Becca. But she didn't believe that the picture was at all clear. More would be revealed about this marriage between "the chemical heir and the equestrienne." Hah, she thought to herself. Every time she remembered the *Times* headline she wanted to *brecht*.

Philippe led Becca and Arlene to another terminal where they boarded the helicopter Philippe had arranged for. It took forever for them to get clearance for takeoff, or so it seemed to Becca.

"What?" Arlene asked, because the clicking of Becca's fingers on her seat's arm was driving her crazy. "What are we doing here?" Arlene put her hand over Becca's, restraining her, forcing her to stop and think.

"Okay," Becca said. "It's like this."

And so she told them her plan.

Edward's father had arrived from the Kazak territory, where he was negotiating the construction of a pipeline, to much adoration and fanfare from the shadow government—that is, the corporate execs, who really ran things.

His helicopter, which freed him from traffic concerns that burdened other poor Manhattan souls, touched down on the landing pad by the chapel. Catherine had rushed out at once to greet her king. Dozens of wedding consultants raced to the scene with a traipsing trail of floral provisions. They had been forced to await Mr. Kirkland's landing before decorating the chapel, as the wind from the helicopter's rotary would have strewn their church bells, flower sprays, and lanterns in its cyclone.

Edward found himself alone in the room with the portrait artist, who was mixing his oils. He and Bunny would sit, this afternoon, for their engagement portrait. Bunny had enough restraint to honor the superstition that she should keep herself—or anyway her dress—concealed from him today. At any rate her dress was a secret to all but Jo-Jo and Adrian; even the bridesmaids didn't know how much of her abdomen would be revealed by its modern design. And Bunny was thrilled that Catherine had approved a small private reception, of even more select intimates, to gather for cocktails in the sitting room while they watched her and Edward sit to be painted. She had never considered herself an artistic muse, but found herself rather well suited to the role.

Edward turned toward the window, wondering if Emily had been taken yet to the stables. He had heard someone mention a riding lesson for her this afternoon. His head was foggy, absent-minded, and tired, and he wished Emily would return to him soon. They had begun reading a new series of fairy tales, and he looked forward each day to the peaceful half hour of putting Emily to bed. He would watch her eyes drop closed as he read the words slowly, drawing them out in a whisper, then folding the book together and replacing it on her nightstand. Her cheeks would be gently flushed and her lips pursed as she rested, a peaceful little rose closed up until morning.

The luxurious sitting room, in which he had spent hours of time as a boy reading a tattered copy of *Treasure Island* by the fireplace, held no comfort for him. He made conversation with the portrait artist, but was thankful that the man seemed content to turn back to his work. Edward's soul was uneasy. He breathed deeply, staring out over the fields toward the stables.

He thought he heard a second helicopter land, but that couldn't be right. Anyway, trailers, sound stages, tents, limousines, parquet dance floors, folding tables, helicopters: What was this place, Las Vegas? Press people crawled the grounds like ants, but his mother had assured him, as if he cared, that all the doors to the house were solidly locked.

So this was the end, he mused, trying to take a detached air. His thoughts turned to his parents. Out on the grass, in front of his helicopter like Patton before his great flag, his father had a crew of fellow club members howling with laughter as he read them the dinner speech he had prepared for the wedding.

Catherine turned her eyes down at her husband's words, but said nothing.

"Some might consider this an occasion of the release of a debt: Edward paying his family back for the effort of raising him as he resolutely commences this new chapter of his Kirkland manhood with the lovely Roberta Stirrup by his side. I say"—he paused, laughing in red-faced cheer as he downed a sip of scotch—"I say, this day is no such thing. For Edward could never repay his debt to the Kirkland family. *All that he is, we have given to him.*"

At this comment, Horace's contemporaries yelped and howled, their eyes shining as they reflected on their own ungrateful sons and daughters. The great man laughed uproariously, waving them down as he continued reading from his page, his huge fleshy hands rocking as he laughed.

"I won't keep you by relating everything Edward owes to his family," he said, pausing as his eyes took on a devilish gleam. "We'd be here all night!"

Hurrahs and laughs went up in a great manly bellow, as if Horace had announced a pay raise at the meeting of his company's pipefitters union. As he traveled back toward the house in the pack of his acquaintances, relating from his list the top one hundred things Edward Kirkland owed to his family, the club fellows contributed additional suggestions, one by one, in a chorus that had everyone full of uproarious glee.

"The yacht!"

"The private car!"

"Don't forget the job!" piped up one fellow with a nose for the obvious. "The job! The job!" thundered a chorus of approving cheers.

"What about Harvard?"

"Forget Harvard. Remember the marina you built for St. George's?"

Finding himself rollicking in enjoyment of his club members, Horace had his bags sent up to the house without him, and agreed to join the inner circle at the scotch and cigar tables set up beside the pond, to relate the enviable success of his Kazak venture.

While his father chewed his cigar, Edward paced back and forth, his hands at his sides, his eyes traveling over the carved oak paneling of the room where he had been told to wait. There was no place to go from here. It was beautiful today, a warm seventy degrees, unseasonably sunny with a salty breeze coming in off the water. But every refuge he could see outside the house was animated with guests and decorations; his exit would be an entrance, requiring false cheer he did not feel able to muster. He caught a reflection of himself in the gilded mirror that hung over the mantel, a drawn, unhappy figure, starched, hemmed, and tucked into his morning coat and tails, his bow tie the absurd grace note of his formal captivity.

And so he remained, ignorant that help was on the way.

Becca was the first out of the helicopter. She did not pay any attention to the small group of people who ran from the chapel, implements in hand, to let her know how much trouble the helicopter had caused for the decorators. She did not notice the pack of older men, an army all dressed alike and all smoking cigars. Behind her she heard Arlene and Philippe running and the helicopter taking off.

She was tackled by Emily, who rushed into Becca's legs and was nearly lost in the great fluffy folds of her orange bridesmaid's dress. Emily's eyes, wide and dazzled, took in Becca's flouncy A-line tutu dress with awe.

"My fairy godmother!" the child said, leaping into her arms.

Forgetting that they were supposed to be quiet, Becca cried and hugged her daughter in joyous relief. Emily had not been hurt, but mostly bewildered by Bunny's behavior. Mrs. Carter, furious at Bunny's behavior, had helped Emily dress in play clothes and brought her to the stable, which Mr. Edward had wanted for the child hours ago. Henry, the Kirkland groom, had spent the last few hours giving Emily a basic riding lesson on one of the polo ponies Horace Kirkland kept for show, and had fallen in love with the chatty child. The reunion between mother and child did not leave him cold. On the contrary, he was the father of six children, each precious. Henry had put together the pieces of the little girl's story and he announced that he would help in any way he could. "And damn"—he looked at Emily in Becca's arms—"I mean darn the consequences. There's plenty of stable jobs here."

"Well, if not, you'll have a job with me," Becca exclaimed.

What is this, *Crocodile Dundee?* her mother thought, but she stayed mum.

Poor, desperate little Emily had pulled herself as close to Becca as she could. Becca had to pry Emily's head back from her shoulder long enough to tell her the secret. They were pretending to run away from Eddie's party.

"Let's go!" said Emily, pressing her cheek against Becca with all her might.

Becca raced toward the line of cars she had passed on her way in.

When she found Edward's driver, she told him he was wanted at the house. She asked for his key ring, claiming she needed to see if Edward had put the apartment key on there for her, as he had said. Shrugging, James headed for the house, agreeing to meet Becca and Emily back at the car. Before he was halfway across the horseshoe driveway toward the door, he heard the sound of his engine. He stood, scratching his head, while his car tore down the driveway.

Philippe met James at the entrance to Sternwood, where the driver was politely waiting to be admitted. He persuaded him with lots of money that, when James entered, Philippe would follow him in. If anyone asked, he was "with the driver."

The driver assured him he would cooperate. His naturally accepting personality had always served him well, and James counted his money as he waited by the door.

Edward's heart surged when he saw Philippe enter the room. *Becca!*

He grabbed the note Philippe handed him and read it eagerly. His hands shook as he recognized Becca's handwriting, and he devoured her words with starved eyes. Philippe walked out before anyone even noticed he was there.

*Edward. I have taken Emily away from Bunny. I can't
let her go. I love her more than anything I know. Please
don't follow me. I hope you understand. Becca.*

Then he noticed a note scribbled at the bottom of the
page, an afterthought. She had written:

P.S. Eddie, I just wonder—why aren't you happy?

His hand shook as his eyes flew over the note. He felt
the dullness, the aching of his head clear as if peeled away.
His thoughts crystallized, sharpened into vivid flashing
images; he felt a rush of energy. Becca.

He saw her name shining through memories that triggered in him the need to act. He saw her holding Emily
against her chest, stroking the child's hair, saw her laughing, then remembered her graceful neck yielding,
collapsing for a moment in tenderness as she kissed him
good-bye on her way to the airport, the last time he had
seen her. He caught his breath as the desire for her returned
to him, and closed his eyes, weighed with his longing for
her and the regret he felt for letting her go.

She had come back!

"Why aren't you happy?" her note asked. He gripped the
paper, feeling his mind sharpen into precision. Purpose
seared through Edward's soul. He felt alive; he felt the
energy of a thousand of Becca's glances, laughs, and
motions alive within him. He felt a hand drop down on his
shoulder.

Bunny's voice whispered into his ear.

"James told me what happened, Edward." He whirled to
face her, and her ice-blue eyes rested on him possessively.
"She's taken the child, has she?"

He looked at Bunny silently, his mind racing. Slowly he
crumpled the note in his hand. He slid it, with his hand,

into his pocket, and watched her in silence. His life, he felt, had moved on a slow course to this surprising moment, as the distance runner, eventually, turns from his resting pace to glorious striving, the end in sight. Remembering his obligations: his promise, such as it was, to his mother to accept a future with Bunny, he stood still, listening to her without interruption.

The portrait painter scurried from the room, cast out at once by the cold stare she flung at him. Edward had forgotten the painter, but Bunny, he saw, missed nothing.

"I have to go," Edward said, his eyes meeting hers directly.

"Edward," Bunny breathed, "let's not be hasty." She slid her cold, smooth hand around his neck to give him a little massage.

"That's a joke," he said. He gave a sarcastic laugh as he stepped away from her touch, indicating the extravagant wedding decorations that spoiled the house in every direction. "You seem to have jumped into marriage with both feet."

"I want us *both* to," she said, drawing him to her in an embrace. She held him firmly for a minute, feeling his tense muscles tighten even further. She could not console him. Not yet. He would learn to love her as he grew accustomed to the charms of their privileged life.

"Your friend Becca has nothing," she said, fluttering her eyes with sympathy, entranced by her own graciousness. Charity sounded so sweet, spilling off her pampered lips. She could really give so much, when she wanted to.

He shuddered to hear Becca's name from her lips. "What do you mean?"

"I mean the child might be better off with her."

"What?" He shook with revulsion at the thought of abandoning his daughter, his special joy. Just minutes before, Emily had been the consolation he relied upon in this circus. Soon he would tuck her in, read her a story. When the tents were pulled down, the decorations packed up, they would go hiking on the horse trails, row the boat into the pond, where he would tell her stories about all the magic that hid among the elm trees, climb the trees with low branches, feed the horses, visit the kennel. . . . Lose Emily? This woman knew nothing of him.

While Edward marveled at her ignorance, Bunny delivered the speech she had prepared for precisely this moment.

"Without the child, Edward, we would have the time we need to be together. To love each other. To *enjoy* each other." She pursed her lips into a sensual pout, and glanced up from under her lowered lids. "To give ourselves to each other, completely." Bunny breathed deeply. In her ears, it sounded just right. She felt as if a wind machine would blow her hair and a chorus of angels would sing on cue. She had delivered the enticement perfectly. So self-absorbed was Bunny Stirrup at that moment, she failed to perceive Edward's look of increasing disgust.

She leaned down, rolling her shoulders forward to create a graceful pose as she reached into her briefcase and withdrew a document of three or four pages. Now is the time to hit him with the waiver, she thought. I will lose the kid, keep her assets, and cut my wedding cake in six hours.

He stared, thunderstruck, at her cold-blooded poise. Where did the briefcase come from? Her beauty meant nothing to him, suddenly; it was sharp and false. He saw her trying to hide the triumphant smile that played at the corners of her mouth. There was nothing real about her.

With effort, she adopted a low, compassionate tone. "I took the liberty of having this drafted," she began, handing him the paper with a smile.

His eyes widened as he accepted the document, but dropped it to his side without reading a word.

"I understand," she spoke, as directly as she had rehearsed, to get it over with, "that you might be struggling with some conflicting feelings right now. But if you take a minute to read this, I think you'll agree with me that it's the right thing to do."

"What is it?" he asked her. His voice and eyes were suspicious. He would not let her off so easily. "This is quite unusual," he said, adopting a teasing tone of voice. "You've never asked me to sign anything before. Please explain, my dear."

She smiled with confidence. "It's a waiver of parental authority. I got it from a lawyer over at Weil, Gotshal & Manges. It's airtight, he assured me. Just sign here," she said, grabbing the document with excitement, and flipping it hurriedly to the last page, "and permanent custody of Emily Stearns will be transferred to Becca Reinhart. Bing, bang, boom! Everybody wins," she promised, beaming with a victorious smile.

He shuddered with revulsion. Bunny stood exposed before him as if for the first time.

Her eyes widened with fear. She sensed she had gone wrong with the waiver. Her mind raced as she considered the contact she might be forced to have with the child. She would still have her sent to Zurich, she consoled herself, and the staff would keep her most of the time.

Edward stared at her firmly, watching the clouds that drifted into her glowing blue eyes. Her selfish, steely eyes. He would not give up Emily.

With his eyes locked on hers, Edward said the kindest thing he could find in his heart for her.

"Enjoy the party, Bunny. It's all yours."

Shaking off the touch of her hand on his shoulder, Edward ran out the door. Becca would have taken Emily back into town. He'd have to ask his driver to hurry.

*

During the ride into the city "Bubbe" Arlene finally got to meet her grandchild. Emily had heard about Bubbe. Becca didn't yet refer to her as her mother, to avoid triggering Emily's grief. And now the two leaned close together whispering. Whatever secrets they were sharing must have been whoppers, because every so often there would be an outburst of hysterical laughter. Becca had known this meeting would be as smooth as the creamy peanut butter on the sandwiches Bubbe had thoughtfully packed and fed them now.

"I can have chocolate after this," Emily said, looking straight into Arlene's eyes.

"I don't think so, over my dead body." Arlene and Becca spoke at the same time. Then Becca picked up her phone to make an urgent call.

Chapter 31

Something Borrowed

Becca had not realized it was Sunday until Judge Jones picked up the phone in chambers; she never noticed the particular day anymore except to check it against Emily's activity schedule. On Sunday afternoons the judge would duck into chambers to read quietly and prepare for the week ahead. She was surprised to hear the phone but thought it might be her husband, so she picked it up without introducing herself.

Hearing the urgency in Becca's voice, she agreed to conduct a hearing, at once, to assess Emily's custody in light of a grave and immediate danger to the child.

Becca was driving Edward's great wide-bodied Bentley, and had hung up quickly to negotiate through road construction before Judge Jones thought to remind her to notify Edward of the hearing.

Arlene had pushed to come with her but there were some times in life when it's better to negotiate the shoals alone. So Becca dropped Arlene at her own apartment, promising to tell her exactly, verbatim, what the judge said.

"Be insistent," her mother had said as she was exiting the Bentley, "and don't leave the courtroom without Emily."

Right—Arlene was right on the money.

Becca knew by the time she returned her mother would

have come up with ways to warm up the judge. If the hearing took long enough, it was probable that Arlene would find the closest Pottery Barn and stock up on dishes and pots that would never be used. Becca would not come back without Emily and, further, she intended to live with Emily in the Stearns apartment, which was now Emily's. Edward and his bride could find another place to return to from their honeymoon—Bermuda she had heard. (Philippe got all the gossip everywhere he went!) A Bermuda honeymoon—how unimaginative can you get!

Pouring a cup of coffee, the judge sighed with anticipation of the end of the year, when she would rotate off the emotional JDR docket and back into the bread and butter of civil practice. Landlords, contracts, and zoning variances: it would be bliss after the frustration of family law.

She slipped into her black robe, picked up the file labeled In Re Emily Stearns, and headed for her courtroom to wait.

Becca's hope had flared with the stimulant of escaping, but as she neared the courthouse, mentally making her case for custody of Emily, she felt more and more doubtful. What did she have? What was so dangerous about Bunny Stirrup?

She planned to ship Emily right off to Zurich—but when Becca regarded it with the awful clarity of hindsight, it was at best a nasty little piece of gossip. And who was her source? She breathed deeply, her confidence sinking like a stone. She imagined calling testimony forth from Adrian Parish, the flouncy feather-collared wedding consultant who couldn't open his mouth but to exaggerate.

Becca reddened with anger. She knew—she felt certain that she had to protect Emily. But Adrian's piece of gossip would be no use at all. She had not stopped, before she rushed home from Brazil in a panic, to think that Adrian might not be telling the truth. Bunny was his client, and by his own description quite a demanding one. She worked him like a slave to put her wedding together, he said. Becca's analysts, toiling with her on contentious deals at three o'clock in the morning, had said worse about her own clients. Adrian had as much as admitted that his bias made him critical of Bunny, she recalled: It's just that I hate her so.

No, it wouldn't help to mention Adrian at all. But Becca had set the judge up to hear something: some emergency, some grave danger to Emily.

It's my intuition, Your Honor, she imagined saying, and actually laughed at herself. She was not Emily's mother. She would have to invent a new phenomenon for that argument to fly. It's my legal guardian's intuition, Your Honor, a very powerful sixth sense I have developed in the past several weeks.

It would all come down to Bunny Stirrup, so Becca marshaled her facts. The judge wouldn't like sending Emily to Zurich. She had thought it important to keep Emily in the apartment where she was secure. That was something.

As vividly as she imagined making the journey to Zurich sound like an unspeakable torture, Becca knew it was possible for the judge to take a different view. Compared to the pile of preschool rejection letters she and Edward had managed to collect for Emily, Bunny had at least gotten her *in* somewhere. The judge might see that fact to the child's advantage, Becca realized with dread.

And they were almost at three months, when the judge was supposed to make a permanent decision on custody. Maybe they were outside the window of vulnerability, when the judge wanted Emily to stay in the apartment, to minimize the harm of change. After all, in a stable, married, two-parent family. . . .

Becca sank her forehead into the palm of her hand as she waited to turn the car down an alley into a parking garage. She had lost. She knew it right now. Why even bother, when Edward and Bunny would have that nice two-parent home the judge wanted for Emily?

"What's wrong, Becca?" Emily asked.

Becca looked in the rearview mirror at Emily's innocent, questioning eyes. She smiled to notice, for the first time, that the interior of the car was covered with pink and red rainbows, flowers, birds, and smiley faces, traced in the lipstick Emily took from her purse. She sighed. What did it matter? Today was all.

She stopped herself. She couldn't think that way. She would tell the truth, and hope the judge understood her.

"I'm just thinking," she responded to Emily, who had asked again, "what I should tell the judge so she lets you stay with me forever. So you don't go away with Bunny."

Emily poked her head into the front seat. "I'll tell her," she chirped. "Don't I get to pick?"

Becca laughed. "I hope so," she answered. Enlivened by Emily's simple confidence, she led her into the courthouse.

"The judge will love your dress," Emily told her.

Becca hung her head. The borrowed bridesmaid's dress, hanging around her calves like a lampshade, crushed from the airplane seat, stained by the horse, and plainly ridiculous to begin with, floated around her like a divine joke. The judge would think she was a maniac.

Chapter 32

Edward Makes His Case

What Judge Jones thought, when she first saw Becca, was that she was desperate. She was familiar with Emily's custody case from her review of the file, and remembered Becca's lively personality from the first hearing, but she couldn't recall ever seeing such an extraordinary gown at a custody hearing.

The judge handed Emily a few packs of Smarties left over from a staff party, and watched her lie on her stomach on one of the courtroom benches, stacking the candy into towers, which she ate one "floor" at a time, from the penthouse to the basement.

While Becca used the excuse of assembling a few papers from her bag to buy herself some time, the judge walked to a window over the street. There was a huge traffic disturbance below: A large white horse trailer obstructed the street, drawing a great commotion of beeps, yelling, and profanity, from cabbies in particular. Its driver had apparently left the trailer, which was carrying a horse, blocking the street in front of the courthouse.

If there's a misdemeanor charge, she told herself with a laugh, at least it won't be on my docket. Judge Hammill was on his rotation through traffic court this fall.

She turned, startled by the sudden entrance of Edward Kirkland into the courtroom.

Becca's eyes flew open with surprise. Seeing Jerry Garcia would have startled her less than seeing Edward Kirkland at that moment. He was in her every thought, but her mind had cast Edward in very different images. She thought he would be taking his marriage vows about now, grinning easily, shrugging his shoulders and accepting his fate in the loping, relaxed manner in which he agreeably met the challenges of life. But he was not behaving as she pictured him. He strode into the courtroom with quick, firm steps. He walked directly to the judge, his eyes blazing and fixed intensely on her.

He was dressed in a morning coat and tails, with a white bow tie. The judge was starting to feel underdressed.

"Edward," she said, assuming Becca had notified him as she was required to under the statute. "Hello. We were expecting you."

She turned to Becca, whose shocked expression made it obvious that Edward had learned of this hearing on his own.

"Hi, Eddie," mumbled Emily, her mouth half full of candy.

Becca watched him soften, his shoulders relaxing for the moment that he smiled back at the child. She caught her breath. Edward loved Emily, and she knew, as she gazed at him standing before her, that she loved him. She turned her head away, trying to focus on anything else she could see: her purse, some papers to shuffle. She had called this hearing, she had led them all here, and now what? She felt utterly lost. Her eyes welled with tears, which she hid by staring at the floor.

The judge cleared her throat. "Well, shall we begin?"

Edward spoke, clearly and directly, to the judge.

"Your Honor," he said, nodding his head in a polite bow before continuing. "We're here—Becca and I—" he said, and his voice trailed off as he paused to turn toward Becca. His eyes rested upon her for a silent minute.

When Edward looked back at the judge, Becca studied him. He was standing in the center of the courtroom, with no wall to lean against, no table on which to rest his hands, no diversion, and no aid.

Standing still, intense and purposeful, Edward spoke.

"We are here, Your Honor," he repeated, "Becca and I, *together*, to seek permanent custody of Emily Stearns."

For a moment, the shock made her feel dizzy and she moved over to a bench to support herself. She knew now what it felt like to "swoon." As she pulled herself together, she had time to grasp Edward's intent. She smiled and watched him tenderly, in silence.

Edward glanced back at Becca, and her beautiful expression of consent filled him with courage. She understood; she was with him. He stopped for a moment, feeling the very air was alive with his joy.

"We are here to seek permanent custody of Emily," he repeated, smiling broadly. His eyes flashed suddenly with humor. "Can I take the stand?"

"If you like," replied Judge Jones gently. She realized she had fallen into a private moment and that it had happened by accident. She didn't swear Edward in as he walked up a step to the wooden witness box. She could see that the truth within him was leading him to speak.

Edward looked at Becca.

"I couldn't let you leave," he said. "Becca, I can't even remember my life before I met you. I tried to go back to it," he said, shaking his head, "but I don't know what it is. I don't know who I am, except with you," he said, his eyes filled with all he felt for her. He did not notice, with his stare fixed on Becca, that Emily had stood up on the bench, and was absorbed in watching him speak.

"I love you, Becca," said Edward, "and whatever is to come, the joy of knowing you will be the meaning of my life and that is all I want."

Her eyes filled with tears and she was flooded with happiness. She admired him so much, his patience, his kindness, his quiet strength. She knew he had come here at the sacrifice of much that was once important to him.

"I love you, Edward," she whispered, smiling at the sound of his name on her lips.

He closed his eyes, breathing in her words with pleasure. When he opened them again, he looked right into her beautiful, animated face, watching her eyes shine with tears.

"Will you marry me, Becca?" he asked simply.

"Yes!" Emily shouted from her bench.

They both turned to her with surprise, laughing. Enraptured by what was taking place between her guardians, she looked at Becca.

"Pleeeeease?" she asked.

Becca nodded. Turning slowly toward Edward, who had stepped down from the witness stand to be near her, Becca gave a great happy smile.

"Yes," she said, her eyes sparkling with joy.

She threw her arms around Edward as he rushed to hold her, and for a minute they embraced in celebration and relief, laughing tenderly.

The judge wiped her tears, thinking family law wasn't all bad. Emily ran to hug her parents, who cuddled her and tousled her hair.

After a whisper to Becca, Edward approached Judge Jones with a smile.

"You see, Your Honor," he said, "we'd like you to marry us. Then Emily can stay with us permanently. Our little girl."

Becca nodded, wiping her eyes.

Approval shone on the judge's face. "Sure, guys, you're dressed for it," she said. "Why don't you follow me into my chambers? I have the papers in there. Don't anybody change your minds," she added with a smile.

"This is where we started," Becca said, suddenly remembering the first time they met, at this courthouse and in this room. She was so hung up about whether he had a job, she didn't even see what kind of man he was: his strong sincerity, his gentle consideration and quiet selflessness, so evident in his patient love for Emily.

"I will never trust my first impression again!"

He shrugged. "I stand by my first impression," he said, looking at her with admiration. He reached for her hand and she offered it to him with joy.

When they walked down the hall behind the judge, Emily was no longer between them. Becca was in the middle, holding Edward's hand warmly, and with her other hand returning Emily's excited squeeze.

On the street Becca looked for Edward's car but instead he led her toward a double-parked station wagon pulling a horse trailer

"This is our chariot," Edward said. "Hope you don't mind that we'll have to squeeze in."

"But . . ."

"I had little choice. You had Dad's Bentley, my car was here, and I didn't think under the circumstances that I should ask Bunny for the loan of hers."

Emily let go of Becca's hand and was jumping up on Eddie like a puppy wanting to play. He picked her up and walked to the window of the trailer so she could see the horse's head within.

"The horse?" So much had happened in the last few hours that Becca was suffering from meltdown. Completing a sentence was tough.

"Oh, why the horse? Well, I could not find Henry and I was in a rush. It's impossible to get this mare out of the trailer without assistance. So, I just got onto the expressway dragging the horse behind me. It's perfectly legal."

"Expressway's pretty popular these days," Becca managed to say.

At this point, Emily was squirming in Edward's arms to be let down, to be allowed to pet the horse's rump, to go into the car and see if the horse was visible from there.

"Just a second, Em," Becca found her tongue. "In a little bit, we'll be unloading the horse and then you'll get to pet her." At this she turned to Edward with a baffled expression. "But"—she swept her arm to indicate the car and trailer—"where?" As usual, Becca needed a plan.

Edward understood all of this as he understood all of Becca and so he placed his forefinger over her lips. "Don't worry. Paul Novograd is a friend. And I'm sure there is space in Claremont."

The picturesque stable on the west side of Manhattan was home to all the most chichi horses in Manhattan. Many a business deal had been cut by two equestriennes on the bridle path through Central Park.

"And," he finished, "perhaps we can get a certain girl some lessons—the mare is a sweetheart when she's not being moved in and out of the trailer."

Emily, proof of the maxim that "little pitchers have big ears," began to cheer, "Horse lessons, horse lessons."

"That's what she needs. More appointments." Becca smiled.

"We'll ask her which ones she wants to keep and which we should cancel. I think Emily has been trained long enough, do you agree?"

Becca shook her head. "Absolutely. From now on it's chocolate in the morning and fancy dresses to play in the dirt."

They hugged, Becca's dress snagged on a rebellious piece of broken concrete sticking up from the sidewalk. She was unmindful of the tear that ripped one section of the dress in the back up to her waist.

"I see London, I see France," Emily sang, and Edward joined her. "I see Becca's underpants."

But she didn't care. The former Becca Reinhart was no more. In her place was Becca Kirkland. And along with that came a softer, more loving and tolerant world.

The other drivers were still forced to veer around the trailer and Edward was worried they would draw the attention of the police. "Let's go, guys, before we end up in the pokey. Do people still say that?"

"What's a pokey?" Emily and Becca spoke at the same time.

"Come with me, my two beautiful women, and we will discuss the pokey."

With that, he took both their hands and escorted them into the passenger side of the station wagon. They pulled away from the curb into Manhattan's traffic. Edward did not know if driving a horse trailer through the city was legal or not, and he saw a cop car pull out behind them. But luck was with them and the cop turned his siren on and rushed past them, on to bigger, more serious criminal acts, no doubt.

And no doubt about it—this was his lucky day.

Legally Blonde

Chapter One

ELLE WOODS GLANCED AT THE reflections of her bickering sorority sisters Margot and Serena in her vanity mirror. She sat on a pink-skirted stool with faux fur trim that matched the comforter on her bed, where her Chihuahua, Underdog, was comfortably resting.

'At least mine won't sag!' Serena pointed to her saline-enhanced chest. 'My boobs are as perky as the day I put them on my credit card!'

'So what if they'll never sag,' Margot said, unimpressed. 'They're as hard as rocks.'

'They're also blocking the only natural light in this room,' Elle whispered to Underdog, who looked up sympathetically. Both Underdog and Elle had heard Serena and Margot's argument countless times before. Elle refused to get involved, because her father, the trendy Beverly Hills plastic surgeon Dr. Wyatt Woods, known among the nip and tuck crowd as a 'Best for Breasts,' had done Serena's work. Anyhow, Elle had a more pressing concern.

'They're not hard. They're firm!' Serena said, and stamped her foot. There wasn't half an inch between Serena and Margot, squared off chest to chest.

Margot's lips, pouty from last year's lip injections, were set in a glossy purple smile that matched the Nike swoosh on her little-used cross-trainers. Despite the fact that Margot had undergone enough plastic surgery to be on a

1

frequent-slicer plan, she told Elle that she prided herself on the fact that she had never let a doctor touch her boobs. Clinically anyway.

'Have you guys totally forgotten? Tonight could be the night!' Elle shouted to get Serena's and Margot's attention. 'I need to look *perfect*. I want everything to be exactly right tonight!'

'Of course I didn't forget,' Serena said, turning her back on Margot. 'I even have a *Cosmo* tip for you. I read that you can totally put someone at ease by matching their body language. The article said that Jennifer did that with Brad and it made it a lot easier for him to pop the question, since he was kind of nervous beforehand.'

'Warner *has* to propose to you tonight, Elle,' Margot chimed in. 'Not only is tonight your third anniversary, but I checked your chart and masterful Saturn has begun a long transit through Taurus. It's your time to make life-altering decisions.'

Elle appraised her appearance once again in the mirror and decided she needed a bit more blush. Her long blonde hair gleamed and framed her heart-shaped face. Her flaw-less fair complexion was set off by huge deep blue eyes that shone with kindness, and her size 2 figure was poured per-fectly into her red slip-dress.

'In fact, I'm way ahead of you, Elle,' Serena said. 'Look what I picked up today!' She held up a copy of *In Style Weddings* with a shot of J-Lo on the cover.

'Oh my God!' Margot shrieked. 'Not that one. Don't you know anything? J-Lo never should have done that cover! There's an *In Style Weddings* curse. Like three of their cover brides, including Courtney Thorne-Smith, were divorced before the issue hit the stand!'

'That's true,' Elle said, 'but that was totally sweet of you Serena.'

A voice over the sorority house intercom suddenly interrupted them just as Margot pulled out the latest issue of *Brides* magazine: 'Warner's here, Elle.'

'Keep your fingers crossed!' Elle said to Serena and Margot as she checked her reflection again, still unsure about the dress she had chosen. 'Are you *sure* this is it?' she asked her friends for the fourth time.

'Maybe you should go with pink. It is your signature color,' Serena said. 'Ow!' Margot had given her a sharp elbow to the ribs.

Elle stood frozen, suddenly unsure of her choice. Would it be the dress she would want to tell her great-grandchildren about when she regaled them with stories about the night Warner proposed? What if it looked dated and stupid by then?

'No, Elle, that's it,' Margot said. 'I'm positive! Red is the color of confidence and it matches your aura.'

'Well, I don't want to look like I expect anything.' Elle tucked her smooth golden blonde hair behind her ears, checking that the diamond earrings Warner had given her for her birthday were securely in place.

'He'll ask. You *know* it's coming, Elle,' Serena said, sounding mildly annoyed. 'Anyway, Margot's right. Red is better.'

'Group hug!' Margot announced, and suddenly Elle was sandwiched between the biggest and most expensive boobs in the Delta Gamma house.

Warner stood waiting in the foyer of the Delta Gamma house. His tall, blond, and handsome looks never failed to leave all of Elle's sorority sisters in a stunned silence. As Elle approached him, he pulled her close to him with one arm while smoothly holding a dozen long-stemmed shell pink roses in the other.

Elle snuggled against him; her smile lit up the room as

her delight to be with him radiated from her. She was completely absorbed in the moment. 'Mar, will you put these in a vase for me?' she absently asked her friend, who was standing at the bottom of the stairs with the rest of the Delta Gamma house, all trying to look casual while inspecting the couple with magnified intensity and not a little envy.

'I'll do it,' Serena said, stepping in front of Margot and making an obvious show for her sorority sisters of tucking *In Style Weddings* under her arm before she reached for the flowers. 'Warner, you look fantastic. Anything special planned for tonight?'

Warner looked slightly amused by Serena's comment and gave her a devastating smile.

'Every night with Elle is special,' he said. He gave Elle a smile, and squeezed her hand. 'C'mon, Elle. I don't want to be late.'

As Warner guided her through the Delta Gamma front door, Elle looked back over her shoulder at Serena and Margot, who were giving her a big thumbs-up.

Chapter Two

WARNER HELD THE DOOR OF his black Mercedes convertible for Elle, and she slid into the plush oyster-colored leather seat. She gazed up at the sky to make sure the stars were in alignment, as *Cosmo* had promised they would be. They were. Suddenly she felt completely sure that tonight was *the* night. They drove for a while in contented silence, the cool air of a California October night blowing the golden blow-dried strands of her hair.

'I hope you won't be disappointed, Elle,' Warner said as he exited the freeway. 'I know you wanted to go to our favorite place, the Beach House, but I thought we should go to the Ivy tonight, since it's the place where this all began.' He smiled at Elle in all his perfection and placed his hand high on her thigh.

'You could never disappoint me,' Elle purred back. She glowed as she placed her unadorned left hand on top of his. 'Our first date was one of the most amazing nights of my life.'

They were stuck in Los Angeles traffic under a Calvin Klein billboard. The model loomed over them, a bronzed work of art. Elle stared at Warner's golden profile with adoration and thought how lucky she was and how she'd be even luckier by the end of this glorious night. There could be nothing better than spending the rest of her life with Warner Huntington III.

*

Elle's entrance into the Ivy caused a stir. Even here, where every night the restaurant was filled with long-legged blondes and movie stars, her radiant beauty and sweet smile made her stand out. Several men tried to get her attention as she and Warner made their way to their table. Warner wore a look of satisfaction as he observed the other men admiring Elle.

A waiter of the L.A. variety, who really considered himself an actor, came to take their order with an annoying dramatic flair. 'Hi, I'm Zach and I've gotta tell ya, we've got some fresh fish tonight so good it oughta be against the law!'

'Actually, we're ready to order,' Warner said abruptly without looking at the menu or the waiter. Elle and the waiter exchanged puzzled glances, and she began to protest, but was silenced when Warner ordered a bottle of Cristal. He must be so nervous, she thought, and immediately felt sorry for him as he got ready to ask the biggest question of his life. She lowered her head and looked up through her Chanel-enhanced lashes.

'Tonight is so wonderful, Warner, and you should know, I plan to keep the celebration going *all night*.' She leaned forward seductively, expecting Warner's ice blue eyes to meet her smoky stare, but to her amazement, he was gazing distractedly around the room.

'Is something wrong, lovebug?' Elle asked as the waiter headed toward their table with the champagne.

'Nothing at all, Elle,' Warner replied, patting her hand as his attention returned to her. He motioned the waiter to pour the champagne. 'In fact, things couldn't be better.' He smiled and took a deep breath.

Elle just knew this was it. Maybe it was a little odd that Warner wasn't waiting until after dinner, when the ring could be nestled in crème brûlée, but, she reasoned, he must be too overcome with nerves to wait.

'Elle,' he began in a low, confident voice, 'the last three years with you have been perfect.' Elle sighed in agreement. 'Tonight, I want to share the best possible news with you.'

Elle's heart skipped a beat, and she took a deep breath to control the urge to blurt out, 'Yes! Yes I will marry you!' Warner paused and waited until the waiter finished filling their glasses and left them alone again. 'Well first, darling, I have something I want to give to you.'

Elle closed her eyes and tremulously extended her left hand to Warner, hoping this would help him slip that 'something' on her finger. She could hear the pealing of wedding bells in her head and was wondering if she should go with Vera Wang or a completely unknown but soon-to-be-famous dress designer when Warner's voice invaded her reverie. 'I want to give you this reminder of our time together,' he said gently.

Elle frowned, somewhat disconcerted by the use of the word 'reminder.' Why would he call an engagement ring a 'reminder?' she wondered. Then she remembered what Serena said *Cosmo* said about how nervous Brad Pitt had been when he asked Jennifer to marry him, and she smiled at his clumsy word choice. It was so adorable! She closed her eyes again, only to open them again in confusion as she felt Warner turn her left hand over so the palm faced up.

'Warner, what are you doing?' Elle demanded as she stared at the Cartier ID bracelet she had given to him on their second anniversary. It had been engraved *Elle and Warner forever*.

'I thought you'd want me to return it,' he replied sweetly as he closed her palm and brought it to his lips.

'Return it?' Elle said, jerking her hand back. 'Why would you do that?'

7

'Well, I knew when you gave it to me that I could never *return* your feelings, so I thought . . .' He let his words trail off and licked his lips as he looked around. Elle stared at him in disbelief. His words began to blur and she shook her head to clear her thoughts.

'What I mean is, I thought now would be a good time to give it back. We're not going to be together forever Elle. You know that. It was a sweet thought, but I've decided to turn my life around and get serious. I think we should make a clean break before I leave for Stanford Law School.' He paused, waiting for her to respond. When she didn't and just stared at him he continued quickly. 'Oh, right, did I forget to tell you I've decided to go to law school next year? That's the good news I wanted to tell you.'

Elle's mouth was dry. She reached for the champagne flute, but realized her hands were shaking and she couldn't safely hold the glass without risk of spilling on her dress.

'What are you *talking* about?' Elle's voice was louder than she intended. Warner looked around the restaurant nervously.

'When you said you'd always love me were you just being *optimistic*? And when you said you'd never felt this way about anyone before were you lying? And how could you make a decision about your life, *our lives*, like law school without telling me? How long have you known?' Her voice was shaky and suddenly her sobbing was uncontrollable.

'I didn't lie, Elle,' Warner whispered, trying to make sure Will Smith and Jada Pinkett, seated two tables away, couldn't hear them. 'I never told you that I felt the same way *you* did, did I? Think about it.' Before Elle could respond he took her hands in his. 'Listen, honeybun, this is really hard on me. Can't you see that? You know how much my family expects of me and the high standards I have for myself—'

Elle interrupted him by yanking her hands away from him. She glared at him in anger and disbelief, but Warner continued on.

'I had to ask myself, "Warner, is it worth it to go through any more of my life with a girl who will never be *serious* enough to be my wife or the mother of my children?" Do you know the courage this took, Elle? How hard it was for me?' He paused for a moment and appraised her cleavage. '*Really* hard,' he added. He looked down, apparently wounded by his own high standards.

Elle left the table and turned angrily on her heel, leaving Warner fumbling for his wallet so he could escape the restaurant without any further embarrassment. He threw some money on the table and hurried after her.

Outside, the valet looked up from the screenplay he was writing long enough to give Elle an appreciative once-over in spite of her tear-blotched face. She was about to ask him to call a cab for her when Warner cleared his throat audibly behind them, and the valet jumped up and ran to get the car.

'C'mon, Elle,' Warner said. 'Let me take you home.' At that moment home was just where she wanted to be, and the faster she could get there, the better. Sullenly, she agreed.

After what seemed like an eternity to Elle, the car screeched up. Warner barely gave Elle time to close her door before he turned up the volume on the radio and merged into the Friday night traffic on Robertson.

Elle could not believe what had happened. She stared at Warner's perfect profile. 'This is not happening,' she said to herself. 'It's 2002. It's the time of *Buffy*, *Charmed*, and *Charlie's Angels*. Be strong.' Elle imagined Warner meeting up with Buffy in a dark alley and felt a tiny bit better until the violence of the image was shattered by a glimpse of her still-unadorned left hand. She felt trapped in an Aaron Spelling drama where bad things happen to good-looking people.

Warner had pulled up in front of the Delta Gamma house. When he noticed Elle waiting for him to come around and open her car door as he always had before, he leaned across her, opened the door, and gave her a quick kiss on the cheek.

'See ya, Elle,' he said with his hand resting on the shift already in first gear.

Elle stumbled out of the car and into the house entirely devastated, completely un-Buffy, and resoundingly un-Elle.

Chapter Three

TRYING HARD TO HIDE HER devastation, Elle Woods entered the spacious TV room of the University of Southern California Delta Gamma house. Not expecting Elle to come home for at least a few more hours, Margot and Serena were completely engrossed in *The Osbournes*.

'I heard Kelly Osbourne has an MTV veejay who is seriously into her,' Serena said.

'Hmmm . . . that's cool,' Margot responded, pursing her lips the way she did when she was thinking really hard.

Glued to the television, they didn't even hear Elle's sniffling noises or see her tear-stained face until finally Elle blurted out, 'Some sisterhood . . . you're supposed to be my best friends. Maybe I should have been a Theta.'

Serena and Margot looked at their friend and gasped. Mascara streaked Elle's blotchy, anguished face as she fell onto the couch.

'Warner . . . broke . . . up . . . with . . . me!' Elle shouted, her words broken by uncontrollable sobs.

'You didn't get the rock?' Margot asked, astonished. She looked as if she might start crying too.

'It's not a Kappa, is it?' Serena shrieked, falling to Elle's side. 'I'll kill them!'

'No, no.' Elle shook her head. 'It's not another girl . . . it couldn't be.'

As the Delta Gamma social chair, Margot vigorously agreed. 'I hereby cancel our annual mixer with Sigma Chi.'

Elle smiled at Margot, but shook her head sadly. 'Margot, forget it. It's too late.' She sank deeper into the floral chintz couch, resting her chin on her knees, her eyes brimming with tears. 'It's o-o-o-over.'

Serena and Margot stared at Elle, then at each other in genuine disbelief. If Elle and Warner weren't getting married, what would become of the rest of them? Everyone knew Elle and Warner were perfect together. They went together like shampoo and conditioner.

Chapter Four

ELLE, SERENA, AND MARGOT WENT upstairs to Elle's room, which only a few hours before had been filled with bridal expectations. The room's cotton-candy-pink walls were almost covered by photos of smiling blonde Delta Gammas at sorority yacht trips and black-tie formals. Tonight, however, the girls looked nothing like their upbeat, glamorous counterparts in the photos.

'Everything was normal, at first,' Elle began after Margot served them her famous pink Margotita with a pink crazy straw. 'We were at the Ivy and the mood was perfect. The Cristal had just been poured when Warner basically told me: "Elle, when I start law school, I think we should stop seeing each other." Boom! Moving off to Stanford Law School, and he told me he needs to find someone more "serious."'

'More serious!' Margot huffed with her pouty MAC Glaze lips. 'What's that supposed to mean? Serious about what?' she asked.

'I don't know what it means!' Elle said angrily. 'That's what he told me. He said, "Elle, I'm ready for someone more serious." Just like that. I think maybe he's grown out of this' – she motioned around the room – 'this scene . . . and out of me!' Elle wiped a stray tear as Margot poured more pink slush from the blender.

'Who the hell does he think he is?' Margot demanded. 'There is no better girl, no better Delta Gamma, no better wife for Warner Huntington III.'

'Right!' agreed Serena. 'When did he decide that he was too good for Miss June?' Serena mocked. 'You were certainly fine for him at his all-important Sigma Chi rat-frat parties.'

Elle had been Miss June on the USC calendar for three consecutive years. She was president of Delta Gamma and of the Intersorority Council. She had practically *invented* her major in sociopolitical jewelry design by merging technical classes at the architecture school with sociological research on tribal ornamentation and feminist critiques of beauty myths.

She remembered Warner's pride when she won homecoming queen last October. She was driven around the stadium in her own BMW convertible, the white car glittering with freshly painted USC war stripes, draped in crimson and gold as Elle and homecoming king Warner Huntington waved from the car.

'There are way better guys around here than Warner, Elle,' Serena said. 'You know how Javier is dying to date you.' Serena's ex-boyfriend Javier was moneyed through his family's investment firm, which had wisely bought California's largest cement manufacturer and celebrated enthusiastically after every earthquake.

Thinking about Serena's sloppy seconds made Elle cry harder. Her perfectly tanned shoulders shook with every sob. 'I was just positive Warner was going to propose to me tonight! I feel so humiliated!' She looked sadly at her left hand. 'I thought the Huntington Rock of Gibraltar was mine for sure. You remember the Rock? The family six-carat?' Margot and Serena nodded solemnly. 'Why would he tell me about that ring if he wasn't going to marry me?'

'Elle, he's such an operator,' Serena said. 'I don't mean to say I told you so, but he doesn't care about anything other than himself and his résumé.' Warner was president of the student senate and had been a first boat rower in prep school and a pitcher on USC's baseball team, which had played in the College World Series the previous spring. Warner often joked about how impressive his college résumé would sound when he ran for president, but he was only half joking.

In fact, Elle remembered, when she wanted to bring Warner down a peg, she would gently mock his political ambitions. 'Oh, Warner,' she would coo, 'you have the makings of a great vice president.' This would infuriate him. The second son in his family, he had come west primarily because he didn't want to follow his older brother to Harvard. He was tired of running second.

'Wasn't his grandfather a senator or something?' Margot asked.

Elle nodded, sipping her drink. 'Mmm-hmm, from Connecticut. For like fifty years or something.' Warner had often told Elle that family tradition would lead him into politics and that public service was a Huntington family legacy. His Grandmummy Huntington was DAR Newport, Rhode Island, a grande dame with tremendous influence over her family since the death of Warner's grandfather three decades earlier. She never let Warner forget that his blood ran blue.

'I should have seen it coming when Grandmummy Huntington came to L.A. for Warner's birthday last month,' Elle conceded. 'Warner hasn't been the same since. Grandmummy ignored me through the entire dinner and then, as she was leaving, told me that I reminded her of Pamela Anderson!'

'Ewww! Pamela Anderson!' Serena and Margot said in unison. That was the ultimate insult.

Underdog hopped up on the couch, and Elle tugged

15

his soft ears and stared into his devoted deep brown eyes. 'You still love me, Underdog,' she cooed to him as she fixed the pink satin bow attached to his rhinestone collar.

Chapter Five

ELLE'S TEARS GAVE WAY TO resolve as she and her two best friends worked late into the evening devising plans to bring Warner to his senses.

Elle decided around 3:00 A.M. that she would go to law school and beat Warner at his own game. Decided, maybe, after one too many pink Margotitas. Tequila-induced or not, the idea stuck. If Warner was going to Stanford Law School to find someone 'serious,' he was going to find one serious Elle Woods.

Elle spent the rest of the fall semester in hibernation, studying for the Law School Aptitude Test, which she had scheduled to take in January. Everyone attributed her social disappearance to her breakup with Warner.

Three months later, Elle was positively beaming as she emerged from the LSAT. Not only were the required sections a breeze, but the extra section, 'Logic Games,' allowed her to use what she considered to be among her greatest strengths: abstract organization. Ever since high school Elle had been a wiz at seating arrangements for parties, saving events that could have been diversity disasters without her strategic social skills. She was famous for the dinner parties to which she would invite sorority sisters with open rivalries or roommates on the outs. She partnered talkers with listeners and athletes with beauties, with dazzling success.

So when she encountered the silly time-zone puzzles in

the 'Logic Games' section she finished four minutes ahead of the clock. Nothing on the exam came close to approaching the subtleties and entanglements of Elle's social world.

Days after the exam, Elle sauntered into her mother's contemporary Los Angeles art gallery on La Brea. The walls had been sponged in rich vegetable-dye pigments and deep brushed metal. The redwood-stained floor shone, and the lighting in the gallery was set to flatter her mother more than the art.

'Kiss noise!' Elle's mother said when she saw her. Elle leaned across her mother's desk and they exchanged air kisses to avoid smudging each other's artfully applied makeup.

'Mother, I've got some news that may surprise you,' Elle announced nervously as she settled into a comfortless straight-backed chair.

'Oh, darling! You're finally marrying Warner!' Eva guessed. Elle had always told her mother everything, but hadn't had the guts to tell her about the awful October night when Warner dumped her. She knew her mother would be devastated. Although her mother ran one of L.A.'s most successful galleries, she had always told Elle that a woman's most exalted achievement was in landing a moneyed husband and maintaining a successful marriage.

'No, Mother,' Elle said, 'um, not yet. The news is, I've decided not to work in the gallery this fall. I'm, uh, well, I've decided to go back to school.'

Eva smiled and turned stiffly back to her work looking at slide submissions from new artists. Elle could sense her disappointment. 'Design or film, dear?' she asked.

'I'm going to law school.'

Eva bolted out of her chair. She was teetering from shock in her Gucci stilettos and was afraid she might faint.

She quickly reached for her chair, and once she was seated, she stared at Elle for several moments before she could speak. 'Law school? What are you talking about? Darling, one must pass tests for that sort of nonsense and—'

Elle interrupted. 'Oh, I know,' she said, and giggled nervously, tugging at the quilted Chanel fabric of her pale-pink-and-white checked micromini. 'I've already taken the test and I think I aced it. It may seem sudden, I know, Mother, but I just totally want to be a lawyer.' She shuffled her perfectly coordinated pink-and-white spectator pumps on the gleaming floor and tried to think of a reason that would satisfy her mother.

'I see,' Eva said. 'Have you applied to schools already?'

'Well, of course! I applied to Harvard, and Pepperdine as a backup. And, um, Stanford too, I think.' She paused. 'Yes, those three, definitely,' Elle lied. She had only applied to Stanford. After all why would she set foot on a campus that didn't have Warner on it?

'Well, your father will be devastated!' Eva said. 'Do you have any idea how much his medical malpractice insurance was last year?'

Elle thought about telling her about the nobler pursuits of the law that she had recently brushed up on to help her write her personal-essay part of the Stanford application, but decided it would be a waste of time. Ultimately, she would get Warner back and both of her parents would be happy.

In late April, while standing in the foyer of the Delta Gamma house leafing through her mail, Elle found a very thin envelope from Stanford. As was typical for a sunny day, the house was empty. Elle ran up the winding green carpeted staircase to her room, gripping the white railing painted with delicate gold anchors with one hand and holding the letter in her other, praying it was a letter of acceptance. She listed all of her credentials in her head before she opened the letter to try to calm her nerves. She had a 4.0 grade point average, a perfect LSAT score, and tons of extracurricular activities. She just hoped that Stanford had liked her personal statement.

Leaning against the inside of her bedroom door, Elle opened the letter with trembling hands and began to read aloud. Her eyes began to fill with tears of joy after she read the letter's first sentence. 'Dear Ms. Woods, we are pleased to extend a spot to you in our first-year class.'

After graduation Elle moved back to her parents', and from that day on, with Underdog faithfully at her side, she began the project of becoming someone she was sure Warner would regard as 'serious.'

Her first instinct, as always, was to turn to *Cosmo* for advice. The magazine, ripe with articles with titles such as 'How to Make Sure He's Ga-Ga for You!,' had been virtually foolproof in the past. However, when Serena found Warner's brother and his bride featured in *Town & Country*, Elle knew that was her new bible.

With *Glamour* and *Allure* tucked safely under her bed, and *Town & Country* under her arm, Elle headed for Laura Ashley, traded in her BMW convertible for a Range Rover, and bought a pair of Oliver Peoples wire-rim glasses (without prescription lenses of course). She began wearing pearls.

In August, after a month of daily six-hour shopping excursions, Elle Woods was ready. She packed her flowery sundresses, tartan headbands, and pink furry slippers, zipped her Louis Vuittons, and headed north with Underdog.

Chapter Six

ELLE COULDN'T BELIEVE HOW demoralizing the Crothers Dormitory was. Her dorm room was less than half the size of her walk-in closet at home and had a low ceiling, dingy gray walls, and a tile floor of an undeterminable color. A solitary window provided the only light.

Elle looked at her watch and realized she was already late. She left her dorm room and the moving men who were grappling with how to wedge in at least three times the amount of clothing and personal items as the room was meant to hold, and drove hurriedly to orientation. She parked the Range Rover and considered what to do with Underdog.

'Sorry, precious,' Elle said, rubbing the dog's head. 'I'll take care of this really fast and you can guard the car.' She poured Evian into his pink inflatable travel dish, cracked the windows, turned on his favorite Cole Porter CD, and blew him a kiss as she darted off.

The melee in the courtyard in front of Stanford Law School reminded her of the first day of summer camp. Groups of proud parents stood around cooing to their embarking prodigies, who brandished dreadful 'Hello My Name Is' tags on their chests. Elle thought about her parents, who couldn't bear to see her 'wasting her talents at law school.' Second-year law students worked at tables hawking Stanford Law bumper stickers, T-shirts, sweatshirts, coffee mugs, pens, notebooks, backpacks, and shoelaces to eager buyers. Elle declined the opportunity to purchase Stanford Law paraphernalia and looked for an alphabetical line to guide her, but Stanford had a markedly different organization than civilized activities like sorority rush.

'If you went to Harvard, pick up your name tag here,' read the sign in front of a crowded table of students pushing each other to get their tags. 'If you went to Brown,' a busy table of Euro wanna-bes beckoned, 'pick up your name tag here.' The MIT/Cal Tech table was teeming with PowerBook-flourishing techies and Trekkies. The Smith table resembled a NOW convention of 'Before' candidates for beauty makeovers. Elle approached the 'State Schools, except Penn, which really is an Ivy' table with a nervous glance, uncertain whether the University of Southern California actually counted as a state school. There was no name tag for her there.

Drifting past the sign for 'Cornell, which is not really an Ivy,' Elle felt a creeping sense of horror. Maybe the acceptance letter had been a joke, a terrible mistake. At the far end of the swarm stood a single card table with the sign that she knew was meant for her alone.

'If you went to Santa Monica Community College for summer school, pick up your name tag here,' read a sign at a table so distant it was the equivalent of being seated by the kitchen at Lutece. Nobody was staffing this table, on which lay Elle's lone sticker with her name and an orientation schedule anchored by a rock. 'Very funny,' Elle said, blushing. She had passed her math requirement at Santa Monica but certainly didn't count it as her alma mater. She shoved the hideous name tag into her Prada bag and departed quickly for a second row of tables.

Pushing past people from among whom Blackwell would have found it impossible to pick out the ten worst dressed, she found a relatively calm-looking woman who wasn't accompanied by her parents or carrying a Powerbook, and asked her if she knew where she was supposed to go next.

'I don't know.' The woman looked her up and down and gave an uninterested shrug. 'I'm waiting for my fiancé.'

'Thanks.' Elle moved to a nearby table and surveyed its collection of pamphlets on date rape, drug and alcohol abuse, and sexual harassment. The table workers were also aggressively distributing brochures for psychiatric care at Stanford. A lengthy pamphlet on substance abuse among graduate students was shoved into Elle's hand from the unmanicured clutches of a do-gooder.

Finally, making her way to an unoccupied wooden bench, Elle sat down to read her orientation schedule for the following day.

Tuesday:

   9:00 A.M.–10:00 A.M. Registration
10:00 A.M.–12:00 P.M. Book Purchase
12:00 P.M.–1:30 P.M. Westward-Ho 'Bar'-b-que
  1:30 P.M.–3:00 P.M. Campus Tour (including Law
                 Library)
  3:00 P.M.–5:00 P.M. You and Others: Meet and
                 Greet
  5:00 P.M.–7:00 P.M. Dean's Welcome
  7:00 P.M.   Pizza Party, followed by 'Bar' Revue

'*Bar*baric,' Elle said and groaned. As if greasy pizza and a 'Bar'-b-que, where they were likely to serve Sloppy Joes, weren't bad enough, the schedule covered every minute of the day with law-themed activities. How could she even begin to color-code her closet (pinks first, of course) before classes began on Thursday? She thought of Underdog and decided to beat the scheduled book-purchase rush the next day and go straight to the bookstore.

Elle returned to the Range Rover, grabbed Underdog, and hurried to the bookstore. She located the Law section by approaching the already familiar crowd of beaming, chattering parents. While Stanford med students and engineers had their own bookstore on University Avenue, law books were sold on the bottom level of the campus bookstore, a dingy dungeon with a gray-lit stairwell and linoleum floors. Elle had naively thought that she would beat the long lines by arriving ahead of the preprinted schedule for book buying. No such luck: dozens of law students, eager to get an edge on their classmates, were staring lustfully at the casebooks they would soon own.

Elle gathered her unwieldy casebooks, twelve in all, thinking how inconvenient they would make vacation travel, and took her place behind yet another set of proud parents and a law student whose stiff demeanor and signature J. Press uniform of khakis, a white shirt, and a navy blazer left no doubt that he had gone to Yale and had never ventured outside of New Haven for shopping trips.

An MP3 player and sunglasses would have been a good call, thought Elle as she tried to ignore the student's father loudly reminiscing about his days at Harvard Law. An MP3's volume couldn't have gone high enough to drown him out, not even if she had played Kid Rock. Elle soon learned that his name was actually Mr. Daniel Baxter III. Tripp, to his friends, as he was greeted by an old Princeton classmate whose pants were sprinkled with alligators and whose belt was embroidered with tiny Princeton crests. His daughter was starting Stanford undergrad, he told Mr. Baxter, with a hearty pat on the back and a quick mention of what he had shot at the club last week.

Baxter's son, a poor imitation of his father and probably his grandfather before him, smiled and nodded at appropriate times as his father boomed his thoughts like a drill sergeant. 'Anne, doesn't this remind you of when we took Edward to Choate? And then Yale? A heavyweight rower and an all-American squash player!' Tripp Baxter broadcast, punching Edward on the shoulder. Elle's classmate must not have been the first son, since his mother addressed him not as 'Daniel' or even 'Dan' but 'Edward.'

Mr. and Mrs. Baxter weren't buying sweatshirts or bumper stickers, and their haughty expressions revealed that they had as little in common with the sweatshirt buyers as with the linoleum floor beneath Mrs. Baxter's bright yellow espadrilles.

Mrs. Baxter smiled at Edward and pushed him along, her eyes twinkling amid crow's-feet and wrinkles that came from too much time on the tennis court without a visor. Elle realized with horror that Anne Baxter's dress was a Lily Pulitzer almost exactly like the one Elle had purchased at Barneys after seeing it in the 'What's Hot' column in *Allure*. Squinting at the flamingo pink print, Elle made a mental note to start a Goodwill pile immediately.

'Edward,' his father began, 'did I ever tell you about John Kaplan, a Harvard Law classmate of mine?' Tripp glanced down at his green-and-blue happy whale pants, a color eruption thankfully ending at his brown L.L. Bean shoes.

Ed's mouth hung open and silent in what Elle saw as an indication that his thoughts were as dishwater-bland as his hair. But he didn't have time to answer before his father regaled all but the deaf with the tale of the illustrious John Kaplan.

'He was brilliant! Or at least he used to be,' Mr. Baxter

paused, 'before he left the East to teach at *Stanford*, if you can imagine,' he said between eruptions of laughter. 'Well, anyway, you should have seen him at *Harvard*. We'd sit there in Professor Gluck's class; boy, he could shake you up. And Kaplan . . . when he bothered to show up to class . . . would take absolutely no notes. Not a word! He just turned his back to the professor and stared at the wall. He never even bought his books, the rascal. But when he was called on, he'd give the correct answer along with such keen insight that even the professor was stunned. What a genius, that Kaplan!'

'Terrible what happened to him,' Anne said as she arranged her headband.

'Yes, terrible.' Ed's father nodded sadly.

'What happened?' Ed asked, his voice tremulous.

'Terrible,' Elle said under her breath. And sadder still that with all of these casebooks . . . all of the reading she would have ahead of her, she would probably have to miss Conan O'Brien.

Elle pulled out *Allure*'s September issue and noisily turned the pages in an attempt to let Tripp Baxter know that he was interrupting important reading. Her annoyance went unnoticed, so there was no choice but to find out what tragic event had happened to John Kaplan.

'Well one tragedy, for you, Edward, is that he wrote your Criminal Law text,' his father said, laughing. Ed looked down over his overdeveloped chest at the enormous book with such tiny print that it should have come with a magnifying glass.

Elle glanced at Kaplan's name on the red Criminal Law text that she was holding.

'He died at a very young age. Around fifty, I think,' Anne answered sadly, shooting a nasty look in her husband's direction.

'If he never studied, how could he teach?' Edward said.

'Well, he found a way, I tell you,' Daniel Baxter III answered with a resounding boom.

Elle stepped out of line, deciding the moral of Kaplan's story was that if he never even bought his books and still managed to become a professor, there was no need for her to worry about missing her regular manicure time, which would fall during Criminal Law.

Chapter Seven

AT NINE O'CLOCK THE FOLLOWING morning, Elle was back at the law school for registration. 'Elle!' Warner exclaimed with what was clearly surprise. Elle noticed that his yellow shirt matched his sun-bleached hair. He pulled a pale, frowning brunette standing beside him closer. 'What are *you* doing here?' He looked with curiosity at Elle's Laura Ashley pastel sundress and sensible string of pearls.

She hadn't seen Warner approaching, and his simple question caught her off guard. 'I'm registering. Like everybody else.' Elle had thought of a million lines to say to Warner alone, but the sight of him with another woman evaporated her confidence and repertoire of snappy Warner witticisms.

'Registering for what? This *isn't* the textiles department, Elle.' Warner laughed.

'Really? I'm thrilled to hear that! Otherwise I would have been standing in the wrong line for hours to register for, like, fashion design when I came all the way here to enter *law* school,' Elle answered, smiling. She glanced at the preppie woman who was pulling Warner's sleeve, anxious for his attention.

'This is . . . Sarah,' Warner said, turning toward his companion. Her mousy brown hair was bobbed and cemented in place by a navy blue headband with appliquéd daisies. Elle stared at Sarah through the pink tinted lenses of her Oliver Peoples sunglasses and managed a weak smile.

'We prepped together,' Warner said, in a pathetic attempt to break the tension. Elle remembered pictures of Sarah from Warner's Groton yearbook. She had to admit, Warner had landed a prize preppie. Her grandfather was immortalized on a postage stamp. Grandmummy Huntington must already be selecting the paper stock for the wedding invitations.

Elle extended her hand toward Sarah. 'I'm sure Warner's told you about me.'

Sarah reached out tentatively and shook Elle's hand limply as she surveyed Elle with contempt, deciding that Warner must have been blinded by Elle's lustrous blonde hair. She was certainly nothing like the decent friends he'd had at Groton.

Warner had told Sarah about Elle, but he hadn't needed to. Sarah would have found out at any number of events, such as Harriman Cup or Far Hills. Everyone they prepped with knew about Warner's foolish college fling, the unsuitability of which was his grandmother's favorite topic of conversation.

'Mark my words, that . . . that woman will never, *never* call herself a Huntington,' she would often tell her friends when they gathered at her beach club in Newport.

In theory, before she had seen her, Sarah had accepted Elle as within the tolerable bounds of Warner's youthful randiness. A college fling. Now, gawking at what Sarah surmised to be a Barbie doll with a pulse, in her flower-print sundress, she realized she had underestimated the depths to which Warner had sunk since he left Groton. Wrenching her hand from Elle's, Sarah adjusted her headband to display the massive diamond on her left hand.

'I'm Sarah Knottingham. Warner's fiancée,' she stated pointedly in her best Groton drawl.

Elle couldn't believe it. She stared openmouthed as Sarah, the Rock, and Warner spun around in her head while she tried to process what had just happened. She thought she might be having a nightmare and shut her eyes tightly, hoping that when she opened them, the whole scene would disappear. But it didn't.

Elle went back to her dorm room, plopped on the bed, and patted it so Underdog would jump up. 'Underdog, you've got to keep quiet,' Elle warned, clamping his tiny mouth to stifle a bark. 'You're not allowed, but I need a friend here.' She pulled her dog's soft ears affectionately.

Elle sighed. Casting aside the dress she would never have worn a year ago, she slid into her more comfortable Delta Gamma Anchorsplash T-shirt to begin unpacking. She glared at the chipper dress where it lay on her bed and scowled at its floral explosion as if the dress were at fault.

'What am I doing here?' Elle sighed, sinking to the floor, her life scattered amid the boxes. A narrow twin bed, a desk, and a chair were the only furniture in her gloomy new room. A year ago, she had pictured her life after college so differently.

Elle had been sure that at this very time, her world would revolve around planning her wedding. She had thought that deciding whether she should have tulle or silk organza for the skirt of her wedding dress would be her biggest concern.

Instead, she found herself in a law school dorm. Elle trembled. 'What have I done?' she moaned again as she dropped her head into her hands. She sobbed remembering Sarah's brunette bob and her pale hand brandishing the

Rock of Gibraltar, the family jewel that should have been Elle's.

'Well, I'm here now,' Elle decided, forcing her agony into resolve. 'Warner, Sarah, and for that matter, my parents better not write me off just yet.' She stood up to search for the telephone.

Chapter Eight

AFTER FINALLY LOCATING HER fuzzy pink Princess-style phone in a box labeled 'Lifelines,' Elle sank into her bed and held Underdog tight. Looking for solace, she decided to call Margot and Serena. She knew they would be home, as they never missed an episode of their favorite soap, *Passions*. Margot was convinced every week that something was actually going to happen. The fact that nothing had changed in the story line since the show's beginning didn't bother her, eternal soap optimist that she was. Elle smiled as she thought of her friends.

Margot picked up right away. 'It's Elle,' she called out, putting the phone on speaker.

'Hi, you guys!' Elle was so happy to hear their friendly and familiar voices.

'Elle! How are you? We miss you already!' Serena said.

'I miss you guys too! You can't imagine—' Elle began, but was cut off by Margot.

'How is the Neiman's up there?' Margot asked. 'Is it as good as the one down here?'

Elle started to say that she hadn't had a chance to set foot inside a store, much less to make comparisons, when Serena burst in.

'Elle! How's Warner? Was he surprised to see you? Did you get the Rock yet?' she asked in rapid succession.

Elle didn't know where to begin, and it was just too demoralizing to repeat the horrible turn of events over a speakerphone. 'Warner's fine, but no Rock just yet,' Elle lied. 'I'm getting ready for classes though and you wouldn't believe how many books I have.' She sighed heavily.

'Oh, you poor thing!' the girls cooed together. "We are so glad to be out of school,' Margot added, speaking for both of them.

'Well, we're dying to hear more, but we're late for a meeting.'

'Meeting?' Elle was skeptical.

'Jesus is the Weigh!' the girls chimed together.

'It's a new spiritual weight-loss program,' Serena said.

'You have to come with us next time you are in L.A. We've only been once and already we feel thinner and more at peace with the universe,' Margot said.

'Gotta go! Much love and send Warner a kiss!' they said in unison.

Elle hung up feeling worse than ever. Serena and Margot had found Jesus and Sarah had the Rock. She collapsed into a heap of pink silk pillows and cried until she had to get ready for her first law school event.

Elle tried to think of something positive as she walked across the Stanford campus on her way to the Dean's Welcome. She noticed that a few political tables had been set up, and Elle approached one with interest. The table's sign read 'Burn Your Bra,' and though Elle was worried that the woman with the frizzy brown bandanna-tied hair clutching a clipboard was a movie extra for a sixties movie, she was still glad to see something she thought she recognized.

She smiled as she remembered the bra-burning party she'd given for Serena after her augmentation. An L.A. post-surgery tradition, all of the guests brought lingerie for the guest of honor in her new cup size.

As Elle neared the table, the table worker jumped up to yell at a couple of fraternity pledges who had dropped a few *Playboy* magazines on her table and then run away laughing. Elle noticed with distaste that the woman definitely hadn't replaced the bra that she had burned.

'Bra burning is a political statement!' the gender warrior exploded.

Elle squinted, puzzled. 'Are you talking to me?' she asked her.

'Liberate womyn from the dominance of male-imposed body image, force-fed by capitalists! Boycott the Wonderbra!'

Elle left quickly, deciding that her first overture to Stanford activists would be her last.

Students and parents filled the law school's auditorium in giddy anticipation of the dean's speech. Dean Haus was known around campus as 'Great Haus,' a compliment to his warm personality and sense of humor, as well as his fabulous ten-bedroom, six-bath residence, courtesy of Stanford.

Dean Haus himself looked the part of a next-door neighbor on a sitcom: fiftyish, tall, thin, and kindly-looking, with faded blue eyes behind horn-rims that were perched on his long, thin nose. But Elle didn't find the Dean's Welcome was welcoming for long.

Dean Haus began by touting the achievements of the 180 students chosen from thousands of applicants for an exalted place in Stanford's first-year class. Expressing his pride in the tremendous diversity of his students, Dean Haus treated the audience to a brief description of the law school's new shining stars, pointing out a special few.

First a member of the Joffrey Ballet was recognized.

Then two surgeons, one cardiac and one orthopedic,

stood up to take their bows. Next, the dean introduced a Rhodes scholar, a Harvard English professor, a cellist from the Boston Symphony Orchestra, and two Pulitzer Prize winners. A mechanical engineer who held twenty-six patents was booed by the four electrical engineers as he stood up. Elle was intrigued by this evidence of engineer snobbery, similar, she mused, to the way San Franciscans felt about Los Angeles. After the world record holder in pole vaulting stretched his spider arms in a victory cheer, the dean paused dramatically.

Elle's gaze had searched out Warner somewhere between the introductions of the English professor and the patent collector. He was seated with Sarah two rows in front and to the left of her. She cringed when she saw they were wearing matching cardigans. Elle watched him to see if he would look in her direction, and she was so involved in trying to catch his eye that she was astounded by the dean's next introduction.

'And now, ladies and gentleman, what class would be complete without a sorority president?' the dean smirked to a scattering of boos and laughter. Even Warner was among them. 'Ms. Elle Woods' – he gestured for her to stand – 'also has the distinction of being, among thousands of applicants, our only *homecoming queen*!'

Elle reddened as Dean Haus continued. 'Appropriate to Silicon Valley, our own Pentium blonde!'

Elle had never heard of a shade called pentium but suspected it must be a horrible color from the outburst of laughs. Declining the opportunity to take a bow, she gathered her things and exited with hasty steps.

Chapter Nine

ELLE'S FIRST DAY WAS A DISASTER. When she arrived at Criminal Law, the first class on her preprinted schedule, Elle realized she had forgotten to bring her name card. Each seat had a special desktop slot that was designed for the display of these large cardboard cards, which enabled professors to humiliate you by name. Elle was alone in her anonymity: all her fellow students were impeccably labeled. Elle groaned as Sarah walked into the room and sat down behind a card which read 'Knottingham, S.'

'At least it doesn't say Huntington yet,' Elle mumbled to herself.

Sarah was chatting with Claire Caldwell-Boulaine, whose card was printed 'Caldwell, C.' but had been crossed out and changed in angry Magic Marker to the appropriate hyphenated form. A white cotton cardigan hung neatly from the back of her chair.

'Like a talking *Barbie*,' Elle overheard Sarah whisper. Claire shushed her friend, tapping her pearl-studded ear and indicating Elle. She flipped open her monogrammed Bermuda Bag to scribble notes instead. She passed a note to Sarah on which the words *HOMECOMING QUEEN!* could easily be read by Elle.

'Wait and see!' promised Sarah.

The prematurely balding boy next to Elle, labeled 'Garney, T.,' busily tapped away on his laptop computer. Elle wondered what he could possibly be taking notes about already as she looked around the PowerBook-filled room.

Her neighbor paused to check the time on his enormous twenty-four-function digital watch and glanced around the room. A perturbed scowl emerged on his face when he found that no professor had yet arrived. Unnerved, he compared his watch with the wall clock. Four Hi-Liters in a rainbow of neon hues were lined up next to his open casebook.

Out of the corner of his eye, he caught Elle's pink legal pad and fuzzy pink pen topped with a feather. Shocked, he asked her, 'Where is your PowerBook?'

Ignoring Garney, T., Elle glanced again at her schedule, hoping it would show she was in the wrong room, in the way people irrationally look twice into an empty refrigerator on the chance that chocolate mousse has appeared. 'Nope,' she said. 'This is the right room.' Looks like I'll be seeing a lot of Sarah, she thought as she watched Sarah pass the folded note back to Claire.

After four years of arranging her college schedule in a creative, now-and-then pattern, Elle had been crushed to learn three things about her law school classes: they were prescheduled, mandatory, and daily, five days a week. 'Warner could walk in any minute,' she reminded herself, glad she had taken the time to dry her hair. She glanced back hopefully when the door swung open.

Her heart plunged when Sidney Ugman rushed through the entryway. Elle had known and avoided Sidney Ugman for years. He was her next-door neighbor in Bel Air and they had attended the same grade school. Sidney had circled her for years, returning like a bad dream, an evil Weeble who could not be knocked down.

Sidney's father, Lee Ugman, was a major client of Eva's gallery. He decorated every office of his sixty-lawyer law firm with paintings and sculptures Eva had sold him. Sidney long ago took advantage of this business relationship by being more intimate with Elle at dinners and gallery events than she ever, ever would have tolerated in public.

His parents often boasted at social events where Sidney and Elle were both present that Sidney and Elle had a 'special relationship,' which is why Lee Ugman bought so loyally from Eva's gallery. 'Might as well keep it in the family,' he speculated. Of course, the idea of this 'special relationship' was created by Sidney alone. Recognizing his friend the digital watch wearer tap-tapping his keyboard next to Elle, Sidney took the other open seat in the row.

'What's on your PowerBook?' Elle heard Sidney joke with the watch wearer. They exchanged some sort of Trekkie handshake.

Finally, Professor Kiki 'Slaughter-Haus' made her entrance. Catherine 'Kiki' Haus was a package deal, a Stanford Law School professor by virtue of the fact that she was the wife of the dean, whom Stanford had wooed away from Harvard. While her husband was known around Stanford as Professor Great Haus, Kiki had been tagged 'Slaughter-Haus' years ago, when she taught Constitutional Law, after the infamous Supreme Court *Slaughterhouse* cases.

Even after Kiki switched to teaching Criminal Law, the 'Slaughter-Haus' nickname stuck because her class was reputed to be unendurable. Especially among the male students. The professor was also nicknamed 'Three-C Kiki' because of rumors that at grade time she evened out her perceived social injustices by giving three Cs, always to three men, especially golden-boy fraternity types.

When Elle heard this 'Three-C' rumor from Bianca, a sorority sister whose boyfriend, John Brooks, had graduated from Stanford the year before, she imagined Stanford

Law would be full of interesting, golden John Brooks types; but looking around, Elle couldn't figure out who would get the Cs in this crowd.

Kiki's class represented in a particularly blunt manner what Elle was just learning about law school: everything was upside-down from her previous life. Sidney had a whole gaggle of pasty-faced twenty-four-function digital watch wearers jabbering about *Deep Space Nine* with him. Claire and Sarah were already chummy with the exclusive East Coast preppies in Add-a-Bead necklaces. The Ben & Jerry's herd had more left-wing causes than it knew what to do with, though the revolutionary tables would be certain to disappear when law firms came to interview. Humanities Ph.D.s met at coffeehouses to fill out crossword puzzles in foreign languages. Science Ph.D.s compared the merits of researching on Westlaw versus Lexis and encrypted their phone numbers. But Elle had no one. She was arriving at the harsh realization that she, Elle Woods, was unpopular.

Chapter Ten

KIKI SLAUGHTER-HAUS, WIDE-FACED, fortyish, and sturdily built, began circling the podium with her eyes anchored to her notes. She spouted a stale stream of Gloria Steinem-era feminism interrupted with a lengthy 'uh' between every few words. 'All law ... uh ... is biased. Um ... against women. Uh ... institutionally,' she droned.

This was Criminal Law? Elle had looked forward to this class as compared to the others. She thought they'd talk about lawyers, guns, and money, like the Warren Zevon song.

Kiki called only on women. In her introductory mono-tone she was making the point that women have to balance work and family life, whereas men, presumably like her husband, are free from this dual responsibility. Nobody had any idea what this had to do with criminal law, but the tap-tap-tapping keyboards took down every word.

'Uh, you, without the, uh, name card.' Slaughter-Haus pointed at Elle. 'Uh, what's your name?'

'Elle Woods.'

'Uh, Ms. Woods, why did you, uh, come to law school?'

First question, first day. A softball.

Sarah turned around with interest. The room grew quiet.

'To be a lawyer?' Elle guessed.

Kiki went in for the slaughter.

'And, uh, why do *you*, uh, want to be a lawyer?'

40

'So I can do my own divorce,' Elle answered candidly, smiling. 'Without getting taken to the bank.'

She shot a glance in the direction of Sarah and Claire, to see if her casual mention of divorce had any effect on them. She caught Claire's eye and added a cool shrug.

'I see,' Kiki said. 'You all want to be lawyers, but first you have to pass my class. And last year only half of the students who sat in these seats made it out alive.'

Kiki turned her back to write on the board. Sarah stuck her tongue out at Elle, at which Claire giggled. 'I told you so,' Sarah said.

Elle was picked out again in Torts class for a question based on the reading. There was no settling into law school, Elle discovered. Reading was actually assigned before the first class, but Elle hadn't gotten to it yet, and didn't even have her books with her. With no name card and no books, Elle was an easy target.

Torts was the class of basic personal-injury law. A 'tort' described not a cream-filled dessert wheeled in on a cart, but an injury over which you could sue somebody. Any sob story with a price tag was a tort. The class focused on everyday grievances like car accidents or harassing phone calls, the stuff of daytime talk shows.

The basic rule was one you might see behind a cash register: 'You break it, you pay for it.' But law school had a way of complicating even the simplest rule. 'Actionable tortious infliction of emotional distress,' for example, meant 'being mean enough to get sued for it.' The point of torts, Elle decided, was to learn how petty squabbles can be dressed up multisyllabically.

Today's word, which Elle might have known had she read the assigned chapter, was 'subrogation,' a neat way for the bad guy to escape paying damages by suing somebody else. Insurance companies are quite fond of the concept.

'You, without the PowerBook or a name card . . .' Professor Glenn, a white-haired red-nosed Harvard lion tortiously inflicting a terrible mix of plaids with a brown tie, pointed at Elle. 'What do you think of subrogation?'

Elle wondered if this professor had a feminist theme too, like Kiki Slaughter-Haus. 'Well,' she attempted, 'it's endemic in our society. Especially the subjugation of women.'

The class fell apart in laughter, leaving Elle to wonder alone what was so funny. Professor Glenn, whom the wags had renamed Professor Glenn-Fiddich in recognition of the obvious difference between his lucid morning classes and his rambling, red-nosed afternoons, shook his head sadly. He was sober today and appeared to regret it.

'Thank you, Ms. Woods. Let's turn to somebody who's done the reading.'

An arm shot up. It was impossible to tell whether the arm belonged to a man or a woman. Elle now realized that the time she had spent reading *Cosmopolitan*'s *Life After College* issue had been a total waste. The 'Law School Revue' article hadn't mentioned anything remotely resembling the law school life she was experiencing. She acknowledged she might need a new source of advice.

Elle suspected she might learn more by staying home and watching Oprah anyway. She began daydreaming.

If I were president, I'd put Oprah on the Supreme Court. Phil's too liberal, Geraldo's too insensitive. Larry King wouldn't take the pay cut. Rikki Lake? She paused, considering. *No. Wouldn't get confirmed. But Oprah . . . everyone knows she's fair. She's got enough cash to retire from TV. And maybe the tabloids would lay off her weight fluctuations if they only saw her in the black robe.* Elle smiled. Definitely Oprah.

She gasped and drew back as if shocked when Sidney's clammy hand gripped her arm. 'C'mon Elle, beam yourself back down,' he said. 'Class is over.'

'Beam yourself someplace else, Sidney,' Elle snapped. Turning to leave the room, Elle heard whispers behind her back. Sidney zipped his black vinyl PowerBook pack and followed her out.

'Elle' – he caught her arm in the hall, gloating – 'this isn't Bel Air. You're not so popular here, you know. People don't even like you.' He tightened his grip as she twisted to get away.

Sidney held on to her arm as Elle moved down the hall, still trying to shake him. 'I have soooo many friends here already, Elle. You should be nicer to me. . . . I *might* let you into my study group,' Sidney snarled.

Elle spun around and faced Sidney, finally yanking her arm free. 'Sidney, don't make this worse than it already is for me,' she said. 'Please.' Sidney's laugh was her answer.

Elle tensed. 'Do me a favor, Sidney? You and your whole study group?'

'What?'

Though she knew her efforts would be futile, she looked at him. 'Please, Sidney, just leave me alone.'

She regretted her words as soon as the grin crossed Sidney's face. The tables had turned and he relished her misery. He was the king and she was a standing joke. Law school was his chance to make her pay, and he was going to enjoy every minute of it.

Hating herself for having attempted to appeal to his better nature, Elle turned on her heel and stormed off.

Chapter Eleven

ELLE WENT IMMEDIATELY AFTER class to Savoir-Vivre, the salon which she had found during orientation week when she skipped the Westward-Ho Bar-b-que. The salon was located in the Stanford Shopping Center and she had found a darling French manicurist who served as her link to a saner world, the world that read *W* and never gave a thought to subrogation or the writing of briefs.

Sighing deeply, Elle leaned back into the soft black-and-white raw silk pillows and put her left hand under the air dryer. 'Josette, it got even worse.'

Josette went to work on Elle's right hand, shaping her thumbnail with short, rapid strokes of the file. Her shiny black corkscrew curls bounced as she worked. 'Worse? Elle, what you told me before . . . it was already horrible!' Her delicate features scrunched up at the thought, making her look like a perplexed Kewpie doll. Josette said 'horrible' in a Frenchified way, 'hor-*ree*-bil.' It was fun to hear her talk. Elle had booked enough time for a pedicure as well as a manicure; she was starved to talk to someone with discerning taste, and would have stayed longer if she could.

Elle glanced around the salon, noting that the only woman within hearing distance had her hair wrapped in foil and was sitting under a noisy hair dryer. 'See, I *have* to go to class because I don't have any friends and I don't know who would take notes for me if I took "vacations" now and then,' she admitted in an embarrassed manner.

'You should make a friend then,' Josette advised.

'No, Josette, wait till you hear what these people are like! This one guy from MIT, the Gummi Bear Man . . .' Elle shuddered as the vision of his computer-lab pallor, orange hair, and long, pimply neck invaded her thoughts. 'He sits behind me in Civil Procedure and he claims to be doing some kind of scientific experiment about congestion or combustion . . . whatever. Anyway, this scientific experiment involves his utterly disgusting habit of sucking on Gummi bears all through class. When the professor turns his back, he spits them out and flicks them up so they stick on the ceiling.'

'Eeeeew!' Josette exclaimed. 'And you must sit in front of thees, thees *man*?'

'Not only that, Josette, but in the line of fire! See, Gummy Bear Man's plan is for the Gummi bears to turn into downward missiles in the spring, when it gets warm, so they'll drip down on somebody in that seat second semester. But since it's Indian summer, his Gummi bears have been melting already!'

'Eeeeeew,' Josette repeated. 'Do they dreep on you?'

'Josette, I can't even attend class when the temperature is over seventy-five degrees. I would be pelted by chewed-up Gummi bears!'

'Do you want me to do a design?' Josette asked, nodding in reference to Elle's nails.

Please, how tacky. 'No thanks, I always do pinks. I've brought a bottle of my favorite Chanel pink to keep here.'

'What about the other students?'

'Well, there's Gramm Hallman. He wastes everyone's time by somehow managing to turn every class discussion into a whiny explanation of the Spanish Succession, blow by blow. It was his thesis topic at Yale, which he'll inform you within the first fifteen seconds of meeting him.'

'He sounds very boring.'

'Boring? He's not half as bad as Ben! Ben *lives* for law school. He watches Court TV when he's not reading the *Legal Times* or briefing cases. He reads the *Stanford Law Review* in the library when we have an hour break between classes. He looks like he's going to collapse under the pile of casebooks he carries around. He loves law school so much, he wants to stick around for more! He told me that ever since he was seven years old he wanted to be a law *professor*!'

'I think I wanted to be a ballerina when I was a little girl,' Josette mused. 'Or a princess. What about you?'

'I wanted to be one of Charlie's Angels! Chris, of course.'

'What about zee women in your school?' Josette asked.

Elle examined her fingernails and put both hands under the air dryer. Stretching out her feet for the finishing touches, she sighed wearily. 'Josette, if they are any indication, the future of America looks bleak and poorly dressed.'

Josette giggled. 'Why are *you* in law school, Elle?'

Elle thought about it and wondered if she should tell her. 'I followed my college boyfriend, Warner, here,' Elle admitted. 'He broke up with me before he came to Stanford, and I thought I'd go to law school too, you know, to win him back. But now he's engaged to this awful woman named Sarah and I'm stuck here and I'm going to have to finish. To show him, at least, that a woman doesn't have to be a mousy brown-haired headband wearer in frumpy Lanz nightgowns to be serious.' She stopped and looked at Josette, then continued shyly. 'And smart and competent. I'm sure as soon as he figures that out, Sarah will be history.'

'Maybe you should see another man?' Josette suggested.

'I know, I'm pathetic.'

Josette needed to get to another client. She tapped Elle's hand, directing her to move to the front of the salon by the window.

'Do you want the same time next week?' Josette said.

'What? Sorry,' Elle answered. 'I was zoning there for a minute. Yes, please, the same time next week.' She slipped on her sandals without smudging her polish and headed toward a career-counseling seminar. The seminars were offered once a week after classes, from the very beginning of the semester. Elle had signed up to see what the future promised. She also hoped to run into Warner there, but neither he nor Sarah was anywhere to be seen.

Judging from the lecture, her future boded nothing promising. The career counselor advised a solid diet of alienation from the outside world during the quest called 'résumé building.' As if it weren't bad enough that law students scorned direct contact with life in three years of ostrichlike submersion. No wonder nonlawyers peeled away from law students like a sunburn.

The prize for law school success was this: an opportunity to slave away in a law firm library researching obscure legal issues, perfecting a nervous twitch, and checking the clock in obsessive fixation on billable hours in order to make money for someone else, more specifically, a partner. This was called the 'partnership track.' You sold your right to light and freedom for seven to eight good years, all in the name of an equity share and free time for golf.

Upon returning from the lecture, Elle found an official-looking note taped to her door at Crothers. The Housing Office had been notified that she was keeping a dog in her room, which was not permitted by the regulations. Elle was requested to find a new home for the dog, or find a new home for herself and the dog. Her rent would

47

be prorated if she chose to vacate student housing altogether.

'So much for animal rights,' Elle sighed. 'Guess we've got to find a new home, Underdog.' She collared her exuberant pet and took him outside.

Chapter Twelve

MOST CLASSES IN LAW SCHOOL were an exercise in intellectual torture. Civil Procedure laid out the ground rules for litigating cases in court. Anyone who could read and follow directions could understand Civil Procedure. You had to memorize concepts in order to bandy them around with other law insiders or spit them back on exams, but beyond that, Elle reasoned, there was no reason to know the law by heart. Also, it would be malpractice to practice off the top of your head.

Elle was engrossed in a magazine and winced when Professor Erie called on Ben to answer a procedural question. They would be in for another marathon of 'Ben Unplugged.' Elle was glad she'd brought the new *Vogue*.

Ben earned a wide chorus of laughs when he changed the names in the casebook from A, B, and C to D, E, and F, 'to pro-*tect* the *in*-no-cent.' It was a matter of lawyer-client confidentiality, he explained to a smiling Professor Erie.

Ben's 'abstract legal problem solving' involved applying what *he* saw as a 'categorical benchmark' from one class to another. As if sitting through Civil Procedure weren't bad enough, Ben wanted to concentrate all five law school classes into every hour.

Elle noticed that Ben was wearing a bulky digital watch. She glanced at the ceiling, worried that all his hot air would melt the Gummi bears. They appeared to be holding their position.

The woman next to her offered her a piece of gum. 'It's Snappin' Apple,' the woman whispered, 'my favorite.'

'No thanks,' Elle said, smiling. The woman wasn't a headband wearer, and unlike most of her classmates, didn't carry a coffee Thermos with the emblem of her Ivy League alma mater. She was J. Crew fresh-faced pretty with ivory skin and clear blue eyes. Plus she was sort of blonde, or could be, with some better highlights.

'It all sounds like alphabet soup to me!' she whispered again with a grin.

Elle looked at her neighbor curiously.

'A can serve process on B, but not on C; A can implead D, but has no personal jurisdiction over F. What the hell is *quasi in rem* jurisdiction?' She scribbled this note on a paper, which she passed to Elle.

'I don't know, sorry,' Elle scribbled back. 'I skip this class a lot to avoid falling Gummi bears.' She slid the paper over tentatively.

'Isn't that GROSS? I think I'll come early and stick a piece of GUM on his seat!' came back the response. 'By the way, my name is Eugenia.'

Elle laughed. She not only knew about the Gummi Bear Man, she was fighting back! This girl was all right.

'Miss Iliakis?' The note passing was interrupted. 'Is Miss Iliakis here today?'

Eugenia gulped, sliding the piece of Snappin' Apple to her cheek, causing it to bulge slightly. 'Uh, yes.' She waved her hand. 'Back here.'

'Miss Iliakis, here in the second problem, A' – Professor Erie turned to Ben – 'you don't mind if I call him A, do you, Counsel?' This attempt at humor was smashingly successful with Ben and his watch-wearing pals.

'No, that will be fine, Your Hon-or,' Ben played along. Tittering giggles could be heard around the room.

50

'Good. Now that we've got our dramatis personae down, Miss Iliakis, let's see if we can help them get into court.'

Eugenia looked helplessly at Elle.

Professor Erie turned to his favored 'counsel,' Ben, who happily demonstrated his civil procedure acumen for the benefit of his growing law student following. His twenty-four-function digital watch, which looked as if it also functioned as a data bank, showed 11:45. Another peak tanning hour wasted.

In the hall, Eugenia caught up with Elle. 'Do you want to grab some lunch with me before Torts?'

'If we can leave this dungeon,' Elle answered, shocked that someone was actually speaking to her, much less asking her to lunch.

'Sure,' Eugenia agreed. 'Wherever.'

The margaritas at lunch were irresistible. Eugenia suggested they call it a day. 'I can get the notes from Claire or somebody.'

'Cool.' Elle had lucked out.

Over lunch Eugenia told Elle she was from a Greek neighborhood in Pittsburgh, grew up among Eastern Rite Catholics, in particular the Warhola family. Elle listened with interest. 'My mother used to see Andy Warhol at church when she was a little girl, before he went to New York and produced the Velvet Underground and all that.'

'At church?' Elle imagined an improbable entourage of transvestites in kimonos.

'Growing up in Pittsburgh, and then going to Yale, I thought once I'd landed in California I'd hit the creative world, you know? The art scene: air kisses and egos.'

Elle laughed. 'You're like Christopher Columbus. Right direction, but you landed about five hundred miles too far north!'

Eugenia was impressed when Elle told her that her mother ran an art gallery in L.A. and even more intrigued that Elle wanted to be a jewelry designer, not a lawyer. She didn't even ask why Elle was at Stanford Law.

Elle marveled. Had she actually found a friend in law school?

Chapter Thirteen

IT WAS EARLY OCTOBER and Elle was confined within the gray walls of her Crothers Dorm studying when the phone rang. She glanced idly at the ringing phone. She decided to let her machine pick up, the safest strategy to pursue in a hostile environment.

She froze when Warner's voice began speaking. Of course, he didn't identify himself. He didn't need to.

'Elle, uh, I meant to call you earlier to see how things were going for you at law school. I've got to say I still can't get over the fact that you're here! Especially *Stanford*! As you probably know, Sarah, my fiancée, is in your section and from what she tells me, you're still the same old Elle!'

Elle glared at the machine. I'll bet Sarah has plenty to say, she thought.

'Anyway, I should have called before, but listen, Daniel's coming to visit and I promised I'd show him our videotape from Vegas. If you can lend it to me, I can make a copy, or just borrow it. Okay, honey?'

Elle warmed at his use of the word 'honey.'

There was a pause in Warner's voice, which stiffened momentarily. 'Thanks, Elle. 854-STUD.' He cracked up. 'Really, that's the number. I thought you'd prefer the acronym. Call me soon.'

Elle collapsed into her pillow. 'Oh, God, the Vegas tape!' She rolled over, laughing, and stared dreamily up at the ceiling.

Unbeknownst to his upper-crust family, and probably to Sarah, Warner's secret, persistent ambition was to direct films. He was an adulator of Martin Scorsese. For three years he had dragged Elle to film after film, and when he got a camcorder of his own, he began 'directing documentaries' of their adventures.

Warner was plagued with his East Coast conviction that the film industry was flaky, disreputable work. Elle encouraged Warner's creative spirit, arguing that film was the art medium of their generation. Nonetheless, Warner never applied to film school or advanced beyond filming a few weekend sprees.

The videotape he asked about was a hilarious, bumpy ride through the high-rolling weekend expedition of Elle, Warner, and Warner's old prep-school friend, Daniel, on the streets and in the casinos of Las Vegas. With only Daniel and Elle in the picture most of the time, except when Warner turned the camera on himself, the eyewitness camera traveled from Siegfried & Roy's white tigers prowling their Mirage jungle to a lost kid crying in front of the Treasure Island ship; from a zoom-in on the $100,000 minimum poker table, interrupted by an unidentified hand and some shuffling bodies, to a sorry pile of ignored porn leaflets littering the dirty street; from Elle, suggestively exposing her cleavage across the blackjack table in a Badgley Mischka dress, luminescent with Stoli and cash and the glow of winning after hitting on eighteen; to Daniel, arching one eyebrow, doubling down and betting smart.

The video wrapped up with a panorama of the gamblers' erstwhile home in the Imperial Palace, an inelegant 'love suite' with tacky faux-shogun decor. The room was, in fact, creatively engineered. The grand bed with its counterfeit bamboo posts was raised on a tremendous platform off to the side of the room, graced overtop with a massive ceiling mirror. Adjoining the bed was a Jacuzzi, also up a step, surrounded by glass doors because, as an investigation of the bathroom revealed, the Jacuzzi was the room's only shower. The camera traveled up to the shower nozzle installed in the bedroom wall, and finally to the mirror over the Jacuzzi, which reflected either the Jacuzzi or the bed, depending on your seat.

The 'documentary' ended with the Jacuzzi mirror reproducing upside down three wobbly revelers: Warner, his shirt undone, with the camcorder over his eye; Elle, leaning sleepily on Daniel; and Daniel, winking, supporting Elle's drowsy blonde head on his shoulder.

Elle picked up the phone, immediately reproached herself, and hung up. A smile reasserted itself across her face as she beat the urge to call Warner back. 'I'll make him wait awhile. I'll make him wait until Daniel's in town.'

Instead, Elle returned the call from her new landlord. He'd left a message approving her request to move in immediately. The crazy old man didn't seem to recognize her, though she had met with him in the past two days.

'Mr. Hopson, Elle Woods. I'm moving into the unit . . . with the carpet . . . problem . . . today?'

The only decent condominium development Elle could find that allowed pets was mysteriously named 'the Mediterranean.' It had a vacancy because of some bizarre flying-carpet occurrence. Adjoining construction had interfered with water pressure to the Jacuzzi bath in the master bedroom, resulting in air jets that broke the carpet loose from its tacks and blew it, together with several pieces of furniture, in billowing surges across the room. Lacking better options for immediate occupancy, Elle took her chances with carpet surfing.

'The jeweler?' the crackly old voice finally recognized Elle. She had thought it best to describe herself as a jewelry designer, since it was most proprietors' unwritten policy not to rent to litigation-prone law students. A good policy, in general.

'Right, right, sir, exactly. The jewelry designer. I just wanted to make sure you know I'm bringing my dog.'

'Dog? You have to pay an extra deposit for pets!'

'Yes, we discussed that before, Mr. Hopson. I wrote you a check.'

'You did?'

'Yes I did. Yesterday.'

The voice on the other end grumbled. 'When do you want to move in?'

'Mr. Hopson, I picked up the key yesterday. You said you'd skip the repainting so I could move in today. I just wanted to tell you I'm coming this afternoon, so you can tell the man at the security gate.'

'What? You're coming today?'

'Yes,' Elle repeated, frustrated. 'Tell him to let in Elle Woods. W-o-o-d-s. Thank you.'

Chapter Fourteen

Elle glanced around her dorm room at the clutter of her remaining possessions. She had packed most of her things the previous night. She had sent home boxes of china, glassware, and framed paintings with the movers in September, when she discovered the shoebox size of the dorm room, but nevertheless, Elle never quite achieved minimalism.

She sighed, exhausted at the prospect of heavy lifting, which she *never* would have had to do herself at chivalric USC, where sorority girls had fraternity boys who had pledges for just this sort of activity. Warner and his various pledge-serfs had carried his share of Elle's furniture and boxes in the past.

What an idea! Elle smiled and picked up the phone. She had absolutely nothing to lose and freedom from broken nails to gain. 854-STUD.

She frowned when Sarah's voice chirped a message on Warner's behalf. 'Answering-machine possessiveness,' Elle sighed, 'the mark of a threatened woman.'

'Warner, honey,' Elle cooed, drawing out her voice intentionally. 'So darling of you to call. I have that videotape of us . . . in Las Vegas . . . right here with me at school. I think it's your best documentary!'

She shifted her tone to serious. 'The problem, Warner, is that I'm moving, and all my things are packed in boxes; it's in a box around here, I'm just not sure which one. I'll try to get them moved soon enough to dig out the videotape for Daniel, but it takes so long . . . doing this by myself . . .' Elle thought quickly. 'Maybe you could give me a hand, if you need the tape quickly.

'Anyway, sweetie, give me a call; you have my number already!'

Elle opened her desk drawer and pulled out the videotape labeled 'Vegas.' She held the tape cradled against her chest. *This is my ticket*. She began to pack the tape in a box within boxes, like the precious doll-within-dolls she was given as a child. 'Nobody'll find this box for a while.'

Within the hour, Sarah's white Volvo station wagon pulled into the Crothers parking lot next to Elle's Range Rover, the back of which was overflowing with boxes and garment bags.

Elle looked suspiciously at the Connecticut-tagged Volvo as she labored toward her car, balancing a lamp in one hand and a mirror in the other. She recognized flowery Sarah climbing out of the driver's seat.

'Come to help me move?' Elle said.

Sarah crossed her arms, staring at Elle without speaking.

'I'd invite you in, but I didn't invite you over,' Elle said. 'Besides, I'm busy moving.'

'I heard a little message from you on Warner's machine. What videotape are you talking about?'

'Ah, how little you know about your fiancé.' Elle relished the jealousy that consumed Sarah's serious face. She lifted a garment bag to make room for more belongings, ignoring Sarah, who paced impatiently behind her.

With the mirror safely packed, Elle stepped away from the Range Rover and turned the palm of her hand out to check her fingernails for chips or smudges. 'Moving can pose *such* a threat to your manicure,' Elle observed momentously, remembering the first day of class when she overheard Sarah call her a 'talking Barbie.' Satisfied that her manicure was holding up, Elle sauntered back inside, pursued all the way to her room by a flustered, furious Sarah.

Elle grinned. 'Be a sport and grab a box on your way out, would ya, Sarah?'

Sarah turned viciously. 'No, I will not be . . . a sport! And I will not carry your boxes. Listen, I have just one thing to say to you, Elle Woods, and I'll make it as painless as I can.'

Elle flopped on her bed and pulled Underdog onto her lap. 'Ooooh, Underdog, Sarah's here to make a threat.' She pulled Underdog's ears up like a bunny rabbit's. 'Listen up!' She and rabbit-eared Underdog looked expectantly at Sarah.

Sarah reddened with anger, then proceeded in a low, snarling voice. 'It is rather obvious, Elle, to anyone with half a brain at Stanford Law School, that you are having some trouble adjusting.' Elle gasped in mock amazement, parting Underdog's jaws with her hands so the dog, too, peered at Sarah with openmouthed surprise.

'We're having trouble adjusting!' Elle said to her dog.

'Basically, Elle, you're the laughingstock of this school. I think there's a betting pool already with odds out on whether you make it through finals. Considering you have no friends, and absolutely no chance of success as a law student, you might be looking for a shoulder to cry on right about now. So I came over to tell you one thing: *Don't let it be Warner's.*'

It sounded to Elle like Sarah had rehearsed this speech on the drive over, more or less, and the smug look on her face revealed that it had come out sounding better than she had expected. She turned to exit grandly.

'Don't worry, Sarah. I'm not interested in Warner's shoulder at all.'

Sarah turned around tentatively. 'You're not?'

'No, I'm not. Not at all.' Elle smiled and stood up from the bed with Underdog cradled in her arms. 'Not one bit.' Then she slammed the door in Sarah's face.

Chapter Fifteen

WARNER HADN'T CALLED BACK. Elle checked her watch. Civil Procedure was dragging on. The professor had turned to the board, drawing another worthless map to illustrate federal court jurisdiction based on diversity of citizenship.

Elle glanced around the room at the two or three hands raised already, in advance of a question. The twins in the class, Jeremy and Halley, were waving fitfully, as usual. These irrepressible class volunteers impressed and competed with each other by firing instant half-brained speeches before anyone could suggest a thoughtful answer, a practice they referred to as 'clutch thinking.'

'Miss Caldwell-Boulaine,' Professor Erie said. Elle looked up from her copy of *Vanity Fair.* She had read the cases for today's class, but found them so boring that she had a whisper of hope that Claire, too, might be confused.

'The corporation being sued does business in Arizona, which is where the plaintiff bought his car. But the car exploded in California, injuring only California residents. Since the subject matter of the lawsuit is a tort, how would the parties get into federal court?'

'On diversity jurisdiction, Professor Erie,' Claire said with confidence. Claire was not only correct, she was chipper, and Elle didn't know which she found more annoying.

'Correct.' The professor smiled, turning again to the board. 'In which state would the defendant be served with a subpoena?'

Before Claire could answer, Fran interrupted.

'Professor,' she said, waving, 'I have an objection.'

Her voice startled Elle. It was a hoarse whiskey voice that should have belonged to an elegant woman who chain-smoked with an ivory cigarette holder rather than to a frizzy-haired brunette feminist with unshaved legs, a scrawny body, a unibrow, and huge, rough hands.

'An objection.' Professor Erie arched an eyebrow, playing along. 'Okay, Counselor. Proceed.'

Fran shifted uncomfortably in her seat and tugged nervously at her skirt, which looked like the 'Indian' bedspreads sold at Pier 1. 'It's just that . . . I wish you'd stop using that word.'

'What word is that, Miss Anthony?'

'Mizzz,' Fran corrected, scowling. 'The word sub-*poena*. It has no place in an emancipated society.'

'I think she's suffering from subpoena envy,' Aaron said as he elbowed Tim.

Doug overheard Aaron's comment and snorted with laughter. 'She *wishes* she had a subpoena!' He poked Sidney, who gave him a high-five. The Trekkies were in an uproar, and Fran spun around angrily.

'See?' Fran shrieked.

Pointing at Doug, Fran accused, 'That's *exactly* the testosterone oppression that women have to fight! Look! He has pornographic materials in class!'

Doug had a color printer in his dorm room and provided the Trekkies with erotic pictures he downloaded from the Internet. He shoved a 'Starship Intercourse' file into his notebook, reddening like a beet. 'I don't know what you're talking about,' Doug sputtered. The Trekkies turned guilty stares to the floor.

Professor Erie raised his voice with exasperation. He finally asked a question that Elle liked. 'When does this nonsense stop?' It was getting to the point where men at Stanford couldn't speak an unobjectionable word. 'Class, enough! Mizzz Anthony,' he drew the word out with irony, 'what would you prefer I call the subpoena? After all, that's what the *courts* call it.'

Fran shrugged. 'Call it a writ. That's what they call it in England, where they have some sensitivity about these things.'

Leslie nodded vigorously.

'Fine, Ms. Anthony. A writ.'

He turned back to Claire, who seemed a little shaken by the commotion. She answered correctly that the 'writ' should be served in Arizona, and Elle crossed the word 'subpoena' out of her notes.

Elle was hurrying out of class when a hand on her shoulder spun her around. Warner stood before her, out of breath, in a great show of the effort.

'Elle, wait a minute! I tried to call you back last night, but I got your machine.'

Elle looked doubtfully at him. He hadn't left a message. 'I was home most of the night,' she said, 'packing.'

'Okay, I didn't leave a message,' he admitted.

'Oh, yeah, I forgot.' Elle brightened. 'I drove a couple of boxes over to my new condo. My mondo condo,' she laughed. 'It's cool. You should come see it.'

'I'd like to,' Warner offered. 'Have you moved your stuff completely in yet?'

She had moved almost all of the boxes already.

'No, no, I've got a lot left to move,' Elle lied. 'I couldn't lift the heavy boxes by myself and I'm sure you remember how heavy my trunks are. I'd love some help, Warner. If you can get away,' she added in a lower tone, checking behind her in case Sarah was nearby. She could bring some boxes back to the dorm this afternoon, while everyone was in class, she thought quickly to herself. That way he'd have a lot to carry.

They started walking toward the front door of the building and Warner paused and cracked a smile. 'Great. I'd be happy to help you,' he said.

Elle shrugged and walked ahead of him knowing the effect her pale pink cashmere sweater and tight silk skirt would have on him.

He followed her outside. 'Listen, I'd love to get away, Elle,' he said quietly, 'but not for lunch.' Elle laughed.

He glanced back over his shoulder to the law school. 'I've got plans. Sarah, you know.'

Elle grinned and pulled on her sunglasses. 'I didn't mean for lunch, Warner, sweetie. I simply need some good Sigma Chi muscle. Call me when you can come over tonight.' Impulsively, she kissed Warner on the cheek, then spun around and walked away.

Elle had no doubt that he was looking forward to helping her move, even if Sarah would be furious.

Chapter Sixteen

'Thanks for taking me, Josette.' Elle looked around at the empty salon. 'I know it's late. I don't need a full manicure, just a couple of silk wraps to fix these.' She indicated two broken nails on her right hand. 'You don't even have to paint the others. I mean, you just gave me a manicure, what, Tuesday?'

Josette's ringlets shook briskly. 'No pwob-wem, no pwob-wem. But we must do the whole hand. Painting coats over these two only,' she explained, 'ees no good. It will be uneven. Ter-*ree*-ble! Here' – she tapped the table – 'thees hand.'

Elle, relieved, dropped her hand down on the table. Josette looked disapprovingly at Elle's ragged nails.

'I know, they're a mess,' Elle said, following Josette's stare. 'I had to move over twenty boxes today. This afternoon. That's why I couldn't get in until so late.'

'Again?' Josette interjected. 'Just a few days ago . . . you were almost done with your move.' Elle nodded, but wasn't sure how to explain.

'So you're moving again?'

Elle blushed. 'Josette,' she began, looking anxiously around her. The only other person in the salon was the receptionist, who, as usual, was excitably occupied on the phone. 'Remember that guy, my old boyfriend, who I told you I followed up to this place they call a law school?'

'Yes, hees name was Warner, I think. Right?'

'Right. Warner.' Elle smiled. 'Ow!' Her fingernails burned under Josette's vigorous filing.

Josette let up on the filing and brushed Elle's nail with a purplish oil, which tingled pleasantly. 'Warner, with the fiancée?'

'Sarah Knottingham.' The smile died from Elle's face.

'Is thees' – Josette glanced at Elle's bottle of pink nail polish meaningfully – 'for Sarah . . . or for Warner?'

Elle looked puzzled.

Josette gripped Elle's hand and held it up for emphasis. 'Why do we make your nails beautiful?' She lowered Elle's hand into a dish of moisturizing lotion and began massaging her fingers as she unraveled the mystery she had posed. 'For him? Does he like zee pretty hands? Or to show her, maybe?'

How French, Elle thought. 'No, it's not to show up Sarah. But I am seeing Warner tonight. He's coming over to help me move.'

'Move!' Josette rolled her eyes. 'You will break zees all again!'

'I don't think so. This time I'll have some help. See, Josette' – Elle glanced around again surreptitiously – 'I called Warner. I wanted to see him, so I told him I was moving, and I sort of hinted that I could use his help.'

'You'll never get him back with nails like that!' Josette wrinkled her brow and indicated Elle's broken nails. 'Don't worry. I will fix them.'

'Thanks, Josette.' Elle blushed. 'You won't believe this. I'm just going to stop saying "This is the most idiotic thing I've ever done," because every time I say that, I run out and get myself into something worse.'

'Yes, yes, what is it? What did you do?' Josette motioned impatiently with the brush for Elle to get to the point.

Elle grinned sheepishly. 'Okay, okay, this is pretty embarrassing. Today I skipped my afternoon classes and moved some boxes and furniture out of my new condo. The stuff I just moved yesterday. I moved it right back into my dorm room. It took a few hours; that's why I couldn't get here till late. Tonight I have to move it back to the condo all over again, but now Warner will help me!'

Elle couldn't see the broad smile breaking across Josette's face as she worked to keep the nail-polish brush steady. Josette whipped the brush up above Elle's hand to avoid smudging the polish as she shook with laughter. A pink stripe drew itself across the table underneath the arc of the flying nail polish. 'You must be very much in love,' she said.

Elle, face-to-face with her own desperate romantic ploy, gave herself over to the giddy truth. She tossed her head back against the manicurist's chair and laughed openly, feeling a gleeful absence of shame. She was in love. The bulb-framed mirrors, Amber Valleta wall prints, and Kiehl's products swirled together with her pink nail polish into one preposterous joke, with herself as the punch line.

'You're right!' Elle said. 'Josette, I'm a mess. I'm a lovesick fool!'

Chapter Seventeen

ELLE COLLAPSED ON THE COUCH in her new condo, surrounded by a multitude of thrice-moved boxes.

'Warner, my arms and legs are aching! Whatever's left, I don't even want it. I'm exhausted. Please, let's call it a day.'

She lifted her hand to let Warner examine the damage. 'See? I've already broken a fingernail.'

Warner took the examination of Elle's fingernail as an opportunity to hold her hand.

'Elle, this place looks like the basement of a museum! I can't believe all these things ever fit into your dorm room.' After a pause, he said, 'I don't guess we'll dig out that video-tape tonight.'

'No.' Elle smiled. 'Not tonight.' The Vegas tape was the one string she still had tied to Warner. 'Warner, it's going to kill me to part with that videotape,' she said dreamily. Her head tilted back and she let her eyes travel over the ceiling. Then she began to reminisce. 'That tacky Imperial Palace. I'll always love it, all of it, the ceiling mirrors and plastic bamboo. Las Vegas, of all places. Still, it was our palace.' Her eyes sparkled with the memory. He was still her prince.

The time had passed when it still made sense for Warner to be holding Elle's hand. He dropped to his knees, level with the couch, interrupting her words with a long kiss. She looked into his half-closed eyes with wide, adoring delight. And then, suddenly, to her surprise, she giggled.

All of her pointed yearning for this moment, all the tension of waiting, evaporated into dizzy girlishness. Covering her mouth with her hands, Elle brushed Warner's face accidentally.

'I'm sorry,' she gasped as she watched him draw back, looking perplexed and slightly angry.

Warner stood up brusquely and moved to the door, trying not to show his anger and embarrassment. Elle had *never* laughed at him before. 'I should have left when we finished moving. Just leave the videotape in my mailbox at school, okay? Sarah would kill me if she knew I was here.'

At the mention of Sarah's name, Elle's mood changed abruptly. She shook her head in self-reproach. 'What was I thinking, Warner? You don't want to be here, you've got a life, practically a wife! All you want from me is that tape. Well you don't have to kiss me for it.'

'Elle,' Warner protested, moving back to her, his eyes slowly traveling up her body. 'It's not like that at all. I'm not here just for the tape. I wanted to see you.' She quieted, but stared at him suspiciously.

'Elle,' Warner explained, holding her shoulders, 'I have a lot to lose. Sarah's very sensitive about this. She doesn't want me to have anything to do with you.'

Elle backed out of Warner's grip. 'Please just go, Warner,' she said. She crossed her arms and stared miserably at the door, avoiding his eyes, humiliated by her own tears and the fact that she thought about him every day.

Elle choked back quiet sobs until she heard the door close, then listened intently to Warner's footsteps departing in a hurry outside. Once certain he had left, she dropped her head into her hands, confused.

What a disaster. Underdog jumped playfully up on the couch. 'Hey there, Underdog,' Elle said, scratching his head. 'I'd better start getting serious about all of this reading for Contracts. I think I just blew my marriage chances.' She had chased Warner to law school, she hated law school, law school hated her, and Warner was hog-tied by his fiancée. On top of that, she had become romantically challenged, reacting like a giddy teenager when Warner made his move.

Her boxes were packed, and she considered moving them all the way back to L.A., escaping and saving herself while she could. She didn't know what she wanted anymore. Yes, she still loved Warner, but she wanted him to love her and only her. If she couldn't tear him away from Sarah, she'd have to think of something else.

Elle imagined how satisfied Sarah and her friends would be to see her parachuting out of law school, scared and beaten. The Barbie doll who couldn't take it. Elle scowled, recalling Sarah and Claire's whispered joke on the first day of class, remembering Dean Haus's mockery of her homecoming queen crown. They would all love to see her fail. And oh, wouldn't it kill them to see her graduate.

Setting her jaw with renewed determination, Elle tousled Underdog's fur. 'We'll both be underdogs,' she said, encouraged by her dog's calm, devoted eyes.

Chapter Eighteen

BALANCING THE EMPTY COFFEE mug that she had drained during Contracts class, Elle did her once-a-week law school mailbox check, prepared to throw away all of the law-related flyers. In the nearly two months that Elle had been at Stanford, she hadn't found anything more in her mailbox than notices of student meetings or the occasional Barbie doll ripped from an ad to tease her. But today her mailbox was stuffed with an enormous stack of papers tied with a red ribbon. A small envelope addressed 'Elle' lay at the top of the papers.

She peeled the envelope open and withdrew a single page of white bond stationery. A poem, marked with calligraphy, done in strange scrawls of fountain-pen ink, caused her to gasp.

> I'm staring at your picture now,
> Don't be alarmed or nervous.
> I'm not some weirdo off the street –
> I plan to do you service.
>
> I am your Secret Angel
> And I'm sure you will agree
> That as I stare into your eyes
> The pressure is on me
> To give you gifts of cunning
> To give you gifts of grace

To give you presents worthy
Of the beauty in your face.

What better way to win your heart
Than with a simple rhyme?
What better way to keep you here
Than with a class outline!

Don't leave law school, Elle. You are one of a kind.

Your Secret Angel.

Elle leaned against the row of mailboxes, stunned by the cryptic offering. With an astonished quiver, she untied the stack of papers and read the thick black type on the top page. 'Criminal Law, Slaughterhaus, Fall '01.' Set apart by a cardboard divider was a second title page atop a separate stack. 'Torts, Glenn [Fiddich], Fall '01.' A quick peek at the pages confirmed what the poem had promised. Someone had given her class outlines, the key to law school success!

Week one discussed subrogation, the same topic Professor Glenn had led with this semester. The outline followed the same format as her class. At that Elle grinned broadly, tucking the papers into her Prada bag with confidence. Elle wondered who could have sent her such a gift.

'Take that, Sarah,' Elle said defiantly. 'You haven't beaten me yet.'

Mr. Heigh had brought his wife to Criminal Law again today, Elle noticed, as she stared at the woman who was poking through her cooler to grab a snack before the lecture began. A late-in-life achiever, Mr. Heigh decided while running a health food store in Berkeley that he was 'smarter than any of the damn lawyers I deal with.' Smart enough, of course, to become what he despised.

A marketing genius, Mr. Heigh dressed frequently in promotional items from his store, which was called, imaginatively, Heigh on Health. When he was low on laundry, he also fancied running shorts about two sizes too small and vulgar tank tops, expressing sentiments like 'How do you spell relief? S-E-X' or, Elle's personal favorite, 'Sexy Grandpa.'

Mr. Heigh brought his wife to class because they believed in 'sharing their experiences.' Mrs. Heigh seemed to enjoy the field trips, packing bean-sprout pita pockets with carrot or prune juice in a Heigh on Health cooler that never left her side.

Professor Kiki Slaughter-Haus sputtered through another episode of Criminal Law. Elle was relieved to see that at least today Kiki had the sense to work with a visual aid, in the form of a diagram on the chalkboard:

'Another day in the slaughterhouse,' Eugenia said, prompting a shushing noise from fixated Gummi Bear Man. As usual, he had Gummi bears and a *New Republic* lying highlighted in front of him, ready to cite.

'Uh . . . the uh . . . Speedy Trial Act, has what as its goal?' Kiki trailed off, and Halley, always trigger-happy, piped up, 'A speedy trial!' Her twin nodded in agreement.

This *would* be their issue, thought Elle, glancing at the speed demons. The Speedy Trial Act directed prosecutors to bring defendants to trial within a fixed amount of time from indictment.

'There are . . . uh . . . different incentives that operate at different times in the process.' Professor Slaughter-Haus moved her pointer to the word 'Crime.' 'To require a speedy trial from the time of the crime would put pressure on the investigation. The incentives would be on the police to work quickly. Why might we not want a trial . . . uh, to start up that soon?'

Professor Slaughter-Haus turned to Cari, who answered promptly. 'The incentive might make prosecutors charge the defendant too quickly. We don't want to put that kind of pressure on prosecutors; we don't want them to prosecute until their case is solid. Right after the crime, if they had to bring a speedy trial, it might trigger premature prosecution.'

Eugenia poked Elle in the shoulder and said, 'Premature prosecution! I hear with love and understanding you can work together and make it last long enough for both of you.'

Elle burst out laughing, then whispered back: 'I think you can get counseling for that.' Kiki glared but ignored them.

'Yes, Cari, but . . . um, there is also delay to consider. The defendant wants a prosecution to be triggered so it will be over sooner. As the delay gets longer and longer, the defendant will object. The innocent defendant might want a speedy prosecution.'

'The poor prosecutor,' Eugenia whispered, 'maybe he just has performance anxiety.' Elle hid her face in her hands, shaking with held-in giggles.

Jeremy butted in, unable to attract Kiki's call with his jumping-frog routine. 'The prosecutor doesn't have forever,' he declared. 'The defendant's in jail all this time, okay, while the prosecutor gets his case ready to go. Nobody wants to trigger premature prosecution, but sooner or later the defendant will start objecting and the prosecutor will have to pull out.'

Elle exploded when she caught Eugenia's flashing eyes, and her laughter echoed through the quiet room.

'Ms. um . . . Woods, do you have something to add, uh, about the, um . . . the problem of delay? We have time for one more comment.'

Elle noticed Jeremy's scowl and imagined it was because she had stolen his limelight.

'It's not just the length of the delay,' Elle said, 'it's what the prosecution does with it that counts.'

Elle glanced at Eugenia, who looked as if she could hold out no longer. They grabbed their books to make a speedy exit.

Chapter Nineteen

'I DON'T KNOW IF I CAN take it anymore,' Elle said, turning her hand over so Josette could massage the silky cream into her palm. 'I'm getting calluses from writing so much.' She pointed to the nail-polish bottle on the end.

'Not zee black?'

Elle shrugged. 'It's Halloween, Josette. I've got a costume party tonight. You're an angel for taking me on your lunch hour.'

'Ees it a school party?'

'Well, maybe. There's a law school costume party I was thinking about stopping by.' Warner might be there, and Elle wanted to show him she was unscathed, beautifully cool, and over him.

'You are sure you want zee black?' Josette repeated. 'Are you dressing up like a weetch?'

'No, I'll leave that to Sarah,' Elle sniped. 'I'll dress in this ultratight black getup that I actually used to wear to parties, back when all that techno-industrial music was hip.'

Josette smiled. 'You zee boss.' She applied a single coat of heavy tar-colored polish, and within an hour Elle was hurrying back to school.

Looking around at her classmates in Torts, Elle realized that any day could have been Halloween at Stanford Law School. If anyone had showed up at her sorority house wearing a polyester undershirt with iron-on dragons, she'd have handed them a piece of candy and closed the door.

76

Layer-dressing was also popular, maybe because the school's central heating system was so out of whack. The temperature du jour was a warm one, yielding a panorama of T-shirts even beyond the standard Ben & Jerry's selection. T-shirts with a message, like twenty-four-function digital watches, were a trendy Stanford Law School item. The point was often to display some grand devotion to a worthy cause or fabulous accomplishment like a summer in Guatemala building 'infrastructure,' whatever that meant. Gramm Hallman, devotee of the Spanish Succession, had today opted for 'Yale, Bored of Education.'

Fran paraded her 'Peace Corps Sarajevo '99' gear for maybe the third time in as many weeks.

Andrew Walton, the Harvard M.B.A. who carried a Motorola flip phone that never rang, wore 'Harvard Business School . . . There's Nothing Quite Like It.' For that, Elle decided Andrew Walton got the Honesty Award of the day.

Professor Glenn-Fiddich arrived a full fifteen minutes late. Elle sniffed a strong odor of scotch as the professor wobbled down the steps to the front of the room.

'Another lengthy liquid lunch,' Eugenia whispered, nodding at Glenn as he fumbled through his lecture notes.

'If I taught Torts, I'd drink too, Elle said.

'Sorry I'm late, class.' Professor Glenn stood gazing aimlessly in front of him. His white hair was plastered against his forehead, as if he had been sweating. His olive-and-brown plaid jacket seemed hastily thrown on. The collar was raised in the back, causing one lapel to turn inside out. He seemed to have grown thinner since the previous class, so his eyes appeared large in his rosy face. A fly woke him from his haze, and he swatted the air around his head. 'Damn fly.'

Suddenly Professor Glenn announced the class topic.

'*Palsgraf!*' His eyes darted around the room as if someone would challenge him. Satisfied, he continued. '*Palsgraf's* the case for today, class.' He laughed, shaking his head. 'This one's a beauty. The kind of tort you just won't see every day. My compliments to the lawyer who had the guts to bring this one, I tell you.'

Having neglected to bring his seating chart, Glenn looked around the room for a student he recognized and could call on. 'You,' he pointed at Ben. 'Tell me what Judge Cardozo says in this case.'

'Car-*do*-zo?' Ben scowled at the professor, who was proceeding out of cherished law school order. Facts were always supposed to come first. 'Don't you want me to describe the *facts* first, before the *leg*-al *iss*-ue?'

'What the hell, you read it. Some idiot had a package with explosives in it, and the train stopped, and this lady bumped into somebody, and ten other things happened, and then all the minks Miss Palsgraf raised on her mink farm went crazy and ate their young.'

Ben couldn't take it. 'The *mink* farm was in the *Madsen* case, Professor,' he corrected. 'Palsgraf—'

'I was speaking hypothetically!' Professor Glenn snapped. 'Whatever happened, the important thing is what Cardozo held. What did the judge say in this case? How about you?' He pointed to Jeremy, snubbing Ben.

'Cardozo said Ms. Palsgraf was out of the zone of danger, and so he denied recovery. He said her damages were unforeseeable. He said the railroad has a duty of care only to people within a foreseeable zone of danger.' Elle scribbled 'no money for the plaintiff.'

'Duty of care,' Professor Glenn repeated, staggering to the chalkboard. He drew two wiggly lines across the board, then crossed them with a series of tracks. 'This is the Long Island Rail Road.' He stepped back, observing his picture.

'The zone of danger describes the limit of people who are within the railroad's duty of care.'

'Like passengers,' Halley interjected. 'And passersby, too, people at the crossings, maybe in the station.'

'Right,' Professor Glenn started, forgetting what he meant to ask. 'So we understand *Palsgraf*, then. Any questions, see me during my office hours. I've got an appointment.' The sodden professor collected his papers and teetered out the door.

Chapter Twenty

Elle parked her Range Rover on the quiet street and pulled down the vanity mirror. Scary. Underneath a kinked blonde mop stared vicious circles of heavy black eyeliner and two cruel streaks arching from her eyelids upward in a Cleopatra motif. Elle pulled out the cheap Wet 'n' Wild lipstick found only in lesser drugstores and traced a shocking black smile. She grinned devilishly.

Adjusting the metal-spiked dog collar, Elle surveyed her extreme getup. Not to be toyed with, she laughed, feeling bold. She kept the light on long enough to read the directions she had scribbled on the back of a class syllabus. Warner had called her early that morning while she was out walking Underdog, leaving a message on her machine that tempted her to believe she still had a chance.

'Elle, come to the party tonight,' he had said. 'I'll get away if I can. I know you hate the law school stuff, but I'd love to see you there.' It was then that she decided to go to the party, although she wasn't sure what to say to him. Her costume, at least, would remind him of what he was missing.

Confidently Elle and Underdog strolled across the lawn. Underdog was dressed as Dogzilla in a green-scaled one-piece costume. She wore hip-length vinyl boots, a peek of fishnet on the inch of her thigh still visible beneath the leather micromini. Studded skulls and cross-bones on Elle's plunging leather vest gleamed in the porchlight. Although she hadn't written down the address, she knew the party was in the third house from the corner. It was awfully quiet. The partyers were probably in the basement. Anyway – she shrugged – she didn't expect a wild crowd.

After she rang the doorbell a second time, the porch door creaked open. A gray-haired man holding a *TV Guide* and a remote control stepped from the dark foyer.

'Can I help you?' The middle-aged man peered with great interest at the chain that attached Elle's dog collar to her waist.

Elle froze, dumbstruck. Then, looking down at her costume, she faltered, afraid he would call the police.

'Oh my God!' Elle said, horrified. 'This must be . . . the wrong house.' She shifted nervously and held her directions up for him to see. 'I, uh . . . I must have gotten the address wrong. I'm looking for some . . . for some law students?' Underdog shifted nervously at her feet.

The man smiled at Elle. He strolled out onto the porch and stood facing her.

'I like your outfit,' he smiled. He made no move to return to his TV dinner. 'Maybe I can be your party?'

Elle flushed crimson when she realized this creepy old man assumed she was for hire. 'Oh no . . . it's no . . . it's not what you think. It's Halloween!'

'Of course not,' he said, playing along.

Elle backed up with Underdog under her arm and scurried toward her car.

After her humiliating brush with the solitary TV watcher, Elle was actually relieved to get to the party. As it happened, the house was the third from the next intersection with Oxford Street. Following directions had never been Elle's forte. She was still blushing when she approached the open front door and headed for the noisy blend of music and chatter inside.

She and Underdog clanked down the stairs in a racket of chains and boot heels, and grimaced when the fever-pitched whine of yammering law students assured her that she had found the right house. Immediately she stood face-to-face with Sidney: or a head above Sidney, whose frame appeared even more dwarfed than usual in a costume of flowing black robes.

Had she been behind him, Elle would have noticed that Sidney's old graduation robe was emblazoned in gold lamé with the name 'Chief Justice Rehnquist.'

Too familiar as always, Sidney reached out to grab hold of Elle's spiked leather wrist-cuff. From the orange stains around his mouth, Elle surmised that he had been at the punch bowl frequently that evening. She yanked her hand free from his grasp.

'You look sooooo hot,' Sidney whimpered. 'You drive me bananas.' He gawked at Elle, swaying, a bit off balance, almost stepping on Underdog's front left paw.

'Save it, Sidney.'

'Beam yourself into the chamber.' Sidney pointed inside. 'But I'm not going back in until my brother Justice Scalia arrives.'

'Thank God.' Elle had no interest in who was dressed as Scalia. She surveyed the room for a sign of Warner.

Cari barged by in a severe navy suit and wig of tight black poodle curls, briefcase in hand. Marcia Clark. Elle looked critically at Cari's imitation of the avenging prose-cutor, certain that O.J. would have been convicted if Cari had been at the helm.

Sidney was groping again for Elle's arm. 'I can't believe you didn't come as one of your *Star Trek* . . . figures,' Elle remarked, stepping safely beyond his reach.

Sidney's glassy eyes lit up. 'Well I am. I'm Captain Kirk, you know.' He stood proudly in his graduation robe.

'Of course.' Elle wouldn't recognize Captain Kirk anyway.

'Not tonight, Elle. I mean in the great enterprise of life, I am the captain. Aaron said he was coming as Captain Kirk,' Sidney blurted, 'and he insisted I would have to be Scotty. Scotty!' he spat, insulted. Elle walked away fast. Braving the rest of her law school peers seemed the better option.

'I am greater than Captain Kirk,' she heard him slur behind her. 'The only man greater than the captain of the *Enterprise* . . . Rehnquist!'

At least I should shake things up a little bit, Elle figured, turning the corner to make her entrance. Striding through orange and black streamers that draped the doorway, she did look out of place. Two *Star Trek*-clad figures stared noticeably.

Fran, dressed as Gloria Steinem with a hippie middle-parted wig and an 'ERA Now!' button, dropped her drink. 'Look who graced us with her presence,' she hissed, typically talking about Elle, but not to her. Picking up the empty plastic cup, Fran scowled at Elle's cleavage spilling out of the leathery bra beneath her studded vest. 'I can't believe that *even* you, Elle, would wear an outfit like that. It is *so* degrading to womyn.'

Claire, who seemed to have taken up with Fran, stared with wide-eyed amazement at Elle's costume.

'If I wanted to degrade myself, Fran darling, I'd have come as a brunette,' Elle shot back in Claire's direction.

Claire was outfitted in a poor copy of Elle's favorite pink quilted Chanel suit as 'Lawyer Barbie.' A recording played from her Dictaphone, repeating in falsetto the phrase 'Law school is really hard!' Claire pushed the play button and smiled victoriously at Elle.

Brushing by her toward the punch bowl, Elle tugged on Claire's fake blonde wig. 'Don't you wish,' she laughed without turning around.

If Elle had been making predictions, she would have assumed Michael would come as Count Dracula or some such hero of gore. Instead, she was amazed to encounter Michael at the punch bowl dressed as Andy Warhol. His typically slicked-back hair was powdered into a gray mop, and he had somewhere found a black wool turtleneck and tight Studio 54-era jeans. He peered through round-eyed spectacles approvingly at Elle's dark getup, and silently offered her the drink he had poured.

Elle took the cup gratefully. Maybe some people around here do have a little imagination, she thought. But the appearance of Dastardly Dr. Dan shattered her charitable mood.

Dr. Dan, formerly a cardiac surgeon, had come to law school to launch a second career. He attended class in his scrubs as if he had just left the operating room, claiming not only that they were 'comfortable,' but that he had a lot of old scrubs that he didn't think should go to waste. He often paired his scrubs with too tight T-shirts that he believed showed off his overdeveloped chest and disguised his short stature. He ran his fingers through his too black to be real and obviously blow-dried hair constantly, as if he couldn't get over his own beauty. Elle suspected that Dan was picking up premeds over at the main campus. Even after losing his medical license for malpractice, Dan could not rid himself of that personality trait of self-intoxication peculiar to doctors. The insufferable doctor of ego headed straight in Elle's direction.

Elle almost giggled when she realized that Dr. Dan, draped front and back with posterboard playing cards, was dressed as the King of Hearts. He eyed Elle through his tinted contact lenses. 'Good thing there's a cardiac surgeon here, Elle,' Dan joked. 'Your outfit might give someone a heart attack.'

'An ex-cardiac surgeon,' Elle pointed out. She looked dismally around the crowd for Warner.

Another Trekkie approached. 'Captain Kirk here,' Aaron introduced himself, sticking out his hand to greet Elle. She sighed and managed a half-smile, scrutinizing Aaron's bizarre neon stretch suit with the mark of the starship *Enterprise*. She offered her free hand. 'I heard.'

Sidney, ever possessive, rushed over.

'You know, Sidney,' Aaron began, 'I think it is just splendid that you have come as the Chief. Rehnquist.'

'Well,' Sidney whined, 'you should not have tried to be the Captain. Kirk. You are much more a Scotty figure.'

Aaron cocked his head but didn't respond.

'Scotty is not the leader,' Sidney continued, 'and not terribly eloquent. But he works harder, and in the end he knows how the *Enterprise* operates.'

Not to be one-upped by Sidney's taunt, Aaron rejoined, 'Well, you are well suited to be Chief Justice Rehnquist. The reason is because he is Darth Vader: an evil, dark force of power used to destroy the constitutional enterprise.'

A. Lawrence Hesterton, who had been staring over Aaron's shoulder waiting for a lull in the conversation to compare Elle to a harlot in *The Canterbury Tales*, was not entertained by the lowbrow discussion. Also known as Literary Larry, A. Lawrence was like a soft-voiced teddy bear with wavy brown hair and warm brown eyes so deeply set behind his round spectacles that they appeared almost sunken. A two-time Pulitzer Prize nominee, Larry had left his English professorship at Harvard when his tenure was denied. He considered himself superior to any conversational allusions that derived from nonliterary sources.

Aaron, still chortling at his joke, turned to Larry. 'What would you wear if you were a justice?' he challenged.

Larry arched his bushy left eyebrow superciliously. 'I am precisely as amused by this conversation as Queen Victoria by peasants.'

Elle took this as her cue to leave since the conversation was taking a turn for the worse.

Elle departed amid a chorus of 'May the force be with you's from the Trekkie Admiration Society. Ben, greeting Elle with a surprised stare, was dressed in suit and tie, white socks poking out underneath the high-water hems of his ill-fitting pants.

'Why aren't you dressed up?' she asked.

Ben had been waiting for the question. 'I am,' he cackled, pointing at his outfit: 'I'm a *law suit*!' He erupted into another fit of laughs.

Distraught, Elle looked at the unromantic downbeat setting. She noticed that Mr. Heigh and his wife were dressed like Lyle and Erik Menendez. She had the toupee; they were both in tennis clothes, and he carried a plastic gun. Heather, complete with frizzy blonde wig, scribbled notes on a yellow legal pad and introduced herself as the brothers' lawyer, Leslie Abramson.

'How witty,' Elle addressed no one in particular. She glanced around again with mounting despair. Of course Warner's not here, she thought. I don't even see Sarah. They probably have a date. She sniffed. And here I am, flanked by the entire starship *Enterprise,* Lawyer Barbie, half the Supreme Court, Gloria Steinem, Marcia Clark, and even the Menendez brothers. Everybody but Warner Huntington.

As Elle turned to leave she noticed Fran launching another offended tirade near the door. 'O.J.! What an outrage! You *would* sympathize with that wife-beating murderer!'

'It's a good thing Sarah's not here to see this,' Claire chimed in.

Elle's ears perked up. Warner, in a USC football uniform, number 32, was dragging a ball and chain on his foot as he headed for the punch bowl. O.J.! He had not strayed too far from L.A. after all. He smiled at the insulted women and pacified Claire with a kiss on the cheek. 'He was acquitted,' he pointed out, silencing even Fran, who stared agitated at the floor.

Elle, obvious in her excitement, rushed to the punch bowl. 'Warner!' she exclaimed.

'Jesus, Elle,' Warner gasped, looking her outlandish costume up and down several times.

'Well' – she shrugged – 'I don't have you to monitor my wardrobe anymore.'

'You look really hot,' he whispered, motioning with his head for Elle to join him away from the crowd. A keg out on the back patio was spent and unoccupied. Elle and Underdog walked out and were joined quickly by Warner. Underdog greeted him as enthusiastically as his costume would allow. He couldn't jump as high as usual in his Dogzilla costume.

'What are you supposed to be?' he asked, pulling gently on Elle's dog collar.

'Whatever you want me to be,' she whispered back in her smokiest 1-900 voice.

Warner smiled. 'Did you get my message?'

Elle nodded. 'Where's your other ball and chain?' she said, pointing at the shackle on his leg.

'Home.'

Elle smiled wide like a child. 'Home?' She paused thoughtfully. 'Postparty at my mondo condo,' she offered, thinking that this time Warner wouldn't leave her apartment until the morning. 'This one goes all night.'

'It's a little dicey, Elle. Sarah's feeling kind of sick. She has a cold, and I don't know, I've been sort of tending to her.'

'Nursing a *cold*?' Elle asked, amazed. '*You*?' That was so un-Warner. It really was all over. She turned to leave.

'It's not really the cold that's got her down.' Warner stopped her, grabbing her arm. 'See, her dog . . . back in Greenwich, the one she's had since she was a kid . . . well, her parents finally put it to sleep. I mean, it was really old, I don't know, I swear it's been in and out of the vet every weekend since I've known her. But she's bummed out. That's why she didn't come to the party.'

'Oh that's terrible,' Elle replied, dejected. 'Postmortem dog blues.' She looked at Underdog and felt sympathetic. 'But you came here anyway?' she asked more hopefully.

'Yeah. I needed some new faces. See, Sarah doesn't think I need to go out anymore. Since we're getting married and all.' He paused, a little exasperated. 'But I wanted to see you tonight.'

Elle glanced back at the party and saw Claire glaring at them. 'We probably shouldn't stay here together much longer.'

'You're right.' He looked inside at the motley assortment of gossiping law students.

Elle shook her head, reminding herself she had planned to act cool. 'Anyway, I need to go, Warner. I've got another party in the city,' she lied. 'Unless you're coming over. It's your call.'

'I'll be fifteen minutes behind you,' he whispered quickly. 'If you promise not to behave like a laughing hyena.'

She beamed and fought the urge to wrap her arms around him. 'Oh, Warner, I promise! I'll tell the doorman.'

Chapter Twenty-One

WARNER WAS TRUE TO HIS WORD. And Elle was true to hers. He had not stepped even a foot inside the doorway to Elle's apartment when she smothered him with kisses.

Underdog hopped sideways to avoid being pummeled by the flurry of clothes that fell in a trail from the door to the couch. Elle had tears in her eyes as Warner's lips traveled down her neck to her bare shoulder. Suddenly he paused, laid his head on Elle's chest, and sighed deeply.

'Elle,' he murmured. 'Elle, what am I doing with Sarah?' He raised his head and stared into her eyes.

Annoyed that Sarah's name had intruded so quickly, Elle pushed his hand away from her cheek. 'I don't know, Warner. You tell me. What does she want from you?'

'She has what she wants from me.'

'Which is?'

'A ring.'

The Rock, of course. 'Almost,' he said. 'She has almost everything she wants. I guess she wants my name, too. Soon.'

Huntington. Elle Huntington. How many times had she whispered it to herself, even practiced her new signature? She gazed at Warner, feeling the poison rivalry with Sarah seeping in.

'Well? Do you love her?'

'Yes, I love Sarah,' he responded mechanically. Elle was doubtful. After all, Warner's credibility was a little low given where he lay cradled in her chest.

'Sarah loves *me*, Elle. We'll be happy in Greenwich or Newport. Her father wants me in his firm, of course, or I could work for my father's firm. Until I run for office. Sarah supports anything I do. Well, I mean, *either* thing. I don't know, Elle, I'm just so confused. You know I really want to direct . . . my documentaries, you know. She'd never understand that.'

Warner stroked Elle's soft hair, seeking solace from his trauma.

'Let me get this straight, Warner.' She sat up, pulling a blanket around her shoulders and sliding away from him across the couch. 'Your *darling* fiancée, who loves you more than anything, and is flexible about whether you work for her family or yours, doesn't let you go out anymore because she simply adores being with you alone. Right? She will support whatever is best for you, work around your decisions, as long as they merge with the life she wants, correct? Your education and family connections have poised you for work in a white-shoe firm or a Fortune 100 corporation, either of which will pay you obscene amounts of money. But this life doesn't fulfill your artistic ambitions.'

'Elle, I knew you would be the one to understand.' Warner reached for her. 'You're the only one who really gets me. I—'

Only minutes before, she had been overwhelmed with long-awaited joy. Now, Elle could barely hold back her newfound wrath and disgust.

'Warner, I do understand!' she said emotionally. 'God do I understand! How can you struggle from day to day? The jobs, the loving wife, the political career . . . it's lined up for you, sure, but you deserve more out of life, don't you? Money, prestige . . . that's not enough. Oh no. You should also be a director, make movies, create. As long as you can maintain a solid reputation in Newport, Rhode Island, and stay securely in Grandmummy's will.'

Warner's blond head bent toward the floor, beaten. 'Okay, okay, point well taken. Are you done yet?'

Her voice softened. 'Yes, Warner. I am.' With that she looked up at him. 'Until you are true to yourself, you won't be able to love anyone. I think you'd better leave.'

He looked up into her eyes. 'Can I kiss you before I leave Elle?'

'No,' Elle replied sadly.

After Warner left, Elle wrapped herself in her favorite blanket and went to bed, but she didn't sleep very well. Instead she and Underdog watched *When Harry Met Sally* on TV. Convinced by the movie that Warner would figure things out just like Harry did, Elle finally fell asleep dreaming of that day.

For the first time since September Elle couldn't wait to get to class. She backed into the curb with a thud that she didn't even hear, her gleeful voice-over of the very un-November Bob Marley filling the world sealed inside the Range Rover. 'Let's get together and feel all . . . right!' she finished in her best Rasta, hopping out of the heated front cushion with first-day-of-school enthusiasm. She was actually early, ready to take on classes that now seemed a small hurdle in the path to a possible reunited bliss with Warner.

Checking her mailbox, she found a second package, ribbon-tied by her Secret Angel. Another poem, she guessed, opening the envelope curiously.

> *An exhale empties out the heart*
> *An inhale fills the soul*
> *Of all the dreams that I hold dear*
> *To kiss her is my goal*

A loving theft, a pilfering
A joining of the lips
A trade of moisture, warmth and breath
In soft and tiny sips

How slim my chances for this dream
I'll blindly roll the dice
And if she will not have me
Then a handshake will suffice

One time she'll fill her chest with air
A trifle, just to say
'Nice meeting you,' and with this breeze
She'd blow my heart away.

I belong to you, mon cherie.

S.A.

Elle fought a chill at her Secret Angel's intimacy. Too bad he didn't introduce himself today, she thought with a shrug. I feel like kissing the world!

Elle tossed her mailbox's week-old mélange of flyers and student notices into the 'Paper Only' wastebasket. She hesitated, smiling despite herself at the painstaking swirls of her Angel's fountain-pen ink. After a moment she folded the letter and returned it to its envelope, which she tucked into a casebook. She flipped open the outline hopefully. 'Professional Responsibility, Pfisak, Fall '01.'

He's gonna help me beat this place. Elle tingled with relief. Impulsively, she planted her coveted kiss on the title page, leaving a pink heart-shaped imprint on the top margin. Fate had returned to fight in her corner.

Chapter Twenty-Two

IN THE BATHROOM, WHERE Elle ducked to check her Chanel 'Pink-Alert' lipstick between classes, she was surprised to encounter a crowd of mirror-peerers. Typically, while there were lines for the Xerox machine and the laser printers, the path to the bathroom mirror was always free of law students.

Claire was struggling with her headband. Elle watched her tuck an errant strand of hair behind her ear, noting that the headband did nothing to disguise the fact that Claire had hair the texture of a Brillo pad. Once she conquered the headband, Claire pulled her white turtleneck snug and fixed her glasses.

Elle tried to muscle into a space in front of the mirror to apply lip liner. Meanwhile, Claire complained to an unidentified person in the bathroom stall.

'Today is yearbook picture day. I can't believe I forgot! This is the picture that follows you *forever*,' Claire whined to the stall dweller.

Dissatisfied with the work she had done on her headband, Claire finally announced that she 'simply was not ready.' She was going to ask the registrar if she could make a special trip over to the studio and be photographed there.

'Why don't you just send over your portfolio?' Elle couldn't help but inquire.

'Portfolio?'

'*Everybody* in California has a portfolio, Claire.' Elle smacked her lips and blotted her pink smile against the back of her hand.

Claire rolled her eyes. Elle had once overheard Claire tell Sarah that it was a 'constant torment' to her that while she had sat up nights amid a dozen coffee cups reworking her honors thesis 'to satisfy some crusty, pedantic old adviser, Elle had been waving at the homecoming crowd from the back of a convertible with a crown on her head.'

The way Claire saw it, Elle figured, was that it was just simply unfair that she had worked for a prestigious degree from Harvard only to wind up with the same postgrad credentials as a fruity bimbo from The University of Spoiled Children.

So every Monday, just to annoy Claire, Elle waited until halfway through class to tap Claire on the shoulder and announce: 'Only seven and a half hours until *Ally McBeal*!'

'Do they want a full body or a head shot?' she now asked Claire's worried reflection. 'Because if it's full body, I'll just send my ad series for Perfect Tan.' Elle grinned and shrugged at Claire.

'Perfect Tan. Perfect Barbie,' Elle heard Claire mutter venomously.

Chapter Twenty-Three

LAW SCHOOL PUT A STRANGLEHOLD on Elle's social life that Jesse Ventura would have envied. Feeling as if she had no life to speak of or about, she decided that she should get out more at night and read the Angel's outlines during the day.

She picked up the cordless phone to call Margot. With finals approaching, her classmates had become the Typhoid Marys of stress, and she needed a break. She had pored over the outlines from her Secret Angel, and had picked up Emanuel outlines on a tip. Still she was nervous. She needed to talk to someone outside the law world.

Elle dialed Margot, but before she could even say hello Margot was practically shrieking her good news.

'Wedding bells are ringing, Elle! And they're ringing in my condo!'

Elle pictured Margot's latest boyfriend and tried to see them growing old together. A romantic at heart, she loved the vision, funny as it was to think of Margot or Snuff mature and married.

'So Cupid struck in Malibu?'

Margot had moved into a Malibu condo after graduation, and had thrown a BYOK party in the fall. Bring your own karma. Elle had skipped the party. She had just started law school, and all she'd had to bring was negative energy.

'You got it, Elle,' Margot cried. 'I'll be a bride by next year!'

'Marg, that is absolutely fabulous.' Elle tried to disguise the note of discouragement that she felt, having expected to beat Margot to the altar. 'I couldn't be happier for you,' she added. 'When's the big day for you and Snuff?' She smiled more easily at the vision of Snuff, a twice-divorced record producer who was Margot's whirlwind summer lover and now fiancé.

'Well, you know Snuff's gotten me really into Zen,' Margot chirped. 'I have to figure out how they do the whole wedding thing. I was thinking we could have it at that church in Sedona that overlooks the Arizona Vortex.'

'Funky!' Elle applauded the choice. 'Barefoot like Cindy Crawford?'

'Oh God no,' Margot protested immediately. 'I mean, I want a real dress and everything. And one for you too, beautiful. Of course I insist you be my maiden of honor.'

Elle flinched at the word 'maiden.' Always the bridesmaid, never the bride. It was still a compliment. 'Thanks, Marg,' she sighed.

As if reading her mind, Margot softened. 'I never thought I'd get married before you, Elle. Not in a million years.'

Elle shrugged. 'It's not a race, silly.'

'I hear Bebe's divorcing already, after only six weeks!' Margot giggled, referring to the first of their sorority sisters to tie the knot. 'Not Snuff and me. We're totally in love,' she crooned.

'I'm honored, Marg. Really. Maiden of honor in the Zen Vortex, who could ask for more?'

'Can you come home this weekend? I know it's a rush, but I want you and Serena to get fitted for dresses. Plus I haven't seen you since you left for law school.'

'Sure.' Elle knew she should probably study, but with her tapes she'd be set.

She turned the stereo on to check out her first install-ment of *Torts on Tape* while she began to pack. 'Welcome to *Torts on Tape*,' mumbled the professor's voice from Elle's stereo speakers. Underdog whined, dropping his head beneath his paws.

'I know, Underdog.' Elle consoled her pet with a vigor-ous rub. 'But I'll try anything.' She dug through a heap of flashcards she had emptied on the couch, locating the stereo remote where she had used it to mark her place in a *Cosmo* quiz. 'Somebody has to keep Emanuel outlines in business,' she laughed, gazing at two enormous shopping bags bursting with commercial study guides.

Smoothing out a hanging bag, she tried to focus on the tort du jour, 'negligent infliction of emotional distress.' The gory tale involved a man suing the hospital that had sent him an amputated leg in the mail, rather than the personal belongings of his deceased father, which he had requested.

Elle cringed, imagining the UPS package. *This tape should have a warning label.*

Chapter Twenty-Four

'WELCOME . . . TO *TORTS ON TAPE*,' the now familiar voice began as Elle buzzed along the freeway on the five-hour drive from Palo Alto to L.A. She had heard the story about the amputated leg so many times that she had developed a definite fear of delivery men by the time she pulled into the driveway of her parents' house.

Elle greeted her parents and then called Serena and Margot. They arrived as she was unpacking the books she had brought home with her. They hugged her, but quickly exchanged glances at the sight of their pale, tired friend.

'We haven't seen you once since you left for law school,' Margot said. She gave Elle a circumspect look. 'And look! You have black rings under your eyes.'

Serena nodded. 'Elle, what are you doing to yourself?'

'You try amusing yourself with flash cards for sixteen hours,' Elle said.

'Tell us. You've been out partying with some gorgeous Stanford man, I know it. Come on, don't keep secrets.' Obviously Serena hadn't seen the Stanford face book.

'I don't believe you brought books with you,' Serena said, looking at Elle's bedroom turned library.

'Well, leave them here,' Margot directed. 'We've got shopping to do.'

Elle agreed and the three girls squeezed into Margot's tiny Carrera parked outside.

The valet took their keys at the Valentino boutique. 'Isn't a Valentino wedding the best?' Margot poked Elle.

Elle laughed. 'Explain to me again how this works with the Zen theme.'

'Okay.' Margot cleared her throat. 'It all makes total sense. See, the wedding's in the Vortex, right?'

'Right.'

'Well, Vortex and Valentino both begin with V! It's so harmonious! I had this fully positive rush the moment it hit me!'

Serena held the door and Margot hurried inside. 'She's over the edge,' Serena whispered to Elle. 'Wait till you see what she dreamed up for the bridesmaids.'

Margot rushed to a hanging rack behind the counter and slid it across the floor. A row of black dresses swung together as Margot pulled the rack to a halt.

'Black?' Elle looked at Margot with confusion.

'It's Zen, black and white . . . yin and yang!' Margot exclaimed, mixing her metaphors. 'See, I was watching MTV, and I saw the Robert Palmer video "Addicted to Love." And since I'm addicted to love, and it's so romantic, you know . . . I had this idea. You, and Serena, and all of my bridesmaids . . . you're going to be the Robert Palmer girls. Skintight black dresses, red lips, and guitars.'

'Guitars?'

Serena mouthed the words 'I told you so.'

'Yeah, Snuff knows a zillion bands. We'll just borrow some guitars. Anyway, it'll be just like the video, except you guys will be all tan and blonde,' Margot piped over the shutter door where Elle was changing into her dress.

'The *rest* of us will, anyway.' Serena folded her arms and stared at Elle, who hopped out of the dressing room pulling a sock off her foot.

Margot's animated expression disappeared instantly.

99

'Morticia!' she shrieked, covering her face with her hands. Elle leaned against the wall, kicking her sock across the floor. She glanced at her reflection in the harsh light. 'What? Is this too tight?'

Margot started to cry. 'Elle, you just can't look like that at my wedding. Oh, no, forget it.' She shooed away the seamstress who had begun to pin the hem of Elle's dress.

'Look like what?' Elle glanced from the mirror and the reflection she had grown used to seeing to the horrified faces of her friends.

'Your skin! Oh my God, she does look like Morticia,' Serena observed sadly.

'If you were a plant you would die!' Margot wiped her eyes. 'Elle, your skin has become so . . . so shallow.'

'Shallow?' Elle didn't bother to correct Margot.

'Totally shallow,' Serena agreed. 'It's disgusting.'

Serena put an arm around Margot to comfort her. 'Don't worry, we won't let her go like that. She can fake bake or something.'

Margot was somewhat consoled. 'Maybe since you'll be so busy with law school you could even use tan-in-a-can and look decent for my wedding.'

'I'm sure,' Serena said, directing her words at Elle. 'She'll be studying, or whatever, but she'll still be tan one way or another.'

They compromised: she would sit in the tanning booth while listening to her school outlines on the MP3. It was unspoken but also decided that Serena would replace Elle as the maiden of honor. Elle's appearance wouldn't be so noticed if she were just another guitar-swinging brides-maid. Hopefully she'd be able to find a Wolff tanning bed within the city limits of Palo Alto.

Margot called her at school frequently to make sure she

100

wasn't skipping her appointments in the tanning room. In December Margot told Elle she was worried that she might be studying and fading into a paler tone, and came to visit her at Stanford.

Margot approved of Elle's living arrangement. Still, she frowned to see the books and papers that littered her condo. Elle admitted she had been working hard to catch up in school, and really hadn't done much else since she last saw her friends in L.A.

'So what's going on in LA-LA land?' Elle said, joining Margot on the couch. 'How's Malibu? Still the valley of other people's rumors?'

'Totally,' Margot announced. 'Well, you know all about Holly Finch.'

'Who's Holly Finch?' Elle asked as she collapsed on her bed, staring listlessly at the ceiling.

'*Who* is Holly Finch? Elle, tell me you're kidding.'

Elle breathed 'No' quietly and didn't make an excuse for herself. Margot was perpetually the victim of her last conversation. Something new, something five minutes ago, must have been rumored over cocktails at one of Snuff's promotions.

'Elle! She's topic numero uno in L.A., baby. The *virtual vixen*. She's caused a total cyber-uproar.'

'Are you into computers now?' Elle asked skeptically. She needed an AP wire to keep up with Margot's fads.

'Well, no. Not me, but a lot of industry people are on-line. It's all the rage. It's not like they're Trekkie types or something. They're keyed into a whole virtual world. Multimedia.'

Margot was speaking a language she had obviously overheard in some Viacom hospitality suite.

'So what's the "cyber-uproar"?' Elle asked, a touch sarcastically.

'Well, Holly Finch's dad owns this big multimedia firm and a record distributorship. He had a database of *major* industry connections and Holly got a hold of it. She set up this totally shady, all anonymous electronic bulletin board so people could sign on with false names. It was totally L.A. exclusive. You could only join if someone died or quit . . . or if your net worth added up to the right numbers.'

'So why is the, uh, virtual vixen in trouble?'

'Well, it seems she used her network to zap around more than just *information*.' Margot paused for a moment to let her hint sink in. 'Everyone was on-line in fantasy mode, you know, talking about *how they like it*.' She lowered her voice to a conspiratorial hush. 'Elle, from what I hear, they had some major perversions. A totally mangy scene.'

'So what?' Elle yawned.

'No,' Margot insisted, 'that's not all. See, the on-line routine was just, like, an opener to get hooked up to the real thing. S-E-X, whatever kinky way they wrote about in their network profiles. Drugs, too. It was like mail order from fantasyland! Key your dream girl into the computer, and tomorrow she's ribbon-tied on your doorstep.'

'But I thought everyone used pseudonyms.' Elle hesitated, confused.

'Totally. They used everything. Heroin, acid, X.'

'What?' Elle interrupted. 'What are you talking about?'

Margot paused, reconsidering. 'Well, not so much X. That's passé. But I'm sure you're right. They must have had a lot of orders for the one you just said.'

'No, Marg,' Elle laughed. 'Pseudonyms . . . uh, false names.'

'Oh.' Margot quieted. She paused for a second to absorb the new word. 'Pseudonyms.' Then she continued. 'The thing is, Holly kept a master list. For every fake name, she has the real identity, plus a practical *directory* of their sick turn-ons. *Highly placed* industry people, and she's threatening to publish the list if she goes to trial.'

'What's she charged with?'

Margot laughed shrilly. 'Holly Finch won't see the light of day for years when the feds get through with her. She's up on distribution charges for every drug under the sun, and even something about sex with *panda bears*!'

'Panda bears?'

'Yeah, pandering, I think it's called. I'm telling you, Elle, these people are sick cookies.'

Elle walked to the kitchen, offering to get Margot an iced tea rather than chance laughing out loud at her friend.

'And then, even I still can't *believe* the most major crime happened right near my condo. It wasn't random, or anything, it was a total hit. Chutney *Vandermark*'s father is dead and her stepmonster did it. If you were already a Malibu lawyer, you'd be really busy!'

Elle had long since ceased reading the newspaper or even *People*, but the name did strike her as familiar. 'Who?'

Margot kicked a pile of Elle's casebooks aside, ignoring her question and looking for the remote control. She approached the TV set and poked a few buttons in vain. 'How do you do this without the remote?'

'Uh, I don't know,' Elle admitted. 'Wait, here it is.'

Margot grabbed the device out of her hand and flipped the channels until she found *Hard Copy*. 'God, Elle, it's all over the major media.'

The voice-over told a grim tale as a dramatic reenactment of the crime scene appeared on the screen. 'Heyworth Vandermark, seventy-four-year-old tycoon. His life taken not by his heart condition, but by a cold-blooded assassin.' An actress portraying the dead man's daughter wailed to police investigators, 'I found his body, right here—' she pointed to a chalk outline – 'and his wife was bent over the body, trying to move it!'

The narrator continued. 'Twenty-three-year-old Brooke Vandermark, sixth wife of the slain multimillionaire, stands accused of the chilling . . . Murder in Malibu. An exclusive eyewitness interview with Heyworth Vandermark's only daughter, Chutney Vandermark, on this week's *Hard Copy*.'

'Oh, Margot, turn that trash off,' Elle complained. 'I can't fill my head with this stuff before exams.'

'Well, while your head is full of that *Tarts on Tape*, the rest of Southern California is filling up with the Vandermark murder,' Margot snapped. 'It even made *Vogue*.' Margot muted the TV show. 'Chutney went to USC, Elle.'

'Wait, I remember a Chutney from rush. Wasn't she a Theta?'

'Delta Gamma,' Margot said. 'But get this, her step-mother, the murderer . . . *she* was a Theta. Typical.'

Elle giggled. 'That's a little strong, don't you think, Marg?'

'I don't know. The whole scene is so gnarly. Did you know that the stepmonster, Brooke, is a year *younger* than Chutney? Twenty-three. Shot the old geezer point-blank.'

'That's so awful,' Elle gasped.

'I know. I would just die if my father married somebody younger than I am.'

Elle shook her head. 'No, I mean, it's awful about her father being killed.'

Margot looked puzzled. 'Oh, that. If you think that's bad, I hear he left all his money to his wife.'

Chapter Twenty-Five

BEFORE SHE LEFT, MARGOT told Elle about a 'darling plastic surgeon' who was living in the Palo Alto area. His name was Austin. Serena had met him in Aspen, and was anxious to get him together with Elle. 'Serena says he's gorgeous,' she promised. 'Can we give him your number?' Looking critically at Elle's book-littered condo, she added, 'You really should get out more.'

Elle shrugged, a bit embarrassed, since things weren't working out with Warner. 'But I haven't been on a date for ages. I'm totally out of practice.'

'All the more reason,' Margot said, turning to leave. 'He'll call you soon. He's dying to meet you.'

From Margot's brief description, Elle couldn't tell if a date with Austin would violate any of her rules about dating. There were three types of men she would not date: men with pinkie rings, men with more than one alimony obligation, and men with children older than she was. She figured she'd give Austin a try.

And he did call quickly, before the week's end. Whether he was dying to meet her or just plain hard up, she couldn't tell. They agreed to meet for drinks.

Elle wasn't sure at first how she was going to pick out Austin at the restaurant. All she had to go on was what Margot had told her, he was a 'darling plastic surgeon'; but it didn't take a minute for her to recognize the 'status doc' sitting at the bar. He wore a big Breitling watch around a dark, hairy wrist, and a snug Prada suit. His Porsche keys were prominently displayed next to his cellular phone, and he was drinking Campari and soda. His complexion was dark and he swam in hair gel: just the type Serena would swoon over.

'Austin,' Elle said as she approached him and offered her hand. He nodded, looking slightly surprised, but extended his hand in return. 'Elle?'

She nodded. The doctor looked approvingly at her little black dress and the figure that filled it. 'Nice to meet you, Elle. Allow me to say that you are *great* raw material.'

'Raw material,' Elle muttered under her breath, dreading the time she would have to spend with him.

The flashy couple drew stares as they headed together for a table. The waiter scowled when Elle announced she could only stay for drinks. She was actually glad that she had a twenty-page memo due the next day. She explained this to Austin, saying she'd have a late night ahead.

He nodded, understanding a busy schedule.

When Austin was seated, Elle excused herself to 'powder her nose.' In the ladies' room Elle glanced at her Wolff-bed tan, which looked a bit yellowish in the light. Hurriedly she whipped the Chanel compact from her bag and dotted powder on her cheeks, smoothing it across her face to even her flesh tone. In her rush the narrow, almond-shaped nail on her ring finger caught the tip of her nose with a sting.

'Ow.' Elle drew back sharply, and the bathroom attendant, who had been sitting quietly, leaped up with a hand towel to lend her assistance. That was when Elle realized her nose had started bleeding.

'Oh, God,' Elle gasped in the mirror as a thin red line trickled above her lip. She grabbed the towel thankfully and pressed it against the cut.

'Use cold water,' the attendant advised. Elle nodded and dipped one end of the towel in the sink. She replaced the chilly corner against her nose and held it there, peeking every so often until the bleeding stopped.

'Thanks,' she said, tipping the attendant, whose job, she thought, might possibly be more boring than law school. With an anxious glance in the mirror, she dashed nervously back to the table. She had been in the bathroom about ten minutes, and Austin had finished his drink. He looked at her with curiosity, but resumed conversation easily when she asked him about himself.

Elle learned that Austin, though never married, was being stalked by a woman who had offered herself under his surgeon's knife after sending to his home a card signed, 'Your canvas.' At the time, he considered her formalities to be a little weird, but he decided to perform the operation anyway. He changed his mind when the woman ripped off her hospital gown and threw herself on the operating table, declaring: 'My love, cut anywhere! This will prove that I trust you completely!'

'Business took the backseat,' Austin laughed, 'after that exhibition.' He had his nurse escort the humiliated patient to a changing room, with orders not to return.

Elle threw her hands to her mouth and laughed. 'Oh, Austin, how terrible,' she said. She reached for her drink and noticed a small red streak on her index finger. Austin noticed it also.

'Oh no,' she said, reaching into her purse for her compact. She opened it quickly and confirmed that her small bathroom gash had reopened. Her eyes darted up to Austin.

'Excuse me,' she said, and hurried back to the 'powder' room. The attendant rolled her eyes but obligingly provided Elle with a fresh towel.

Elle returned to the table thankful to see Austin standing, claiming his beeper had gone off. 'I know you'll be up late tonight anyway,' he said. Elle blushed. She was sure he had a certain suspicion about her sudden nosebleeds, but she didn't feel the need to explain she had merely injured herself in spastic application of face powder. He wouldn't believe her anyway.

In the lull before the waiter returned with his credit card slip, Austin reached out his hand and held Elle's arm gently. 'Elle,' he smiled, 'are you seeing anyone right now?'

Elle knew she didn't want to date Austin again, but didn't want to admit to her life as a law school hermit. 'Yes, Austin, I'm seeing a few people.'

He looked puzzled but interested. Gripping her arm with fatherly concern, he asked, 'Why do you see more than one therapist at a time?'

'Oh,' she said, realizing that Austin had been asking about psychiatrists. She shrugged her shoulders. 'I'm more complicated than I look.'

'I see,' he said. From the tone of his voice, Austin seemed doubtful.

'Two heads are better than one?' she tried again.

'Sure,' he said. Clearly she'd need to add a new rule to her dating commandments: Never date men named after cities in Texas.

Chapter Twenty-Six

ONE RULE ELLE WAS LEARNING fast was this: Blondes do not have more fun in law school. Her unsuccessful day in Professional Responsibility was a prime example of Stanford's antiblonde snobbery.

Professor Pfisak had asked the students to write a two-page 'mini-essay' in which they were to invent a legal organization that would serve the public interest. They could choose any cause they felt was neglected in the 'corporate capitalistic status quo.' In the context of this imaginary group, Pfisak asked the class to discuss the Model Rules of Professional Responsibility governing formation of the attorney-client relationship.

Elle turned in a mini-essay describing her public interest vision: the Blonde Legal Defense Fund (BLDF). Its mission would be to combat antiblonde discrimination in all its forms. At the same time it would be a full-service law firm by and for blondes, providing positive blonde role models, focusing on community outreach in high-blonde areas like beaches. The BLDF would be particularly aggressive vindicating claims of hair salon malpractice.

The firm's decor would memorialize great strides in blonde history. It would feature sizzling Jean Harlow and Marilyn prints and an exhibit of Christie Brinkley's magazine covers through the years. The BLDF would have an ongoing display of the artwork of famous blondes, starting with one of Princess Grace's pressed-flower arrangements.

Absolutely nothing by Madonna, though, since she could not be considered a true blonde.

Elle went to some trouble in her mini-essay to explain the distinction between a true blonde and a natural blonde. The BLDF would take cases of brunettes who had been discriminated against, but only those who could be considered blonde at heart. True blondes, whether natural or not, could be identified by their inner light of buoyant, charmed confidence. Andre Agassi, for example, had the beacon of a true blond despite the atrocious things he had done to his hair. On the other hand, Madonna's light was snuffed out for good when she turned her platinum hair to that icky black color. The change meant Madonna wasn't blonde at heart, since no true blonde would ever go back. Billy Idol would still be okay.

Elle discussed the difficulty of finding blondes who are established intellectual role models, one effect of anti-blonde discrimination. Male blond intellectuals seemed particularly scarce. She could invite Robert Redford to serve on the BLDF board of directors, or maybe get an endorsement from Andrew McCarthy, but Elle was having trouble coming up with famous blond men who weren't actors or surfers. Dan Quayle was the highest-ranking blond Elle could think of, but he might have to be disqualified for making fun of Candice Bergen, another blonde.

The scarcity of respected blonde business leaders would be evidence to use in workplace discrimination claims of BLDF clients. Elle could just see squirming employers justifying the promotion of a brunette over an equally competent blonde: 'But, Your Honor, it's only fair – blondes have more fun.' And herself, lead counsel, fighting on: 'Objection. Irrelevant and prejudicial.'

When Professor Pfisak began reading Elle's essay to the class, it was clear that his idea of reforming the capitalist status quo did not start with the Blonde Legal Defense Fund. Voice heavy with sarcasm, the professor paused several times to shake his head in apparent disbelief. He repeated phrases that especially struck him: 'Did you get that, class? Madonna is not a true blonde because she turned her platinum hair to that icky black color. *Icky black.*'

Amid her classmates' jeers and her professor's ridicule of the Blonde Legal Defense Fund, Elle held steadily to her vision.

Chapter Twenty-Seven

STANFORD SADISTICALLY SCHEDULED its exams after the winter vacation, stealing Christmas and New Year in one fell swoop. Even the Grinch stopped after Christmas. Elle parked the Range Rover in the driveway of her Bel Air home, then dragged heavy casebooks and Emanuel study guides to the doorstep.

Underdog had jumped from the passenger seat, over-joyed to be home. 'Well, it's good to be back, even if I have to study over vacation,' Elle said, the yipping dog lifting her spirits.

Elle's mother, Eva, was a holiday fanatic. She always went to extra lengths during the Christmas season, spoiling Elle wonderfully. The year that Tori Spelling's 'White Christmas' was the talk of the town, Eva became irritated every time she heard it mentioned. *She* should have thought of flying in enough snow to blanket their yard, she rebuked herself. The truth was that Eva, a native Angeleno, associated snow with skiing and not Christmas.

Elle didn't have to wonder for long what gimmick her mother would think up this year. As soon as she entered the front hallway she was greeted by a preposterous 'Elle Tree' that dwarfed the diminutive Eva and even Elle's lanky father, Wyatt. He beamed at Elle in his place beside his wife. His bland club-tennis-pro-blond good looks and agreeable ways were a perfect counterpoint to Eva's wacky and vivacious personality.

A twenty-five-foot fir tree, twinkling with elaborate five-by-seven ornaments, stood in the foyer. Elle gasped as Eva led her excitedly to the tree.

'Oh, Mother,' Elle said, and laughed. She hugged her giggling mother and gazed dumbfounded at the unique tree trimmings. Each was a reproduction of a famous painting, copied by artists from Eva's gallery. Each featured Elle's own face in the most unlikely of settings.

'Look, look, darling,' Eva said, reaching out to one of the images. 'My favorite is the *Birth of Elle*!'

'Mother.' Elle blushed, mortified to see her face on the plump, naked body of Botticelli's Venus. 'Oh my God! That's *me*, and she's so *fat*!'

The *Mona Elsa* wasn't so bad, since only the shoulders gave away the grande dame of da Vinci, and the artist had been nice enough to leave Elle's hair blonde on the reproduction. Elle's sky blue eyes replaced the art-book gazes of women from the imaginations of painters of centuries. She smiled flawlessly from Matisse to Modigliani, Rubens to Renoir, Gainsborough to Gauguin to Goya. 'Mother,' Elle said as she embraced Eva warmly, 'you are without doubt the craziest Santa on the block.'

'Never boring!' Eva exclaimed.

'Never boring,' Wyatt said, winking at Eva. 'Here, Elle, my favorite is the *American Gothic*. I think it suits you.'

Grant Wood's famous pitchfork-wielding couple had been transformed, with Elle's face atop the matronly dress of the midwesterness, and a simple question mark on the blank face of the man standing beside her.

'You answer the question mark any way you want.'

'Daddy, you know whose face *I'd* like to see there!' Elle hugged her father gleefully.

She retired to her room, leaving word with her parents that she wasn't taking calls, not even from Serena or

Margot. 'They'll just report the party schedule. I don't even want to be tempted. Tell them I'm sick or something, okay?'

Eva sighed and glanced worriedly at Wyatt.

'Please, Mom. I don't want to fail my exams.'

'All right, honey,' Eva said. 'I'll call you for dinner.'

Stress meters were running high the week of final exams, the library packed to capacity with students trying to make sense of a four-month blur of rules and procedures in a not-English not-Latin vocabulary called legalese. The Secret Angel had kept Elle, and through her Eugenia, supplied with accurate outlines, but the wear of living in a pressure cooker made exams almost welcome.

Reading furiously through byzantine Civil Procedure cases, Elle actually happened upon a useful bit of information. When creditors sue a debtor, they cannot take things that are 'essential to everyday life.' So Elle was consoled that if she ever hit rock bottom, she would be spared her wardrobe, make-up, telephone, and standing manicure appointment.

Chapter Twenty-Eight

EUGENIA PRESSED HER FACE against the screen of the window next to Elle's door and rang the bell a third time. She detected the muffled sound of a hair dryer blowing in the bathroom.

'Well, at least she's up,' she said. Eugenia shifted the package that was making her arm tired. The blow-dryer stopped for a minute, and Eugenia gave the doorbell a long ring. 'Elle!'

Elle peeked around the corner in her pink-and-white-striped terry-cloth robe. 'Genie?'

'Hey, Elle, I came to make sure you got to your first exam on time. I'll drive you over if you want.'

'Oh, great,' Elle said, opening the front door. 'Coffee's on in the kitchen. French roast.'

'Thanks,' said Eugenia. 'Can't get enough of the stuff.'

Elle hurried back to the bathroom. 'Come talk to me while I get ready. I'm totally nervous.'

Eugenia sank down Indian-style on the floor in the hallway and set her coffee cup down. 'The doorman asked me to bring this in to you.' She indicated the package. 'Here.' Eugenia carried the box to the kitchen with Elle trailing behind her. 'You might want to open it. It's from Warner.'

'That's so sweet!' Elle exclaimed. 'It's probably a good-luck present. I should have sent him something, too. I was thinking about it.' She cut through the masking tape eagerly with a steak knife.

A note was taped to a second box inside. Elle read it aloud as Eugenia sipped her coffee.

'Dear Elle,

I guess I should have sent these to you a while ago. Sarah finally insisted that I get rid of them. She doesn't like to be reminded of you, and I guess it's not right for me to have them anymore. How many married men do you know who keep pictures of their ex-girlfriends? I can remember you without pictures anyway. Whenever I go to the beach I think of you doing the ad for Perfect Tan. (Even sometimes when I see you at school!) Good luck on your exams.

Love, Warner.'

Eugenia put her cup down slowly. 'Pictures?'

Elle opened the box, stunned, and spilled a pile of photographs across the kitchen counter. She picked them up one by one, growing increasingly shaky. Eugenia walked over and didn't speak.

'Delta Gamma Crush party, 1999. Homecoming, 1999. Sigma Chi Bahamas party, 2000.' She paused. 'God, we kept Chuck Lane photography in business. Derby Days. I don't believe it, here's us in Aspen. On Valentine's Day.' She smiled sadly, tears welling up in her eyes. 'Some good-luck present.'

'What a cretin.' Eugenia cursed harsher words in a low voice. 'Elle, come here.' She put her arms around Elle, who sank her head on Eugenia's shoulder.

Elle shook weakly, leaning on the counter. 'Why did he have to send them back? I've got copies of all these.' She stared at the images of her face and Warner's, fanned across the white countertop like so many playing cards. 'Why now? How could Warner do this to me? Oh, God, Eugenia, I can't go to the exam today. I just can't do it.'

Eugenia shook her head angrily. 'Warner? He's as sensitive as a block of wood. It's Sarah who sent these.'

'What do you mean, Sarah?' Elle gulped, her eyes dull, morose and unfocused. She hadn't even thought to blame Sarah for Warner's ill-timed delivery. What good was all this studying? Night after night spent poring over Emanuel outlines was supposed to have taught her how to spot a hidden legal issue when it snuck up on the exam. Had she destroyed her own mind in the process? Chasing after elusive subtleties, missing the obvious culprit? 'Of course, it must be Sarah,' Elle realized with a sigh of misery. Sarah was behind everything Warner did wrong. But still, 'Warner wrote the letter, didn't he? Those were his words.'

'Elle, don't you get it?' Eugenia persisted. 'It's no coincidence that you got these pictures now. Sarah "insisted," did she? I'll bet she insisted. Damn it, she's got him jumping through hoops.'

'Eugenia,' Elle began, but Eugenia waved her off.

'I'll say this for Sarah, she plays hardball. Elle, she doesn't want you to make it. You've been working your heart out for these exams, and you're ready. I know you are. She's just trying to shake you up. She wants to get you out of law school. Don't let her win.'

Shivering, Elle pulled her robe tight around her.

'Elle, I mean it.' Eugenia grabbed Elle's shoulders, straightening her with a vigorous shake. 'You go get dressed and put this out of your head. Don't let Sarah or Warner . . . don't let either of them ruin what you've worked all semester for.'

Elle dropped her head and stared at the floor. 'I don't care if Sarah made him do it or not. I came here for Warner,

117

Eugenia. He's who I've worked all semester for! Nobody else. I only wanted to show him that I could finish. . . .' Elle's quivering voice broke into a sob.

Eugenia released Elle's arms and collected the pictures on the counter. She shoved them back into the package and glared at Elle without speaking. Elle hid her face, unable to stand the black reflection of her own weakness in Eugenia's withering stare. Eugenia sighed, seeming to soften, but when she spoke again she spoke gravely.

'Warner and Sarah won't be thinking about you today, Elle. They'll be thinking about Contracts. Before your memory is five minutes old, they'll be framing their law degrees. Do whatever you want, leave if you feel like it, but don't forget: at least one of them will be thrilled to see you fail.'

Elle bristled. 'Try to see what I see, Eugenia. I made an incredible mistake coming here.' She reached for the letter, an anxious flush coloring her pale face, spotting her neck with crimson patches. 'Look, for every single case I read, for every class outline I fell asleep with my face on top of, what does Warner think when he sees me at school? Does he care that I've got a brain, that I can do anything his fiancée can do? That I'm as serious as any preppie from Groton? No, he thinks Perfect Tan! My bikini shot!' Elle restrained her voice with an effort, wiping a tear angrily from her burning scarlet cheek. 'What difference will passing an exam make? Warner doesn't care and he never will. It won't change the fact that I'm not from Greenwich. I'll never be a Knottingham. I'll never be what he wants. And its just become clear to me that I'll never be a Huntington! What's the point of keeping this up anymore?'

'Finish because you can, Elle,' Eugenia answered in a firm tone. 'Leave on your terms, not theirs. Not *hers*.'

Elle peered sheepishly at Eugenia, then shook her head in the negative. 'Who are you kidding, Eugenia? I can't even remember what a contract is anymore.'

'Offer and acceptance,' fired Eugenia.

'Don't forget consideration.' Elle smiled meekly, and Eugenia laughed out loud.

'See? You know this stuff better than I do. Come on, Elle, don't flake out now.'

Elle gave an uncertain glance at the clock over the stove. 'There's still time.'

Eugenia smiled. 'I'll drive. You can read the outline in the car, if it won't make you sick. Elle, it will *kill* Sarah if this little stunt doesn't faze you.'

'Warner, too, huh?' Elle looked mischievous.

'Definitely.' Eugenia opened the cupboard. 'Want a Pop-Tart?'

'Gross!' Elle giggled. 'Those are left over from the ones you bought before. I don't know how you can eat that stuff.'

'Fine, have a rice cake. But get ready. This is your day.'

The first exam, Contracts, began at 9:00 A.M. Elle finished the four-hour test a full hour early because, in her panic, she misread the clock.

Having raced under the pressure of her own deadline, Elle realized that with a full hour to go she had nothing to add to the thoughts scribbled in her test book. In fact, a weird postexam amnesia erased whatever random ideas she had just assembled into arguments.

One down, Elle thought with relief, floating happily down the aisle to drop her exam with a smack on the front desk. As she turned to leave, Elle caught a glimpse of dozens of hapless, furtive eyes shooting to the wall clock in fear that they were behind schedule. Watching her classmates' nervous heads and shaky hands jerk to work faster was so delightful that Elle decided she would try to finish all her exams first.

Civil Procedure was the only exam that Elle didn't finish an hour early. One question involving jurisdiction reminded Elle of the Secret Angel's outline, which was sixty pages in rhyming verse on the Federal Rules of Civil Procedure. The verse, called 'Jurisdiction Diction,' was a takeoff of Schoolhouse Rock's 'Conjunction Junction,' a mnemonic approach to memorizing that turned out to hurt more than it helped.

While trying to remember the difference between *in rem* and *in personam* jurisdiction, Elle visualized the 'Conjunction Junction' episode instead. 'Hmm hmm hmm hmm, phrases and clauses,' she sang to herself, annoyed that she couldn't remember the first line. She mixed the episode up with 'Lolly lolly lolly get your adverbs here,' and in the next minute remembered her favorite, 'Interplanet Janet.' As precious minutes ticked by, Elle, worlds away, was humming 'She went to the sun, it's a lot of fun – it's a hot spot, it's a gas. Hydrogen and helium, in a big bright glowing mass.'

She had to fight to get the tune to 'I'm Just a Bill' cleared from her head as she stared dismally at the blank page in her test book. Indecisively, Elle settled on an argument that the plaintiff had *quasi-in-rem* jurisdiction, which she thought was iffy enough for half credit.

What was worse, Elle noticed as she glanced back over her essay that she had written 'queasy' instead of 'quasi' every time she used the key phrase. 'Freudian slip,' she muttered, scratching out each offending word. Serena was in Aspen and Margot was comparing wedding dresses in the Valentino boutique; Elle was rushing to eke out a miserable essay on jurisdiction amid a sweaty throng of grademongers. She felt queasy, all right. Elle paused and left the word 'queasy' uncorrected once, on principle.

The week after finals might have been some measure of vacation, since classes didn't begin for another ten days, at any place other than Stanford Law. But here 'vacation' defined time to study or write papers. The law school scheduled interviews for spring internships and summer jobs during that hiatus, just to ensure that its captives lived and breathed law school stress constantly.

Eugenia had made plans to spend half of the time at home and then meet her college boyfriend, Kenneth, and some other friends from Yale in Vermont to go skiing. 'These early interviews are a waste of time,' Eugenia explained. 'Grades aren't even out. The first round is just where they weed out severe social misfits.'

Elle laughed. 'Who's left?'

Eugenia was admirably unconcerned with the pressures of job hunting. Her thesis adviser wanted her to do research for him in New Haven over the summer, still trying to encourage her to pursue a Ph.D. in literature. She had a safety net, so she walked on the employment tightrope with casual grace.

Elle noticed with interest that Christopher Miles, a well-known defense attorney in San Francisco, was interviewing first-year students for spring semester internships. The January issue of *Architectural Digest* had named his firm, Miles & Slocum, among the top ten law firms in the country for its office design. It was the only California firm to have made the list.

Naturally, Elle's first instinct had been to drop by the offices with business cards from her mother's art gallery. But when Eugenia told her that Christopher Miles was interviewing for research assistants on the Vandermark case, Elle developed a keen interest in getting the job; and when she saw Warner's name among the forty-odd students on the interview list, she made the internship her first priority.

Elle was eager to talk to Eugenia about the interview. So far, the only interview advice she had came from a *Cosmopolitan* quiz, 'Are You a Savvy Job Interviewee?' She thought advice from someone who had actually held a few jobs might prove more helpful. Eugenia's tips proved her right.

Seeing Elle's name on the interview sheet for the coveted internship, Sidney added his name in bold print and then hunted Elle down. Seeing her coming out of the law lounge with Eugenia, he was characteristically armed and ready with an insult.

'Elle, *why* don't you just get married and go play tennis at the club like you are *supposed* to?' His snide comment drew thundering laughter from the other Trekkies standing with him.

Sidney broke into a new set of hysterics, appreciating his own witticism. Even Sidney knew of Elle's desperation to break up Sarah and Warner, a topic that had apparently become common knowledge at the law school.

Less bothered than she would have expected to be by Sidney's comment, she walked right past him.

'What luck,' she said to her mother on the phone that evening. The 'Murder in Malibu!' Margot would flip if she heard Elle might be working on the hottest case in L.A. She might even forgive her for going to law school, Elle ventured optimistically. But when Serena called, Elle realized that even a stylish lawyerly debut would play to no applause from the roving bons vivants she called her friends. Law school was still an unacceptable alternative lifestyle.

Serena had invited Elle to join her in Aspen during the week of Elle's interview, and couldn't believe it when Elle turned her down. 'Come on, Elle, has that sickhouse poisoned you? Do you hear what I'm saying? Absolutely everybody is here this week. I mean, it's a practical *reunion*. Davis asked about you, and Vince is here. And Charles . . . Charles still *adores* you. He's always asking about you.'

'Serena, it's not just any interview,' Elle protested, playing the card she thought would win Serena over. 'Listen, you heard about the Vandermark murder. I mean, it made *Vogue*. It was all Margot could talk about when she came up here to visit.'

'Yeah, of course.' Serena recognized the hot topic. 'Everybody's talking about Brooke "the blonde butcher" Vandermark. Her picture's been on the front of every tabloid. You know she was a Theta? Typical.'

Serena was beginning to sound more and more like Margot.

'Right,' Elle said. 'Well, this big-deal defense lawyer took Brooke's case, and he's here, see? I have a chance at an internship on the "Murder in Malibu." Isn't that exciting? He's interviewing here to get some law students to help him do research or something. Or get him coffee. I don't care, I think Brooke Vandermark is getting a bad rap. I want to help her.'

'A Theta?' Serena sneered. 'What are you all concerned about a Theta for? Don't you remember when they beat us in the swimsuit competition at Derby Days? Jesus, Elle, I mean, it would be one thing if she were one of *our* sorority sisters. Then maybe I'd get it. But a Theta?'

'Who cares, Serena. It's a great opportunity.'

'Elle, what's up? Are you totally gone?' She tried to reason with her friend. 'I'm in a hot tub right now, chiquita.' Elle visualized Serena's parents' eighteen-thousand-square-foot 'log cabin' and sighed. 'You could be here too, babe. What's with you?'

'Okay, okay, Serena, don't make this harder than it is. Would the interview make more sense if I told you it had to do with Warner?' Elle heard Serena burst into laughter.

'Oh God, Elle, I almost dropped the phone,' Serena giggled. 'I could get electrocuted!' Elle heard a man's voice explaining how cordless phones work. 'What? No, Nathan, it has electricity. Shut up.' Elle heard splashing. 'It doesn't run on air. Hee-hee-hee. Cut it out! You'll zap us!'

'Serena. Serena,' Elle said. 'Warner's interviewing too. I hardly ever see him. We don't have classes together. We could work together on this, you know. If I get the job. Then I could talk to him, talk some sense into him.'

Serena quieted. 'Oh, you poor thing. Elle, there are so many other fish . . . on the slopes.'

'Fish on the slopes?' Serena sounded drunk.

'Hee-hee. On the slopes. Elle, what about Charles? He's just dying to see you again.' One man was as good as another to Serena.

'Serena, listen. I'm all the way up here in this hellhole. I came here for Warner. I might as well give it the old college try.'

'Will you *please* come home if he doesn't come to his senses soon, Elle? Please? This is getting ridiculous.'

Elle sighed. 'I'll come home. Serena, I just took exams. I mean, I *totally* studied. I worked harder than I've ever worked before. I'll finish this year, okay? Just trust me on this one. This interview is my last chance, and I'm giving it everything I've got.' Elle cradled the phone in her shoulder and walked across the room to her closet.

'Well,' Serena reconsidered, 'I'll set up my crystals for you, then. Direct some good karma your way.'

'You fruitcake,' Elle laughed affectionately. 'Thanks.'

Serena squealed and splashed her Jacuzzi companion. 'It's not voodoo, you geek. Naaathan! Elle, I'll catch up with you later, sweetie. Love you!'

'Miss you, Serena. Later.' Elle clicked the phone off and reached into her closet to pick out an interview suit.

'I've got to look perfect tomorrow.' She flung open her closet doors and began frantically searching for the perfect outfit. She paused at a navy Armani. Holding the suit up in front of her body, she glanced at Underdog's reflection behind her in the three-way mirror. 'Navy?' The dog curled unenthusiastically on the floor. Elle swore she saw him yawn.

'You're right. Boring. Sarah would wear navy.' She pulled out a cheerful Chanel whose gold buttons twinkled. 'Better,' she smiled. 'Think pink, Underdog,' she said. Underdog breathed a contented sigh.

Chapter Twenty-Nine

JOSETTE HAD ACCOMMODATED yet another last-minute appointment, and Elle strode in to meet Christopher Miles confident, rosy and polished to the tips of her fingers. 'Ingenue,' the Italian-suited defense attorney said to her, grinning, as he sat behind a Formica table in the law lounge and watched Elle's legs cross under her narrow pink skirt.

Not to be outdone, Elle spoke back in French. 'Comme il faut! As it should be.'

He had his own reasons for calling her in, which were trivial. '*Mon petit bijou*' – he smiled smoothly – 'I imagined you less . . . sophisticated.'

She scowled. 'Indeed.'

'Elle,' he explained, still smiling, 'I see a lot of résumés. Never a pink one.'

'Stands out?' she said.

He nodded.

'It's my life there, on that page.' She pointed at the résumé where it lay on the desk. 'How much can you say on a page?'

'Engraved?'

'Why not? You engrave a new shipment of stationery every time your address changes, and don't think twice about it. And then people Xerox . . . Xerox!' she said, grimacing, 'their résumé, the one piece of paper that must be right!' She paused, wondering if she should be talking about stationery.

'Engraved, rose-colored résumés . . . almost a medieval script. You could send one to the House of Windsor. If the royals were hiring sociopolitical jewelry-design majors, with awards in—'

Christopher stopped in midsentence.

'Elle, under Honors and Awards' – the lawyer leaned across the table and turned the blush paper sideways so they could both read it; Elle peered cautiously at her life-on-a-page – 'you have here: Homecoming Queen, '00; Greek Goddess, '99 . . .'

She smiled and traced the honors with her fingernail as he read. 'President, Delta Gamma sorority, USC; Chair, Intersorority Council, USC; Spokesmodel, Perfect Tan skin products, Los Angeles.' The lawyer paused. 'Spokesmodel?'

Elle shrugged. 'Well, as for the awards, I took some off, you know, the older crowns. Princess of this and that. Those are the most recent.'

'I've never seen anything like this résumé. I had to meet you, Elle.'

'Here I am, then. Let's talk about the job you're going to offer me, shall we?'

'Of course,' he said, half mocking her. 'What do you know about this project?'

What Elle knew she didn't want to say. She knew, thanks to Eugenia, that Christopher Miles, a Stanford Law graduate, was a famous defense attorney, and he had a quid pro quo going with the top law schools. When he had a big case, he would provide the school with name recognition and press.

In turn, the students would provide him with limitless free research for academic credit and trial experience that would help them in later interviews.

Christopher Miles would be trying Brooke Vandermark's case in San Francisco, and when he had turned to Stanford

Law for research assistants, Dean Haus had welcomed him warmly. Over forty students had become rivals for one of the four spots on the lawyer's defense team. If Dean Haus had rolled out anything but a red carpet, the halls of Stanford would soon be bloody anyway.

It was said that students weren't above telling lies about the last student they saw interviewing. 'I probably shouldn't say this, but the woman you just spoke to is a manic depressive. One day without her lithium and you don't know what could happen. I think this case might be too much for her.' Treachery started early in the ambitious.

Elle's interest in the job was manifold.

'I'm interested in criminal-defense work,' Elle lied. 'You're defending a woman who is said to have killed her husband. That's all I know. What else can you tell me?' she asked, sitting back in her chair.

'Brooke Vandermark,' he began after a lengthy pause, 'twenty-three, sixth wife of Heyworth Vandermark, who was in failing health at seventy-four. Heart condition. It didn't matter, though. He was shot at very close range. His health goes to motive. . . . Brooke had just married him. Multimillionaire. His will left everything to his wife.'

Elle raised her eyebrows and leaned forward. 'Blonde?'

'I'm sorry?'

'Nothing,' she said. 'Please,' she said with an inviting wave of her manicured hand, 'please continue.'

'Brooke's been charged with the murder. There's not a lot of physical evidence: no scuffle and no murder weapon.'

'What happened to the gun?'

The lawyer shrugged. 'Your guess is as good as mine. The police never found it. But an eyewitness saw Brooke at the scene.'

'Eyewitness?'

Christopher nodded gravely. 'Heyworth's daughter, his

only child, walked in on the gory aftermath. She was in the house . . . the estate . . . and when she came downstairs she caught Brooke covered with her father's blood, bent over his body, trying to move it. She took Brooke completely by surprise.'

Elle drew in her breath, cringing. 'What happened then?'

'The daughter says Brooke pleaded with her, but she ran into the kitchen to call the police. Brooke chased after her, begging her to stop. When the police arrived, Brooke had fainted in the kitchen. The gun was not on the scene, and the police didn't find it in a search of the house and the grounds. So there's no evidence to dispute the eyewitness's testimony. Brooke's fingerprints were all over Heyworth's body, his blood was all over her, and she has no alibi.' After a moment the lawyer shook his head with exasperation. 'Well, no alibi that holds, anyway.'

'What's her alibi?'

'She's a difficult one, this Brooke. When I interviewed her, she told me she was at a group meeting. A support group for Home Shopping Network addicts. Shopper Stoppers Anonymous.'

'How sad!' Elle said.

'See, according to Brooke, there were a good fifteen other people who spent all afternoon with her. However, she refuses to name them because that would reveal their addiction. So her "anonymous" alibi is as good as no alibi at all.'

'Well if I, God forbid, went to a "Shopper Stoppers" meeting, I sure wouldn't want the world to know.'

Christopher Miles tapped his pen again, appearing agitated. 'Well, the group members have nothing to fear. Brooke says the same thing. Apparently there are all sorts of executives, reputable types, you name it, who have

129

this . . . problem. She won't breathe a word about who was at this meeting.'

'Of course not,' Elle stated with conviction.

'Everyone says it's an open-and-shut case, Elle. The murder, I mean. The prosecution faces an even greater immediate challenge though. That's what I'm working on right now, and that's what I need my defense team to help me with.' He drummed his fat black Montblanc pen against his legal pad.

'Worse than *that*?' Elle marveled. Brooke's lot sounded bad enough with the murder charge.

'Heyworth's daughter has already presented his will for probate. Under California law, what's known as the Slayer Statute, a will beneficiary cannot take a legacy if that beneficiary caused the death of the donor.'

'So if Brooke killed him, she's cut out.'

'Right,' he said, and smiled.

'Why is that worse? Losing the money . . . that's pretty bad, but I'd be worried about going to jail.' Elle shuddered at the thought.

'Worse from a legal standpoint. The burden of proof in a criminal prosecution is, as you know, beyond a reasonable doubt. The burden of proof in a civil case, the burden for will probate, is lower.'

'Preponderance,' Elle finished. Thanks to her Secret Angel for the Civil Procedure outline.

'Preponderance,' he repeated. 'More likely than not. The plaintiff, Chutney, need only show that it is more likely than not that Brooke is guilty of the murder for purposes of defeating her gift . . . cutting her out of the will.'

'Who is Chutney?' Elle asked, eyes innocently careful to conceal that she already knew who Chutney Vandermark was. A Delta Gamma who, according to Margot, had a terrible nose job and was probably named after a spice.

'Oh, sorry. Chutney Vandermark. That's his daughter, who, by the way, is a year older than Brooke.'

'Blonde?' Elle asked the lawyer.

'I'm sorry?' Christopher Miles asked, puzzled.

'Is Chutney blonde?' Elle couldn't remember, and anyway, that could change.

'Uh, no. No. Why?' He looked at the pink homecoming queen with curiosity.

Elle knew where her sympathies lay. Smiling, she announced: 'Then I am perfect for this job.'

'I'm not sure I understand.'

Elle beamed. 'It's my ambition. That's why I'm in law school,' she proclaimed momentously. 'One day in Professional Responsibility . . . John . . . he's very judgmental. He started this thing . . .' Elle got sidetracked for a moment, the enthusiasm of her public-service vision taking center stage.

'Go on,' Christopher encouraged with interest.

'We had to describe, you know, our idea of a public-service project in the law. So this girl Rebel, she has something for Native American alcoholics, and Cari . . . well, she just wants to send all men to the gas chamber.' Elle paused.

'When my turn came around I told the class that I was going to found the BLDF. The Blonde Legal Defense Fund. My professor read my essay to the class.'

Christopher Miles burst out laughing.

'Come on . . . I'm serious,' Elle frowned. 'There's a lot of antiblonde prejudice in the professional world. Believe me, I know. Not the jokes. I mean, that's just envy, you know? Not actionable. But I was thinking about it. Look at the world's blonde role models. Can you name a blond president?'

He paused. 'I guess not.'

'Dan Quayle. He's the closest we've gotten. And look what happened to him!'

131

'So the Blonde Legal Defense Fund . . .'

'Will stand up for blondes everywhere!' Elle finished. 'Public service! Starting with Brooke Vandermark.'

Christopher Miles smiled. There had been a time when he was at Stanford and had plans to fight the system, long before he accepted that all of his clients were guilty.

Elle, a minute before effusive with the reformist zeal of youth, suddenly halted and then spoke gravely, as if telling a secret. 'Anyway, Brooke didn't do it. She didn't kill Heyworth Vandermark.'

He paused, surveying Elle with care, but skeptically. 'Oh? How convenient. Do you also know who did it?'

'Chutney did it,' Elle declared, already on the side of wholesome blonde innocence.

'His daughter? What makes you so sure, Elle?' The lawyer squinted at her. It was odd to accuse the victim's own daughter, and though Elle sounded certain, she didn't know any facts.

'Chutney did it,' Elle said again.

'I've told you very little about Brooke,' he said, his voice a calm contrast to her impulsiveness. 'And I really couldn't tell you much of anything about Chutney. Neither of them has been deposed. Perhaps it would restrain your enthusiasm to know that witnesses are coming out of the woodwork already to testify against Brooke when the murder charge goes to trial after probate.'

Elle sat sullenly without responding.

'Chutney has already given statements to the police that are very damaging. I have no doubt that she will testify against Brooke. Brooke's personal trainer, the gardener, the maid, and the interior designer, among others, are all pointing at Brooke as the murderer.'

Elle didn't speak, but she looked offended. She folded her arms and glared as if the charges were against her personally.

'Remember, Elle,' the lawyer pointed out, more to restate the facts to himself than to debate the matter, 'Chutney is the man's daughter. She is his blood. Brooke only married Heyworth Vandermark about a year ago, and it's pretty clear she did it for the money.'

'See, you take the wrong inference from that,' Elle protested. 'A woman my age who marries a man that old on the hope that he doesn't write her out of his will and leave it all to his daughter anyway, that's a woman who's willing to work for her money. That man had been married almost as many times as Larry King, for God's sake! He knew how to file divorce papers. But he kept Brooke around. That's honest work, hard work: keeping a rich man happy. Anyone who marries for money ends up earning it.'

Christopher looked at Elle, tapped his pen, and then scribbled something on his legal pad. Now he realized that, weird as it sounded, the girl had an inkling of a defense theory. It was more than he had heard in twenty interviews during which law students had tried to sell their legal ambitions like brokers peddling tax-deferred annuities.

'And what about Chutney?'

'Well,' Elle said, 'I only know a little of the facts. But from what you've told me, it's got to be Brooke or Chutney. Brooke, I tell you, was making honest money putting up with a testy old dinosaur who married and divorced on a whim. Chutney, though, the late-in-life kid: those kind think they're entitled. They never see their parents struggle, or grow up. They just see this old lump between them and their inheritance, breathing its last intolerable breaths.'

'God, Elle, that's pretty cynical.'

'I am from L.A.,' she said, and smiled. 'Have you been to California Cafe? If you'd like to test my theory, let's talk about it over dinner.'

'Shall we invite the other interviewing students?' the lawyer teased.

Elle glared at him. 'I have this phobia. I can't eat in company greater than two.'

'You should get that checked out. Why don't I meet you there, say at five-thirty?'

'Why don't you pick me up, say at six?' Elle scribbled her address and phone number on a finely lined pink sheet of paper. 'Call if you get lost.' Elle crossed her fingers and turned to leave the room.

'It's casual,' she called back from the doorway, impatient to change out of her suit.

The heat of the day was suspended in a sultry dusk, and the terrace tables at California Cafe, only recently open for outside dining, were lively with the appreciative buzz of shoppers enjoying the early hint of spring after Palo Alto's rainy winter. Not a few garment bags lay slung over chair backs. Elle saw a Neiman Marcus bag draped across the back of a chair at the table of a lone woman who was attacking her taco salad with too much enthusiasm.

She might have met Christopher here, instead of driving over with him, Elle thought to herself, if only she had remembered that Lancôme was doing Hydradermie facials at Neiman's. A Belgian aesthetician who had pioneered the use of mild electric currents to rejuvenate the eye and neck area was visiting the store until the week's end. The postcard that announced this event was the one piece of unsolicited mail she had received this month that escaped an instant trashing. It was never too early to exfoliate, Elle believed.

Maybe another time, she thought. Elle folded her sunglasses and slipped them into their case, blinking with an anxious smile. She noticed soft glints of gray that streaked

Christopher Miles's dark hair about the temples. She wondered if he had been divorced, thought it likely as a matter of odds, but at the same time instinctively doubted it. He was exceedingly graceful; his gaze rested easily wherever he turned it; the air about him was that of a man who belonged. He was successful, welcome, and unhurried. He had the maturity of calm knowledge without the vinegar of hard experience. Elle had never dated an older man who did not fancy himself a young one. She did not realize until the waiter approached that she had been staring into his steady hazel eyes.

Her eyes flashed when she became conscious of herself. She looked down abruptly and busied her hands in the folds of the silk sarong that skirted her bare legs. She clicked her left heel in and out of her mule with apprehension. She felt entirely inappropriate.

Christopher's sleeves were rolled back and his collar was unbuttoned at the neck under a loosened Hermès tie whose print featured rabbits being pulled out of top hats. He hadn't had time to change from his suit, however. Elle remembered suggesting California Cafe specifically for its casual atmosphere, but Christopher, in his professional formality, had missed the hint. The restaurant was in the Stanford Shopping Center, for God's sake, in a mall. Nobody wore suits in malls, she insisted to herself, gulping when she noticed the table of happy-hour revelers who might have been tax accountants, bankers, or lawyers . . . pin-striped to the last. Well, nobody should be wearing suits, Elle decided. If she knew anything, she knew what to wear to the mall.

'It's a nice night to sit outside,' she attempted, extending a shaky hand to her water glass.

Christopher smiled broadly. 'I wish I'd had time to change out of my suit,' he said. 'I envy your comfort.'

135

Elle laughed. 'I'm not the least bit comfortable,' she admitted. She hadn't even grabbed a snack before Christopher arrived, and now, on top of everything, she was starving. Elle had wanted to be prepared to discuss Brooke's case, so she had researched in the obsolete manner of the computer illiterate: she talked to people who knew, or knew of, Brooke Vandermark. She had spent hours on the phone with sorority sisters, gathering gossip about Brooke's USC days, making notes like a tabloid reporter of reliable, if secondhand, details. As Elle should have expected, the best rumors came from Margot, the human Internet. She had even tracked down Dookie Dean, who was president of Theta when Brooke lived in the sorority house, which was some trouble, since the recent divorcée was still living under her married name. Elle found out in the first breath that Dookie Dean didn't go by the nickname 'Doo-Dee' anymore, an offending gaffe that thwarted Elle's friendly attempts to gain information.

Elle ordered a diet Coke and Christopher ordered a single-malt scotch. Elle was familiar enough with the menu to ignore the gesticulating waiter who made up for the lack of variety in the day's specials by painstaking description of the manner in which each was prepared. Elle suspected he was a chef at heart, stuck in a second-string job. She ordered grilled mahimahi, with instructions that the fillet be accompanied by two lemon wedges and not be touched by one drop of butter. 'I mean it, if I see any butter, I'll send it back,' she cautioned, requesting her salad dressing on the side.

'The Trappist monk will endure her fast alone,' Christopher said, and smiled. 'I'd like the giant T-bone steak,' he announced, 'and I want enough butter on the baked potato to drown a mule.'

Elle laughed. 'I don't know how you manage to eat like that,' she said.

'I'm from the Midwest,' he answered with a shrug. 'We've advanced beyond gathering nuts and berries. No ice in the scotch,' he called after the departing waiter.

'Glenn Fiddich,' Elle smiled, relaxing, 'is what we call my Torts professor.'

'Don't tell me old man Glenn is still teaching!' Christopher shook his head incredulously. 'He must be a hundred years old. I thought his liver would go before the end of my first year! Still knocking them back in the afternoons, is he?'

Elle paused, wrinkling her brow. It was odd to imagine the stylish Christopher Miles at Stanford. Maybe law school was different then.

'I can't imagine you at Stanford.'

Christopher smiled. 'The feeling is mutual, Miss Woods.'

'What, you can't imagine yourself there either? I guess it's been a while.'

'Easy, young one,' the lawyer cautioned. 'It wasn't so long ago. I meant I can't imagine you there. Stanford must be very proud to count you in its ranks.'

'Well, I doubt that it's changed very much.' Elle caught herself on the verge of trotting out her grievances with law school, the bulk of which were aesthetic. 'People just study mainly, and worry.' She shrugged. 'Stanford Law is not a proud place.'

'You're right, then. It hasn't changed.' Christopher winked. 'There's no pride in practicing law either.'

Elle shook her head vigorously. 'I don't believe that. I don't believe that or I wouldn't be here. I think you should be very proud of what you're doing for Brooke. She needs someone to believe in her, and you're standing up for her.

137

I want to help her too. That's why I want to work on her case.'

'Quite noble, Miss Woods. A lawyer who wants to be of help.' He cocked his head slyly, but his skeptical words were at odds with his soft eyes, looking back on a musty old feeling. He had wanted to be of help too, when he started. Students encouraged him when he felt they had not lost faith.

'Tell me, Elle,' he asked mischievously, 'would you take this job if I told you I would not, in any event, act as a reference? Not call around to help you get a clerkship? Not even confirm that you worked for me? Just let you . . . help?'

'Absolutely,' Elle said. 'If we get Brooke out of trouble, I'll just have people call her instead.'

'And if we don't,' Christopher sighed, 'they'll have to call the warden.'

Elle scowled. 'That's a bad attitude.'

'Realistic,' the lawyer said with a shrug, nodding thanks to the waiter for his scotch. 'The way it looks now, this case is the toughest of my career. Like I said, the criminal defense will be easier than the will contest. Brooke has no alibi, and if it comes down to credibility . . .' Christopher trailed off, not wanting to predict his own defeat.

'Brooke didn't do it,' Elle declared firmly. 'She didn't need the money. She believed in perfection. She worked very hard. She was nice to animals. She used to brush her dog every day and she gave him mints. She was . . .' Elle thought of what she had heard, and halted. It still seemed rude to mention. She blushed, taking her cocktail stirrer from the tablecloth. Christopher was in good shape. Maybe he wouldn't understand.

'She was what, Elle?' He leaned forward, setting his drink aside, staring expectantly, his hands kneading together in the manner of prayer. 'What do you know about Brooke?'

'Well, I hate to say it,' Elle said, grimacing, 'but she was really fat.'

'Fat?' Christopher settled back in his chair, breathing a heavy, disappointed sigh. 'Elle, I just don't see how that makes any difference now. By the way, she's in great shape now. She's absolutely outraged that there wasn't a StairMaster in the L.A. County Jail. She was sure her rights were being violated.'

Elle frowned with impatience. It was as if men never thought about the struggle women endured, daily, to stay thin. They thought about the results, all right, when they wanted the feminine trophy of their success. As if women came from cookie cutters. She would bet her life that Christopher Miles never dated a fat girl. Warner certainly hadn't, she thought in gentle reproach. It must have been hard for Brooke.

'Don't you see, she made something of herself,' Elle protested. 'She's worked for every pound. She's not a woman who takes the easy way.'

'You talk about her as if you know her,' Christopher said, puzzled but still unconvinced.

Elle nodded. 'I do. She was my step-aerobics instructor at USC. It was the hardest class I ever took!'

'She taught an aerobics class in jail,' Christopher said. '"Felon-o-robics," she called it. I'm sure there was some disappointment when she made bail. She told the ladies to keep themselves together, to use the time they had as a project to shed those few extra pounds. She said to think of it like going away to a spa and surprising your friends with the beautiful new you on your trial date. It was a pretrial confinement, so she didn't have to deal with any hopeless long-termers. She was very popular.'

Elle smiled warmly, more convinced than ever by Brooke's vigorous optimism that she was on the side of truth and healthy blonde energy.

'I wasn't sure that Brooke was the same one I knew at USC when I interviewed with you this afternoon,' Elle allowed, 'but I made some calls. She was Brooke Rayburn then. She was a year ahead of me, but I remember the big controversy she caused at the Theta house.'

Christopher raised his eyes with concern. 'Controversy? That's all she needs.'

'She almost moved out. See, she was a double legacy. Her mother and her grandmother were Kappa Alpha Thetas, and her mom is still really active, a chapter president or something. So when Brooke showed up at rush, she was pretty much a given. And that didn't make the Thetas real happy, since she was so fat. On top of being a legacy, her mom gives a lot of money, so there was no way they could blackball her.'

'That's awful.' Christopher cringed. The viciousness of pretty women never failed to take him by surprise. 'So Brooke comes from money?' The lawyer grew interested. 'Brooke told me that she put herself through school. Brooke seemed to say nothing to me that wasn't self-defeating. It seems as if she wants to play against the highest odds.'

'Well, she did. Come from money, that is. Her dad was a real estate developer who made a fortune building strip malls, but in her sophomore year, her parents went through a divorce. Brooke found out in the worst way that her father was having an affair. One of the guys on the swim team was at a Theta crush party and he mentioned to Brooke that he'd had breakfast with her father, Mr. Rayburn, just that morning. Brooke thought he must have been interviewing for a job with her dad's real estate company, so she asked him how the interview went. He just laughed and said it was no interview, Mr. Rayburn just liked his mother's blueberry pancakes. It turned out that this guy's mother lived down the street from the Rayburns in Pasadena. She was divorced, living off of a generous settlement, and spending most of her time with her horses, playing tennis at the Valley Hunt Club, and being a friendly neighbor.'

Elle took a sip of her diet Coke and looked around the restaurant.

'Anyway, she met Brooke's dad because she got some of his mail by mistake, and she brought it over to the house. Brooke's mom was away on business. She was a fashion photographer and was in Paris photographing the spring collections. I guess Mr. Rayburn was lonely.'

'Don't tell me.' Christopher swatted the air with his hand.

'You guessed it,' Elle sighed. 'The rat started sleeping with his neighbor. Brooke's mother said she was a photographer because of her love of art, but she must have known something about her husband's once lucrative so-called real estate company. It went Chapter Eleven right after the divorce.'

'So I guess Brooke told her mother about the affair?'

'It was terrible. Injustice should be Brooke's middle name.'

The waiter arrived with an enormous tray, carrying the salads and dinner together, evidently to hurry the meal along. How mercenary, Elle thought with a scowl, resolving to eat her rice grain by grain and occupy the table all night. If she could get to it without knocking something over, she thought, surveying the cluttered table for the best angle from which to approach her salad. The waiter placed Elle's dish in front of her with a grand, affected

bow. 'The lady will find not one ounce of butter to dis-
please her,' he said.

Elle rolled her eyes. 'How grand,' she answered, forcing
a smile.

Christopher tapped his foot impatiently. 'We would also
like a bottle of Evian, please.'

The lawyer grinned and stared at Elle a bit too intensely
before catching himself. 'I won't let that waiter rush us out
of here,' he said.

'I'm in no rush,' she said.

She began to toss her salad in the little room that the
delicate bowl allowed, forgetting in her hunger what she
had been saying before.

'Well, did Brooke tell her mother?'

'Sorry,' Elle smiled. 'It's just unforgivable, what happened. Brooke told her mother as soon as she returned
from Paris, and told her everything. Her mother called
Brooke a liar and a wretched, dumpy little failure. She said
all these awful things. She even said that Brooke was jealous of her mother's beauty. She wouldn't take her calls and
told her to move out of the house.'

'The poor thing,' Christopher gasped. He was incredu-
lous.

'Wait' – Elle held up her finger – 'it gets worse. Her
mother had to say something to explain Brooke's being
thrown out of the house, so she told her husband of the
awful rumors Brooke was spreading about his misdeeds.
He denied it, of course, and they cut Brooke off. He said
that the little brat tried to ruin him. He threatened to sue
her for slander, but she didn't have a penny that wasn't his,
so he just went about calling her a lying wretch.'

'Did they divorce anyway?' Christopher asked.

'Oh,' Elle said, 'they did, but not for a while. Basically,
they divorced Brooke instead. They held up the facade of

their marriage for another year and then divorced when *W* ran a spread of the Riviera that had the indelicacy of picturing Brooke's mother asleep in the sand with her head on the chest of one of Lagerfeld's financiers. She's married him since, and she's living in France. I don't know where her father is. This happened in the fall of Brooke's sophomore year.'

Christopher shook his head. He had worked in California as the natural progression of his time at Stanford, but he would never call it home. He had grown up in a small town in Iowa, where divorce was neither so common nor so ugly, and certainly not so public. His own parents, both alive, had just celebrated their golden anniversary.

'After that, she started losing weight,' Elle concluded, and turned back to her plate.

After a moment Christopher halted, a question in his eyes. 'So the controversy that you mentioned at her sorority . . . that was this terrible divorce?'

Elle shook her head. 'No, that was about the picture. See, Brooke started on this grazing diet, and she went to the gym constantly. Her own mother called her a dumpy failure! Can you imagine?'

'Grazing? Elle, I'm surprised at you. You make Brooke sound like some kind of a cow.'

'No, the grazing diet. That's just what it's called. It got really popular in L.A., but nobody I knew had heard of it before Brooke published it. The idea is to graze; to nibble now and then, but not really eat. I think it was six meals a day; tiny ones, like airplane-sized.'

She glanced down at her own meal and wondered if California Cafe had trained its cook at the USC Theta house.

'Brooke lived in the sorority house at the time, and she

143

insisted that the Theta house cook use baby food to prepare all the baked goods, and nonfat yogurt for anything with a cream base. She had this whole regimen planned out. She ate barley with skim milk every morning. She had tofu-potato mash twice a day, before her afternoon and evening aerobics. For a treat, she had strained-prune-and-carob brownies.'

Christopher's steak looked more attractive to Elle when she considered the third-world alternatives fashioned by Brooke.

'So the controversy was over the house cook?'

'No, that went over really well. All of the Thetas lost a lot of weight. The controversy was over the Model Wall.'

'I can hardly keep track of Brooke's troubles as it is,' the lawyer said. 'What's this about a Model Wall?'

'See, a lot of Thetas have been models. Not as many as the Delta Gammas, though.'

'You were a Delta Gamma?'

Elle looked down at the table. 'Right.' With all this talk about the Thetas, she didn't feel so proud of it now. 'Anyway,' she continued, 'it's sort of a tradition to have a wall with all the sorority sisters' best modeling shots. Keeps up the house image that they have the most beautiful girls on campus.'

'You added to the Model Wall, no doubt?' Christopher said.

'Sure,' Elle said, not eager to emphasize the similarity of her sorority house to Brooke's. She was sorry she had mentioned the Delta Gamma house at all.

'The Thetas have a pretty good wall, I've got to admit. Anyway, Brooke insisted on putting this picture of herself on the wall from before she lost any weight, and Doo-Dee, the Theta president, said no way. I guess Brooke kept putting pictures up, and they kept disappearing. It caused a major conflict within the sisterhood.'

'Doo-Dee?' Christopher shook his head slowly. 'Are you kidding?'

'Dookie Dean, but she doesn't go by Doo-Dee anymore,' Elle said. Christopher was grinning.

'It's not important,' Elle said. 'What matters is that Brooke finally moved out, and I think she even deactivated. She had lost enough weight by then to get a job teaching aerobics at Mega-Muscle. That's where I met her. She taught this head-banger aerobics class, with trash-metal music. The sit-ups were twice as fast as in any other class. It was one long hour!

'She was all the rage with her aerobics class. She started sponsoring competitions, and whoever did the most sit-ups got a little half T-shirt or a free tattoo on her stomach. She published her grazing diet and it went into a second printing almost immediately. Then she went membership-only with a wellness center–restaurant she set up.'

Elle tried to signal the waiter for some lemon wedges, but he refused to make eye contact.

'Anyway, at the wellness center she planned all of the menus for the restaurant. It started to become a really trendy place to go. She expanded it to include a huge multiplex fitness center featuring her famous aerobics classes. All kinds of people worked out and ate there, from the trendy L.A. crowd to older people with health problems. That's how she met Heyworth. He went there under doctor's orders for her cardiac-rehab class and the food.'

Christopher laughed and moved closer to the table.

'Eventually she sold forty-nine percent of the wellness center to some investors from Texas, and it has since become a chain. I hear it's a hot stock, and she still has the

145

controlling interest. So she did tell you the truth. She put herself through school using student loans at first, and then with the money from the wellness center.'

'I wonder why she didn't tell me that,' Christopher said, swirling a cut of his potato in a generous golden pool of butter.

'Please,' Elle frowned, 'she's gorgeous now. Why would she tell you she used to look like the Blueberry Girl in *Charlie and the Chocolate Factory*?'

'Talk to her, Elle,' Christopher said hurriedly. 'She'll tell you things she wouldn't tell me. You've already made her a more likable witness, much less like someone who would marry or kill for money, since she already had her own.'

Elle raised her water glass in a toast. 'I've got a job, I take it?'

Christopher smiled. 'You'll do well, my friend. I didn't realize I had made you an offer.'

'Well?' Elle paused, her glass hanging uncertainly in the air.

'You've got a job,' he agreed, reaching for his own glass and raising to hers. 'Sealed with a toast.'

Elle's heart leaped. '*Magnifique.*' She smiled. 'You won't regret it.' She felt impulsively like making a pitch for Warner, but decided not to push her luck. Either way, she was a winner. If he got the job, she'd finally get some time with him. If he didn't, she thought impishly, who would be the 'serious' lawyer then?

Christopher leaned back in his chair, folding his hands and squinting thoughtfully. 'I'd like you to meet Brooke soon. She's moving up to San Francisco to be closer to my office, and to get away from L.A., from the memories.'

'And the rumors,' Elle added.

The lawyer nodded. 'Keep up on those rumors, Elle.

146

Rest assured I'll be mining your brain constantly between now and the trial date.'

Elle gazed gratefully at Christopher Miles. She had never heard herself and her brain mentioned together in a sentence without a punch line.

Chapter Thirty

EUGENIA CALLED WHEN SHE RETURNED early from her visit home and promised Elle she had significant news that she must relay in person. Though Elle was impatient to tell Eugenia more about Christopher Miles on the phone, she accepted her friend's congratulations and agreed to meet her on Stanford's main campus with Underdog in tow.

She hung up the phone, threw on one of Warner's old sweatshirts, and put Underdog's collar on, all the while wondering what the news could be.

Underdog ran to meet Eugenia. Elle didn't recognize her friend at first. She was wearing a ribbed white mock turtleneck sweater of a beautiful cashmere. The contrast made her blue-black bob resplendent. Her nose was chapped with a fading ski tan.

'Warholesque!' Eugenia said, and winked.

Elle gripped Eugenia in an excited hug. 'You look gorgeous,' she said. 'Very Liv Tyler.' Eugenia blushed happily. Though Elle would rather she had highlighted her ash-blonde hair, she had to admit that against Eugenia's flawless ivory complexion and her blue eyes, her newly black hair was stunning. Elle had thought many times about bringing Eugenia under the masterful painting hand of Che-Che at Savoir-Vivre, but she knew Eugenia labored under the debt of heavy student loans and avoided putting her friend in an uncomfortable position. She had found a good colorist, wherever she had gone.

'You look gorgeous!' Elle repeated. 'Did you get it done while you were home?'

'I did!'

'What gave you the nerve to do it?'

'I went to Vermont knowing that I was going to break up with Kenneth, and I wanted to look my best.'

Elle grinned at her steely friend with admiration. 'Better to drop the ax than to suffer it, I guess.'

'He wanted us to get married,' Eugenia said with disgust.

'Eugenia!' Elle felt the melancholy that usually afflicted her with any mention of someone else's marriage. 'Why don't you want to marry him? He was your college sweetheart!'

'Elle,' Eugenia chided, amused with her friend's sensitive naïveté, 'we went to Yale, remember? Nobody has a college sweetheart at Yale. People don't even date. They just go out drinking in groups and sleep together at night because it's freezing cold.'

'Gross.' Elle wrinkled her nose, finding a new reason for distaste with the Ivy League.

'He told me I broke his heart,' Eugenia said with pride, 'and I told him it was never mine to break.'

'Saucy,' Elle said. 'I thought you missed him.'

'No, but MCI sure will.' Eugenia shrugged. 'I guess now he's neither friend nor family. No more long-distance love for me. I can't believe I spent so much time on the phone with him in the first place. All he talked about was college and our college friends. He's boring, Elle.'

'We'll have to get you out on the scene,' Elle began, but she halted with the quick recollection that she had no social life in Palo Alto. 'If you don't mind the trip to L.A.,' she said.

'That's the other thing I need to tell you,' Eugenia said. She was smiling. 'Come here.' She motioned to the bench of a picnic table and sat down across from Elle, gathering Underdog in her arms. 'My favorite laptop,' she said, stroking the dog's ears.

'Underdog missed you!'

'Remember the writer I told you about? The one that I met at the Slack and White Ball? The one who kept calling me?'

'Coerte,' Elle said, intentionally drawing his name out in an affected manner. 'It would be hard to forget, since you haven't stopped talking about him since.'

'Changed names aside, he seems really cool. I've talked to him a lot, and now that I'm Kenneth-free, I'm going out with him tonight.'

'That's great! Where are you guys going? A poetry reading or something?'

'No, you're gonna like the name of the restaurant he picked. The Elite Cafe. Maybe he's more for you!'

'Well, I can't wait to meet him, but I'm going to be pretty booked up with this internship. I was going to ask you about Nexis, that on-line thing.' Elle looked embarrassed.

Eugenia arched a surprised eyebrow.

'Really,' Elle continued, 'I want to read all of the articles about the case. I don't want to miss a word. I'm going to help Brooke Vandermark.'

'We can go over to the law library and I'll show you now,' Eugenia offered, but her tone was hesitant and insincere.

'Not on your life,' Elle said. 'Here.' She patted the picnic bench. 'Put out your hand.'

Wondering what her hand had to do with Nexis, Eugenia removed her hand from Underdog's head and placed it on the table with an open palm.

'Flip it over,' Elle directed, fishing in her overstuffed bag. 'There, Cotton Candy. I jumped the gun a bit on summer nail polish, but it'll flatter your skin tone. And pastels are all the rage this season.'

'No way!' Eugenia drew her hand back to the appreciative Underdog. 'The only pastel I'll wear will be the horrible bridesmaid dress you pick out when you marry Warner.'

'Then you'll be wearing red-black for a while. I've got a bottle of Urban Decay Gash at my condo. Fashion is rich with alternatives.'

'If you're as much help to Brooke as you are to me, she'll skate,' Eugenia said. 'Look, today I'm newly single and about to be manicured, with a gorgeous dinner companion for tonight. Not bad for a struggling law student.'

'Struggling? I wouldn't have made it through exams if it weren't for you, forgetful,' Elle said. 'Let's hit the Woods Salon.'

'The Woods Salon. It's got a nice ring,' Eugenia said.

'*Sarah's* got the nice ring!' Elle said quickly, clipping Underdog's leash onto his collar.

Eugenia paused, folding her arms across her chest and gazing at the academic village that housed such diverse dreams. Warner was so pitifully ordinary. 'If I were you' – she looked past Elle as she spoke – 'nothing in the world could make me trade places with Sarah Knottingham.'

Elle followed Eugenia's stare to the buildings around the empty park where they stood. 'Eugenia, a month ago I would have given anything to be just like Sarah.'

'And now?'

Elle sat back down on the bench and dropped her chin into her hands without speaking. After a moment, she lifted her head and tapped her fingernails briskly on the wooden table. She drew a deep breath. 'Now I've finished exams, and I studied my heart out, and when I took my first breath clear of that dungeon, I felt like I had passed. I've got an internship that's worth more to me than a week in Aspen with Serena. Now I've got somebody with her fortune and her freedom in the balance and an opportunity to help her. And I'm working for a respected lawyer who listens to what I think, and spends a whole dinner keeping his hands to himself.' Elle halted, surprised by her own words. 'I've got a lot ahead of me,' she said.

Eugenia nodded her head quietly, then broke into a grin. 'I've just got a date ahead of me and I'm pretty excited.'

'You'll have to tell me every detail tomorrow,' Elle said. 'I've forgotten what a date is like. I'll be at home, picking out my outfit for tomorrow's meeting with Christopher Miles.'

Nervous and excited to see Christopher Miles again, Elle was the first to arrive the next morning. When Warner took the seat next to her, Elle blushed nervously, her heart pounding with excitement.

'Warner!' she said. 'I'm so glad to see you.' She gave him what he used to call her 'megawatt' smile, glad she had chosen to wear her red cashmere twinset. *Marie Claire* was right, red was a 'confidence color.'

Sarah was Brooks Brothered from head to toe in a navy knee-length skirt-and-jacket ensemble worn with an ivory-colored high-necked silk blouse and sensible navy heels. Padding like a dog behind Warner, she entered the room, pulled a chair close to him, and linked her arm into his with a nod in Elle's direction.

'Sarah,' Elle said curtly.

Cari Zellwether entered next wearing a black wool double-breasted blazer with huge square shoulder pads over a severe knee-length dress. Her short straight hair was parted at the side and pulled tightly back at the nape of her neck with a plain rubber band. After a brusque general hello, she sat and opened a huge black briefcase from which she pulled out a casebook. Placing it in her lap, she began scanning the highlighted pages with a busy air.

Elle shifted uncomfortably. The February issue of *Harper's Bazaar* had a retrospective on Bergdorf Goodman ball gowns through the ages. To keep up appearances, Elle left the magazine in her bag, removing a pink legal pad instead. She clicked her heel against the tiny chair leg, feigning inattention to the chummy conversation between Sarah and Warner.

Until Christopher Miles arrived, the couple noisily compared class schedules, Cari scribbled notes in her casebook, and Elle counted the lines on her legal pad with a vacant stare.

The lawyer swept across the tiny interview room, offering apologies for keeping them waiting and shaking hands with the four students in turn.

'You've all been notified that there are no more interviews,' Christopher said, 'so relax. You've made it.' Elle traced a design on her paper to avoid staring at Warner, whose hand Sarah was clasping excitedly.

The lawyer continued with enthusiasm. 'Out of the forty or so applicants I interviewed, I've chosen the four of you to work with me on this case. None of you have gotten your first semester grades back, so you might be wondering why you were selected. We're in confidence, so permit me to tell you exactly why.'

Christopher surveyed the room. 'Cari, your particular interest is criminal law, and I see that you've worked in some clinics. This will be good experience for you if Brooke is brought up on murder charges, which I think will happen soon.

'Sarah, I went to law school with your father. If you've got half of his work ethic, you could try this case yourself.

'Warner, your father and I go all the way back to prep

school. And I didn't want to get accused of working with only beautiful women!'

Warner and Christopher snickered together, Cari scowled, and Sarah smiled sweetly, glad to be called 'beautiful.'

'And Elle . . .'

Everyone, including Elle, looked curiously at Christopher Miles. She wondered if he'd mention their dinner, which she knew Sarah and Cari, at least, would regard with suspicion. To her relief, he spoke in innocent generalities.

'You said something to me in your interview that reminded me of an axiom by Oliver Wendell Holmes . . . one that I have always considered to be the bedrock of my criminal defense practice. Justice Holmes said, wisely, "To look at the law you must look at it as a bad man."'

Cari cleared her throat so Christopher would add 'or woman,' but the lawyer didn't notice her protest. 'Do you recall what you said about my client, Elle?'

'She didn't do it,' Elle said nervously. 'I told you that.'

Christopher nodded. 'You said you felt sorry for Brooke and you asked me if she was a blonde.'

Sarah rolled her eyes and Cari looked angrily at Christopher Miles, who she thought was flirting with Elle.

'She is.' Elle smiled. 'I knew she was. I could tell. Any twenty-three-year-old married to a seventy-four-year-old with a heart condition is a blonde, I guarantee it.'

Christopher Miles grinned broadly.

'Elle, I have a feeling you will be able to identify with my client. Maybe you will understand her . . . predicament. I'd like you to sit in on the next deposition in the case so you can meet Brooke yourself. It's next week.'

The lawyer pulled a file from his soft-sided camel-colored leather briefcase.

'I have some research questions that I'd like the rest of you to get started on,' Christopher said, laying several papers in a thin pile on the table. 'We're on a tight schedule, so don't waste a minute. Elle, call my secretary, Mia, on Monday for the deposition schedule.'

Chapter Thirty-One

IF IT WEREN'T FOR that interview, Elle thought, gazing exhausted at the clock on the classroom wall, there is no way I'd be sitting here at this hour of the morning. What a waste of my only elective.

Maybe it was his eyes, or maybe his tone, which shifted from gentle to firm without being intimidating. Probably the eyes, Elle laughed to herself. The eyes have it. She trusted Christopher Miles and believed him that she could help on Brooke's case.

She thought she understood Brooke and Chutney. At the very least, she knew where they came from. Chutney was far from the only girl in Los Angeles with a stepmother younger than she was. Elle was familiar with the way these people lived, and Christopher, at least, seemed to take her perspective seriously. She laughed at the irony: it was the first time she had considered that Sarah's narrow, field-hockey world put her at a disadvantage. Elle could tap the Los Angeles rumor mills with a phone call. She could find out the name of Brooke's gardener, every ingredient of her grazing diet, every step of her aerobics regime. Could Sarah do that?

Elle watched glumly as Professor Gilbreath walked from the board up the stairs to the back of the classroom. Her hopes were momentarily raised, thinking that he might be leaving.

The gaunt professor pulled the door closed with more

force than appeared natural for his frame. Turning to the class, he began his first-day intimidation routine.

'This door shuts promptly at nine. If it opens again before nine-fifty, it will be because I open it. Not you. No late arrivals; no excuses. If any of your friends are considering adding into this class, please pass the word along to them.'

Elle doubted anybody who was not already present would decide on a whim to take a class about dead people at nine o'clock in the morning. Especially with Professor Gilbreath, the Grim Reaper of black humor. Elle would need her afternoons free for the internship, so she was stuck waking up to 'Death with Gilbreath.'

Satisfied that the door was secure, the scarecrow walked back to the podium. 'Welcome.' Indicating the door, he explained, 'I don't like my monologue to be interrupted.'

Who does he think he is, Jay Leno? Elle wondered.

'This class is about two things,' Gilbreath began. 'Death, number one. Death.' He paused, surveying the room's quiet audience. 'Number two is money. This class is about death and money.'

Professor Gilbreath smiled. A brave laugh erupted somewhere behind Elle, which she guessed was probably Michael's. He would surely tell his diabolical sweetheart Cari to sign up for Death with Gilbreath. Elle suspected this class was going to turn into a bad replay of *The Munsters*.

'First, let's talk about money.'

Elle did not join the excited laughs of a scattering of would-be ambulance chasers. The humor of greed was pretty well worn, considering that every class, from the spills and bills of Torts to the kills and bills of Criminal Law, could boast the same theme.

'There are three ways to make money,' continued

Professor Pallbearer. 'You can earn it, inherit it, or marry it. I've done all three. If you're a wills lawyer, you can earn it whenever other people inherit it.'

Better off marrying it, Elle mused wistfully.

'A wills lawyer sees people at their ugliest. The cases you will read in this class all concern the two things that awaken abhorrent qualities lying buried within the human spirit. Those two things, class, are . . .'

'Death and money,' several students answered promptly.

'Very good. Now' – the professor smiled – 'we can talk about death. This class will be your easiest class, because it is based entirely on a single rule.'

Furious keyboard pecking subsided as students prepared to capture the Rule.

'Dead people can't own money.'

Elle remembered Warner's grandmother and wished that she could take her whole infernal fortune to her grave.

Professor Gilbreath stepped back from the podium. 'That rule is the heart and soul of the law of wills. Dead people can't own money.' The room was silent as he gathered papers casually and turned to leave. 'That's all I have for today.'

The blunt professor walked to the door. 'Any questions?'

Nobody dared.

'Very good. See you tomorrow at nine, then.'

Elle glanced at the wall clock, which read 9:11. She had prejudged Gilbreath. This could turn out to be her favorite class.

Elle decided to make a rare morning appearance in both Wills and Property this morning in case Christopher asked her about law school on the way to Los Angeles.

She was uncomfortable at having skipped Property class all week, concerned that a property-law issue might be important in the buzzards' fight to dish out the Vandermark estate. When she got to Property class, she seated herself in the safest back corner of the room.

All four feet eleven of Whitman Hightower, Barrister, disappeared behind the podium. 'He should have stayed at Oxford,' Elle muttered. In his first lecture, Hightower had directed the class to refer to him as Barrister, his proper title as a counselor admitted to the King's Court of Exchequer.

'I think they still wear powdered wigs over there,' Eugenia whispered. 'Maybe if he wore one here we'd be able to see him.'

At least Hightower was aware of the language barrier that separated baffled students from the vocabulary of centuries-old English property law. He would often dart to the chalkboard midsentence to scribble peculiar words that formed, he insisted, the 'law's living lexicography.' By the end of class, the board looked like a Christmas tree decorated by children on only the low branches, an exotic language scrawled in the space within Hightower's reach.

Elle felt her head spinning as she copied down the phrase *Quicquid plantatur solo, solo cedit.*

Wizened Barrister Hightower popped suddenly from the podium and tapped his chalk on the board. 'Whatsoever is affixed to the soil, belongs to the soil. An estimable maxim. Why, my apprentices, does this not end our dispute?' Elle rolled her eyes. They had been through this last week.

Larry Hesterton and Gramm Hallman were already battling with Drew for primacy with Hightower, the only professor at Stanford caught in their medieval time warp. Today Gramm edged Larry out.

'Both the fox and the land, Barrister Hightower, are wild.'

'The land, Counselor? Wild?'

'More accurately, Barrister, the land is public. As we discussed last week, the vested rights of the landowner are inapplicable to this case. At any rate, the fox being wild, it is not affixed to the soil.'

'Born free,' mumbled Elle, wondering what she would learn about marital property from the law of fox hunting. She was right to have skipped this class last week to get her hair highlighted. One scrawny fox was nothing to go to court about. When class ended, Elle gathered her belongings and headed for Christopher's office with nervous anticipation.

Chapter Thirty-Two

THANK GOD FOR THE Tight Skirt Button in her Range Rover, Elle thought, surveying her reflection in the elevator door. This button adjusted the driver's seat to minimize skirt wrinkles, especially important during the warmer linen-wearing months.

The Vandermark case was becoming more complex every day. Witnesses and details were coming out of the woodwork. Elle felt a slight shiver, excited to be a part of it. Her parents had never pushed her toward one career or another, but the cardinal sin of the Woods family was to be 'boring.' Elle considered this case to be definitely cutting-edge.

The elevator door opened to the sheer moneyed luster of Miles & Slocum. The floors of the enormous grand entrance were marble of the smoothest silver-gray; the furniture was modern and beautifully crafted, and its scale was perfect. The room was bathed in light, which streamed in through an entire wall of huge vaulted windows that gave a fabulous view of the bay.

'I'm Elle Woods. I have an appointment with Christopher Miles,' she said to the prim-looking receptionist.

'Elle Woods.' The librarian-like receptionist repeated Elle's name with disdain as she looked Elle up and down through eyeglasses perched at the end of her long nose. 'I saw your name on Mr. Miles's appointment calendar. Is this a *personal* appointment?'

'No, no,' Elle protested a bit too quickly. 'I'm working on the Vandermark case. I'm one of the interns from Stanford.'

The secretary looked dubiously at Elle and asked her to take a seat in the waiting room while she rang through to Mia, Christopher's secretary.

Elle gazed out a vaulted window overlooking the water and remembered the spread on Miles & Slocum in *Architectural Digest*. 'Best-looking firm in the country,' Christopher had said in reference to it. Looking around, Elle didn't doubt it.

Christopher's secretary joined Elle moments later, greeting her with cheerleader enthusiasm.

'Sorry to have kept you waiting,' Mia said. 'Martha' – she glanced toward the receptionist – 'is a bit of a mother hen when it comes to Christopher.'

On the way to Christopher's office, Mia conducted a brief tour, dashing with Elle through halls decorated with stunning contemporary art.

The interns' office was a stark contrast to the rest of the office. It was barren, with the exception of a Keith Haring print, four standard black desk chairs, and two heavy wooden desks, one of which was covered with documents. Elle glanced uneasily at the surroundings.

'Don't worry, that's Sarah Knottingham's pile.' Mia seemed to have read her mind. 'She's coming back in later for document review. Her secretary is on vacation, so I've had to walk her through her schedule.'

Elle tried to maintain a poker face as she noticed a bottle of Advil on Sarah's desk, thinking of the throbbing headaches that Sarah had caused her.

'You're to wait for Mr. Miles in his office. He called from the car. He'll be here shortly. He's expecting you.'

Mia led Elle into a sitting room adjoining Christopher's

corner office. Elle wondered if she would get her own secretary like Sarah. She sat in a low armchair with a curving black back and leafed through a Rothko art book, the only book on an exquisite coffee table. When she heard Christopher approaching, she pulled out her Wills book and opened it to a page in the middle.

'Have important calls forwarded to my car. I'm running late for the deposition,' Christopher Miles barked at Mia as he swept into the office. Elle stood up to greet the lawyer, who was busy packing thick files into an accordion litigation bag.

'Elle.' He looked up, startled. 'You were so quiet I didn't even know you were here. We have to leave now, so gather whatever you need and let's go.'

Elle quickly shoved her Wills book inside her suede Cartier briefcase, a present from her parents, who thought that if she was going to be a lawyer she should look the part.

'I'm glad you're going to sit in on this deposition,' he said, locking his briefcase. 'I just wish it weren't at Henry Kohn's Los Angeles office. This is the third deposition he's taken in L.A. I think he does it just to annoy me, since his main office is only five blocks from here. I'll be glad when I'm deposing the witnesses and I can do it right here.' He surveyed the office as if completing a mental checklist. 'Right. Come on, Elle, we're running late.'

Elle caught a glimpse of Cari looking up suspiciously from behind a paper mountain as she and Christopher flashed through the hall. Elle waited until they stepped into the elevator to mention the other interns.

'Cari seems to have a lot of documents to read,' Elle said.

Christopher smiled. 'I have Cari researching a venue issue. She was probably reading cases. As for you, Elle, I want to make sure you meet all of the witnesses. With your background, I think you'll have the best handle on the facts.'

'I thought I went to law school to learn the law.'

'You might be right, but cases are won and lost on the facts.'

The elevator opened to the parking garage. Christopher opened the passenger door of his racing green Jaguar convertible and Elle slid into the low leather seat. She noticed that he was thoughtful enough to put up the top before he started the car. She felt the car lurch forward as Christopher sped out of the garage.

Christopher weaved from lane to lane, speeding toward the freeway. 'I'm worried we'll miss the flight,' he said, narrowly missing a car in the next lane as he forged ahead of it.

'Not with you driving,' Elle said. Christopher was tracing figure eights through traffic. 'If Chutney's lawyer likes to hold all of his depositions in L.A., why isn't the whole trial being held in L.A. anyway?'

'Because the old man's broker, and most of his assets including the Vandermark Vineyards, are in Northern California. They could have offered the will for probate anywhere in California, so Chutney filed suit in San Francisco. Under advice of counsel I'm sure.'

'Why, is the judge better up here for her or something?'

'No, better for her lawyer. Henry Kohn, Chutney's lawyer, has a branch office in Century City, but his main office is in San Francisco. I'm sure he gave the kid sound legal advice to keep the proceedings convenient to his corner office at Kohn & Siglery. He'll bill her for all of his flights and time to and from L.A. anyway.'

'Sleazy!'

'Welcome to private practice, Elle. And speaking of

private,' Christopher added quietly, 'let me tell you about our witness, while we're still in confidence.'

He sighed at the thought of the scheduled witness. 'The good news first: it should be brief. The witness despises Brooke, and what's worse, he speaks flamboyantly, tends to use the word "murder" a lot, on the record. He was Brooke's interior designer, until he quit. He says she's got "murderous" taste. According to him, she "murdered" the sitting room, "ravaged" the library, and "had intent to kill" the foyer. You name the room and he'll say she killed it. As it stands, the guy's a perfect plaintiff's witness. Trenton Davis, the name gives me nightmares.'

'Trent? *Not* Trent Davis. He is an absolute doll! I've known Trent since I was a little girl,' Elle said. 'My mother owns an art gallery, so she works with a lot of designers. Trent is her absolute favorite designer and mine too! Our only regret is that we don't get to see enough of him. He's not only the best designer around, he's absolutely charming! Clients are always jetting him off . . . Paris, Hong Kong . . . you name a cosmopolitan city and he's a designer and a dinner party guest in demand.'

Christopher leaned over to turn up the volume of the car stereo, as if he were unable to stand hearing any more. Elle just spoke louder.

'You're just lucky you're not deposing one of the new breed of designers who insist on being called "interior dramatists." They usually carry small dogs with them, which they use like Kleenex, crying into their fur that something is *missing* or *lacking*.'

'I can't believe you *know* Trenton Davis!' Christopher shook his head as if he felt sorry for Elle.

'Know him? He is a perfect gem! He redid our house in Bel Air after the earthquake, and I thought at the time that I might be interested in becoming a designer, so he took me everywhere with him to let me get a real view of the business. I remember this one completely wild woman . . . oh, what's her name . . .' Elle frowned briefly. 'Anyway, she had him on an absolute yesterday deadline to move all of her furniture out and stage the scene with theme furniture because she was giving this party. Trent, caterers, florists, artists, party and art consultants . . . you name it. Everyone was working day and night. She was having a theme party – Tequila Sunrise – so she wanted the wallpaper stripped so she could have the walls of the house painted like a sunrise. What's worse, the woman had a terrible sense of direction and insisted that the sun rose in the west. So for her party at least, it did.'

Christopher stopped his chatterbox passenger. 'Art consultants?'

Perplexed, Elle wrinkled her nose at the lawyer. 'Of *course* she had art consultants! What a weird question to ask. Anyway, this lady told everyone working on the house to bring their swimsuits. She *insisted*. She liked to swim, but hated to swim alone. So at exactly noon, she had everyone from Trent to the painters suit up and splash around with her for an hour.'

'And I thought lawyers worked hard for their money.'

'Well, on this case you certainly have,' Elle said.

'Trenton Davis is going to make me work a little harder, Elle. He may have adjusted to his other clients' idiosyncrasies, but not to Brooke's. Right now he is an ideal plaintiff's witness.'

'Chutney is the plaintiff, right?' Elle wanted to make sure.

'Well, she's attacking the will in probate, and we're arguing that the legacy to Brooke stands. Wills procedure is a little different, since the interested parties are not strictly adversarial. I've thought of her as the plaintiff out of habit.'

Christopher glanced at Elle. 'You keep me on my toes, Miss Woods.'

He looked back at the road and his smile disappeared. 'I don't know if being on my toes is going to be enough for this case,' he admitted. 'It was high-risk to begin with, but plaintiff's witnesses just keep coming out of the woodwork, Elle. Her entire household staff, her personal shopper, her personal trainer, even her shrink.'

'Her psychiatrist,' Elle gasped. 'How horrible! What about doctor-patient confidentiality?'

'The court can subpoena those records,' Christopher said grimly. He pulled into the valet parking lot, worriedly checking his watch. 'Grab one of these files, Elle, would you?'

Elle hopped out of the car with the case file and dashed after Christopher, making a mental note never to trust a psychiatrist, much less a personal shopper.

Chapter Thirty-Three

A WAITING CAR AND DRIVER used surface streets to whisk Elle and Christopher to the law office in record time, but Trent, arriving from Laguna Niguel, called from his car phone to complain that he was 'stuck on the 405 parking lot.' Even after he arrived, Henry Kohn was tied up in a conference for another twenty minutes. So as it turned out, their driver had risked the wrath of the California Highway Patrol for nothing.

Kohn & Siglery was no Miles & Slocum, Elle thought. Although the soaring modern architecture of the building was impressive, once on the inside it was horrendous.

Elle overheard Trent talking to the receptionist from the waiting room, where she was sitting in an itchy Louis XIV chair covered in zebra skin. 'I'll let your attorney know that you're waiting for him,' she said, pointing the cherub-faced designer around the corner.

Short, pudgy Trent had gained another few pounds, Elle noticed. She stood up to greet him.

'Elle Woods!' Trent was surprised to see her. His eyes crinkled at the corners as he grinned widely. 'Are you in trouble, you little devil? Or maybe here to sign a prenup?' he asked, kissing both of Elle's cheeks, a lock of nearly white blond hair brushing his forehead.

Elle jumped up, happy to see him and anxious to get out of the itchy throne. 'No, Trent, I'm actually here with the lawyers, not to see one,' she said, and laughed.

'Coco Chanel would turn in her grave! Your mother told me about law school, but I simply cannot believe my eyes.' He covered his lively blue eyes and peeked through his fingers like he was watching a horror movie and was too afraid to look at the full screen. 'You, with all of your creativity, my darling . . . a lawyer?'

'Well, not yet. I lucked into helping a lawyer,' Elle admitted humbly, indicating Christopher, who introduced himself as Brooke Vandermark's attorney. 'I heard about the murder' – Christopher cleared his throat audibly – 'uh, the alleged murder,' she corrected herself, 'over Christmas. Mr. Miles is kind enough to give us law students a little real-world experience through an internship.'

'And you're still doing pinks.' He eyed Elle's light pink Escada suit, noticing the details, the white collar and cuffs and chunky gold buttons. 'Thank heavens you still find fashion exciting.' Trent breathed a long sigh of relief. As always, he was as interested in what Elle was wearing as in what she was saying.

Elle smiled and glanced down at the narrow Manolo slingbacks, which were already killing her feet. She motioned to the black leather Roche Bobois couch, which wouldn't make her itch. 'Let's sit down and get caught up. Are you working in Laguna now?' She loved Trent's stories.

Trent gave the couch a disapproving once-over and perched himself on the edge as if he didn't want the offending object to contaminate his aesthetic sensibilities. 'Elle.' He threw his arms skyward like a televangelist and then brought them down, hiding his face in his plump hands. 'My stars! This home is an atrocity. And what she wanted me to do . . . it was even worse.' Trent rolled his eyes. 'I say it should be a *crime*!'

'What did she want, Trent?'

'This woman, I kid you not, was in love with this notion of bubble-gum pink tile over black grout. Not just in the bathroom, which would have been bad enough. She led me around the house wearing a purple turban like she was something out of *The Arabian Nights* and told me that she wanted this bubble-gum explosion to cover the entire house and the garage! She wanted me to *murder* this house. Elle, I would never have decorated in this town again!'

Christopher cringed visibly at Trent's use of the m word.

'So you turned her down?' Elle said.

'Absolutely. I told her she had such vision, that she was so fabulously talented, that I would only serve to hinder her creative process.'

'Trent, how do you make a living if you only design when it suits you?'

'Elle, I have my standards. With the exception of Brooke Vandermark's monstrosity, I'd have to say it was the worst idea I'd ever heard.'

'Be nice,' Elle chastised. 'Was Brooke's place so awful? I thought it was written up.'

'It was. Her house was written up under the "Enough Already" column in *L.A. Whispers*. As she kept adding more square feet, it became a preposterous joke. The house was approaching the size of Candy Spelling's, and the only thing bigger than the Spelling house is Brooke Vandermark's ego. I *never* should have taken the job, even the walk-through. I was the sixth designer. All of the others had quit or been fired. The woman's impossible.'

'Well, at least she didn't make you go swimming,' Elle said.

'True.' Trent cringed at the memory. 'But Brooke's house was swimming in black lacquer. I could have drowned! The walls . . . I had to get rid of those *murderous* black lacquer walls. They nearly *killed* me! She said they were from

170

her "reflective phase." Some little Shinto book from one of her support groups had struck her fancy so, she insisted on turning the place into *Shogun*! She butchered what could have been a lovely foyer with gargoyles and vases and horrendous bonsai trees. Oh, Elle, it's indescribable.'

Henry Kohn and Chutney entered the waiting room. Elle glanced at Chutney's tight black dress with gold lettering around her waist, which read, 'Waist of Money.' She looked more confident than her lawyer, who in his rumpled, stained suit looked as if he had been pulling a lot of all-nighters.

'You shouldn't talk to lawyers about the case until I'm present,' Henry Kohn cautioned Trent, exchanging a weary handshake with Christopher.

Chutney glared at the entire group, her arms crossed.

Trent shrugged his shoulder. 'My little doll, Elle Woods, has brightened up an otherwise tiresome event,' he said. Elle introduced herself to Henry Kohn and, feeling as if she had been chastised, told the lawyer that she had known Trent since childhood.

'We were just catching up,' she said, blushing faintly.

'Of course,' Henry said, with a second glance at Christopher that suggested he was not convinced. Elle followed the lawyers into a conference room as Trent, heading for the bathroom, promised to join them after he 'freshened up.'

Brooke Vandermark was sitting at a conference table long enough to span several zip codes. Across the table sat a stenographer. Christopher turned to Henry Kohn with obvious displeasure.

'Your receptionist did not tell me that my client had already arrived,' he said, indicating Brooke.

Henry Kohn ignored the comment. 'Perhaps Mrs. Vandermark would like another cup of coffee,' Henry replied, nodding at the white, lipstick-smudged mug in front of Brooke on the table. 'By all means, help yourself.'

On another long table across the room were a tall silver coffee service, several mugs and glasses, a row of canned sodas, and a bucket of ice.

Christopher approached Brooke with a concerned, almost fatherly air. She stood up to greet him, and Elle saw him grip Brooke's arm firmly at the elbow when he shook her hand.

Brooke's head reached no higher than Christopher's shoulder when she stood next to him, Elle noticed with surprise. She had expected Brooke to be taller. She had always seemed so controlling at the head of aerobics class. Now she didn't appear a head taller than a parking meter.

The neutral of Brooke's sleeveless linen Empire dress melded almost imperceptibly into her straw-colored hair. Elle recognized the dress, which she had considered ordering from J. Crew in a color other than this year's 'grain' or 'almond,' shades fit only for the suntanned. A turquoise patent leather backpack that lay slouched by her chair and matching patent sandals provided the only shimmer of color until Elle caught Brooke's curious stare. Her eyes, which mirrored Elle's own, were a keen, inquisitive aqua blue.

'Brooke, I would have offered to have my driver pick you up, but I was running late. Almost missed the plane,' Christopher said.

'I'm glad to hear you have a driver, Christopher. I've driven with you before and I think I was safer in jail,' Brooke said. She gave Christopher a quiet smile, but when she sat back down, she was anything but relaxed. Her posture was rocket straight, her back not touching the chair back, her hands fidgeting nervously in her lap.

Christopher smiled. 'Mea culpa. Brooke, this is my assistant, Elle Woods. She's a student at Stanford Law School.'

Brooke nodded at Elle without standing.

Elle blushed, clearing her throat. 'Hello, Brooke. I'm very pleased to see you. I went to USC.' Elle glanced at Chutney's grumpy lawyer, who stood at his seat arranging a notepad next to a manila folder and a foam coffee cup. This was the wrong time for small talk. Christopher had introduced her as his assistant, and there she went talking about college right off the bat, as if this were a punch bowl at a college reunion.

This is serious, Elle instructed herself. Act like it. Don't say anything. Nod and take notes. Brooke, apparently advised to do the same, hardly budged when Trent entered the room with a sulky glare. She acknowledged him, then set her gaze imperiously beyond him, a stiff pose she maintained throughout the designer's testimony.

Elle smiled at Trent and sat down silently next to Christopher, backing her chair from the table to balance the legal pad in her lap. While she waited for Henry Kohn's secretary to pour water into glasses from a heat-condensed silver pitcher, Elle began sketching Brooke's earrings. Dangling from each of Brooke's ears were small hoops in which two identical naked twins linked arms. Twins.

'Gemini,' Elle thought to herself. 'Ruled by the planet Mercury. Longs for affection and understanding.' Good thing she had taken 'Zodiac and You' for her planetary science requirement at school. When she had finished Brooke's earrings, she began sketching Pisces earrings and wondered how to distinguish them from Aquarius. It occurred to her that Aquarius was an air sign, but rather than puzzle over it any longer, she drew a bull, which was definitely a Taurus. She never considered Taurus a woman's sign, but figured she could market the earrings to men and women in Miami Beach or San Francisco.

The Libra scales reminded her of law school, and Elle began drawing earrings with a legal theme, which she felt was more appropriate given the circumstances. By the time the deposition ended, a model resembling Brooke was scribbled on Elle's legal pad, adorned with Libra-scale earrings, a necklace pendant in the shape of a gavel, and a bracelet with various casebooks for charms.

Christopher had been right; the deposition was brief, though it was hardly as damaging as he had feared. Trent did use the offending term 'murder' to describe Brooke's assault on the interior of her house, but when asked about her personally, he only said that he found her 'immature, and pitifully nouveau'; he said it almost apologetically, glancing at her Isaac Mizrahi patent leather backpack as if to prove his point.

Elle winked at Trent on the way out and promised to call him the next time she was in L.A. She followed Christopher and Brooke to the building lobby, not speaking because nobody else did. When they stepped outside into the sunlight, Brooke sighed with relief.

'You did great,' Christopher answered the question in Brooke's eyes.

'Thanks.' Brooke swallowed hard. 'I can't believe what he said about my house. You should have heard him rave about my "genius" when I proposed the idea. The mercenary! He even praised my velvet paintings, insisting that they were more than just kitsch, that such paintings were found by Marco Polo in Kashmir, where velvet was first woven by monks in the Middle Ages.'

Elle bristled, her formal allegiance to Brooke uncomfortably set against her natural affection for flamboyant, lively Trent. 'Trent did my family's house in Bel Air,' Elle said.

Brooke shot a surprised look at Elle, as if she hadn't until that moment been visible.

'You're from Bel Air?'

Elle nodded. 'I wanted to say something to you before, but I felt weird chatting at the deposition, in front of the lawyers and especially Chutney. I went to USC, Brooke, and I took your aerobics class at Mega-Muscle.'

'And lived to tell?' Brooke said, and laughed gleefully.

'Barely,' Elle said. 'It was the toughest workout.'

In the flurry of name exchanging that followed, Christopher stepped aside. He watched with approval as Elle and Brooke began to build a firm bridge toward each other on the mortar of common acquaintances, classes, enemies, and memories. Before he could suggest it, Elle had already promised to show Brooke around San Francisco, where Brooke would be moving for the duration of the trial.

They parted at the elevator, Brooke heading for her car in the garage and Elle and Christopher heading for their waiting car. Brooke folded Elle's phone number on a piece of paper, which she tucked into her tiny turquoise back-pack. 'Are you sure you don't mind my staying with you? I won't be but a day or so until I find a place, but if you don't have room or something . . .'

'Of course you can stay,' Elle said firmly. 'Underdog, my Chihuahua, will be thrilled to have some company.'

After the deposition, Elle was surprised to find the driver headed in the opposite direction from the airport.

'I hope you like sushi, Elle. You've been working so hard, I thought I'd surprise you and take you to dinner away from Palo Alto, on a school night.'

Elle was equally pleased by Christopher's recognition of her dedication to the internship.

When they pulled up to Ginza Sushi-Ko, a three-table,

twenty-two-seat restaurant located on posh Via Rodeo just above Tiffany, Elle knew that Christopher had put some thought into where to take her.

Nervous, Elle launched into a story about Everett, a particularly unappealing entertainment lawyer she had a date with just before she started college. He had worked in the Fox Building, where the deposition was taken, so Elle figured it was a timely tale. Elle told Christopher how the boasting associate mentioned at least a dozen times that the Fox Building was where *Die Hard* was filmed.

'I met him at the office in order to preserve the freedom of having my own car, since Everett had gotten mixed reviews from friends of mine whom he had wined and dined. I didn't expect a ninety-minute office tour where my date pointed out the desk Michael Jackson danced on, the Montblanc pen Harrison Ford wrote with, the chair Fabio sat in, and other unremarkable celebrity fingerprints. The only area he didn't point out was the cubicle that served as his office. "What do you think of the office?" he asked at dinner. I told him the office was lovely, but he should apply for a job as a tour guide at Universal Studios.'

Christopher laughed at the story. 'You've got some tall tales, Elle Woods!'

Chapter Thirty-Four

WHEN HER ALARM CLOCK JINGLED at 6:30, Elle felt as if she had just fallen asleep. The one thing she could say for property law was that it made great bedtime reading. Fretful and anxious the night before, Elle had only to glance at the phrase 'livery of seisin' before she was out like a light.

Elle had plunged headlong into the sea of current events after Eugenia showed her how to search newspaper articles on LexisNexis. Her desk was a dumping ground for littered white papers with VANDERMARK highlighted in bold type. In an expanding 'court corner' of her bedroom, piles of dog-eared textbooks and outlines on the will probate procedure were strewn. Whether Brooke won or lost, Elle was dead set on stealing Sarah's professional turf in the process. She attacked these courtroom manuals night after night, hoping to gain a home-field advantage.

As she got out of bed, she gazed at the court corner listlessly. Some way to spend Valentine's Day.

It was the first Valentine's Day that Elle had not looked forward to. Stanford Law School distributed first-semester grades on February 14, a practice known as the Valentine's Day Massacre. To make matters worse, Sarah would be spending the evening with Warner, and Elle hadn't even lined up a date.

'Oh, Underdog,' Elle yawned, looking at her beloved pet whom the dog groomer had decorated with a red-and-white heart-trimmed bow. 'Today's the horrible day.' She slipped on her running shoes to take Underdog for a walk.

A short time later Elle dragged herself to class, wishing that she were somewhere . . . anywhere else. She lingered in the parking lot, gathering resolve in the safety of her Range Rover to enter the halls of Stanford Law. She checked her ruby lipstick in the vanity mirror and adjusted the red bow with white hearts that she had tied in her hair to match Underdog. At least she didn't look as if Valentine's Day filled her with dread. The giant red heart on her snug white T-shirt even made her smile.

'Got to keep up appearances,' she said to herself, straightening her red velvet miniskirt as she walked inside. The halls were buzzing with students engaged in the socially ungracious activity of comparing grades. Heading for the student lounge, where law students met to gossip and caffeinate, Elle narrowly missed being blindsided by Aaron.

'I cannot believe it!' Aaron was springing up and down spastically, waving a piece of paper in the air. He blocked Elle's entrance to the lounge, thrusting the paper, his report card, in front of her face.

'Three point one four! Do you have any idea what this means?'

Elle didn't know and didn't care. 'Excuse me, Aaron. I'd like to get a cup of coffee.' Elle was looking for Eugenia, a coffee addict and permanent solitary fixture who read in the law lounge.

'My GPA is pi! It's an absolute mathematical phenomenon!'

'Congratulations, Aaron.' Elle glanced around, seeing no pie or any other dessert offered for Valentine's Day.

'I just can't wait until Sidney finds out that I achieved pi! He will be so jealous. This gives new meaning to the Valentine's Day Massacre!'

Elle gave up on finding Eugenia in the lounge and headed to her mailbox instead.

Two bouquets of flowers had been delivered to the registrar's office in Elle's name. A note in her mailbox, stuffed amid a stack of cards, read: 'Come to the Registrar! You have flowers!'

Elle beamed, and hurried to the front office. Just maybe, she hoped. At least flowers would soften the blow, since her report card was lurking at the same office.

One bright bouquet was from Trent with a card saying it was nice to see her; the other, strangely, was from Austin, the 'darling' plastic surgeon she had dated only once. Yellow roses. 'You will find nothing yellow about me except my roses,' read the card. 'Signature Texas. Fondly, Austin.' He probably used the same cheesy line every year.

'What was I thinking?' Elle chastised herself. 'Like Warner would send me flowers here. Or at all.'

She stuck the report card unopened into her heart-shaped bag and leafed through her cards. Dr. Dan had sent an enormous red heart inscribed with the phrase 'Your heart is my business.' He probably had them left over from before the board yanked his license to practice.

Wearily, she glanced inside a card featuring the crew of the starship *Enterprise*, the same one Sidney sent every year. 'Our enterprise awaits,' wrote the Trekkie. 'I sent your *reel* present to your home. Love, Sidney.'

'Our enterprise? Vile.' Elle shivered at the thought of what Sidney could have sent her. Probably a *Star Trek* home video for them to watch together.

A 'secret admirer' card in Eugenia's handwriting promised to stalk and assassinate all professors at Stanford Law to win Elle's love. Elle giggled.

Next, she peeled open a pink envelope that contained her last card. 'Have a great Valentine's Day, alone! Sarah.'

'Lovely of her to think of me,' Elle sniped.

Expecting to find Claire and Sarah in the hallway by the registrar's office rejoicing over their grades, Elle turned quickly in the opposite direction and headed for the phone booth. She figured that she could check her messages. Even though she had left her condo less than an hour ago, she wanted to stay occupied until it was time for class to begin. Long enough to avoid the Grade Question from any uppity law student who might dare to ask her.

To her dismay, Elle found herself walking directly behind the twosome, but when she noticed Sarah was wiping her eyes and sniffling, Elle paused with curiosity.

What could Sarah possibly have to cry about? I'm the one without a date on Valentine's Day. She leaned against the wall, partially obscured by a plant, and began fishing through her purse as if looking for something. She wanted to hear Sarah.

'*Nobody* gets kicked out of Stanford. You know that, Sarah,' Claire said in the exasperated tone of one whose consoling advice was falling on deaf ears.

Sarah squeezed her report card in one hand and clutched several crumpled Kleenex in the other. Elle gasped.

'Her grades!' A rush of excitement consumed Elle. Sarah was crying over her grades. She strained her ears to hear more information with the singular concentration of an animal bent on its prey. If Sarah had failed her classes, and if Elle had managed to squeak by, then Elle would have Warner all to herself. It was as if a genie had appeared from a magic lamp and granted her most impassioned wish. Sarah could be gone in a poof of Stanford's harsh air. Peeking at Sarah, who was blubbering in woe, it seemed too good to be true.

Claire escorted Sarah down the bloodred carpet that had been rolled through the hallway, a devilish tradition that signified the blood of the grade massacre more than the ardent flame of Valentine's Day. To Elle it was the red of revolution, of victory. Finally, she thought with satisfaction, imagining herself and Warner next semester, linking arms in the very halls she had found such a torture alone. Finally they would be together.

She padded after Sarah and Claire on her tiptoes, craning to overhear every word. With Claire's next comment, Elle's hopes were dashed into confusion.

'You should be thrilled with your own grades, Sarah! I'm sure you're at the top of our class,' Claire gushed. 'I don't know anybody whose grades are as high as yours. Be happy for yourself, at least. Warner will find his way.'

Claire paused, and then said with hesitation, 'Warner can't be good at everything, Sarah. Maybe law school just isn't his thing.'

Sarah shook her head cheerlessly.

'What if it's just a rumor that Stanford doesn't kick anyone out? Warner's barely coping with the shock of his grades now, but if he had to go back to Newport under a cloud like that, the black sheep . . .' Sarah choked, 'I don't know what would happen to him. To be honest, I don't know what would happen to us.' Tears began to pour down Sarah's blotchy cheeks.

Elle's heart plunged. This was no wish from a genie lamp. It was the worst possible turn of events. It was *Warner* who was in danger of failing out, and if Elle stayed in school, he would be as far out of reach as ever. Farther. He would be gone, and she'd be left with Sarah reveling at the top of the class. Suddenly her mind jumped to the unopened report card in her red patent leather bag. Maybe she had done no better.

She withdrew the envelope with tentative curiosity, but changing her mind, returned it unopened into her purse. There was no reason to inflict bad news on herself so early in the day. Warner might be a failed law student, but it wouldn't console him to marry another.

'Your father will still hire him, won't he, Sarah?'

Sarah shrugged. 'I don't know. He's not so sure about him. Nobody is, after he dated that mannequin for three years. This won't help anything. I mean, it's not like Warner's ruined,' she said, but she spoke in a hollow voice, as if to convince herself of something she didn't believe.

'He'll recover,' Sarah said, folding her arms in a cool, conclusive gesture. 'I'd really have to lean on Daddy to hire him, but even if he works somewhere else, that won't rule out his running for office. He could spin it differently, like he dropped out because law school didn't serve his ideals,' she said, her eyes darting as if searching for a new plan. Then she stopped walking and turned Claire by her arm to face her.

'The problem is, I can't tell him that now, Claire, and he's pressuring me for reassurance from Daddy. Warner's totally devastated. I'm just going to try to avoid the subject entirely. Nobody likes to be reminded of failure.' Sarah spat the last word with venom, and Elle guessed she didn't like to be reminded of it either.

'He didn't even come to class today,' Sarah babbled. 'As if it'll do him any good to skip classes now. He ought to be here. I think he's acting irresponsibly.'

'Definitely,' Claire agreed. 'He shouldn't be thinking of himself. I mean, your career looks splendid, but he is going to marry you and he ought to be thinking about how to provide for you aside from his trust fund. It's not just his failure now, it's both of yours. He should take a lesson from you and get serious about school.'

Sarah scowled, but the mention of her own impressive grades seemed to mollify her. She adjusted her backpack on her shoulders and idled there in the hallway, not walking toward her classroom, but not heading home to console Warner either: just waiting, indecisive.

'I've got obligations to Warner too, I guess. Part of me says I should be with him, but I don't want to give him the idea he can just lean on me when we get married. I'll be fully supportive of him, but I *won't* carry him!'

Sarah whined and threw her hands up in frustration. 'I don't know how to handle this, Claire. I didn't plan on propping up Warner, but I don't think he'd think me much of a partner if I sat in class like nothing happened when he's miserable, sitting at home. I should be with him now. That's what he would want his wife to do. That Barbie doll is just waiting for her chance,' she added, her eyes narrowing. 'I won't let Warner have the chance to turn to her.'

Elle thought of Sarah's reference to her, plotting, waiting to move in on Warner, and smiled with the recognition that she still had the ability to threaten their relationship. Sarah didn't know her, either. She was waiting for her chance, all right, but she knew Warner well enough to let him lick his wounds in solitude.

Elle remembered when USC lost the College World Series, when Warner had been thrown out at the plate. He wanted to be left alone then. If his grades were as bad as they sounded, he'd feel like a loser and would rather be alone.

'Well, don't miss your classes,' Claire said. 'That won't help him, and it can only hurt you. I say we go to my apartment after school and bake him some chocolate chip cookies! You know the way to a man's heart is through his stomach,' Claire said, and then gave Sarah the biggest, most insincere smile Elle thought she'd ever seen.

183

Elle called home to check her messages, of which there were none. She didn't notice in the relative safety of the phone booth that Sarah had parted ways with Claire. She stood alone in the hallway, gazing at the wall.

Impulsively, Elle called out Sarah's name.

The puffy-eyed girl turned with surprise to face her. Elle noticed Sarah staring at her cheerful holiday outfit, cringing to see Elle's curves emphasized under the enormous red heart, which decorated her clingy stretch T-shirt. Elle's red velvet micromini blared the words LOVE, PEACE, and HARMONY, which reminded Elle, when she was dressing, of Warner.

Elle gave a mischievous grin and walked toward Sarah. Her white tights descended to a flash of red patent leather loafers that matched her showy purse.

'Thanks for the Valentine,' Elle said, looking at Sarah's outfit, red wide-wale cords, white turtleneck with tiny red hearts around the neck, and the ever present wool cardigan, which today was red.

Elle's intense blue stare pierced Sarah, who bowed her head toward her tasseled loafers, shuffling her feet on the linoleum floor. Her shoulders drooped; she looked beaten. Elle smiled.

'I'm sorry, Elle,' Sarah said peering at her. She spoke in a muffled voice. 'I acted like a child. I feel so stupid.'

Elle squinted, skeptical of the convenient apology from her otherwise hateful adversary. Sarah sniffled and turned her eyes back to the floor.

'Don't worry about it,' Elle said. 'Anyway, what makes you think I'm spending my Valentine's Day alone?' Elle laughed then, her eyes sparkling, her dimples young and soft, looking more the mischievous imp than the notorious femme fatale.

'You know what I meant by that,' Sarah said, with an

almost imperceptible smile. She checked the time on her sensible Seiko.

'Elle, we have ten minutes before class, can I talk to you?'

Elle accepted the invitation with a dubious shrug, wondering where Claire was lurking. She followed Sarah to a vacant room.

'We'll have some privacy here,' Sarah said, holding the door to their Property classroom open for Elle to enter. 'Nobody spends a minute more in Property than they have to.'

Elle stared at Sarah's fingers playing nervously with her headband while she marshaled her thoughts. She braced herself for a mean-spirited speech, imagining Sarah warning her not to interfere if Warner and Sarah left for Rhode Island sooner than expected.

Adjusting her headband for the umpteenth time, Sarah finally cleared her throat to speak. Elle stretched her long legs on an adjoining chair with nonchalance, her gaze passing over Sarah with the impassive air of a shrink who's heard it all.

'Look' – Sarah choked back a sob – 'I know I have no right to ask you this, but I need your help. Elle, I don't mean this condescendingly, so please, don't take it wrong.'

Elle arched her eyebrows, but didn't respond.

'I see you in class . . . when you go to class, you hardly bother to show up. I see you reading those magazines or filing your nails, and you don't seem to give it any thought. But your grades,' Sarah said with a tired slouch, 'are probably better than Warner's.'

Elle thought of her unopened report card, but didn't say a thing.

'Well, it's not about me anymore, Sarah,' Elle said coolly, her eyes on the Rock that adorned Sarah's clenched hand.

'No, Elle, you're right. It's about me. I haven't told Warner, but my grades are excellent. I'll be at the top of our class.'

'You must be very proud.'

'Elle, Warner's grades will put him at the bottom of the barrel if he's even allowed to stay here, they're so bad,' Sarah whined. 'I'm afraid it will be hard for him to live with my success. But Warner's different, isn't he? He says he admires my serious attitude toward school, my dedication.'

Elle cringed.

'I tell myself he'll love me even more when he finds out about my grades.' Sarah halted, resting her head in her hands. 'I don't know, Elle,' she spoke toward the floor.

Elle wondered if Sarah was setting up to interrogate her about whether *Cosmo* might have an answer. But Sarah turned her eyes to Elle imploringly.

'You know Warner, Elle,' she said. 'You dated him. You know what he's like, and he always tells me how you know what he likes.' She halted, blushing that she had admitted that Warner talked about Elle. 'Will he be happy for my success, even if he fails at the same thing?'

With a heavy sigh, Elle decided to tell Sarah the truth. 'Warner does admire your dedication, Sarah. He values your seriousness, you're right about that. And more than anything, he admires your background,' she added, flashing Sarah an icy glare. 'But Warner loves competition. He's not "different" like you hope he is. He despises losing. He'd be happy for you if he had done well himself. Then, you'd be a prosperous, shining couple, the envy of your set. That hasn't happened.'

'So what does that mean?'

'Warner wants accompaniment from a woman,' Elle said, raising her chin with a haughty gesture. 'He doesn't want to be graced by your success.'

Sarah stared at the floor and didn't respond.

'Warner won't love you because you did better than he did,' Elle said. 'He won't love you because you've succeeded.' She paused, then added quietly, 'Sarah, if he does love you, he'll love you in spite of that.'

Sarah smiled, but her solace was a momentary light, obscured in the next moment by the reality of the unpleasant task that lay ahead. 'What should I say to him then, Elle?' Sarah said. 'What would *you* do?'

Elle sat up in her chair. 'You want to know how to make him love you more?'

Sarah nodded sheepishly.

'You can't.'

Sarah sat motionless, but Elle felt her rival had grown skeptical. Elle knew that what she had said about Warner was true. She sat forward, leaning her elbows on the desk, and explained.

'Sarah, don't you see that Warner loves himself as much as he has room to love anything? He won't love you one bit more for your achievement. It didn't do anything for him.'

Sarah took off her wool cardigan, placing it on the chair back.

'You want Warner's love? I'll tell you how to get it. Make him believe you think the sun waits to rise until he gets up,' Elle said matter-of-factly. 'Unqualified admiration. That's what keeps Warner going.'

She turned a steely glance to Sarah, whose eyes avoided her. Sarah adjusted her headband, and neither of them said another word.

The dense quiet was broken by the swing of the door behind them. The Trekkie Tribe of Five charged into the room, armed with PowerBooks. Sarah stared down at the desk and began aligning her Hi-Liters. Elle examined her

187

fingernails for chips. It appeared to nobody that they had been speaking.

Property class flew by as Elle's mind whirled through the strange events that had just occurred. Sarah, making an overture to her for advice about Warner. She considered what she had told Sarah. In some measure, she regretted giving away any insight that might help Sarah smooth out a tension in their relationship, which, if played wrong, could have given Warner doubts about his bride-to-be. But part of her was laughing, imagining Sarah taking her advice. Sarah, humbly attending to Warner's almighty ego; Sarah, hiding her own success like a fault. For once, Elle didn't envy her.

Hightower's lecture left no more impression on Elle than an evanescent dream forgotten in the foggy morning. Sidney was still packing up his PowerBook when Elle tried to walk past him.

'Elle, did you get my present? It's reeeeeeely great,' announced Sidney, beaming proudly.

'No, Sidney, but thank you in advance,' Elle answered as she hurried away.

She went all day without checking her grades, fearing the worst. By the time she got home, her condo looked like a florist's shop. Her landlord, Mr. Hopson, had apparently used his key to let the delivery men inside. Nice of him, she thought warmly. Saved her several trips.

She cleared a place for her bag on the coffee table and fished inside nervously for her report card. 'Get up here, Underdog.' She patted the couch. 'Let's see if we have to move again.'

Elle looked at the row of Ps and breathed a tremendous sigh of relief. She jumped to the phone to call Eugenia, who she had already heard had placed first in their class.

'Genie.'

'What's the word?'

'I passed everything.'

'I knew you would! What were your grades?'

Elle paused. 'Well, they were all Ps.'

'Ps?' Eugenia was stunned.

'Yeah,' Elle admitted, laughing. 'I took all my classes pass-fail.'

'You took everything pass-fail? Are you serious? I didn't know you could do that!'

'All you have to do is ask.'

Elle congratulated Eugenia on her grades, which came as no surprise. 'You're a Eugenius, you know.'

'I made it, Underdog,' she announced happily. Reaching to the table, she read a card from Serena and Margot. 'We still love you, even if you do want to be a lawyer.'

She flipped on the television, and Robert Redford in *The Way We Were* momentarily captured her attention. 'Redford,' she said. 'Great blond of the strawberry variety. Well, I guess this is what people do who don't have a date for Valentine's Day.' Elle pulled an Afghan blanket around herself, settling in to watch the movie. In two minutes, the opening scene changed her mind.

With every image of Robert Redford, Elle buried her face further in the pillow. Redford in dress whites. Oh, God, that looked like Billy. Redford rowing crew. The image of Charles. Redford in a letter sweater. Oh, Warner, and . . . how many times had she fallen for the BMOC, how trite. Elle felt as if she were looking into the mirror of her love life, and it was the common fare of a mushy movie. She flipped off the switch and headed to the kitchen.

A dozen shell pink roses sat on the counter. She rushed to open the card, positive that these flowers, finally, came from Warner. The card read, simply, 'To remembrance of flings past.' Elle jumped, clapping her hands together with glee. Clearly it wasn't in the past, or he wouldn't have sent her the same roses as always.

Elle froze when she glimpsed a huge aesthetic atrocity sitting on her kitchen table. Placed there because it was too enormous to fit anywhere else was a basket stuffed with styrofoam, fanned by twenty wooden sticks. A cookie was attached to the top of each stick; the whole bouquet reached at least three feet into the air. Each cookie was shaped like a fish, with a pink 'girl' fish in the center. Elle pulled a note off the 'girl' cookie, which was iced with a Stanford banner, yellow hair and blue eyes.

The note was signed by Sidney, and it read, 'WAY TO REEL IN FIRST SEMESTER.'

Elle didn't know whether to laugh or cry. She crumbled a fish cookie and fed it to Underdog.

She knew she wouldn't catch Margot or Serena at home on Valentine's, so Elle called the next morning to thank them for their flowers. Elle thought Margot would flip when she found out that she was actually working for Brooke Vandermark. She began searching for Margot's new phone number under a mountain of 'Murder in Malibu' articles printed off Lexis at law school expense.

Elle located the envelope with Margot's new number scribbled next to a note which read 'current . . . Feb. 5th.' Margot changed her phone number capriciously and often, her preferred means of distancing herself from men who grew tiresome. Now that she had Snuff, Elle figured this number would last at least a few more months, so she set the new number on memory to avoid future scavenger hunts, then dialed.

'House of Zen,' Margot sang.

Elle groaned. 'Zen again? Hey, it's the Dolly Parton Lama!'

'Elle, baby.'

Elle cringed to hear that Margot was already picking up Snuff's record industry jargon. She'd make a good wife, functioning basically as a mirror for Snuff, who, if not looking in one, was looking for one. 'Marg, baby,' Elle mimicked. 'Thanks for the roses. Even if I am in law school, it's nice to know you guys still love me.'

Margot laughed. 'We think you're kooky, but we love you just the same.'

Chapter Thirty-Five

AFTER HANGING UP WITH MARGOT, Elle decided she'd pen Serena a thank-you note for the flowers rather than listen to more thirdhand scandals associated with Snuff and the record industry. She opened her Wills textbook to the emery board that served as a bookmark, beginning where she had left off last night in her pre-nailfiling ambition to read the book cover to cover.

Studying with the fervor of a practitioner, as an advocate for a real-life blonde, Elle didn't notice just how interested she had become in at least this area of law. She was also intent on proving herself to Christopher Miles.

She even found herself getting to Wills class early, a move that didn't result in added class time. Gory Professor Gilbreath had a habit of appalling the student audience with his tactless death humor, then frightening questions out of them so he could end class prematurely, as if weary of his own voice.

The next morning Professor Gilbreath finished his lecture gruffly, snarling the rhetorical 'Any questions?' as he stomped to the door.

Expecting two packages from Christopher Miles, Elle rushed from class to her mailbox. Chutney Vandermark had been deposed by Christopher, and Christopher had sent copies of her deposition transcripts as well as the transcripts from Trent's deposition by messenger to Stanford Law School for his interns to review.

Elle assumed the transcripts would be stuck with flyers in her mailbox. She was puzzled to find a note instead, directing her to the copy center.

Elle figured out soon enough that Chutney's deposition was far lengthier than Brooke's and far too thick to fit into her law school mailbox. It ran over three hundred pages, scuttling Elle's prior plan to skim over the cumbersome deposition while sitting in her Property class. With an empty half hour thanks to Professor Gilbreath's early break, she headed for the law lounge to read what Chutney had had to say to the lawyers. Within the first few pages of Chutney's deposition, it was obvious to Elle the girl was ready for a knock-down-drag-out fight for her father's fortune.

In the short recess between Wills and Property classes, Eugenia entered the law lounge and recognized Elle's head bent over her reading. 'Hey, Elle,' she yelled from the line where she waited for a coffee refill. Elle looked up and smiled.

'Coming to Property class today, Princess?' Eugenia kidded, beckoning with her bag of peanut M&M's toward the hallway. 'Maybe it's changed rooms since you last showed your face.'

Elle felt a rush of anxiety, having missed days of classes to focus on a self-taught course in will probate practice, preparing for Brooke's trial. 'It's still in the same place, isn't it?' she asked, startled.

'Yeah, silly.' Eugenia smiled, shaking her head as if at a child. 'I'm just giving you a hard time.'

'Okay, only if you share your candy,' Elle joked, standing to join Eugenia in line. 'Hope you brought enough for everybody.'

'Enough for everybody I like.'

'Thanks.' Elle accepted a handful of M&M's before walking to Property class, where she and Eugenia sat together.

Elle poked her friend when she saw Sarah enter the room. 'Check out the power suit,' she giggled, indicating Sarah's severe figure approaching in her navy Brooks Brothers uniform with a paisley bow strangling her neck.

'Hey, is this dress-like-your-mother day?' Eugenia whispered.

'Certainly not my mother!' Elle laughed.

Sarah made a point of walking by Elle's seat. 'I was at Christopher Miles's office this morning,' she said. She looked quizzically at Elle. 'He's already got me doing document review,' she said with an air of self-importance.

'Have *you* had a meeting at Miles & Slocum yet?' Nosy Claire said, having just joined Sarah. They were both quite unaware that Elle had been to one deposition in L.A. and out to dinner with Christopher twice. During both dinners they had discussed the case in detail, and Elle felt she was gaining an edge on Sarah and the other interns.

Elle smiled. She told them that Trent's deposition had been a great way for her to dive right into the case, that she was convinced of Brooke's innocence, and that today 'her client' would be coming to stay with her.

By this point she had all but given up class reading and attendance, keeping abreast with Eugenia's notes and her two Secret Angels, the poet and Emanuel. She was devoting all of her time and tremendous effort to the case, which genuinely interested and challenged her.

'There's more to this case than document review,' she added.

Elle's confidence came through in her voice, and Claire

looked discouraged. Claire turned abruptly, and Sarah clomped behind her in heavy, thick heels to her seat.

Elle peered at the phrase '*Fructus perceptos villae non esse constat*,' Barrister Hightower's lexicon lesson of the day. Another worldly-wise word for the collection, Elle thought despondently, remembering torturous grade-school vocabulary books as she copied the phrase into her notes. Barrister Hightower was crouched invisibly behind the podium, preparing his lecture.

The enormous deposition could not be hidden even from wee Whitman Hightower, so Elle opened *Interview* magazine under the desk and began reading an article on Stella McCartney's latest collection.

Elle's reading was rudely interrupted when Witless Hightower called her name. She looked up, surprised, as he bounded from the chalkboard back to his notes.

'Well, Ms. Woods, we are waiting for an answer.' Hightower weaved back and forth, probably on his tiptoes, beady eyes peeking over the podium.

'I'm sorry, I'm afraid I didn't hear the question,' Elle mumbled.

Hightower persisted. 'Ms. Woods, the query posed for your comment relates, as I have said, to this maxim.' He waved impatiently at the board behind him. '*Fructus naturales*, Ms. Woods. The products of nature alone,' Hightower muttered. Sarah turned around, disappointed.

'Gathered fruits do not make a part of the farm,' interjected Drew Drexler, the irrepressible Rhodes scholar. He was translating the bizarre phrase on the board, and the professor nodded with satisfaction.

'The question, Barrister,' Drew continued, 'is whether they belong to the farmer. It is my judgment that they do.'

'Excellent, Counselor,' Hightower said.

195

Grateful to be spared further humiliation, Elle returned to reading her magazine.

Brooke's one-day planned visit turned into six days, on the last of which Elle and Eugenia skipped their classes to spend the morning with Brooke at the Museum of Modern Art. Brooke was terribly homesick for her life and friends in Malibu, especially her support group. Elle and Brooke arrived that afternoon at the office of Miles & Slocum in a wave of breathless and cheerful chatter. The intern and the client had become fast friends. From the kitchen, Elle got a diet Coke and Brooke poured herself a cup of black coffee before they made their way to Elle's tiny office.

'I still think Eugenia was right about *Tied Tubes*,' Brooke said, taking a seat. Her reference was to a sculpture in which the barrels of two handguns were twisted together. 'It was a socially critical piece about birth control. She's right, it's a tool to limit our life force. If I had seen it a year ago, maybe I would have had Heyworth's child. He wanted to, you know.' She began to cry softly.

'Well, you had his love,' Elle said gently. 'Better to have loved and lost,' she added softly. So easy to tell somebody else. It never consoled her when she thought about Warner. 'And anyway,' Elle changed the subject as much to dodge her own maudlin sentiment as to avoid upsetting Brooke, 'what about *Madonna and Twins in Jell-O*? How could you want to have children after seeing that?' The painting portrayed a mother dressed in an apron that read 'EAT JELL-O' gazing distantly at the television while stirring a bowl of green slime. A set of twins were hanging limply by fangs implanted in her bloody neck.

'I'm telling you, it had nothing to do with children,' Brooke said. 'It was an exposé on the use of animal gelatin in Jell-O products. People think it's a family food, but it gets its consistency from animal fat. Eating Jell-O is as cruel as eating veal!'

Brooke was a vegetarian. Elle doubted her critical analysis, but found herself increasingly confident that Brooke lacked the heart of a murderer.

'You're like the calorie Rain Man, Brooke. Do me a favor and leave my lunch quotient a mystery today. Please?'

'Knowledge is power,' Brooke said.

'Then tell me who was at your Shopper Stoppers meeting, Brooke, so we can prove that you didn't kill Heyworth.' Elle narrowed her eyes. 'Please, Brooke, you don't have a single alibi witness,' she said in a whisper.

Now it was Brooke who spoke gravely. 'Shut the door,' she motioned.

Elle jumped from behind her desk and pulled the door closed. How proud Christopher would be if she got the name of an alibi witness out of Brooke! Brooke trusted her, she thought; Brooke knew Elle believed she was innocent. She returned to her desk as casually as she could manage, restraining an anticipatory quiver with great effort.

'Please, Brooke, who can testify for you?'

'Elle, you don't understand,' Brooke said, her voice definite. 'I won't hurt the people who have helped me. I won't embarrass them, and I won't set their lives back. The only people who knew where I was when my husband was shot are in my support group in Los Angeles, and I won't expose them. Even if nobody will testify for me.'

Elle's heart plunged. She cursed herself for being too forceful. Brooke had been so close to telling her something.

'Elle, I have what they call an addictive personality. That's why I had the discipline to lose all that weight. I committed all of my energy to that single goal. In that direction it was useful, but when I got hooked on the

Home Shopping Network, I turned all of my commitment and energy to the power of spending. It's immediate, but it's transitory. I lost sight of the future,' she said, her eyes dimming from sharp turquoise gems to the pale, blank blue of a faded day.

Elle drooped in her chair, and for a moment neither of them spoke. Then suddenly, like a mood ring, Brooke's face lit up again.

'That was before I met the life leaders,' Brooke said. 'The group leaders at the Shopper Stoppers meetings . . . they gave my future back to me. I regained what Heyworth loved about me, and he was so happy.'

'What do you mean?'

'When Heyworth met me at the wellness center, he was trying to get in shape, and I made him my project. His whole attitude had to change. He was almost ready to die. He was so world-weary at first, and I couldn't blame him. Everyone treated him like some old patriarch with all of his achievements behind him like ghosts.'

Elle reached for her diet Coke while she listened intently.

'It wasn't his past that I cared about. His companies, equity shares, or vineyards weren't my interests. We started working out together, and he was like a child, with all of the energy that made him his millions turned toward improving his health and getting stronger. That's what I cared about. He clung to his life after that. He felt vigorous, and capable. Together, we had our eyes set on the future. On our future.'

'What does that have to do with your alibi, Brooke?' Elle said with exasperation. 'What would Heyworth want you to do?' she said. 'Just give up?'

'We understood loyalty and support, Elle. He'd want me to stand by my friends. He'd want me to do just what I'm doing, which is moving forward. I'll face this trial and I'll tell the judge and jury the truth. I won't involve anyone who I'll hurt. Come what may.'

Elle thought of Warner, and how hard she had tried to resurrect the love of their past days. Brooke was crazy. Loyalty was fleeting. Look what Warner had done to her, even if she had changed her entire life to match his like a newly fashionable tie. Sarah was his future, and what was hers? What was Brooke's?

'Your future doesn't look so bright, Brooke. You're going to have your entire life, not just your alleged involvement in the murder, put on trial, I can promise you that.'

Brooke dropped her head into her hands. 'Elle, I lost both of my parents when I dug up their business. They're like strangers to me now. Without Heyworth, the only people who care about my future' – she paused, glancing at Elle – 'besides you and Christopher, who I'm *paying*, are the Shopper Stoppers. So I won't bring them down by exposing them, even to save myself. They still have families. And they're my family.'

Brooke wouldn't budge. She clung to the last family she had. She wouldn't sacrifice her friends on the altar of self-preservation, and yet she had everything to lose.

Elle thought of Serena and Margot. They ridiculed her for taking this job, defending a Theta . . . an unpardonable crime, forgetting the primacy of her Greek letter label. Their paths were separating. But Elle also had the misgiving that she too had filled her college days with superficial judgments. Good fraternities, bad fraternities, whispers about sisters, china pattern dreams. Her old friends seemed so remote now.

Margot was a 'we,' having ceased to refer to herself in the first person since she became a charm bracelet on Snuff's arm. Serena, always the same, was a scattering of crystals, drugs, dates, and diets. They were the friends of habit and memory, to which she now clung like lint. She sensed that she had lost them, coming to law school, maybe for good, but then maybe inevitably. Either way, she was left with a sense of loss.

She had strayed from her old life and had found fulfillment where she least expected it, but she still hadn't given up on getting Warner back. Law school had not changed her in Warner's eyes, so she'd found a way to get him, with Brooke's case as a front and the Elle he had loved as the bait.

She'd see Warner after class, and she'd be holding a Property textbook in one hand and a deposition in the other, but to him she might as well be holding a dog-eared copy of *Cosmo*. So *Cosmo* it would be. Elle had a plan to work out at the gym available to Miles & Slocum employees. Positive that she'd run into Warner there, she dutifully packed her gym clothes and the latest *Cosmo* to read while she was on the StairMaster.

The rest of her class looked upon her like an alien. Barbie paraphernalia still made its cowardly, anonymous assault on her school mailbox. She found herself bored in classes, which she attended with less and less frequency. She sighed, and Brooke's obstinate expression caught her eye. It reminded her of Eugenia, and she smiled. Eugenia was as stubborn as a mule.

Eugenia was a miracle who strengthened her resolve to get through law school and, as hard as it was, helped her see Warner for what he really was. A happenstance of a seating chart. Another gift was her lovelorn Angel, sending her aid and comfort in ribbon-tied outlines. There were people who wanted to see her make it.

Elle set her jaw. Brooke believed in herself and Elle believed in Brooke. The underdog.

'Take me to a meeting,' Elle said all of a sudden. 'I won't say a word to Christopher or anyone. I want to meet your friends.'

'If you'll take me to law school. I want to see what your prison is like.'

Chapter Thirty-Six

THAT NIGHT ELLE WONDERED which would be more bizarre, Brooke at law school or a Shopper Stoppers meeting. Her mind wandered from the Rule of Perpetuities. It was impossible for anything else to be this boring, Elle thought, slamming her Property book shut. The phone rang, and figuring nobody could have anything worse to say than the words printed in her casebook, she answered the phone without even screening.

'So what's up on the job scene . . . or should I say job scheme?' Eugenia asked, always amused by Elle's romantic ploys.

'The internship is great . . . and it's actually yielding a way to see Warner!' Elle exclaimed enthusiastically. 'The firm is adjacent to a building that has a gym, and we're allowed to use it. Warner works out twice a day, so I'm sure he'll take advantage of it. My lit bag and my gym bag are dutifully packed for tomorrow, and I've been working out every day.'

'So have you seen him there yet?'

'Not yet. It's only been two weeks, and I hadn't figured out his schedule yet, but now I've got it. I'm positive I'll see him there tomorrow. We used to work out together every day,' she added in a dreamy tone.

'Well I was just calling to catch up, since I never see you anymore,' Eugenia said, but Coerte beeped in on call waiting before any good gossip could be exchanged.

Elle giggled as she hung up the phone. Elle was genuinely happy for her friend. Exhausted from her desperate, useless attempt at trying to understand her Property reading, she fell asleep immediately.

The next day, Elle got to the gym around 4:30, figuring from the schedule she saw pinned to Mia's bulletin board that Warner would arrive around 5:00.

The usual crew of secretaries and paralegals were on the StairMasters while bankers, lawyers, and other businessmen pedaled the Lifecycles that were strategically located behind the StairMasters.

Five o'clock arrived, and as Elle looked up from a compromising position on one of the machines, the unlikeliest candidate entered the gym. Sarah. 'Great, now it's *Sarah* and Warner who work out together,' she muttered; but he was nowhere to be seen.

Sarah took a nervous glance around, her pale arms clutching her *Property book*! Elle couldn't believe it. Noticing that the Lifecycles were all being used, Sarah headed for a StairMaster. Elle watched her. Clearly Sarah hadn't seen her yet.

Elle stood up, and Sarah's mouth gaped open. Elle's blonde hair was still hanging perfectly, her makeup unsmudged, and her pink leotard, cut to show maximum cleavage, was clinging to all the right places.

Elle's usual stiletto-gouging walk was now a long athletic stride. All eyes shifted to watch her athletic beauty as soon as she hit the floor. 'Sarah!' Elle exclaimed in mock surprise as she approached the StairMasters. 'I didn't know you worked out here.'

'Well, today's my first day,' Sarah admitted. She was maintaining an unsteady balance as she tried to keep up with the advanced level she had set the machine on.

StairMaster ruin stared her in the face. 'I'm not used to these things,' Sarah said as she gasped for air.

Elle reached over and lowered the level to novice. 'Maybe I can help you,' she said tentatively.

'Warner wrote out a schedule for me to follow,' she said, and indicated a piece of paper with Warner's unmistakable scrawly handwriting sticking out of her casebook. 'He said you used to do it twice a day, but I'm so exhausted from this . . . I don't know if I can do . . . step aerobics.' She glanced at the sheet dubiously.

'Step aerobics? I can't believe I ever put myself through that torture. Did Warner mention my step aerobics instructor was Brooke Vandermark?' Elle asked.

'You're kidding!' Sarah exclaimed. 'Not that she doesn't look like she could have been.' Sarah poked irregularly at the buttons until the machine stopped.

'I'm really glad Warner doesn't work out here. He's dying to use this gym, but he doesn't want Christopher to think he's a slacker. I would have died if Warner had seen me! But I'm even more embarrassed that you did, to be honest,' Sarah said.

'There's nothing to be embarrassed about. You've seen my answers in Property,' Elle joked, glancing down at Sarah's casebook. 'How about we make a trade?' Elle offered.

'Well . . . what kind of trade?'

'I'll show you how to find your way around the gym and work out with you, minus the step aerobics, if you'll help me out in Property. I'll need your notes and some tutoring weekly and your outline at the end of the semester.'

'It's a deal,' Sarah agreed, 'but only if we can start tomorrow with the gym tutoring.'

Elle laughed. 'No problem.'

The two girls showered and then headed back to Miles & Slocum for Elle's first Property session. Although Elle had passed all of her first-semester classes and was feeling increasingly confident, Property, only a second-semester course, was still a stumbling block. Sarah helped Elle with the cases that weren't covered by the commercial outlines, and Elle even withstood briefing a case for class the following day. She was determined to succeed at the entire law school game, Property included.

Chapter Thirty-Seven

ELLE REMEMBERED A TIME so distant it seemed prehistoric when the week after spring break was dedicated to the wholesome activity of comparing tan lines, piña coladas, and stories from Mexican jails.

Over the March vacation, selections for the *Stanford Law Review* had been made on the basis of first-semester grades and a writing competition that had taken place in February.

On the morning of her first day back, Elle found Eugenia by the coffee machine. Eugenia watched the excited members jump around as if they were on speed while the rejects muttered plastic congratulations. Eugenia shook her head and motioned for Elle to follow her to the dreaded law library.

On the way upstairs, it occurred to Elle that Eugenia's straight As should have earned her a spot on this *Law Review*. 'Did you make it, Genie?'

Eugenia grinned. 'Yeah, thanks but no thanks. If I wanted to be a librarian, I would have been.' She maneuvered expertly through the bookcases to a shelf of *Stanford Law Reviews*. 'Open it at random, Elle.' Eugenia picked out a recent volume. 'I think you'll agree that there are better ways to spend your time.'

'Probably few worse,' Elle laughed, cracking the heavy book open to a worn interior page. She leafed through the vacuum of time and talent.

Eugenia sighed suddenly. 'You'd think with all their

economic analyses, the inefficiency of spending twenty hours a week checking somebody else's homework would occur to one of these people. Oh, by the way, Sarah made it, but Warner didn't.'

Sensing that everyone would be so caught up in the *Law Review* excitement, Elle decided that a massage and a facial would be a better way to use the next few hours than attending class. She didn't notice that Larry had followed her out until he caught up with her in the hall.

'Elle, wait up.'

She turned around surprised. Larry stared intensely at Elle, walking next to her. She fished in her purse for her car keys, nearing the parking space where her trusty Range Rover was primed for exit.

'Elle,' Larry said as he placed a hand on his hip and watched her struggle through the clinking contents of her bag. 'You're too sexy for law school.'

'Larry, my mom's Volvo is too sexy for law school.'

Larry laughed and agreed with her, but added that it didn't make Elle any less sexy.

'Jezebel, my painted Jezebel,' Larry shifted lyrically into the Old Testament, extending one arm as if heralding Elle to a royal audience. '"See to this accursed woman, and give her burial; after all, she was a king's daughter."'

Elle glanced up from her purse, surprised. 'Jezebel? What on earth are you talking about?'

Larry leaned against the Range Rover, gazing at Elle with a dreamy, quiet calm. 'A loving theft, a pilfering, a joining of the lips. A trade of moisture, warmth and breath, in soft and tiny sips.' He paused, watching her mouth drop in astonishment.

'You're the Secret Angel!' Elle cried, recognizing the verse from her outlines.

'Every true romantic needs his Guinevere, Elle.' Larry's gaze seemed detached, his John Lennon sunglasses hiding a world only glimpsed by his eyes.

'Oh, Larry, they're so . . . unique,' she said. 'Your poems . . . you're inspired!' She paused, gazing at the English professor gone wrong. 'But why on earth are you wasting your talents in law school?'

'Elle,' he smiled, 'my talents aren't wasted.' A. Lawrence Hesterton turned back toward the house of law. 'A poet needs but one,' he said quietly.

Elle rested her weight against the car door and watched her Secret Angel depart. The unlikeliest people, she thought to herself, confounded by this flash of Larry's private mind. Now that she knew that it was someone who was with her and saw how she had struggled in all of her classes, she decided that if she was his Guinevere, he was her Palo Alto Knight.

Chapter Thirty-Eight

ELLE AWOKE THE NEXT MORNING feeling tense. She was feeling the pressure of finals approaching again even though they were still quite a long time away. Dragging herself out of bed, she wondered how she would fare this time. She took Underdog for a long walk, ultimately arriving to Professional Responsibility a half hour late.

Elle wondered why she ever bothered to take notes on the zany antics of Charley Client, given that Professor Pfisak's ethical conclusions were foregone and unassailable. She slid the April issue of *Vogue* under her desk. After reading the 'Fitness' section, she decided to tear it out for Sarah. Although Sarah was improving at the gym, she was still having trouble with crunches. Elle hoped the article on abdominal toners, with pictures, would be helpful. She genuinely wanted to see Sarah succeed at the gym.

Elle glanced up from the magazine long enough to focus on the class and ascertain that, simply put, today's ethical duty was to withhold information from paying clients. She peered into her casebook to see what rule created this Kafkaesque bureaucratic parody.

Fran volunteered to answer a hypothetical, which involved gun-wielding Charley Client racing paranoid into his lawyer's office, asking whether the state has to find a corpse within state lines in order to bring a murder charge. Indignant, Fran repeated that the lawyer's duty was to avoid at all costs giving information that would clue Charley in to his legal rights.

Also call the police and bill him for the time, no doubt, thought Elle with increasing impatience.

Finally, on Charley's third misadventure, Elle raised her hand. 'Ms. Woods,' Pfisak noticed her with surprise. 'I presume you've caught up with the class discussion, as most of it preceded your entrance.'

Elle glowered amid her classmates' smug chuckles. 'Maybe I haven't caught on,' she said. 'Because what I hear is that we're supposed to learn all this law so we can lock it up in our offices and decide *for* people what the "interest of justice" will permit them to know.'

'She must think Charley is a blond,' Claire whispered to Sarah.

'Thank you for your contribution, Ms. Woods,' Professor Pfisak said. He turned to John Matthews. 'Mr. Matthews, perhaps you can tell us how a lawyer would handle the next situation and not risk *disbarment*.'

This class would bankrupt them all if it had any relevance past the exam. Elle turned back to *Vogue* to learn something that mattered. She had a scheduled date with Brooke later that day.

Chapter Thirty-Nine

ELLE GAZED SULLENLY AROUND at the student audience of Wills and Estate Planning, cheered only by the fact that Brooke was out on bail and visiting her today after class. Another grim morning of Death with Gilbreath, then maybe she'd talk Brooke into a shopping spree, nontelevised of course.

Behind her she could hear Cari and Michael exchanging death jokes. 'Did you hear the one about the lawyer who believed in reincarnation? In his will he left everything to himself!' Michael laughed uproariously.

Dr. Dan dropped his head to the desk. 'What I don't know won't hurt me,' he declared, justifying a morning nap.

Mr. Heigh and his wife arrived carrying Thermoses of Chinese tea made from dried figs. Mr. Heigh's gray-haired chest was bared in a tank top that read: 'It took me FORTY YEARS to look this good!'

Elle pulled out *Self* just as Professor Gilbreath shut the door to begin class. While Ben ar-tic-u-lat-ed an interminable theory of 'partial will republication by holographic codicil,' Elle immersed herself in 'The Politics of Hair.' It was an interesting article, but not entirely favorable to blondes, she noted with concern.

Elle was pleased when she noticed that 'The Politics of Hair' had engrossed her throughout Gilbreath's entire lecture. She knew without checking the clock that class would be over in exactly two minutes, since Claire had begun to attack her split ends.

On the dot, exactly two minutes before the end of every class, Claire would start arranging her unruly hair just so, preparing to approach the law school hallway as if it were her great debut. Elle used Claire's hair-poking as the signal to pack up her books.

Elle strolled toward the front entrance, where Brooke stood waiting. She looked stunning in an emerald green slinky silk knit tank top and a knee-length linen skirt with a thigh-high side slit.

'So you're at large again,' Elle laughed, greeting the jail-bird with a happy embrace. 'Congratulations.'

'What a relief,' Brooke gushed. 'Christopher's so great, you should have heard him at the bail hearing!'

'Come on.' Elle linked her arm with Brooke's. 'Now you can see what *my* prison is like.' Together they walked to the law lounge.

'I'll have to warn you, the caffeine syrup they call "coffee" here might keep you up for days.'

Drawing glares from law students immersed in their casebooks, Brooke rattled briskly through the events of the last few days. 'I've been so busy, Elle, I wanted to come see you sooner. Everything's been so crazy, trying to get back to my normal life.'

'As if you ever *had* a normal life!'

'Hey, we aren't all lucky enough to go to law school,' Brooke giggled. She sipped the smoking black tar and grimaced. 'Eeew, you're right about the coffee. Swamp syrup!'

Elle agreed, adding a pack of Equal to hers.

'Let's go get a latte someplace decent,' Brooke offered. 'Can you skip out of class? I want you to see my new Mercedes.'

'Already?' Elle choked on her coffee, laughing. 'Oh, Brooke!'

'Heyworth wanted to get rid of the Jag, anyway,' Brooke justified her purchase casually. 'His British stocks weren't doing so hot, and he said we should boycott the queen's economy.'

'Respecting his wishes,' Elle said, smiling. 'What loyalty. You would have made a great Delta Gamma.'

'I was cut in prefs,' Brooke snapped back, remembering her first social trauma. 'I got a Theta bid. They didn't have a choice and neither did I, since I was a legacy. If I'd had my way, I would have been a Pi-Phi.'

'Oh.' Elle covered her face, embarrassed. 'Oops. Theta's cool, though.'

'Ancient history.' Brooke dismissed it with a manicured wave. 'Pi-Phi had the scariest rush, though, I'll never forget it. They made us eat this dessert of ice cream scooped in the middle of a doughnut. It's *impossible* to eat, because if you use a fork you can't shake hands, but if you lift it up the ice cream drools all over the place. That's how they weed 'em out. They cut the droolers and the forkers.'

Elle rolled her eyes. 'I remember that. I think I was actually a forker *and* a drooler!' She looked curiously at Brooke. 'How'd you . . . approach the doughnut?'

'Oh, I just told everyone that I was on a macrobiotic diet that didn't include dairy products. I got a plain doughnut.'

'Bonus!'

'Yeah, those were the days.' Brooke beamed at her sorority coup. 'But I've made something of myself without Pi-Phi or Delta Gamma!'

'Touché,' Elle laughed. 'So what are you going to do now?'

'What do you mean?' Brooke asked. 'After the trial?'

Elle nodded.

213

'Well, if Christopher keeps me out of jail, I'll get married again.' Brooke wrinkled her nose and squinted at Elle quizzically. 'Of course.'

'Any prospects?' said Elle, grinning.

'That's the silliest thing I ever heard.' Brooke shook her head, struck by Elle's naïveté. 'What else would I do? I'll be married by year's end, no question. Aren't you going to get married?'

Elle grew quiet. 'Not by year's end,' she admitted. 'Well, anyway,' she added, 'probably not.' Suddenly she dug into her white Kate Spade tote and produced a jewelry box, which she handed to Brooke.

'I don't want to marry you!' Brooke squealed.

'Of course not! It's a present. Open it!'

Brooke dangled a gold earring and peered at its delicate italic carving. 'One, Elle?'

'It's my jewelry line!' Elle exclaimed, clapping her hands. 'Brooke, you're going to flip when you hear this, but I met some people from the Home Shopping Network, you know, when we were investigating your alibi.'

Brooke scowled. 'Leeches.'

'Listen, listen.' Elle grabbed for the earring, nearly spilling her coffee. 'See, I was a jewelry design major in college, before' – she glanced dubiously around the lounge – 'before I gave it all up for this. Anyway, some of the Home Shopping executives met me when I had to go over some of your receipts at their offices, and they actually wanted me to audition or interview . . . whatever, to be a legal correspondent – they actually called it that. It was for a proposed show called *Fashion Crimes*!'

'So you're going to be like a fashion rehabilitator?' Brooke asked skeptically.

'Exactly! Plus, I'm going to design a whole line of legal-themed jewelry and advise people, on air, which pieces to buy! Home Shopping loves the idea and I've already gotten started.'

Elle reached for a tiny velvet box and handed it to Brooke. 'I designed one piece with you in mind. This fabulous diamond "shackle" on a gold chain bracelet. You don't have to wear it around your ankle this time,' Elle laughed.

Brooke unhooked the dainty bracelet still in the box. 'What a riot! An artist's original! Hey, Elle, I hope you sell your jewelry in stores, because you know I can't order anything off TV.' Suddenly she shot from her chair, checking her watch. 'Oh, Elle, I didn't realize how late it was. You just reminded me, I've got to get to my meeting.'

Elle grinned. 'Shopper Stoppers Anonymous?'

'Former Home Shoppers,' Brooke corrected meekly. 'Addicted.'

Elle followed Brooke to the parking lot, where the Mercedes' owner was obvious from its license plates alone: ISO SWM.

Chapter Forty

'HOP INTO MY CHARIOT!' Suddenly Brooke vaulted into the driver's seat of her sparkling gold convertible as if she were mounting a charger.

Elle giggled, opening the passenger door. Vaulting would have been impossible given the narrow dimensions of her white piqué halter dress.

Brooke looked somewhat disappointed by Elle's conventional entrance, but that didn't slow her down as she merged into the freeway traffic, heading north toward the airport.

'The color of your car really complements our hair,' Elle said, thoughtfully examining a strand of her own hair as she pulled it back into a ponytail.

Brooke nodded silently.

'I'm dying to know where these anonymous meetings are held,' Elle said.

'The meetings aren't anonymous at all, Elle. It's the members' identities that must be kept anonymous.'

'Right. Sorry,' Elle said. She realized once again how seriously Brooke took these meetings and the group members.

'Sometimes I feel like even you make fun of my addiction, Elle.'

Elle looked away from Brooke, pretending to check her makeup in the side mirror of the car. 'I'm so sorry, Brooke,' Elle said. 'I'm not making fun of your addiction. It's just hard to imagine anyone, *especially* you, with your sense of style and elegance, ordering something like porcelain commemorative dolls of the nation's first ladies.'

'Those were pretty scary,' Brooke admitted as she screeched the convertible to a halt in front of the airport Hilton.

The Hilton. Elle wondered if one of the members rented a suite under a false name.

Brooke and Elle pulled out hairbrushes to fix their windblown hair and then entered the hotel. Elle followed Brooke to a second-floor suite called the Archibald Room. The only furnishings were cheap plastic chairs placed around a long Formica table and oddly mismatched paintings and prints.

Several people, the most eclectic mix Elle had ever seen, were sitting around the table. They seemed to be at ease with one another and were conversing in a casual manner. A few others were gathered around an enormous coffee machine or had taken seats in extra chairs around the edges of the room. From their wide range of looks, they seemed to be everything from housewives, to mechanics, to doctors, to CEOs.

When Brooke and Elle entered, Brooke announced that Elle was there as a guest and not a member. This had the effect of quieting the nervous murmurs and stares of the nine or ten people present. Brooke suggested that they introduce themselves to Elle, and when nobody volunteered, Elle gave a wave of her hand generally around the smoke-filled room.

'My name is Elle Woods. I'm a friend of Brooke's from college, and I wanted to meet the people who have helped her so much,' she said with a smile.

'I'm Miranda,' said a tiny dark-haired woman. 'Welcome.'

Brooke tapped Elle's arm. 'She's the life leader,' she whispered into Elle's ear.

Miranda stood up and closed the door behind Elle. 'We're all here,' she said, returning to her seat. 'Yves, why don't you begin by introducing yourself to our guest.'

A wrinkled man sitting closest to the door, wearing a starched, collarless denim shirt, squinted through wire-rimmed glasses, then removed them from his small face. 'My name is Yves Muir,' he said.

Elle, having taken a seat next to Brooke at the other end of the table, waved from her chair. 'Hi, Yves.'

'I'm from Citrus Heights, California,' the little man continued. 'Last month I was rolling my shopping debt over on five credit cards, three in my wife's name, and she's been deceased for several years.' He nervously reached for a cigarette and lit it.

Elle heard a sympathetic murmur from several people in the room.

'Yves is our most recent member,' Miranda said. She then turned to the woman seated by the wall next to Yves who was loudly crunching her way through a bag of Cheetos. 'Veronica, why don't you introduce yourself next?'

'My name is Veronica,' said a garish woman with a lemon yellow bouffant. Her cheeks and lips were streaked with the same bloodred color, giving her white face the appearance of a checkered gingham cloth. She was dressed in a prune-colored sweater that exposed one shoulder like Jennifer Beals in *Flashdance*. Elle wondered if her penchant was for high-volume cosmetic purchases.

'I'm a florist, originally from Bentonville, Arkansas,' she said. 'That's where the original Wal-Mart store is located, you know. I always did love a bargain!' She smiled engagingly and revealed that she had ordered enough scented soaps and oils to take baths every hour for twenty years. Elle giggled, but drew a scowl from Yves and Veronica together. She straightened her face into a more appropriate look of concern.

'Nice to meet you, Veronica,' she said, and was relieved when the woman returned her smile.

Without prompting from the life leader, a scruffy-haired man in a black T-shirt who was seated at the table introduced himself. 'I'm Jeff,' he said in a deep baritone that sounded incongruous with his youthful grin. 'I play bass for the Funeral Pyre. We've got a gig tonight in the city at the Cat House. I can put you on the guest list if you want.'

Brooke laughed out loud. 'Jeff, you're out of luck. She's hopelessly in love!'

Elle blushed. 'Brooke!'

'No secrets here,' Brooke said, poking Elle in the shoulder.

The rest of the people seated around the table introduced themselves to Elle one by one. There was Walter, a CEO; Gloria, a dental hygienist; Anne, an interior designer; Carolyn, a school principal; Jean, a legal secretary; and Nicolette, whom Elle recognized as the evening anchor-woman on Channel 4.

Brooke thanked the group for allowing Elle to be there. 'You all know how hard it is to find someone to understand our addiction, and even though Elle never even watched Home Shopping before she met me, she's been my greatest support outside of the group. I wanted to bring her today so that she can fully understand the importance of these meetings and what the meetings and the members mean to me.'

Suddenly Miranda jumped up from her chair and called the meeting to order.

Elle pulled a compact out of her purse to make sure that her mascara hadn't been smudged from her watering eyes. The room was dense with cigarette smoke. At least ten people in the room had replaced one addiction with another. Satisfied with her mascara, she looked doubtfully at Miranda.

'For those of you who don't know me, I'm Miranda,' she began. 'I'm a recovering home shopper. As your life leader, I've spent a lot of time telling you how I overcame Home Shopping and what Shopper Stoppers has done for me, but today I'd like to tell you something more important.'

'Hi, Miranda. Tell us your story!' the group said warmly in a loud, unified chorus.

'I used to be lonely. Now I'm not lonely, but I know that if I do get lonely, shopping won't fill that aching void. I have to turn to you . . . my friends. That is what recovery is all about. It's about friendship, support, and *anonymity*. It's about coming to people whom I can share my worst fears and secrets with and know that they'll never, under any circumstances, be revealed. That is friendship to me, and it's why I've been Home Shopping-free for one year, two months, and three days!'

Elle looked at Brooke's tear-splotched face and knew that she would never, under any circumstances, reveal the identity of her group members in L.A.

Chapter Forty-One

'CATCHY LITTLE TUNE.' Elle noticed she had been humming 'You must pay the rent, I can't pay the rent' as she collared Underdog for his afternoon walk. 'I'll pay the rent.' She opened Underdog's dainty jaws to mouth each booming word.

'My hero!' she answered gaily, fluffing her puppy's crown of wispy fur. Underdog whined and trotted around in a circle, impatient to go out.

'Poor thing, I've been neglecting you.' Elle glared at the pile of deposition transcripts littered about the couch. 'I'll take this afternoon off, handsome, and we'll go for a walk.'

When they returned, fresh-faced from the brisk spring wind, Elle warily inspected her answering machine. She shifted Underdog where he was cradled in her arms and reached to play the tape.

'Elle.' Warner still didn't bother to introduce himself, knowing his voice would always be familiar. Elle gave Underdog a hopeful squeeze.

'I'm calling from the office.' He paused. 'From Miles & Slocum, I mean. I, uh, hoped you'd be here today. Listen, I know this is short notice, but I've had sort of a weird couple of days, and I really wanted to talk to you. Can we have dinner, maybe, tonight?'

Warner lowered his voice, speaking tenderly. 'You're still the only . . . the only person, I think, who understands . . .

what I want in my life. I've had so little time for what's important.' Elle moved her ear closer to the machine.

'Anyway,' Warner sighed after a moment of thought, 'I'm making some changes. Listen, sweetie, call me here. Sarah's not coming in today. Maybe we can meet downtown.'

Elle pounced anxiously for the phone, dropping her contented pet with a thud. 'Oh, sorry, Underdog,' she gulped, dialing rapidly. 'It's Elle Woods calling. Can you connect me with Warner, please?'

She held her breath, feeling her heart pound as she tried to restrain the excitement in her voice.

'Elle on oh-two,' Warner said in falsetto, imitating Mia. 'Just what I wanted to hear.'

'Oh, Warner,' Elle cooed despite her effort to act composed. 'It's so great to hear from you.' She hadn't seen him nearly as much as she had hoped through this internship. 'What's up?'

'Listen, Elle, I can't really talk here. I'll be downtown working on this brief for a while, and I wanted to see you. Not in the office, though. Can we meet for dinner? My treat. There's something I wanted to talk over with you. You alone.'

Elle jumped with delight, nearly dropping the phone. 'Warner, of course,' she answered breathlessly. 'Time and place.'

He paused, collecting his thoughts. 'It's been too long, Elle. Let's do this right. How about Masa's?'

'Warner, that's my favorite!'

'Perfect,' he decided. 'Seven-thirty, then. I'll reserve a table, under Huntington. Table for two.'

'Huntington,' Elle repeated dreamily. 'Table for two.'

'Right.' Warner was businesslike. 'Looking forward to it.'

'Seven-thirty,' Elle smiled, charmed. She started to ask Warner for a hint, but he had already hung up. 'Never mind,' she thought, envisioning Warner reserving a table for two: 'Huntington. Two Huntingtons.' She had been so busy she had hardly thought about Warner, but his voice brought all of her dreams crashing back. She knew from his air of mystery that this sudden dinner invitation could only mean one thing.

Her next call was to Josette.

'Eet eez always a new story,' Josette said, and laughed, graciously waving off Elle's repeated thank-yous for taking her without an appointment.

'Warner's taking me to dinner tonight!' Elle was beaming.

'I knew eet was Warner.' The manicurist smiled, one eye fluttering into a coquette's wink. 'Ees eet a special occasion?'

'You bet it is.' Elle nodded. 'Josette . . .' She paused. 'I think . . . In spite of myself, I'm hoping he'll come back to me tonight. For good.'

Josette arched her eyebrow. 'Eesn't there a woman already his fiancée?'

'I think it's over,' Elle admitted. 'He called me and said he had to see me alone. He said he's been thinking over his life, and he's making some changes. He wants to tell me about them at dinner.'

Elle's enthusiasm didn't quite convince Josette. 'Are you sure that's what he means?'

Elle nodded eagerly. 'He was totally mysterious, but he hinted at it, you know? He's reserving a Huntington table for two! That's exactly what he said,' she gushed, launching the hand Josette had finished into a victory sign of two shining fingernails. 'Two. Two Huntingtons, but not Sarah. Finally, it's Warner and Elle.'

Chapter Forty-Two

ELLE IDLED IN HER parking space, pondering the mechanics of car energy. 'If I turn it off but leave the CD player on, that drains the battery. But I'll probably be asphyxiated soon if I sit in here any longer.' She surveyed the dark interior of the parking garage and turned the engine off.

She peeked at her watch again, annoyed at its holding pattern. It had been 7:30 last time she checked, and was only 7:32 now – 7:33 if she looked down from the top of her hand at an angle, but that was cheating. Elle checked her lipstick in the vanity mirror.

'One more song,' she decided, and flipped the Styx CD to 'Babe,' a song she loved when in love. 'You know it's *you, babe*,' Elle sang blissfully, ranging far from the tune. Singing had never been her strength.

She finished her operetta and sat again in the quiet, warmly envisioning a link that defied circumstance, a reunion stronger for the separation. In her heart, she had waited for Warner, never losing faith. He was her Velveteen Rabbit, finally opening his eyes to love's constancy. She breathed deeply, dreaming of their future.

Deciding that fifteen minutes satisfied the feminine necessity of tardiness, Elle entered the low-lit restaurant. Her silver Gucci mules clicked quietly but steadily with each hasty step, an apology ready on her lips to console her waiting date. 'Huntington, table for two,' she beamed to the maître d'.

'Yes, madam,' he crooned, leading Elle to an empty table. She was oblivious of the admiring stares taking in her beauty and her silver metal-mesh dress with plunging neckline and green rhinestone straps.

'Would you care for something to drink while you wait?' He motioned to a server.

Elle sighed, downcast. She ordered mineral water, gazing uninterestedly at the menu. Warner had beaten her at the delay game, so he started with the upper hand.

'Elle!' Warner rushed to the table just as her drink arrived. She didn't stand to greet him. 'Hello, Warner,' she nodded, feigning indifference. He leaned around the table to kiss her cheek.

'I'm sorry I'm late. Traffic was heavy,' Warner said with a shrug. As if she hadn't driven in the same.

'I just sat down, don't worry.' Elle sipped her water nonchalantly. But her eyes defied her attempt at composure, shining with delight.

'You look beautiful' – he reached for her hand – 'as always.'

Elle smiled. 'Thanks.' She stirred the ice around her drink, chasing the lime about with the red plastic straw, apprehending it finally with a poke. Winning lines she had rehearsed in the car emptied from her mind as if through a sieve. 'It's been too long,' she attempted.

'Definitely,' Warner agreed, opening the menu. 'Much too long. I'm starved.'

Elle turned to her own menu and commented stupidly on the range of appetizers. She felt like cornering him, asking what this was all about. *Don't push him.*

Warner motioned to the server to bring a wine list. 'It's great to see you, Elle. It's so nice to get together again.'

'It's wonderful.' Elle smiled eagerly. Nothing had changed after all.

Elle began chatting about the Vandermark case, asking Warner politely about his research. He frowned, waving his hand to dismiss the topic. 'Elle, you never did care about that stuff.'

Elle retreated. She had spent such energy on Brooke's case, thinking that she and Warner would have that, at least, in common.

'But, Warner, I care about it now. I've become totally involved in this case.'

'You're full of surprises, Elle.' Warner laughed. 'How about this for a surprise . . . I'll have a steak tonight. And rare!' He beckoned for a waiter and ordered a red wine without consulting her.

'But you always have it rare.' Elle squinted, puzzled. '"I want something that took its last breath in the kitchen,"' she imitated Warner's old line.

'Elle, you're right,' Warner smiled. 'It has been too long. God, I haven't said that in ages. I forgot . . . I guess you wouldn't know. I hardly ever eat red meat anymore.'

'Since when?' Elle arched one eyebrow suspiciously.

Warner hid behind the menu, playing embarrassed. 'You'll laugh. . . . I've been a different man lately. Sarah says red meat is bad for my heart, you know, so when I'm with her I never eat it anymore.'

'Sarah's bad for your heart,' Elle said. She shook the ice in her glass, more angry than nervous.

'Ha-ha, you've got me there,' said Warner, winking. When he saw her disappointment, his tone dropped and he spoke seriously.

'Okay, Elle, I've let a lot of things change me. It took me a while to notice it myself. I thought I had to grow up, you know, into this new life. But I caught myself!

'See, I took a look around,' he continued, 'at what I was becoming . . . no, at what I was letting myself become.' At that Warner shook his head abruptly, and his grin returned. 'No more, though, baby: I'm a new man. A new, steak-eating man.'

'How daring,' Elle muttered, not loud enough to be heard.

The server arrived and poured wine for Warner to sample. 'I've had it before.' He motioned for the man to keep pouring. 'Anyway, Elle's the epicure. Let the lady taste it, please.'

Obligingly, the server handed a sharply fluted glass to Elle, who sipped and nodded her approval. Red, as if he didn't know she would have chicken or fish. She scanned the menu hastily for tomato-based pasta.

'I think a toast is in order,' Warner said as he hoisted his brimming glass.

'Allow me,' Elle agreed. 'To the old Warner. The old, steak-eating, USC golden boy.' With his USC golden girl, she added mentally.

'I'll drink to that.' Warner clinked Elle's glass. 'In solidarity.'

Elle smiled shyly. 'To Poland?'

'To what?' Warner set his glass on the table and squinted at Elle, not sure if he had heard her right. 'Oh, right,' he chortled, toasting anew. 'Why not? Here's to Poland.'

Elle frowned, unsatisfied.

'I mean it, Elle.' Warner spoke naturally, soft with instinctive charm. 'Since I've seen you again, through this internship, and around school . . . it's made me think about the things we used to do, when we were together.'

Elle sighed, her tender eyes anchored to Warner. 'Warner, I think about it all the time. Things were good back then. Why . . .' She trailed off, shook the crimson pool of wine like brandy in her glass, wondering why Warner had left her last spring.

'"Why" is right,' Warner agreed with a hearty nod. 'Why, just because we checked ourselves into law school, why should anything be different?'

'"Checked in,"' Elle repeated. 'That's the way to describe it. It's a madhouse, law school. A regular cuckoo's nest.'

'Elle, that's what makes you so lovable. Your charm is that you'll never change. You're a homecoming queen, even among toads. I didn't know what to think when you showed up at registration. It was so . . . unlikely.' Warner smiled, gazing at Elle's captivated face.

'Man. I couldn't bear to see you waste . . . what you've *got*' – he dropped his gaze beneath her eyes – 'at a dull place like Stanford. Law school can suck the life out of you, Elle. And you were always so full of life.'

'Warner,' Elle gushed, 'oh, I know. I *know*. I felt the same way about you. Your films! Remember how you directed documentaries? Remember Vegas?' She paused, tracing patterns on the tablecloth with her fork. 'You had such joie de vivre. Then one day' – her eyes narrowed – 'you just traded it all in.' She imagined Warner buying Sarah a toaster, and shuddered.

Warner reached for her hand. 'Elle, you've known me better than anyone. What you say about me . . .' He drew back, shaking his head with self-reproach. 'Elle, it's true. I bought into this law school routine. I put other things . . . more important things . . . on the shelf. But I'm not going to live that way anymore, and I guess I should thank you.'

Elle gasped, blushing. She waited for the words she dreamed Warner would say, wondering whether he had taken the Rock back from Sarah, or maybe gotten another ring for now. She was too excited to speak.

'Maybe that doesn't make sense.' Warner hesitated, releasing her hand. 'I'd like to think I would have come around even if you weren't in law school, but I don't know. It doesn't matter. It was you who made the difference. Seeing you just be yourself, *my* Elle from college, the calendar girl . . . taking the same exams as anyone else.' He smiled. 'Elle, you've taught me a lesson.'

'What do you mean?' she prodded, thinking he had gotten a little off track.

Warner laughed. 'I mean you haven't changed, Elle. And you shouldn't, and neither should I, just because of law school. It's a damn degree, that's all. Everything can be just the way it was before.'

'Oh, Warner,' Elle cried, 'I've wanted so much to hear you say that!'

'I know, Elle. I can't believe it took me this long.' He reached under the table, fishing for something. 'I should have realized this when I first saw you at Stanford.' Warner stood up suddenly, reaching deep into his pocket.

Elle shivered, knowing what moment was at hand. 'Warner, thank God, you're back!'

'Listen, Elle, the old Warner *is* back. What was important to me before law school is important to me again. No matter what Sarah says.' He pulled his hand from his pocket and sat back down, resting his fist, clenched, upon the table.

Elle gasped as Warner's fist opened with a flourish. She expected the Rock! Instead, two white golf tees spilled onto the tablecloth.

'I played golf in college, and I'm going to make time for it again. Law school or no law school. I don't care *what* Sarah says,' Warner stated firmly, sitting back with satisfaction.

Elle gaped in shock at the golf tees. She stared at Warner for a moment, then shot from her chair, almost upending it. 'Ladies' room,' she explained, forcing a smile. Warner

229

shrugged, and was glad to see his steak arriving. Elle managed to stifle her tears only until the bathroom door closed behind her.

Elle replayed the voice mail that directed her to the office of Kohn & Siglery in San Francisco. Chutney Vandermark was to be deposed at 10:30 that morning. It was the last deposition scheduled before the will probate proceeding.

'Sorry I can't drive over with you, Elle,' Christopher Miles said. 'Try to meet me there a little early, around ten.'

Elle looked at her watch and jumped from her seat, which was a tubular creation, more artful than cozy. She caught her knee beneath the desk and winced.

Drawing back, Elle rubbed her knee and noticed a small run in her nylons. 'Great,' she said, reaching for her purse. She didn't have time to change, and she didn't want Chutney to see her lugging binders around with a run in her hose, like a harried proletarian. She'd disgrace the Delta Gamma house.

In her emptied bag she found only Chanel's nearly black blue polish, an annoyingly trendy purchase that she never should have made, and 'Pink Alert,' which she kept in her bag to touch up her manicure. A woman should always carry clear nail polish for these blunders.

She hobbled to Mia's desk, careful not to put stress on her right leg and lengthen the run. 'Mia,' she pleaded, 'tell me you have some clear nail polish.'

Mia opened the drawer of her desk and began removing its contents. Behind the pink and green Great Lash mascara and a blue jar of Nivea moisturizing cream, Mia grabbed a nail polish and brandished it happily. 'Ultra Glaze Nail Enamel,' she said with a smile, but Elle's heart dropped when she saw the bottle's color.

'Mauve-black. That won't work,' she sighed.

'Sorry, it's all I've got.' Mia shrugged.

'That's okay,' Elle said. 'I guess I could dot it with mauve. At least I'd match.'

'I'd just leave it,' Mia advised, leaning over to assess the damage. 'You don't want a big spot there.' Elle's nylons were white, and either course was a bad one.

'I've got clear polish, Elle, if you want to borrow it.' Elle heard Sarah's voice behind her and turned around with surprise.

'It's in my office,' Sarah offered simply. She started down the hall and motioned with her hand for Elle to follow her.

She walked meekly behind Sarah into her office, where she was prepared with a bottle of nail polish in her top drawer. 'I keep it in here,' Sarah said. 'I should keep an extra pair of nylons, too, for the really bad runs.'

Elle smiled in agreement. 'Those horrible ones that rip down your leg before you know what hit you,' she laughed. 'They're the worst.' She took the nail polish from Sarah's hand and stretched her leg out across the arm rest of a chair to determine the best place to paint.

'I've had some like cartoons, I swear.' Sarah smiled. 'Like those cartoons where somebody catches a sweater by its thread and runs away and the whole thing unravels?'

Elle paused, tapping the bottle against her hand to shake it.

'I don't know why we have to wear these silly things, anyway,' she muttered, balancing on one heel while dotting her knee with Sarah's nail polish. 'I mean, the old ladies wear them to hide their varicose veins. But when you're young, what's the point?'

'Maybe because your shoes would hurt otherwise.' Sarah shrugged.

'You're right,' Elle said, glancing at Sarah. 'Which raises the question of these painful shoes.'

'I don't wear heels that narrow,' Sarah replied. 'I don't know how you can even stand in them.'

'Slave to fashion,' Elle said, noticing Sarah's steady Ferragamo pumps and considering that she might have a point. Neither spoke for a minute as Elle waited for the polish to harden.

'I've gotta run,' Elle said as she stood to leave.

'I'll say, but it's not such a bad one now.'

Elle turned around to look with surprise at Warner's serious fiancée suddenly turned punster. 'Yeah, thanks to you,' she said and grinned, then left in a rush.

'You're welcome,' Sarah said quietly.

Elle hesitated.

'Elle, will you wait a minute?' Sarah asked suddenly, gathering her papers. 'I'm on my way too. Christopher asked me to go to the deposition.'

Elle waited at the entrance to Sarah's office while Sarah grabbed a highlighted street map from her shiny briefcase. Unclipping from the map a sheet that had directions scribbled on it, Sarah frowned.

'I hope the office isn't too hard to find,' she said, hurrying toward the hall where Elle stood.

Elle glanced down at the floor. She turned and started to walk away, then turned back as if she had remembered something.

'I know where it is,' Elle said quietly, not looking at Sarah.

Sarah didn't respond.

'I'll give you a ride over.' Elle shrugged her shoulders, insecure at having made the offer. 'If you want.' Elle bit her lip and glanced uncertainly at the brunette.

Sarah turned her attention to the Brooks Brothers button on her navy blazer, which she fastened and unfastened. 'That would be nice,' she said. 'I don't really know my way around the city yet.'

Elle tossed her hair behind her shoulders and walked ahead. 'Let's go, then,' she said, waving for Sarah to follow her.

On the drive over, Elle found out that not all of the interns were attending the deposition.

'Warner's preparing witness books,' Sarah said, sensing Elle's silent question. 'It's just you and me,' she added.

'His loss,' Elle said sarcastically, turning up the stereo.

Chutney Vandermark was extremely well coached, so the deposition was an exercise in futility. She would not reply to a question without first turning for a nod or motion from her lawyer, Henry Kohn, and even then she mumbled terse replies under her breath. Several times the stenographer, who was straining to hear her, had to ask Chutney to repeat herself. She balked even when Christopher Miles asked her for background facts about her education, scowling and behaving like a spoiled child. Most of the time she sat sullenly with her arms crossed.

During one of the several breaks in which Chutney asked to 'be excused to the hallway to consult with counsel,' Christopher Miles left to check his messages. Elle sat alone in the room with Sarah.

'She seems really upset,' Sarah said, finally breaking the heavy silence. 'I can't imagine what it must have been like. She actually found his body.' Sarah quivered, dropping her gaze to the floor.

Elle studied her fingernails for a minute, then shook her head in a sharp motion. 'She's not crying.'

'No, she's not,' Sarah agreed. 'Poor thing, she seems bewildered. I bet she's just shocked, losing her father like that. She found his body! Can you imagine?'

'No,' Elle admitted, 'but still, I expected her to cry.' She paused, wrinkling her face, unsatisfied. 'So she was working out at the gym and then home taking a shower when it happened.' Elle traced on her legal pad and spoke rather absently, repeated these facts as if to herself. 'Must have happened awfully fast.'

'Yeah,' Sarah agreed. 'God, I bet he was still bleeding. Can you picture that?'

'No,' Elle said, shaking with a cold shudder. 'No, I really can't. It must have been horrible.'

Christopher Miles reentered the room and pulled his interns aside.

'We've got a transcript,' he said, glancing at the stenographer to make sure he was off the record, 'so you don't have to take everything down. Listen' – he dropped his voice to a whisper – 'take note on her demeanor. Her motions, where she pauses, that sort of thing. The transcript won't pick that up. Record anything that strikes you as odd. It'll give me an idea where to go on cross-examination. Right now,' he muttered, 'I wouldn't know where to start.'

The lawyer shook his head and returned to the table across from Chutney's seat, hunching his shoulders in a weary slouch.

Tapping heels in the hallway announced Chutney's return. Straightening, Christopher checked his watch and motioned to Henry Kohn as he stepped into the room with the solemn girl at his elbow.

'Henry.' Christopher stood up, smiling with light charisma and confidence. 'Thanks for your patience. We'll only be another fifteen minutes or so. I've got just about everything I need.'

Chapter Forty-Three

WHEN CHRISTOPHER MILES WAS ALONE with Brooke in the room set aside for witness prep, his famously calm sea of patience burst as if through a dam.

'They will crucify you with this . . . with this so-called alibi of yours,' he said angrily, slamming her deposition with his open hand.

She stared at the lawyer silently.

'Jesus, Brooke, why do you have to make this so difficult? Do you know how close you came to spending your twenty-fourth birthday making license plates?'

'Thanks for getting me out on bail,' Brooke sighed, eyes fixed on the floor. 'I hated that place.' She paused, then glanced up sorrowfully at the baffled lawyer. 'I didn't do it, Christopher, I told you,' she protested. 'Poor Heyworth was . . .' she choked, wiping her eyes. 'I found him on the floor, lying there, and blood everywhere.' Brooke hid her face in her hands, shaking, unable to continue.

'Brooke,' Christopher repeated with frustration, 'if you could just tell me who was at that meeting, I'll move for a continuance. You don't seem to understand how serious this is. You have no witnesses, Brooke. None. Nobody can corroborate what you say. You will lose everything that's yours under his will, and unless you plead to a lesser charge, your chances—'

Brooke rose from her chair, indignant. 'I *will not* plead to anything. I *did not do it*. Don't you see? I can't rat on the support group, I mean . . . we swore, you know? These people have an addiction. They were the only people who helped me get my life together. Christopher, I have an *attic* full of Norman Rockwell plates and china figurines and music boxes, synthetic rugs, juicers. . . . I spent almost one hundred thousand dollars and hours and hours of my life just to hear those gentle voices take my orders. The Home Shopping Network has turned people's lives upside down like that, and Shopper Stoppers came together for help. I can't turn on them.'

'Brooke.' The lawyer shook his head wearily. 'We've been over this ground before. They'd understand . . . Anyone would understand.'

'No.' She sat back down. 'Please, why can't I just tell the truth? Why won't anyone believe me? Heyworth was the sweetest soul. I'd never lift a finger against him. He was my husband, and nobody understands that I really loved him.' She stared past Christopher, crying softly. 'I lost my husband. I saw him dead, horribly, viciously murdered . . .' Her voice trailed off and the room was still.

'I believe you, Brooke,' he said. 'I do believe you. I was only trying to prepare you for what I know will happen if you testify. They'll string you up, Brooke. You have to understand that if you don't give more information about where you were when your husband was murdered' – he paused gravely – 'I might be the only one who believes you. And your inheritance will go to Chutney, or to one of his other wives.'

'Ex-wives,' Brooke corrected. 'But why? I don't get it. His will left everything to me. I know, he showed it to me. He cut that daughter of his right out when he changed his will. "Chutney will grow up," he said, "when she has to earn something."'

Christopher began pacing again, going over the facts in

his own mind. 'He didn't do it very well, Brooke. His will leaves his fortune to his "most beautiful wife." Not to Brooke Vandermark.'

'He called *me* that!' Brooke exclaimed. '"Hello, my most beautiful wife,"' she impersonated. 'Oh, Christopher, he just wrote it that way to be *romantic*.'

'Well, there's a regular beauty contest outside of former Mrs. Vandermarks who think they fit the bill, Brooke.' Christopher threw his hands up in despair.

'If Heyworth knew that, he would turn in his grave.' Brooke scowled.

'This case could be the end of an illustrious career,' the lawyer muttered, already imagining the headlines. He sighed with fatigue, picking up his notes to walk Brooke through her doomed testimony.

Sarah chatted nervously with Warner, glancing at the crowd of hostile ex-Mrs. Vandermarks who were primping in compact mirrors to avoid speaking to one another. 'Some first case,' she remarked.

'Yeah,' he responded. 'Looks grim.' He searched the courtroom for Elle, who had not arrived yet. 'Wonder where Elle is.'

Sarah had noticed Warner 'wondering' about Elle a lot and was not oblivious of the fact that when it wasn't Elle, he would still wonder about and wander toward other women. She felt weighted down by the Rock.

Cari shuffled papers importantly as she entered the courtroom, escorted by an especially morbid, black-suited Michael. She took her seat next to the other interns, leaving empty chairs at either end of the long table. Michael sat in the gallery amid a growing mass of Stanford law students whom the judge had allowed to sit in on the hearing. Judge Carol Morgan had closed her courtroom to the media but had permitted students to watch the proceeding for its educational value.

Mr. Heigh, characteristically sharing the experience with his wife, had arrived a full hour early to get a front seat. Mrs. Heigh had packed a lunch for them to share consisting of her famous sprout-and-pickle sandwiches, which she had reluctantly agreed to leave with the bailiff.

Fran was seated with John Matthews, complaining about the 'false consciousness' that led Heyworth's lineup of ex-wives to paint 'tribal sex indicators' on their cheeks and lips.

Sidney had snuck in a Nintendo Game Boy, making him the envy of Aaron and Doug, who sat on either side of him. They had to be satisfied to peer over Sidney's shoulder and participate as voyeurs, sitting behind him twitching their fingers on imaginary electronic buttons.

Claire and Ben sat together arranging a sign-up sheet for refreshments at the 'Welcome to *Law Review*' party.

A. Lawrence Hesterton leafed through the *New York Review of Books*, tapping his foot idly. Gramm Hallman and Drew Drexler, seated with Larry toward the back of the courtroom, were engaged in a rapid, eager discussion of the Spanish Succession and how it compared to the English War of the Roses. Neither had the least bit of interest in what the other was saying, but both were happy to corner a willing ear for their thesis-topic expertise.

Elle surveyed the ragtag crowd of spectators, trying to decide where Eugenia could tolerably sit. She found a seat close to the front.

As Eugenia left to take a seat, Henry Kohn entered the courtroom. The confident lawyer strode to his table, opened a briefcase, and began removing stacks of files. Chutney followed her lawyer and took her seat behind him. She seemed apprehensive, nervously twisting a strand of chemically enhanced hair around her finger as she glanced at her mother sitting behind her.

'Mother,' Chutney greeted stiffly.

'Please, call me Emerald. You're looking well, Chutney.'

'That's not a compliment, Mother. That's a second opinion.' Chutney turned her back on her mother, who sat near the end of the painted group.

Wittingly or unwittingly, the women had assembled chronologically in order of their marriages. Elle surveyed the troupe and decided they should be the first women to appear on *Fashion Crimes*, with charges ranging from reckless accessorizing to excessive use of cosmetic force.

Chutney's mother, now Emerald Vandermark-Klein-Tearston-Allen-Meyers, was an artful self-made social climber. If she remarried, Emerald could pull into a tie with six-wife Heyworth.

Like windup dolls gone wrong, Chutney and Emerald, equally high-strung and difficult, avoided looking at each other. Objectionable first names were not all that Emerald and Chutney had in common. Heyworth's third wife looked exactly like Chutney, though neither would admit it.

Beyond their achingly auburn mall-girl perms, both she and Chutney wore the signature ski-jump noses of Dr. Binky Blass, but on Emerald the pert nose of a teenager merely highlighted the taut, weary compression of the rest of her features. A fortune spent on surgeries fought years of wearying failed marriages for control of Emerald's tight-as-a-trampoline face, and science had failed comically.

Nor was Emerald the only ex-Vandermark guilty of compulsive surgical attempts to imprison her youth. It looked as if Heyworth's wives would rather repeatedly face the surgeon's knife than face gravity. Heyworth's first wife, now Dawn Vandermark-Kirkland-Schaffer-Price, stared fastidiously into her compact, caking whitish powder onto her nearly translucent skin. With jet-black hair, ghostlike skin, and bloodred lips, the woman was a dead ringer for Snow White's wicked stepmother.

Whitney Vandermark-Warren-Sands, Heyworth's second wife, had the sole distinction of a successful remarriage. 'Three's a charm,' Whitney sniped at Chutney's mother.

'No, dear. Bad things come in threes,' Emerald responded.

Ignoring Emerald's remark, Whitney adjusted the aggressive squared shoulders of her blazer. Her silver eye shadow was ferociously applied: when combined with the flaming magenta of her cheeks and lips, Whitney was the apparition of a maniacal clown.

Heyworth's fourth wife, Sonia Vandermark, appeared to be suffering from spandorexia. Her purple spandex cat suit left nothing to the imagination. Along with her tawdry jewelry, she had clearly overplayed her hand.

Heyworth's fifth wife, Angela Vandermark, was a drastic contrast to the spandex stunner beside her. Pointedly simple in a Talbots dress and polished Ferragamo loafers, the Atherton suburbanite suggested Heyworth's rebound marriage.

Elle took the empty seat at the end of the table directly across from Brooke, who looked pale, tired, and diminutive in the oversize courtroom chairs. Elle leafed through the pink pages of her legal pad to avoid looking at Warner.

Satisfied with the layout of his paperwork, Mr. Kohn approached the bench to speak with Christopher Miles.

Chapter Forty-Four

AFTER CONSULTING WITH THE LAWYERS, Judge Morgan pounded her gavel to call the court to order. 'In the matter of Estate of Heyworth Vandermark.' She peered at the stenographer, who nodded to indicate that he was ready.

'First, petitioner's motion to consolidate claims for relief is denied. The instant proceeding decides only the validity of the Vandermark will entered as Exhibit A. Without objection, so ordered.' The gathering of lawyers at the bench murmured but dispersed without filing any objection.

'You aren't going to object?' Chutney said loudly enough for Henry Kohn to hear. 'What am I paying you for? I could have done that for free!'

'So ordered.' The judge glared at Chutney, but did not comment on her outburst. 'I'll recess for five minutes or so to allow you' – she indicated the lawyers behind Henry Kohn – 'to explain to your clients that they are free to leave today if they'd like. If I don't admit the will to probate, we'll evaluate their claims at that stage.'

The Vandermark vultures blinked like dazzled Christmas trees, stammering, demanding explanations from their attorneys.

'A five-minute recess is ordered.' With another pound of the gavel, the judge turned to depart for her chambers. Elle crowded with the other interns around Christopher Miles to find out what had happened.

'That ruling is standard,' he explained to the students. 'In an uncontested situation, the court may consolidate petitions for relief. The lawyers for the Mrs. Vandermark pageant over there' – Elle giggled as she glanced at a petulant few arguing with their attorneys – 'made a routine motion to consolidate their claims. They wanted Judge Morgan to combine the estate administration with today's will probate proceeding.'

Sarah scribbled notes as if Christopher were planning to quiz the interns on these facts at the next recess. Cari, who had researched several issues of procedure, nodded vigorously to show that she understood. 'Today we're only concerned with the Slayer Statute, then,' Cari announced. 'Whether the will is to be enforced as written, or whether the judge will throw it out, since it leaves everything to the slayer.'

Christopher scowled and glanced over his shoulder. 'To the *alleged* slayer.'

Cari gulped. 'Didn't I say "alleged"? I meant "alleged."'

'Warner, can I have that witness list?' Warner sifted through document files on the desk while Christopher returned to his explanation of the court's ruling. 'Probate is a relatively informal proceeding. The judge has discretion to combine all matters of interpretation, appointment of a personal representative, and distribution of assets in one proceeding. She might still do it today, if they renew their motion after her decision on whether the will stands.'

Elle glanced at an uproar that was taking place between Chutney's mother and her lawyer, who were leaving the courtroom to confer out in the hallway. 'Wait, Christopher.' She waved her hand to get his attention. 'I'm not sure I get all this.' Elle tilted her head to indicate the hubbub of quarreling women.

Sarah rolled her eyes and sighed with obvious exasperation. During the internship and their tutoring sessions she had seen how quickly Elle caught on when something was explained to her. She had gained a certain respect for Elle, watching her work, but she wasn't about to show it in front of Warner. 'Elle, please, can we have the remedial class some other time?' She smiled condescendingly at Warner, who ignored her.

Frowning briefly at Sarah, Christopher turned to Elle, who, knowing exactly what Sarah was doing, ignored her completely. 'What is it you don't understand, Elle?'

'Okay,' Elle began. 'The only question for today, in the, um, probate part . . .' She hesitated, glancing at Christopher for confirmation. He nodded. 'The question is whether Brooke did it. Whether she shot him. Right? And if the judge thinks she did, then she throws out the will, and then the estate is distributed by, um, you know, by statute.'

'By intestacy,' Christopher clarified. 'Right. If the judge finds that Brooke feloniously and intentionally killed Heyworth.'

'And if the judge believes Brooke, then we have to deal with the will. Like, what it means, that he left everything to his most beautiful wife, but not exactly to Brooke by name.'

Cari tapped a Bic pen on her legal pad, impatient. 'Thanks for the recap, Elle,' she scoffed.

'No, wait, that's not my question.' Elle frowned. 'Those women, the ex-wives . . . which side are they on?'

'What do you mean, which side?'

'Well, do they get anything under the intestacy statute, even though they're divorced?'

'Chutney's mother would,' answered the lawyer, 'by law. A one-third share goes automatically to a former spouse who had children by the decedent. The rest of the wives didn't bear Heyworth any kids, so their arguments will all

243

be equitable claims, based on their contributions during marriage to the estate. Those are mushy, unlikely to win.'

'So they're on Brooke's side, then,' Elle concluded. 'I mean, sort of. They want the will to be valid.'

'Well, that's true, Elle, but if the will is valid then they're out of her corner. Then we have to deal with the words Heyworth used to bequeath his estate.' The lawyer sighed, frustrated. 'If he had just said "wife," that would mean Brooke, his wife at the time of his death. But thanks to Heyworth's fancy description, we've got a beauty pageant of spouses who say he meant to refer to them.'

Warner handed Christopher the lengthy witness list just as Judge Morgan reentered the courtroom. 'Thanks. Sarah, get those witness books in the order of names on this list, please. Right here.' He pointed to the desk. 'Cari, do you have that brief on the Slayer Statute?'

Judge Morgan's gavel called the court to order. Sidney's beeping Game Boy subsided as the room grew quiet. Elle turned anxiously to look for Eugenia, who gave her a thumbs-up from the third row.

The day looked to be a grim one for Brooke, judging from the testimony of Thom Romeo, the first witness called by Chutney's lawyer. Brooke's personal trainer, Thomas Romero, had dropped his first name, going only by his changed last name, Romeo, after his first victory as Mr. Muscle Beach. As much of Romeo's body as was visible was stained with a greasy surface tan so thick Elle wondered if he'd leave an orange ring on the seat. He had rolled up his sleeves to display his bulging forearms, and Elle marveled that the gym rat even owned a pair of long pants. Most likely he usually wore only an indecent Speedo.

Romeo described his regular house calls to the Vandermarks' basement spa, where he sculpted Brooke's body with exhausting weight tortures and had recently begun coaching Heyworth. When Henry Kohn asked him to describe Heyworth's workouts, Romeo's deep voice boomed low and ominous.

'Heyworth Vandermark told me Brooke was going to kill him. Like a stuck pig.'

It wasn't until Christopher Miles's cross-examination that the full story was revealed. Before Heyworth took up jogwalking, more to thwart his cardiologist than for his health, the old man had agreed to undergo various tests of his body's fat content.

One such morning, while Heyworth was wrenching with fat-measurement devices poking him at every angle, Brooke popped into the weight room to check on him. Groaning, Heyworth complained to Romeo that Brooke was going to kill him like a stuck pig. So Brooke's beleaguered husband had only been chafing under Romeo's fitness tortures.

Henry Kohn insisted that Brooke's physical persecution of her husband went 'to motive.' Images of a contorted, miserable Heyworth begging for mercy in the weight room cut the heart out of Christopher's argument that Brooke had encouraged exercise to prolong her husband's life. A crafty move, the lawyer had to concede, crossing Romeo off the short list of witnesses he planned to call on direct.

After Henry Kohn called the mailman, Judge Morgan drew the line. The parade of doomsayers, whose collective antipathy toward Brooke had established that she was a meddlesome terror to work for, had become tedious. Henry Kohn's repeated assurances that 'it goes to motive' were growing increasingly far-fetched.

Carmen Marisca, the heavyset cook who had worked in the Vandermark home for twelve years before Brooke fired her, testified that Brooke tried to starve her husband to death with recipes from Oprah's cookbook. Insisting that a man could not survive on dishes prepared from Gerber baby food, Carmen snuck Heyworth desserts on the sly. The ruse ended when Brooke found Moon Pies in her kitchen. She replaced Carmen with a chef from Olaf's Organic Garden.

Neither the gardener, the cat trainer, nor the florist had a kind word for Brooke. Without supporting evidence, the florist claimed Brooke had been pricing funeral bouquets just prior to Heyworth's death. On cross-examination, he admitted that she hadn't exactly *priced* the RIP arrangement, merely *eyed* it, but he could tell what was on her mind. Christopher Miles didn't even get the word 'speculation' out of his mouth before Judge Morgan sustained his objection.

The mailman wore his dress blues to emphasize that he was, in some manner, a representative of the United States of America. He described mountains of Heyworth's letters piling up untouched in the mailbox, a dilemma that forced him to brave the landscaper's trenches and deliver door-to-door. Brooke picked up her own catalogs, but left her husband's mail to rot, the mailman said, glowering, 'as if he were already dead.'

Holding that further testimony from the veterinarian who treated Chutney's Persian cat, which was in Brooke's home and care during the time she was married to Heyworth, would be 'cumulative, if even conceivably relevant,' Judge Morgan ordered a recess.

Elle encountered Warner alone in the hallway. 'Elle, how's it going?' He waved to call her over.

'Well, terrible, if you're Brooke.' She shrugged with fatigue. 'She hasn't exactly *endeared* herself to the community. And the worst is yet to come. Henry still has to call Chutney.' Elle groaned in dread of Chutney's eyewitness tale.

'Do you have a minute?' Warner motioned toward the witness room. Elle nodded, following him curiously. He shut the door behind them.

'What's up, Warner?'

'Elle, I don't know, it's been so weird to see you,' he pointed, 'all suited up like this. And asking these legal questions, these *basic* questions.'

Elle frowned. 'What do you mean, "basic"?'

He approached her more delicately. 'Elle, for God's sake. You're so creative, remember all the jewelry stuff you used to be into? I don't know . . . are you even keeping up?'

'What do you mean, Warner?' Elle retorted. Her stare was sharp, pointed. 'What about all that you said at dinner?' She recounted his words bitterly, all to Warner's quiet acknowledgment.

'Remember?' she goaded, desperate to shake any response from his terrible silence. 'Remember how you were so impressed, seeing me in law school, but not caving? Not blending into this horrible herd? "Being *yourself*"?' Elle imitated Warner's low voice. She sneered as if swallowing something acidic. 'What about that, Warner?'

'Get over yourself, Elle.' Warner ended the barrage of questions. 'That had to do with me, not you.' He glared at her, annoyed. She suddenly realized she had had the effect of raising self-doubts within him. He hadn't asked her to come to law school, to make trouble for him. Elle lost her patience with him. With the whole situation. She had more important things and people to think about.

'Take your own advice and get over *yourself*, Warner. I certainly have.' Elle turned and began walking away from him.

He grabbed her shoulder and tried what he thought was a flattering approach. 'Elle, listen, this law school thing is ridiculous for you. I mean, let's face it. Who are you trying to impress? Really, women like Sarah, *they* go to law school. They *belong* in law school. Come on, do you really see yourself as a lawyer?'

'Maybe.' She eyed Warner with suspicion. 'Why do you think I came to law school?'

'Uh, maybe on a whim?' Warner laughed at his own joke. 'Really, Elle, you came because I was here. Listen, you told me that much yourself at Halloween. Don't let your memory get so selective.'

'I got the same internship as you, Warner Huntington,' Elle spat. 'And as your precious Sarah. What makes you think I'm not as *serious*?'

Warner smiled at Elle, who grew more and more livid with his mocking tone. 'Elle, I have something to say to you.'

'Say anything you want to, Warner. You're the only one who's listening.'

With that, she turned toward the courtroom and followed Christopher inside.

Henry Kohn practically skipped into the courtroom, tasting blood already. The only remaining witnesses were Brooke and Chutney. 'Your Honor,' he began after Judge Morgan gaveled to recommence the hearing, 'May it please the court, I call Brooke Vandermark to the stand.'

Brooke swore her oath and sat glaring sullenly in Chutney's direction.

'Brooke' – Elle noticed Henry was licking his lips – 'tell the court where you were at the approximate time of day, about four in the afternoon, when your husband was murdered.'

Brooke glanced at Christopher, who pleaded desperately with his eyes. 'I was out of the house. I was at a meeting. And it's Mrs. Vandermark to you,' she snapped at the lawyer.

'Mrs. Vandermark.' Henry smiled inappropriately. 'What meeting, Mrs. Vandermark, was that?'

She tilted her head, annoyed. 'You know what meeting it was. I told you already,' Brooke hissed. Christopher Miles dropped his head into his hands, wondering why he bothered with witness prep.

Henry Kohn paced toward the bench. 'Your Honor, for the record, there was no outside communication with the witness. She refers to her deposition, I believe.'

Judge Morgan peered at Brooke. 'When did you tell Mr. Kohn about this meeting, Mrs. Vandermark?'

Brooke whirled around to face the judge. 'At that thing they dragged me to, with all the lawyers. They had someone taking notes,' she accused the stenographer, 'like him.'

'At your deposition?' the judge clarified.

'Yeah, that.'

Henry Kohn swooped back toward Brooke like a bird of prey. 'Please tell the court, Mrs. Vandermark, about this . . . meeting.'

Brooke heaved a weary sigh. 'Okay, for the hundredth time, I was at my support group.' She peeked furtively at the crowd of Stanford spectators. 'Shopper Stoppers Anonymous.'

Elle heard a yelp from the gallery that she was sure came from Sidney. Other chuckles were quickly muffled as Judge Morgan glared forward, then turned back to Brooke.

'Shopper Stoppers Anonymous,' Chutney's lawyer said, suppressing his own smile with effort. 'I take it, Mrs. Vandermark, that this group helped you with some sort of problem . . . associated with the Home Shopping Network.'

'Not a problem, a *dependency*,' Brooke corrected. 'I was addicted to the thing, okay? I was totally attached to those people, the shopper-helpers, the ones who took your orders,' she rambled, as if opening a twelve-step sob story.

'Heyworth was always so busy, and I used to order all these things, sometimes just to talk to the shopper-helpers. They have the gentlest, sweetest way about them. . . .' She trailed off dreamily.

'This addiction filled, then, an emotional void in your life? In your marriage?'

'Objection, Your Honor.' Christopher Miles rose from his chair. 'Pure speculation.'

'Sustained.' Judge Morgan scowled at Henry Kohn. 'What's the relevance of Brooke's . . . addiction, Counsel?'

'It goes to motive, Your Honor. Her commitment to the Home Shopping Network is evidence that her marriage to Heyworth was emotionally unfulfilling, and—'

'That's not true!' Brooke interrupted angrily. 'Heyworth was everything to me, and first I started watching it to buy him things. But he didn't really seem to like the Norman Rockwell plates' – she paused sadly – 'and I kept trying to watch to find something he'd like better. Then I was watching it all the time, and I even stopped going to malls.'

Several Mrs. Vandermarks gasped, horrified. Chutney's mother hid her face, toying nervously with the leather tassels of a Chanel key chain. Elle glared at Henry Kohn's self-satisfied face, feeling Brooke's frustration.

'I am not convinced you have shown a link between Mrs. Vandermark's shopping habits, Counselor, and her marriage. Objection sustained. You may ask about the meeting, but only as it relates to Mrs. Vandermark's location at the time in question.'

'Well, then. Mrs. Vandermark,' Henry continued eagerly, 'one final question about the meeting. Did you attend this . . . counseling alone?'

'No,' Brooke sighed. 'The rest of them were there, too. The other group members. About fifteen, maybe even twenty people, including the life leaders.'

'The life leaders?' Brooke had not gone into this detail in her deposition, or even in conference with Christopher, who looked increasingly gloomy. Henry Kohn bristled, sensing a surprise attack.

'Who are the life leaders, Mrs. Vandermark?'

'That's what we call the group captains. They have the same rank as the psychiatrist—' She caught herself. 'Oops, I mean, the, uh, person who runs the program. See, anyone can be a life leader who overcomes the power of their addiction, and takes charge of their life. The support group is very egalitarian. The meetings are, like, totally life-affirming. They made such a difference for me.'

Henry Kohn didn't like talk of life-affirming from the supposed murderess and directed his line of questioning to the main point. 'Mrs. Vandermark, can any of the life leaders, or any group member, corroborate the fact that you were in attendance on the day in question?' Henry asked the rhetorical question slowly, savoring every word.

'They could,' Brooke began angrily, 'and they *would* be here for me, I know it. We're so committed to helping each other. But, see' – she shrugged – 'the thing is, I can't tell you who they are. It's anonymous, an anonymous group. We all promised to protect that.'

'So I take it that you, Mrs. Vandermark, are the only person who will testify that you attended this . . . anonymous meeting? Although you claim there were ten, maybe twenty people in attendance? Is that correct, Mrs. Vandermark?'

Christopher slumped in his chair, not even bothering to object.

'Well, yeah,' Brooke admitted. 'I mean, I'm stuck. I have my loyalty to the group, and I won't turn on them.'

'Answer the question, please, Mrs. Vandermark,' directed Judge Morgan.

'He's right,' Brooke said, and sighed. 'I mean, yes. I'm the only one who will tell you that I was gone from the house, at my meeting.' Christopher made a cutting motion against his neck, but Brooke continued, exasperated. 'So you got me. There's not a soul here who will back me up. Okay?' she glared at Henry Kohn, standing up in a huff.

'Mrs. Vandermark, you haven't been excused.' Judge Morgan motioned with her hand for Brooke to remain seated. 'Are there any further questions, Mr. Kohn?'

'Just one, Your Honor.' Henry Kohn turned to the witness. 'Would you please tell the court what your license plate reads, Mrs. Vandermark?'

'Objection, irrelevant.' Christopher Miles stood by reflex, staring puzzled at opposing counsel.

'Lay a foundation, Mr. Kohn.'

'Your Honor, Mrs. Vandermark will testify that her license plate on her Mercedes, purchased only weeks after the death of her husband, solicits new male companionship. It goes to state of mind.'

Judge Morgan narrowed her eyes into skeptical slits. 'You may proceed,' she allowed.

'Mrs. Vandermark, what are the letters on your license plate, please?'

'California: I-S-O S-W-M. California,' Brooke added at the end, smiling at her spelling-bee imitation.

'Would you please tell the court what those letters signify?'

'Oh, everybody knows that,' Brooke dismissed.

Henry Kohn turned his palms skyward in a great affected shrug. Lawyers always knew the answers to their questions.

'Oh, *excuse me*,' Brooke said sarcastically. 'Anyone who reads the *personals*. The in-search-of pages, in the classifieds. ISO SWM stands for "in search of single white male."'

Henry Kohn arched one eyebrow, suggesting Brooke had retired her widow's veil too early. She took the wrong inference.

'I couldn't fit "*no lawyers*" on the tag,' she sniped.

Christopher collapsed heavily into his seat.

Eyes glinting, Henry Kohn took pleasure in stating the obvious. 'So you are, now, after the tragic death of your husband Heyworth Vandermark . . . on the market, so to speak? In the classifieds?'

Fran cleared her throat with a thunderous cough that echoed through the courtroom. Brooke cocked her head, staring coldly at Henry Kohn.

'Yes, in fact I am, as you say, "on the market." Not in the classifieds, just on my car. But I didn't plan to be!' She scowled at law students hiding their chuckling faces, feeling her feminine allure had been questioned.

'I'm doing my best, Mr. Kohn,' Brooke explained, 'to put together a new life thanks to some *sicko* who gunned down my husband.' She glared at Chutney, who stared indifferently at the floor.

'And anyway, Heyworth would have wanted me to remarry,' the witness sniffed, eyes rolling to heaven as if imploring his ghost. 'All he ever wanted was for me to be happy.' Brooke's shoulders shook with a sob. She peered red-eyed at the judge, quivering.

'Thank you, Mrs. Vandermark, I have no further questions,' cut in the lawyer, cursing himself for allowing Brooke to show tenderness.

'Your witness,' he motioned to Christopher.

'Your Honor' – Christopher rose – 'I'd like Mrs. Vandermark to describe what she saw when she came home from her meeting.' He stepped gingerly toward Brooke. 'Please,' he invited, 'if it's not too painful.'

'I'll tell you,' Brooke nodded, wiping tears from her

streaky face. She breathed deeply, gathering strength. 'Oh God' – she cringed – 'it was so frightening. I came home from my meeting, and the first thing I saw when I walked through the door was Heyworth. Oh, Heyworth!' she shook with a wail, face whitening as if witnessing the sight. Christopher stood frozen in passive sympathy, waiting, patient and practiced.

'I . . . I didn't know at first. I couldn't tell what had happened.' Brooke struggled to continue. 'I saw him flat on the floor. I thought he might have had a stroke. When I got closer, I saw there was blood everywhere, and I knelt down. I tried to shake him but he didn't move, and his eyes just stared.' Brooke halted, shuddering. She drew her breath but said no more, gazing blankly, the courtroom still.

'Brooke,' Christopher spoke gently, 'I know this is hard. Please try to remember. Can you tell the court if you saw anything, or anyone, else in the room.'

'No.' Brooke dropped her weary head. 'No, Heyworth was alone. I dropped to the floor and I grabbed him.' Her hands shot in front of her, cupped as if around her husband's shoulders. 'I shook him, like this, I tried to bring him to.' She choked, a sob gurgling in her throat. She stared blankly for a horrible, still moment.

She looked up to see Christopher nod his head, guiding her.

'Nothing worked,' Brooke sighed. 'He was white, his face was empty, like a shell. His eyes were open, but he was . . . he was not there.'

The image before her eyes, Brooke's face screwed up into a sour grimace. 'Oh God, I kept talking to him, crazy, like he was playing a joke or something. I think I sat there with him for a while, I'm not sure.'

At that Brooke raised her head abruptly. Her eyes blinked quickly, as if opening for the first time into light.

'He must have been jogging!' Brooke exclaimed, slapping her forehead. She laughed, a strange, chilling cackle that resounded through the courtroom. Christopher's jaw dropped.

'Of course! He was wearing his Adidas sweat suit. It looked so ridiculous on him. Oh, the poor thing, he was trying to stay in shape, because I was so much younger. He used to kid about it, taking up jog-walking, he said he'd outlast me. I think he did it just to spite the doctors!'

Brooke smiled warmly, the chummy joke remembered as if she sat among tennis partners or at Thanksgiving dinner. Deaf to the urgent throat clearing of her lawyer, Brooke seemed to forget it was a dead man she was kidding about, a dead man she stood accused of killing.

'Brooke. Brooke, please.' Christopher tried to pull his witness back to the crime scene, where her grief spoke with such compelling sincerity. Her vague, casual smile was unbearable.

'He bought it himself,' she shook her head sadly. 'Oh, silly Heyworth! He thought it was cool to wear what the kids wore.' Accidentally, it seemed, the thought jolted Brooke. 'Aieeee! Heyworth *never* could shop for himself!' she howled, plunging her head into her hands.

'Brooke.' Christopher raised his voice.

'It's horrible!' Brooke shrieked, the crowning indignity of dying without style sending her into a spasm. 'Heartless! My poor Heyworth, shot in that awful Adidas sweat suit!'

'Mrs. Vandermark!' Christopher yelled over her erupting wail.

Brooke turned to the lawyer, sobbing. 'What?' she choked.

'Brooke, please, try to remember what happened *after* you saw Heyworth.' If he never saw an Adidas sweat suit again, Christopher thought, mopping his own sweat, it would be too soon. 'Please, I know it must have been a terrible shock. I know it was,' he repeated, softening his voice with an effort. 'But please, if you can remember what happened next, I'd like you to tell the court what you did. What you saw. Anything you remember.'

Brooke sniffed noisily, her face blotchy, agitated. 'I'll try,' she promised in a weak voice.

'Take your time, Brooke. I know this is difficult.'

Brooke trembled silently for a moment. 'Okay' – she raised her head – 'but I was so scared, after I realized . . . what happened.'

'That's understandable, Brooke.'

'Okay.' Brooke gathered her arms around her body as if a wind blew through her.

'I guess at some point it hit me to call the police, so I went to the kitchen, where the telephone is. Chutney was in the kitchen, and she looked fine, you know, a little frizzy, but she wasn't crying or anything. She was at the sink, washing her hands. I didn't know how to tell her.' Brooke swallowed hard, another sob garbling in her throat. 'I . . . I tried so hard to say something, but I was shaking, I was terrified. I couldn't even make a word come out.'

'What did Chutney do then?' the lawyer prodded.

At that Brooke shot upright, staring wide-eyed at Christopher. She quivered with choppy breaths.

'Everything went crazy then,' Brooke gasped, still disbelieving. 'Chutney started yelling things at me, she ran out of the room, and I don't know what happened. I fainted, I think, in the kitchen. The police woke me up, and the next thing I knew I was handcuffed, and there were all these people in my house, marking things around my Heyworth . . .' Brooke's shrill lament resonated through the room: 'Oh, my husband, my poor Heyworth! How could anyone hurt you? My Heyworth, Heyworth . . .' Brooke murmured Heyworth's name like a mantra.

For a long moment Christopher stood still. 'Thank you, Mrs. Vandermark,' he sighed finally. 'I have no further questions, Your Honor.'

Judge Morgan glanced uneasily at Brooke. The witness had embraced her knees like a child, swaying as if to a lullaby, repeating Heyworth's name in a distant voice. Henry Kohn approached the bench with slow steps, wary of rousing another demented vision in the fragile witness.

'I'll postpone cross,' he whispered to the judge, 'but I ask your permission to call Brooke again later, if I need to.'

Judge Morgan looked at Christopher Miles, who nodded. 'I have no problem with that, Henry,' Christopher agreed collegially. 'I'd like Brooke to be able to pay attention to the witnesses, though, if she'll be called again. Your Honor, can you break for a few minutes? Give Brooke a chance to pull herself together?'

Judge Morgan was more than happy to oblige, anxious to avoid another hair-trigger catharsis from Brooke. 'Any objection, Counselor?'

Henry Kohn shook his head no. He intended to maintain a sympathetic appearance.

Judge Morgan's pounding gavel startled Brooke out of her eerie meditation.

'Mrs. Vandermark,' Judge Morgan spoke, 'you may take your seat. The court will recess for five minutes.'

Brooke accepted Christopher's arm gratefully, following his steady steps past the interns to the private witness prep room outside.

Chapter Forty-Five

CHUTNEY'S HAIR AND EYEBROWS were exactly the color of Romeo's uneven burnt orange tan-in-a-can, Elle decided, staring at Chutney's frizzy halo as she took her seat in the witness stand.

'With reference to the exhibits produced by Mr. LeBlanc and Ms. Maximillian, Chutney, please describe to the court where you were on the day of your father's death.'

To corroborate Chutney's activities on the day in question, Henry Kohn had called Philippe LeBlanc, the head stylist at Frize of Beverly Hills. Philippe had verified a page from the salon's appointment calendar, showing that Chutney had been scheduled to get a permanent wave that morning. He had rolled her hair himself, and he testified that Chutney acted perfectly normal, no different from any of the several times he had styled her hair over the years.

Maxine Maximillian, of Max Fitness Center, had spoken with Chutney at the gym in the afternoon. She placed the time around 3:00, since she had just finished teaching her marathon step aerobics class, which ran two hours and began at 1:00.

Chutney testified that she had returned home to an empty house after working out on the StairMaster. She went upstairs to take a shower and ran downstairs to grab a drink from the kitchen. That was when she found Brooke, who was shaking, paralyzed with fright, trying to move Heyworth's body. She surprised Brooke, who must not have heard her upstairs, and Brooke ran in a frenzy to the kitchen, where she fainted. Chutney called the police while Brooke was passed out. When she revived, they arrested her in the kitchen.

As her lawyer had advised, Chutney kept it short, leaving little territory for opposing counsel to investigate on cross.

When Christopher Miles began questioning the witness, his questions were unfocused, as if he were hoping for inspiration to strike him on his feet.

He asked Chutney to describe the layout of the massive house, a ploy to buy him time; then suddenly Christopher seized on something.

'You were surprised, you said, Ms. Vandermark, when you encountered your father downstairs.'

'I'd say so!' Chutney gasped. 'For God's sake, my father was . . . he was dead!'

'So you didn't notice anything unusual, then, before you came downstairs.' The lawyer spoke methodically, getting the facts straight, it seemed, for himself.

'Mr. Miles, are you going anywhere with this?' Judge Morgan leaned forward with annoyance.

Absorbed, the lawyer didn't respond immediately.

'And nobody was there when you got home,' he mused. 'So . . . so it happened while you were upstairs.' His mind raced for another question, for anything to keep Chutney on the stand. Delay beat defeat, and he was down to the final witness.

Chutney glanced at her lawyer, who shrugged. Judge Morgan, losing patience, peered expectantly at Christopher Miles.

'Counselor?'

He held a finger in the air, motioning for the judge to wait, rubbing his chin as if deep in thought.

Elle twirled her hair, wondering if she should braid it to keep herself awake. Better not. She didn't want it to frizz like Chutney's. Glancing at Chutney, Elle remembered her first and only perm and wondered why anyone paid money to have her hair ironed into wrinkles.

Suddenly, Elle shot from her chair, knocking it backward with a crash. 'Wait!' she exclaimed.

Judge Morgan glared and pounded her gavel. 'Order. Order.'

Christopher, thankful for any excuse to delay, made no move to restrain his intern.

'Your Honor,' Elle implored the bench, 'I'm an intern for Mrs. Vandermark's defense team. May I ask Chutney a question?'

Judge Morgan, glancing at the student audience, decided to play to the crowd. She wanted an article in the *Law Review*, and it was so hard to get will probate research published in the current academic climate.

'Mr. Miles?' she asked. 'Will you defer to co-counsel?'

Elle clasped her hands, pleading like a child yearning for one present on Christmas Eve.

All was lost already, the lawyer figured. This way, he could chalk the defeat up to an experimental inclusion of student lawyers.

'A fine idea, Miss Woods.' He smiled. Sarah gaped in horror.

'Your Honor' – Elle nodded seriously – 'it's relevant, I promise.'

She turned to Chutney, who grinned, more comfortable with the Intersorority Council than with a lawyer asking her questions.

'It's about your hair,' Elle began. 'It looks nice.'

'Thanks.' Chutney stared at Elle with curiosity.

'Did you just get a perm?'

'Yeah, before the trial. Philippe did it.' Chutney indicated the smug Philippe, who bowed his head to the gallery.

'I'll have to get his card,' Elle commented, laughing. 'He did your hair during college too, didn't he?'

'Oh, yes,' Chutney answered, 'he's permed my hair since the first time I went with Emerald.' Chutney's mother nodded proudly from her seat. 'In fact, I got Philippe to teach a hair-care class to the Kappas. Kappa Kappa Gamma. My sorority sisters,' Chutney explained to the judge. 'Remember, Philippe, the THM class?'

'What's THM?' Elle asked.

'Total hair management. It was my idea,' bragged the witness, tugging on her hair. 'See, Philippe's always done my hair, and he's the best! He goes to hair shows in Paris, and he comes back with all these tips. I never do a thing to my hair unless he tells me it's okay. And I do absolutely everything he tells me. He's a total professional,' Chutney rattled on.

'And you've gotten, oh, I don't know,' Elle wondered aloud, 'how many perms?'

'Well, one every six months since I was about ten, when I tried out to be Little Orphan Annie in the school play.' Chutney scowled, remembering she hadn't gotten the part. 'Tons,' she changed the subject quickly, 'like twenty at least.'

'And you got a perm the day that Heyworth . . . your father was murdered.' Elle walked toward Philippe, her back to Chutney.

'Yes,' Chutney answered. 'It's in the books, I was at Frize.'

'But your father was shot a little later, after you got home,' Elle recapped.

Sarah poked Warner with an annoyed frown. 'Do we

261

need to go through this until Elle gets it straight?' she hissed.

Elle wheeled around, approached the witness stand with her hands on her hips.

'But you didn't hear anything, not even a *gunshot*.' Elle punctuated the word loud and sharp, like a shot.

'Yes. For God's sake, I told you. I was in the shower. I worked out after I left Frize, and when I got home, I took a shower. I'm sure I didn't hear anything, any shot, because I was washing my hair. I wash it every day.' Chutney glared at Elle, her story tight. She saw no need to repeat it.

Elle walked casually toward the court gallery, smiling at Philippe. 'Chutney, veteran of twenty-odd perms, graduate of total hair management' – she spun to face the witness – 'it is absolutely *elementary*, absolutely the *first rule* of hair care, that you can't wash your hair for *twenty-four hours* after a perm.'

Chutney gasped, raising her hand to cover her open mouth. Philippe nodded excitedly.

'Is that not a fact?' Elle demanded. 'Chutney?'

'Yes,' Chutney sputtered, beginning to cry. 'Never. You have to wait twenty-four hours.'

'And you were *washing your hair*?' Elle prodded the witness. 'Three hours after you walked out of Frize?'

'No!' Chutney choked, hiding behind both hands.

Henry Kohn shot from his chair, objecting.

'You would *never* wash your hair right after getting a perm, would you, Chutney?' Elle persisted over Henry Kohn's furious shouts.

Judge Morgan pounded her gavel. 'Let her answer the question, Mr. Kohn.'

'No, no, no,' Chutney sobbed, 'never! I wasn't in the shower, of course not. *I just got a perm!*'

'You lied then, Chutney.' Elle folded her arms, staring at

the witness. 'Tell the court again where you were when your father was shot.'

Chutney spun violently in her chair, pointing at Brooke. 'She is *younger* than I am!' she shrieked. 'She was in my *geology* class, and she moved in with my *father*!'

Henry Kohn had begun jumping up and down, desperate to silence Chutney's outburst, but the demon of her savagery was unleashed.

Chutney attacked Brooke relentlessly: 'You stole my father! You ruined him! You ruined my life!'

She stood up, rushed recklessly across the courtroom in pursuit of Brooke, who leaped from her chair. 'I didn't mean to shoot him,' Chutney screamed, swiping air as the bailiff seized her. '*I meant to shoot you!*'

Chapter Forty-Six

WHEN THE FUROR SUBSIDED, the lawyer for Mrs. Whitney
Vandermark-Warren-Sands renewed his motion for the
court to consolidate the claim of his client, on the theory
that the will was valid, and Whitney was unquestionably
Heyworth's most beautiful wife.

Without the least inclination to evaluate the cosmetic
merits of five Mrs. Vandermarks preening excitedly in their
seats, Judge Morgan ruled swiftly.

'Motion granted. There being no competent evidence
that Brooke feloniously and intentionally killed
Heyworth Vandermark, the will is admitted to probate.
As a matter of law, the phrase "most beautiful wife"
employed by Heyworth Vandermark refers to his wife at
the time of his death. Matters of taste *aside*.' She directed
the comment to Whitney in particular, who had stood up
furiously.

'The parties have stipulated that Brooke was married
to Heyworth at the time of his death,' Judge Morgan continued, 'and there is no further ambiguity. Pending
appointment of a personal administrator to distribute
assets' – she pounded her gavel several times to be heard
over Whitney's sobs – 'the matter of the Estate of Heyworth
Vandermark is hereby dismissed.'

Henry Kohn hung his head.

Eugenia practically scaled the railing that separated the
lawyers' seats from the gallery, rushing to embrace Elle

amid the pandemonium of wailing wives and cheering students that erupted. Brooke, free and happy, grabbed and swung Elle's hand like a child.

'Oh, today I'm free to be me, free to be me, there goes Chutney, said it was me,' Brooke sang, bouncing along with her flowery little cheer. Elle burst out laughing.

'God, Brooke, it's a miracle you weren't so goofy on the stand.' Elle poked Eugenia, grinning with wide-eyed relief. 'Meet Eugenius,' she announced to Brooke, 'the smartest girl in Stanford Law School. I wouldn't have made it here without her.'

'Group hug!' announced Brooke, hauling Eugenia into a merry circle.

'*You're* the smartest girl in law school!' Eugenia declared, freeing her hand to rustle Elle's hair into a white moppy mess.

Elle shook a lock from her eyes with a grin. Sarah was involved in a heated conversation with Warner at the far end of the lawyers' table. 'Not bad for a Barbie doll,' she said.

'Ken should be proud,' Eugenia replied, pointing at Warner's blonde head.

Elle pinched Eugenia's arm and lowered her tone. 'Ken's on the shelf now, Genie. With the rest of the dolls.'

Eugenia wrinkled her nose, confused.

'I'll tell you later,' Elle promised.

Brooke was pulling on Elle's arm with another jingle. 'Free, free, always me, always gonna be me!'

Eugenia laughed and turned her tousling hand to Brooke's hair. 'You oughtta take that show on the road!'

'Hey, I can do anything now,' Brooke declared happily.

Elle had turned to pack up her legal pad. Brooke turned to thank her 'other lawyer Christopher,' hopping away with another chorus of 'free to be me.'

'I'll go get the car, Elle-o-rama,' said Eugenia. 'Time to party!'

Elle glanced around the clearing room and agreed. 'I'll meet you out front.'

She turned to look for Christopher, who was nowhere to be seen. Maybe he's out in the hall, Elle decided, picking up the closest two witness books to carry back with her. Acknowledging Dan's congratulations with a smile, she glided into the hallway, where Christopher stood surrounded by reporters. Out of the corner of his eye he caught Elle, and pulled her to his side. 'Here' – he beamed at Elle – 'is the real star!' Cameras were flashing, placing Elle securely in her element. The reporters had a lot of questions, many of them for Elle, which she answered beautifully. The last question, however, was directed at Christopher.

'Mr. Miles, how do you feel about being upstaged by your intern?' one of the reporters asked.

'Proud! Thanks, Elle.'

At the door of the courthouse she saw Warner standing alone. 'I guess this is my exit cue,' Christopher said, and gave Elle a wink before heading out the door.

'Elle!' Warner reached to hug her. His open arms caught air as Elle saluted him sarcastically, ducking through the door.

She couldn't resist peeking back when she heard Warner rush out behind her. Over his shoulder, she noticed Sarah standing at the doorway with her arms folded indignantly.

'Elle, stop, please,' he said as she turned to face him. 'God, let a man admit his mistake. That joke was all wrong. I *underestimated* you, Elle.'

Elle thought she noticed Sarah look away, pretending she didn't hear her fiancé's confession. Making an effort not to catch Sarah's eye, Elle drew closer to Warner.

'How's that, Warner?'

'Elle, come on, you know. I thought I'd have to marry *Sarah*, because she . . . oh God, Elle, she had the *brains* and everything. You know my family. I mean, I wanted to be with you, really, but everyone . . . everyone thought you were so flaky.' Warner laughed heartily with Elle, who encouraged him with a warm gasp to continue.

'A frosted flake? Me?' Elle giggled in faux humility, glancing to assure herself that Sarah heard. 'Little ol' Barbie doll me?'

'Oh, Elle, come on, you *act* like the biggest bimbo around.' Warner chuckled, positive that Elle shared his humor. 'I mean, you should just hear what people say about you at law school!'

Confident that he had won her back, he put his arm around her shoulder and jostled her like a friend. 'I'm so glad they're wrong! You showed everybody! I'm so glad I can be with you again now.' Warner pulled Elle close to him.

'You want me back, Warner?' Elle peered up from her old love's embrace with sweet doe eyes, trying not to laugh.

'Elle, I'll leave Sarah,' he gushed. 'I don't need her anymore. You are smart! Christopher and my father go all the way back to prep school, and with the glowing description he'll give of you, my family will have to love you! You've got the brains *and* the body. Thank God! Why did it take me so long?' He smacked his head jokingly. 'Right here all the time. The one woman who really knows me.'

Elle saw Sarah glaring furiously at Warner, and for the first time thought she and Sarah might have something in common.

'Warner, I do know you now. I didn't know you at all before,' she pronounced in a cool, even tone, lifting his hand and dropping it from her shoulder.

His smile dropped into a confused stare.

'No, Warner. I didn't *know* you,' Elle repeated. 'I loved some image that you never really were. It's not your fault. "That had to do with me, not you,"' she hissed, imitating his words from their fight in the witness room.

'But, Elle, we spent so many years together,' he protested. 'You'll never find anyone like me again, Elle.'

'I certainly hope not!' Elle answered genuinely. 'By the way, your brainy fiancée looks lonely.' She pointed behind him at Sarah, who was tapping her foot in a brisk allegro.

Warner wheeled around to face Sarah, his mind racing to explain what he had just declared with such indiscretion.

'Good-bye, Warner,' Elle said as she started down the steps. She paused, turning back with a smile. 'I'll see you around.'

Chapter Forty-Seven

EUGENIA DROVE BACK to the office of Miles & Slocum, where Elle dropped off her witness books and Brooke jumped around like a hummingbird. After waiting fruitlessly for Christopher to return, Elle decided to leave. It was Thursday, the spring days were beginning to warm and lengthen, and already she was savoring the indulgence of a long weekend.

'You'll have a summer job waiting,' Eugenia beamed.

'Heyworth's ex-wives certainly had some potential hair salon malpractice,' Elle said.

Brooke quieted, and Elle gulped a quick apology. 'I'm sorry to bring up Heyworth, Brooke.'

'That's okay.' The widow shrugged, collecting herself.

'He's been avenged!' Eugenia blurted, thumping her fist on Elle's desk. 'That despicable daughter of his won't see the inside of a hair salon for a long, long time.'

'Fitting,' Brooke said, nodding with satisfaction. Elle glanced at her curiously.

'She's got her permanent now, the wretch,' Brooke said with a smile. 'A permanent prison sentence.'

Elle giggled. 'Hey, Brooke,' she said, tugging on her client's arm. 'You up for partying with us tonight? I won't promise you much in Palo Alto, but I think it's time for you to get back on the scene. In search of . . .'

'Single white male,' Brooke finished, smiling. 'Definitely. Do you know any cute law students?'

'No!' Elle and Eugenia exclaimed in unison.

'We'll see about that.' Brooke winked, trotting out the office door.

In an hour they were toasting the future around the cactus-legged table in Elle's condo. Flushed with champagne and giggling madly, the gathering was reminiscent of 'Margotitaville' days at USC. Underdog leaped toward Elle's lap, missing her slightly, a bit dizzy from the champagne that Brooke had poured into his dog dish.

Brooke gave the first toast, encouraging them both to graduate early so she could finance the Blonde Legal Defense Fund with her Vandermark fortune.

Elle raised her glass. 'To being a Ken-free Barbie!' Shouts and applause went all the way around.

'I wondered about that,' Eugenia said, nodding. 'What's up with Warner?'

'Finishing law school, then a life in Newport with Sarah, I guess.' Elle shrugged. 'I'm too busy thinking about all of the things I want to do to think about him. Like getting the Barbie trademark and designing an entire jewelry line in her honor.'

'To Barbie,' Brooke announced, raising her glass. 'Forever in pink.'

'To Visa,' Eugenia grinned, 'living pink in the red.'

'Okay,' Elle acknowledged Brooke's waving invitation, 'my turn. To underdogs!' The drooping eyes of her faithful Chihuahua fluttered open at the sound of his name, then dropped contentedly shut. The three girls clinked glasses, drinking the remaining champagne.

Eugenia's glass struck the table first. 'Let's hit University Avenue!' she chirped.

In a minute's time, only one Underdog was left. He curled his head under his paws to sleep.

Brooke's credit card flashed as gold as the microbrewed lagers they drank, as yellow as the cab, and as blonde as the heads of Brooke and Elle who staggered back to Elle's condo and wilted like morning glories.

Class was out of the picture on the lazy Friday when they awoke; Eugenia and Brooke headed to the city to shop, and Elle, wrapped in the warmth of her bathrobe, set to the task of cleaning her littered bedroom. She discarded piles of articles on the 'Murder in Malibu,' trimming the raggedy edges of a few that were scrapbook worthy. In particular, one, which had a picture of Elle and Christopher on the courthouse steps.

She filed a few *Law Review* articles with her notes from Gilbreath's Wills class, in case they would help her study for the final exam, which was approaching fast. She answered the knock at her door still swaddled in terry cloth, sure that Eugenia or Brooke had forgotten something.

When she swung the door open she froze, gasping in disbelief. Before her stood Sarah Knottingham, redolent with the fragrance of salon products; smiling, blushing, and nervously tugging at a strand of her newly styled and highlighted hair, finally free from a headband.

'Oh my God,' Elle stuttered, supporting herself with one hand against the wall. She stared without speaking, and Sarah grinned mischievously.

'Does it look that bad?' The preppie laughed anxiously and stared down at her espadrilles.

'Oh my God, Sarah. You're . . . you're . . .'

'Mind if I come in?' Sarah asked.

Underdog stared at Sarah suspiciously, and Elle took an unsteady hungover step backward.

'No, come in,' she managed. 'Sarah, you got rid of your bob and that . . . that headband,' Elle said in victorious shock.

'Yeah, I pulled an Elle Woods,' Sarah laughed. 'I skipped class and went to the beauty salon. It seemed to work okay for you,' she added. 'Manicured and winning in court, I figured you had a secret.'

Elle regained some measure of composure when she sat down on the couch. 'No secret,' she said. 'Just habit, I guess. Manicures relax me.'

Sarah was still standing, and Elle stared noticeably at her visitor's empty left hand.

'I gave the ring back.' Sarah shrugged her shoulders. 'Now Warner has two ex-girlfriends making the law school curve worse for him. What do you think of that?'

Elle gulped, then smiled. 'I've finally quit thinking about Warner,' she said, shaking her head as if waking from a dream. 'Anyway, I think your hair looks so much better. I can't believe you even got a few highlights!'

Sarah stroked her shiny coiffure. 'I think it's worth the upkeep.'

'Definitely.' Elle nodded with vigor. 'Did you get a good conditioner?'

'Kiehls,' Sarah answered. 'That's what the stylist recommended.'

'Perfect.' Elle smiled.

Sarah handed Elle a bound outline from her shaky hand. 'I'm finished with my Property outline,' she said. 'I'm wondering if I can mine you for the answers for the Wills final? I saw some books you brought to the office one day on your desk and it looked like you could teach the class!' Sarah was highlighted, but still brunettely sensible.

'Of course,' Elle smiled, standing. 'I'm almost done with my outline. Warner's out of luck, but I'll cut you in.' Elle couldn't resist tugging at a strand of Sarah's highlighted hair. 'After all, you're blonde at heart now.'

'A *true* blonde,' Sarah laughed, remembering Elle's mini-essay.

'Naturally,' Elle said.

If you've enjoyed *Legally Blonde*, you'll love:

Family Trust by Amanda Brown

Chapter One: All Business

Becca Reinhart laughed. Her eyes were bright, shining with humor as she listened to her telephone call. Her loose black hair brushed her shoulders as she shook her head in protest. She laughed, but her answer was firm. No way.

She stood leaning against her desk, her long, graceful arms supporting her tall figure as she turned her eyes towards Central Park. In a second she had absorbed the lush view of dewy treetops surrounding the pond. She breathed deeply, adjusting her headset. She began to pace.

Worn into the border of her Turkish carpet was a visible footpath, the wake of her intense relationship with the telephone. The carpet was now a vague crushed pattern of scarlet, gold and cobalt in that rectangular path, once a meticulously designed border, hand-woven and delicate. It was, perhaps, a mismatch from the start. Nothing about Becca Reinhart or her restless, money-drenched world was delicate.

'A thousand times no!' Becca insisted, grinning with amusement. 'Listen, I've met him. The guy's rude to his own shadow. Abby Joseph Cohen wouldn't give him a buy.'

She stood in front of her brass-studded leather chair, which functioned mainly as a padded shelf for her incoming files and faxes. Becca Reinhart was a pacer: she lived on her feet. If she had a nickel for every lawyer her mother wanted her to date!

'Not even a hold, Mom,' she said firmly. 'He's an absolute sell.' Becca glanced down at her open desk calendar searching it quickly for an excuse. 'Anyway, I'm out of town. I'm in Hong Kong next week through Saturday.'

Abruptly Becca paused. Her feet were still; with a stray pen she scribbled idly on the Saturday block of her calendar.

'I know it's a holy day, Mom,' she said. She hung her head.

Her gaze traveled out the northern window of her West 57th Street office, resting once more on the untouchable extravagance of Central Park. She took a deep breath, drawing comfort from the anomaly of this city jewel. It pleased Becca to think that the Park, though inviting to all, was available to none. Manhattan's great, enduring, beckoning heart, it outlasted all the striving in which it was encircled: it could not be won. Inhaling the view like pure oxygen, Becca spoke with renewed confidence.

'I'm meeting with the finance minister, Mom. What was I supposed to do, reschedule?'

She leaned against her desk, staring at its scattered papers with a quiet glance of understanding. She looked at the screen of her computer, which indicated several dozen new messages had arrived. All were first priority.

'All right, Mom. I'll try,' she promised.

Becca waved her hand as the quick little figure of Philippe, her secretary, popped his head into her office. His hair, until recently jet black, had been highlighted with some gray, achieving a salt-and-pepper look that people typically paid to erase. With a gesture of welcome, she invited him to take a seat on her couch.

Philippe returned her smile and reclined on the couch to wait. He began to page through an issue of *The Economist*, the only reading material displayed on Becca's coffee table, noticing with a wry smile that the magazine was dated the second week of June. Today was the third of September.

It felt like June, thought Philippe, glancing out the

window behind Becca, who was tapping a pen impatiently against her desk. A dull haze hung in the thick, humid air. The sun seemed to have ripened, swelling in intensity as if to remind the city masses that summer held court for another three weeks.

Philippe looked affectionately at Becca, who had resumed pacing as she laughed into the telephone. Her restless energy had made him nervous when he first met her, but Philippe had come to appreciate, even to crave, the warmth of Becca's confidence. Her teeth, white and even, gleamed as she laughed out loud. She was incredible.

Between board meetings, speaking tours, conferences and the usual round of deal negotiations, Becca had been traveling every week this summer. It was natural to her; travel suited her pace. There were days at a time when she was nothing but a blur to Philippe, racing past his desk with her Pullman suitcase bumping and rolling behind her, hurrying to finish the call on her headset before she lost cellular service in the elevator.

Becca had fire, the effects of which he saw reflected in the faces of the clients and hopefuls that revolved through her office. Sometimes their worn lines of anticipatory tension were soothed, warmed by her competence, her iron reliablity. And other times he ducked to search for imaginary files under his desk, unwilling to meet the violent eyes of the seekers of capital who came away burned.

Philippe was amazed that Becca could survive the physical pressure of travel on top of her intense load of back-to-back meetings. She changed time zones with chameleon-like agility. Every day she met with companies at the make-or-break stage and handled their urgent pleading with integrity and dispatch. He wondered, sometimes, what Becca would have done without a job. Would she run marathons? Climb mountains? Pile up credit card debt? He knew she was cut out for something extraordinary.

He smiled to see her suitcase by the door, standing at

the ready. Becca pre-packed her bags for different climates and labeled each piece of luggage for maximum travel efficiency. A brass-rimmed tag which dangled on the Louis Vuitton rolling bag that leaned against the wall read 'London, Autumn'.

Philippe had booked her a flight on Virgin Atlantic. She would hardly have time to adjust to the six-hour time change before she was supposed to conduct a meeting to evaluate an offer for the shares of Machovia, a Davis Capital portfolio company in whom she was the single largest private investor. Most people took at least three days on the ground before returning from business in London. Becca would be three days door-to-door.

She had succeeded quickly in this unyielding world, thanks to the gamble Dick Davis had made on her when he'd given her the chance to join the partnership five years ago. She had been leading the technology group at Morgan Stanley at the time, a young analyst with a sterling reputation for her exhaustive, personally diligent research and an iron stomach for risk. Her returns, even in the bear market, were unbeatable.

Dick Davis, the founding partner of Davis Capital, had left the Bear Stearn partnership nearly twenty years ago to found his venture capital firm. He had seeded it at first with the fortune that his wife had inherited from her grandfather's piece of Standard Oil. Today the firm managed eleven billion dollars of invested capital.

Becca would never forget what Dick Davis had made possible for her: to enter the elite, private partnership of Davis Capital as a relative *child*. She was twenty-six years old when she started with the firm. Dick's confidence in Becca was aggressive, and she soon proved it to be well-placed.

Though it carried the Davis flag, the name that came to mind when anyone thought of Davis Capital was Becca Reinhart. At thirty-one years old, Becca Reinhart was still the firm's youngest partner, and on their portfolio compensation scheme she was also the best paid. Her own portfolio made up nearly forty per cent of revenues and over half the profits of the firm. Becca had high visibility from her very first day at Davis Capital.

Her brash entry into the firm was a legend. The day she accepted Dick's offer, Becca got his secretary, Philippe, on the phone, asked him what he made and offered him more money to come and work for her. She wanted somebody who knew the business, she said, and who better than her boss' secretary?

'Poached my secretary,' Dick would laugh, pretending to complain about her hard bargaining, 'and she didn't even blink an eye!' He told the story all over Wall Street. He had wisely chosen not to fight her, though: with a knowing smile he told Philippe to pack up his desk. Dick knew that Becca's confidence was going to make the partnership rich.

Philippe was happy with the switch, as he had never been fond of Dick Davis' overbearing wife. For Becca, as long as he could talk fast, type fast and schedule every ten minutes precisely for the next three months, he stayed above the water. He managed Becca's calendar and her travel, copied the reports for her meetings and trotted in with her faxes, sorted her mail and kept her files secure. She had another assistant on full-time to handle the phones, and the analysts took care of her research. The clippings service prepared its own news summaries.

Becca could have a staff of fifty, Philippe marvelled, and she wouldn't know what to do with it. She had never quite learned how to delegate. She put a bear-hug on her own companies and served on dozens of their boards. For travel, however, she had learned to lean on Philippe.

In a moment she was rushing towards the couch to join him.

'Did you get my message?' She held her breath, glancing

at the Eastern Standard clock on the wall. Eleven-thirty her time. Her eyes shone with energy as she turned towards Philippe for his answer.

'Check,' he said, nodding simply. 'Consider it done.'

He stroked his hair, intending to draw her attention to it. This color was a big change for him. Alexander, his partner, who ran a fashionable Upper East Side salon, had worked for days to get just the right silver tone in the gray on his temples.

She paused. 'I'm in London till Tuesday; I arrive in New York at six-thirty in the morning. We're doing an eight o'clock meeting at Wasserstein; I won't have time to get back here after the flight.'

He ran a hand over his salt-and-pepper hair. 'Of course I know, Becca. I booked your ticket. I *love* to wait on you in my spare time.'

'What *is* spare time?' she shot back with a laugh.

She dug the J.F.K. locker key from her desk drawer, being careful not to confuse it with the La Guardia key, and scribbled down her combination to the electronically secured file room in which she kept the permanent records for her portfolio companies.

She began to describe the precise location of the Wasserstein files when Philippe waved impatiently.

'I filed them, sweetie, I know,' Philippe assured her. He was practically pointing to his hair with both hands in his eagerness for her to notice it. He tried to catch Becca's eyes and saw that her glance had passed him already. She was moving again, headed towards the coffee bar.

Philippe began to feel a little testy, and paused to console himself that his *hair* was not at fault in her failure to notice him: it was Becca's fundamental lack of attention to appearances. He remembered the day, just a few months ago when they were working late in the office on the Celex deal, she'd asked Dick Davis when he'd started wearing glasses.

'Nineteen-ninety-two,' Dick had informed her, to Becca's enormous surprise. Dick still laughed about that.

Philippe declined the latte that Becca, standing in front of her coffee bar, offered him. Her imposing black coffee machine, mounted into the wall, featured over thirty small silver buttons that produced on demand an infinite variety of coffees. For herself she pushed the espresso button five times before placing a large mug below the coffee spout.

Philippe broke down. 'Look at my hair, Becca,' he pleaded.

She turned her head at once. 'Philippe,' she said, smiling broadly, 'it's great!'

'The Old Economy's back in,' he boasted, sauntering towards her. 'Alexander says people are *rushing* into the salon for gray temples and sideburns. *Gravitas* is hot, you know. Credibility is back.'

Becca put the coffee in the refrigerator to cool so she could drink it quickly.

'Good thing,' she said, grinning. 'Now, how do we sell it?'

She closed the door behind Philippe, turning quickly to answer a call that the temp had put through. Changing into her nylon warm-ups and a jogging bra, she said hello to David Sheffer, the external lending director of the European Investment Bank. Becca was in a hurry: she had scheduled herself to take a run at twelve-fifteen, and so far she had stuck to her schedule.

Becca had known David when he ran the European equities platform at Morgan Stanley. It was a strange time to call from Luxemburg, she said; he replied that he was in New York. He had a German paper company he wanted to put her on to, which the EIB wouldn't fund because of his family's stake in the business. She agreed to meet with the German CEO next week, if she could get a translator, and appreciated him sending over the company's information.

She tapped an email on her computer asking Philippe to adjust her schedule to leave open a half-hour next Thursday.

David held for a second while Becca slipped a T-shirt carefully over her headset. Her eyes roved around her office. There were a half-dozen stacks of paper to read, all top priority. The messages and faxes piled up by the minute; if she had an impromptu social conversation in the hall it knocked her off schedule. Empty mugs lined the wet bar, alternating with empty Evian bottles: now and again one pile of mugs would disappear and clean ones would appear in their place.

Becca glanced at the bagels, still untouched, which she had delivered to her office every morning to guard against the real possibility of starvation. She tried to keep a bagel in her purse for the times when she ran to get a cab and felt the sidewalk spinning.

Becca used time as efficiently as she thought it could be used.

Marking the time on the clock, Becca started the treadmill on Alpine Walk, making conclusory remarks into her headset to let David know she had no more business with him. Then David got to the real point of his phone call.

He had a nephew that he would like her to meet for dinner this week.

She cranked the machine up to Hard Jog. Not another nephew!

Becca did her best to listen politely, since she did want to check out the German paper firm as a possible investment, but the setup was difficult to endure. Was she wearing a sign – Desperate Single Girl? Marry Me Please? She pounded through her workout, fueled by indignity.

'He's thirty-four,' David offered, a bit tragically. 'Lawyer at Simpson Thatcher, good practice, good prospects. Never married.'

'Tell him to call my office sometime,' Becca offered,

without enthusiasm. Why did David think that her life was incomplete? Did anything suggest she was looking for a crutch?

'Frankly, David,' she told him flatly, 'I'm more interested in the business piece. I'll let you know how the paper company looks after we talk.' She cut off the call and ran for several minutes as hard as she could.

Becca couldn't understand why capable professionals, with whom she had a solid business relationship, were always trying to marry her off. She didn't ask after their prospects. She didn't comment on their divorces, their affairs. Why was her personal life so interesting to them? Didn't they see how busy she was?

It had gotten worse since she turned thirty-one last year. Even her mother, for whom marriage had never done any favors, was constantly after her to give a nice boy like Gary Yahkzen a chance. Everybody had something to offer, her mother would point out, despite apparent shortcomings. Who says it's not nice to be a urologist?

Her father must have found something useful in the state of marriage, Becca reflected with the spite she reserved for the man who had abandoned her mother. He had tried it twice. While her mother was being treated – successfully, thank God – for her cancer, Becca's father and the chemo nurse had begun an ongoing affair. He had married her, Becca was told: needless to say she did not attend the ceremony. Her father's betrayal had never lost its bitterness.

He had left her mother when Becca was only ten, and for all practical purposes she considered her father to be dead. She never spoke of him. But Becca's mother had more than filled the void he'd left in her life. To Becca her mother was both parents and a dear friend, not to mention a conscience.

Becca tried to get to Brooklyn on Fridays for Shabbat dinner with her mom, but she only made it every other month or two. Things were all right between them, though, in spite of Becca's absence. She always remembered to call. Becca and her mother were secure in their love for one another, and both were good friends to the telephone.

Becca was her mother's sole source of financial support, outside of the part-time work Arlene did at her temple, where really she went just to hear things. Lately Arlene had been hearing about everybody's grandchildren. If Becca had spent an afternoon kibbutzing with Arlene's friends, she would understand the logic which motivated Arlene's sudden interest in matchmaking. But for Becca to take an afternoon off was unthinkable. Becca had people depending on her, and they were uniquely well-served. She was tireless in her devotion to her job.

She felt the muscles in her calves stretching from the pull of racing with the treadmill. The workout was an extreme one. Becca tried to exhaust her natural intensity before she conducted client meetings. She hoped she would appear mellow and reasonable if she conducted the meetings in a state of physical exhaustion. Her feet and mind raced together as Becca rehearsed the speech she was giving at the Capital Markets meeting next week.

Becca tugged a Sergio Valente pantsuit from her closet and folded it in a tight, sleeping bag-style roll. She stuffed it into her shoulder bag, intending to change for the flight to London after she had showered at Virgin's airport lounge. She pulled her office door closed and hurried down the hall, her suitcase bumping behind her. She glanced at her watch. The car would be downstairs by now.

Becca quickened her step as she hurried past Sam Wattenberg's office. Sam's door was open.

'Becca,' he called, leaping from his desk chair.

She kept walking. Sam followed her.

'Sam, I've got a meeting at the airport at three and a flight at six,' she told him over her shoulder.

'I've got a press conference in ten minutes. Any recessionary expectations?'

Stepping sideways towards the elevator, Becca ticked off a few suggestions.

'Venezuela, Peru and Colombia plunge this year. Russia's always in recession, so throw it in. Egypt looks bad, Czech Republic is slipping. Japan may make it, but I'd put it in the slide category. Argentina probably goes with Peru. I've got to go, Sam!'

Becca blew Philippe a little kiss of thanks for shuttling her files to the airport. The elevator doors closed and she smiled broadly, taking a deep breath as she dug her hand in her Prada bag to check for her Palm, her phone, her ticket confirmation and her cash wallet.

She could feel her heart beating eagerly as she thought ahead to the meeting in London. The offer for her British company was likely to get approved; Becca would recommend accepting it and she thought she had the votes on her side. She had always liked that company, and she had a good feeling about this deal. It was proving to be a smart investment. She could bet on getting tapped for a spot on the holding company's board of directors, if she wanted one.

She smiled, looking forward to the manicure she would get from Virgin's in-flight spa therapist. Becca felt a surge of enthusiasm as the elevator doors opened in the lobby. She saw the Davis car waiting to take her to the airport. She could start calling the American directors right away and get a count of their votes. She had assumed the board was accepting proxies, but she should get that into the minutes of the meeting. She'd move for that at once; she'd have to make sure she had a second to back her up. Who should she call? Who had the next largest investment? Her mind began to race: she had little time and much to do.

Becca Reinhart breathed deeply. She loved her job.